SHADOWS OVER

UTOPIA

Book Two of the UTOPIAN DREAMS Series

Alan M. Atkinson

Cover by Nevena Jevtić

IngramSpark™ Edition

Second Printing

2022

I0600959

Disclaimer:
While this story is entirely a work of fiction, it is also a work of alternate history, referencing recent real-world events. Every effort has been made to show all due respect to any person or persons, living or dead, who may be peripherally or overtly referenced regarding the real-world or associated fictional events within this book. No living person will be directly named* within this book. Any resemblance of a commercial trade name to a real-world trademark is likewise accidental and is in no way intended to portray any link to the company holding that trademark. The author, their agents and publishers cannot be held responsible for any claim otherwise and take no responsibility for any such coincidence.

* Referenced by birth name, as opposed to a superheroic pseudonym or other nickname.

This book written in Palatino Linotype, using Office 365™.

Title: Shadows Over Utopia
Author: Alan M. Atkinson (1970—)
Subjects: Superheroes, Science Fiction, Alternate History, Non-Binary Characters, Social
            Issues, Crime, Romance.

First Printing: 2022

Printed and distributed by IngramSpark (www.ingramspark.com)

ISBN: 978-0-6487296-6-2

Alan M. Atkinson
Words on Paper (Ink)
Townsville, QLD 4810
words.on.paper.ink@gmail.com

Edited using Grammarly™

Cover design and layout by Nevena Jevtić at https://www.deviantart.com/u-svetu-maste
Cover image © Nevena Jevtić and Alan M. Atkinson

Author image created using Sketch Camera™

The American Captain™ font (used in the Force Majeure logo) created by The Fontry™
(https://thefontry.com)

Dedication

To my best mate Batts—

acerbic and abrasive;

incisive and insightful;

staunch and steadfast;

brilliant and insightful GM;

the most grounded individual I know;

who has demonstrated that not only
is it *possible* to make a leap of faith …

but it's also sometimes *necessary*.

Best of luck, mate.

Preface

I stand once more upon the precipice of writing a book.

This is both easier and harder than it was the first time around; easier because I know I've done it once, and so it's possible. Harder because I didn't know then how much time and effort and dedication would have to go into making it work. All the rewrites and moving plot elements around, wondering *will this work?* and *am I overthinking that?* and of course *have I given away the reveal too soon?*

Well, nobody's told me yet that they figured out the reveal before they reached it, so I got that bit right at least. I'm hoping the next one goes off as well.

But this isn't supposed to be about me, or about the last book. It's supposed to give you a taste of what's in *this* book. To tell you why you should be putting everything aside to settle down and read what's between these covers.

So, let's get to it.

Shadows Over Utopia is not going to be the same as *Welcome to Utopia*. Even apart from the shift from 9-point font to 10-point (you're welcome), it's not intended to be. Some things will remain constant; Jericho Hansen will be front and center in the action, along with many of the secondary characters from the first book. Some, though, will be fading into the background while others move forward into the limelight. Characters mentioned only in passing in *Welcome* are going to get top billing (at least for a while), and we will learn more about them in the process.

As the story progresses, the world itself will change. I'm sorry if you wanted to read an idyllic story about a technological Utopia in modern-day America, but a good story requires change and conflict, and I'm hoping to present both of these in amounts that satisfy the palate; not an easy task in today's action-movie saturated reality.

Once more, Jericho will be forced to consider his place in the world and where he wants to be. I will not say more than that for fear of betraying the plot before it gets properly started, but I can assure you that these are not off-the-cuff audience shockers pulled out to justify a sequel. I've been planning all of this from the beginning. Do you have any idea how hard it is to plant the seeds for a future reveal without giving the game away altogether or making it too obscure? I have a whole new appreciation for my favorite authors now.

One unavoidable aspect of the ongoing plot is that this book (unlike *Welcome*) will end with somewhat less of a satisfying wrap-up of the major threads. There will be an endpoint, and it won't be the type of cliffhanger that leaves the reader wondering 'how are they going to get out of *this*?' but it rather clearly sets things up for the next book.

I understand that some readers will be disappointed that the big issues aren't being resolved *right now,* but the fact remains that big issues are *big.* As in, they take a while to resolve. Also, a lot of effort. A whole book's worth, in fact. This was always intended to be a multi-volume series and, while each novel tells its own section of the story, the narrative must be ongoing and continuous. That said, I can't resolve everything all at once. Some things need to run on and be dealt with in their own time. This is one of those things.

Important Note:

If anyone reading this book lost loved ones in the 1986 Challenger disaster, be aware that the alternate-history version of that event alluded to in the first book will be expanded in this story; specifically, that the disaster caused one of the crew to develop super-powers, with which they saved the day (and the rest of the crew). This is not intended to cheapen the serious nature of the tragedy, or minimize the real-life sacrifice made by those seven brave men and women.

I have deliberately avoided revealing the true identity of Challenger, and I will continue to do so. That decision is up to the individual reader; Challenger is (or was) whichever member of the crew you want them to be.

Anyway, I hope you enjoy the read.

Alan M. Atkinson
April, 2020

Previously ...

If you've already read the first book in the UTOPIAN DREAMS series, *Welcome to Utopia*, then you can skip this section.

If you have not, I suggest you put this book down right now and read that one. There is much detail there which will be referenced but not necessarily explained in the text of this one.

However, if you don't have access to *Welcome to Utopia* right now, or you're okay with the no-frills version, we can do that too. Buckle your seatbelt, this is gonna be a bumpy ride. (A more complete timeline can be found at the back of the book.)

This is a superhero novel.
The main character, Jericho Hansen, is gay.
People with powers are called "Enabled".

There are three basic powersets: Dynamic, Prodigy, Artificer.
Dynamic covers overt powers, such as flight or laser vision.
Prodigy covers "peak human condition" characters who do everything normal people can do, but *better.*
Artificer covers people who build impossible machines.
These are also known as Capes, Cowls or Cogs, especially in the media. The alliteration is deliberate.

1986: (January) Space Shuttle Challenger incident. A crewmember on board manifests Dynamic powers and saves the rest of the crew. Ends up as the superhero Challenger.

1988: Challenger founds the first superhero team (Inspire), along with British artificer Arfogwyr.

1990s: A series of particularly nasty villains become known as the 'terror villains of the Nineties'. In alphabetical order, these are: Carnifex, Charnel, the Darksider, Doc Iridium, False Flag, Guillotine, Kraken, Mindscrew (previously 'Mind-fucker'), the Minotaur, Mutilator & Devastator, Raider, Seismic and Singularity. None survive the end of the decade.

1990: Charnel captured by two independent heroes; Adam Power and the Tesseract. This signals the beginning of an unofficial team-up (and ongoing relationship) between the pair.

The Minotaur takes the families of government officials hostage to enforce the release of Charnel. He is broken free by other villains, and the Minotaur murders his hostages anyway.

1991: Inspire recruits Castellan, a prodigy.

1994: A radical activist group called Unmask tries to blackmail Adam Power and the Tesseract with knowledge of her secret identity. They defy the group, and Adam unmasks as well. They announce the formation of Team Power, and are married shortly after.

1997: (January) The Minotaur murders the newly elected Vice President, provoking the US into declaring war on the terror villains by way of Executive Order.

(March) After Carnifex is hunted down and killed, the President and his successor are murdered in retaliation. Following that, the Executive Order is rescinded.

(July) The Minotaur kills Arfogwyr and puts Challenger into a coma. Castellan hunts him down and kills him, then retires.

The Challenger Act, which makes it a Federal offence to expose the identity of a recognized superhero, is finalized into law.

1998-99: A new team, Force Majeure, goes after the terror villains. They take out all but Doc Iridium, who threatens to 'blow up Manhattan' if the members of Force Majeure are not arrested and summarily executed. His bomb (placed in Manhattan, *Kansas*) goes off prematurely, taking him with it. 91,473 innocent people are killed and a thousand square miles irradiated. With the blessing of the US government, Force Majeure reclaims the land and begins the construction of an ultra-tech metropolis called Utopia City on the site, with the centerpiece being a mile-and-a-half tall building called the Spire. Force Majeure's core membership consists of Relentless, Independence, the Technologist, Transit, Silent Knight, Lady Quantum and Tourbillon.

2011: Vanessa Power, daughter of Adam and Tesseract Power, accuses her father of attempted rape. She flees in her powered armor suit. It crashes, and she vanishes.

2013: ...

Welcome to Utopia

Jericho Hansen, AKA G-Man, a gay superhero residing in Savannah, Georgia, applies to join Force Majeure. His boyfriend Stephen doesn't want him to go. He goes anyway, with his cousin Luke, on the high-tech maglev (another Force Majeure product). On the way, Luke reveals that Stephen has been cheating on him. They also meet Bobbi, an empath who wants to prove that Adam Power had nothing to do with his daughter's disappearance.

On arrival in Utopia City, they meet a personable young man called Thomas, who helps them out and shares an air taxi to the accommodation complex where they've chosen to stay. There's a brief encounter with the police that indicates people with criminal records are under surveillance in Utopia City. Thomas goes on his way, leaving Jericho confused about his feelings.

That night, Jericho goes on patrol. After encountering Transit, he intervenes in an assault which turns out to be an undercover police operation, allowing the arrestees (including Thomas) to escape. He later encounters Thomas again and finds out about the Survivors, would-be heroes turned petty criminals who just want to get out of town. He offers to help.

Still wrestling with his feelings for Thomas, he gets back to the accommodation block to find that Luke and Bobbi have been murdered. Cops arrive, he breaks down, then learns that the murderer was Bobbi's boyfriend. Goes to the roof to brood, meets an enigmatic Enabled called Smokeshadow.

The interview to join Force Majeure doesn't go well (his emotions are still running high, and Independence is hostile), but he gets Smokeshadow to help with Thomas and the Survivors. His uncle Leroy comes to Utopia to claim Luke's body. They go back to Savannah for the wake and funeral. Jericho breaks up with Stephen, then returns to Utopia where Thomas and Smokeshadow help track down the killer of Luke and Bobbi.

Relentless offers Jericho a place in Force Majeure (which he accepts) then invites Jericho back to his rooms in the Spire and makes a pass. Jericho turns him down in favor of Thomas. At Smokeshadow's urging, Jericho and Thomas spend the night together.

In the morning, Jericho deduces that Thomas is Vanessa (who gained shape-changing powers from her ordeal). He convinces her that her father didn't attack her. She goes home and reunites with her family. Smokeshadow indicates she will be taking over the local crime scene. Jericho is given a power-enhancement harness that allows him to fly.

In the epilogues, a New York team called Manhattan Justice has a new recruit, and Relentless reveals that he got a mysterious note fourteen years previously (long before Jericho even got his powers), telling him to "*trust G-Man*", because "*he will save Utopia*".

And now you're up to date ... mostly. Enjoy.

Contents

Part Three: The Façade Crack'd

Part Four: The Final Act Unveiled

PROLOGUES

Prologue One
Castellan

The spike trap came out of nowhere. Castellan caught the merest whisper of razor-edged steel splitting the dust-filled air and brought his sword up, but his reaction time was an instant slow. Even as the Arfogwyr-forged blade sliced the deadly mechanism in two, a single spike flickered past his defenses. He grunted as it punched through a part of his armor that had been damaged by an earlier trap, stabbing deep into his shoulder.

He kept the sword moving, slicing away the last of the treacherous device until there was just one piece of metal protruding from his armor; it glowed a dull red where his sword had cut it. From the feel of the wound as he moved his arm gingerly, no major blood vessels were damaged, though that could change if he left it in place.

He knew what he had to do; re-sheathing his sword on his back, he grasped the severed end of the spike in his gauntleted hand. Metal grated against metal as he wrenched it out of his shoulder and flipped it end for end. Before he could talk himself out of it, he set his jaw and jammed the still red-hot metal stub in through the hole in his armor, searing the torn flesh within and cauterizing the wound.

Just for a moment, he stood there, half doubled over, air hissing between his teeth as jagged lightning bolts of pain lanced into his skull and slammed their way through his nervous system. It hurt as severely as anything he'd experienced before in his life, certainly more than the AK round he'd taken through the thigh in Vietnam an eternity ago. Flesh sizzled, and acrid smoke rose, but he held firm until the blood vessels were sealed shut.

Finally, breathing heavily, he discarded the bloodstained, blackened metal spike with a clatter on the flagstone floor. It was no longer glowing, and there were ugly scraps of burned flesh adhering to it, but it had served its purpose. He wouldn't bleed out, not from that wound, anyway. Working his arm back and forth, he decided he could live with the pain. He drew his sword once more as he moved on down the passageway.

I'll rest and heal once the Minotaur is done with.

At that moment, the villain of the piece decided to make himself known. **"Hello, Castellan,"** he gloated, the electronically modulated voice booming from the speakers hidden here and there in the stonework. **"That looked like it left a mark. How's your shoulder? A little sore?"**

Gritting his teeth, Castellan chose to ignore the taunting. He couldn't afford to forget that the Minotaur had every foot of these passages wired for both audio and video, as had been the villain's practice with all the murder mazes he'd constructed to date. After all, how else was a sadistic monster supposed to broadcast the gruesome deaths of his victims to their friends and loved ones for maximum pain and suffering?

The term 'terror villain', applied to the Minotaur and those like him who went all-out with their powers and abilities to hurt people, was not one Castellan tended to use. It had gained popularity over the last few years, presumably to differentiate them from the run-of-the-mill robbery and murder villains that most heroes faced. He simply called them 'suspects', a habit from his life before donning the mask. This kept matters straight in his head and denied them the recognition they craved.

"Why are you even bothering?" Despite the masking overtones, the Minotaur's voice managed to come across as both bored and confident. **"You know you'll never find me. And if you do find me, I'll just kill you, just like I killed Arfogwyr and Challenger. They couldn't even put up a good fight. I wouldn't blame you for walking away now."**

No, but I would. The temptation to lash out verbally at the Minotaur was strong, but Castellan's innate discipline stifled that importunate urge before it could ever see the light of day. A brasher man might have let slip the fact of Challenger's continued survival (albeit with critical injuries) or betrayed his knowledge of exactly how to locate his foe, just to have the satisfaction of throwing something back in the villain's face. But he gave away nothing and kept moving, his head on a swivel, the sword up and ready.

The Minotaur's voyeuristic greed for recording every last gasp of pain and suffering generated within his murder mazes was about to backfire on him. While the cameras and speakers were discreet and not always apparent to the untrained eye, they required wires for both power and signal transmission to and from a single monitor room. In a more mundane construction that would not have mattered so much, as standard drywall can be utilized to cover a multitude of sins. But this labyrinth, as with all the Minotaur's creations, had been hacked from the living rock, then smoothed over and tiled—walls and floor—with slabs of carefully fitted stone. No matter the artisan's level of proficiency and care, there was only so much discreet concealment that could be achieved with rock.

This wasn't to say the Minotaur hadn't tried. The cables were stashed away in an overhead recess in the ten-foot-high tunnel roof, making it difficult to spot by any viewer previously unaware of its presence. Lights were affixed to the ceiling at semi-regular intervals directly over this recess, precisely so the glare would render it even harder for a casual observer to notice it. Castellan only knew about the recess and its significance because he was one of the few living people who could claim previous experience with the Minotaur's mazes.

As the various wires converged on the control room where the Minotaur lurked in the center of the labyrinth, the bundles became thicker and more distinct. For the average person, this particular data point would have done little to guide them to safety, but Castellan wasn't trying to get *out* of the maze. In a grim reversal of Greek myth, he was following a series of cords to track the monster down, not escape from him.

At any other time, knowing the Minotaur lacked innocents to hide behind, his plan of action would have been to hold position outside and call up reinforcements to surround the maze. With all exits located and blocked, the Minotaur would be called upon to surrender. If he did not, a controlled detonation could then be carried out on the demolition charges Castellan *knew* were buried in the walls.

But here and now, it was intensely personal. Blood cried out for blood. For what the Minotaur had done—*again*—he was going to have to either surrender to lawful authority or die, and he'd long since proven he wasn't the surrendering type. Which suited Castellan right down to the ground.

Death, it is.

For all his determination on that score, Castellan's emotions were ice-cold, his movements measured and precise. The last thing he wanted was for intemperate anger to risk allowing his quarry to escape yet again and carry on with his reign of terror. Castellan's pursuit of the Minotaur had gone on far too long to accept even half a chance of that happening. Too many innocents—and heroes—had already fallen to the villain's hand. No matter what else happened in this maze, the Minotaur was not leaving it a free man.

Castellan moved on, keeping a watchful eye out for the telltale signs of more deathtraps. As if by accident, he let the tip of his sword score against the smooth-polished wall of the labyrinth, the plasma generators within the Artificer-created blade leaving a line of molten rock behind it. The glowing orange line crossed a gap from one stone panel to the next, and just so happened to slice through a not-discreet-enough wire set between them.

While cutting the camera or speaker lines would've risked tipping his hand with how he was closing in on the Minotaur, he'd figured out which were the ones connected to the demolition charges seeded throughout the maze. He wouldn't put it past the villain to have linked up some sort of life-signs detector to a self-destruct signal as one final screw-you, and he certainly intended to interrupt the Minotaur's life signs permanently. Accordingly, he was severing the wires whenever he spotted them. Putting an end to the Minotaur was his ultimate aim, but he had no intention of it being his *last* act on Earth.

Long ago, while he was still making his mark in the Department of Justice, his world had been turned inside out when he'd lost virtually everyone he held dear to a murder maze very much like this one. Worse than that, he'd *witnessed* their deaths, broadcast live when the Minotaur triggered the self-destruct charges: more from pure spite, it appeared, than anything else. The experience had scarred him deeply, searing his soul to the core. Where a lesser man would have been forever shattered and lost, he found a more profound strength and endured, moving forward, calling for justice.

Something *needed* to be done about the terror villains; attacking the innocent in this fashion was thoroughly unconscionable. He'd spoken to many people about this, up and down his chain of command. Unofficially, they'd agreed with him.

However, the official stance (quite often from the same people) was something else again. The response to this new breed of villain had somehow evolved overnight in the face of the Minotaur's demonstrated ruthlessness into something akin to *'if we don't push them, maybe they won't push back'*. While nobody in the administration would even come close to admitting appeasement was on the agenda—multiple thesauri were undoubtedly scoured for phrasing that could convey the concept without actually *saying* it—the bottom line was simple.

There would be no justice for the Minotaur's actions.

To add insult to injury, Charnel's escape from custody (which had been the entire reason for the Minotaur's actions) led to only a cursory manhunt, called off all too soon. While those in the field were still dedicated to their jobs, the sudden downturn in political will from above was tying their hands. It didn't help that crucial resources aimed at tracing and capturing other villains of the same ilk were being redirected toward less problematic targets, and the villains in question were taking full advantage of the new hands-off attitude.

Disgusted by what he saw as an abject surrender to the forces of crime and corruption, he'd walked away from his career, putting aside years of seniority in the process. Officially, he retired in protest; unofficially, he became Castellan. Years had passed since he first donned the mask, but he still held one truth sacred.

Nobody is above the law.

Now, after many false leads, he was on the verge of getting closure at long last. Of ending this.

To keep the Minotaur guessing, he took a couple of wrong turns, then doubled back once he considered the false trail established. At the next junction he came to, he stopped and looked one way, then the other. He knew which direction he needed to go, but if he betrayed that fact too early, the Minotaur was entirely too likely to slip out through a previously prepared escape route. Turning toward the way he knew led to the exit, he took three purposeful steps.

Let's see if …

"Oh, come on, Castellan!" The arrogant voice boomed out through the speakers. **"I slaughtered your whole team! You can't tell me you're giving up already!"**

The Minotaur had made errors before. His most egregious one to date had been to kill people Castellan cared for: not once, but twice. This was a whole new level of miscalculation. Specifically, the villain had taken Castellan's bait, betraying his confidence that the armored hero had no idea where his foe was.

The electronically amplified voice sounded precisely the same as it had earlier, which meant that for all his braggadocio, the Minotaur was still broadcasting from the monitor room. When it came down to it, the terror villain was just as much a bully and a coward as he was a sadistic murderer. He was happy to attack and kill people weaker than him or strike down an unsuspecting victim from behind, but he'd never had the stomach for facing up to someone who might beat him in a fair fight.

Turning on his heel, Castellan pushed himself into a run. He was beaten and bruised from the Minotaur's prior traps, and his injured shoulder sent stabs of pain through his body with each step, but he didn't care. This was one reckoning the Minotaur wasn't going to slip away from.

Not this time.

He dashed down the rock-lined corridor, following the bundled cables and trusting the infrared sensors built into his helmet to save him from running headlong into a lethal trap. A turn loomed ahead, the larger cable bundles going to the right. He went right as well, then the IR outlined a section of floor with lower heat an instant before he would've run straight over the top of it. *Pit trap.* Aided by the powerful actuators built into the legs of his armor, he hurdled it and kept going. He was in the zone now, his focus unwavering. Every step was taking him closer to his goal.

"Wrong way, Castellan," the Minotaur's voice taunted him as he turned left down another corridor, slashing the wires to yet more of the demolition charges. **"Might want to go back and try again."**

Castellan ignored the content of the words; they were only chosen to irritate and upset him. The tone, on the other hand, revealed a great deal. However much the Minotaur tried to conceal it, there was a new level of tension in his voice. The monster lurking in the center of the maze was becoming less and less comfortable with how close his nemesis was getting.

To his right, the thin stone tiles covering the wall shattered, another spike trap erupting from the purpose-built cavity in a blatant attempt by the Minotaur to skewer him and end the threat before he got any closer. The previous one had nearly gotten him, but his reactions were faster now; at the first crack in the stone façade, he sliced his sword across the spikes and sent them clattering to the ground. Ignoring the red-glowing stubs, he kept running.

The corridor he was in continued onward, broad and inviting, with just a single narrow passage to the left. He slowed all the same, having learned to beware of the apparently innocuous. A single glance down the unlit side passage, his sword at the ready in case of ambush or traps, assured him it was empty. In fact, it only went in five or six yards and stopped dead, serving no visible purpose.

He was about to move on, but the question nagged at him: *why would he have a useless dead-end passage?* It didn't fit the Minotaur's style. Then he looked up at the roof, and the question was answered; while the recess in the ceiling also continued onward, the bundle of cables diverting down the side-passage was far thicker than anything in the main corridor.

I see you now.

Taking a few steps into the side-passage, switching entirely to infrared in the absence of light, he examined the far wall. Up ahead, the passageway ended abruptly, but the recess holding the cables fed directly into a hole in the wall. Acting on a hunch, he turned the IR off and spotted the faintest sliver of light peeking through the hole, past the bundled cables.

There was no question about it. The 'wall' ahead was a concealed door of some kind, with a room beyond. And with all those cables coming through, Castellan figured he knew what the room contained. He didn't have time to search for the opening mechanism, but it wasn't really an issue.

He'd brought a key of his own.

Up came his sword, the tip dragging across the ceiling, slicing through stone and electrical conduits with equal ease. The lights in the broad corridor behind went out altogether as sparks showered from the destroyed cables above him. There was no danger of electrocution; even if the sword itself hadn't been insulated against far worse shocks than this, his armor certainly was. He continued the stroke onward and downward, the Artificer-created blade slashing in a diagonal stroke across where he figured the concealed door to be. The resistance was nowhere near what a solid stone wall would have provided, and he smiled grimly inside his helmet.

The edges of the bifurcated stone panel were still glowing when he pulled the sword from the cut and smashed a brutal kick into the middle of the obstacle. It shattered away from him, revealing a room outfitted with the latest surveillance technology. He stepped inside, looking around, scanning with both infrared and visible light.

Bank after bank of screens showed images from throughout the labyrinth, though about half of them were now dead and blank thanks to the severed cables outside. There was more to see, but the most critical aspect of the room was what *wasn't* there: specifically, the Minotaur.

Standing over eight feet tall in his thematically designed power armor if one counted the horns, the master of the maze had no chance of hiding behind any of the equipment in this room. However, the slowly closing door at the far end of the chamber provided a clue as to his whereabouts. True to his nature if not his name, the Minotaur had chosen to flee rather than face his well-deserved fate.

Spurred into motion, Castellan lunged across the room and out through the doorway, sword held in a defensive posture in case of ambush. None eventuated; he paused, listening to the heavy footsteps receding into the distance. Steel-clad mechanical hooves—the Minotaur had gone all-out when it came to the design of his power armor—were not overly stealthy at the best of times. When the suit they were attached to massed in the region of five hundred pounds, trying to run quietly on rock was an exercise in futility.

Turning his head from side to side, he attempted to discern which way the sounds were coming from, but they stopped before he could get a fix on them. The problem was, although the Minotaur couldn't help but make noise when he moved quickly, Castellan wouldn't be able to move fast *and* pick the right noises out of the echoes in the maze. If he had to stop and listen each time to pick up the trail, he would quickly fall behind.

Unless ...

His eyes lowered to the floor, and his lips pulled briefly back from his teeth. While each flagstone had been carefully placed to maximize the chance of camouflaging the various deathtraps in the maze until it was too late, in doing so the Minotaur had perpetrated his third mistake. His suit's hooves were not just steel-clad; they were also exceedingly sharp-edged. And the suit was *heavy*.

Using low-light vision, it was easy to pick up the trail of the fleeing villain. Every running step, bringing all that weight down on the thin stone slabs, had left behind radiating cracks in a distinctive semi-circular pattern. He may as well have left a trail of neon signs shouting, '*this way!*'.

Sheathing his sword, Castellan broke once more into a run. He was close, very close. Justice was what he desired, not vengeance, but either way, he would've pursued the Minotaur to the ends of the Earth for what the monster had done. His internalized duty demanded it.

Nobody is above the law.

Whatever else was wrong with his head, the Minotaur wasn't stupid. As Castellan got close enough to hear the heavy footsteps of his quarry, they slowed then stopped. Either he'd realized he couldn't outrun his pursuer and was attempting to reduce the evidence of his passage, or he was trying for an ambush.

All things considered, the latter tactic wasn't a bad idea. The Minotaur was also armed with an Artificer-created weapon, one with which he was adept. One significant difference between them was that where Castellan hadn't bothered naming the sword gifted him by Arfogwyr, the Minotaur had the luridly titled Blood Rose: a horrific weapon that suited his bloodthirsty personality right down to the bedrock.

Castellan had never observed the other blade in action, but he'd borne witness to its aftermath more than once before. To slash with it opened dozens of wounds, while a stab caused catastrophic trauma to every vital organ and blood vessel even vaguely close to the blade. In contrast, the plasma generators in Castellan's sword merely allowed it to slice through anything the edge encountered.

The armor Arfogwyr had built for him, designed more for speed and agility than brute power, gave him the option to move silently when he needed to. As he neared the spot where he'd last heard the Minotaur, the cracked tiles gave way to merely chipped stone. The fresh damage led around the corner up ahead. Just barely, through the enhanced auditory capabilities of the suit, he could hear the tiny scraping sounds as the villain shifted his weight from foot to foot.

The Minotaur had been hunting people through his murder mazes to satiate his own sick appetites for nearly a decade now. Now, at long last, the tables were turned. It would've been funny, but Castellan wasn't laughing, and he was confident the Minotaur wasn't either.

Drawing his sword and bringing the blade to a guard position in one fluid movement, Castellan stepped around the corner. The Minotaur stood facing him, Blood Rose held ready in a defensive posture. He was just far enough back from the corner to have room to retreat before a charge, which confirmed once more that the villain didn't want to fight.

There should've been a little more satisfaction involved at this moment, but all Castellan felt was the need to finish the job. To deliver justice for the fallen. He'd been pursuing the Minotaur for far too long already; it was time to bring it to an end.

For a long moment, hunter and quarry sized one another up. Both were wearing invested power armor, but where Castellan's hands and feet extended into the gauntlets and boots of his metallic integument, he strongly suspected that the Minotaur's didn't.

The villain's armor stood over seven feet tall, not counting the heavy curving horns that added another foot to its height. All but the hooves and the horns were a metallic bronze in color, with those particular accouterments bearing a blued steel sheen. Where some power armor owners went with a stylized face or a blank faceplate, the Minotaur had gone all the way with an animatronic bull's head, complete with glowing red eyes and sharp steel teeth in the bronze jaws. There were three fingers on each hand, significantly larger than would be ordinarily comfortable if worn as gloves, which bore out Castellan's conclusions about the partial investment. Neither were the feet merely replaced by hooves; the armor's legs were digitigrade in configuration, which explained much of the extra height. The way the armor was shaped, the Minotaur's heels had to be at least a foot above the ground. That still left him somewhere over six feet tall, which told Castellan that whatever the reason for the Minotaur's reign of terror, it wasn't down to any size-related complex.

In other words, he was just a criminal. And criminals existed to be taken down.

"**Castellan.**" The Minotaur's voice sounded amused, for all that it had been electronically modified. "**You've been a pain in the ass for far too long. It's about time I get to put you out of my misery.**"

Refusing to be baited, Castellan took a careful step forward, watching his foe intently. Every hint and tell he could glean before the final battle commenced would contribute toward victory. "Minotaur, you're under arrest," he said bluntly. "Drop the weapon. Exit your armor. On your knees with your hands behind your head. I'm only going to tell you once."

Even as he spoke the words, Castellan was fully aware that he was only doing it to satisfy the letter of the law. He'd been following in the Minotaur's back-trail long enough that he knew the chance of actually getting a genuine surrender from the brutal mass murderer was somewhere south of 'negligible'. When the bull-headed power armor let out a realistic-sounding snort, he knew his surmise was correct.

"You don't honestly think I'm just going to roll over for you, do you?" The Minotaur shook his head disbelievingly. "Before you got in on the act, nobody touched my mazes. Nobody messed with my people. Nobody got in my way at all. Why do you think I came after Inspire? I might've had problems with Challenger and the armor bitch on your side. Just you, on your own? Dream on, buddy." He hefted the heavy weapon in his hand.

The Blood Rose, Castellan noted, didn't look all that sharp on its own. It had a two-foot haft and a three-foot 'blade' composed of reddish metal. At this range, he could see the multiple tiny grooves that indicated where it would split apart into a multitude of razor-sharp sub-blades. These were arranged so they could extend outward by about sixty degrees once the weapon had been stabbed into its victim, or so he'd surmised from his examination of the injury reports. To make matters worse, the flared blades were then able to spin around the weapon's axis, leaving a series of concentric circular cuts on the surface that vaguely resembled a rose. Within the body, the damage would be much worse.

Any sort of upper torso hit was certain death, while a strike to the lower torso would theoretically be survivable if the victim could be gotten to a trauma ward before everything crashed and they bled out. He'd heard rumors of people living through attacks by the Minotaur, but those were hard to verify.

Fortunately (for a given definition of the word), Challenger had taken a slash rather than a stab wound before powering up. Even then, due to the horrific nature of the weapon, the blood loss had been considerable *before* the destroyed base had collapsed on the veteran hero. Castellan had left his teammate in the hands of emergency responders, making all speed toward the nearest hospital, but Challenger's fate was literally down to a coin toss now.

"Have it your way," he said quietly. "How did you even find Arfogwyr? I know exactly how seriously she took her security."

The Minotaur laughed, briefly and harshly. At no time did he take his attention away from Castellan. "Well, you're going to die here, so I may as well tell you. A couple of local cops are members of Unmask. They got hold of the information with some excuse or other, then put out feelers and sold it on to me. Where she lived, what she looked like." He tilted his head slightly. "She had a nice house. Nicer than I ever owned. How did working with Inspire earn her money like that, or pay for the stupid base I blew up?"

"We get paid a government stipend," Castellan said curtly. He only kept enough to live on; the rest went to a charity benefiting the sufferers of spina bifida. He was unwilling to share either fact with the serial killer before him, though the revelation about the dirty cops was something he filed away for later attention.

"Huh. Nice racket if you can get it, I guess. Me, I always found it easier to just take the cash. More fun, too." The Minotaur spun the Blood Rose lightly in his hands, making it hum through the air. "So, we gonna do this?"

"If you're not going to surrender; yes, we are." Castellan watched his adversary's stance and pretended to mimic the Minotaur's flashy move. The instant his blade moved out of line, the massive power armor lunged forward. He heard a sinister metallic hiss from the sub-blades on the Blood Rose as they separated—it wouldn't have surprised him in the slightest if that aspect had been deliberately engineered in—and the lethal weapon lashed out at him.

Shifting his weight, Castellan changed his grip on the massive sword, pivoting it around its own center of mass. The great blade sliced through the air, its plasma-infused cutting edge leaving a faint trace of ozone behind, and deflected the Minotaur's attempt at a surprise attack. Undeterred, the Minotaur brought his free hand around in a formidable blow, the three-fingered metallic gauntlet folded into a solid fist. With the sword out of position, Castellan couldn't block the attack with a slice, but he managed to deflect it with his forearm anyway. The massive fist skidded up his bicep and jolted into his right shoulder just where the spike had gone in, sending a flare of agony through his body and forcing him backward a couple of steps.

"Well, well, fuckin' *well*." The ugly laugh was pure Minotaur. "So, the famous Castellan *can* feel pain. I was starting to wonder."

Castellan was not a fan of hero-villain banter at the best of times. His personal philosophy involved self-discipline in all matters, and pretending a vicious killer was someone with whom to pass casual chatter had no part in that. Grimly, seeking an opening, he stepped back in. The Minotaur had height and reach on him, but he'd beaten bigger opponents before.

He brought the sword around, but it was deflected by the Blood Rose. With professional interest, he noted that the red-hued metal survived the encounter with only light scorching, which made him wonder what it had been crafted from and by whom. Possibly the same mystery artificer who had built the villain's power armor to order.

I'll follow that up later, he decided, turning to launch a vicious side-kick at the Minotaur's leg. His boot struck home with a resounding *clang*, making the villain stagger sideways. If he could get the Minotaur on the ground even once, the fight would be over then and there. He'd cut his opponent's armor off him piece by piece if he had to.

Recovering his balance (and proving the efficacy of the suit's gyrostabilizers), the Minotaur came back strong. He launched a slash that scored Castellan's armor deeply and knocked his sword out of line, capitalizing on the lapse with a punch that slammed into Castellan's upper chest and drove the breath from his lungs. There was a soft *pop* as a rib went. Castellan barely evaded the following back-kick, which would've caved in the armor over his abdomen all the way through to his spinal column.

His head was ringing as he recovered his balance, the threat of his sword the only thing keeping the Minotaur honest. As rugged as Arfogwyr had constructed his armor, the malfunction messages were building up in his HUD. The battering it had taken to get through the deathtraps, compounded by the abuse being handed to it by the Minotaur, was giving it problems. While the actuator next to his wounded shoulder was still working—for now—it was beginning to show an intermittent fault.

But he couldn't think about that now. The Minotaur might look like he had Castellan on the ropes, but he was laboring under one huge disadvantage: he didn't know he could lose. He couldn't conceive that the fight could turn against him, so he had no exit plan. And even discounting his armor and sword, Castellan was a prodigy. Prodigies, above all else, were past masters at dragging victory from the jaws of defeat.

Besides, there was a single factor that Castellan had confided to one other person: Arfogwyr, who'd been murdered by the Minotaur. Although it had colored every aspect of his life since donning the mask, it usually lay quiescent. Until now. Now … it roared forth and demanded its due.

Every prodigy had a focus, something they based their career around. Castellan's was simple.

Bring the Minotaur down.

It had taken him years of effort, gradually working his way through the layers of security with which the serial killer had surrounded himself. Once he'd gotten to the point where he could locate the murder mazes before they were destroyed, he'd thought interfering with them would draw the Minotaur to come after him and him alone. It had been a fatal miscalculation. Arfogwyr was dead and Challenger horrifically injured, and that was on him.

He couldn't make it right, but he *could* destroy the Minotaur.

It was all he had left, his defining goal.

Sparks flew as their weapons clashed back and forth. The air rasped in Castellan's lungs, but he had the stubborn resilience of the prodigy to fall back on; his armor would fail before he did. More than once, his blade sliced through the rock around them instead of the foe before him, leaving streaks of molten stone in its wake.

He thought he saw an opening; the sword came down in a killing blow, only to clash with the Blood Rose in a shriek of protesting metal. They separated to stand a few yards apart, breathing hard. His weapon now had a notch where they'd smashed into one another, while the Blood Rose had lost a few sub-blades.

Their eyes met, and the Minotaur snarled: a primal sound, for all that it was electronically synthesized. By unspoken mutual agreement, they surged forward, each one determined to best his foe.

Castellan felt himself slipping into the zone again. His thought processes were crystal clear, every movement preordained, the coppery taste of blood in his throat a mere afterthought. The sword was a blur in the dusty air, hammering at the Minotaur's guard, slicing into the armor, showering sparks across the passageway. The villain gave ground, defending as well as he could, but the ornate power armor was beginning to shed some of its metal plating. A high swing sliced off one of the horns when the Minotaur ducked just in time, leaving the stub glowing red-hot.

He deflected a lunge with the Blood Rose toward his faceplate, then kicked aside the follow-up hoof strike. This opened a gap in the Minotaur's guard, and he exploited it with a vicious chopping blow downward at the joint of his opponent's left shoulder. The bronzed armor plates exploded off the suit but the villain evaded most of the blow with a rapid retreat, heavy hooves shattering the tiles underfoot instead of merely cracking them. Still, blood was now trickling down the Minotaur's side; Castellan pressed his advantage.

It was not his enemy's fear that drove him on. There was no sense of impending revenge. He only knew that he was on the verge of righting a wrong that had torn at his heart for seven years. Implacable, unyielding, he strode forward. The sword flickered in his grasp, more like a living silver flame than a length of steel. A feint to the left drew the Blood Rose off-line and took him through the Minotaur's guard again, then he shifted his weight and swung hard in an eye-defying arc from right to left.

"**Motherfucker!**" Moving faster than Castellan would've given him credit for, the Minotaur fell back yet again. The sword bit in, but not as deeply as Castellan would've liked. More plating clattered to the stone tiles, the severed edges glowing red. "**Getting a bit personal there, aren't you?**"

The entire front of his adversary's armor was down to an under-mesh, bloodstained and tattered. While Castellan had scored once more with the swing, the wound wasn't deep enough to bleed the Minotaur out or even seriously hamper his movements. Not that it mattered; with the torso armor out of commission, Castellan had his pick of targets. Any vital organ would do.

He took one step forward, aware of the Blood Rose coming up in defense. Deep in the zone, his mind's eye sketched out the movements necessary to flick it aside, then bury his blade in the Minotaur's black heart once and for all—

His foot came down on a piece of the Minotaur's armor. Skidding out from underfoot, this disrupted his balance and drew his sword out of line for a fatal instant. With strength born of desperation, as if aware of how close he'd just come to death, the Minotaur slashed the Blood Rose down on Castellan's injured shoulder. The damaged plating shrieked as it was torn away; a dozen of the blades bit into the muscles of his right arm, rendering it useless.

He dropped the sword.

As if in slow motion, he watched it fall, having shifted his grip at just the wrong instant, not quite believing what was happening right now. He couldn't go down after it, not with the threat of the Blood Rose right in his face. But he'd long since perfected a maneuver where he kicked the blade and flipped the hilt up into his hand. All he had to do was let the Minotaur decide that it was no longer a factor, defend against one or two attacks, bring it back into play—

The sword landed point first, rebounded, clattered to the uneven flooring, and the Minotaur smashed his steel hoof down on the cross-guard. Arfogwyr had built it tough; for a moment, Castellan held out hope that it would survive the treatment, but then there was a metallic *crunch*. The animatronic eyes gleamed redly with anticipation as the Minotaur snarled in triumph.

"**You're fuckin'** *done*," the villain gloated. He moved forward, arrogance and confidence rapidly returning to his posture. "**I am gonna carve you up like a—**"

Blades beginning to flare outwards, the Blood Rose lashed out toward Castellan's chest. A solid hit would punch through; he knew that by now, but this wasn't the first time he'd been in this situation. Back before he even knew he had powers, when he'd first put on a mask and commenced the crusade that eventually ended up in this place, he'd possessed neither armor nor sword. All he had was preternatural fighting skill, combined with reflexes that an Olympic-level martial artist would've wept tears of envy to see. That had been enough then, and it would have to be enough now.

The world became crystal clear once more. As the thought passed through his mind that perhaps he'd been allowing himself to depend too much on the hardware, he pivoted to allow the Blood Rose to scrape past his chest. His left hand took hold of the haft of the weapon, twisting it in *just* the right way to remove it from the Minotaur's grasp before the villain quite realized what he was doing. The three-fingered hand may have made for an excellent striking fist, but what it gained in strength it lost in finesse.

"Hey, what—"

Ignoring the Minotaur's startled exclamation, he kept turning, moving as fluidly as he knew how. The villain's left fist whistled past as he ducked around the blow, the villain swinging at where he'd been instead of where he was going to be. He settled the captured weapon in his gauntleted hand, then dropped and rolled as a massive steel hoof came driving down at him, sending stone shards flying in all directions. When he came to his feet this time, he was inside the Minotaur's guard. Right where he needed to be.

Taking away an enemy's weapon before defeating them had been a favored tactic at one time. Amusingly enough, he'd run out of enemies with easily grabbed weapons before he ran out of room to display them on his 'wall of weapons', back in the now-destroyed Caerwyn. But this was the first time he'd set out to kill the foe with their own weapon.

The multiple blades of the Blood Rose drove in with all the power he could muster, slicing easily through the armor underlayer, the preternaturally tough skin, and the abdominal muscles beneath. The Minotaur's expression was hidden to Castellan, but the animatronic bovine features managed to convey an equivalent representation of astonishment just the same. He wasn't sure if the Blood Rose was controlled by an automatic detection system or if there was a grip sensor, but once the majority of the weapon was buried inside his foe's torso, the blades began to spin with a high-pitched shriek. With sickened fascination, he watched as the ones still outside the Minotaur's body shredded the remains of the flexible underlayer and carved the weapon's gory trademark into the villain's very flesh. What was happening inside ... he really didn't want to know.

The Minotaur gaped mutely, then tried to grab him; ducking away, Castellan pulled the Blood Rose from the horrific wound with a slurping sound that he just *knew* would haunt his dreams. He would've left it there, but the Minotaur wasn't dead *yet*, and there was no way he was going to leave a weapon like that in his enemy's hands. Lurching forward, the Minotaur flailed at him, then fell headlong. Castellan stepped back warily in case this was a ruse, but the spreading pool of blood beneath his foe's body told a different story.

And then the first demolition charge went off. It was distant, but quickly followed by another and another. The maze began to shudder, dust sifting down from the rock ceiling. Castellan grimaced; he'd wanted to unmask the Minotaur and see at last the face of the man who had destroyed his life twice over. But it would take far too long to get the armor off him, even with the assistance of the Blood Rose, and it seemed his fears of a final screw-you had been accurate.

Turning, he started back toward the monitor room. His left leg had taken a hit at some point, and now the knee actuator was beginning to go. The flesh and bone underneath weren't feeling especially good, either. In fact, his whole body was now one big ache, but he didn't slow down. It wasn't in him to give up, now or ever.

By the time he had the monitor room door in sight, leaning on the Blood Rose like a crutch, chunks of rock were tumbling down from the ceiling. The detonations were getting closer, and he was reasonably sure he could hear bits of the maze sliding into the ocean as the cliff it was built into fell away. And then the entire floor shifted beneath him, a crack almost instantly becoming a gaping crevice, and reasonable certainty gave way to an absolute guarantee.

Kicking off with his right leg, he landed awkwardly on the far side. His gyros gave out; he tripped and fell full-length, then struggled to his feet and stumbled on. There was a coppery taste in his mouth, and he spat blood into his helmet. More explosions sounded, deeper in the complex, and more rocks rebounded from his armor as he lurched through the open door.

Within the control room, it wasn't much better. More debris had fallen from the ceiling, and the electronics were trying to either wipe themselves or short themselves out; it wasn't Castellan's area of expertise. But he recognized the smell of frying insulation, and knew the computer system would be of no use to him.

Ignoring it all, he crossed the room to get to the other doorway. The broken door looked like a set of shelves from this side; no doubt the intent had been for him to come storming in through the main entrance while the Minotaur slipped out the back way, leaving him none the wiser.

Once he pulled away some of the rubble blocking the once-concealed doorway, he realized that he had a problem. Explosions had dropped rocks and debris in the broad passageway, some of it spilling into the narrower one. The demolition charges had ceased blowing, but the rumbling hadn't stopped; in fact, it was getting more pronounced by the second.

Pausing just for a moment, he took a breath and tried to center himself. Panicking would do him no good. Trying to dig his way through with only one working arm would get him all of two yards before the ceiling pancaked him into the floor, the whole section subsided into the Pacific Ocean, or both. The Minotaur had been paranoid enough to build one bolt-hole, but had he constructed a second one?

Stepping away from the useless doorway, Castellan surveyed the control console for any way out. The room shuddered more violently and the lights flickered and died, but he switched to infra-red and kept looking.

What would he have done if people were coming in from both directions?

And there, right in the middle of the control console, he saw it. Amid the keyboards and the pan-tilt-zoom joysticks, almost directly behind the microphone the Minotaur had been taunting him with, there was a large mushroom-shaped button under a transparent plastic flip-cover. Limping across the room—his leg was getting worse, not better—he flicked the cover out of the way and jammed his palm down on the button.

For just a moment, nothing happened. He braced himself as part of the wall collapsed, revealing a churning abyss full of rocks. Then explosive bolts blew away a section of the ceiling. Rubble thundered into the room. And from above, daylight glared in his IR readout.

Climbing up was not the easiest thing he'd ever done. More than once, he had to wedge the Blood Rose between two rocks and lever himself forward. But he persevered as the rumbling from below increased, and minor rockslides within the escape tunnel threatened to deposit him down below once more. Halfway up, the suit died altogether, the last warning light wavering despairingly before blinking out for good. With only one functional arm and a damaged leg, he couldn't stop to remove it, not in these surroundings. So he just kept climbing, carrying the weight of the suit, refusing to give up. Refusing to let the Minotaur get one last victory.

It took him an eternity to cover an ascent that he customarily would've scrambled up for light exercise. One lung wasn't working, and he was reasonably sure that he'd taken enough hits to put an ordinary man into a hospital bed. But he wasn't an ordinary man and hadn't been one for quite some time. It was his honor and duty to be a prodigy, with all that entailed. His was the burden to get up and keep going, to fulfill his purpose when all others faltered and failed. So, on he struggled, foot by agonizing foot.

Finally, with what felt like his last reserves of strength, he clambered over the edge of the hole, fell to his knees, and looked up into the muzzles of at least a dozen firearms. A helicopter circled overhead, and he thought he saw more gun muzzles protruding out the side.

"Friendly," he rasped, aware that the grime and damage wouldn't be helping with their identification of his armor. "Castellan." Driving the tip of the Blood Rose into the ground, he struggled to push himself to his feet. A glance over his shoulder confirmed what he'd already assumed. Everything past the room had collapsed, along with the cliff face itself. Where his adversary had taken the fatal wound was now hundreds of feet below, being washed by the surf. There was no sign of the villain's body, but he hadn't expected to see one. The heavy metal armor would have pulled the Minotaur deep underwater, even if he hadn't simply been buried in the rockslide.

As people recognized him, weapons were raised and put on safe. The local FBI Special Agent in Charge came forward to give him a hand up. "The Minotaur?" she asked in an undertone.

All of a sudden, he felt exhausted. "I gave him a chance to surrender. He chose not to take it. Challenger?"

"Under heavy guard. They're still operating, but ..." The FBI woman grimaced and shook her head. "It's not looking good."

Castellan digested that as he moved away from the new cliff edge. He didn't know if it was stable or not; finding out the hard way wasn't in his plans. "Thanks," he said eventually. "You'll let me know if anything changes?"

"Absolutely."

"Good." He gestured toward the cliff edge. "If I were you, I'd put divers down there to dig through the rubble. Throw a cordon around the whole area, check the local currents to see where the body might have drifted, and search for a few miles up and down the coast. If nothing else, it's a good idea to make sure someone like the Clone Arranger doesn't get hold of it first."

"But he's dead." It wasn't a question.

Castellan braced his injured leg and hefted the Blood Rose. "You've *seen* what this does to people. The angle it went in, it would've shredded his liver, both kidneys, and most of both intestines. After that, the maze collapsed on him, then it dumped him in the ocean. If he had a strong Prodigy rating or a team standing by to rescue him, those last two would give a chance of survival, however slim. All three, especially with the Blood Rose involved?" He shook his head. The odds weren't even worth talking about.

"Good." The FBI SAC smiled. It wasn't a happy smile; although this was only the second terror villain they'd gotten this close to, it was self-evidently preferable to have a body to show to the higher-ups. But in this case, she'd clearly decided she'd take what she could get. "I'll give the orders. And if they do find him, standing orders will involve a double-tap to the head before doing anything else, just in case. But from the way you're walking, you need to be in the hospital."

"I'll be fine." Castellan knew he was stretching the truth, but it had to be said, for form's sake. Leaning on the Blood Rose again, he coughed, tasting blood.

"If the damage to your armor's any indication of the shape you're in, you're a damned liar." The SAC gestured toward a pair of paramedics. "Now, you're going to go with those nice people, and they're going to put you in a soft hospital bed and see what's wrong with you. Because I'm not going to lose *three* of you if I can help it. Don't worry about the cost; Uncle Sam will be covering the bill, like always."

Castellan didn't bother arguing anymore. A hospital bed sounded wonderful right about then. He wouldn't be there for long, he knew. Injuries that would've usually had him laid up for six months would barely last two weeks since he'd gotten his powers. He would be walking out under his own steam sooner rather than later.

And after that … he'd achieved his goal. With the Minotaur dead, his focus was satisfied. Castellan had reached the end of his purpose. Even if Challenger survived, there would be no resurrecting this incarnation of Inspire. They'd had a good run, and he would mourn the loss of Arfogwyr, but now it was over. He was done.

Perhaps it was time to hang up the mask and rejoin the human race in their nine-to-five routine. He didn't know if his security clearances were still valid, but perhaps he could go into teaching law instead of enforcing it. After all, Richard Miller didn't need to be a superhero to change the world for the better, one student at a time.

- End of Prologue One -

Prologue Two
Camping Trip

Anchorage, Alaska
Monday, December 2, 2013
10:46 AM Alaska Standard Time

Seabirds swooped and called in the sky above, while the smell of fish and dead seaweed permeated the air. The floatplane, moored fore and aft, occasionally rocked on the gentle waves that made it past the breakwater. Derek Saunders dropped the backpack at the edge of the dock and moved away, pressing his hands to the small of his back and lifting his chin to breathe in the chill salt breeze. As he exhaled, he watched the long streamer of vapor flutter away in the wind.

Standing on the near-side float and holding onto the door-frame with one hand, Troll reached down and hefted Derek's backpack with the other, then tossed it lightly inside the aircraft. The pack weighed at least eighty pounds—Derek had brought along enough food and warm clothing for the next eight days—but he knew Troll by now and refused to be impressed by the casual display of strength. Inspecting the engine at the front of the plane, their pilot said something to Troll that Derek didn't hear, and Troll nodded.

Drone and Splendid (or rather, Conrad and Nina, as they were out of costume at the moment) were standing a little way down the dock, their breath also visible in the sub-zero air, and Derek went back over to them. "Well, this is about it," he said quietly. "Troll says we'll be back in a week or so. Think you'll be okay until then?"

Conrad gave him a raised eyebrow and pulled the heavy jacket more closely around himself. In his identity as All-Star, Derek was the fourth (and most junior) member of Manhattan Justice, and Troll and Drone rarely let him forget it. "Splendid and I have been protecting the city since you were in high school, young man," Conrad retorted in cultured tones. "It's your own well-being you need to be looking out for, not ours. I still cannot understand why you could not have done this in upstate New York rather than the very ends of the earth, especially in winter. Surely one camping location is as good as another." He glowered at the oily gray water of the Knik Arm and the intemperate gulls as though they existed solely to irritate him.

Nina rolled her eyes dramatically as she held a happily panting bundle of fur in her arms, neither of them showing problems from the cold. A thin hard-light carapace to hold warm air in and keep cold air out didn't have to be *visible*, after all. "You've got no sense of adventure," she said brightly. "I just wish *I* was going. It sounds like a lot of fun." She scratched her dog behind the ear. "Yes, Mister Fluffikins, it does, doesn't it?" It yapped agreeably and licked her face.

Derek didn't have her particular power, but his Prodigy-based endurance and Dynamic environmental adaptation made it much easier to withstand the knife-sharp cold. The light coat he was wearing helped a lot, though. Troll wasn't even pretending that far; the older prodigy's leather vest left his ridiculously brawny arms exposed to the sub-zero temperatures, the dense hair on his forearms standing up like fur.

It was Conrad's turn to roll his eyes. "You *have* met Troll, right?" he asked, keeping his voice down in case of eavesdroppers. "If he took that furball of yours camping, it would be eaten by a bear on the first night. And on the second night, the bear would be on the menu." He chuckled dryly to show he was joking.

Derek wasn't so sure. He'd never encountered a bear in real life, but he'd seen Troll in action, which had been impressive enough in its own right. A moment later, he realized that Conrad was insinuating that Troll would use the yappy little dog as *bait* for the bear.

Nina twigged at the same time he did. "That's mean!" she exclaimed, clutching her fuzzy companion even closer. "I'm not going to let any nasty old bear eat Mister Fluffikins!"

Derek shook his head. "Ignore him," he advised. "It would've been good to have you along, but Troll said no." In the seven weeks he'd been part of Manhattan Justice, she'd been the friendliest to him. Nobody had been actively *unpleasant*, but Troll seemed intent on doing an excellent impression of a drill sergeant (and Derek had to admit, he'd never been fitter), and Drone had been a little distant.

Not that the artificer was the most sociable of people overall, Derek had to admit. The man wasn't really nice to anyone, except maybe Nina. He'd met people like that before; they were *capable* of reaching out to others but just didn't see the point in doing so. Troll was much the same, with an extra helping of crusty on top. How people could get like that still puzzled Derek.

Troll stumped on over to them as the pilot began to clamber into the floatplane cockpit. "Okay, enough lazin' around, junior. We're burnin' daylight. Time to make a move."

"I still wish I could come along," Nina said immediately. "It sounds like so much fun."

"An' I'll invite you along sometime," Troll said. "Just not today. Junior here needs to do some catchin' up on what it's really like to be a prodigy." He gave her an avuncular smile, the expression rare to his features. "I'll try an' bring him back in one piece."

"We'll be *fine*." Derek did his best to inject surety into his voice. "Chelatna Lake's what, a hundred miles from Anchorage? And some towns are a lot closer. If anything goes wrong, we can hike that distance easily." This was not an idle boast. Just as his powers let him endure the biting cold with little hardship, he figured he could make a fifty-mile hike in maybe two days through the worst weather conditions Alaska could throw at him, if he really had to. He gave Conrad a nod and Nina a smile. "See you in a week."

Nina stepped up to him and kissed him on the cheek. "Take care of yourself," she whispered. "And don't let him push you around too much,"

He chuckled hollowly. "I'll try." His first encounter with Troll had been a real wake-up call on how untrained he really was. As a result, he was willing to accept a significant amount of physical discomfort if it meant honing his skills and capabilities to a level the veteran hero considered worthwhile. The good thing about having a Prodigy rating was that he didn't have to work nearly as hard to maintain the improvements he'd already gained.

He headed over and stepped onto the seaplane float, grabbing the door-frame to steady his balance before climbing in. It was extremely cramped and was likely to get more so with Troll's breadth of shoulder. But he'd agreed to this, so he was going to see it through. And who knew; it might even be fun.

Troll climbed in alongside him as he was getting the five-point restraints sorted out. The side door was pulled shut and the latch clicked into place, then the pilot called back, "You boys strapped in back there?"

"Will be in a moment," Troll said, wrestling with his restraints. Derek turned partly side-on to give him extra room, earning a grunt of thanks.

"Who's going to untie us from the dock?" asked Derek, remembering the mooring lines. They weren't going to go far with those still attached.

"Did it before I got in," Troll said, just as the plane's motor burst into life. He clicked the restraint into place, then nodded to Derek. They settled in, shoulder to shoulder, as the plane started to taxi across the expanse of water before them.

He'd never been on a floatplane before, or any other light aircraft. Once, when he was very young, his family had flown across the country to visit his grandparents in LA; apart from that, his flying experience was minimal. He found it noisy, bumpy, and more than a little frightening. While his powers would allow him to adapt to new environmental circumstances given a little time, he wasn't at all sure that if something went wrong, the few seconds before hitting the ground would count as enough time.

Engine shrieking like a banshee, the plane jolted steadily as it raced across the water, each jolt more intense than the last. Intellectually, he knew they had to get up to flying speed before they could lift off. Emotionally, the far shore of the Knik Arm looked way too close, and some part of his brain was sure they were going to pile up in a heap of flaming wreckage.

And then the jolting was done, the floatplane lifting off smoothly and pressing Derek down in the seat as the pilot pulled a long climbing turn. Even the engine note sounded deeper and more triumphant once they were in the air. He kind of wished he was in the co-pilot's seat so he could see what the pilot was doing. A prodigy's fast-learning capability wasn't on par with actual formal training, but it was amazing what he could fake with just a few minutes of observation.

Still, on this trip, it wasn't to be. Troll wanted him to concentrate on the camping experience, so flying lessons would have to wait for another day. He settled down in his seat, as much as he could in the cramped surroundings, and craned his neck to look out the window. If nothing else, he could enjoy the scenery.

Before they were even out of the city limits, he watched the silver line of the maglev rail pass beneath them. If Nina and Conrad were not already back on the train by now, they soon would be, riding in ease and comfort back to Manhattan. He felt a momentary stab of envy, then shook his head to stave it off. Now was far too late for second thoughts. The camping trip was a done deal, and he was committed to it.

Time passed.

The floatplane droned northward, as far as he could estimate the direction. He was on the right-hand side of the plane, so he could see the sun steadily sliding backward as it rose toward what this latitude laughingly called noon. Eventually, he couldn't even see it if he turned his head and pressed his cheek against the window. This made him frown.

"Hey!" he shouted to Troll over the engine noise. "Weren't we supposed to be there by now?" He was sure they'd been in the air for more than an hour now, and floatplanes weren't *that* slow.

Troll seemed grumpy to have been woken out of a doze—seriously, how could *anyone* sleep through that racket?—and shouted something back about a headwind and "we'll get there when we get there". Then he turned away from Derek, making it quite plain that he was ignoring the younger man.

Fine. Be that way.

Derek turned back to the window and decided that if Troll could ignore him for the whole flight, he could do the same right back.

I suppose it could be worse; if we had more room, he'd have me doing push-ups.

However, looking out the window to pass the time became rapidly less interesting, as quite a lot of the landscape below was covered in the white of new-fallen snow. That wasn't totally surprising; winter started early and finished late in the far northern latitudes. Satisfied with that observation, he sat back in his seat and did his best to relax … right up until a mountain loomed just outside the window, or so it seemed.

"What the hell?" he yelled, nudging Troll's shoulder with his.

Troll woke up again, looking more irritated than the last time. "What's up your ass this time?" he bellowed.

"Mountains!" Derek shouted back, pointing out the window. Slowly but steadily, the tiny aircraft was threading its way between the massive peaks. "Why are we in the mountains?" He hadn't taken more than a cursory look at the map, but he was sure the mountains were a lot farther north than the lake they'd been going to camp at. "We're way past Chelatna Lake!"

Troll peered out the window, then shrugged. "Yeah, and?"

"Wasn't that where we were going?"

It had seemed like an obvious question when he asked it, but the look Troll gave him made it seem like he'd overlooked something that he should've worked out for himself. "Don't look like it, does it?"

Which was, he had to admit, a fair point. Troll never missed *anything*. If the pilot was overshooting their original landing point, and Troll didn't have a problem with it, then it was because that had been the plan all along. If he was being honest with himself, he'd readily agreed to the camping trip because it had seemed a simple jaunt into the wilderness, at a lake with a lodge already on it in case anything went wrong. He doubted that anything *would* have, but it was better to be prepared.

The conclusion was both inescapable and straightforward. This whole thing had been a bait and switch. He still would've agreed to go if he knew the real agenda; he knew that, and he was certain Troll did as well. But he probably would've packed more survival gear if he'd known.

It was a dirty trick. It was also a very Troll thing to do.

"What about the others?" he yelled.

"What about 'em?"

"If we're not back in a week, they're likely to come looking for us!" And he didn't want Nina trudging around in the wilderness hundreds of miles away from his actual location.

"Left 'em a letter back at base!"

Which also made sense, though it didn't make him any happier about the situation. He wasn't sure which part he disliked more: that the easy vacation he'd been expecting had just turned into a much tougher one, or the sheer unconcern Troll felt about lying to him so blatantly.

Well, he did *say he'd be the meanest motherfucker I ever met. And if I complain, he'll just ask me if I want him to kick me into shape or not.*

With a sigh, he leaned back into the thinly padded seat. It seemed he was destined to be toughened up, whether he liked it or not. Nina was going to be upset with Troll, which … probably wouldn't bother the man overmuch, one way or the other. If he knew Conrad, which he suspected he did, the artificer would be more inclined toward amusement over the whole thing. It also neatly answered the question as to why they hadn't done this in upstate New York, and why Troll had vetoed Nina from coming along.

He figured it was past midday, with the northward-reaching shadows on the landscape below beginning to stretch to the right, by the time the plane began to angle downward. They'd passed through the mountains, then flown onward for what seemed an inordinate amount of time. Derek estimated that they were as far north of the mountain range as the range was north of Anchorage. He was *reasonably* sure they hadn't crossed the Arctic Circle yet, but he wouldn't have bet money on it.

The landscape ahead had enough snow blown off it that he could tell what was rocks and trees … and what had to be a lake. A vaguely rounded oblong, dead flat, surrounded by trees. The pilot flew low over it, banking steeply to get a good look, then opened the window (letting in a blast of

Arctic air) and tossed something out. Derek saw a bright orange ribbon unravel as it fell.

On the next pass, Derek eyeballed the ribbon. It was on a vertical stand, just barely sticking out of the snow, with the ribbon itself blowing sideways. Turning to face them, the pilot gave Troll a thumb's up, which the burly prodigy returned. Nodding, the pilot took one more turn around the lake, setting up what had to be a landing approach.

Derek couldn't see it happening. That was thick snow over what was clearly a frozen lake. Technically, he supposed a floatplane could land on snow, but he'd never heard of one lifting off again. Floats weren't skis, after all. And the wheels wouldn't help in any real depth of snow.

Then, Troll took his harness off.

Derek stared at him. "What are you doing?" he yelled. "Aren't we landing?"

"Hell, nope!" bellowed Troll. "We're chucking the stuff out! Get ready to hand it to me!" He pointed at Derek's restraints, indicating that he should also undo his harness.

I suppose it's a slightly less suicidal act than just plain landing.

The pilot was now pulling the plane around into the wind and throttling back until they had to be just above stall speed. Troll shoved the side door open against the howling gale and kept it there with brute strength as he stepped out onto the float. He gestured at Derek and their packs and made a 'hurry up' gesture.

Screw it. In for a penny, in for a pound.

As the plane swooped in over the near edge of the frozen lake with the floats barely skimming the snow, Derek unlatched his safety harness and stood up in the cramped cabin. Just as he turned to reach back and grab his pack, a question occurred to him.

If the plane can't land to drop us off, how will it pick us up?

That was when Troll reached across, grabbed him by the front of his jacket, and hauled him bodily from the aircraft. Powerful muscles propelled them both outward into the slipstream before he had a chance to realize what had happened, and long before he could yell in protest.

Craaaaap!

Reflexes took over, and he hit the snow-covered ice in a curled-up ball. His world went white, the cushioning ice particles showering in all directions as he tumbled over and over. After a few seconds of letting the thick snow bring his speed down, he spreadeagled his arms and legs, the better to stop more quickly and not break through the ice. Snow went *everywhere*: up his nose, into his ears, down his jacket, up his sleeves, and into his pants' legs. He visualized it spraying in the air in a giant rooster-tail as he sledded to a halt.

As he carefully stood up, the ice thankfully not so much as creaking underfoot, he found he was caked in white from head to foot. Troll, similarly covered in the abundant white crystals, had begun to extract himself from a nearby snowbank of his own creation, making a sound that Derek had never heard from him before.

After a few moments, Derek figured it out. Troll was *laughing*.

Augering the snow out from his ear canal with his pinky finger and brushing it vigorously from his hair, Derek looked up as the floatplane came around for one last pass. Still chuckling, Troll waved as it zoomed overhead then watched as it disappeared to the south, seeking the sun.

"What's so goddamn hilarious?" Derek snarled, trudging through the calf-deep snow toward the stocky Enabled.

It better not be the look on my face when he yanked me out of the plane, or so help me …

"That was the most fun I've had in fuckin' *years*, junior," chuckled Troll. "Don't tell me it wasn't fun, because I'll call you a damn liar if you do." He paused. "That, an' the look on your face was classic." His expression dared Derek to say something: *Go ahead. What are you gonna do about it?*

Derek didn't know what was more aggravating, knowing there was no way in hell he could wipe the irritating expression off his mentor's face, or having to admit that Troll was right. Jumping out of the plane—or rather, being thrown out—and landing in the snow had been the wildest ride he'd ever been on. He wanted to go up there and do it again, damn it!

"You realize we left the packs behind in the plane, right?" he asked instead. "That's all our food. Our canteens. Firelighters. Sleeping bags. Tents. Everything we needed to survive out here!" He flung his arms wide, dislodging more snow, knowing his voice was getting louder by the second and not giving a good goddamn for once. "And we're stranded here, because he's not coming back for us, is he? I hope you've got a plan B for this shit-show because I'm not seeing it!"

"Pfft." Troll rolled his eyes. "Tinned food, canteens, all that stuff, you know what they are? They're *things*. Crutches. We're *prodigies*. The average person'd die out here, but we're not gonna. You can use that stuff, but you don't need it, not when you've got your most important piece of survival gear *right here*." Reaching up, he tapped Derek on the side of the head. "Feller I once knew, he pulled this sort of shit on me one time. Told me it was all in my head. Everything I needed was right there. So, I learned how. It wasn't easy, an' it wasn't fun, but I learned anyways. An' you know something? One fine day when I was least expectin' it, I found out he was right, an' I never bitched about his ways an' means of teachin' me, ever again."

Derek stared at him, then shook his head. "So … the whole plan was to teach me how to live off the land? That was the basis behind this bullshit so-called camping trip?"

Troll slapped him on the back, sending more snow showering off him like dandruff turned up to eleven. "*Now* you're gettin' it. So, you ever have anyone teach you how to find flint an' iron ore?"

Derek blinked. "They didn't exactly cover that in school."

Troll snorted. "Kinda school *you* went to, maybe. Okay, were you ever in the Scouts? Learn how to make a bow drill?"

"What … for hunting?" Derek shook his head. "No."

"Actually, it's for makin' fire." Troll sighed theatrically. "Welp, looks like we're gonna freeze out here. Unless you had a plan for figurin' out how to get a fire started before the sun sets altogether." He gestured toward the diminishing glow on the horizon.

Derek looked around and came up with precisely no ideas. "I was going to use matches," he said blankly. "But my matches are in my pack, on the plane."

"Here." Troll dug a small box from his pants pocket and tossed it toward him. "Think fast."

Derek caught the matchbox, which rattled. He opened it and found three safety matches inside. When he looked up, Troll was grinning at him.

"You got three nights to learn how to make fire on your own, junior."

The last of the sun's rays winked out, and darkness began to spread over the landscape. Derek looked down at the matches, then toward the south where Anchorage lay, hundreds of miles away. Nina and Conrad were no doubt most of the way back home to New York by now. Meanwhile, he was stuck in the untracked wilds of Alaska with three matches to his name and a mentor who was determined to teach him how to subsist in the wilderness if it killed him.

They'd survive; he knew that implicitly. Prodigies were notoriously hard to kill, especially when two were working in tandem. But as Troll had said, it wasn't going to be easy, and it wasn't going to be fun.

Some vacation this *turned out to be.*

- End of Prologue Two -

Prologue Three
From the Shadows

Utopia City, Kansas
UCPD Precinct House
Tuesday, December 24, 2013
12:46 PM Central Standard Time

Everyone was looking at her.
Nobody could see her as she actually was.
Just the way she liked it.

A little way down the street from the front steps of the precinct house, she'd located a security camera blind spot, right next to a bus shelter. She paused at the correct location in her patented *'I'm not here'* mode, waited for the few seconds it took for everyone within sight to ignore her existence, then changed her entire outfit and manner. Moving forward again, she started up the steps into the precinct house.

The MagCard in her right hand was genuine, while both the zippered case under her left arm and the police uniform she wore were realistic fakes generated by her hyperweave costume. Moving with near-military precision, she didn't slow down once she reached the top of the stairs.

The identity patch she'd installed in the system would last for precisely fifteen minutes, then delete itself without a trace. If anyone tried to backtrack it before then, they would find a trail of spoofed proxies leading right into the Spire itself. She wondered if anyone in the UCPD would have the stones to try and push for an electronic search warrant.

As far as the civil administrators of Utopia City were concerned, Force Majeure and any potentially affiliated Enabled were a protected species, which would make that a definite *hell, no*. Nobody messed with the people who unofficially ran the city, not if they wanted to keep their job. While this might have been an irritating obstacle to someone lacking her imagination, she had instead turned it into an asset.

The heavy doors, made of something that looked like glass but almost certainly wasn't, rumbled aside at her approach; she entered without breaking step. A subtle aura of authority drew every eye as she walked into the room, just as intended. Not a single person there would be able to describe *her*, but they would all later state categorically that she had been the most significant person in the room. She called this her *'visiting VIP'* mode.

Maybe she was overdoing it slightly, as the place already had an air of moderately frantic activity. In a city as monitored and regimented as Utopia, she found this somewhat comforting. Certainly, the average Utopian was less likely than usual to go nuts on Christmas Eve, but even here it was a hectic time of year. Which meant every able-bodied officer was out on the streets, maintaining order. Those left to hold the fort down, keep the home fires burning, and carry out all those other tired clichés ... were the remainder. The ones who were less enthused about doing their jobs well. Or if they could get away with it, doing their jobs at all.

She loved dealing with that sort of person. With the right kind of persuasion, they could be convinced to overlook nearly *anything*. And she was very good at persuasion. Almost criminally good, in fact.

There was a judge in Ohio willing to contest the 'almost' aspect of that descriptor, but she was fine with letting him challenge it all he liked. She wasn't about to argue the point with him, especially face-to-face. Handcuffs just weren't her scene.

She ignored the discreetly placed tinsel, the muted carols playing over the PA system, the restrained Christmas banner that looped above the counter, and the artificial tree lurking in the corner with a single fake present hiding under it. Reaching out as she passed by, she gave the reader on the reception desk a disdainful tap with her MagCard. The override patch did its work, and the door alongside the desk clicked open. At the same time, her assumed identity would be flashing up on the security screen. She was apparently Captain Beatrice Lombard, a person with whom the current officer riding the desk was entirely unfamiliar. The real Captain Lombard was, at this time, taking an hour off to go home and freshen up.

Timing, after all, was everything.

Walking through the door, she let it click shut behind her and tapped the reader on the elevator, just a short way down the corridor. So deeply entrenched was she in her role that when another officer stepped up alongside her, she didn't even side-eye him.

"Hell of a day," he observed as the doors opened and they stepped inside.

"Hell of a week," she agreed noncommittally. Using the verbal exchange as an excuse to give him a polite glance, she identified him as a Lieutenant Frobisher, someone who worked on the same floor as Captain Lombard. He would know Lombard by sight, which meant it was time to improvise on the fly.

Fortunately, she was good at that. She subtly adjusted her 'uniform' while he was looking toward the button panel. At the same time, her Prodigy-enhanced body language dropped several notches down to '*someone who works under you, but you can't quite place right now*'. "Seventh floor, thanks."

"Now, now," he chided. "We each tap the panel. That lets the system keep track of us. You should know that by now." He used the corner of his MagCard to tap the number seven. Was he suspicious, or had he intended to go there all along?

"Sorry, sir, my head was elsewhere," she said disarmingly, mimicking his action. Jericho had once told her that his powers let him detect the movement of Utopia City elevators, especially inside the Spire, but it didn't work that way with her. There was no sensation of motion at all; the doors shut, and then a fraction of a second later opened again on the seventh floor.

They started down the corridor, moving almost in lockstep. She noted this and subtly adjusted her gait to kill the impression that they were marching side by side. Captain Lombard's office was just up ahead; she slowed a little to let Frobisher lose interest and outpace her.

He slowed as well. *Damn, this guy's persistent.* "So, where were you heading?" His tone and body language still showed curiosity, not suspicion. So far, anyway. "I don't think I've seen you on this floor before."

It was amazing how often just going for broke actually worked. Glancing around theatrically, she lowered her voice a touch; simultaneously, she changed up her body language to '*I'm letting you in on a secret*'. "You'll need to keep this quiet, sir, but I've been sent to give Captain Lombard's computer a security check. There have been some concerns, and they think someone might be proxying in through her external connection."

His eyebrows rose toward his hairline. "Well, damn," he muttered. "That's … very concerning. Is the Captain meeting you there?"

Now, that was interesting. From Frobisher's intonation and stance, he knew damn well that Lombard was offsite. But *still* he wasn't suspicious, so much as discreetly trying to determine if Lombard herself was under suspicion.

Office politics made life *so* much more fun.

"No, sir," she said. "I just got told to go in, do the check, plug any holes, and report the results. No more, and no less." *In other words, we have yet to determine who's under suspicion.*

Most people would've made an excuse to walk away by now, anxious to avoid any trace of such a scandal attaching to them. Not so the oblivious Lieutenant Frobisher. He wasn't questioning her utterly non-existent right to be there; her deception was holding firm in that regard. But he seemed to want to *help*.

"That's understandable," he said. "I'll escort you in, so if anyone else queries your presence, I'll be able to vouch for you." It wasn't phrased as a question.

She didn't want to push him away in case it (finally) tripped his bullshit meter. Getting into an argument would cause him to wonder more deeply about the holes in her extemporized story and maybe remind him to ask her for the appropriate credentials. Which she didn't have, because her skillset just didn't lie in those directions. As she'd told Jericho not so long ago, she was more about audacity over idiocy. Which was why she was infiltrating the precinct house rather than the Spire itself.

"That would be amazing, thanks. But you really don't have to." She gave him a beaming smile, noting with an internal smirk the way his chest puffed out. Her power finished filling in the blanks and gave her the reason why Frobisher was on duty at the precinct house rather than out on the road. While a stickler for the rules and somewhat of a busybody, he tended to get flustered under pressure and make bad decisions. She could just imagine how this would go if he was out on the road at this time of year.

"It's entirely my pleasure," he insisted, heading over to Captain Lombard's office and tapping the door reader with his MagCard. "I'm authorized to go in. You tap as well, so we have a record of you going in and out."

Well, I'm getting in anyway, so I may as well see how this goes.

She tapped the reader in her turn; it started reading her biosignature, encountered the patch, rerouted to Captain Lombard's stored template where it verified her alleged right to be there, then beeped agreeably.

With a confident stride, she moved past him into the office. The computer built into the desk was both slimline and powerful, not the latest model that Force Majeure's tech division had brought out, but right up there all the same. She knew quite well that the screen was a holographic construct that would be generated once the computer was powered up, and could be adjusted to any size, shape, and orientation the user desired. The keyboard, similarly generated, would be an interactive hard-light sculpture with literally dozens of variant and innovative configurations available.

She really, really wanted one of her own.

Right now, she was going to have to settle for borrowing Captain Lombard's system for a while. Settling into the ergonomically perfect office chair, she pulled out the drawer she'd known would be there; or rather, what looked like one. Within were connector ports for virtually any external data drive that might be passed around in the precinct house.

The 'zipper bag' went on top of the desk, her left hand never moving from it. With her right hand, she tucked away her MagCard and made the motions of unzipping the bag.

Inside were two things. One was a perfectly ordinary (though somewhat upscale) tablet computer with its connector cord. The other was the universal hacking tool that she called the 'discus', mainly because it looked like one. She'd gotten that from Gimmick by way of thanks for helping the Survivors flee Utopia, and had been putting it to good use ever since.

Well, *her* definition of 'good', anyway.

Moving with unhurried precision, she plugged in the discus and the tablet, then powered the latter on; the former already had lights blinking on it in a steady fashion. Once the 'bag' was no longer needed, she mimed placing it on the floor next to her feet but instead reabsorbed it into her costume when it was no longer in Frobisher's line of sight.

"Uh, what's that?" asked the lieutenant, pointing at the discus.

"Improved firewall," she lied shamelessly, already tapping at the keys of the tablet. "This will prevent any hacking tools from getting into the system while I'm checking it out."

She had seven minutes left on the identity patch, and eight and a half on the discus. When the patch ran out, swiping a MagCard would present the system with *her* biosignature, rather than Captain Lombard's. Worse, running out of time on the discus would allow Force Majeure's horrifically powerful anti-intrusion software to zero in on her precise location. Once it was discovered that the hack was coming from within the precinct house, the building would be remotely locked down within seconds. They would then physically clear it, room by room, one forcible biosignature at a time, until they located her. All the body language in the world wouldn't save her at that point.

There was indeed a data conduit into the Spire from the precinct house, just as she'd figured. However, Captain Lombard's clearances only covered access to a few essential areas relevant to precinct business. With the discus attached, she had carte blanche, able to travel anywhere in the system she wanted to go. This was the first time she'd managed to hack into the Spire, a heady feeling. At the back of her mind, a pessimistic voice reminded her that any repeat attempts would probably be rendered impossible once they discovered the means of her intrusion, so she needed to make the most of it.

"Hm," she murmured. "That's interesting."

"What?" asked Frobisher. "What's interesting?"

She pointed at a random line on the screen. "Looks like someone's been accessing this system from outside, alright. I'm going to need to do a deep-dive, so if I ignore you, that's why."

He looked so serious, she wanted to pinch his cheek and tell him that everything was going to be okay. "Understood," he said. "Do you think they got very far?"

"That's what I'm trying to find out." She started typing again, painfully aware of the timers running down.

Her first look at the servers governing the Spire was awe-inspiring. There was no way in hell she'd be able to siphon off one-thousandth of one percent of all the information contained in there, and even if she'd brought the truckload of solid-state hard drives which would be required to pull off such a stunt, she didn't have the days she'd need to do it.

She flicked past medical, power generation, personnel, and security footage. Even if there was something interesting in there, she lacked the hours it would take to trawl through it all.

I'm starting to think this is a bust.

Force Majeure's projected rosters and itinerary over the next month popped up; it was better than nothing, so she snagged it. *Maybe I can do something with this.* On she went, browsing for anything remotely worthwhile.

And then, just as she was pulling an interesting file from the MagCard registry, she saw the one tab that was grayed out, as if invisible to the rest of the network. It was blank, without anything more than an alphanumeric designator to define it. Her eyes narrowed, and she looked more closely. Not even people who had admin access to the entire Spire system could so much as *see* this particular server bank. Concealing a smile, she tapped the icon.

It unfolded into a new list of files, and her momentary excitement fizzled, then built up again. Each one had a title consisting of a time-date stamp, and a file type that she didn't recognize.

I have no idea what these are, but they must be worth something.

This was precisely what her fishing expedition here was all about; if she was going to seriously present herself as a criminal underlord in the world's most superhero-guarded city, she needed all the possible dirt on the opposition she could find.

The problem was, she had no way to personally decrypt the files. Going unseen was her schtick: tricking others into believing what wasn't there, or ignoring what was there. It was her focus, and she was very good at it. For her, getting the files was a lot easier than figuring out what was in them.

Still, she had other resources to fall back on.

She'd given herself five minutes to walk out before the identity patch deleted itself, and her timer was cutting perilously close to that limit. Methodically, she began to transfer files onto the tablet. When she ran out of room, she ruthlessly culled data she knew she had elsewhere, then jammed more on.

Finally, having gone thirty seconds over her self-appointed time, she shut down the tablet and unplugged it, then pulled the discus connector free. "Done," she said without having to fake her satisfaction.

"So, did you find out who was getting in?" asked Frobisher. Before she could answer, his phone rang. He pulled it out as she came around from behind the desk. "Hello?" There was a brief pause. "Oh, uh, Captain Lombard, hello."

Shit. That's in no way good.

She stepped forward, adjusting her body language to '*out of the way, I'm coming through*'. He instinctively moved aside for her as he kept talking. "What do you mean, your MagCard doesn't work?"

Captain Lombard must have raised her voice considerably because what she said next was clearly audible. **"I mean, it won't open the door to my patrol cruiser! And that when I rang the front desk, they refused to believe that I am who I say I am because apparently, I signed into my office seven minutes ago! And so did you! Are you in my office right now? Who else is in there with you?"**

That was a clear sign to get out of Dodge. It was hard to maintain the air of casually sauntering while power-walking, but she managed it. As she neared the elevator, she heard Frobisher call out hesitantly. "Uh ... excuse me? Uh ... hey, you! Come back!"

Yeah, that's gonna happen.

Taking the elevator was a calculated risk, but it was also the fastest way to get to the ground floor. She tapped the reader, and the doors opened. In one smooth move, she stepped inside and tapped the button for the first floor. Obediently, the doors closed. One second later, they started opening on the first floor … then they began to close again.

Forming a pocket to drop the tablet into so she could free her hands up, she pressed the discus against the button panel, waited for the 'door open' button to light up, then hit it. The doors sprang wide open, and she came out fast. Alarms were starting to sound, and flashing lights were everywhere.

Even as she started toward the door out into the lobby, she heard it lock with a distinctive *ch-chak*. Turning, she pushed through another door into the area behind the reception desk. She knew from her research that the desk had a gravity-based repulsion field that prevented people from jumping or even leaning over the desk. The officer behind the desk was just reaching for the stereotypical big red button that would lock down the whole lobby. She spoke to forestall him, her voice crackling with authority. "Hold it right there!"

He froze and looked around at her. "But ma'am, I just got orders to—"

Before he could continue, she went straight past him. Vaulting over the desk into the lobby area, she hit the floor at a dead run. "Make a hole!" she shouted. "The intruder's getting away!"

Again, instinct reigned over conscious thought as people obeyed her without even understanding why. The solid doors of not-glass had just opened to admit a couple of civilians, who gaped as she bolted past them to safety. As she leaped down the stairs three and four at a time, she heard the doors slam shut behind her.

She ducked around the corner at the bottom of the steps and moved briskly back into the camera blind spot next to the bus shelter. As she came to a complete halt, her hyperweave costume was already reshaping itself into a jacket and jeans and a Christmas hat complete with bobble. Unhurriedly, she slid the discus into a pocket her outfit formed for the purpose, then she cranked her video jammer to its highest rating, turned around and headed back in the other direction.

When she sauntered past the building frontage once more, her body language was adjusted to *'nobody important, don't mind me'*. The part of her mind that was always on alert noted the first drifting snowflakes of the day, right on time.

She was almost past the steps again when the doors slammed open, and several UCPD officers ran out. Led by Lieutenant Frobisher, they descended the stairs *en masse* then congregated on the sidewalk, pointing down the street in the general direction of the bus shelter.

Hands in pockets, she turned to look at them. "What's going on?" she asked.

"Miss, you'd better move along," Frobisher told her firmly. "Police business."

"Okay," she replied agreeably. "Merry Christmas."

She didn't hear his answer as she headed up the street a short distance to where her car was parked. As she climbed in, a fleet of police cruisers flashed past, sirens blaring and lights flashing, with hexes crowding the airspace above. She started the car and retracted the landing struts, keeping her movements casual and steady. Checking her maneuvering cameras, she eased the car out sideways onto the street; once she was clear of the other vehicles, she smoothly applied acceleration and drove off.

All the way back to her apartment building, she kept a careful eye on the street behind her and the sky above. The snowfall wasn't thick enough to obscure vision at street level, but anything in the air would have as much trouble spotting her as she would with it.

This had factored into her decision to make the run on the police precinct today; once she'd taken the measure of the people who ran Utopia City's weather control apparatus, it was easy to predict and exploit their procedures. No snow fell in the city without their say-so, but it *was* Christmas, so they'd been allowing frequent falls on and off over the weeks leading up to the big day itself.

The snowfall was designed to give the buildings just enough of a dusting to make them look pretty, but to fall more thickly over the parks so children could have fun with toboggans and snowball fights, as children had done with snow since time immemorial. Just as impressive, the intermittent thaws revealed that the grass beneath was just as green as ever. Because of *course* it was a UCIAT-developed cold-resistant strain that could handle a few days of being buried under snow without any problem.

Utopia City. Their motto should be 'and why the hell not?'.

Addressing her more immediate concerns, no vehicles seemed to be following her for any significant length of time, and the body language of the drivers indicated no interest in her. While the hexagonal police drones were spreading out over the city, none of them were cutting across her path any more often than random chance would suggest.

She was *almost* sure nobody had her face on camera; the jammers she carried negated that possibility for audio and video recordings both. Neither would a sketch artist be of any use. Frobisher simply hadn't recognized her at the bottom of the steps, even though she'd spoken to him face-to-face at some length before her incursion had been detected.

Parking her car in the underground garage, she took the elevator to her apartment. The door opened to the tap of her MagCard, and she let herself in. Even then, she refused to let herself relax until she'd checked every last intrusion detector she'd left guarding the place.

Nothing.

Letting out a long sigh, she took the laptop from the kitchen table and settled down on the sofa. First, she transferred the mystery files from the tablet onto the computer, then she shut down the tablet, connected up her proprietary signal-scrambler, and activated her wi-fi. Finally, she allowed the laptop to go online.

A few sites here and there purported to dislike Force Majeure and all it stood for. She'd sounded them out one at a time, and settled on a couple that actually seemed to be serious. Still thinking through her intended spiel, she logged onto a site called **UTOPI***ANSWERS* under her customary username: CampfireAtNight.

Hey, guys, she typed. **Was trawling the dark web and found some files that might've come off a FoxtrotMike server. Trouble is, they're encrypted all to hell. Anyone want to lend a buddy a hand?**

Leaving that to percolate, she went and took a long, hot shower to try to work out some of the residual nerves. She fixed herself a snack afterward, then wandered back to the sofa to check on the laptop. There were three hits. The first was from someone she strongly suspected to be an FBI plant, the second was from a new guy on the scene, but the third came back from someone called PowerSlammer81.

If it'll show up Frankenstein's Monster for the frauds they are, I'll give it my best shot, Campfire. I know a guy who knows how to crack stuff like that.

She nodded as she composed a private message in reply. PowerSlammer might come across as more than a little pretentious from time to time, but he never made claims he couldn't back up. When it came to digging up dirt on Force Majeure, he was a true believer.

Sounds good, Slammer. I'll send you the lot in a zip file. Just remember, this stuff is hotter than magma. Once you've got it cracked, don't spread it around. Just send it straight back.

It took a little more time to prep the file, then she sent it away. Finally, she connected the discus and carefully swept her electronic back-trail, ensuring nobody could trace anything back to her even if they started at Slammer's end.

That, she decided, was enough subversion and insurrection for one day. After shutting down her laptop and unplugging it from the internet, she found the TV remote and turned on the cheesiest Christmas romantic comedy she could find.

Later, Smokeshadow decided, she would go down to the Market and get something to eat. Her evening would be spent sitting out on the balcony and centering her mind by watching the fresh snowfall gently settle over the city.

But right now, the head of Utopia City's newest up-and-coming underground criminal empire needed some 'me' time.

- End of Prologue Three -

Prologue Four
A Most Dedicated Companion

The Spire
Utopia City, Kansas
Friday, January 3, 2014

Holding the MagCard between his knuckles, Relentless tapped the reader outside the R&D lab that the Technologist had sequestered for his personal use. The door slid aside immediately, and he stepped through. He always enjoyed finding out what new toys his old friend and ally had created for him to play with.

This one wasn't for him per se, but he was going to get use out of it anyway. Arms and legs splayed like a high-tech rendition of the Vitruvian Man, the humanoid robot was secured to a large standing frame in the middle of the lab. It looked to measure about seven feet from head to toe, and was built like a tank. The matte black steel armor it sported was faceted in the manner of a stealth fighter. Cables and connectors were linked into sockets that (he guessed) would usually be covered by the smaller armor pieces lying on a bench nearby. Attached to the frame, small screens displayed innumerable readouts.

Transit and the Technologist were peering at it critically as he entered, though the white-clad artificer waved one hand in a distracted greeting. "Separate those two components and reverse the alignment of the one on the left," the Technologist said, pointing at a display on the screen.

Relentless knew enough about Artificer work to understand that the request hadn't been addressed to him. Transit was far more suited to carry it out; as well as possessing the Artificer powerset, she also had a Dynamic ability which allowed her to control and reshape any machinery she was in physical contact with. This allowed for some *fantastic* synergy.

Placing her hand on the robot's arm, Transit seemed to concentrate briefly. There was a series of whirring and clicking noises within the humanoid construct, then a final *clunk*. An access panel shifted, then clicked back into place.

Looking down at his tablet, the Technologist tapped some data into it, and the readout changed from amber to green. "That's better," he murmured.

"I'm glad to hear it," Relentless said bluntly. "Have you got some good news for *me*? After last Tuesday's shit-show, something better be going right."

"I am still at a loss as to how the data breach may have occurred, but I assure you that I have ramped up my countermeasures since then," the Technologist shot back. He'd been on the defensive ever since the hack had taken place, repeatedly claiming that whatever had happened, *it wasn't his fault.*

Relentless wasn't having any of it. "And why weren't they ramped up before now?"

The Technologist let out a long, aggravated breath through his nostrils. "I had them finely balanced so that the requisite processing power and the inconvenience involved were negligible, compared to the requirements of the Spire for high-speed external connections. Now, our responsiveness to the outside world is not as prompt as it used to be, and I cannot be certain that this will even help, not without knowing how the intruder effected the hole in our defenses the first time around." He reached up to his steampunk-style multi-lens goggles and flicked the extra lenses out of the way to look Relentless in the eye. "What have we deduced about the infiltrator?"

Relentless nodded in acknowledgment of the question. "She walked straight into the precinct house, went directly to Lombard's office, and left again when Lombard called. All indications are that she'd finished the hack by that point and was preparing to leave anyway."

"So, the infiltration and data acquisition may well have gone entirely undetected, had the good Captain Lombard been marginally less conscientious about her duties," observed the Technologist, not sounding even remotely happy about that particular state of affairs. "What about the officer whom Lombard actually spoke to about the matter? Did he have any hand in her gaining entry to the building? I seem to recall him being the one who admitted the infiltrator into Lombard's office."

"Frobisher?" asked Relentless rhetorically, then shook his head in negation. "He's been questioned extensively, and his background's been investigated all the way back to first grade. They found nothing. He didn't even walk her into the building proper. She used a MagCard that pinged with Lombard's account, cutting the real Lombard temporarily out of the loop. I remember you telling me those things were impossible to hack. Between those damned kids slipping through our fingers and now *this*, I'm frankly starting to fuckin' wonder."

"They *are* unhackable, by anyone but me!" snapped the Technologist.

"Well, unless *you* did it, I'm gonna have to call bullshit!" Relentless shouted back.

"Can we just cool our jets and back things up a second?" Transit held up her hands in a 'slow down' gesture. "Are they sure it was a woman? None of the cameras came up with a workable image. Even the audio's so distorted we can't unravel it."

"Frobisher *claimed* it was a woman." Relentless made a dissatisfied noise deep in his throat. "But he also thought she was someone from his department, and that's simply not the case. The movements of everyone belonging to that precinct house have been checked and traced. Nothing."

"So, we've got no actionable data to work with." Transit looked from Relentless to the Technologist. "Do you think she's got anything to do with the person who assisted G-Man with the Survivors? We also had trouble getting any sort of verifiable information on that one, remember?"

That was a connection Relentless hadn't made. "That's ... entirely likely. It would mean whoever this is, they never left Utopia. This is a problem we will have to deal with, once we get a line on her. Or him, if Frobisher's mistaken." He took a deep breath, changing gears in his brain and gesturing at the figure on the rack. "So how much longer before this thing's operational?"

"Well, the chassis is ready to roll," Transit said, apparently relieved at the reduction in tension in the room. "It's powered by a micro-fusion plant that lets it run at up to sixty miles per hour on the flat, or thirty over broken terrain. Horizontal leaping capability of one hundred sixty feet with a run-up, vertical jump of forty feet. This can be augmented via the direct cycle turbojets on the back, heating air via the fusion plant to boost jumping distance by fifty percent."

"Fifty percent doesn't sound like much." Relentless frowned. "So, it can't actually fly?"

"Not like that, no," allowed Transit. "But in an emergency, the robot can override the heat exchanger safety protocols, draw air into the reactor itself and superheat it into a high-intensity plasma jet. Much more thrust will be obtained when this is vented, but it *will* set fire to anything behind it, and the vented plasma will be radioactive, so I'd recommend restricting its use."

Relentless nodded. "We can work with that. Sensory capabilities?"

Transit ticked points off on her fingers. "Far infrared and ultraviolet, plus complete access to the visible spectrum. Up to ten times visual magnification, microscopic and telescopic. Full audio input capabilities, from ultrasonic to infrasonic, and directional hearing."

"Mm-hmm." Relentless reached forward and flicked the angled black armor with a fingertip. The metal gave back a dull thud that spoke of durability and density. "I can see you've given it defensive capability. How about offensive?"

Transit tapped an icon on the tablet she was holding, and the armor on the figure's right arm folded away. Dangerous-looking apertures were revealed, then vanished again as she tapped the icon a second time and the covers slid back into place. Another icon caused the left hand to angle backward on the wrist. He watched as an eighteen-inch blade emerged briefly, then retracted.

"It's got a railgun firing four-millimeter gravity-accelerated rounds and an anti-personnel laser. The blade can be electrified as needed. There are targeting designators incorporated into the visual sensors." She gestured to the figure. "External weaponry can be attached via those sockets as needed."

He nodded, satisfied. If anyone could make a bipedal war-bot work, it was Transit. "Nicely done." He turned to the Technologist. "And the programming?"

"For all intents and purposes, its programming is complete." The white-clad artificer pulled down a menu on his tablet, then tapped several buttons in a row. One at a time, the cables and connectors disconnected and retracted, then the eyes of the figure lit up, glowing a deep blue. They flickered, blinked a few times, then changed to green. Bending forward at the waist, the robot stepped forward off the rack and stood before them, arms at its sides.

Relentless evaluated its posture. It wasn't rock-steady but swayed almost infinitesimally, its arms moving gently to maintain its balance. The green-glowing eyes seemed to fix on Transit, moved to Relentless himself, then stopped on the Technologist.

"Identify yourself," the Technologist ordered.

A speaker crackled to life, somewhere in the vicinity of the robot's chest or face. **"Unit Alpha one four nine three. Designation 'Sidekick Zero One'."** The voice was harsh and synthesized.

Relentless folded his arms. "So far, not impressed."

The Technologist cleared his throat. "Sidekick Zero One, what is your primary function?"

"Primary directive: to protect Enabled identified as G-Man and assist him in saving Utopia City." As it spoke, the robot's eyes shifted from green to amber.

That was definitely more like it. Far from the mechanical-sounding identification, the robot's speech was now fluid and precise. Allowing himself a tiny smile of triumph, the Technologist spoke once more. "And your secondary function?"

"Secondary directive: if Enabled identified as G-Man attempts to betray Utopia City, *destroy G-Man*." The dark-armored figure's eyes shifted to a burning red with the last two words.

"Really?" Transit shook her head. "You built in a kill command?"

In perfect agreement with her, Relentless glared at the Technologist. "You just had to put that last bit in, didn't you? He joined us in good faith."

"I understand that both of you hold more trust in the boy than the rest of us," the artificer replied in an unruffled tone. "Try to see it from my perspective. You know precisely why I find it difficult to trust anyone who's not an original member of Force Majeure. If G-Man never attacks us in any way, he will not come to harm."

"Hmm." Arms still folded, Relentless looked from his white-clad colleague to the waiting robot. The red eyes had faded back to amber again as if waiting for further input. "It's not an ideal scenario, but I suppose I can live with it."

Transit was still unhappy. "I don't like it either, but I'm guessing you're not about to change your mind on this. So, I'll make you a deal. We go ahead with it as it is, and if G-Man hasn't even tried to make a move against us in one year, you take out that ridiculous kill command."

"Or what?" challenged the Technologist. "Certainly, your expertise in programming is better than most, but I remain your superior in that and many other disciplines."

"I built the chassis," she retorted. "I can shut it down at any time. And yeah, I know ways to crash it so hard, you'd need to reconstruct the whole thing from the ground up to get it working again."

Relentless chuckled. "She's got you there. Her idea has merit, so we'll make it one year. Agreed?"

Sourly, the Technologist nodded. "I believe both of you are perpetrating an egregious mistake, but yes, one year is acceptable."

"We can all make mistakes. Including you." Transit slid her tablet into a leg pouch. "So, how were you intending to attach your robot to G-Man without raising his suspicions? He's nice, not stupid."

The Technologist never hesitated. "I shall consult with our esteemed head of surgery. They already possess a significant rapport. If there is a method to achieve this, she will find it."

"Excellent." Relentless looked the armored figure over again. "Kill command aside, you've both done well."

Amber eyes surveyed him right back, but the robot said nothing at all.

- End of Prologue Four -

PART ONE

OBLIGATIONS

The price always demands payment.
- Sarah Owens, Deputy Head of Surgery, the Spire

1
Heroes

A chill breeze cut briefly across the open ground of the cemetery, then died away again. There had been a recent snowfall, and the leaf-bare trees stood out starkly against the smooth white blanket, itself marred only by three sets of footprints coming in from the roadside.

Each upright gravestone sported a layer of snow, while impossibly razor-thin deposits had built up on the overhead high-tension power lines. Even now, more white flakes were drifting down out of the low-hanging clouds, settling gently on the shoulders of all present and on the one headstone that had been brushed clean.

ROBERTA 'BOBBI' REYNOLDS
May 19th 1981 to October 6th 2013
BELOVED DAUGHTER AND SISTER
SHE BORE THE TORCH OF TRUTH

Clad in his new costume, Jericho stood next to the grave with Vanessa at his side. She held a single red rose in her hand. On the other side of the burial plot stood Vanessa's parents, Adam and Tesseract Power. Like Jericho, they were in costume, their matching blue and gold power armor standing out vividly against the winter backdrop. Vanessa was the only one wearing civilian clothing: specifically, jeans and a plain gray jacket with the hood pushed back to allow her long red hair to spill out.

Buddy, her brother, had opted to keep an eye on the Team Power jet, a long, sleek, dangerous-looking aircraft that had dropped them off before departing again. Despite it being fully VTOL capable, Jericho gathered that the Indianapolis authorities hadn't given permission for them to park it anywhere but at a legitimate airport.

Dusting the last of the snow from his gloves, he restrained the impulse to rub his arms for warmth. Between his Prodigy-based endurance and the new costume, the cold was more imagined than felt. "I didn't know Bobbi for very long," he said, trying to put his emotions into words, difficult at the best of times. "But she was a good person. Luke and I both liked her. She was determined to do the right thing, to be a hero, no matter what it cost her." He took a deep breath of the freezing air. "Even though coming to Utopia ended up costing her everything, in the end." The lump that swelled in his throat prevented him from saying more.

Vanessa took him by the hand, pressing the stem of the rose between their palms. "She had no idea how it would turn out, but she did it anyway. She put the idea into your head, so when you made the final connection, you believed it strongly enough to convince me." Her head went down, and she squeezed his fingers tightly. "Without her insight, I'd still be convinced that Dad was a dangerous predator. Even *with* it, I nearly discounted everything you were telling me." She shook her head; he could tell that her eyes were squeezed tightly closed. "I was an idiot. A gullible moron. I should've known Dad *just wouldn't do that.*"

"We've already established that whoever masqueraded as your father was undoubtedly a master of impersonation." Tesseract's voice was firm, though the glint in her eye promised mayhem to the person who'd sought to drag her husband's name through the mud and destroy her family. "You were in what you considered to be a safe place. Nobody expected something like that to happen."

Adam shook his head. "We should have. *I* should have. That was my failure. I designed and built Power Plaza, and I was the one who installed the security systems. We'd just dealt with one False Flag copycat, for God's sake. I should've figured there could be *more.*"

Jericho knew the name but hadn't heard of the incident in question. False Flag, dead for over a decade now, had been one of the more notorious members of that nebulous fraternity known as the 'terror villains of the Nineties'. Possessing a Dynamic shape-changing ability, the man's best-known crime had been to assassinate the newly sworn-in President while impersonating the head of his Secret Service protection detail.

Great. And this new one's still out there somewhere.

"That doesn't follow," argued Tesseract. To Jericho, it sounded as though they were going once more over well-trodden ground. "The one we caught had an Artificer device that allowed him to change his face. We know the one who attacked Vanessa had Dynamic powers because she got *her* powers from him, via the Proximity Principle. There's no way you could've anticipated two separate villains, using the same type of power via two entirely different powersets, showing up in such a short time."

"Mom, Dad, can we please drop it?" asked Vanessa plaintively. "We can all try to grab the blame for what happened, but at the end of the day, it's done. Whoever did this was clearly trying to screw Team Power over, but they *failed.* And between Dad and me, we've got security in the Plaza sewn up tighter than a drum. So, they're not going to have a second opportunity. And if they *do* try, we'll catch them and kick their tailbones up between their ears. Okay?"

Tesseract pursed her lips as though she had more to say on the subject but was choosing not to. Instead, she nodded sharply. "Yes. I agree this is not the time and place for that discussion." She opened a flat canister-style carrying case on her hip and took out a small wreath. Moving with more agility and dexterity than someone wearing powered armor had a right to, she placed it up against the headstone. "Bobbi, we never knew you, but you had more faith in us than we had in ourselves. For that, we will forever be in your debt."

As his wife stood up and stepped away from the gravesite, Adam took a knee; an armored Titan, humbling himself to show respect for the dead. "There are no words I could say that someone else here hasn't said better than I could. So I'll say this instead: as co-founder and leader of Team Power, I hereby induct Bobbi Reynolds posthumously into the team, to be kept on our rolls in perpetuity as a mark of our respect and gratitude."

He pointed his arm at the gravestone and tilted his hand upward. Jericho watched as a cover on the underside of his arm folded to one side and revealed a small cylindrical mechanism. When the laser beam ignited, it was bluish in hue but so bright it was almost white. Shading his eyes, Jericho still had to look away; the surrounding snow reflected back the actinic glare, while the gravestones cast long, exaggerated shadows in every direction. Ozone and the smell of burning stone stung his nostrils as the high-intensity beam did its work.

When the laser shut off, leaving the heated stone popping and crackling as it cooled, he had to blink a couple of times; the daylight suddenly seemed a lot dimmer than it had before. Leaning in as Adam regained his feet, Jericho peered at the gravestone. His eyes adjusted quickly enough, allowing him to see that the Team Power logo and the words 'HONORARY MEMBER' had been incised into the stone beneath the original inscription.

"Yeah," he said, finding his voice again. "I think Bobbi would've liked that a lot."

Vanessa nodded in agreement and bent down. He leaned over with her, holding her hand, and helped her place the rose over the wreath. "Rest in peace," Vanessa murmured.

By unspoken agreement, Adam and Tesseract Power inclined their heads in respect, then turned and started back toward the road. Vanessa and Jericho followed them, still holding hands. "The jet's on the way," Adam announced. "Buddy says he'll be here in a minute or so."

"Mm-hmm." Vanessa turned to Jericho. "I've been meaning to ask. Your costume looks a bit different. Did you get a new one?"

"Total upgrade." A little self-consciously, Jericho plucked at the black outfit he wore. "Force Majeure set me up with a blend that includes Kevlar and Nomex to give me personal protection and some fire resistance. It's even got a water-shedding layer so I can stay mostly dry in the rain." He thumped his chest with his hand. "My costume jacket had plastic plates sewn into the lining for protection. This one's got the same thing, but in advanced polycarbonate. Just as light, ten times as strong. Plus, there's a high-end utility belt, with more pouches than I've got stuff to put in them." Tapping the side of his head, he grinned. "On top of that, they replaced my mask with a lightweight helmet that takes a Bluetooth earpiece on the right side and a radio earpiece on the left. Anytime I'm in the same city as another Force Majeure member, we automatically tie into the same radio net."

"Okay, I can appreciate the technology," she said. "But when you've got an earpiece in both ears, how can you hear anything?"

His grin widening, Jericho tapped his helmet again, this time indicating the tiny holes in the high-impact plastic over his ear. "External microphones. They feed sounds through to the earpieces so I can hear if someone's talking to me, even if I'm listening to music at the time." He found it funny because he'd asked the same question back when they'd issued him the helmet.

"Nice," she said approvingly. "I'm guessing the logo on the front is new, too? I seem to recall it was only on the back."

"Yeah." He'd almost forgotten that detail. Reflexively, he looked down at the symbol on his chest, an angular white 'G' bracketed by vertical chevrons. "Apparently, having your logo up front is a PR bonus. I never did it with my jacket because I was worried about having the halves match up. But having access to an on-call professional costumier is just one of the many perks of being part of a big team like that."

"So I see," she observed with a grin. "I hope you didn't just trash the old one, though. That would be a pity."

"Well, no." There was no sense in getting rid of something that worked perfectly well, just because he'd upgraded. "I've got someone I trust holding on to it." To some, Leroy might have been an odd choice for such a crucial position, but his uncle was a shady underworld character second and his kinsman first. Family trumped everything else where Jericho was concerned. He knew damn well if he ever needed that costume back for anything, it would be there.

"Oh, good." She smiled. "Not gonna lie, you looked pretty badass in it."

"Thanks." Reaching up, he flicked at the shoulder of her hoodie. "Talking about costumes, you don't seem to be wearing yours."

She rolled her eyes. "Well, you know I had to ditch my last set of armor in the Missouri River. Dad's working on a new outfit that he says will be able to actually shape change with me. The prototype should be done in a week or so."

"That'll be cool," Jericho said. "It'll be good to see you back in action with your family. Shut the doubters down *hard*."

"I'm definitely okay with that." She heaved a sigh, puffing out a white cloud. "Oh, and I told Mom and Dad about the money I took to feed the Survivors while I was in Utopia. I kept notes on everyone I ripped off, and they're helping me locate the people and pay it all back. On the quiet, you know?"

"Good, good." Jericho nodded. He knew how much it had been weighing on Vanessa's mind. "I'm glad."

"Me too." Her mouth took on a wry twist, and she rolled her eyes. "Dad says I'm using up my team pay from now until twenty-twenty, but I *think* he's joking."

Before Jericho could agree with her that her father was probably pulling her leg, there was a distant rumble. He looked around and spotted the incoming jet. "Your ride's here."

"Yeah." Vanessa bit her lip and turned to her father. "Um, Dad, could we give Jericho a lift back to Utopia in the jet?"

Before Adam could speak, Jericho hastily shook his head. "Thanks for the offer, but that's more or less in the exact opposite direction you need to be going. I'll be fine." He really would've enjoyed spending more time with Thomas, but between Tesseract and Buddy, he didn't think there would be much room for privacy on the Team Power jet. Putting his hand on Vanessa's shoulder, he looked her in the eyes. "We'll be fine," he insisted in a lower tone of voice. "I'll see you again, as soon as I can."

Adam nodded in acknowledgment. "So long as you're covered. Anytime you need a hand, though, feel free to ask."

With a rumble of engines and a swirl of jet-wash that scattered flurries of snow here and there, the Team Power aircraft arrived overhead. It slowed to a hover, then descended to about thirty feet up and held position there. Jericho would've thought there'd be a lot more noise, but regular expectations went clear out the window when dealing with something constructed using Artificer capabilities. He felt momentarily envious that Buddy Power, still only eleven or twelve, got to fly something like that. At that age, he hadn't even known how to drive a *car*, let alone fly a plane. Luke, on the other hand ...

The unexpected reminder of his cousin made him grit his teeth. It had been three months since the funeral—*most of which I missed because I'm a dumbass*—but the pain of the memory still wasn't any easier to deal with. Taking a deep breath of the chilly air, he tried to distract himself, with only middling success.

"You okay?" asked Vanessa quietly, glancing sideways at him. No matter who she was at the moment, she was altogether too perceptive.

"I will be," he said, which was true. Eventually, he'd learn how to deal with it. He could've told her he was all good right then, but that would be a lie, and he didn't want to ever set foot on that slippery slope. Besides, he knew she'd just call him out on it.

A hatch slid open in the belly of the hovering aircraft, and a cable unspooled downward. Almost as though they'd planned it, Adam and Tesseract Power turned to look at Vanessa. The unspoken message was clear; she had to go first.

"Fine," she grumped. "Give me a minute with Jericho, okay?"

Again, her parents glanced at each other, then her father nodded.

"Good. *Thank* you. First chance I get to see my boyfriend in *way* too long, and you just want me to jump right back in the plane without even properly saying goodbye? Yeah, *that's* gonna happen."

As she spoke, Vanessa pulled her hood up and tucked her long red hair inside, then loosened her belt. Jericho watched her take a deep breath, then the change began. It seemed … smoother, perhaps. More natural. Or maybe it was just down to the fact that he was used to it now. Over the next thirty seconds, Vanessa's body bulked out and got taller, then somewhere along the way she stopped being Vanessa and he started being Thomas.

"Hi." Artfully tousled black hair stuck out from under his hood as he stepped up to Jericho.

"Hi," Jericho replied wittily, putting his arms around Thomas and holding him close. The first kiss was gentle, almost teasing, then he closed his eyes and let his boyfriend take the initiative.

It had been, he decided as his head spun, *definitely* worth the wait. If the kiss went on a little bit longer than absolutely necessary, he wasn't complaining in the slightest. Strong arms held him up as his knees went wobbly, then Thomas let it end just as Adam ostentatiously cleared his throat.

"Much as I hate to break up you two lovebirds," the older man said in an amused tone, "we'd like to get back to Chicago *today.*"

"Oh, that's fine, Dad," Thomas offered. "I can always take the maglev home." Jericho heard the half-joking tone in his boyfriend's voice but knew damn well Thomas would jump at the opportunity if they took him up on it. More time to make out in a taxi before they took the maglev out of Indianapolis, one going north and one west? That would be a definite 'yes, please'.

"No, you will not be doing that, young man." If Thomas' mother hadn't already been on Jericho's '*do not mess with*' list, the glint in her eye and the tone of her voice would've put her there. "Someone's already tried to get at us through you once already. I wouldn't put it past them to try again, in a more lethal fashion. So, until we *know* who targeted you and we've put them either behind bars or six feet under …" She let the rest of the sentence trail off. Jericho didn't need her to connect the rest of the dots. Nor did he think the implied intent to kill the mystery perp to be anything but deadly serious (pun intended). Tesseract Power didn't play.

"I know, I know, I'm basically grounded." Thomas rolled his eyes. "Seriously, I had more freedom in Utopia, with the Survivors."

"With a set of crosshairs painted on your back by every hero and cop whenever you went outside," Jericho reminded him, more for his own amusement than from any specific need to set the record straight. "I mean, holy crap, you literally had to fight your way out of a police hex cordon."

Thomas gave him a dirty look, then shook his head in mock disgust. "Exactly whose side are you on, anyway?"

"Ours," Jericho said firmly. "Just remember, at least here and now, you still get to go out and about. And I'll definitely come to visit when I get the chance."

"You better, you hear me?" Thomas kissed him again, hard, then held him close.

Through their mutual embrace, Jericho felt his boyfriend sigh. It wasn't hard to figure out what Thomas was feeling; Jericho had much the same turmoil going on within his own heart. "I know, I know," he murmured. "It sucks. I just wish I could call you from Utopia."

"Not worth it." Thomas rested his forehead against Jericho's mask. "If they ever decide to check up on communications by Force Majeure members and they've got a voiceprint on file for me, then our relationship would sink your chances of staying on the team deeper than Kraken's sub. Text me instead, on this number. It's one of our anonymous ones." He pressed a folded Post-It note into Jericho's hand.

"*Ugghh.*" Jericho's sigh came out more like a groan as he tucked the paper into a pouch. "Fine. But we'll see each other again. Soon, if I've got anything to say about it."

"Won't be soon enough." Thomas pulled back just far enough to surprise Jericho with a tender kiss on the tip of the nose. "Give me a boost?"

Jericho read Thomas' intent immediately. "Sure." Reaching down, he took hold of one *extremely* well-muscled buttock and squeezed it, not missing the shudder of enjoyment that went through Thomas' body as he did so. Using his grasp as a point of contact, he exerted his power and reduced the effect of gravity on his boyfriend by a factor of ten. Then he kissed Thomas one more time. "Done."

With a grin, Thomas stepped onto a patch of previously undisturbed snow, his feet barely breaking the surface, and performed an impromptu dance routine across it—involving a lot of booty shaking—until he stood under the open hatchway. Then he gathered himself and leaped upward, leaving two perfect footprints in the otherwise almost pristine expanse.

While Thomas was impressively athletic by definition—his Prodigy powerset saw to that—he would typically have been unable to achieve anywhere near a twenty-foot standing vertical jump. The power boost Jericho had given him changed all that; soaring upward, he caught the cable just shy of the open hatch. Refusing to use his legs, he hauled himself up the last few feet and scrambled inside, while Jericho didn't even pretend not to watch the play of muscles in his arms and back.

It's not skeevy if he's already my boyfriend.

Once aboard the aircraft, Thomas paused to pull something out of his pocket and wave it over the opening. A handkerchief. The same square of cloth, in fact, that Jericho had given him in the maglev station back in Utopia. Thomas' message was clear: *I've still got this.* Jericho nodded and waved back, then watched as his boyfriend vanished from sight, probably to find a seat and strap in.

"G-Man." Tesseract's voice pulled his attention away from the hovering jet, and his boyfriend within. She knew Jericho's real name—Thomas had shared that information with his parents, with Jericho's blessing—so this was either an operational security thing, or she had something serious to say. Or perhaps both.

"Yes, ma'am?" he asked. Even if he hadn't learned Southern courtesy at his daddy's knee, he would've said the same thing regardless. Being polite to one's boyfriend's mom was *always* a good idea.

She clasped her hands behind her back, which was probably better than folding her arms, though the tone of her voice didn't make her words any less ominous. "You make Vanessa … Thomas … happy. I approve of this, though I'm having trouble making sense of your … arrangement."

He couldn't blame her. Her daughter had come back out of the blue after a two-year absence, with the ability to become a young man, in an ongoing relationship with *another* man. This had to be straining her understanding of how the world functioned. "We're both working at it," he offered candidly. "Thanks for not kicking me to the curb."

"I'll be frank." She gave him a hard stare. "When I first heard about you, I was considerably less than pleased. *Nobody* wants to find out that their missing daughter has been spending time, unsupervised, with a grown man who they haven't even met."

Jericho gave a half-shrug of apology. "Well, it was Thomas I was spending time with, not Vanessa, if that helps."

"And that's another thing." Tesseract barely paused as she changed conversational gears. "The next time I hear about parents of transitioning teenagers complaining about not knowing what to call their kids, I swear I'm going to laugh out loud. At least they only have to deal with it *once*."

"Yeah, well, I like them both," Jericho said. "Though Thomas is the one I prefer to spend time with, for obvious reasons. Anyway, I know him better than I know Vanessa."

"Yes. I'm fully aware of that." Tesseract gave him an unamused stare, as though suspecting him of deliberately tweaking her sensibilities. "So long as you don't upset either one, you'll be fine. Are we on the same page?"

"Absolutely, ma'am," Jericho assured her. Not only was she his potential mother-in-law, but he had no doubt she could also kick his tailbone up between his ears (as Vanessa had so eloquently put it) without breaking a sweat. No matter *what* Dynamic powers he tried to bring into play.

"Good," she said with a tight smile. She patted him lightly on the cheek, then turned and grabbed the cable. This time, it retracted up into the hatch as she held on, leaving him facing Thomas' father.

Back in the day, Arfogwyr of Inspire had been lauded as *the* pre-eminent heroic artificer in the world, outfitting herself and Castellan with the best of her work, and constructing Caerwyn as their home base. Following her demise at the hands of the Minotaur, Adam Power had taken up the mantle and borne it ably for the next few years. The only reason he no longer held the title was that the Technologist had taken over the spot following the construction of Utopia City from 1999 through into the two-thousands, and had yet to relinquish it.

The public reputation of Adam Power and PowerTech Industries had suffered a negative backlash following the rumors surrounding Vanessa's disappearance, but that was all in the past now. Revitalized following her very public return, Adam had already made significant progress in regaining PowerTech's market share where it came to selling high-tech equipment to the military and civilian markets. The man was just that good.

"So," he said. Fortunately for Jericho's peace of mind, his expression was more amicable than Tesseract's had been.

"So," Jericho repeated awkwardly.

Adam chuckled and slapped Jericho on the shoulder with his metal gauntlet, driving the younger man's heels into the packed snow. "Relax, son. Tess has already given you the shovel speech, so I'm not going to bother. As far as I'm concerned, you've already proven yourself ten times over. But I meant what I said. Just in case you ever need help in a hurry—and trust me, I *know* how that feels—I want you to take this." He reached to his waist; there was a *click* as something dispensed into his hand.

Jericho didn't know what the device was until Adam passed it over to him, and even then he wasn't sure. "A radio?" he hazarded, looking at the palm-sized object, made of polished blue and gold metal. It had a single light and a bright red recessed button, which made the identification easy … unless it was something else altogether. Artificer tech was funny like that.

"PowerTech emergency beacon," the older hero corrected him. "Waterproof, shockproof, EMP hardened, five-year battery. Hold down the button for five seconds or less to check the power status, more than five seconds to start transmitting a continuous SOS on our dedicated band."

"Uh, wow, thanks," Jericho said, staring at the beacon in his gloved hand. "I really mean it. Thanks."

"It's not a problem. Go be the best hero you can be. And if you're ever in Chicago, don't hesitate to drop by." Adam stepped back away from Jericho, raised his hand in a lazy approximation of a salute, then lit off his suit's thrusters. As with the plane, Jericho wasn't sure what principle they worked on but then again, neither of his powersets involved building devices that made physics go and cry in the corner. He watched as the veteran hero lifted straight up off the ground, spraying snow everywhere, and into the open hatch of the jet.

The hatch slid shut, then the jet ignited its main thrusters with a flare of violet energy. Within moments, it had accelerated out of sight to the east, curving around to the north. He looked down at the beacon still in his hand, then picked a pouch of about the correct size. Given that he had a direct line to Force Majeure at all times, he didn't think he'd ever need the Team Power device, but there was always the old saying about it being better to have and not need than the other way around. So he carefully put the beacon away, making sure the waterproof magnetic seal on the pouch clicked into place, then activated his enhancement harness.

Just as he had with Thomas, he could use his gravity powers to reduce the effect of gravity on himself to one-tenth normal. The gliding surfaces on his original costume had been replicated in the current iteration for the sake of completeness, though he hadn't needed to use them since he got the new version.

Before he'd joined Force Majeure, the stretched fabric under his arms had (in conjunction with his power) allowed him to ride the wind currents to his heart's content, but only insofar as to glide. Much to his frustration, true flight had ever been beyond his reach. His harness, supplied by the Technologist once he joined Force Majeure, had changed *everything*.

He could feel it energizing, drawing on his Dynamic abilities to form midnight-black wings from pure shaped gravity. As they unfurled outward from his arms, he lifted off the ground and gained speed with somewhat less fuss than the jet, though with nowhere near the acceleration. Flying back to Utopia from Indianapolis would be possible, as far as he was aware, but excruciatingly dull; however, there was a simpler way.

Turning in a lazy circle over the cemetery, he reacquainted himself with where the maglev station was, and set out in that direction.

Why fly for hours at highway speeds in freezing winter temperatures when I can ride in style?

2
Reassignment

Unlike the airlines it had supplanted, the maglev didn't have first class, business class, or any other separate ticket pricing. All seats cost the same, and all train cars were as near to being identical as Artificer ingenuity could make them. One hundred twenty feet long, counting streamlining; roomy, comfortable seats on the lower deck; café-style tables on the upper deck; restrooms at one end; vending machines at the other. Riding on a magnetic cushion over a cylindrical rail and stabilized by gravity generators, the automated cars were linked together into trains which played a never-ending game of musical chairs all over America, twenty-four hours a day.

Due to Utopia Maglev Lines being a wholly-owned subsidiary of Utopia City Holdings LLC, which was in turn owned and operated by the core membership of Force Majeure, all team members rode for free. They were encouraged to do so in costume, as this was good for PR in two different ways. One: people liked superheroes, and signing a few autographs went a long way toward making the team look good. Two: having a costumed hero on the train made it feel safer.

Jericho had never ridden the maglev before the fateful day he set out to attend his interview in Utopia City. Since then, he'd lost count of the number of trips he'd taken, but he would never forget that first journey with Luke where they'd met Bobbi on the train. The camaraderie established over the course of the transit to Utopia had been shattered by their later murders; however, he preferred to recall them as they had been in life, not in death.

Once he tapped his MagCard and was scanned through onto the platform, it was his habit to go directly to the upper deck. His favorite seating location was to the rear of the car, on the right-hand side of the aisle. With the privacy bubble engaged, he could be alone with his thoughts or listen to music while keeping an eye on what was going on around him. One stroll forward at St. Louis and a second at Kansas City, and he'd be back in Utopia before he knew it.

An hour and a quarter, two short walks, home again, jiggity jig.

As he settled into his seat, he reflected on how weird things sometimes played out. If that False Flag copycat hadn't targeted Vanessa, she wouldn't have gotten powers and run away and become Thomas.

And I wouldn't have met Thomas in Utopia.

From what Thomas had told him, it wasn't uncommon for the terror villains to have others emulating them, even fifteen years after Doc Iridium died to his own nuclear explosion.

What was the last thing that went through his mind? The clock tower.

Morbid humor aside, he acknowledged the problem, though it was hard to determine a guaranteed solution that didn't boil down to 'paranoid readiness'. The public was fully aware of Force Majeure's stance against anyone even attempting to take up the bloodstained mantle of the original terror villains, and copycats fell squarely into the proscribed category. As an indicator of the team's effectiveness, no new terror villains had established themselves since nine-twenty, which had to be a good track record.

The downside of this success was that the public was becoming (in his opinion) dangerously complacent. Why bother keeping an eye out for random sickos fixing to be the next Seismic when the heroes were right there to do it for them? Admittedly, inside the United States, they had a point. Any villains aspiring to escalate their activities in that direction ran into a Force-Majeure-shaped wall before they ever really got off the ground.

Unfortunately for Jericho's peace of mind, the United States wasn't the only place in the world where people could become Enabled. Nor had American foreign policy made it (or its citizens) overly popular in some quarters overseas. The reign of the terror villains had inspired levels of security capable of stopping mundane terrorists in their tracks; this much was true. However, those precautions would do little to prevent an Enabled with a real or imagined grudge from honing their talents on their home turf, then entering the United States as a random tourist to spread death and destruction.

But if I studied how they did things back then, I could maybe see the signs coming the next time around.

He snorted derisively, fully aware of how his own motives extended beyond the altruistic.

And, of course, it's got nothing to do with distracting myself from how crappy I feel about being away from Thomas.

Taking out his phone, he searched for videos about False Flag. There were several, but most of them dealt with the aftermath of the vicious killer's exploits. He tried searching for pictures of the villain but quickly gave up. The problem wasn't a lack of images, but too *many*, none of which were guaranteed to be False Flag's original face. In retrospect, this was something he should've anticipated when dealing with a person who could change his face more readily than his socks.

One particularly emotion-charged clip showed a sobbing businessman telling a sympathetic reporter about how he'd come home from work to find his wife had murdered their children then cut her own throat. In a twist that had Jericho performing a double-take, a report appended to the video revealed that the actual husband's body had been found later; far from being the sole survivor, he'd actually been the first victim.

Wait, what again now?

Even re-watching the video with full knowledge of who the man really was, Jericho was entirely incapable of discerning the monster lurking beneath the surface. There were no tells, not even a subtle hint. The man's act was utterly flawless, down to the tears running down his face.

Jericho had trouble getting his head around the sheer depraved malevolence of the mindset. Someone like that surely saw people more as playthings, toys to be destroyed and discarded at a whim. It was sobering and not a little terrifying.

The only thing to be grateful for was that shape-changing to the level of being able to fool friends and loved ones, coupled with the requisite acting skills, were a relatively unlikely combination. The chance of someone like that *also* being a psychotic killer had to be minimal, which hopefully reduced the likelihood of another False Flag copycat appearing any time soon.

It was just Vanessa's bad luck that one of them happened to target her. I wish the asshat would try the same trick on Independence. She might be a b-word, but she'd totally kick his tailbone up between his ears and down the other side.

He scrolled onward in search of videos to give him more insight into people like that, but the phone rang before he found anything promising. Grumbling a little to himself, he checked the name on the screen, at which point his complaints dried up faster than lizard spit in the Mojave.

Samantha Colburn was executive assistant to Relentless himself; the number of conversations he'd had with her could be counted on the fingers of one hand with enough left over to perform any rude hand gestures he cared to think about.

Taking a breath to compose himself, he double-checked the privacy bubble—still engaged—and swiped to answer the call. "G-Man here, Ms. Colburn. What's the problem?"

That there *was* a problem, he had no doubt. Second in authority only to Relentless himself, Ms. Colburn was not in the habit of calling up relatively new recruits to pass the time of day.

"There's been a murder in Savannah," she replied with her customary brevity. "What is your location?"

"I'm on the maglev, ma'am, just out of Indianapolis, heading for St. Louis. I presume you want me to attend?" The question came automatically as the adrenaline began pumping through his system. On top of that came the questions. *Who's the vic?* And then, *Why am I being called in?*

A flash of worry went through him about his parents, but he hadn't gotten any calls, and his family was very tight-knit about that sort of thing. In any case, his amateur detective skills were no match for the resources available to a properly staffed police department.

"Yes, I do." Her tone was firm. "The victim is a Franklin Tucker. His next of kin specifically requested your presence. What is your connection to him?"

Jericho frowned. "To be honest, ma'am, I don't know anyone called Frank Tucker, in Savannah or outside of it." He rubbed his chin, trying to jog his thought processes. "Wait. Is he gay? I mean, *was* he gay?"

Stephen, his ex from Savannah, had been sleeping around before Jericho dumped him; it happened to be one of the primary reasons for their breakup. If he'd bragged on G-Man's heroic capabilities a little too much during pillow talk, this Tucker guy might have a boyfriend who remembered whatever wild tales Stephen had spun. This was unfortunate, because while Jericho was good at what he did, he was no world-class Hollywood-style detective.

"Not unless he's only recently come out," Ms. Colburn observed candidly. "He had a live-in lady friend named Chantelle Green, and the two of them had a child. Mother and child are alive and well. Ms. Green is the one who requested your presence."

This was getting more bizarre by the second. "I'm not questioning the decision to send me, ma'am, but why are they requesting me, and why is this request even being considered? I'm not exactly certain what I can contribute. Because I really don't know these people."

Ms. Colburn's voice became even more clipped and precise. "You were requested because you're the only Enabled from Georgia, much less Savannah, with current membership in Force Majeure. You're going because it's easier to determine whether you can help or not on the spot, rather than from a thousand miles away. And finally: Mr. Tucker, among other things, was a conspiracy theorist focusing exclusively on anything damaging to Force Majeure. Not only do we wish to avoid any accusations of discriminatory treatment, but we also want you to vet the information he had on hand when he died."

"I can totally do that, ma'am," Jericho said, trying to keep the dubious tone out of his voice. He wasn't entirely sure how he was supposed to go about vetting a bunch of conspiracy theories. Still, he had no intention of letting down Ms. Colburn (and, by extension, Relentless and Force Majeure) if he could possibly help it. "Though there may be a slight problem with the timing. Unless you can convince the Savannah PD to hold off for the next two hours, they'll be done and dusted by the time I get there."

"We have that aspect, at least, under control," Ms. Colburn said. "Leave the maglev at St. Louis. Tourbillon will be meeting you there."

In that moment, he knew exactly how serious it was. Tourbillon was a big name in a team of big names. One of the seven core members of Force Majeure, the androgynous teleporter undoubtedly had many demands on their time. Jericho had been transported by them exactly once before, at the request of Relentless himself. Calling on them at a moment's notice to get Jericho to Savannah made it very important indeed.

"Understood," he replied. "So, what … exactly … should I be looking for with this conspiracy theory information, anyway?" Even as he voiced it, the question sounded stupid, but he knew he had to ask.

"Force Majeure is a large organization," Ms. Colburn replied crisply. Apparently, she didn't think the question was so stupid. "There exists the possibility that we are inadvertently harboring rogue elements who are acting outside the boundaries of our procedures, or even the law itself. As a conspiracy theorist, Mr. Tucker almost certainly had access to information channels that we do not. It would be useful if you could obtain copies of any such information before it's sequestered away by local law enforcement. The Savannah PD can deal with the legal side of things, but we need to know what loopholes in our procedures require nailing shut, and if anyone's gone off the reservation." She paused. "Do you have any other questions?"

He thought hard, scouring his brain for ideas, and came up blank. "No, ma'am. I've got the picture."

"Good." The call ended.

Jericho shut the phone down and slid it back into its pouch. Placing his hands flat on the table, he closed his eyes and breathed deeply, in and out. In and out.

Great. My first big case with Force Majeure is another damn murder. In Savannah, no less. A stab of dark humor went through his chest. *Well, at least it's nobody I know this time.*

On the other hand, it was in Savannah. Which meant, if he was in any way unlucky, Stephen might just find out he was there before he managed to wrap up his business and leave. That was a can of worms he was anxious to avoid dealing with all over again. Giving his ex yet another chance to get under his skin was to be avoided at all costs.

The maglev upon which he rode was a wonderful invention which, as he understood things, transported millions of people around America every day in ease and comfort. The less visible side of it was the cargo transport: maglev cars that looked like passenger cars but transported other things. Any single cargo car could make it across the US far more cheaply and quickly than could be achieved by ordinary rolling stock or even eighteen-wheeler, though the actual bulk transport was still left to the old-style trains. But smaller things, such as the mail, could definitely go via maglev, which was why the USPS and FedEx and most other carriers had had ongoing contracts with Utopia Maglev Lines for the last few years.

Moreover, the letters and packages were automatically screened for dangerous substances or explosives before being disseminated quickly and conveniently across the nation. This also meant that a letter or parcel posted anywhere in the United States would show up at its destination within twenty-four hours, night or day, any day of the week. 'Express' simply meant that there would be no more than a half-hour lag on either end of the trip.

Jericho understood all this and accepted that it was a good thing, except for one tiny but irritating problem. Specifically, the fact that his post office box had been getting inundated with mail from his ex-boyfriend ever since Jericho blocked Stephen's phone number.

Getting a PO box hadn't been his idea; he'd never rented one in the past and hadn't intended to when he moved to Utopia City. But once he took up residence in the Spire, he found out one had been opened in his name—paid for via his membership in Force Majeure—so as to keep it on the down-low that he was indeed living in the Spire. Not that this would be an immediate giveaway, of course. Many civilian employees also resided in their own apartments within the building. But every little bit helped.

Of course, he hadn't told Stephen his new postal address. The only members of his family whom Stephen even knew had disliked him from the get-go, so he'd been unlikely to get it from them. But his ex had shown a degree of cunning that drew Jericho's reluctant admiration. By addressing the mail to the apartment building (where Jericho no longer resided) with Jericho's name as the header, Stephen was forcing the post office to redirect it to Jericho's actual address, where it arrived at his doorstep with unerring accuracy.

At first, it had been just letters. He had to admit, Stephen's meticulous penmanship was vastly superior to his own half-assed chicken-scratching. The handwritten missives admitted to everything Jericho had charged him with, and pleaded for a second chance. These had ranged from cute to embarrassing, but none had swayed him. For one thing, Stephen had indeed cheated. Equally important, Jericho was with Thomas now. There was no more to be said.

When the letters didn't work, Stephen had started sending thumb drives bearing image collections and video clips. Jericho had told himself that he shouldn't view them. There was no way he would take Stephen back; *that* ship had long since sailed, struck a reef in the middle of a hurricane, and been lost with all hands. However, a lingering sense of duty compelled him to at least acknowledge the effort the man was putting into them.

The pictures weren't so bad, at first. Images of the apartment made him feel a little nostalgic. Photos of Stephen himself *in* the apartment or around Savannah, in the places they'd used to frequent, not so great. He'd had to stop looking at those because the memories brought tears to his eyes. How could Stephen have been so stupid as to throw away everything they'd had together?

Because he didn't think he'd get caught.

The videos started out cute but quickly became … problematic. After the second one, he was intensely grateful that he'd put some of his pay toward a laptop which he'd ensured wasn't tied into the Spire's insanely fast WiFi network. He didn't want *anyone* else viewing what Stephen was saying and doing to get him back. When the third and fourth ones turned out to be more of the same, he ceased viewing them past the first ten seconds.

And then there were the kooky ones. These weren't so much an attempt to bring him back by showing him what he was missing, as they were a direct effort to drive him away from Force Majeure altogether. Sometimes it was a Manila envelope full of tabloid articles, and other times a thumb drive with clips from conspiracy theorist websites, the type that used odd fonts and far too many exclamation points. Each such package was accompanied by a brief note urging him to '*look at the TRUTH about the people you're working for!*'

In retrospect, it may have been a mistake, but he'd tried to be fair. He'd looked. Each time, it had taken him mere minutes online to debunk every single extravagant claim made by each of the articles and websites that Stephen kept sending him. Then he'd send the rebuttals back to his ex-boyfriend, hoping that being faced with the *actual* truth of the matter would cause Stephen to reconsider his position.

It really, really, hadn't. If anything, it had encouraged the man. So he'd stopped responding, but he couldn't bring himself to simply throw everything out. He hadn't even opened the last two deliveries from Stephen: a letter and an ominously thick Manila envelope. He'd just dropped them into the same bottom drawer where he'd been storing everything else.

Now, he was going back to Savannah to investigate the death of a conspiracy theorist, because that was how his life was going. He just hoped he could be in and out before his ex caught wind that he was back in town.

Of course, since when has my luck been that good?

3
Partnered

The St. Louis maglev rail came in from the four points of the compass, cutting between the buildings in three of these directions and crossing the Mississippi River from the east. In terms of size and complexity, the station struck a balance between Savannah and Utopia. It had a two-level platform but failed to rival or even approach the sheer opulence and capacity of the Utopia station. For one thing, it lacked skylights, not to mention the integral food vending kiosks.

What it *did* have that the Utopia station lacked was about two square miles of parking lot, or so Jericho estimated.

He walked out of the station and had just enough time to pick out the curve of the Gateway Arch between some buildings before the radio earpiece clicked and buzzed. As he'd mentioned to Vanessa, that was the signal indicating the presence of another Force Majeure member within radio range.

"G-Man here, over," he reported.

"Tourbillon," he heard in response. "Triangulating your position. Report when the immediate area is clear, over." As always, the teleporter's voice was as androgynous as their appearance, though there was a faint but noticeable French accent.

Jericho looked around, then moved sideways out of the main flow of foot traffic. It was a point of procedure when dealing with Tourbillon to have five yards' clearance in all directions; as soon as he had that, he said, "All clear."

"Incoming," Tourbillon answered. About two seconds later, the telltale vertical swirl of darkness began to form precisely three yards to Jericho's left. Expanding rapidly to eight feet high, it looked like a giant whirlpool turned on its side but was in fact a portal to wherever Tourbillon desired it to go.

Jericho stayed where he was as the charcoal-robed hero stepped through. Pushed back as if absently, the epicene hero's cowl revealed their masked face beneath, complete with the silver circlet around their brow. The black gemstone over their forehead caught the same weak winter sunlight that gleamed off the circlet.

They nodded to Jericho in a formal yet distant fashion, which didn't surprise him; they tended to be standoffish (and occasionally judgmental) in demeanor. What did surprise him was the identity of the person who followed Tourbillon through the portal.

"What?" Jericho immediately recognized the newcomer but hadn't expected to see her here. In brutal honesty, he hadn't expected her to make it into Force Majeure, period. He tried again. "What are *you* doing here?"

"Heeyyy, G-bitch!" The blonde teenager was wearing a black domino mask and a costume of the same color that appeared to have been carefully constructed out of leather, spandex, and metal rings. It covered her in all the places she needed to be covered, plus a good bit besides, but gave the impression she'd stopped by on the way to an S&M event. "Fancy seeing you here! Whassuup?"

"She's been assigned as your partner for this mission," Tourbillon explained. What might have been a smile tugged at the corner of their mouth, then vanished again. "Feel free to test her on knowledge of official procedure while in the field. We'll be expecting a full report."

"Understood." Jericho sighed and looked at the girl. "Are you still going by Black Dragon, or have you changed your name up for something else?"

"*Hell* nope," she demurred. "I'm still the baddest with the mostest, and any motherfucker tries it on with me is gonna get their ass sliced, diced, and *fried.*"

That answered the unspoken question about her swearing habits. She was clearly as foul-mouthed as ever, which gave Jericho reason to wonder if Relentless was still holding a grudge against him.

Or maybe this is Transit's doing. I managed to keep Black Dragon in line once before, and she wants to see if I can repeat the miracle.

Whichever it was, he was sure of two things. One: he didn't need this crap. Two: what he did or didn't need along these lines didn't matter to the core members of Force Majeure.

Something else she'd said caught his attention, but Tourbillon dismissed the swirl and created another one before he could ask. "This will get you through to Savannah. The details of the case have been emailed to your phone. Watch that first step."

Jericho very much doubted that they would rate a return trip by 'Tourbillon express', which meant that he was facing hours on the maglev with Black Dragon on the way back. Specifically, a Black Dragon with the same foul mouth and low impulse control as when he'd first met her.

Yeah. Relentless is still pissed at me.

Still, he'd signed up to do the job, so there was nothing for it but to step on through.

The first red flag came when his ears popped. The second was when his leading foot came down on nothing, and he tumbled forward with wind whistling around him. His vision cleared about that time, and the first impression was verified. He was falling. Down below, several thousand feet away—but closing at a steadily increasing rate of knots—was the city of Savannah, Georgia.

Fortunately, using his powers un-enhanced was like riding a bicycle; the reflexes never entirely went away. Without even thinking about it, he used his power to reduce the effect gravity had on him to one-tenth normal, then turned his fall into a glide by spreading his arms to bring the spandex flight surfaces into play.

Once that was under control, he activated his power harness. Drawing on his ambient gravity manipulation, the shaped-gravity wings unfurled in less time than it took to think about it, converting the glide into a casual hover. Turning his head, he looked around for Black Dragon.

When he'd first encountered the girl, she'd said she was able to partially morph into a human-sized dragon. Complete transformation, she'd told him, was only possible when suffering from emotional extremes, such as fear or anger. No matter how irritating she could be, he didn't want to find out too late that her instinctive responses weren't enough to get her out of this predicament.

Angling downward, he started scanning to spot her falling body … just as a black-scaled figure flashed past, borne up by widespread batlike wings and laughing uproariously. As he watched, unsure how to react, the apparition pulled a sharp loop then came flying back down toward where he was holding steady in mid-air. It had stopped laughing but was grinning all over its muzzle; with the impressive amount of dentition it was displaying, its grin was very effective.

It was a black dragon. A *human-sized* black dragon, wearing black spandex and leather pieces held together by metal rings. Jericho only needed a few seconds to make the obvious connection. "Okay, then," he said with considerable relief; his heart rate was still elevated from the initial fright. "So, you can transform fully now. Good to know."

"Damn right." The girl's voice was about an octave deeper and quite a bit rougher when coming out of a dragon's throat, but he could still hear the sheer smugness of the teenager underneath. "El Techmeister fitted me out with a power booster, so *boom*, baby! I can go full dragon anytime I like!"

"I bet he doesn't let you call him that, though," Jericho answered absently, concentrating on separating his arms from the gravity-wings.

It was one of the minor downsides of his power harness; whenever he activated his flight ability, the shaped-gravity wings always formed over his arms. This gave him improved control over his aerial agility if he left them there, but at the same time denied him the use of his hands. Freeing them from the midnight-black pseudo-matter always felt like extracting them from thick, clinging tar: possible, but it took a little effort.

Right now, he needed his hands more than he needed the ability to pull an Immelmann turn. Wrenching his arms clear, he retrieved his phone, then tapped in the code to wake up the electronic device.

"Yeah, sure he—hey, are you callin' him to snitch on me? Shit, no, don't do *that*!" Black Dragon, her voice raised in concern, swooped closer as if to grab the phone away from him.

Tightening his lips, he held it out of her reach. "No, I'm not calling him, yet. I need to check my emails so I know where we're going, so chill."

"Oh. Right." The scaled form angled away from him then turned back. "Hey, wasn't your power cock-blocking you from flying too? I thought you could only glide."

"That was true, but then I joined Force Majeure. Take a wild guess what happened next." With a grin, he turned his attention back to the phone. His emails came up, and he opened the one from Force Majeure. The name came up—Franklin Tucker—and the address. It was a neighborhood he knew. In fact, he was sure he'd delivered pizzas to that street back in the day. Then a picture came up, and he frowned.

"Wait, wait, I know this one." Black Dragon was either suffering from constipation, or she was concentrating hard. Then the lightbulb came on over her head like a supernova. "Oh, wait. He gave *you* a fuckin' power booster too?"

"I'm pretty sure everyone gets one, but that's not important." He stared at the image on his phone. "I think I know this guy. At least, his face is familiar. But I'm damned if I know where I've seen him."

"How the hell do *you* know the guy? Did he visit Utopia City sometime recently?" Black Dragon flew around and up, craning her neck to peer over Jericho's shoulder. "Wow, how redneck's that guy? I can practically hear the banjos from here." She cast a disapproving eye over the city below. "Not really surprised, mind you. There's probably a Klan mask hangin' on every backyard line."

Jericho sighed. He'd known this would be problematic, but he hadn't expected to be regretting the situation already. Black Dragon, it seemed, was an overachiever in that way. "First, not everyone in the South is a redneck. Some folk just dress like it. Second, I'll need you to tone down on the swearing. Force Majeure requires us to present a positive image, and that sort of thing won't cut it. And third ... this is my hometown. So cool it, okay?"

Not very much to his surprise, Black Dragon had been burring up as he spoke—it was straightforward enough to interpret draconic irritation—but the look of shock as he dropped the last bombshell was also clearly visible. "Ah. Uh. Crap. Sorry?"

Rubbing the back of his neck, Jericho sighed again. "It's okay. Just ... do me a favor and don't make a habit of saying things like that. And I meant it about the swearing. Three strikes and you might as well get on the maglev back to Utopia. This is my town. Folks *know* me here. Give them the wrong impression, and you'll mess it up for me *and* Force Majeure in this town. If that happens, I won't need to drop a dime on you to the Technologist. You'll be in enough trouble without it."

"Yeah, okay, jeez," growled Black Dragon, making a surrender motion with her forepaws. The razor-sharp claws he remembered from their first meeting were retracted, which was a good thing. It seemed her power was capable of more restraint than she was. "No fuckin' swearing while I'm talking to your cop friends."

Jericho nodded. "Thank you. I appreciate the effort." He put the phone away then looked over the city below them. If the river was *there*, then … "Okay, it's this way." Angling around, he swooped away to the northwest. The sooner he got this over and done with, the sooner he'd be able to get back to Utopia.

Grumbling just loudly enough for him to hear, Black Dragon stretched out her wings and followed along.

4
Investigation

From the air, it was easy to pick out the exact address. Two police cars and an ambulance sat outside with their bubblegum lights flashing away steadily, plus an unmarked sedan with a detachable light on top. Police tape had already been strung around the front of the house. Jericho could see civilians being questioned by uniformed officers, but the only one inside the tape was a woman with a child in her arms.

The ambulance pulled away as they came in for a landing in the middle of the street. Allowing the grav-wings to dissipate, Jericho watched Black Dragon as the scales receded and her draconic features reverted to a regular human aspect.

The teenage girl stood before him in less than a minute, smirking broadly. Then she leaned in with her hand alongside her mouth as if passing on a secret. To her credit, she even lowered her voice as she did it. "Uh, not to diss your hometown, G, but this does kind of look like redneck central. I swear, I counted four cars up on blocks on this street alone."

"Yes, well, stereotypes exist for a reason." He grimaced, keeping his voice down as well. "Sometimes they're even true. But just remember, one word out of place, and these people will lock down faster than an oyster at low tide. And they asked for me by name, so that's got to mean something."

"Yeah, it means you're the only superhero they know the name of." But she kept her voice down for that as well, so the plainclothes detective who'd just ducked under the police tape didn't hear. Or if he had, he didn't show any signs of it.

"Detective Villanova," Jericho said with a warm smile, reaching out to shake the man's hand. Raul Villanova was the closest he had to a regular contact with the Savannah PD, which made him wonder about the coincidence. "Did you put in the request to get me here? Because I do need to see the crime scene, but you know my powers don't really work that way." Though, thinking about it, he knew some people in the UCPD forensics department who could probably blow this case wide open, if they could make time in their busy schedules.

"Not exactly." Villanova had black hair and a permanent tan, along with a brilliant smile of his own. "When I heard that Force Majeure had okayed the request, I pulled strings and got myself put on the case. After all, Savannah PD doesn't have an official liaison with Force Majeure." Jericho could hear the unspoken *yet* hanging in the air as the charm came out in full force, directed at both of them in equal measure. "And who's the young lady?"

As far as Jericho knew, Villanova was a good cop. He liked the guy, but only as a friend. With his open nature, average height, and slender build, the detective didn't really tick any of Jericho's boxes. They'd consulted on cases before; or rather, Villanova had consulted with him. He hadn't really been able to help that much, but the detective had kept calling on him. It wasn't until Luke had explained that Villanova was gay that the penny finally dropped.

'Gordoning' was the practice of passing on information to a superhero to help solve a crime; to be Gordoned was the ultimate sign of trust between law enforcement and heroes. Villanova, however, had been showing all the signs of 'Trevoring' him. The difference between Gordoning and Trevoring was that with Trevoring, solving the crime was less important than spending quality time with the superhero, with the ultimate aim of getting into their pants. Luke's revelation had cleared the air in that regard, though Jericho still didn't know whether to be flattered, amused, or annoyed.

"I'm Black Dragon," the girl said, stepping forward and looking Villanova in the eye. "So, what do we got?"

Villanova glanced at Jericho, who raised his eyebrows and tilted his head slightly toward Black Dragon. The teenager was irritating as hell when she wanted to be and more than a little immature, but he was *damned* if he would let anyone treat her like she was invisible just because she was a girl.

"Oh, uh, right," the detective said, rallying gamely. "So, male vic, forty-seven years of age. His name's Franklin Tucker; our best guess at the cause of death is a single GSW to the back of the head, through-and-through. We're going with a nine-millimeter for the moment. There's no sign of the murder weapon, though the bullet was extracted from the vic's computer monitor. It didn't suffer much deformation, so if the gun's on file …" He trailed off with a shrug. Jericho knew as well as he did that the chance of it being from a firearm of interest was minimal to zero.

"So, he was shot in the back of the head while sitting at his computer," Jericho clarified. "Which means that he either knew his killer, or was really zoning out when it happened."

Black Dragon snickered, and he mentally grimaced. He was almost sure that he knew what she thought was funny—*the guy was probably watching porn*—but this was neither the time nor the place for that sort of joke to come out. *Any* time was the wrong time, really. The man probably hadn't even been dead an hour.

He cleared his throat. "We were told there was a significant other and a child. I'm surprised they're still alive. Someone who can cold-bloodedly put a bullet through someone's head from behind isn't going to balk at killing a witness."

"Oh, they weren't in the house at the time," Villanova explained. "Apparently, he'd been arguing with her over something, bad enough that she's been living at her sister's and only coming over to cook for him occasionally."

"Ooh," Black Dragon piped up. "Maybe *she* popped that cap in his ass. What were they arguing about? 'Cause if she caught him seeing another woman, I can totally see her doing it."

Villanova shook his head. "We looked at that, and it doesn't fit. Our best estimate of the time of death is about five minutes before she showed up. Neighbors report hearing a gunshot about then, but nobody knew where it came from. Her sister gave her a lift, which also serves as her alibi."

"G-Man!" called a voice. Jericho looked around to see the woman approaching them, holding the infant with one arm as she let the police tape drop down behind her. "I didn't think you'd come! You've got to help us, please! You've got to find out who killed my Franklin!"

Again, he was struck with a strong sense of *déjà vu*. Her face was somehow familiar to him, but he wasn't sure where he knew her from. About ten years older than him, she was a little pudgy, with bleached blonde hair showing dark roots. Her mascara was smudged to hell and gone, but she didn't notice, continually dabbing at tear-swollen eyes with a tissue that had definitely seen better days. The kid, a little boy, looked to be not much more than a year old. Recalling the truncated briefing, Jericho dredged up a name. "Ma'am, I reckon you'd be Chantelle Green?"

She nodded, then blew her nose with the same tissue. He hoped she'd change it out before she wiped her eyes again.

"Yes, that's me. Can y'all find out who done this?" Her gaze fastened hopefully onto Jericho and Black Dragon, flicking from one to the other.

A little self-consciously, Jericho cleared his throat. "I'll do my best, ma'am, though I haven't seen the crime scene yet. Also, my powers don't really lend themselves to forensic investigation."

"Mine do," Black Dragon put in unexpectedly. The front of her face morphed and pushed outward, black scales emerging from the skin. In another moment, she sported a reptilian muzzle which bore an abundance of needle-sharp teeth, as well as a prominent pair of slitted nostrils.

Chantelle Green let out a strangled yelp and took a step back, and even Villanova paled noticeably. Black Dragon let out a sigh, as if this kind of reaction was not unknown to her, though Jericho strongly suspected her of deliberately setting out to evoke just such a response. She struck him as someone who'd do that sort of thing.

"I'm *saying* that I can give the crime scene a good sniff an' tell you who was there if you want," she explained patiently. To demonstrate, she flared her nostrils wide and inhaled deeply.

"Yeah, th-that might be of some assistance," the detective agreed. "Come on, follow me." Lifting the police tape, he let them duck through then led the way into the house. Jericho noticed that the bereaved woman didn't follow them inside.

The room they ended up in had clearly been a spare bedroom at one time before it had been refitted as the luckless Franklin's computer study.

The body had been removed, but the gory spatter all over the ruined monitor and keyboard made it abundantly clear where the crime had happened.

Fortunately, the day was cool, and the blood hadn't been sitting long enough to really start to smell, but it was still sufficient to flash him back to that night in the Oaklands when he'd entered the shared apartment to find that Bobbi and Luke had been brutally murdered while he'd been out and about. He closed his eyes and turned his head away, pressing his lips together and breathing out through his nostrils. Wrapping his arms around himself, he barely managed to bring the knuckles of his left hand up to his lips in a vague imitation of a thinking pose.

Black Dragon either didn't notice his distress or didn't care. Pushing his power through his G-sense, Jericho 'watched' her take a few steps into the room. Raising her muzzle, she sniffed loudly. "Okay, got th' gun smell," she said. "Couldn't smell it in the rest of the house, but that's prob'ly because everyone's been walkin' around so much." She paused. "Huh."

"Huh?" asked Villanova. "What's 'huh'?"

Jericho made himself take a breath in through his mouth, trying not to register the coppery smell of the blood. If he wimped out every time he ran into blood at a crime scene, it would severely hamper his ability to pull his own weight in the team. Forcing his eyes open again, he did his best to straighten up and appear interested and untroubled.

"Shooter was a woman, and there was another one along with her," announced Black Dragon, then sniffed again. "I didn't see any lady cops on site, so we got two chicks in the picture, over an' above Miss Savannah Two Thousand Fourteen out there."

"Wait, two *women*?" Villanova looked and sounded startled, but he was scribbling in his notepad as fast as his pen could move. "Can you verify that?"

Black Dragon gave him an irritated look. "Yeah, soon as my nose c'n take pictures, sure thing. Until then, you're just gonna hafta take my word for it."

"Okay, okay, keep your hair on." Villanova shook his head. "Jesus. This is getting complicated. Any idea of how they got in and out?"

"Not through the window," Jericho said, not wanting to sound totally useless. The sole window was covered with a heavy blind, but he could tell the glass was intact behind it. Stepping over to it, he pulled the blind out a little to confirm his supposition. "Looks like it was painted shut years ago."

Black Dragon stepped out into the hallway, sniffing sporadically. "Yeah, no, they came this way …"

This was the first time Jericho had actually watched her walking, and he frowned as he saw her moving awkwardly, like she had a cramp. "Uh, you okay?"

She turned her head and glared at him. "What?"

"Are you okay?" he asked again. "You're walking … I dunno, funny, I guess."

"*You're* walking funny," she retorted. "I'm fine. You do your thing; I'll do mine." She inhaled again, deeply. "Yeah, definitely this way ... huh."

Moving back and forth, she kept testing the air, then led the way down the corridor. Jericho opted to stay behind in the room, determined to push his way past the discomfort.

"You keep saying 'huh', but you keep failing to explain," Villanova said, following her. Jericho could hear the pen still scratching across the pad.

"Hey, it's my nose. I'm allowed to say 'huh' if I want," retorted Black Dragon. Jericho was irritated at her lack of respect, but Villanova seemed to be taking it in his stride. Besides, he'd just found what Ms. Colburn had tasked him to locate.

On the wall, alongside the computer desk, was a giant corkboard *covered* in material. Headlines, photos, news clippings, and pencil drawings had dates and locations appended, with strings of three different colors forming an intricate webwork between them. It was a genuinely magnificent example of a classic conspiracy theory diagram. Jericho was forced to admit that this took everything Stephen had ever sent him, beat it like a red-headed stepchild, and sent it crying home to Mama.

Taking his phone out, he took several photos, one of the entire display before zooming in on each section to pick out the finer details. He wanted to take a closer look at some of the more bizarre sections but feared he'd be sucked into the rabbit hole if he followed any of those colored strings too far. So instead, he put his phone away and closed his eyes again. Letting his G-sense spread out and permeate the walls of the room, he *felt* for anything out of place.

At first there was nothing, but then he felt a tiny spark of denser mass where there shouldn't be one. Opening his eyes, he looked to where his power was indicating: a skirting board, identical to any other. After making sure he wasn't stepping in any blood-spatter, he moved closer and crouched to look more closely at it. There was nothing that he could see. No marks at all.

"—*telling* you, they dusted the back door handle, and nobody had touched it." That was Villanova, sounding exasperated. This was a familiar feeling with Jericho when it came to Black Dragon.

"And I'm tellin' *you* that the scents go up to the back door, an' trail off straight after," Black Dragon snapped back. "So you can take that '*nobody touched it*' BS an' shove it—"

"Detective Villanova!" Jericho called out hastily. "I think I found something!"

Fortunately, the girl took the hint. When Villanova hurried back into the room, she was trailing along with a sullen air and a face that was fully human again. Her expression was only just short of actual rebellion, but she wasn't talking anymore. When she saw him watching, she straightened up and almost marched toward him, as if daring him to make a comment about her gait.

"What is it?" asked the detective. "What have you found?"

Jericho pointed at the skirting board. "There's something behind there. Small and metallic. It's not connected to any wiring."

Villanova raised his eyebrows. "And you thought you said your powers wouldn't be useful." He stepped closer to the wall and knelt down. "Where, exactly?"

"Put your hand on the wall," Jericho instructed him. "Move it left a few inches. Down to floor level. Right there. It's just inside the wall."

"Okay, then." Villanova pulled out a multitool, opened a large blade from it, then carefully wriggled the tip down behind the skirting board. After a few creaks and cracks, a previously invisible division appeared, then an entire section slid out with almost soundless ease. Villanova leaned down and investigated the space thus revealed with his phone in hand, then took a photo. "Whoa, jackpot ... I think." Pulling on a glove, he reached in and retrieved two items. When he turned around, Jericho could see he held a thumb drive and a folded piece of notepaper.

"Well, come on, what's on them?" demanded Black Dragon, miraculously overcoming her snit with both men. "Give with the deets!"

Meticulously, Villanova dropped the drive into an evidence baggie. Then he unfolded the notepaper, careful not to tear it. "It's ... a list of email addresses," he said, frowning. "That's interesting, but it doesn't exactly tell us what they're for."

"Yeah, that's probably what the drive is all about," Jericho said.

"Probably. Computer guys will get this." Refolding the paper, Villanova dropped it into the baggie with the drive and sealed it in.

"Oh, come *on*," Black Dragon said, pointing at the computer. "Don't be a pussy. Plug it in, and let's see what's on that bad boy."

"Dragon, dial it back a notch," Jericho said curtly. His experience with the girl had left him painfully aware that politeness rarely worked. "For one thing, that monitor is ruined. For another, we have no idea what's on the drive. It might be a virus that wrecks any system except one that's set up to deal with it."

"Exactly." Villanova tapped the baggie. "Though I think one of the email addresses belongs to a boxer or something similar. It's got 'slammer' in the name, anyway."

"It takes all types," Jericho acknowledged. He took a deep breath, keeping his eyes averted from the blood spray on the wall and monitor, and dusted his hands off. "Well, I think that's us done here. If there's anything on the drive or computer that impacts Force Majeure, I'd appreciate it if you could forward it to us once you've had it checked out."

"I can do that," Villanova confirmed. "Now that we know for sure there were two women and they went out the back door, we'll be canvassing the neighbors behind the house to see if anyone saw anything. And we definitely wouldn't have found the other stuff if you hadn't pointed it out."

"Yeah, well, we're here to help." Inside, belying his casual façade, Jericho felt a swell of pride. This was one of the main reasons he enjoyed being a superhero. Helping others, making the world a better place, was what it was all about. He knew he wasn't always going to succeed, but he was damn well going to keep trying.

I can't wait to tell Thomas about this one. Minus all the gory bits, of course.

5
Atonement

Chantelle looked around as the two superheroes made their way out of the house. Shifting little Richie on her hip, she looked pleadingly at the officer who was taking her statement, asking her the same damn questions over and over, like he was looking for a different answer. "Can I go talk to 'em before they take off?" she asked.

He sighed and closed his notebook. "Sure thing. Go ahead. I'll be right here."

"Thanks." She hurried over to where the heroes were ducking under the police tape. "Did you find out who killed him?" she asked urgently. "Are you fixin' to arrest 'em?"

"Not right at this moment, ma'am," G-Man said, but in a way that gave her hope. "We spoke to Detective Villanova, and he's got some promising leads. Rest assured, whoever did this will be behind bars really soon. I've worked with these officers before, and they're the best in the country." Somehow she doubted that last qualifier, but he was plainly trying to make her feel better, and she appreciated the effort.

"Oh, good." She dabbed at her eyes with a fresh tissue. "Do y'all know why I wasn't here?" She lowered her voice and glanced around. "Why I was a-fussin' an' a-fightin' with Franklin?" This would be the hard part, but she had to tell *someone*, and he was one of the people she'd sinned against. Making it right with the folks she'd wronged was a big part of her pastor's sermons in church.

G-Man tilted his head. "I'm afraid I have no idea, ma'am," he said. "That there's your business, not mine."

"No, no, if the lady wants to talk about it, I'm listenin'." Chantelle didn't know who the teenage girl was, except that she could make her face look like something out of a horror movie, but she seemed to be normal again now. Also, it sounded like she really wanted to know.

"Thank you kindly, honeychild." Chantelle gave the girl a grateful smile, then took a deep breath. This was going to be painful to talk about. "Y'all gotta know this. I ain't a good person."

"You can't judge yourself like that," G-Man said, predictably enough. "We've all done stuff—"

"Not like this, I bet," Chantelle said, cutting him off. She looked at him and the girl both. Interestingly, the teenager didn't try to chip in with her own emo bullshit. She just watched Chantelle thoughtfully. Patiently.

"I'm sorry for making assumptions." G-Man's tone was apologetic. "Go ahead; we're listening."

That was a first for her, having a superhero apologize for saying the wrong thing. Hell, this was the first time she'd ever gotten to *talk* to a superhero, even Pickup. But she had stuff to say, so she got back to it. "Like I said, I ain't a good person. Time was, I'd look at a colored person an' think they weren't nothing." She nodded toward G-Man. "When I found out you were, you know, like *that* …" Her voice trailed off. Even now, with all her resolve, she just couldn't say the damn word.

"Gay, you mean?" He had no problem at all with it. And he didn't even sound angry. Just … disappointed.

"Yeah …" She tried again. "Gay. Yeah. When I found that out, me an' Franklin, we started makin' jokes about you. Anytime you were on the news, we'd change the channel. You weren't a *real* superhero, we told each other. Real superheroes don't suck other men's dicks." Even thinking about the way she'd been made her cringe a little bit inside.

The girl in the domino mask half-raised her hand. "Hey, what about—"

"Don't even go there!" snapped G-Man; to her credit, the girl stopped talking, though she gave him a filthy look. He ignored it as he turned back to Chantelle. "I'm sorry. I believe you were trying to tell us something before you were so rudely interrupted?"

Richie started fussing, so Chantelle bounced him on her hip a couple of times to settle him. That gave her time to get her composure back. "Yeah, so that's how we were until last year when that Hansen boy got hisself kilt out yonder in that Utopia City place all you superheroes live in. See, I wouldn't'a known him from Adam, but I'd met him earlier that day when he saved li'l Richmond here from fallin' under th' maglev."

G-Man caught his breath as if taken by surprise. He seemed to swallow hard before clearing his throat. "So … that changed things?"

"Well, not at first." She had to be honest, after all. Pastor Timothy was very much in favor of honesty. "To start with, I tried to put it out of my head. A body don't like to think they're wrong about stuff, you know?"

The rueful huff from G-Man sounded altogether too genuine. "Oh, trust me. I know *that* story from go to whoa. Been there too many times."

Chantelle nodded gratefully. *He gets it.* "Yeah, but when I saw the news about him gittin' kilt tryin' to save that white girl, it got thrown in my face all of a piece. Like everythin' I ever thought about colored folk was wrong. And then I started wonderin', if I was wrong about that, what else was I wrong about? There's a piece in the Bible about scales bein' lifted from a body's eyes, an' that's what it felt like. Seein' clearly for the first time." It was a relief to finally say it all and not have folk look at her like she was addled.

With a smirk on her face, the teenage girl mumbled a line from a song Chantelle knew vaguely, something to do with being able to see clearly because the rain was gone.

G-Man cleared his throat again and gave an exasperated sigh. "Sorry about that. Black Dragon and I are overdue for a discussion on what's appropriate to say at times like this. That's not one of those things." Stepping forward, he lowered his voice sympathetically. "But I appreciate you sharing that with us. It gives me hope for people to be more tolerant of others in future."

Black Dragon, for her part, treated him to a condescending sneer but didn't say anything.

"No, there's more," Chantelle said. In truth, she wasn't even annoyed at the girl. Cracking a joke about what she'd said was better than making comments behind her back. "I tried to talk to Franklin about what I'd figured out, but he wouldn't listen to me. It was like headbuttin' a brick wall. Between the way he was an' his hate-on for Force Majeure, he wouldn't pay me no mind nohow. So, we started arguin' an' fussin' an' fightin', an' I moved out to my sister's. An' that's where we were 'til today."

"Today? What happened today?" G-Man had gone from polite to interested, and even Black Dragon was paying attention again now.

Chantelle knew precisely what they were thinking: that she was about to reveal why Franklin was murdered. But she didn't share their optimism. It just plumb didn't add up. "I wasn't gonna be comin' over, but Franklin called me. He was all excited about how he'd finally gotten the goods on Force Majeure and how he was fixin' to bring 'em down for good an' all. He wanted me to see it; that's how het up he was."

G-Man raised his eyebrows, a visible movement even behind the helmet eyeholes, while Black Dragon leaned forward with laser-focused interest. Belatedly, Chantelle recalled that the two superheroes in front of her were part of Force Majeure, the same team Franklin had been fixing to eighty-six.

"I saw the corkboard," G-Man noted. "Was it something on there that was going to bring us down? Because I really didn't see anything worth worrying about." He didn't even sound blustery. It was a simple, matter-of-fact statement.

"No, I reckon he hadn't had time to update it," Chantelle said. She couldn't be certain-sure, of course, but it hadn't *looked* like there was anything new on the board. "Since he started this whole thing, he's gone all-in on learning encryption an' decryption an' stuff, an' he got pretty good. There's all sorts of resources online for a body who don't mind spendin' a lot of time an' a little money to learn how to do that sorta thing. From what he was sayin', there was some new project, a thing one of his online buddies had sent to him so's he could look into it. And sometime between that gettin' done an' me showin' up, someone done shot him."

"So, wait." Black Dragon's voice was full of sarcasm. "He had a coded file that he thought would embarrass Force Majeure, and he told you that he'd cracked it? That sort of thing gets around. Five gets you ten that if he told you, he told other people. More than a few people would love to see us go down hard, and I figure some of them wouldn't hesitate to do something like this just so they're the only ones with their hands on that information."

Chantelle was nowhere near an expert at that sort of thing, but it sounded about right, and she figured the girl knew what she was talking about. "I reckon you're right," she conceded. "I wish he'd never gotten into all of that." She recalled that it had started with a stupid pistol and Franklin's goddamn stubborn insistence that he had a right to carry it on the maglev. *Now look where it got him.* "I should oughta have done more."

"You couldn't have known," G-Man assured her. "There's a lesson it took me a while to learn, but it's stood me in good stead ever since I lost my best friend. Sometimes, it really isn't your fault. Simple as that."

She stared at him as if he'd just started speaking Latin, or one of those other old languages that nobody knew anymore. "But ... I should've been able to do *something.* I didn't even *try.*"

"Because you didn't know." He put his hand on her shoulder. What she could see of his expression below the mask was pure compassion. "If you'd known what was going to happen and still didn't do anything, that would've been your fault. But you *didn't* know. You couldn't. Which means you're not to blame. Simple as that."

"Oh." This was almost as crazy a brain-twister as when she'd first had her epiphany about colored folk. It knocked what she'd been thinking just thirty seconds ago all cattywampus, but the worst bit was, *it made sense.* Which in turn meant that before, she'd been thinking stuff that was wrong.

Well, it's not like it's the first time.

Part of her still wanted to beat herself up for not being better, not being perfect, not having done *something* to save Franklin, but G-Man's words pushed back against that. She shook her head, wondering how she could've been such an idiot.

"You okay?" G-Man asked quietly.

She pulled a new tissue out of her bag and blew her nose. "No," she admitted. "But I think I'm gonna be. Thank you kindly."

For listening, she meant. For being there and not calling her crazy. And for accepting what she'd had to say.

G-Man smiled tightly. She got the impression he'd heard everything she hadn't said. "No, Ms. Green. Thank *you.*" He turned to Black Dragon. "I think we're done here. Let's go."

"All-*righty!*" she declared. "Time to up, up and away!"

He snorted and shook his head. "Whatever floats your boat." Taking a couple of steps away, he held his arms out from his body. Chantelle watched as long dark wing-shapes formed out of nothing, spreading out to a span of twenty feet in just a few seconds.

At the same time, the teenage girl went through a metamorphosis of her own, though much more dramatic. Shiny black scales came out of nowhere, and her body started twisting and changing. By the time she was finished, she had lots of teeth, a massive pair of wings, and a long whippy tail. Chantelle hadn't been paying attention when the girl had landed and changed, but she sure as shootin' was now.

Richie pointed at the dragon-girl as she flapped her wings to get airborne—G-Man was already fifty feet up, hovering as he waited for Black

Dragon to take off—and gurgled happily. Chantelle still thought the girl looked like something out of a nightmare, though she wasn't fixing to say so out loud.

They were disappearing over the rooftops when that nice Detective Villanova stepped up alongside her. "Did they … did they just … *leave*?" He sounded a little put out.

"Looks like it," she said.

"Did they say anything about coming back?"

She shook her head. "No, sir. G-Man said they were done here."

"Ah." He let out what may have been a sigh before he turned and looked at her. "Did it help you, calling them in?"

She nodded absently. "Yeah. I think it did." There was a lightness in her chest that hadn't been there before.

It turned out confession really was good for the soul. That was another thing Pastor Timothy had gotten right.

6
Revelation

Black Dragon flew up alongside Jericho as they soared over the Savannah skyline toward the T-intersection of the two gleaming cylindrical maglev rails—north-south and east-west—that marked out the local station. "So, that Villanova guy. How long the two of you been bangin'?"

"What?" He turned to stare at her. "We've *never* … wait. You can tell he's gay?"

"Well, *duh*." She made a rude noise with her lips. Which, considering her current shape, was impressive. "He was fuckin' you with his eyes from the moment we walked up. You didn't know he was into guys?"

"I knew." Jericho sighed, trying to slide past the memory of Luke telling him just that. "He was Trevoring me for about a year before I joined Force Majeure, but I was already in a relationship." Which was the truth, but not necessarily *all* of it. "Anyway, I'm pretty sure none of that's any kind of a fit topic for conversation."

"Dude," she said. "Dude. Dude. *Duuuuude*. What happens in the phone box *stays* in the phone box. Even I know that. I mean, I mighta got a bit drunk and partied hard last night, but the public doesn't ever need to know anything about that. You can only really celebrate joining Force Majeure once, you know."

"What, you joined *yesterday*?" He'd known she was new to the team, but not *that* new. Also, the whole underage drinking thing was technically illegal. On the other hand, while he'd never really indulged until his twenty-first birthday (which had been a night for *several* firsts), it was something he'd seen more than once and didn't have a particular problem with. So long as folks were sensible about it and nobody got hurt, it wasn't something to get all frazzled over.

"Nah, nah," she laughed, sculling through the air with her oversized wings. "Joined a week ago, came back to pick up my power harness from el Techno-dude. Worked like a dream, and I didn't feel like headin' back to my empty apartment, so me an' Relentless got down an' partied like it was twenty ninety-nine."

"You … and Relentless." He tried to make his comment sound unconcerned, but all he could hear was the voice of Force Majeure's leader, the last time they'd spoken face-to-face. *I just like to fuck any new recruits that are interested.*

At the time, he'd made the automatic assumption that Relentless only made the offer to those recruits who were of age. It appeared he'd been in error.

He didn't want to think about it, but tiny details kept cropping up in his mind, like the odd hitch to her step as she walked through the house. Initially, he'd thought she might've exercised or sparred too hard and pulled something. Now, he fervently hoped his current assumption was wrong and it was what he'd assumed at first. Even if Black Dragon was eighteen, as she claimed, Relentless had to be twice her age, *and* he was her superior in the team, *and* he'd gotten her drunk. There were so many wrong things with that situation that he'd have to take a run-up to cover them all.

"Ooooh, *fuck* yeah," she purred, a very odd sound to hear coming out of a dragon's throat. "That man is *all* man; I'll tell you that for free."

And there went any chance of pretending nothing had happened. "Uh … you know that kind of thing violates several ethics statutes, right? Just the fact that he's the boss is bad enough without bringing the drinking into it."

"What the hell do I care?" she asked snidely. "You're just pissed because I've had that, and the big guy doesn't swing your way." She let out a single brief cackle of laughter. "You're butt-hurt because you're *not* butt-hurt."

It took Jericho a second to figure out what she meant, then he wanted to facepalm. Worse, she was wrong in every way a person could be, and didn't even know it. Relentless *had* made a advance, but Jericho had turned him down … which was almost certainly *why* that was the last time they'd spoken face-to-face.

Okay, so Black Dragon had sex with Relentless. Now, what am I supposed to do about it?

It was a simple question, but any potential answers were likely to be insanely complicated, if not outright impossible to implement. Confronting Relentless directly would accomplish nothing, and Jericho doubted going over his head to the civilian leadership of Utopia would do much better. Even ignoring Force Majeure's de facto position of power within the city, Relentless was the leader of Force Majeure and one of *the* major players in the Enabled scene, both within the US and abroad. He was bulletproof, in more ways than one.

Force Majeure owned the entire maglev network, and *sold* electricity to the American power grid. Jericho was willing to bet Relentless had more favors banked up with the movers and shakers of American politics than any other two people. So, taking it to the federal authorities probably wouldn't work either. Even if someone were willing to accept the case, it would likely vanish into legal limbo, never to be heard from again. Whatever scandal it generated would be gone by the beginning of the next news cycle.

With a sinking feeling, he recognized the symptoms of incipient surrender within himself. Already, part of his brain was manufacturing the rationalization that it was all consensual and nobody was being harmed (*except morally*, he insisted to himself). Nobody would be willing to testify, and all he had was his own experience and the reported hearsay from Black Dragon, which she could flat-out deny at any time.

His choices, as he saw them, were simple. He could quit Force Majeure in protest and probably achieve nothing except ruin his chances of being taken seriously as a superhero (and *there* was the self-serving impulse, right on cue). Or he could stay on and use the organization's resources to help far more people than he could as a solo vigilante while doing his best to ignore his boss' shenanigans with the new recruits.

Trying to determine how to ease his conscience over the matter, he reminded himself that Relentless wasn't actively forcing himself on the recruits. While pissed at the rejection he got from Jericho, the head of Force Majeure had merely told him to leave (albeit *much* more forcefully than that). The offer of a place on the team had been honored, and apart from Independence sneering at him (which was a pre-existing situation), Jericho's treatment had been entirely equitable from all concerned. It was like the miscommunication had never happened, except that he hadn't seen or spoken to Relentless since.

In the grand scheme of things, Relentless' actions were immoral, unethical, and almost certainly illegal, but were also likely to be ignored or dismissed by everyone in a position to do something about them. Things Jericho could do something about happened every day of the week; this wasn't one of them. He wanted to push harder and force attention to the issue, but there was the old saying about *'shitting in one hand and wishing in the other'* to consider.

A piece of Luke's wisdom drifted across the back of his mind: *Cuz, sometimes ya gotta pick your fights. 'Cause if ya don't, your fights will sure as hell pick you.*

It was a bitter pill to swallow, and he was still working on it when his phone rang, the Bluetooth earpiece rendering it as a steady series of chimes in his ear. With a grimace, he pulled to a hover so that he could work his arm out of the right-hand grav-wing and press the clicker up under the rim of his helmet, thus allowing the earpiece to accept the call.

A recorded message began to play: **"This is a redirected call from ..."**

It could only be from his regular phone, still sitting in his apartment back in the Spire, so he hit the clicker again to jump to the call. "Hello?"

"Hey, boy. You near a TV?" It was his uncle Leroy: Luke's father, and a good man in a tight spot.

"Not right this second. Why?" While he and Leroy tried to keep in touch, especially since Luke's passing, they'd never made a practice of calling each other out of the blue like this. Though, if he was being honest with himself, he welcomed the distraction.

"Somethin' you're gonna wanna see. There's a building on fire. It's where you useta be when you were still livin' in Savannah. Goin' up like the Fourth of July."

He paused, staring at nothing. "I ... *what* again, now?" The information came from so far out in left field from what he'd just been thinking that he had to mentally change gears to comprehend it. "On fire? The apartment building?"

Oh crap. Stephen's going to be devastated.

Just because he'd dumped his ex-boyfriend for persistent and repeated infidelity didn't mean he wanted to see the guy lose everything. The apartment and contents were comprehensively insured, but it would still be a tremendous blow.

"Yeah." Leroy's tone was heavy. "It's lookin' bad. Dunno if everyone got out. They say there's folks on the roof."

"Okay, thanks. I appreciate it." Jericho clicked the switch to end the call. Turning his head, he tried to spot the plume of smoke … and there it was, right where he'd thought it would be. "Dragon, how are you against fire?"

"I'm immune to it; why?" She pulled a loop. "Did you want something set on fire? I can do that, too." By way of demonstration, she blew a long plume of flame from her nostrils.

He stared briefly, then got his reactions back under control. "Right. We've got a building fire to go to, and people to save. You up for it?"

She flared her wings. "Oh, hell to the yeah! Let's go show these country hicks how it's *done!*"

Jericho stifled a sigh as he spread his 'wings and made his best speed toward the distant plume. He'd bring her around, eventually.

But right now, it was time to go be a hero.

7
Rescue

Leroy hadn't been kidding. By the time they got on site, the apartment building was ablaze from top to bottom. Flames were coming out of most of the windows, and there were indeed people trapped on the roof. He didn't know why they weren't using the fire escape, and there really wasn't time to find out. Fire tenders were pulling onto the site, but the landscaping around the building was hampering the ladder trucks in their efforts to get close enough.

Plan B it is, then. Half and half.

"How many people can you carry at once?" he called out to Black Dragon as they neared the building.

Almost instinctively, his eyes flicked to Stephen's parking space. It was empty, which was a blessing. Dealing with this and Stephen's crap all at the same time was the *last* thing he wanted, right now.

He's probably heard I'm attending the Tucker murder, and he's gone there to try to intercept me. Hopefully, we'll be done and gone by the time he gets back.

"One big kid, or two little ones," she yelled back. "Flying at this size isn't exactly easy!"

That was the problem with being a superhero that nobody ever talked about. Sure, it was possible to do amazing things, but physics was always lurking in the background, and Murphy claimed his due whenever he could.

Great. Okay. Let's hope Plan C works, because I'm running out of plans.

"Right then, we got this. Follow my lead." Hoping he sounded more confident than he felt, he arrowed toward the rooftop, pulling his arms from the grav-wings.

Once they were free, he delved into two of his belt pouches. One held nose filters, which he pushed into place in his nostrils. The other had a pair of HUD goggles, which he usually only wore in Utopia, but would serve to protect his eyes from the smoke. Made to fit over the eyeholes of his helmet, they had a strap that would lock into a corresponding groove running around the back of the headpiece.

Over the crackling of the flames and the warbling of the sirens, he could hear the frantic refugees calling for help. Their hands reached out to him, visible even through the heat distortion of the fire and the billowing smoke. A rough tally put it at fifteen to twenty people. Even with Black Dragon, this was going to be touch and go.

Taking a deep breath, he swooped through the wave of heat and curtain of smoke that surrounded the building. He didn't land immediately; Force Majeure training films had portrayed would-be flying rescuers being overwhelmed by everyone trying to grab them at once. That sort of hysteria had led to tragedy on more than one occasion.

"All y'all, listen up!" he shouted, expending some of his precious oxygen. "Women and children first! Women and children first!" Shutting his mouth, he dragged air in through the nose filters. They weren't perfect—they never were—but the amount of smoke that made it in was minimal.

Black Dragon was hovering over the crowd, her wings blowing smoke and ash around and making it even harder to see. Jericho didn't know if she'd seen the same training films as he had or if she was just naturally cautious in situations like this. Either way, the smoke and ash aside, she was doing the right thing.

It appeared they'd heard him, as several women came forward. Two were holding young children; he thought he recognized them from his time in the apartment block. Firmly, he put that thought away. Right now, he had to get it right. First time and every time.

Dropping to the rooftop, he gestured them over, wary of a rush. Only the women came to him, so he looked up at Black Dragon and waved her down. Reaching out to the two women and their children, he reduced their effective weight to one-tenth normal apiece.

He could affect a single object of up to two tons without his harness to boost his powers, for a maximum duration of about five minutes. His harness extended the mass limit to four tons, and pushed the duration to nearly ten minutes. However, the time interval was significantly reduced if there were multiple recipients, dramatically so if they left his immediate vicinity and moved in different directions once he'd placed the effect on them.

"Take them," he said to Black Dragon, pushing them toward her. "Go!"

"But I—" protested the dragon girl.

Caught in the middle of forcing his nose filters to deliver more clean oxygen to his lungs, Jericho didn't have the air to shout. He opened his mouth to inhale, and immediately regretted it. The air was hot and ashy, and the smoke stung his breathing passages all the way down to the bottom of his lungs. But he took it in anyway, then bellowed, "*Take them!*"

Turning toward the other women and suppressing the cough that followed, he gritted his teeth and dragged more air in through his nostrils. It wasn't enough. It would never be enough.

Out of the corner of his eye, his vision distorted by the goggles, he saw Black Dragon enfold the women with her forelimbs and fight her way into the air. Jericho's estimate was that two adults and two children made up roughly the mass of ten kids; she'd have trouble, but she could make it work. Briefly, he wondered if he shouldn't have lightened her as well, but now was not the time to introduce yet another variable.

The crackling was louder, and he could hear ominous cracks and crashes in the building below. If load-bearing structures were giving way, the roof could collapse at any moment. There were nine women left, and six men.

Moving quickly, he went from person to person, making a clean contact each time to bestow the benefit of his power on them. The time for care was gone; eschewing the nostril filters, he inhaled the smoky, ash-filled air with the rest of them. As he slapped each man on the shoulder, he shouted, "Jump!" The women, he gathered to him.

Beneath them, the roof shuddered, and he saw a fiery gap open up at one corner. They were out of time. With the terrified women clinging to him, each one affected by just one-tenth normal gravity, he flexed his harness-enhanced power and lifted off the roof. The men had already leaped, soaring out over the void and falling ever so slowly to safety.

Behind them, as they passed over the edge of the rooftop, he heard—and felt, via his G-sense—the surface fragmenting and crumbling into the roaring inferno below. It was just the top floor, though the rest of the apartment building seemed to be still intact, if only for the moment. The women holding onto him were coughing almost nonstop, which wasn't surprising. He'd been exposed to the smoke only briefly, and his throat was already stinging.

After the raging heat of the fire, the cool January air came as a balm and a blessing. He coughed up phlegm and turned his face away from his human cargo to spit out something black and horrible. Already, he could feel his power's grip beginning to erode from the women he wasn't in direct contact with, so he angled his way down toward an as-yet unoccupied section of the parking lot.

This was why he would've preferred to rescue them in smaller lots, to ensure that everyone made it to the ground in one piece. Alternatively, while it would've been technically possible to get them all to jump, as he'd had the men do, it was still a sixty-foot drop. Even reduced to an effective six feet, a fall like that had the potential to go badly wrong, especially if his power failed mid-drop from being stretched too many ways at once.

The landing was rough; some of the women fell over, but he didn't hear any cries of pain. As soon as his G-sense told him everyone was solidly on the ground, he released the last of his power effect and lifted off again. Firefighters and EMTs were already running in the direction of the rescuees, so he took a deep breath of non-smoke-laden air, coughed up some more phlegm, and looked around for Black Dragon.

It wasn't hard to spot the girl. Still in her dragon form, she was posing with the people she'd saved for the cameras. On its own, that would've been fine. Unfortunately, microphones were being thrust at her, and she was happily talking to the reporters.

Oh, crap.

Their mission in Savannah had been to look into the potential fallout from the murder of Franklin Tucker, and that should've been the beginning and end of his responsibility for her. Choosing to go and save people could only be a PR bonus for Force Majeure (and the right thing to do), but he had a sneaking feeling any faux pas she committed here would be laid at his doorstep anyway. Hoping against hope that she was exercising at least some vague level of propriety, he flew in that direction. On the way, he tugged off the goggles and removed the nose filters.

"... so yeah, me an' Relentless are tight," the girl said as he got in earshot. She held up her scaled hand, two of the digits pressed together. "For an older guy, he's a damn good boss. I mean, when I joined —"

"Ah, there you are, Black Dragon." Jericho landed alongside her, not bothering to flex his knees to absorb the jolt of landing. "Mighty fine work saving those civilians. They trained you well." Turning to the reporters, he essayed a charming smile. "She only started today, would you believe? She's one of our most promising recruits."

As he'd planned, the microphones and cameras turned his way. "G-Man!" shouted one reporter, quickly echoed by the others. "Can you tell us anything about this fire? Do you have any suspicions about how it started?"

Drawing on his own public-relations training, Jericho patted the air, still smiling, until the questions died down a little. "Now, now, one at a time. I'm good, but I'm not that good. As for this fire, I just got here, and I'm no expert. The good city of Savannah has assessors who'll be able to tell you exactly how it started and why. Black Dragon and I were in town for another reason altogether, but when we saw the smoke, we decided to help out."

More questions were shouted. Jericho observed the crowd as he waited for the one he knew was coming. If Stephen returned before he and Black Dragon left, it would be just like his ex-boyfriend to pull some move that would embarrass the both of them, then get all pissy when Jericho rejected his advances. If that looked like happening, Jericho figured he'd just fly away and wear the bad publicity. Nothing was worth that sort of aggravation.

Finally, someone asked the right question, and Stephen hadn't yet appeared. Feeling that *something* was going right for once, Jericho acknowledged the question with a smile before he answered. "Yes, I am fixing on coming back to Savannah when I can; it'll always be home to me. But it's way above my pay grade to determine when a Force Majeure team office is due to open in Savannah or who'll be in charge of it. Still, I'll be certain-sure to put my name down for it." He raised his hands in mock surrender. "Now, I know you fine folks would love for me to stay and answer questions all day long, but Black Dragon and I are due back at Utopia, and it's never a good idea to keep Relentless waiting."

He knew he'd hit the right note when they laughed and ceased the barrage of questions. Casually, he reached up as though scratching his left ear, and pressed the helmet clicker on that side. "Okay," he added without moving his lips, just loudly enough for his radio earpiece to transmit to Black Dragon's, "now we take off. Dramatic exit, stage left."

For a long moment, he thought she would ignore him and keep talking to the press. He was very much in the position of the older brother who had been told to keep an eye on his bratty little sister. Unlike when they'd had their first tour of the Spire, the only authority he had over her right now was what she was willing to tolerate.

"All-*righty*!" she declared, stepping back and bringing her wings up. Jericho exerted his power, lifting into the air as the dragon girl flapped hard, sending dust and ash in all directions. Together, they ascended skyward, Black Dragon throwing the occasional barrel roll for the hell of it.

All in all, Jericho figured that could have gone a lot worse. They'd saved a bunch of people, nobody had died, and Stephen hadn't shown up to cause a scene.

I'll take the win.

8
Realization

Jericho had ridden on the maglev quite a few times by now, occasionally with others but mostly on his own. He was happy to journey alone, though he had no issue with being accompanied by friends or family. Unfortunately, his current traveling companion fitted into neither category. Worse, she had the potential of developing into a third classification: 'problem'.

With Black Dragon's propensity toward being irritating and amusing by turns (or even simultaneously), Jericho was worried that the ride back to Utopia would be interminable at best and acutely unpleasant at worst. Technically, he was still responsible for her impact on the public until they reached their destination, and he had no doubt she knew any number of ways to make his life hell without breaking any specific laws.

Somewhat to his surprise, she followed him to the upper deck of the train car with only a moderate sneer at the minimal facilities afforded by the Savannah maglev station. It appeared she shared his preference for the tables over the seating downstairs. While he installed himself in his favored traveling position, she sat across the table from him and turned her back to the window, stretching out her legs and putting her bare feet up on the bench seat to occupy the entire length of it.

"So how long 'til we get back to Utopia?" she asked as she scooted her butt forward to get comfortable. He didn't exactly approve of her feet being where they were, but it wasn't a hill he was prepared to die on. If it kept her from doing something more openly obnoxious, he was willing to ignore it.

"Two and a half hours, more or less," he replied from memory, and flicked on the privacy bubble. "Why? You got somewhere to be?"

"Oh, *man*," she complained, rolling her eyes. "They were running a drill, and I was just getting into it. It'll be over before we get back. Can't this thing go any faster?"

Jericho raised his eyebrows. "We're a thousand miles away from Utopia. The maglev averages four hundred. I doubt they'll speed it up just for you."

"Still sucks," she grumped. "It was fun being a villain for once."

He knew what she was talking about; on a semi-regular occasion, Force Majeure ran 'emergency drills' (closer to full-scale military exercises) to maintain Utopia's readiness for emergency situations. For verisimilitude, members of the team were given a chance to volunteer as opposing forces. The idea of Black Dragon embracing such a role did not surprise him in the slightest.

Neither had he been even remotely taken aback to discover these drills were Relentless' idea. In his experience, the leader of Force Majeure never did anything by halves, whether it was taking down the Madness or preparing a city for worst-case disasters.

To that end, they could be initiated at a moment's notice by any core member. Theoretical scenarios included hostile incursions into Utopia from outside, 'villains' within the city who had to be captured before they did too much (virtual) damage, and so forth. Once initiated, a drill played out to its conclusion. The only thing that could interrupt the fake emergency would be a real one. In addition, Force Majeure ensured that anyone who participated was compensated for their time, including business owners who had to suspend operations for the duration.

He'd been on the team for precisely one week when a 'villain attack' drill alert went off in the middle of the night. Unsure of what was going on or even where he was supposed to be, he'd stepped up anyway. He'd been tagged as a 'hero', while Relentless had been playing the part of one of the 'villains'.

They'd clashed on the rooftops; Jericho was trying to get close enough to use his G-shake while Relentless alternated fluidly between playing keep-away and attacking aggressively. The whole time they were sparring, Jericho's G-sense had been acutely aware of the gravity motor in the head of Relentless' mace, but the weapon had never come into play. On the upside, he'd managed to keep Relentless busy long enough that half a dozen other heroes had been able to come in and dogpile the big guy, ending the drill.

What had deeply impressed him while attending the debriefing the following day was how fast a drill (and its response) could swing into action. Back in Savannah, attempting to implement that kind of city-wide wargame would take days just to get all the pieces into place. Traffic would be tied up for hours while it was going on, and sure as shooting, any number of damn fools would ignore all directives and blunder into the area of operations. Worse, the subsequent lawsuits for loss of business would likely bankrupt the city for years to come.

In Utopia, it had taken half an hour from the initial announcement to the commencement of the exercise, and three hours for the drill to play out to its conclusion. After which, camera harnesses were handed back in to assist with composing the post-exercise debrief, and everything just ... went back to normal.

When he didn't respond to the 'villain' comment—in his opinion, there was no good way that conversation could go—she replaced her radio earpiece with a second earbud, no doubt so she could listen to music on her phone. This was a rules violation, as Force Majeure members were expected to keep their radio earpieces in at all times while costumed up. Again, he wasn't inclined to make a fuss. They were literally face to face; if he wanted to communicate with her, all he needed to do was raise his voice slightly.

As she began to fiddle with her phone, he cleared his throat. She rolled her eyes toward him, in a masterful amalgamation of *'yes, I'm paying attention'* and *'this better be good'*.

"I was fixing to get something from the vending machine," he offered. "Did you want anything?" He was willing to offer her an olive branch for her restraint from earlier. After all, they'd gotten through the public-facing side of their first joint mission with remarkably few hitches, and in his opinion that called for some positive reinforcement.

"Mountain Dew and a dozen cookies," she said at once before turning her attention back to her phone.

Jericho paused, waiting for a 'please' or even a 'thank you', then realized that if he wanted either one, he should've made it clear first. Right now, he was less concerned with his pride and more concerned with getting them both back to Utopia without embarrassing the good name of the team. In the grand scheme of things, a little lack of politeness didn't matter.

Up he got, with an internal sigh—from the rarefied heights of the age of twenty-three—about the insanity of the teenage metabolism.

A dozen cookies? Good God.

Though perhaps, the shape-change between girl and dragon and the exertion of winged flight might actually draw on her physical reserves. He hadn't been briefed on it, and wasn't inclined to speculate.

The vending machines had sugar cookies, water, and a selection of carbonated beverages. Jericho acquired thirteen cookies, the Mountain Dew, and a water bottle for himself. Due to Force Majeure's firm stance on environmental preservation and recycling, the bottles were made of high-impact glass, and the cookies were sealed in greaseproof paper. He 'paid' for them by tapping the reader with his MagCard; given that he and Black Dragon were both in costume, the refreshments would be free of charge, just as the ride was. Such were the benefits of membership in America's most prominent superhero team.

Black Dragon barely glanced up when he slid the Mountain Dew across to her, along with the dozen cookies she'd requested. She did mumble something that sounded vaguely like 'thanks' before unwrapping the first cookie and stuffing it in her mouth. A little touched that she'd made at least a minimal effort, Jericho settled back in his seat with his cookie and bottle of water.

The meal passed by in the almost echoing silence of two people choosing to ignore one another. After he finished his snack, Jericho took out his phone.

Black Dragon was engrossed in whatever her own phone was showing her when he glanced her way, so he decided to get back to his impromptu terror villain history class. This time, he opted to look up Guillotine. *At least with her, I'll know who the bad guy is.*

This indeed turned out to be accurate, though it was problematic in other ways. Guillotine was a slender woman wearing what Jericho would've tentatively described as a 'battle bikini', set off with knee-high boots and elbow-length gloves, all in purple-dyed leather. Over the gloves, she wore silver finger-claw rings daubed with (in the picture) what could easily have been real blood. Her purple hair was shaved and teased up into a long trailing mohawk, and she wore silver skull earrings. Her identity was hidden by a surgical-style face mask and a pair of wraparound sunglasses: again, purple in color. Finally, a row of heavy metal staples around her neck followed the line of a thick red scar, apparently intended to make it look as though her head had been removed and reattached.

This was from one of the few still shots of the woman he'd been able to find. Where she wasn't moving too fast for cameras to capture more than a blurry image, she was generating a pale purple mist from her hands and spreading it around for visual cover. It was effective, too; the purple theme of her costume and hair dye made for effective camouflage, allowing her to consistently never be where the police or superheroes thought she was.

Watching the footage of her rampaging through a shopping mall in Boston, Jericho could see how terrifying she'd been in close quarters. Wispy clouds of purple mist filled almost the entire space, with the shouts and screams of shoppers echoing like the cries of the damned. Appearing and reappearing from the clouds of purple almost at random, she seemed to be the only one who knew where everyone was.

A mall cop, bruised and bleeding, lurched out of the rolling clouds of purple fog, pistol up and finger on the trigger. With a creepy giggle that put chills down Jericho's back—they hadn't mentioned *that* in any of the retrospectives he'd ever seen—Guillotine appeared as if by magic right in front of him. He fired point-blank at her, but somehow he missed; a mall patron went down instead, clutching their stomach.

The fog rolled over him. Silver flashed, and he shrieked a shockingly high note; a second later, it receded again to show the man clutching a blood-spurting stump. Nearby, the guard's hand lay limply on the ground with the pistol alongside. Guillotine gave the man barely long enough to see his severed appendage and to know just how boned he was before the purple mist washed over them again. This time, there wasn't even a scream.

Jericho didn't need to see the casualty count to know the man was dead. The cuts she made were always impossibly precise; some thought it was a monowire blade extending from the flamboyant finger-claw rings, while others proposed a Dynamic ability. He only knew that bone was sliced through with the same ease as flesh and cartilage, and Guillotine always got away, usually leaving a trail of dead and dying behind her in the fading purple mist.

Always ... except for the last time.

One fine evening in Louisville, her luck ran out when she went up against Relentless and Transit. The battle had been long and arduous, but eventually, they'd managed to cut off every last avenue of escape. Transit had tagged Guillotine in the fog with the machine guns on a bulkier and clunkier version of her current sky-cycle, and Relentless went in for the kill with the kinetic hammer he'd carried back then.

It flashed once above the purple shifting clouds, then came down hard. The fog dissipated to show Relentless standing triumphant, the villain's skull gruesomely crushed to ruin. It was a fittingly ignominious end for someone with so little regard for human life.

While Jericho watched more videos along the same line, wincing every now and again, Black Dragon apparently skipped from music to cat videos to whatever else she was doing while chugging Mountain Dew and scarfing cookies. When she ran out, she went and got more for herself.

Each time the maglev passed through a city, passenger cars were dropped off the back and added to the front. When he'd first started riding the high-tech train, Jericho had been irritated by the need to keep moving forward from car to car. Now, he hardly noticed the inconvenience. Not even Black Dragon bothered to complain about it.

They'd just passed through St. Louis, Jericho glancing out the window to get his third view of the Gateway Arch for the day, when Black Dragon stirred and sat up from her bonelessly slumped position. "Well, shit," she said aloud, putting her fourth bottle of Mountain Dew (not that he was keeping count) down on the table. "We missed one."

"Hm?" asked Jericho. Just for a moment, he had the impression she was referring to his studies into terror villain techniques and that somehow one was still alive somewhere.

She turned to face him. "Back at that apartment fire? We missed one."

Oh. Right. Good. Wait, not good.

Jericho's research into Guillotine's tactics had allowed him to avoid thinking too deeply about the fire; this, in turn, had allowed him to keep from dwelling on everything Stephen would've lost in the blaze. But now he had to go right ahead and think about it anyway. *Joy.* "Please tell me you're yanking my chain."

She was just enough of a smart-ass and a button pusher to get in one last dig, and he really hoped it was the case this time. He wouldn't even be mad at her for trying to get a rise out of him. But as he searched her face, there was no smug teenage smirk in evidence.

"No troll, G," she said earnestly, angling her phone to show him. It showed an image of the burning apartment building, with the caption **APARTMENT FIRE CLAIMS ONE LIFE.** Then she turned the screen back toward herself and scrolled downward with a flick of her finger. "Says here firefighters were going through the building to check for spot fires an' they found a dead guy in one of the apartments. Poor schmuck was on the third floor, where the fire started. Never even made it out the door."

An ominous dread began to coil inside Jericho's guts.

No. No. No, no, no.

He knew the third floor well. It was where he'd lived with Stephen. "Have they ... have they identified him?"

"Yeah, his name was Lemonade or something ..." She paused, frowning.

Jericho began to relax. He didn't know anyone called Lemonade. The building had been well alight when they got there, so the chances that they would've been able to save the guy were minimal.

Still, if we'd known he was there, maybe …

"Yeah, here it is," Black Dragon said. "Stephen Lemonade." She held up the phone to show him.

The bad feeling returned in full force, an unexpected tsunami of despair. "LaMonde," he choked out. "It's pronounced LaMonde." He closed his eyes tight and breathed in deeply through his nostrils, trying not to let the sudden tears squeeze out from between his eyelids.

Every casual thought he'd had about the fire now came back to taunt him. How he'd deliberately avoided thinking about Stephen, aside from being relieved that the older man hadn't shown up to the aftermath. But worst of all, he'd *posed* in front of the still-burning building, playing the hero for his admiring public.

"Hey, what the hell? Are you *crying*?" Black Dragon's voice cut into his self-flagellation. "Shit, I thought you were tougher than this. You're a *superhero*. You can't just go bawling your fuckin' eyes out over some guy you didn't even have a chance to save …" She paused for a long and damning moment. "Waaait a minute …"

Rubbing his eyes with his thumbs, Jericho tried to compose himself before she connected any dots he didn't want her connecting. But he was too late. As he opened his mouth to speak, he could see her staring at him with dawning speculation. "It's not …" he began weakly.

"The hell it's not." She pointed at him with a look of triumph. "You an' that Lemonade guy were bangin', right? That's why we went there straight after you got that phone call. Someone you know called you an' told you that your main squeeze's place was on fire. So, you hadda go over there an' try to make sure he was okay." She tilted her head. "How come you thought he was? 'Cause you weren't stressed at all once we got there."

Jericho had to admit one thing: as aggravating as her pushiness was, she'd managed to drag him bodily out of the incipient depression that the news of Stephen's death had drawn him into. He drew a deep breath. "One, he wasn't my boyfriend. He was my ex. He never wanted me to join Force Majeure. We split up before I made it onto the team. Two, I thought he wasn't there because his car wasn't in its usual spot. So yeah, I figured he was fine until …"

Not bothering to finish the statement, he rubbed the heels of his hands up and down his face, careful not to dislodge his helmet. He still felt like crap, but at least he wasn't on the verge of thinking it was somehow his fault anymore. That was a good thing, he supposed.

"Wow, man, that's gotta suck huge donkey balls." Black Dragon shook her head. "Your timing is the fuckin' *worst*. If that shit had gone down half an hour earlier or later, we wouldn't'a even been in town. I mean, it probably still woulda been a shock to find out he was dead, but it wouldn't be like you were right *there* when it happened, know what I mean?"

It seemed to be some kind of cursed gift. As far as Jericho could tell, Black Dragon was trying to comfort him, but even the 'nice' version of her somehow managed to upset him once again.

"Just … stop talking. Please," he managed to say. "Can we … not tell anyone about this?"

What he *didn't* want, or need, was for this to get out in any kind of official fashion. If it came down to it, brooding on a rooftop would be his first stop. It was literally how prodigies like him kept their heads in the game.

Black Dragon's shrug evinced an extreme lack of concern. "Eh, whatevs. You do you, G." Settling back into her seat, she returned her attention to her phone.

Left alone to think at last, Jericho tried to direct his internal meanderings anywhere but the apartment fire, to no avail. Some part of his brain was determined to find out who was to blame for what had happened.

If Stephen wasn't heading for the Tucker place, why wasn't his car in the right parking spot? Maybe he sold it. Maybe it broke down and was in the garage. Or maybe he just left it at someone else's place overnight.

There were a lot of maybes, and no solid facts to go on with. He abandoned that line of thought.

Okay, then. Why couldn't those people get down the fire escape?

That was something he might be able to determine. Taking out his own phone, he scrolled through the news feed until he found the article Black Dragon had pointed out.

The sole casualty was LGBTQA+ rights activist Stephen LaMonde, 32. His next of kin have been informed …

That wasn't helping, except to verify that Jericho was no longer listed as Stephen's next of kin. He scrolled onward.

Piecing together information from witness reports, he learned the fire had indeed started on the third floor and had spread so aggressively that both the interior and the exterior fire escapes had been quickly blocked off by the flames. He wasn't sure *how* such a thing had happened, but that was the report. The building owner, he suspected, was going to have a lot of tough questions to answer. If he and Black Dragon hadn't shown up when they did, a further nineteen people would've almost certainly died.

Well, it's a good thing that we were there. I just wish we could've done more.

He figured he wasn't the first hero to express that desire, and he certainly wouldn't be the last. But dwelling on his failures was painful; he suspected that never changed, either.

I need to talk to Thomas.

Fortunately, now he had a way to do that. He dug in his pouch for the Post-It note, then opened the notepad app on his phone and carefully copied the number across. After triple-checking what he'd typed, he crumpled the note up and ate it, washing it down with a mouthful of water. The last thing he wanted was for the wrong person to get hold of that number. Finally, he pasted it into his texting app and sent a message away.

Hey, are you free to chat?

God, I hope he is. I hope I don't come across as whiny or needy.

The answer came back almost instantly. *Anytime, sexy. What's up?*

A smile came unbidden to Jericho's face, but it slid away again as he tapped out the message. **Something just happened, and I'm not sure how to deal with it.**

In Savannah? I saw you on the news. That apartment fire. Was it bad?

Well, he'd known Thomas wasn't *stupid.* **Yeah. Not everyone got out.**

He'd barely sent the message when Thomas' answer popped up on his screen. *Shit. Want me to call?*

I'd love you to, but I've got to watch the new recruit. While he *could* go elsewhere for privacy, it would be his ass on the line if she got bored and did something problematic.

And let's face it. She probably would.

There was a pause before Thomas' next missive came back. *It says here there was only one death, a Stephen LaMonde. Why does that name sound familiar?*

Shit, I never actually told him Stephen's full name before.

It wasn't something that tended to come up in conversation with one's *current* boyfriend. He dithered for a moment, then bit the bullet. Thomas deserved honesty about something like this.

He was my ex.

There was another pause, longer than the last one.

Was it a mistake to mention Stephen? Has he just put the phone down and walked away?

His phone pinged, and he sagged with relief as he saw what Thomas had to say. *Fuuuck. I can't even.* Before he could even begin to compose his next words, another message popped up. *You okay?*

And isn't that the sixty-four-million-dollar question right now.

I dunno. I feel guilty I couldn't save him. I didn't even know he was home. Only found out afterward.

I shouldn't have said that last bit. It sounds like I'm making excuses for myself.

Thomas' answer overrode his doubts. *Oh, that's terrible. Want me to come meet you? Pretty sure I can manage it, one way or another.*

The temptation was strong. If it hadn't been for Black Dragon, he would've jumped on it. **I wish we could, but I'm on the clock right now.**

Thomas had to be typing like a madman to answer so quickly. *Another time, then. It's not your fault, you understand me? You can't save everyone. That's a fact.*

Jericho nodded slowly as he typed. **Yeah, I know, but it doesn't make it any easier to accept.**

It was *so* good to have someone who actually understood the problem. *Never does. But anytime you want to chat, you reach out, okay?*

A smile crossed his face. **Okay, thanks. I love you. Bye.**

I love you too.

The four simple words were accompanied by half a dozen love-heart emojis and a couple of 'hug' smileys. He sat there just looking at them for nearly a minute before closing the app with a sigh. Even over the impersonal medium of text messages, talking to Thomas had left him in a better mood. More able to handle the travails of the world.

After a few moments, he cleared his phone and went back to where he'd been watching video files.

I might not be able to change the past, but I can surely learn from it.

9
History

Des Moines was ablaze. Or rather, that was what it seemed like to Jericho. Swiveling turrets atop the gigantic multi-legged robot rampaging through the urban landscape fired off explosive payloads seemingly at random, setting buildings alight as far as half a mile away. Others were more precise, targeting anything in the air that got within a certain distance. It didn't seem to matter whether these were military, police, or even news choppers; they all went down, hard. A superhero swooped into view, but Jericho didn't have time to recognize the costume before a sharp detonation took them out of the picture.

He winced as the shockwave damaged two nearby police helicopters; they pinwheeled away, trailing smoke. The image on his phone became a blurred mess as the camera jerked up and sideways. He sat back, breathing deeply and allowing the induced tension to bleed away.

For all that he was watching archived footage from the Nineties, it felt far too real in the moment. This sort of thing had been on the news regularly when he was growing up; time and again, Raider had shown zero remorse over civilian deaths. In fact, the terror villain almost seemed to make a game of it, stomping on fleeing cars and picking off panicked civilians just before they would've made it to safety.

The news chopper filming the feed Jericho was watching finally turned back toward the action, somewhat farther away than before. Evidently, the pilot had decided discretion was the better part of valor. Jericho silently agreed with the choice; there was no sense in the guy throwing his life away for nothing.

A dozen times larger than life, a hologram flickered into existence above the giant robot. It featured the head and upper body of a man in power armor, sporting a helmet in the shape of a steel cowl. The only detail that could be seen of his shadowed features was an orange prosthetic eye, glaring in the left socket.

"THAT'S RIGHT!" he bellowed, the sheer amount of bass in his voice vibrating the speaker in Jericho's ear. *"FLEE BEFORE ME, YOU PUNY, INSIGNIFICANT PIXELS! WHEN THEY ASK YOU WHO HUMBLED YOU HERE TODAY, TELL THEM YOU WERE HONORED BY A VISIT FROM NONE OTHER THAN RAIDER!"*

"Dude, what the *fuck* are you watching?"

Jericho raised his eyes to see Black Dragon sitting up and staring at him quizzically from across the table. He paused the replay, trying to figure out what her problem was. "What?"

"The sound on whatever shit you're watching is so loud I can hear your earpiece buzzing from here," she explained impatiently. "I didn't think people your age even knew music that loud existed anymore."

"It wasn't music," he said, then sighed. "It was footage of the time Raider hit Des Moines. Middle of April, 'ninety-four. Hundreds of people dead, over two thousand injured, billions in property damage, and he basically gutted the local U.S. Bank branch while he was at it. Anyone who tried to get in his way got blown out of the air or stomped into the ground."

This actually seemed to capture her interest. "Sounds like someone it wasn't a good idea to mess with."

He nodded somberly. "You don't know the half of it. Someone managed to take out one of his guns just as it looked like he was fixing to target the Salisbury House Museum, and he apparently didn't like that. So, he turned the whole mecha side-on and launched *everything* in that general direction. The house, the grounds, it all caught fire. Even with all their units on site, they still couldn't save it. Seventy years of history up in smoke, just like that. And they were days putting out the fires over the rest of the city, and *years* in repairing the damage."

It surprised him how passionate he was starting to feel about the matter and how offended he was by the crimes of the terror villains, even twenty years past. He'd started watching the material mainly to take his mind off Stephen's death, but now he was becoming positively immersed in it. In fact, the more of it he watched, the more he understood the emergency drills and tactics Force Majeure used. Explaining to Black Dragon how educational it was, on the other hand ... that would be a whole new challenge in itself.

"So he burned the place down, then," she retorted with an eye-roll, proving his point without ever knowing it. "What do you care about shit done by old dead villains, anyway? They're *dead*."

"Mama always favored a quote she said was by Mark Twain: '*History doesn't repeat itself, but it often rhymes*'." Jericho paused, waiting for a reaction from the girl, but she just looked at him blankly. "That means, while the exact same things aren't gonna happen again, usually because the people who did them are dead, it doesn't mean—"

"—other assholes can't do the same things for the same reasons, yeah, got it." She snorted and shook her head. "Just because I don't go looking up history and shit doesn't mean I'm *stupid*."

"Did I say I thought you were?" It seemed every time Jericho thought he had a handle on dealing with Black Dragon, she showed a whole new prickly side. Sometimes, he wondered half-seriously if she was deliberately screwing with him and pretending to take offense at basically everything, just to keep him on the back foot. He honestly would not have put it past her.

"No, but I saw the look in your eye." She reached for where the cookies had been and wrinkled her nose when her hand slapped empty table space. "Motherfucker. Now I gotta get more cookies."

As if the yellow lights had been waiting for their cue, they began to flash. **"Attention, all passengers. Attention, all passengers. This train will be passing through Kansas City in six minutes. All passengers stopping in Kansas City ..."**

"Get 'em when we're up in the front car," he said, not even bothering to listen to the rest of the announcement. Sliding out of the seat, he put his phone away and started toward the front of the train.

"But what if they're out of cookies there?" He was pleased to see Black Dragon was following him even while she tried to argue.

"One, have you ever seen one of their vending machines run out of *anything*?" He glanced down at her as she trotted along beside him. "And two, big deal. I doubt you'll starve for all of the fifteen minutes it takes us to reach Utopia."

"Hey, you don't know what it's like," she snarked. "I'm still growing. I might need those cookies right now because this is a crucial stage in my physical development or something."

It was his turn to roll his eyes. "Yes, because sugar, butter, and flour are so *very* essential to a growing teenager. Besides, I remember going through a growth spurt myself once upon a time. I know what it's like to suddenly need *all* the food."

"So why are you up in my grille about it?" At least she kept her voice low, so the other passengers might not have heard what she said. While she was very definitely a boundary pusher, she evidently recalled what Tourbillon had said about needing a report on her behavior while in the field with him. So far, she hadn't specifically done anything to embarrass him or make Force Majeure look bad, no matter how close to the line she managed to skate.

"I'm not. You're a big girl now, and you can just plain wait for your cookies." He lengthened his stride, not wanting to get drawn into yet another irritating argument.

As a tactic it worked, though he wasn't looking forward to the backlash. Very few people could be as passively-aggressive annoying as a pissed-off teen who figured they'd been disrespected. Still, it got the pair of them to the front car in the train, so he decided that was a plus.

As soon as they arrived and Jericho settled down in his usual spot, Black Dragon vanished in search of cookies; or rather, he presumed that was the reason why. He could've gone looking, but he chose to not borrow trouble for the moment, instead watching out the window as the landscape whipped past at over four hundred seventy miles per hour.

For a few moments, he allowed his mind to dwell on Thomas. The memory of his boyfriend from that morning was far more pleasant than anything he might want to think about Stephen or Black Dragon. He felt himself relaxing, his mind calming down.

It wasn't long before the branching rails split off to the left and right, with the northbound cars following the ones he could see. The Missouri

River looped around to the north, then the Kansas River flashed by underneath the maglev.

Black Dragon got back to the table at that point, bearing a sizable bounty of cookies. She began to eat them, one at a time, with a very pointed '*these are mine, and you can't have them*' air. Jericho decided not to tell her that this behavior amused him far more than it bothered him. If it let her think she'd scored a win, he was okay with that.

Okay, she's happy for the moment. Back to business.

Reclining in the seat, Jericho closed his eyes, the better to mull over what he'd seen in the footage he'd watched. The tactics used by the different terror villains to get the jump on their victims varied from individual to individual, but they'd all been effective in their way. Sure as hell, they wouldn't work in the current day with Force Majeure on the job, but back then, they'd done just fine.

False Flag had gone the sneaky route, murdering and impersonating one victim after another in a gruesome cross between musical chairs and a conga line. He'd shown inhuman patience and impressive acting skills to get where he wanted to be, whether that was behind the desk of a Fortune 500 CEO or a placement in the Vice President's Secret Service detail. When he wasn't doing either of those, he'd apparently murdered people while masquerading as their loved ones, purely for sadistic kicks.

On the other hand, Raider had gone loud from the start, employing brute-force tactics and widespread damage to dissuade opposition. He'd been both petty and vindictive, going out of his way to murder civilians when he got the chance, and destroying historical monuments for the sheer hell of it.

Guillotine's modus operandi was somewhere in between the other two. She'd enter an area as an ordinary civilian, then employ her terror tactics either to get what she wanted or cover her getaway with panic and chaos. The creepy giggle Jericho had noticed was amazingly effective for spreading fear.

Watching this footage had given him new insights, which was disturbing on the face of it. The concept of murder purely for the sake of murder was not something he could comprehend, except on a strictly hypothetical level. He wouldn't say he *understood* the thought processes that led to them doing the things they did, but the way they performed the crimes had a particular pattern, one he could almost figure out.

Maybe if I look at some more, it'll help me out with that.

Though he was reluctant to admit it even to himself, he also welcomed anything that would continue to take his mind off Stephen, at least for a while.

10
Debriefing

Utopia City's skyline was as spectacular as ever. While Jericho couldn't bring himself to truly appreciate it at the moment, it was nice to be able to get out into the open air again. Having yearned to be able to fly for so long, the experience always gave him a rush, no matter how emotionally battered he felt.

He was wearing the goggles again, this time with the flight control HUD activated so he could keep within the 'lane' he was supposed to be following. As the city with the busiest airspace in the world, Utopia actively enforced the use of flight lanes for its sheer volume of aircars, flight-capable Enabled, police hexes, and other air traffic. Nobody bucked the system if they didn't want to find themselves quite literally grounded.

All around him, exquisitely sculpted buildings reached toward the heavens. By day, they were aesthetically pleasing in a high-tech sort of way. In contrast, once night fell, they came alive with dynamic holographic overlays and decorations, which made flying after dark one of his favorite things to do in Utopia. And while the majority of them would have easily put the average mundane skyscraper to shame, they were all dwarfed by the Spire.

In 1999, the terror villain Doc Iridium had accidentally destroyed the city of Manhattan, Kansas with a nuclear device while attempting to hold it for ransom. Force Majeure, then an up-and-coming superhero team, cleared away the radioactive debris in record time and constructed Utopia City in its place. As its centerpiece, fully one and a half miles tall from base to tip, the Spire was *the* most eye-catching example of architecture in a city full of impressive buildings.

It was also where Force Majeure (and, by extension, Jericho and Black Dragon) had their base of operations, and thus where they were heading.

Black Dragon, wearing goggles of her own, dropped down alongside him. "Hey, old man!" she called out, the deeper draconic tones somehow conveying her cheeky tone perfectly. "Think you can fly any faster? I'd like to get there *today*, y'know?"

With a sigh, he shook his head. "You go on," he said tiredly. "I've got things to think about."

Black Dragon gave him a strange look; as a dragon, she was exceptionally good at this. "Seriously? You're still hung up on that guy? Listen, there was jack shit we coulda done about it, even if we'd known he was there. So toughen up, buttercup. We can't save everyone, every time."

"I'm well aware of that," he retorted, more than a little stung. "This one just hit pretty close to home. You go on. I'll be fine."

"You do you, G. Smell ya later, slowpoke!" Increasing the tempo of her wingbeats, she put on a burst of speed and left him behind. He watched as she banked gracefully around another building ahead of him, passing out of sight.

At least she's not pissed off with me anymore.

That was one good thing about dealing with Black Dragon; there was no chance of encountering mixed messages with her. Whether she was happy, sad, or upset, everyone in the vicinity knew exactly what the situation was.

He flew on, pushing his speed up a notch to remain within Utopian airspace regulations at that altitude, but not so much as to catch up with his erstwhile companion.

A police hex, six feet across with a ducted fan in the middle, cruised up alongside and matched its airspeed with his. He figured its operator was looking him over, probably pinging the user-info chip built into his HUD goggles. Pulling his right arm from the grav-wing, he saluted the hex with a casual wave. It replied with a double flash of its running lights, then peeled off on a tangent, gained altitude, and shot away across the city.

This city ... he mused with a grin and a shake of his head, letting his arm merge back into the 'wing. If that had happened to him six months ago, it would've freaked him out big-time, but now it was just another thing. Onward he flew, repeatedly turning the day's events over in his mind.

He couldn't help but note the weird parallel with the first time he'd taken the maglev; he'd gotten bad news to do with Stephen on that trip, too.

Stephen ...

He and Black Dragon had saved lives by attending the fire. That much was certain. But a lingering sense of loyalty to his ex-boyfriend, although he'd dumped the guy for infidelity, continued to nag at him.

If I hadn't just assumed he was out, could I have saved him?

He couldn't imagine not trying.

His flight path led around one last building, then the Spire came into view. As low as he was, barely five hundred feet in the air, he was looking *up* at the monumental construction rather than *across* at it. The building's circular footprint covered an area maybe two thousand feet across, tapering somewhat as it rose into the air. There was a no-fly zone extending for a thousand feet in all directions from the base of the building, though as a member of Force Majeure, he was exempt.

This close, he was shaded from the afternoon sun by the bulk of the Spire itself; delicate and slender it may have seemed at a distance, but up close, it was *immense*. Looking down, he could see people wandering through the sprawling Challenger Plaza, which took up the area between the main entrance of the Spire and the closest row of air-cab stands. Some were taking pictures of the floating statue of the eponymous hero, while others clustered around the fountain that made up the centerpiece of the Plaza. On his first visit to the Spire, he'd walked in through the front doors. But today, he was setting his sights somewhat higher.

As he gazed upward, he could see clouds parting to flow around the tip of the imposing structure, over seven thousand feet above where he was currently flying. Fortunately, he didn't need to go that high; the Technologist's lab was only half a mile up. Exerting his power, he began to climb in a long, lazy spiral. From prior experience, he knew there was a landing stage that would be perfect for his purposes.

As he ascended, he wondered how many cameras were tracking his flight path. There were people, he knew, who picked a particular Enabled hero and followed their career, posting each and every public exploit on social media. He didn't think he had fans of that type yet (except maybe Thomas, who was a special case), but some just congregated wherever superheroes were likely to go, looking to get whatever photos and footage they could. Undoubtedly there would be people like that in the Plaza, and anyone crossing the bubble of empty air surrounding the Spire would be very quickly spotted and photographed.

Other heroes may have been irritated by this uninvited attention, though he suspected Black Dragon would cheerfully pose for pictures. For his part, Jericho had felt almost stifled in Savannah by the sheer lack of *any* kind of feedback, so he had no problem at all with people taking notice of G-Man as a hero.

He glanced upward and noted that the landing stage was only a short distance above him now, so he broke from the spiral and arrowed directly toward it. Lofting up and over the lip, he flared his grav-wings and touched down, allowing them to dissipate a moment later. Within the laboratory proper was the Technologist, wearing his trademark multi-lens goggles and labcoat-themed costume, intently studying something resting on an ornate cradle before him.

The artificer glanced toward him briefly before returning his attention to the original object of interest. Moving closer, Jericho saw a humanoid robot attached to a stand, the body constructed of angular matte-black metal. He figured it to be maybe seven feet tall; to him, it looked like someone had decided to assemble it out of the offcuts from a stealth fighter.

"Ah, G-Man, you have finally decided to grace us with your presence," the older man remarked acerbically. "Did you perhaps locate another burning apartment building, or did you simply choose to dawdle?"

Jericho took no offense from this; the man treated everyone around him as second fiddle to his technology. "Figured I'd take my time," he said as he powered down his power enhancement harness and removed his HUD goggles. The world became a slightly smaller place as his G-sense lost range and detail. "Had some things bothering me a mite."

The Technologist's head came around. "Are you having difficulties with the harness? Place it over there, on that diagnosis rack. Let us ascertain what unconscionable abuse you've subjected it to this time."

Obediently, Jericho placed the harness on the rack intended for it, alongside the one that held Black Dragon's. Force Majeure's pre-eminent artificer moved to a console next to the stand and activated the holographic displays, humming wordlessly at what he saw. While Jericho considered himself of above-average intelligence, he'd be the first to admit that he could make neither head nor tail of the numbers, graphs, and transforming bands of color projected into the air above the console. In this, he suspected, he was not alone.

"The problem's not with the harness," he said, not sure how much he wanted to tell the man who was very much one of his bosses. "Something happened out there in the field. I'm guessing Black Dragon told you about the apartment fire?"

"If the issue does not originate with the harness, it can wait," the Technologist said brusquely. "How did you fare with the investigation of the Tucker murder?"

Jericho took a deep breath to center himself and get his mind back on track. As abrasive as the Technologist could be at times, he had the sharpest intellect of anyone Jericho knew in Force Majeure—hell, of anyone he knew *period*—and was undoubtedly correct in his priorities.

Deal with the mission first, my problems later.

"He was shot in the back of the head with a nine-millimeter pistol while sitting at his computer," Jericho reported. "Several people in neighboring houses heard it. Black Dragon deduced by scent that both the shooter and the accomplice were women and tracked them to the back door. I located a thumb drive hidden in a wall cavity and asked the detective on the scene to furnish us with a copy of the contents, once they'd had a look at it."

The Technologist turned his head then and gave Jericho an extremely dubious look. "I comprehend the practice of Gordoning, but do you consider that to be even remotely likely to happen?"

To that, Jericho could only shrug. "I used to consult with Detective Villanova back in the day, so maybe?" It wasn't the total truth, but he figured it was close enough for the moment.

"Hmm." Stroking his graying beard, the Technologist turned back to the display. "I will grant that as a possibility, then. Did you glean any other crumbs of information from the crime scene?"

"Uh, yeah." His memory thus jogged, Jericho took out his Force Majeure issue phone. "He had one of those corkboards with pictures and events connected by strings. I took photos."

"Ahh. Now, that may well be of considerable use to us." The Technologist accepted the device and dropped it onto a cradle. Tapping on a virtual keyboard, he called up the photos and merged them together, showing the entire compilation as a holographic image in the middle of the room. Each picture, each note, each string was vividly displayed.

Jericho stared at it. He'd had neither the time nor the will to make sense of it on the wall of the dingy little room back in Savannah, especially with the smell of blood distracting him. But now, it was magnificent in its chaos. From what he could make out, red strings seemed to connect events together, green connected people to one another, and yellow linked events to people.

A piece of paper with **9/20: A PLANNED EVENT?** scrawled in magic marker seemed to connect to half the board in one way or another. Including, for some reason, a note reading **SILENT KNIGHT: CASTELLAN REBRANDED?** with photos of both heroes linked by a green string and notes in pen pointing out supposed similarities in stance and armament. This was repeated on another part of the board with photos of Cherenkov (a fuzzy satellite image, for obvious reasons) and Devastator, of the infamous (and thoroughly defunct) terror villain pairing Mutilator and Devastator. Given that both the named terror villains were long dead, and Castellan even longer since retired, Jericho had zero ideas why those were even up there.

The next thing to catch his eye was a headline apparently cut from a Spanish-language newspaper, with what he assumed to be the translation scribbled over the top in red marker: **SEVERED HEAD FOUND ON DECK OF FISHING TRAWLER.** Appended to this was a note, also scrawled in marker in the same hand: **Is Force Majeure disposing of people who know too much?**

On yet another section of the board was a grainy tabloid photo of the Challenger space shuttle at the point of explosion, along with the headline **WAS THE CREW REPLACED BY ALIEN IMPOSTORS?** If that wasn't bad enough, off toward one corner was an even weirder one: **I WAS A MEMBER OF LADY QUANTUM'S SEX/DEATH CULT!** Down toward the bottom was the one that might have topped them all, so to speak. **THE SPIRE: MODERN-DAY TOWER OF BABEL?** Or it would have if Jericho hadn't spotted yet another one: **MULTINATIONAL CABAL DICTATING TERMS TO FORCE MAJEURE?**

"Holy crap." Jericho shook his head. "Do people even believe any of this stuff, or is it like those flat earth idiots pushing the conspiracy to get hits on their sites?"

"I consider engaging with fanatics of that thoughtless caliber to be the ultimate waste of my time and energy," the Technologist stated. "They are entirely unwilling to listen to anything resembling reason, while being simultaneously incapable of fact-checking their own radical delusions. Lady Quantum seems to enjoy spending her leisure hours either baiting them or flirting with them; I have no idea which, and even less desire to find out. Did you happen to locate any eyewitnesses?"

That went a long way toward explaining how the provocatively dressed Force Majeure member had known so much about the conspiracy theories at Jericho's interview. Also, why people might believe the 'sex/death cult' crap. However, Jericho had other things to think about. "Ah, yeah. Well, not an eyewitness, but his partner. She said he'd told her that he'd been sent some encrypted files which he claimed had stuff in them that would surely bring

Force Majeure down. But the only things I saw on site were the thumb drive and the board."

The Technologist nodded slowly. "There exists a very significant chance that his hard drive was either sanitized or removed entirely before you arrived, which means only the thumb drive has a chance of possessing the relevant information."

"Whatever that is." Jericho frowned. "What could be so damaging?"

"Is your imagination so limited?" The older man shook his head dismissively. "The secret identities of every member of Force Majeure, including your own. Schematics of the Spire, showing the locations of all the classified technology. Control codes allowing access to the traffic computer system, or even the *weather* system. Any one of those could do us, and the city itself, irreparable harm if it fell into the wrong hands."

"What, really?" That sounded downright terrifying. "How could they get any of that stuff? I mean, it's all locked down under airtight security right here in the Spire, isn't it?" The only way he could imagine someone getting their hands on that sort of thing would be to sneak into the building. He recalled from his initial tour with Transit how problematic that approach would be, even for an Enabled.

"Most of that statement is accurate, yes," conceded the Technologist. "Unfortunately, and I absolutely insist you pass this on to *nobody*, we suffered a security breach not long ago. I am still determining exactly what data was accessed, but it is entirely plausible that these stolen files were precisely what Mr. Tucker had been decrypting. Until I locate further information to refute that hypothesis, I intend to use it as our operating model."

"A security breach? Who the hell pulled *that* one off? Did we catch 'em?" Jericho was honestly stunned. The Technologist's revelation sounded impossible on the face of things, but he couldn't think of a reason for the older man to lie to him.

"I'm afraid I possess minimal information in that regard." The grim set to the Technologist's jaw spoke volumes about how much he hated to admit that he had next to nothing. "No physical penetration of the Spire took place—if it had, our security precautions would still be on high alert—but instead, the thief infiltrated the main precinct house and made use of a regular channel into our information systems. Then they activated an override device of heretofore unsuspected capability to bypass our security lockouts, and proceeded to hack directly into our high-security servers. Fortunately, we keep the files encrypted as a matter of course, so while they were able to retrieve copies and spirit them away, they were unable to simply read them right there in secure storage."

Jericho blinked, trying not to react too blatantly. He knew about a device that allowed the user to override any and all security measures. In fact, he'd seen it in action. Still, he could be wrong. He didn't want to end up blaming the wrong person by jumping to conclusions.

"How long did they have to grab stuff? I mean, did your security take much time to realize something was up?" If he recalled correctly, Smokeshadow had told him at one point that the discus could only delay inevitable discovery by eight and a half minutes. After that, all bets were off.

"Hmm. I believe I see where you are going with this line of questioning. The data channel only allowed for a certain bandwidth, after all." The Technologist nodded approvingly. "Our best estimate puts the duration of the intrusion at barely exceeding two minutes. That places a hard limit on what could be extracted from the system in that time. Still, whoever it was, they were extremely competent at their craft."

The sinking feeling in Jericho's stomach didn't go away. This was sounding more and more like Smokeshadow all the time.

"That's bad and good at the same time, I suppose," he conceded. "Good in that they didn't have much time, bad in that they got away. Did you get anything from the precinct house? As I recall, that place's got security cameras out the wazoo."

"Indeed they do, though they may as well have been elaborate fakes for all the actionable data we've received from them." Frustration tinged the Technologist's voice. "Not a single viable image or audio file. The perpetrator presented as a woman. Or rather, two different women: a ranking officer and a junior tech. Security cameras only recorded a blur when it came to her face, if she truly was a woman. Audio recorders were similarly fuzzed. More problematically, their clothing altered itself while moving from one camera to the next."

"That's ... uh, that's a pretty good trick." Jericho was referring to the blurred face and fuzzed audio. He didn't know if Smokeshadow could build something capable of that, but it definitely sounded like her style. The self-adjusting hyperweave costume, unfortunately, was something he *did* know about.

The Technologist wasn't done. "Indeed. Our current hypothesis is that the perpetrator has access to a high-end hard-light emitter which allows them to alter their face, clothing, and apparent height at a moment's notice. In addition, I posit some kind of Dynamic capability that allowed them to effect an escape past half a dozen people without a single attempt to apprehend them. Eyewitness accounts claim that the person was 'too important to stop', whatever *that* is supposed to convey. Once outside, they entered a camera blind spot, from which they apparently never emerged."

"Yeah, that's a problem," Jericho admitted. He knew he was atrocious at lying, especially to people he owed allegiance to. The trouble was that his loyalties were being tugged in two different directions at once, so he did his best to keep his comments as general as possible. "Has anything like this happened before? Inside the Spire, I mean?"

The Technologist shook his head definitively. "Most assuredly not," he declared. "We have in the past *apprehended* people in the act of attempting to gain entry for nefarious purposes, but in no instance have they ever gotten anywhere close to achieving their goal. Even those who attempt it remotely usually find the cuffs being slapped on before they properly get started. The benefits of having advanced security precautions and a teleporter on staff." His expression became even less happy. "I strongly suspect that we have become overly complacent with our ongoing success. It would take an artificer with a breadth and depth of skill rivaling my own to create an override device capable of defeating my security precautions. I have never encountered such a talent before now, and thus I did not account for it."

It had to be Smokeshadow, using the discus. Too many factors were adding up for it to be otherwise. However, Jericho didn't want to just say so out loud, because the matter would be out of his hands about one second after he explained who she was. It would be better if he approached her on the down-low, asked her what the hell she thought she was playing at, and impressed on her the need to leave town 'til the heat died down. But for that, he needed the opportunity to drop off the grid and go looking for her in Utopia *without* anyone breathing down his neck.

"You know, I had me a notion about that ..." he ventured diffidently, not wanting to give the impression he knew something for certain. If they thought all he had was a hunch, they might give him the free rein he needed.

"With all due respect, whatever concepts you are entertaining, I have almost certainly considered and rejected them already." The Technologist's tone was as dry as it was blunt. "Your Prodigy talents, by my recollection, lean more toward directed violence than contemplation and cogitation."

He was incorrect where it counted and correct where it didn't, and Jericho didn't know how to tell him otherwise without flat-out betraying Smokeshadow. There was no way of getting around that without maybe talking to Relentless—*who hates me*—so he decided to shelve it for the moment and deal with the other big issue at hand.

"Okay, uh, the next problem. Who shot Franklin Tucker, and why? If it was the person who sent him the data, they don't have to show up and pop him. They're going to be getting it anyway, yeah?"

The Technologist's voice became even drier. "Surely I do not have to explain the concept of '*no honor among thieves*'? It may be that Tucker was trying to extort more money from his contact. Alternatively, the person who initially stole the data may well have decided to pilfer it without paying the agreed-upon price. That is perhaps the simplest matter of all to explain. Now, you had an issue related to the fire?"

Five minutes previously, Jericho would not have considered a reminder of Stephen's untimely death to be a good thing. But he needed *something* to distract him from his suddenly very complicated life, and this fit the bill perfectly.

"Yeah," sighed Jericho. With a few brief words, he filled the older man in on what had happened at the apartment building, and how he'd found out that Stephen had died in the blaze.

The Technologist stood looking at Jericho once he'd finished, thumb and forefinger smoothing his beard. "And the untimely demise of this man, with whom you were actively seeking to cut ties, still bothers you deeply?"

"It does, yes," Jericho admitted. "I didn't even take the time to look for him in the crowd."

"Because of the unpleasant memories."

Jericho nodded; it was mostly true, after all.

"Well, then." The Technologist dusted his hands off briskly. "I am in no way qualified to assist you in this matter. Thankfully, we have someone who is." He touched the side of his goggles. "Ms. Chandler. Are you currently engaged in matters of any pressing import?"

Meredith Chandler was Force Majeure's in-house head of surgery, though her medical credentials extended far past that. Among other things, she was an excellent listener. She'd helped Jericho a lot already with coming to terms with Luke's death. He thought the world of her, but he didn't want to lay this on her as well. "Uh, I don't really think —"

A raised hand cut him off. "Very good. I have with me G-Man, who is currently suffering what I consider to be a misplaced crisis of conscience. Would you be free to talk with him?" A pause. "Good. He will be down to see you momentarily. Thank you for your time." The Technologist touched his goggles again and turned toward Jericho. "And there you have it."

"I'm to report to Ms. Chandler?" Jericho took a breath and resigned himself to his fate. It seemed as though he'd been left with no choice in the matter. Through his association with the lady, he'd learned that surgeons were called 'Mr.' and 'Ms.' rather than 'Doctor' once they gained their surgical qualifications. It was an odd kind of inverse snobbery, but that was apparently the way of the world.

The older man removed Jericho's phone from its cradle and handed it back. "As you say, you are to report to the lady surgeon. Her analysis of your emotional condition will determine our ongoing course of action."

Jericho tucked his phone into its pouch and left the laboratory. He wasn't looking forward to this, but orders were orders.

Well, best get to it. Next stop, Medical One.

11
Analysis

If Jericho disliked anything about living in one of the temporary accommodations within the Spire, it was the need to take an elevator if he wanted to get somewhere in a hurry. It wasn't that the elevators were slow or clunky or the Muzak was monotonous: quite the opposite, on all three counts. They were lightning-swift and silk-smooth, and there was no elevator music because (as Transit had once put it) nobody was in one long enough to need it.

And therein lay the problem, for him at least. The speed was achieved by using artificial gravity generators to accelerate the elevator cars—and the passengers within—to approximately ninety miles per hour in less than one-tenth of a second, then decelerate them at the destination floor within the same time interval. As everyone and everything in the elevator car shared the car's inertial frame of reference for the trip, nobody was flattened against the floor or ceiling by the acceleration or deceleration. They couldn't even detect the fact that they were moving.

Except that Jericho could.

Whether he had his power enhancement harness on or not, his G-sense was strong enough to detect the gravity field outside the elevator, to the point that he always knew exactly how fast he was going and how far he had traveled. This had the unfortunate effect of clashing with the perceived lack of motion *within* the elevator car, causing a thoroughly uncomfortable bout of cognitive dissonance every time.

Still, he had little in the way of choice. There were stairwells that he could've taken (and he had, a few times), but for the most part he tended to accept the discomfort as an acceptable price for the convenience. And getting where he needed to be in just a few seconds was indeed highly convenient.

Stepping out of the elevator on the appropriate floor (down near ground level, this time), he paused to allow the disorientation to pass, then proceeded on to the door marked 'MEDICAL-1'. Although he knew he was expected, he knocked anyway.

"Come in." It was Ms. Chandler's voice. He tapped the reader with his MagCard to open the door and entered.

Meredith 'Merry' Chandler, MD, DSurg (along with several other qualifications) was a slender woman in her late thirties with wispy blonde hair tied back in a ponytail and tired-looking faded blue eyes. At the moment, she was wearing fresh scrubs, which meant she'd had to change after coming out of surgery. He wondered who had gotten hurt and how badly. There'd been nothing on the news, but that didn't mean anything.

Force Majeure often moved too fast for the news media to keep up with them.

"If this isn't a good time, I can come back later," he offered. 'Later' was a usefully generic term that he could stretch out for quite some time, and he could always go brood on a rooftop until he'd sorted things out in his own head. It had worked for him in the past, and would do so again.

"Nonsense." Ms. Chandler brushed his objections aside and took his hands in hers. "Sarah's just made tea. It's always good to see you, Jericho."

He responded with a respectful nod. "It's good to see you too, ma'am. How've things been around here?"

She closed her eyes briefly and let out a sigh. "Hectic, but you'd already figured that one out, hadn't you? There was a Madness attack in Detroit, and the local team only barely managed to put them down. Half of the team were unconscious and dying, with civilian casualties as well. There was no way for the local medical services to deal with everyone in time, so as soon as we got the emergency signal, Tourbillon opened a portal and my people ferried the critical cases back here. Even then, it was all hands on deck. But they should all recover."

"That's a plus, I guess." Jericho didn't say 'good', because Madness attacks were never good. He briefly squeezed her hands, then let them go.

The Madness (the name referred to both the victims and the affliction) were otherwise ordinary people who inexplicably vanished when nobody was looking. When they returned a few days later, sometimes on the other side of the country, it was always with powers and an insanely murderous attitude.

They popped up in the middle of populated areas and attacked with brutal savagery, never surrendered, and never retreated. Both heroes and civilians were targeted, and the Madness had to be either knocked unconscious or killed before they ceased to fight. While they lost the powers within twenty-four hours of reappearing, just as mysteriously as they'd gained them, in that time they were capable of causing significant death and destruction. And while the powers vanished, the psychosis remained.

Jericho had never gone up against the Madness, but he knew it was only a matter of time. He didn't want to think about it; deliberately setting out to kill an opponent wasn't something he was comfortable doing. If he was ever faced with the decision of taking a life to save a life, he hoped he had the mental fortitude to make the right decision when the time came.

"Yes, but we're not here to talk about that. We're here to talk about *you*. Come on." With a beckoning tilt of her head, Ms. Chandler turned and led the way past the currently quiescent auto-medic tables with their dangling horror-movie array of surgical tools into the back area. This was where she'd set up an ad hoc office area, including a camp bed and a kitchenette. Like him, she had a dedicated apartment of her own within the Spire, but events such as Madness attacks sometimes made it so she couldn't step away for even half an hour; during those times, she slept in the back with one ear out for the alarm buzzer.

Half-heartedly, he tried one more time to wriggle out of the gentle interrogation he knew was coming. "Look, if you want to catch a nap, I'll be fine. I'm just a little down. Once I get in some quality brooding time—"

"Sit," she said firmly, pointing at a folding chair.

"Yes, ma'am." He sat down, just as Ms. Owens brought in the tea tray and set it on the small table.

As the steam rose and the fragrance of the tea permeated the room, Jericho felt himself relaxing into the chair, the tension easing out of him. The aroma redoubled as Ms. Owens poured two cups of tea with—it had to be said—surgical precision, then put down the teapot and stepped back from the table.

Petite and dark-haired, Ms. Chandler's deputy head was quiet and self-effacing, though Jericho understood her to be a competent surgeon in her own right. She seemed content to work under Ms. Chandler for the moment, which in Jericho's opinion was an intelligent move; having been even the deputy head of surgery in the Spire would be a fantastic look for her CV. If Ms. Owens ever decided to broaden her horizons, Jericho knew, basically every hospital in America would be beating down her door with offers.

She also happened to pour a mean cup of tea, a somewhat less recognized skill but just as vital under certain circumstances.

"Thank you, Sarah." Ms. Chandler's words were polite, though the tone was more direct than Jericho would've employed. As Ms. Owens lingered, Ms. Chandler frowned. "Don't you have paperwork to take care of?"

Ms. Owens nodded. "Yes, ma'am. G-Man." Giving them each a nod of acknowledgment, she stepped back to the corner of the room, where she had a laptop on a small folding table. Seating herself, she faded into the background almost as efficiently as Smokeshadow herself could have done.

Jericho briefly considered saying something, then realized he had no context for dealing with the situation, if indeed there was a situation. He'd already proven himself utterly incompetent at understanding workplace politics. For all he knew, this was how they preferred to speak to each other. So, he did the wisest thing he could think of under the circumstances; he kept his yap shut.

With a delicate touch, Ms. Chandler stirred milk and sugar into one of the cups and handed it to Jericho. He hadn't been a big tea drinker before he came to the Spire, but he had to admit the taste was growing on him. The very act of drinking it, especially in Ms. Chandler's presence, was calming on a fundamental level.

She busied herself with her own cup for a few moments before speaking again. "Before we begin, are you comfortable having Sarah in the room? She has her own work to do, but she's been read in on your situation."

"Oh, uh, I'm fine with it." Jericho trusted Ms. Chandler's judgment in the matter. Her advice had panned out well to this point, so he wasn't about to start second-guessing her now.

She nodded to acknowledge his words, both spoken and unspoken. "Very well. One more thing; regarding what you said earlier, do not assume for a moment that I am downplaying the importance of brooding when it comes to your mental health. It has a role in your self-care, and I will happily advise you to find a rooftop and brood away anytime you feel the urge. But all the research the Technologist has shared with me on the matter suggests that it relates more to maintaining your center as regards your powers and your Prodigy focus, as opposed to solving random moral quandaries."

Jericho nodded. "I get that. I really do. But this *is* about my focus. I'm all about loyalty, which is why this here's tearing me up inside."

She took on a thoughtful expression and sipped at her tea. "So noted. Who do you feel you've betrayed, and why?"

And just like that, the tension was back. For a frozen moment, Jericho nearly blurted out what he knew about Smokeshadow and why he'd been keeping her a secret from Relentless and Force Majeure, but then he regained control of his speech centers. That would have to wait until he'd thought it through in detail, preferably on some isolated rooftop. For now, he had to speak about the matter at hand.

"His name was Stephen," he began. "Before I joined Force Majeure, he was my boyfriend. We'd been living together for six months at that point. He didn't want me to join, but I came anyway. Soon after that, I found out he'd been cheating on me ..."

Once more, the sad and sordid story unfolded. Jericho carefully left out any reference to Thomas, just that he'd been happier away from Stephen than with him. When Ms. Chandler refilled his mysteriously empty cup, he stirred more milk and sugar in and kept talking.

"... I only found out he'd been in the apartment the whole time when we were on the maglev, halfway back to Utopia," he concluded. "But I mean, I didn't know he was there. I honestly thought he was across town, trying to catch up with me at the Tucker investigation. Still, I feel bad about it. Like I failed him somehow. I mean, I should've checked anyway, right?"

Ms. Chandler sipped at her tea. "The answer to that one is 'it depends'." With a smile at his irritated glance, she went on. "First, I have to establish some facts outside of what you've already told me. Did he ever leave his car elsewhere for any good reason?"

Of course, Luke chose this moment to stick his oar in.

What, like th' time I caught him down the bayou with that asshole from Augusta an' kicked his teeth in? That kinda good reason?

He decided not to voice the interjection out loud; it would lead to *far* too many questions. Besides, there were other potential reasons. "Well, he *could* have been out shopping, or running other errands, or taking it in for repairs.

It was a rust-bucket at the best of times." He paused. "Why didn't I think of that?"

"Because you had nineteen other potential victims to save at that moment," she reminded him. "So, how finished was this relationship? Were you still seeing him occasionally, or had you cut all ties?"

"All ties," he said immediately. "We were done. If he wanted to sleep with other men, he was welcome to them. Just not to me."

"Hmm," she murmured. "Wise, on several levels. How about emotionally? Did you spend much time thinking about him? Regretting how it had turned out?"

He thought he saw where this was going, and shook his head. "My only real regret was that I let him fool me for so long. I mean, I surely missed *being* with someone, but I wasn't about to let him pull the wool over my eyes again for the sake of a little intimacy. Besides ..." Realizing he'd been about to mention Thomas, he cut himself off.

She raised her eyebrows. "Besides ...?"

Cursing himself for an idiot, he shrugged and gave her a weak grin. "Besides, there's other fish in the sea, right? I'll find someone else."

Well, I already have. But she doesn't need to know that.

From the glance she gave him, he thought she might have read more into his answer than he wanted, but she merely nodded. "That's entirely true. So, let's recap. Your Prodigy focus is all about loyalty, and you've had reason to be loyal to him in the past. Perhaps, because you failed to save him in the present, you feel you're somehow betraying that past loyalty?"

That was a way of looking at it that he hadn't thought about. "I ... I guess. Maybe?"

"Mm-hmm." She took another sip from her tea and changed tack. "Now, given what you said about the building, it was thoroughly on fire. If he'd been on the rooftop, would you have hesitated to save him? He betrayed you and lied to you, after all."

"With all due respect, ma'am, not just 'no' but *hell* no!" He felt vaguely offended at the suggestion. "No matter what he'd done, he didn't deserve *that.*"

"Of course he didn't." She smiled slightly in approval, and he realized she'd been subtly testing him. "Okay, this is the tough one. Suppose you've looked in the window and seen him lying there. The building is on fire. There's fire all around him. Despite your costume, you aren't personally fireproof, and there'll be lots of smoke and heat and very little oxygen in there. There's a significant risk to be assessed in getting him out, and no time to grab an oxygen mask to improve matters. Would you still try to get him out? Even knowing he might already be dead, and being aware you might die in the attempt?"

He pressed his lips together as he thought over his answer. Ms. Chandler was right; this wasn't an easy one. But his response was still the same when it came down to the line. "I reckon I'd try anyway."

She set her cup down and spread her hands. "Why? Why not send Black Dragon in instead? She's far more able to stand those conditions than you are."

"And she couldn't lift and carry him in a hundred years," he said. "He's not … he wasn't exactly light, and she said she can only handle a big kid. Even if she *can* breathe smoke and ignore fire, the building would've been coming down around her before she got him out. No, if anyone could've done it, it was me." By way of demonstration, he infused a rainbow-sparkling push-tag into the teacup and released it. They both watched as the cup drifted gently upward under the influence of its brand-new gravitational frame of reference.

"Impressive," she noted. "Your control's getting better. But what's that in aid of?"

Reaching up, he recaptured the cup and dismissed the G-tag; the tea, which had begun to form a hemispherical bulge in the middle of the cup, flattened out again, albeit with ripples covering the surface of the beverage. "I could've made him light as a feather and flown out with him," he explained. "Thirty seconds, in and out." He sipped at the tea for emphasis.

"And what if the roof fell in while you were right there?" She looked him straight in the eye. "What's to say the apartment itself wouldn't start collapsing? As I said, you're not immune to heat, and a fire-resistant costume only gets you so far. If you'd gone in and been trapped for any amount of time, there's a good chance you never would have made it out."

"I still would've owed it to him to try," he said stubbornly.

She didn't argue back at him. "Keeping that view in mind, let's revisit your original question. Do you see your choice of actions as a betrayal by omission, if not commission?"

He turned his head away at the word 'betrayal', not due to Stephen, but because it resonated too closely with the way he was keeping his cards close to his chest about Smokeshadow. "Yes. No. I dunno."

"Well, that clears things up nicely." She gave him a look strongly reminiscent of maiden aunts he'd known back in Savannah. "When you can make up your mind on that aspect, we'll both know where you stand."

"Yeah, that makes a lick of sense." He finished his tea off and put the cup down. "So, what's the verdict, ma'am? Am I sane?"

She snorted with amusement. "As sane as anyone in this open-air asylum can ever be. But I don't think you were quite over your ex, and you definitely aren't over the way he passed. Especially as you still think you could've done something to save him, despite all the evidence to the contrary."

He didn't want to argue with her, but he couldn't help taking issue with that statement. "Now, hold your horses just one doggone minute. I've gone into dangerous situations before, and come out the other side just fine."

She leaned forward over the table toward him. "Yes, but in this case, there's a good chance you would've let your need to save him override your judgment of how perilous it actually was." Her fingertip prodded him in the chest; he could vaguely feel the pressure past the polycarbonate plates in his costume. "And that may have gotten you killed."

She wasn't *wrong*, but he did think she was maybe overstating the case a little. He wasn't exactly a newbie at the game, after all. However, while he was the superhero in the room, she *was* a medical professional, so he couldn't really argue against her conclusions. The only thing left was to find out what she wanted him to do.

"Possibly." He raised his hands, palm out. "Look, I can see what you're saying, and it's not like it'll ever happen again. Where do we go from here? Am I good to go?"

"Not so fast." Her tone sharpened. "Just because you dodged this bullet doesn't mean you're out of the woods. You might project this onto the next person—or five, or ten—you see in danger, and ignore potentially lethal risks to save them. We need to pull you out of the line of fire, at least temporarily, until I can put together a baseline assessment of your mental condition."

"Wait ... you're *benching* me?" He was on his feet and backing away from her in a heartbeat, unable to believe this was happening. "I can be more careful now that you've pointed this out. I *will* be more careful. It's not gonna catch me by surprise."

Standing up in her turn, she gave him a contemplative gaze. "I'd like to believe that. I know you're a responsible person, and that you perform well in a mentor role."

Jericho shook his head in disbelief as the import of her words registered on him. "You want me to teach new recruits to be superheroes? To do *my* job?" As ridiculous as that sounded, he couldn't figure out any other interpretation of her words. "I'm brand new on the team! The only one I've been in charge of so far is Black Dragon! You might want to go ask her what *she* thinks about that idea! 'Cause I can guarantee you, she won't be a fan!"

She turned her hands palm down, fingers spread, and patted at the air. "Calm down, Jericho. We're not putting you back with Black Dragon. She was a bad fit for you. However, the Technologist has been working on a project that I think would suit your current needs."

The subject change caught Jericho wrong-footed. "Project? What kind of project?"

"I think I'll let him explain it to you. But first, I will need to contact him to ensure this is a good time to bring you in on it. For now, Jericho, take a seat." When he hesitated for a moment, she pointed firmly at the chair, just as she'd done the last time. "*Sit.*"

He sat. There really was no other option.

With a nod of satisfaction, she turned and left the room, presumably searching for a phone.

Almost like a butler in a British comedy, Ms. Owens appeared at his side; Jericho had been so distracted, he hadn't registered her getting up and coming over to the table. "You're finished with this?" she asked, indicating the tea tray.

"Ah, yes, ma'am," Jericho said hastily, scrambling to remember the manners his Mama had impressed on him as a child. "And thanks for making it."

She nodded, clearly pleased at the courtesy. "You're welcome, G-Man." About to leave the room with the tray, she paused. "I have a little advice I could share with you, if you're interested."

"Uh, maybe?" he said, a little taken aback. This was the most Ms. Owens had ever said to him at one time. Though given the previous exchange, he wondered what she would say.

Is this going to be something nasty about her boss?

If she merely intended to pass on malicious office gossip, he was going to have to shut the conversation down hard. Of course, he wouldn't rat her out to Ms. Chandler, just let her know he couldn't listen to stuff like that.

She took a deep breath, clearly steeling herself. "You're not the first person to feel you've let someone down, and you won't be the last. I've been there myself, if you're interested in hearing the story."

That got his attention. He stared at the petite woman, unwilling to believe that someone so diffident and unassuming might stoop so low as to break faith with anyone. "I'm sorry, ma'am. I just can't see it." At the same time, he mentally smacked himself over the back of the head for thinking the worst of her.

Her smile was sad. "Nobody can, not even with themselves, until it's too late. Once upon a time, I was … involved with a man who needed me more than I needed him, but then I was made a better offer."

Unaccountably, he felt a lump forming in his throat. Working his way past it, he searched for words. "What happened? To him, I mean?"

She turned her face away until it was hidden by her hair. "He had a life-threatening condition. As a result, he underwent two dangerous procedures, one after the other. He wouldn't go through with it unless I oversaw it, and I stupidly agreed. There's a reason they don't let surgeons work on their loved ones." She sighed sadly. "I genuinely thought I could pull him through it. Through all of it." Her voice drifted to a halt.

Jericho waited silently.

After a few moments of silent introspection, she shook her head. "The toll on his strength was too great, and he died. I wish now I'd had the strength to cut ties altogether and walk away before it ended like it did." Her voice was almost inaudible.

"I'm sorry." He reached out and put his hand gently on her arm. "I can't imagine what that would be like."

She nodded in acknowledgment. "We all make decisions when we're young and infallible that we excoriate ourselves for in later life. I suppose it's the universe's way of showing us that our actions, no matter how petty they might appear at the time, have consequences. For me, it was thinking I could get what I wanted without having to pay the price. Forgetting, of course, that the price *always* demands payment, and we rarely get to choose the coin we'll be paying it in." She took a deep breath, then let it out slowly. "It's one of the reasons I accepted this position here, in this place, so I might make a difference."

"And you surely do," he said sincerely. Ms. Chandler might be the head of the surgical department, but from what he could see, Ms. Owens was the one who ensured it ran like clockwork.

"Thank you, G-Man. I appreciate that." With another pleased smile, she took the tray away.

He stood there, wondering at the revelation. For all of Ms. Owens' surety as a surgeon, that tragedy seemed to have affected her deeply.

Ms. Chandler reappeared, barely glancing at the cleared table on the way through. "He's given us the all-clear. Let's go and see what this project holds in store for you."

As they headed for the elevator, Jericho glanced at Ms. Chandler. "Don't suppose you'd give me any hints about the project?"

She favored him with a serene smile. "None whatsoever."

12
Sidekick

The matte-black metallic humanoid form loomed over Jericho as he looked up at it. Now that he was paying more attention, the clamps didn't seem to be holding it onto the rack very firmly. The arms and legs were bulkier than he would've expected from a proportionately scaled form, and the eyes glowed a verdant green. He had a distinct feeling that it was watching him. Worse, that it was silently judging him.

"Oh," he said for want of a better thing to say. "*That* project."

"The observational skills of today's youth never cease to astound me." The Technologist's voice was as dry as ever.

"Be nice," Ms. Chandler said mildly. "He's already had to deal with one unpleasant shock today. We don't need to add to his issues."

That gave Jericho time to get his conversational feet under himself. "Okay, so what's it supposed to do? And more importantly, what am I supposed to *do* with it? I don't know anything about robots except what I've seen in movies. Which, I suspect, isn't going to be very helpful here."

Wonder of wonders, the Technologist moderated his tone a little. "What you see before you is the pilot model for what I have dubbed Project Sidekick. It is durable, intelligent, and both reactive and proactive. With the increasing number of obstacles facing heroes in this modern age, it is intended to assist you in performing your duties. Most specifically, it will ensure that you will no longer be required to venture into hazardous scenarios without some kind of backup."

Jericho found himself on the back foot once more. "Wait, so you're putting *me* in charge of your prototype? What if something goes wrong with it? I'm pretty sure I just said that I know exactly nothing useful about robots."

"Even if you *were* an expert, it wouldn't help you here." The artificer's snark was back in full force. "The chassis was constructed, extensively tested, and reinforced to withstand the most extreme stresses. Transit and I are both confident that its onboard diagnostic and self-repair systems can handle ninety-nine-point-nine percent of what can go wrong with it. And in the exceedingly unlikely event that a zero-point-one-percent case emerges, it is programmed to go into sleep mode and transmit an emergency beacon."

"Okay, that's the hardware." Jericho waved at where the glowing green eyes seemed to be still fixed upon him. "What about the software? What if someone hacks it? If whoever hacked the Spire takes a run at this guy, it could cause us a heap more immediate, visible problems than a few pirated files."

While he didn't *think* Smokeshadow would be interested in acquiring a robot sidekick, he wouldn't be doing his due diligence as a member of Force Majeure if he didn't at least mention the possibility.

The Technologist turned sharply toward him. "Of all the potential scenarios, why did you see fit to invoke that particular one?" The irritation was evident in his voice.

"Before you told me about the Spire being hacked, I thought that was impossible too," Jericho pointed out, entirely truthfully.

He was already unsure about Smokeshadow's motives; while he didn't see her as being up to shooting a man in the back of the head in cold blood, the Technologist had made a good case. He *did* want to talk to her about that, while at the same time not wanting to find out he might be wrong about her. And, of course, if he *was* wrong, he didn't want her to also steal the Sidekick robot.

The Technologist's voice carried enough edge to slice tungsten carbide. "That specific incident required the perpetrator to gain physical access to a computer linked into our systems. There is no way for the unit to be accessed wirelessly without it detecting such intrusion and counter-hacking the signal."

"Okay, understood," Jericho said, more to get off dangerous ground than because he actually agreed with the older man. "It can't be hacked. Which means we're back to the question of '*why me*'?"

"We've got two reasons for this," Ms. Chandler noted. "First, you appear to have a knack for mentorship. Twice now, you've been able to deal with Black Dragon at short notice with no significant mishaps. You're both empathetic and sympathetic, and you think on your feet. I'm personally of the opinion that you're more capable of handling something like this than you think you are."

"So long as we're being honest, dealing with Black Dragon sometimes felt like juggling live hand grenades," Jericho said candidly. "But let's say I've got this knack you're talking about. What's the second reason?"

Not at all to his surprise, it was Ms. Chandler who spoke up again. "Your safety."

"Wait, no, seriously. I'm fine, really." But even as he spoke the words, he knew it would do no good.

"As much as you may try to give the impression of slowness, I know there's a brain behind that mask." The Technologist's tone was as cutting as ever. "You heard what the lady surgeon said. Following the events in Savannah, we have concerns about the possibility of you taking unnecessary risks when you go out into the field once more. I happen to agree with her analysis of your mental state, so we will be placing you on light duties for the next few weeks. In the meantime, you will be accompanied by Sidekick Zero One whenever you appear in public as G-Man. Mostly, you will be working to assist in socializing and calibrating its public-interaction software. As a useful coincidence, if you do happen to find yourself in a situation where a lapse in judgment may endanger you, you will have access to immediate and effective backup."

Jericho tried not to feel offended, but it wasn't easy. "So, basically half the time I'll be babysitting it, and the other half it'll be babysitting me. Is that about it?"

Ms. Chandler winced slightly. "That's one way to describe matters, though not precisely accurate. You'll be teaching it how to interact with people, and it will be adding its capabilities to yours when you do have to go into action." She sighed. "Because I *never* bet against superheroes when it comes to finding trouble to get into."

"Right." He really couldn't argue with that. "So how long will these 'light duties' go on for? Because I can't exactly prove a negative. Sooner or later, you'll have to trust that I'm tougher than that."

The surgeon and the artificer looked at one another. Ms. Chandler raised her eyebrows interrogatively. The Technologist nodded, then turned back to Jericho. "As it happens, Relentless has already made it known that he intends for you to represent Force Majeure at the Challenger Commemoration Day ceremony this year at the Kennedy Space Center. In my personal judgment, that should act as a sufficient cut-off point."

That made it just over three weeks that he'd have to do this. The Challenger Commemoration Day was a massive deal for superheroes across America and beyond. A day of celebration of the beginnings of both the first Enabled and superhero culture in general, it was upbeat and optimistic; the sheer volume of superhero-themed fireworks let off across the nation on January twenty-eighth rivaled those for the Fourth of July.

The corresponding event for the death of the iconic superhero, Challenger Memorial Day, took place in late August. Ceremonies were considerably more somber and featured black armbands with Challenger's colors of red and gold rather than fireworks and celebrations. The main one of these took place at the Arlington National Cemetery, where Challenger's headstone was located.

"Wait, what?" Jericho was surprised, but not so much that he couldn't respond. "He wants *me* to represent Force Majeure? But he hates my guts!"

Silence filled the room in the aftermath of his outburst. Neither of the other two said anything for a long moment, then Ms. Chandler shook her head. A delicate snort of amusement escaped her nostrils. "No," she said, tightening her lips to school her expression. "No, he doesn't."

"*I'm* pretty sure he does," Jericho insisted, but he could already feel the certitude of his assurance beginning to erode. "The last time we talked, he wasn't happy with me. At all. And I've never had a chance to speak with him since."

"Have you *asked* for a chance to speak with him?" The Technologist raised an eyebrow. "Or have you assumed that just because he has far too much on his plate to seek you out for casual conversation, he dislikes you for something that has probably already slipped his memory altogether?"

Jericho doubted very much that Relentless had forgotten that particular incident. The rage in the man's face when Jericho turned him down for sex would forever be burned into his memory. Still … it *had* been months.

"Um," he said eloquently.

Holy crap, I've been thinking he hates me all this time, and he couldn't care less.

"More to the point," Ms. Chandler said firmly, "he has spoken to me about you on more than one occasion. I'm not at liberty to tell you the exact topics covered, but his view of you is anything but negative. Relentless holds a high opinion of your capabilities and future with Force Majeure."

Huh. Well, I'll be damned.

Oddly enough, although it was a surprise to hear, the news didn't impact Jericho nearly as much as he'd thought it would.

He had definitely been through a lot since he'd set off as a hopeful applicant to try out for Force Majeure back in October. At the time, he'd been sporting a moderate crush on Relentless that had only intensified each time he met the man. If he'd heard this opinion of him back then, it would've made his entire year and cemented his crush into adoration.

Since then, reality had ensued. The crush was gone, killed by Jericho's relationship with Thomas. Now, the compliment was just a nice thing to hear. A pat on the back from the boss: no more and no less.

But even that was tarnished by his knowledge of what Relentless did behind closed doors with the new recruits. Again, he wondered how to deal with the unwelcome information that he'd learned from his teammate. Black Dragon had seemed positively smug with the revelation that she'd slept with Relentless; there was no sense of victimization there. He wondered if rules existed that even covered this situation within a superhero team. It wasn't as though Relentless was forcing himself on people, like Adam Power had been accused of attempting with Vanessa. However—

"G-Man? Earth to G-Man?" Ms. Chandler waved her hand before his face. "Are you all right? You zoned out for a minute there."

"Yeah, I'm fine," he said. "It was just a bit of a shock to hear that Relentless doesn't hate me."

"Believe me, when Relentless takes a dislike to an individual, they learn all about it in very short order." The Technologist waved his hand through the holographic readout on his tablet. "Under no circumstances do they get the opportunity to spend weeks agonizing over what he really thinks of them." He made a pulling motion, drawing a diagram out to full extension above the tablet. "Now, let us cease this idle banter and return to the actual matter at hand. It is time to bring Sidekick Zero One to full operational status."

Jericho nodded, focusing his attention. This was more important than his half-assed problems. Or rather, this was something he could deal with here and now, rather than having to wait for an opportunity to go rooftop brooding somewhere. He watched as the Technologist flicked holographic switches on the three-dimensional construct hovering over the tablet. The clamps snapped open, one after the other.

As the form on the rack stirred, its glowing eyes shifted to a soft amber. Bending forward at the waist with the sound of articulated armor plates sliding over one another, it pushed itself off the rack and stepped forward onto the laboratory floor. It was surprisingly light on its feet for something that had to weigh as much as a motorcycle.

"Sidekick Zero One reporting for duty." The synthesized vocal tones were clearly artificial, yet also somehow familiar. Far from the halting mechanical voice he'd been subconsciously expecting, it spoke fluently and emphasized words correctly. **"Individuals identified: Technologist. Ms. Meredith Chandler. G-Man. All affiliated with Force Majeure. All designated 'allies'. Are identifications correct?"**

"Your identification protocols are correct, Sidekick Zero One." The Technologist's voice was firm and clear. "Defining new directive: begin. Sidekick Zero One is now partnered with G-Man. As per prior directives, the primary objective of this partnership is to protect G-Man. G-Man is authorized to issue orders to Sidekick Zero One, super-user status level alpha three. New directive: complete. Acknowledge."

"Partnership with G-Man understood." The robot turned its head to look at Jericho, and its eyes went from amber back to green. **"Primary directive: maintain the safety of G-Man. Secondary directive: follow orders given by G-Man. Directive assimilated and acknowledged."**

"Wait, wait," protested Jericho. "Can we swap those two around? I don't want it to spend more time thinking about my safety than what I might want it to do."

"Hmm." The Technologist stroked his beard with forefinger and thumb, then looked over at Ms. Chandler. "Thoughts on the matter?"

She looked from Jericho to the robot and back again. He had the distinct feeling that he was the kid in the room, his choices being judged by the grown-ups. "So long as it still keeps his safety in mind, we can do it that way," she conceded.

The Technologist nodded, then addressed Jericho once more. "If you are entirely certain, I can alter the weightings of those directives. Were there any other concerns you wished to address while I have its command set open for modification?"

Jericho paused for thought. "Actually, yeah. Can we call it something other than 'Sidekick Zero One'? Because that'll sound weird in public."

From the Technologist's voice, he was holding back irritation. "That can certainly be achieved with a minimum of effort. Did you perhaps have a name in mind?"

Just for a second, Jericho was tempted to say 'Luke', but it was still far too soon, and he didn't relish explaining the choice to people who knew him. So, he went with his second option. "Scout."

"Scout?" asked Ms. Chandler. "Where did you get that name from?"

"My cousin Luke's dog," Jericho explained. "Luke had him from a pup, 'til he passed a few years back. He was damn smart for a dog. Luke and I were torn up about it, and he swore he'd never get another one."

"And so, you have decided to apply the name of a common hound to the most advanced robot in the history of artificers." The Technologist shook his head. "And there are some who wonder why I fear for the future of the human race."

"Hey, I liked that dog," protested Jericho. "There was nothing 'common' about him. He once took on a cottonmouth that like to bit Luke when we were just kids. When Uncle Leroy found out how close it got, he tanned both our hides for being down the bayou without telling anyone where we were going."

"Enough," snapped the Technologist with a raised hand. "Kindly cease this maudlin display of sentimentality post-haste. I will take your word that the dog was a suitably effective protector. Sidekick Zero One's official designation will be altered to 'Scout'. Now, do you have any other matters with which you wish to disturb me before I commence the status alteration?"

"No, no, I'm fine." Jericho came to a decision and caught Ms. Chandler's eye. "There was something I wanted to talk to the lady about anyway."

"Very well, then. Confer away. I shall be occupied for at least three minutes." The Technologist almost managed to sound magnanimous as he turned his attention to the tablet he held.

By unspoken agreement, Jericho and Ms. Chandler took several steps away from the artificer. "What's the matter?" asked the surgeon. "I can tell that something else is bothering you but not what, exactly."

Oh, if only you knew.

Jericho took a deep breath, trying to focus his thoughts. As much as he liked and trusted her, there was no way she would forego her allegiance to Force Majeure over his perceived debt to Smokeshadow. It was time to address the problem she *could* help him deal with. At least, he hoped she could.

"Could we ... get us some more privacy?" he asked, flicking his eyes toward the Technologist. The man came across as detached and impersonal, but he was still Relentless' teammate, and airing this in front of him could result in any one of several disastrous outcomes. If they had to step out of the lab and discuss the matter in the hall, that would work for Jericho.

"Well, of course." Ms. Chandler took a palm-sized device from her pocket and pressed the recessed button on it; immediately, all ambient sound cut out. "What did you want to talk about?"

Up until that moment, Jericho hadn't known that hand-held privacy bubble generators even existed, but he had deeper problems to worry about. "It's Relentless," he confessed. "Back when I first joined, he hit on me pretty hard, and told me that he likes to screw the new recruits."

She nodded. "I'm aware of this habit of his," she confirmed. "I won't go into the psychology of it, but it's not an uncommon urge. And yes, I'm also aware that there's a potential ethical problem, given that he holds a position of power over them. They may feel obligated to say yes, after all." She tilted her head. "Did you?"

"Well, no," Jericho admitted. "I'd be lying if I said I wasn't attracted to him, but I had my reasons for turning him down. Which, by the way, was why I thought he hated me. When he opened the window and kicked me out—metaphorically, not literally—he was mad enough to chew up nails and spit out barbed wire. But that's not the part I'm worried about."

"All right, now I'm curious." She opened her hand, inviting him to keep talking.

Now was the time to bite the bullet. Jericho inhaled a sharp, choppy breath and spoke the name on the exhale. "Black Dragon."

Ms. Chandler was silent for a moment. "You believe he made her the same offer because she's a new recruit."

He'd already known she was quick on the uptake. "I *know* he made her the same offer," he corrected her. "She was bragging on it to me. Between that and how she's walking … yeah, it happened."

She tilted her head, clearly thinking about the ramifications of the situation. "Well, as I said, somewhat dubious in the ethical sense, but if she was a willing participant, not actively illegal. Do you believe she was?"

There was only one truthful answer. "Yeah, I think so, but I'm also worried about her being underage. If the news crews get even the slightest idea that the head of Force Majeure is in the practice of making moves on all the new recruits, legal and otherwise, it's gonna open a whole can of worms where it comes to our reputation." And he really didn't want to think about trying to balance his sense of loyalty against the notion of working for someone who was in the habit of breaking the law like that.

"Hm. One second." Sliding the privacy bubble generator into her pocket, Ms. Chandler took out a small holographic tablet. She flicked through 3-D menus for a moment, then nodded with a look of satisfaction on her face. "Worry no more. The girl is eighteen. That's legal right across the United States. I *will* make an appointment to give her a checkup, but again, it's at worst unethical. Not illegal."

"Wait, she's eighteen?" Jericho was startled. "You certain-sure about that?" He'd been running for so long on the belief that the girl was sixteen—at best—that the revelation blew him out of the water.

"The numbers don't lie." Ms. Chandler tapped her finger through the readout, collapsing it. "While normally you would not have access to this information, in the interest of settling this, her paperwork shows that she was born in nineteen ninety-five. Legally, she's an adult." A sigh escaped her. "As much as her behavior would try to convince us otherwise. Apparently, 'late bloomer' applies just as much to emotional maturity as it does to the physical side of things. Who knew?"

He realized she was trying to use humor to defuse what would have otherwise been an intensely awkward moment for him: a courtesy he appreciated. "Okay, got it. But how about the drinking side of things? Sixteen or eighteen; either way, she's still underage for that."

"Relentless hasn't gotten to where he is now by being an idiot," Ms. Chandler reminded him gently. "Kansas law says a legal guardian—and Force Majeure *does* take on guardianship of its underage members—are permitted to supply non-distilled cereal alcohol to a minor. I suspect you'll find he's covered there."

"Non-distilled cereal alcohol?" Jericho tilted his head. "What's that when it's at home?"

"Beer and wine, mostly," she said lightly. "I can't see him drinking wine, but he does strike me as a beer person. If I were a betting person, I'd say that's what he gave her."

"Right." He rubbed the back of his neck, feeling more than a little embarrassed. "Uh, thanks for clearing that up for me. Should I go and apologize to her? Or Relentless? Because I've been thinking unfair things about both of them."

She paused, then shook her head as she slipped the tablet back into her pocket. "As admirable as your motives are, I don't think that's a good idea. Right now, the situation has been resolved. Bringing it up with either one of them is likely to go places that nobody wants it to. You had what you thought was a legitimate concern, but now you know where you went wrong, and you've corrected that. Nothing more needs to be said. Do you understand?"

"Absolutely. And thank you." A flood of relief surged through his chest. While he'd been willing to go and offer his apologies to both Enabled and take whatever lumps were coming his way as a result, being let off the hook was a profoundly liberating sensation.

"You're entirely welcome." She leaned out to look past his shoulder. "Ah, it looks like he's finished."

"Cool." Turning, he saw the Technologist shutting down his tablet while the robot loomed in place, blue-glowing eyes giving way to green. When Jericho stepped forward, he knew the moment he'd left the bounds of the privacy bubble by the sudden influx of sound from around him. "Can I ask a question, sir?"

The Technologist gave him what might have been a superior look. "You *can* ask questions all day long; I am unable to stop you. Whether you *may* ask such questions is another request altogether." He paused, then sighed. "Yes, you may ask a question. What is it that you wish to know?"

Jericho organized his thoughts, pulling himself back from the minefield of asking what the difference was between the two (he knew vaguely, but not definitively). "The eye colors. I know green is probably good and red is probably bad, but what do they really mean?"

"Hm." The artificer frowned. "I would have presumed that you'd already worked that out for yourself. No? Well, the explanation is simplicity itself. Blue is for standby and shutting down. Green is for operational and awaiting orders. Amber is for operational, processing orders, and reacting to non-dangerous stimuli. And red is for reacting to danger, which is also when the weapon systems are activated. Will that suffice, or do you require me to provide a printed manual as well?"

"Eye color, no. Weapon systems, yes." Jericho stared at the robot, trying to determine where it might be hiding weapons. The forearms and legs *did* seem a little bulky. "You might've missed that tiny detail the first time around. Just saying."

The Technologist snorted derisively. "That 'tiny detail' was omitted because nobody with the slightest iota of forethought constructs a robot of this complexity and capability *without* installing offensive and defensive measures. Especially when one of its major directives is to keep its Enabled companion—in this case, you—alive and well. But if you must, feel free to proceed with it to one of the firing ranges and command it to run through its paces."

"Yeah, I think we need to do that. Figure I'll take it to Range Two." Jericho looked up at the renamed Scout. His previous visit to that particular target range, a month previously, had been low-key; he wasn't overly dangerous at a distance, at least in the conventional sense. He suspected that this time around was going to be considerably more exciting. "Hey, big fellow. Ready to go see what you can do?"

The robot's response was almost immediate. **"The Scout unit is ready, G-Man."** While the weird phrasing threw him for a moment, it was something he figured he could work on.

"Let's go do that, then."

13
Testing

They stepped into the elevator. Jericho tapped the display screen with his MagCard to bring up the floors he was authorized to visit, then flicked his fingers past the screen sensors to scroll the list in the direction he wanted. When it reached the level number corresponding to Target Range Two, he selected it with a tap of his finger then hit the OK icon. To distract himself as his powers tried to tell him that the floor was dropping out from under him, he gave the robotic figure beside him his full attention.

At six foot two, he was not used to looking *up* at anyone he was speaking to. The last time that happened had been with Relentless, because the man was freakin' *huge*. Scout was a little taller than the leader of Force Majeure but nowhere near as bulky. Still, the robot probably outweighed Relentless by a factor of three or four, purely due to its metallic construction.

I bet Adam Power would love to have a look at this guy. And Thomas would think he was pretty cool, too.

"So, um ..." he said, more to fill the silence than because he had anything to say. Before he could think of an appropriate conversational subject to bring up with a robot—*so what about those wacky Asimov laws, huh?*—the elevator stopped, and the doors opened.

"Yes, G-Man?" asked the robot, its eyes going from green to amber. Jericho had to give the Technologist props; while he hadn't noticed it at first, Scout's voice sounded just a shade smoother and less mechanical each time it spoke.

Stepping out of the elevator, still trying to think of something to say, Jericho headed for the firing range with Scout walking a steady two paces behind him. This made him deeply, viscerally uncomfortable on a level he found hard to express. The discomfort came not from fear of being attacked but from something far more profound.

Over and over, his mind insisted on drawing parallels between the power he had over Scout and the way life had been in his own hometown just a hundred sixty years before. The only difference he saw was that the control his a-few-generations-removed ancestors had held over their fellow human beings had been enforced by inhumane punishments instead of just a few lines of computer code. Not that he saw this way as being any better.

Finally, he decided to address the matter, no matter how stupid it might make him feel or look. Stopping in the middle of the corridor, he turned to Scout. "I can give you orders, and you have to carry them out, is that correct?"

"Yes, G-Man. The Scout unit's function is to carry out your orders and keep you safe."

If the reply had come back in a flat monotone, he might have felt better about it, but the words were inflected and nuanced in a way that would've sounded downright human if it weren't for the stilted phrasing.

He took a deep breath. "Okay, then. How do you feel about this? Do you enjoy following orders?"

"The Scout unit's function is to carry out your orders and keep you safe. The Scout unit does not experience emotions but can emulate them to improve the quality of interaction with humans."

This time, he could've sworn that the first statement had been repeated with what sounded like impatience. *What part of 'my function is to do what you say and protect you' didn't you get the first time, dumbass?*

"Right," he muttered. "Uh, are you able to use first-person pronouns? Like *'I am'* instead of *'the Scout unit is'*?"

"The Scout unit is capable of doing so. Is that a directive, G-Man?"

Oh, good. I'm not totally failing my 'how to deal with a robot' test.

"Yes, that's a directive. Uh, unless you want to keep talking that way."

"Directive assimilated and acknowledged. I do not have an opinion on the matter. I will employ first-person pronouns until a directive to do otherwise is issued."

"Okay, that's good. That's fine. Uh, can you, uh, walk beside me instead of behind me?"

"I can walk alongside you if directed to do so. However, I will be required to give way to persons walking in the other direction."

"Yeah, definitely," Jericho said with a hasty nod. "I don't want you barreling anyone over. Yeah, that's a directive."

"Directive assimilated and acknowledged."

It still felt weird issuing orders to something that looked and acted so close to human, but he was beginning to suspect that his fleeting thought about this being a test was closer to the truth than he'd realized initially. If Relentless did indeed have a higher opinion of him than he'd thought, maybe he was being groomed for a leadership position? And what better way to analyze someone's leadership capability than to observe their treatment of someone who could not disobey their commands?

Still mulling that one over, Jericho led the way to Target Range Two and tapped his card on the reader to gain entry. The door hissed aside, and he heard rifle fire from within. He was no kind of an expert with firearms, but from what he could tell, they were firing tightly controlled bursts with almost mechanical precision.

A woman with short blonde hair in a Spire Security uniform bearing the nametag BRADLEY came to meet them. Jericho vaguely recalled her from the last time he'd used Range Two. "Corporal Bradley," he greeted her, thankful for the reminder of her name. "Good to see you again."

"G-Man, likewise." Her grip was firm and businesslike as they shook hands. "The Technologist told me you were on the way down. So, who's this?" She looked Scout up and down with a discerning eye. "New recruit?"

"In a manner of speaking," Jericho confirmed. "Scout, this here's Corporal Bradley. She's the range master here. That means you do exactly what she tells you while you're on the target range. Corporal Bradley, this is Scout. You might say he's been assigned as my sidekick."

It was easy to slip into the habit of calling Scout 'him' instead of 'it'. He didn't like deceiving Bradley, but he had no idea if she was cleared to know of Scout's true nature, so he compromised with some half-truths.

"Nice to meet you, Scout," Bradley said, holding her hand out. Scout reciprocated the gesture only a second or so later, but the pause was long enough that Jericho's heart had time to almost stop in his chest.

"I am pleased to meet you also, Corporal Bradley," the robot replied, shaking her hand briefly. **"I will endeavor to follow your instructions."**

Bradley nodded. "That's what I like to hear." She looked them over searchingly. "Did you bring your own weapons, are you using Dynamic abilities, or will you be drawing weapons from the armory?"

"The first, kind of," Jericho noted. He gestured toward the looming robot. "Scout's got built-in armaments that we need to test out."

"That's what we're here for," Bradley said, then addressed herself to Scout. "Low impact, medium impact, or high impact?"

Scout's eyes flickered from amber to green and back again. **"Upon analysis, my onboard weaponry can be categorized as medium to high impact."**

"Copy that." Bradley tilted her head toward the door Jericho knew led through to the target range. "Let's get you two set up."

As they reached the door, it opened from the other side; Independence emerged, slinging her assault rifle over her shoulder opposite the claymore she already wore. Second in command of Force Majeure and icon of Utopia City, Independence had been a superhero since Jericho was eight. Tall and statuesque in her iconic red-and-blue costume, with her platinum-blonde ponytail blowing in the breeze (or so it was portrayed in every publicity shot he'd ever seen), she'd inspired nearly a generation's worth of women, Enabled and otherwise. Hell, she'd encouraged *him*. Her trademark weapons had put an end to terror villains and members of the Madness alike.

Corporal Bradley was fit, moved like someone who could handle her end of a brawl, and was a competent member of the Spire's security detail. By contrast, merely by walking into the room, Independence gave the impression of a tiger looming over a tabby cat.

Nodding briefly to Bradley, Independence turned her attention to Jericho and Scout. Her lip didn't quite curl, but her expression wasn't exactly welcoming either. "G-Man." The tone of her voice was distinctly chillier than the one Bradley had used.

"Good afternoon, Independence, ma'am." For all that he was an established member of Force Majeure, he knew damn well she could make his life difficult in far too many ways, so he was careful not to give her the slightest excuse.

When they'd first officially met during his initial disastrous interview, she had started by beating the hell out of him on the practice mat, then pushed his buttons with deliberately antagonistic questions until he snapped back and stormed out. He wasn't sure if her attitude was a general set against giving new recruits an easy ride, but she hadn't gotten any friendlier since then.

Even though it was Relentless who'd chosen to offer him a second chance, he'd been told that all seven core members had to agree—or at least not *dis*agree—on a prospective recruit before they could be brought on board. With the level of animus she appeared to hold against him, she could've sunk his membership chances without a trace but had clearly opted not to do so, and he had no idea why. Neither had he figured out where all this was coming from. Even Ms. Chandler, sympathetic as she was, had no insights to offer in that regard.

Just as he'd expected, she ignored him and looked Scout up and down. "I see Technologist finally let his latest Tinkertoy out of the lab. Bringing it down to wind up and point at the targets, huh?"

Jericho tried hard not to snap at her. He could handle being picked at himself, but Scout lacked the wherewithal to defend himself against a verbal attack. "Scout's been assigned as my partner, ma'am," he said stiffly. "I'm just bringing him down here to run him through his paces."

"Partner. Right." She snorted. "Gotcha. Yeah, you have fun with that. See you, Bradley." Turning on her heel, she stalked out of the firing range.

Corporal Bradley watched until the door closed behind Independence and let out a quiet breath. "Well, *you're* popular with her today," she murmured, then shook her head when he opened his mouth. "Uh-uh, don't tell me. I don't want to know. This is the sort of thing I stay the hell away from. I *like* having a career."

A minor verbal disagreement between two members of Force Majeure was so far out of her wheelhouse that he wasn't surprised she was washing her hands of it. He couldn't blame her. It wasn't her job to fix his problems or even be his friend. Her function was to ensure security was maintained within her part of the Spire, and she did it well.

"Totally understood," he said, obscurely pleased that she'd at least recognized what was going on, even if she had no way of doing anything about it. "Let's get this here done."

As Bradley headed through to the firing range proper, Scout spoke up. **"Force Majeure member designated as Independence is causing a potential conflict in my directives."**

Jericho looked at him, startled. This was the first time the robot had initiated a conversation. He lowered his voice so that Bradley wouldn't hear, or at least to give her an excuse to pretend she hadn't heard. "What? What do you mean?"

"My primary directive toward you, after following your orders, is to protect your well-being. Members of Force Majeure are automatically designated as allies. Independence has demonstrated hostility toward you. This hostility clashes with her designation as an ally. I predict a conflict in my directives if her hostility escalates to the point that she becomes an active threat to your well-being."

It was almost chilling, the way Scout laid it out in blunt terminology. "Uh … are you having trouble right now? Do you want me to order you not to think about it or something?"

"It is not a situation that will be resolved by ceasing to think about it. Independence will still be hostile toward you."

Jericho took a deep breath, trying to figure a way around this. It would be problematic if Scout decided to shut down because he couldn't resolve the problem. Worse, the robot might opt to attack Independence because he thought she was a direct threat to Jericho. "Uh, right. Well, she isn't about to attack me. She just doesn't like me for some reason, that's all. No cause for alarm. We'll just go our separate ways and not bother each other. The Spire's big enough for that."

"Directive assimilated and acknowledged. I will treat Independence's hostility as non-significant."

"Yeah, that's probably for the best," he agreed. They stopped alongside the row of shooting booths, and he nodded toward the firing lanes. "Okay, you know what you're going to be doing here?"

"I will be discharging my onboard weaponry at targets to determine how effective they are."

Jericho nodded. "That's about it, yeah." He gestured toward the closest shooting booth. "That one's as good as any, I guess."

Obediently, Scout moved into the booth and stopped. Jericho looked over his shoulder at where Corporal Bradley sat in the glass-fronted control booth and, gave her a thumb's up. She nodded in return and picked up a microphone.

"Attention, Scout. I will be generating a human-sized target in your lane. When the buzzer sounds, you may open fire on it. Cease fire when the target is eliminated, or the buzzer sounds a second time. Is that understood?"

"Your directive is understood, Corporal Bradley," Scout replied without turning around. He raised his right arm and extended it forward.

Between one instant and the next, a human form began to take shape at the twenty-yard range. Jericho recognized hard light when he saw it, as Bradley added layers onto the target until it looked altogether too realistic. As a final touch, she gave the menacing form a gun in one hand and a machete in the other. Ragged clothes and a leering mask completed the ensemble.

As the buzzer sounded, the construct began to bring its 'gun' up toward Scout. It never completed the motion as covers slid back on Scout's armored forearm. Accompanied by a high-pitched crackling noise, red bloomed on the target from mid-torso up to the head. The buzzer sounded within seconds, and the word 'HARD KILL' displayed itself above the thoroughly riddled target.

"Well, that was a thing." Bradley's voice was thoroughly deadpan. *"What was that, and what else do you have?"*

"That was a four-millimeter railgun firing at fifty rounds per second on half-second burst mode. I also have an anti-personnel laser."

"Generating new target. Let's try out the laser. Fire on the buzzer."

"Directive understood."

It seemed that Corporal Bradley and Scout were on the same page. Jericho watched as Bradley worked her magic to weave another target to be shot at; this time, it was a render of the Terminator from the 1986 movie, with sections of the human flesh removed so mechanical bits were visible. It started at the back end of the firing range, in a running pose.

The buzzer went off, and the simulacrum of the killer robot broke into a sprint up the firing lane; this time, flashes of light interspersed with whipcrack reports as Scout obliterated the chest region then moved up to the head. Bradley had layered the hard light so that the 'flesh' was blasted away first, then the mechanical chassis was revealed to be destroyed in turn. Jericho was seriously impressed, both by the realism and that Scout demolished the target before it was halfway up the lane toward them.

It quickly became evident that Scout's aim was impeccable and that his reflexes were likewise excellent. Bradley threw up target after target, sometimes requiring Scout to fire across the lanes to hit numbered targets in sequence. By the time he ran out of ammunition for the railgun, he'd proven his combat capability.

"Okay, that was just fun," Bradley declared as she emerged from the control booth. "Come back anytime. It's nice to see a master at work."

"It is good to see that my onboard weaponry works as well as it should," Scout replied. **"I will return if and when my duties allow."**

"We'll do what we can, anyway," Jericho allowed. "That was damned impressive. I didn't know you could generate half those targets."

"It's all force fields and holograms," Bradley pointed out. "The tricky bit is making some parts of it harder than others. See you 'round, G-Man."

"See you 'round, Corporal." With a wave, Jericho led the way from the target range.

Once they were back in the corridor, he looked up at Scout. "That went well. Do you think you learned anything new?"

"I learned about the capabilities of hard-light systems. A few of my weapon specifications were off by a fraction of a percent, but that has been recalibrated. I have also verified that I would be of use in an urban combat scenario."

"Well, *yeah*, you would." Jericho snorted at the understatement. "Hey, can you fly? Because that's how I get around most of the time."

"I am capable of high-speed running and short-range assisted leaping. True flight involves high-temperature radioactive plasma venting and would be dangerous to anything behind me. My current directive is 'do not do this in a city'."

Jericho blinked. "Yeah ... that's definitely not a good idea. But what do you mean by 'assisted leaping'?"

"Direct air cycle turbojets. These add fifty percent to my jump distance. Without them, I am rated as capable of leaping one hundred sixty feet forward, with a forty-foot leap ceiling."

"Really ..." murmured Jericho. While that would easily allow Scout to get around in a city via rooftop running, he was starting to get ideas. "How much do you weigh, exactly?"

"I currently mass one thousand four hundred seventy pounds," Scout informed him. **"Once I have replenished my ammunition store, this will increase by ten pounds."**

Jericho smiled. This, at least, was a problem he could do something about.

14
Flight

The Technologist frowned as he performed calculations on his tablet. "Using your power to reduce his gravitational potential to one-tenth of its usual amount will last how long, precisely?"

Jericho shrugged. "I can't give you a solid number until we try it out. Maybe five to seven minutes, depending on how close together we stay. I haven't experimented much with the harness for that sort of thing. Back in Savannah, when I had nineteen people going every which way at once, it didn't last long at all."

"And while you are capable of using your power to its full effect upon the robot without your harness, the duration is considerably reduced." The Technologist swiped aside a graph, then pulled one up that looked almost identical. Turning his head, he glanced at the third person in the room. "Transit? Your judgment of the situation?"

Due to the reflective faceplate on her helmet, Transit couldn't convey emotion via her expression, but Jericho got the impression she was irritated about something. He just hoped it wasn't on account of his ideas for Scout. She was the first Force Majeure hero he'd ever met, and her opinion was important to him.

She looked every inch the high-tier artificer she happened to be, wearing as her costume of choice a tech-encrusted flight suit in red and silver. Without being blatant about it, this fitted snugly enough to leave no doubt there was a woman within, which also served to raise her popularity with a significant fraction of the population. On the other hand, Jericho liked her simply because she'd gone out of her way from the start to be nice to him, like a cool aunt or the big sister he'd never had.

"We should try it out and see what happens," she said thoughtfully. "We know G-Man can carry Sidekick Zero One if things go wrong—" She broke off as Jericho cleared his throat. "Yes?"

"Uh, his name's officially 'Scout'. In case nobody told you." He gave her an apologetic look. "Sorry."

In return, he got a brief nod of acknowledgment. "Understood. G-Man's capable of carrying Scout if anything does go wrong, but it shouldn't be too hard to adjust the turbojet firmware programming to allow for continuous flight."

"Thus allowing sustainable flight once G-Man's powers are integrated into the loop, yes." The Technologist sounded as close to being excited as he ever did. "Why did we not consider this aspect earlier?"

Transit's reply was dry. "Because we had G-Man's gravity-change powers marked down as 'offensive', and we were both stuck in the mindset of *'assisted jumping isn't flight'*." She turned to Jericho. "Take this as a lesson. Even the smartest of us sometimes forget to think outside the box."

"I figure that's why they call it 'outside the box'," Jericho said carefully. "If everyone thought that way all the time, they wouldn't need a name for it."

She chuckled. "Very true. Just give me a minute here." She started working with her tablet; up on the cradle, Scout's eyes went from blue to green and back again several times. Jericho heard some of the robot's internal components audibly whirring, then everything seemed to shut down again.

Just as he was about to ask if everything was okay, the Technologist tapped something on his tablet. "That appears to have integrated adequately with the rest of the software. I believe the time has come for the first test of the new iteration of the system."

Transit nodded. "Let's do this." She swiped something aside on her tablet, and the clamps snapped open. "Scout, report status."

The robot's eyes flared from blue to green to amber, all in less than a second. **"I am operating at nominal functionality. The assisted jumping system has been modified for use in conjunction with outside gravity assist via G-Man to achieve powered flight without the need for high-temperature plasma venting."**

This time, Transit let out a delighted laugh. "Okay, now I'm impressed. I knew you made it smart, but that's what I call *intuitive*." She tilted her head, then looked around at Scout. "Or did you already know what we had planned?"

Scout's eyes reverted to green. **"G-Man and the Technologist discussed it within my auditory sensory range before I was placed in sleep mode. It was a simple logical step to link that discussion with the modifications to my direct air cycle turbojet system firmware."**

There was a smile in Transit's voice as she nodded. "Hah, nice. Not as intuitive as I'd thought, but still pretty damn smart." She turned to Jericho. "So, are you ready to try out your little idea?"

"Definitely," he replied, attempting to sound more confident than he felt. While he knew his powers backward and forward without the harness, and he understood them reasonably well *with* it, there was still the fact that he'd never tried this specific trick before.

"Indeed." The Technologist nodded austerely. "Scout unit, commence preparations."

"Commencing preparations." Scout stepped off the cradle and stood in front of Jericho. **"I am ready, G-Man."**

"Okay, then." Jericho activated his enhancement harness, then put his hand on Scout's shoulder and exerted his power. "You're set. Like Transit said, let's do this."

Panels on Scout's back and legs moved and adjusted, then Jericho heard the internal mechanisms kick over again. Instead of dying away this time, the whirring transitioned to a whine that became more and more pronounced, rising steadily to a crescendo. Then the panels shifted again; air exploded out from beneath them, creating a wall of heated air that pressed Jericho's costume against his body and pushed back at the spandex inserts under his arms. Gusting out in all directions, the intensity and volume of the hot blast increased as Scout slowly lifted from the floor, holding his arms out for balance.

High-intensity jet-wash blitzed throughout the lab, making the Technologist's labcoat/cape flap behind him. Slowly, the hovering robot turned in a complete circle to the right with his metal boots a good two feet from the floor, then reversed direction to the left. Jericho was pleased that there were no paper notes in the lab; if there had been, they would have been *everywhere* by the time Scout reduced thrust and lowered himself to the floor once more.

The high-pitched whine died away and the airflow tailed off, leaving Jericho feeling somewhat windblown; an unusual sensation for him when he hadn't even been the one moving. **"Initial flight test performed well within projected analyses,"** declared Scout. **"Allowing for ground effect, sustainable flight seems entirely plausible."**

"That sounds good to me," Jericho said. "What now?"

"I think we can try a free flight trial now," Transit decided and looked at the Technologist. "What do you think?"

"The data we have gathered does seem to support the idea of that being an applicable experiment," the senior artificer agreed. "Will you be accompanying them upon one of your airborne vehicles, or do you believe remote monitoring will be sufficient to our needs?"

"Well, G-Man needs to go with Scout anyway to make sure it doesn't fall out of the sky, so I think that's all we really need." Transit tilted her head toward Jericho. "Think you can handle that?"

"I, uh, definitely." The weight of responsibility was almost palpable as it settled on his shoulders once more. He took a deep breath to steady himself. "I've got this. Just a quick lap around the city?"

"Do not proceed beyond fifteen miles from the Spire," the Technologist decreed. "I need to monitor its internal processes at all times." He hefted the tablet he held for emphasis. Already, a three-dimensional model of Scout was floating over the surface of the device.

"Keep inside the Greenway, gotcha. Anything else?" Jericho hadn't been planning to go that far anyway; there was ample room to fly around in Utopia airspace if all they intended to do was get a thorough read on Scout's flight capabilities. If he wanted to hold a race against the robot, the Greenway—a half-mile-wide park that entirely encircled Utopia at the fifteen-mile mark—would be the perfect venue for it, but that would not be on the cards for this particular day.

Transit folded her arms and leaned back against a bench. "I'm good. You've proven you're responsible enough. I trust you to not accidentally break the multi-million-dollar robot." Her tone was light, almost whimsical, though he had no doubt she meant every word.

"Gee, thanks." Wondering if he should ask whether Scout was insured against plowing into skyscrapers, Jericho pulled his goggles on and activated them. A moment later, he paused. "Is he tied into the air traffic net? That might be necessary if we don't want hexes swarming us as soon as we hit the regular flight lanes."

With a tightening of his lips that Jericho interpreted as irritation, the Technologist pulled up another holographic image from the tablet, then tapped a square on it to change the color from red to green. "That is now the case. Air traffic data will be transmitted to its heads-up display, and air traffic control now has access to its onboard IFF."

"Okay, then." Jericho reached out and slapped Scout on the shoulder, replenishing his power effect. "Let's go." He jogged out onto the landing stage, spreading his arms and leaning into his power at the same time. As he ran off the end of the platform, the grav-wings unfurled into place, allowing him to swoop outward in a single smooth movement. He slowed to a hover thirty feet out, then turned to observe Scout's actions.

Moving smoothly and precisely, the matte-black robot proceeded to the edge of the landing stage and stepped off, activating his turbojets a moment later. He seemed to have just as little problem hovering in the open air as he had inside the lab; despite it being half a mile to the ground, he quickly regained Jericho's altitude.

Jericho nodded in approval. "Okay, that's good." He was still relatively new to flying himself, but Scout seemed to be adapting to it with impressive speed. "Let's kick it up a notch. Take a lap around the Spire. You go first; I'll tell you if I can't keep up."

"**Directive received and understood,**" he heard through his radio earpiece.

Ah, right. He's tied into the net.

Scout leaned forward, slowly transitioning from a staggered hover into actual forward motion. At first, it was rough going, but by the time they were a quarter of the way around the towering building, he'd managed to achieve something approximating level flight.

One thing that intrigued Jericho was how Scout had his hands out in front, emulating classic images of both comic-book superheroes and how some Enabled patterned their flight characteristics. He honestly hadn't thought the Technologist would've programmed something like that into a robot that wasn't originally intended to do much in the way of flying.

Maintaining a distance of about ten yards from Scout, Jericho monitored the effect of his power on the robot. It was diminishing, but not too quickly. He figured he had about five minutes before he'd have to replenish it, which left him time to ask the question. "Why are you holding your arms like that?"

Scout's voice was as measured as ever. **"My chassis possesses a rudimentary aerodynamic capability and is only moderately effective as a lifting body. I am using my hands both as control surfaces and for additional lift. The benefit is significant for the former and minimal for the latter, but tangible on both counts."**

"Huh. Right." It wasn't something Jericho would've thought of, but this wasn't surprising. Once his enhancement harness had given him access to actual flight, aerodynamic efficiency had ceased to be one of his concerns. If he wanted to fly somewhere, he flew there.

They continued on around the Spire, Scout gradually increasing speed as he refined his flight technique. Jericho was impressed; for an artificial intelligence that clearly had not been pre-programmed to fly in such a fashion, Scout was a damn quick study. He wondered just how fast the robot would be able to go using the fusion-assisted plasma thrust in this fashion. Given an extra thirteen hundred pounds of thrust to play with, he guessed the appropriate descriptor would be 'very'.

"Okay," he said once the landing stage came back into view. "We can return to the Technologist's lab now, or go for a flight through the city proper. Your choice."

He wasn't just throwing the decision onto Scout's broad metallic shoulders for shits and giggles. Part of him was indeed curious whether the robot could weigh an abstract choice and make a measured judgment. The rest of him wanted to give Scout full rein in what little autonomy he currently enjoyed, because once they returned to the lab, that agency would surely vanish.

"My flight systems are operating within acceptable margins," the robot replied. **"Further testing will assist in gathering additional data and improve current control of aerodynamic capabilities. Extending our flight path into the city proper is an optimal course of action."**

"Okay, let's do that then."

Jericho looked outward at the city surrounding the Spire. Although he could see moving dots in the medium and far distance, he couldn't determine whether they were flight-capable Enabled or airborne vehicles. His HUD goggles gave each one an altitude, compass heading, and ground speed but did not identify them beyond that. However, all the fliers at their altitude had one thing in common: high-speed flight. And the last thing he wanted to do was throw Scout in at the deep end.

"Until we've got a better idea of how well you handle high-end maneuvering, we need to lose some altitude. So, we're going to drop down to about five hundred feet, then you follow my lead from there on out. Got that?"

"Yes. I have got that. We will reduce altitude to five hundred feet above ground level."

Jericho nodded with satisfaction. The robot certainly learned fast, which shouldn't have impressed him as much as it did. He was dealing with the

Technologist's work, after all. "Excellent. Before we go, just hold up a moment, and I'll just refresh my G-effect on you. We do *not* want you crash-landing in front of the tourists. That would not be good optics for Force Majeure. Just saying."

"**Affirmative.**" Scout slowed down then came to a hover. He was getting better at it, Jericho thought.

Extracting his right arm from the grav-wing, Jericho came up on Scout's left side and slapped him on the shoulder to renew the effect of his power. Then, on a whim, he turned off the enhancement harness and let himself drop. Even with his arms spread to give the reinforced spandex its best chance at catching air while his power ensured that gravity only had one-tenth its effect on him, he still found himself building up speed as he fell toward the base of the Spire. He could've gone a lot faster in a dive but right now, he was just choosing to enjoy the freedom of riding down on a cushion of air.

Even without the benefit of the harness, his G-sense picked up the solid mass of Scout at his five o'clock, dropping feet-first and using the turbojets to match his falling speed. "**Are you suffering an equipment malfunction?**" asked the robot, edging closer to him. "**Do you require assistance?**"

And there went the moment. "Nope," Jericho replied. "Just figured to free-fall instead of wasting power to get down to where I need to be. I was gliding a long time before I was flying, after all."

"**Affirmative. Understood.**"

Keeping an eye on the numbers scrolling down in his HUD altimeter, Jericho angled his body and arms just right, turning the near-vertical drop into a long swoop. Scout followed, keeping up nicely despite his minimal aerodynamics. They leveled out at five hundred feet, more or less, and he noted with satisfaction that they were right on the money for airspeed.

Still, gliding was not a self-sustaining flight method, so he activated his harness and smoothly unfurled the 'wings, transitioning to powered flight without so much as a jolt. With Scout still at his five, he set his course down the center of the airspace 'lane' being projected onto his HUD goggles.

Flying between the merely conventionally tall buildings, Jericho put the robot through his paces, regularly refreshing the gravity treatment to keep him in the air. It turned out that while flying straight and level, Scout had reasonable control over his speed and altitude, but any sort of sharp turn needed to be approached with caution. After several attempts that nearly sent Scout skidding out of his 'lane', Jericho decided that the robot required some kind of hand-thrusters like he'd seen on an old comic-book character, or perhaps side-vents for his turbojets.

Still, weaving between buildings was good practice for both of them, and Jericho enjoyed getting out and about for a nice leisurely flight. Keeping an eye on where they were in relation to the Spire, he led Scout around in a broad half-circle through the taller buildings so that when he chose to return, it would be right there. Scout also seemed to enjoy flying, and the longer the practice session went on, the more he seemed to be picking it up.

After about half an hour, Jericho triggered his radio clicker on his helmet. "Okay, we'll pull it up there for today. We'll head on back to the lab and give the Technologist your flight data to play with."

"Affirmative," agreed Scout. He didn't turn and head back immediately though; instead, he waited for Jericho to make the turn so that he could follow along. This showed that the Artificer-designed AI could make judgment calls, which only impressed Jericho all the more.

The voice in his earpiece came through unexpectedly. "Flight Control calling G-Man. Come in, over."

He responded automatically as his eyes searched his HUD for emergency warnings. "G-Man here, Control. What's the problem, over?" With the automated nature of the flight-lane system, it was rare for Control to contact anyone directly.

"Relaying a message from UCPD," Control informed him. "There's been a report of a minor disturbance in Challenger Plaza, near the statue. You're the closest active asset. Investigate, take appropriate action, and report. Control, out."

"I copy, Control. Roger and out." Feeling his heart rate accelerate, Jericho banked toward the Spire as the radio link cut out. "Come on, Scout. Follow my lead, and let's go see what's happening."

"Affirmative. Following your lead."

15
Encounter

It was a given that there would be tourists in Challenger Plaza, especially on a Saturday afternoon. These were usually easy to pick out from the regular workers, in that they stood around the statue or the fountain, or just took pictures of the Spire itself. Employees, by contrast, sat under the auto-adjusting umbrellas and enjoyed their meal breaks in the open air.

As Jericho entered the Spire's airspace and swooped down toward the Plaza with Scout holding steady at his five, he wasn't searching for people eating lunch or taking photos. Control had said the disturbance was near the statue, so he looked carefully in the given direction.

There. That's got to be it.

'That' was the largest group of people currently on the Plaza, consisting of a ring of spectators surrounding two combatants. This was a pattern he recognized with depressing ease, having seen it more than a few times before.

God, I hope it's not a hero-villain thing. Those folks could get badly hurt, being that close if someone lets loose with something damaging.

"Who have we got down there?" he asked. "Next to the statue, I mean. Enabled or normal?"

It only took Scout about half a second to come up with an answer. **"Enhancing image. Analysis indicates two Enabled. Ninety-seven percent match for Troll, of Manhattan Justice. Seventy-five percent match for All-Star, unaffiliated New York superhero."**

Okay, not what I was expecting.

While Utopia City had the largest per-capita population of superheroes in the US, and it wasn't uncommon for them to show up at the Spire on some errand or another, out-of-town heroes rarely attended in costume unless they were seeking to join the team. He'd never heard of All-Star before, but Troll was a founding member of the New-York-based team. Somehow, he couldn't see the wild-man-themed prodigy being interested in jumping ship.

More to the point, he was now distinctly curious as to why the two heroes might be brawling in public. Whatever was going on, he needed to ensure the safety of the civilians first, then deal with the actual situation second.

"Okay, then. Let's head on down there and see what's going on."

"Affirmative. Preparing to investigate the situation."

Down they went, Jericho using his grav-wings to reduce his speed. Scout matched him move for move, the turbojets increasing in volume and pitch as they both decelerated for the landing. Several of the crowd around Troll and

All-Star looked around for the source of the noise; when they found it, camera phones appeared as if by magic.

Jericho touched down with the finesse of a ball of thistledown alighting on a mirror; Scout, on the other hand, landed with a great deal more force. While the robot's effective weight was one-tenth normal, his inertia was the same as his actual mass: nearly fifteen hundred pounds. As such, he was constrained from exerting the level of fine control available to Jericho. He didn't break any pavers, but his metallic boots did come down with a distinctive *clank* an instant before his turbojets would've canceled the last of his downward momentum. This got *everyone's* attention.

As they all turned and looked, Jericho allowed the 'wings to dissipate and took the opportunity to figure out what was really going on here. He was no Smokeshadow, but the bystanders' expressions seemed to show more interest and excitement than fear or anger. There were also a couple of battered-looking rucksacks on the pavers, though he didn't know who owned them.

Moreover, Troll and All-Star—the latter sporting blond hair and the beginnings of a beard, and a spandex costume with torn-off sleeves—seemed to be moving with the calm deliberation of a sparring match rather than the all-out frenetic pace of actual combat. As Jericho watched, Troll swayed aside from a palm strike then converted the movement into a hip throw that dropped All-Star face-first onto the pavers. The engagement ended with All-Star's arm up behind his back, his free hand slapping the ground beside his head.

"Afternoon, everyone," Jericho greeted the crowd politely, then turned his attention to the fighters. "Troll, right? I saw your TV ad back in October."

The stocky, shirtless Enabled released All-Star's arm and came to his feet in a lithe move that would've shouted *prodigy!* to anyone not already in the know. Extending an arm downward, he gave All-Star a hand up, then moved in Jericho's direction.

"Yup," he said, dark eyes giving Jericho a once-over from behind the fanged and horned mask. "G-Man, yeah? Caught that stunt you pulled off around about that time. Pleased to meet ya."

Jericho got the impression that the Manhattan Justice prodigy didn't miss very much at all. He shook the heavily calloused hand that was extended in his direction.

"Likewise." He was by no means lacking in grip strength, but when the handclasp was over, he felt the urge to check for bruising. "This here's Scout. I'm giving him some on-the-job training."

"I am pleased to meet you also, Troll," the robot said politely, offering his hand to shake.

"Whoof, you're a tall one an' no mistake." Troll shook Scout's hand. "Flight lessons, huh?"

Jericho nodded. "Yeah. I'm guessing this was a training session, too?"

"Got it in one." Troll turned and gestured toward the Spire as All-Star joined them. "Me an' junior here just come back from a campin' trip out in th' back of beyond. Turns out he ain't never been through Utopia City, so I thought I'd show him th' Spire on th' way home. Tourists were curious, so we figured we'd put on a show for 'em. We in trouble?"

Jericho glanced at the surrounding crowd, gauging their mood, before answering. He was the primary responder on site, which gave him a fair amount of leeway. As he'd noted before, nobody seemed fearful or upset about the sparring session. It was evident that Troll and All-Star had been careful to keep their sparring session within a small area, ensuring none of the bystanders got in the way. No people had been hurt or property damaged, and entertainment had been given, making it easy for him to reach his decision.

"No." He shook his head. "I haven't got a problem with it. You've got some pretty smooth moves there, but I don't recognize the style."

Troll shrugged massively. "Stuff I've picked up here an' there. You know how it goes." He tilted his head. "Any chance you could set up a tour of the Spire for us?"

With a regretful grimace, Jericho sucked in air through his teeth. "Sorry. I'd love to help you out, but I haven't been given the training to do tours yet, and we only do them in the mornings anyway. Though if you wanted to come back tomorrow, I reckon I could bump you to the front of the line."

Troll appeared to think about it for a moment, then shook his head. "Nah. Wanna be back in New York by tonight. Been away too long as it is."

"And whose idea was it to extend the camping trip?" All-Star raised his eyebrows. "Not mine, that's for sure."

"You enjoyed it, an' you know it," scoffed Troll. He caught Jericho's eye and jerked his head in All-Star's direction. "Needed ta teach junior about bein' a prodigy out in th' wilderness. Took him about three weeks ta git his head around it, and another week ta git good at it."

"And that's the most irritating part," All-Star retorted. "Just as I *was* starting to really enjoy it, that's when you decided it was time to go home. I mean, what sort of camping trip's that?"

"The type of campin' trip that ain't for fun." Behind his mask, Troll rolled his eyes. "I keep tellin' ya, ya don't know what ya don't know 'til ya find out th' hard way ya don't know it."

"You're not wrong there," allowed Jericho. "Sorry you can't stick around for a tour, but I can tell you something about the Spire that most people don't know. You know how tall it is?"

"Yeah." Troll nodded. "Seven thousand nine hundred eighty feet."

Jericho blinked. Not many non-Utopians could call on the exact figure. "Okay, that's correct. But do you know *why* it's that tall?"

Troll grinned. "'Cause the local elevation's a thousand twenty above sea level. Which puts the tip at nine thousand neat."

It took an effort of will for Jericho not to let his jaw drop. "Okay, wow. How did you know *that* one?"

"Because I was here when th' area got surveyed, back in the day." Troll gazed up at the towering edifice, shading his eyes against the afternoon sun. "Reminds me of th' Pyramids, in a way. Started out as a good idea, then they said screw it, let's see how big we can go. Made it into a dick-measuring contest with every other artificer out there."

Jericho was reminded of the tour he'd taken of the Spire with Transit and Black Dragon, where the girl had irreverently likened the building to a deliberately constructed phallic symbol.

That's one way to make it into a dick-measuring contest, all right.

"You never said you'd been to see the Pyramids," All-Star said. "When was that?"

"Long time ago. And ain't none of your business, anyway." Troll gave Jericho a sideways wry glance with a twist of the lips that said quite plainly, *'see what I've got to work with?'* "But if there ain't no more tours today, we might as well get movin' on back to New York. Nice meetin' ya, G-Man, Scout."

"Yeah." All-Star paused. "Hey, uh, G-Man, could I get your autograph?" He flushed slightly as Troll shot him a sharp glance. "It's not for me. I've got a friend who's a Force Majeure fan."

It was amazing how many autographs were 'for a friend'. Jericho had received requests like this almost daily since becoming a member of the team. Between Force Majeure's prominence and his own moderate celebrity status, any number of people wanted a souvenir of having met him but shied away from appearing too eager.

Taking out a pen and a standard publicity card from the appropriate pouch, Jericho glanced at All-Star. "Who do I make it out to?"

"Nina," All-Star blurted, causing Troll to snort slightly.

Under his mask, Jericho's eyebrows raised slightly. Unless the guy's parents had decided on a weird naming convention, it really wasn't for him. Interestingly enough, it seemed Troll also had an opinion on the matter.

Oh, well. As Luke would put it, ain't none of my never-mind.

After checking for the spelling, as he'd been shown—names were *not* always spelled how they sounded—he scribbled, *'To Nina, from G-Man. Being a hero isn't about powers. It's a state of mind'*, on the card, then handed it over.

"Have a good trip back to New York," he said. "Nice meeting the both of you. Kick ass, take names, and look good on the news."

Troll chuckled briefly—All-Star was too busy avidly studying the card to respond—and raised a hand in a brief wave. "Yeah. You, too. See ya 'round. C'mon, junior."

Jericho activated his radio as the two slung their rucksacks over their shoulders and headed toward the air-cab stand. "G-Man to Control, the situation has been investigated and resolved. A pair of out-of-town prodigies decided to put on an impromptu sparring session for the tourists. There were no problems, and everyone enjoyed the show. They've gone on their way, over."

The response wasn't long in coming. "Control to G-Man, I copy. All good. Control, out."

"G-Man, out." He ended the call as the bystanders closed in on the pair of them. Or rather, the tourists gave the imposing seven-foot robot a respectable berth and approached the hero they knew about. Jericho was used to this, and was soon signing bits of paper and posing for selfies. By the time he looked around again, Troll and All-Star were gone.

"Well," he said as the last tourist moved away with his autograph scribbled on a restaurant menu. "That happened. I think we should get you on back to the Spire. That flight data isn't going to analyze itself. What do you reckon?"

"I believe you are correct." Scout glanced around, as did Jericho; nobody was close enough to be a problem. **"Clear for takeoff."**

Jericho reached over and slapped Scout on the arm to renew the gravity effect, then activated his harness and unfurled his grav-wings. "Let's go, then."

Boosted on a thunder of superheated air and soaring on pinions of pure shaped gravity, they rose into the sky.

- End of Part One -

PART TWO

MAKING
CONNECTIONS

Going my way?
- *Thomas*

Ignition.
- *Scout*

16
Unwelcome Reminder

Jericho Hansen's Apartment
The Spire
Utopia City, Kansas
Monday, January 20, 2014
08:05 AM Central Standard Time

River Street was in flames, the historical buildings going up like tinder as Raider's monstrous creation rampaged through downtown Savannah. Screams echoed through the streets from all the people trapped in burning buildings. Jericho felt a surge of hope as Pickup's truck began its modification into the robotic form that most people knew it for. However, it was so laden down with guns of all descriptions that the change was ludicrously slow; he tried to shout a warning, but a series of shots from the hideously grinning robot monster transformed the half-altered vehicle into an unquenchable inferno. Jericho felt tears well in his eyes.

"Dunno what you're bawlin' about, cuz," Luke said, his lip curling with disdain. "That sumbitch was always about one step away from the Klan, anyways."

"He was a hero!" protested Jericho. "He would've helped protect the city from the terror villains!"

"Yeah, but would he've protected 'em from me?*"*

Wondering why Luke would say that, Jericho turned and saw his cousin with one brawny hand wrapped around Thomas' throat, holding him half a foot off the ground. Thomas frantically clawed at Luke's fingers as he turned into Vanessa and back again, but he couldn't get free.

"Let him go!" pleaded Jericho. "Why are you doing this?"

*"You haven't figured it out yet, have you ... cuz?" Luke turned side-on, carrying Thomas with him, and in the distance, Jericho saw something on the ground. Or rather ... some*one*. Luke was lying dead in the street.*

There were two Lukes.

There couldn't be two Lukes.

He swung back to the Luke who was holding Thomas. "You're not Luke," he spat. "You're False Flag."

"Took you long enough." Brandishing an improbably large knife, False Flag sliced across Thomas' throat from ear to ear. Blood splattered far and wide, even as Thomas reached out to Jericho for help.

"Nooo!" screamed Jericho, lunging toward False Flag.

"Uh, uh, uh," giggled Guillotine, appearing in front of Jericho in a burst of purple smoke. The silver claws on her fingertips grew into giant scissor blades that reached out and sliced his hands off.

Without his hands, he couldn't use his powers, couldn't save anyone. He was useless. Savannah was burning up, and there was nothing he could do to stop it. All he could hear was a siren playing the same tune over and over again.

And then the Minotaur stepped up out of nowhere, towering over the blazing city like a vengeful demon. Red eyes glared down at Jericho as the Blood Rose lunged toward him. Each of the blades licked at the air like a razor-sharp tongue, the ghastly weapon emitting an evil hiss as it carved his heart from his chest —

Launching himself from the bed, Jericho landed on the floor and tumbled over in a tangle of sheets. It took him long moments to recollect his nightmare-scattered thoughts and realize that he was supporting himself on his hands. Then he rolled onto his back and scrabbled frantically at his chest, finding unbroken skin rather than the gushing wound he'd half expected. Closing his eyes in relief, he relaxed back against the soft, supporting carpet, drawing in deep, shuddering breaths.

Guillotine hadn't severed his hands, the Minotaur hadn't cut his heart out, and False Flag hadn't murdered Thomas. Aware that his heart was still pounding and that he had sweat cooling on his body, he chose to just lie there for a moment and let his breathing even out.

God damn it. Just a dream.

Dream or not, it had seriously rung his bell.

Was that really what their victims went through? No wonder people called them terror villains.

The tune from his dream played one more time, and only then did his nightmare-addled mind finally recognize it as his door chime.

"Just a minute!" he called. He took a moment to orient himself, then climbed to his feet. Padding out into the living room/kitchenette area in his boxers, he tapped the door panel to trigger the exterior camera. The screen showed that it wasn't a person waiting in the entryway to the apartment, but one of Transit's ubiquitous rolling service robots. This one, SD-0043, acted as a housekeeper for the live-in apartments on Jericho's level of the Spire.

Reassured that he didn't have to worry about donning any more clothing, he tapped the door-open icon; the door unlocked and hissed aside while the outer one stayed closed. "Hey, Forty-Three," he said by way of greeting; he was usually more chipper, but the nightmare had taken its toll on him.

"Good morning, Jericho." The robotic housekeeper's warm, impersonal tone never varied. It probably couldn't even tell he was out of sorts. **"You have mail."**

And indeed, on the tray set into the boxy robot's upper surface, there were three letters. On two of them, the original address had been pasted over with a printed-out label bearing Jericho's Utopia City PO box number, which almost certainly meant they'd been redirected from the (now entirely defunct) apartment address in Savannah. "Thanks, Forty-Three. Appreciate it."

"You are welcome, Jericho. Have a pleasant day." The robot reversed direction and rolled toward the outer door but did not trigger it. Holding the letters, Jericho stepped back into his apartment and let the door slide shut behind him. He saw on the screen that Forty-Three had waited until the inner door was entirely closed before opening the outer door and going on its way. The Spire was the closest thing to an arcology the modern world had yet to boast, even with Artificer technology involved, so privacy was a big deal.

Having more or less recovered his wits by now, he yawned expansively as he stuck the letters together with a glue-tag before tossing them onto the table. Then he wandered toward the small bathroom to deal with the usual morning business. "Morning, Scout," he mumbled as he passed the imposing robot standing motionless in the corner of the living room.

"Good morning, Jericho," Scout replied after a couple of seconds' delay. **"Did you sleep well? I detected higher than normal levels of movement following commencement of sleep patterns, and occasional audible vocalizations. Indications are that you also fell out of bed."**

Jericho didn't answer at first, his attention taken up with using the facilities. Then he washed his hands before splashing water on his face; by the time he emerged from the bathroom, he almost felt human again.

"Had a bad dream. Could've done with another hour." As a prodigy, he only needed four hours of sleep a night. Three, he could handle so long as there was a good reason. Mail call at eight in the morning might not count as a good reason, but it had pulled him out of that nightmare, so he wasn't going to split hairs. He went into the kitchenette and started the coffee machine before sitting down at the small table.

The first letter was a notification of a local election in Savannah, something to do with the city council. He didn't bother reading it all the way through before crumpling the letter and envelope into a ball and tossing it over the kitchenette counter toward the fridge. He'd found if he hit the fridge door just right, he could usually get a rebound into the trash can under the counter. This time around, he was rewarded with a hollow *doonk* as it went in; with a brief grin, he went back to checking the mail.

Next up was a letter from his cousin-in-law Olivia, wanting to know how he was and what Utopia City was like. He picked up a hint of sadness — Livy had been a widow since Luke's funeral in October — but it sounded like she was bearing up and trying to make the best of things. Cousin Serena and Aunt Ellie would be giving her all the support in the world, of course. Kin was kin, whether a body was born into the family or married into it.

He put that letter aside for re-reading later, and picked up the last one. It had been sent to him from the USPS itself, but even then it had been redirected, just like the city council missive. This made him frown; why hadn't the post office sent it straight to him if they already had his mail redirection on file?

Only one way to find out. Tearing off the end, he extracted a printed letter, which he unfolded and began to read through.

"Okay," he muttered once he'd finished, scratching behind his ear in puzzlement. "What the hell?"

According to the USPS, he'd been renting a post office box in Savannah for some time, paying for it via direct debit. Deciphering the official verbiage (which managed to carry a slightly accusatory tone), he gathered that the last payment had failed to clear. Furthermore, the United States Postal Service would really like their money within three weeks, or they would be forced to close the PO box in question and destroy the mail within.

Which only served to raise more questions. Jericho *had* a post office box, but he wasn't paying for it, and it was in Utopia, not Savannah.

I never rented any post office boxes back home ... did I?

No. No, I didn't.

So why did the post office seem to think he had one? If he wasn't the one who'd opened it, who had, and why was it in his name? Mentally he floundered, trying to push past the last lingering cobwebs of sleep and make sense of the situation.

Getting up, he poured himself a cup of coffee and returned to the table. "This can't be right."

And then, with the fresh infusion of caffeine into his system, the metaphorical lightbulb came on over his head. Everything suddenly made sense when he added one extra variable into the mix.

Stephen. Son of a bitch. *It must've been him. Though why put it in* my *name?*

When the breakup first happened, Jericho had thought he was over and done with that chapter of his life. His point had been clearly made, and his ex-boyfriend had accepted it. Or so he'd assumed.

The letters had proven him wrong. Time and again, when he thought he'd *finally* gotten through to the man, yet another one would show up, to be briefly glanced through (Jericho didn't want to miss any admission by Stephen of his wrongdoing), then dropped into the bottom drawer along with all the rest. More than once, he'd made the resolution to clear out that drawer for good and consign the entire mass of correspondence to the same ash-heap the relationship had long since been condemned to. But this had never quite happened; it was easier to just let them keep piling up.

During that stage, tossing the letters would have simply been symbolic of the end of his patience with Stephen's stubbornness. His ex-boyfriend's death had thrown all of that into confusion. If he did it now, he'd be destroying fragments of someone else's *life*.

As if his day hadn't started crappily enough already, the asshat had managed to find yet *another* way to screw with him from beyond the grave. The very fact that Stephen had opened a post office box in Jericho's name was bizarre, but it was the only explanation that made any sense.

Of course, once he was aware of *what* had been done, Jericho found it easy to connect the dots on *how* Stephen had done it. His ex-boyfriend had always been good at photography and image manipulation, and once upon a time (for fun, or so Jericho had thought at the time), he'd created a fake driver's license for Jericho that looked pretty damn real. It would've been child's play for him to put together something good enough for the post office to accept, bearing his photo along with Jericho's name and their mutual address. To back it up, any one of their bills would have both their names on it, as Jericho had been on the lease.

Of course, before the revelation of Stephen's infidelity, Jericho simply would not have believed the man emotionally capable of such a thing. In his opinion, it hadn't been remotely possible. But now …

Yeah, it was. Unfortunately.

With a sigh, he got off the bed and straightened it up as best he could. It was literally Forty-Three's job to come through and clean the place up, empty the trash and suchlike, but he liked to think he was doing his bit by reducing its workload. Even if people thought he was weird for doing so.

Before he'd come to Utopia, he'd never put much thought into such mundane aspects of city infrastructure as garbage disposal. It always happened out of sight; thus, it remained out of mind. But in a building as large as the Spire, much less a city the size of Utopia, such a thing was in no way trivial. Quite the opposite, in fact.

Force Majeure, he'd learned early on, was far more than just a superhero team that had once (re)built a city. They espoused green practices at every level, combined with the technological and political clout to ensure such initiatives didn't get bogged down in committee.

For instance, recycling was one of their top priorities in Utopia and beyond. For the past few years, automated ships constructed by Transit and the Technologist had been trundling back and forth across the Pacific and Atlantic, suctioning up ton after metric ton of floating garbage. While the live sea creatures that had also been caught up (and occasionally trapped) in the trash were carefully released back into the wild, the garbage was parceled up and flown back to Utopia to be recycled into useful goods.

Every consumer item in Utopia was either destined to be re-used somehow or was already part of the cycle. It was why they used glass in their bottles, albeit a modified formula that was significantly lighter and harder to break than usual.

No garbage trucks rumbled through the city in the early hours of the morning; no mounds of landfill filled the air with their dubious fragrance, waiting to be covered over. Every streetside trash can in the metropolis was in reality an access point to an underground transport system that conveyed the collected refuse to one of several reclamation plants. There, it was sorted, disassembled, sterilized, and prepared for re-use. All powered by the 'negative point energy' power core in the base of the Spire.

Of course, instead of trusting in fallible humanity to separate what needed recycling from what needed mulching, each reclamation plant was set up with mechanisms to do it for them. The intricate machinery would separate paper, plastic, and other materials, and even (Jericho had been told) disassemble electronics and computer equipment almost down to their component elements.

For this reason, he was careful about casually dropping things on the floor or into the trash can in the kitchenette. Anything discarded in that fashion was considered by Forty-Three to be written off for good and all; once the housekeeping robot conveyed it to the Spire's dedicated recycling plant, it was *gone.* There was no getting it back.

He'd met Forty-Three on the day he moved in. Once he'd unpacked and put everything away, the robot had been brought in to trundle through the apartment and scan each room for its contents. This had established a baseline for the placement of his possessions, allowing Forty-Three to recognize and return them to their designated locations when necessary, and ensuring the robot didn't steal his shoes. It also meant he could leave his costume out for Forty-Three to take away for cleaning or maintenance, and know he'd get it back.

Stepping into the shower helped him organize his planning for the day ahead. While his primary duties at the moment involved helping socialize Scout under various circumstances, the letter changed everything. He needed to head back to Savannah, involving a five-hour round trip, and straighten this whole mess out. At the very least, whatever was currently stashed in Stephen's illicit post office box had to be retrieved and disposed of accordingly.

I am so not looking forward to this.

The shower done with, he dried himself off and dressed casually: jeans, a black pullover, and a light jacket. Not that he really needed the last item, but the lack would make him stand out. Retrieving his phone, he scrolled through the list of numbers, then tapped the one he'd chosen.

It rang precisely once. "Relentless' office, Samantha Colburn speaking. Please state your name and business."

Jericho had spoken with Ms. Colburn on several occasions (including on the train, a couple weeks back) and even met her a few times. She looked like someone's maiden aunt, but as Relentless' executive assistant, she oversaw the day-to-day business of Force Majeure with ruthless efficiency. If anything was going on within the Spire that she *wasn't* aware of, he couldn't attest to it.

"Good morning, ma'am," he replied. "This is G-Man. I've just found out about a case of identity theft in Savannah, involving my civilian identity. Am I needed for anything that'll stop me from taking the maglev out that way today and sorting it out?"

He told himself he wasn't *really* overstating the case; what Stephen had done was indeed technically identity theft. But if he'd just said he needed to close out a fraudulent post office box and see what was in it, he suspected it wouldn't sound nearly as urgent.

"I am unaware of any pressing situation of that nature, unless the Technologist has an ongoing need for your presence," she said at once, the barest inflection in her voice making the second part of her statement into a question.

"He didn't say anything of the sort yesterday, ma'am." As acerbic as he might be on other matters, Force Majeure's pre-eminent artificer was punctilious with such issues.

"Understood." Her tone shifted slightly. "Will you have a need to deal with law enforcement in your costumed identity while you are there?"

That was also an extremely valid question. Even before joining Force Majeure, he'd been recognized in Savannah as a vigilante hero; as such, he was deliberately given a certain amount of leeway by the police. However, as a gay superhero with a reputation for calling out racial profiling and discrimination whenever he saw it, he wasn't universally well-liked. Even the knowledge of his Force Majeure membership probably wouldn't change some attitudes by a whole lot. *Will you need a partner for backup*, was what Ms. Colburn was asking.

"I'm not intending to," he said, glad to be able to assure her that things weren't about to get needlessly complicated in Savannah. "As I said, it's a personal matter. The perp is deceased. I'll just be cleaning up the mess he left behind. I should be done and dusted in an hour, two at most."

"Understood," she said once more. "I shall double-check with the Technologist, then mark you off as being in Savannah for the day, personal business."

That she would inform him if matters had changed, he had no doubt whatsoever. In the meantime, the commissaries were open all hours, and he hadn't had breakfast yet. There was cereal and milk in the fridge, but that was for when he was in a hurry. "Thank you, ma'am. I'll make plans to leave in an hour if nothing else comes up."

"If something does, you will hear from me before then. Good day to you." She ended the call without further ado.

"Thank you, ma'am," he said again to dead air, then snorted and put the phone in his pocket. Ms. Colburn didn't wait around for thanks. She just went ahead and got the job done.

Which left one other task for him. Strolling out into the apartment's living room, he stopped in front of Scout. "Hey, big guy. I don't know how much of that you heard, but I've got to head back home to Savannah for the day, to deal with personal business. This is a Jericho thing, not a G-Man thing. You understand what that means?"

"I understand. My presence would compromise your secret identity. I will instead report to the Technologist. There is flight data to be analyzed." Scout paused. "Good luck in Savannah."

"Wow, you're really getting there. Thanks. I hope I won't need it." Jericho held up his hand for a fist bump; after a moment, metallic knuckles tapped against his. "See you when I get back."

Scout's eyes flickered to amber, then back to green. **"I will observe you when you are within range of my ocular sensors."**

"Yeah, something like that." Jericho tapped the door panel to open it. Breakfast awaited; from there, he'd be going on to Savannah to unscrew the mess Stephen's death had left for him to deal with.

He could hardly wait.

17
Side Studies

The absence of Black Dragon on this particular trip to Savannah didn't necessarily make it *easier* for Jericho, but he knew he could undoubtedly relax a little more. Not that he ever wanted her to find out the details of why he was going now. Knowing her, she'd find *something* inappropriate to say about the whole situation, possibly more than one thing. She had a distinct talent for it.

He found he couldn't really get settled until the train had passed through Kansas City, as too many questions were flooding into his brain over what he would find once he reached Savannah. With half an hour to go before the maglev got to St. Louis, he made his way to the front car and took up his customary seat; at the rear and to the right side of the train car, where he could lean against the window frame and watch the world flash by at several hundred miles per hour.

Over the past couple of weeks, he'd been more or less fully occupied with socializing Scout and figuring out how to improve the big guy's effectiveness in the field. The imposing robot was becoming more and more capable of holding up his end in a conversation, though the available topics were narrow. All things considered, Jericho was quite pleased with Scout's progress, and even more impressed with the Technologist's skill in creating artificial intelligence.

But Scout wasn't here now. Without the freedom to brood—which usually required a solitary rooftop and uninterrupted time to think—Jericho needed something else to keep his brain from spiraling into ever-decreasing circles until he was tearing his hair out from frustration. Two more hours of that would be no fun at all.

Fortunately, he had a couple of ready-made solutions at hand. The much more attractive one was to get into contact with Thomas. It had been just over two weeks since they'd seen each other, which was *far* too long.

Though now he came to think about it, their time apart felt both good and bad, in a weird kind of way.

He loved Thomas; there was no doubt about that. Thomas, he knew, loved him in return. But he'd become all too accustomed to Stephen's intrusive clinginess, and now it felt oddly liberating to be *allowed* to be apart from his boyfriend. While he wasn't exactly *enjoying* Thomas' absence, having the very option to be apart without tearful recriminations was ... different.

He had no idea what that meant for their relationship. It wasn't like he had anyone to talk to about it, except maybe Thomas himself.

So talk to him, dumbass.

Taking out his phone, he powered it up and accessed Thomas' number in the notepad. Opening the texting app, he started typing.

Hey, sexy. On maglev, heading to Savannah. On my own, this time. Want to chat?

While waiting for an answer, he got up and went to the bathroom, washed his hands, then grabbed a drink and a cookie from the vending machines. The cookie vanished quickly, and the drink followed shortly after. Sitting in front of him, his phone stubbornly refused to come back with any sort of reply. After about five more minutes of watching and waiting, he heaved a sigh.

The pitfalls of having a boyfriend on another team. He's clearly got better things to do than sit around all day waiting for me to contact him. I'm sure he'll text me back or call me.

Taking up the phone, he opened another app. His second option for passing the time was less personally satisfying but more educational. He'd meant to keep up his impromptu history lessons concerning False Flag's ill-gotten ilk, but free time had been sparse on the ground. Now, with Thomas apparently unavailable at the moment, he had nothing *but* free time.

Almost immediately, he had to chuckle when he saw the algorithm had been busy; the first three suggestions were video clips featuring Singularity, Charnel, and Doc Iridium. Beyond that were less well-known terror villains such as Kraken and Carnifex: the former having preyed on Great Lakes shipping in his squid-sub, and the latter bearing the dubious distinction of being the only villain to die under the aegis of the short-lived War on Terror Villains, back in 1997.

Jericho shook his head. It had probably seemed a good idea at the time, almost inevitable perhaps. Unfortunately, in hindsight, the Minotaur's televised murder of the Vice President seemed to have been a calculated provocation. Carnifex had been gunned down by the Texas National Guard (with the assistance of some enthusiastic volunteers), and the nation had cheered. When this resulted just days later in the murder of the President who had signed the Executive Order, followed shortly thereafter by his successor, the silence had been deafening.

False Flag had left a signed note pinned to the chest of the second President to die, via a knife through his heart: '*We can do this all day.*' It was a clear warning for all concerned to butt out of terror villain business, and it held firm for the next four months … right up until Inspire got too close to the Minotaur's operations and he struck back at the team.

With one member dead and another in a coma, Inspire was finished, but Castellan had taken the Minotaur down *permanently*. One month later, Team Power consigned Kraken's squid-sub (along with Kraken himself) to the depths of Lake Michigan. These were just the first stirrings of the backlash to come; over the next two years, Force Majeure declared open season on the remaining terror villains, swiftly dismantling what remained of their façade of invincibility.

This was definitely a rabbit-hole Jericho could see himself falling down, but he restrained himself from launching whole-heartedly into it. He was here to learn from the tactics used by terror villains in the past, not to become an expert on the whole subject. Accordingly, he picked the one at the top of the list: Singularity.

If he had to choose a phrase to describe her appearance, Jericho would've favored 'murder Goth'. She'd gone with a bustier over a high-necked body-stocking, a split skirt, and high-heeled thigh-length boots replete with silver buckles. Long-sleeved opera gloves completed her outfit; all in basic black, of course. Pure white makeup with a single red teardrop under the left eye, along with enough eyeshadow and black lipstick to outfit an entire punk rock band, all under a veil that was just substantial enough to defeat facial recognition software.

But the scary part wasn't her outfit; it was the level of her power tier. A classic flying cannon (even though she also wore a skirt), she could unleash devastating blasts of coruscating yellow energy from her hands. Her defensive capability involved a spherical force field that became darker and more durable as it decreased in size, going dead black at about six feet across. However, since she could shoot her beams out through the shield and her accuracy did not diminish with opacity, it was presumed she could see through it all the time.

Unfortunately for anyone who opted to fight her one-on-one, she could also manifest her force-field around *them* if they were within a few yards of her. Once she had them trapped, she could reduce the size of the field at will, down to some unknown limit. Nobody she'd ever inflicted this on had survived.

The force field could also be used to hurt people in another way, as Jericho discovered when he opened the first video clip, dated April of 1995. He never found out what that particular Atlantic City casino owner had done to offend her, or even if any offense had been given. But he watched in growing horror as she piloted the force field (with her inside) like a wrecking ball, smashing through the building and taking out the supporting pillars even as patrons and staff tried to flee for their lives.

Security cameras showed her bludgeoning the force field into stairwells, smearing would-be escapees over the crumbling concrete, then flying on to destroy more of the building. As with Raider, she appeared to take issue with people trying to avoid death at her hands; Jericho watched as she pursued a bunch of people down the street, detonating them one by one into showers of gore with her energy blast. The last, a woman with a child who had been shielded by several of the men, was crushed into a red splatter on the street by the force field before Singularity flew back to finish demolishing the casino.

Her other trademark behavior involved the serial abduction of young men and women, always good-looking. Videos of the victims were sent out; however, they weren't ransom demands, at least in the traditional sense. Her victims were subjected to horrific tortures on camera, and the message of each video was simple: *'Pay the money, and their suffering ends.'*

Sometimes she got paid, sometimes not. She always followed through if money changed hands; a second video would be posted, showing their timely demise. None of her victims were ever *found*, much less found *alive.*

Jericho only got about thirty seconds into the single ransom video shown on the site before he had to back out again, shuddering. The victims weren't pleading for their lives; they were begging their family members to pay the money and end their agony.

The announcement for St. Louis came as a welcome distraction; he got up to walk forward, the action almost automatic now. Before he settled into his seat in the front car, he used the restroom, washed his hands, then raided the vending machine for a bottle of water and a couple of cookies. While he didn't possess the raging furnace that Black Dragon apparently enjoyed in place of a normal metabolism, he admitted to feeling the need for a snack to pass the time. Basic requirements taken care of, he allowed himself to think over the videos he'd just watched.

As far as he could tell, Singularity had employed tactics somewhere between Raider and Guillotine in severity. The record showed that, between the force field and the flight, she had been insanely hard to pin down. Fighting her would be an absolute nightmare, and several heroes had learned the hard way that engaging her alone was literally suicide. That Independence and Transit had managed it between them merely underlined the skills and capabilities each of them brought to Force Majeure.

If Independence had had to face people like *that* immediately after the founding of Force Majeure, he was not so surprised about her attitude. While it still hurt his feelings, he figured it was less of a personal thing and more a general reaction to what she probably saw as a slackening of the standards that had made Force Majeure into America's premier superhero team.

Maybe I should just keep my head down until she gets over whatever she figures she's got against me.

It would take the maglev three-quarters of an hour to reach Nashville, the last long stretch until Jericho passed through Atlanta. The closer he got to Savannah, the antsier he was like to get, which meant he wouldn't be able to pay attention to what he was watching nohow.

One more video, then.

The top two options on his phone were Doc Iridium … and Charnel. His finger hovered, hesitating between the two. For personal reasons, he wanted to skip Charnel, hopefully for good. But this wasn't about his personal feelings. This was about learning from the lessons of history.

Drawing in a deep breath, he held it for a long moment, then tapped Charnel's image. The thumbnail unfolded before him.

Public consensus presented Charnel as able to change to and from his monster form at will, like a werewolf of legend. But no werewolf ever sported a flexible carapace capable of stopping knives altogether and providing significant protection against bullets. Charnel had no hair, but the carapace featured red-and-black tiger stripes, fading to red on the extravagantly clawed hands and feet. His underbelly, throat, and eyes were also red; the only parts of him that were neither black nor red were his wickedly sharp teeth, crowded into his prominent muzzle to give him a profoundly sinister grin.

As the video panned onto the grin, Jericho hit the pause icon. He closed his eyes and leaned back in the seat, working to contain his shudders of revulsion. When he was about six, he'd seen a film clip of Charnel grinning like that on the news, and it had given him nightmares for a month. Seventeen years later, it still made him want to hide under the table.

I'm not that kid anymore. I'm stronger. I'd kick his ass if he tried that grin on me now.

Jericho wasn't sure if he'd convinced himself, but it sounded good in his head.

When he restarted the video, the image of Charnel spoke; Jericho was forcibly reminded that the one thing worse than Charnel's grin was his *voice.* Whatever changes he went through to attain the monster form clearly wreaked havoc with his larynx. Charnel's speech, though intelligible, sounded like someone trying to gargle broken glass and razor blades marinated in battery acid. Fingernails slowly scraping down an old-fashioned blackboard (Jericho had once listened to this, on a bet with Luke) would be positively restful to the ears by comparison.

The video he was watching wasn't the one he'd seen on the news, but it was close enough in content. Like in the Guillotine footage, Charnel had trapped his victims in a shopping mall … but he wasn't trying to get away. One by one, apparently in near-pitch darkness after he pulled the breaker switch, he hunted them down. The security cameras had a low-light mode, which allowed Jericho to watch each murder; the grainy footage and lack of precise detail didn't make it any easier to witness. Some tried to fight back, while others attempted to run and hide, but nothing worked. Implacable and unstoppable, his manner positively *gloating*, Charnel caught up with them and killed each one in a way calculated to be as painful and lingering as possible.

Perhaps the scariest (as opposed to the most stomach-turning) moment came when a group of people was feeling their way through the corridors, and Charnel literally sneaked up behind them and took the last one in line *with nobody hearing a thing.* That spoke to some very effective stealth skills, along with a profound level of arrogance. Though if someone really *was* all that, perhaps it wasn't arrogance after all?

Just as he looked up from the screen, the privacy bubble cut out, and the Nashville station announcement came across the speakers. This was as good an excuse as any to put the videos on hold for the time being. Although it had all been for a good cause, he felt soiled to his very core for having waded through such horror and sadism.

He checked his phone to see if Thomas had tried to contact him anyway, and came up blank. Sliding it into his pocket, he got up from his seat and started forward through the train. One brisk walk later, he settled himself into his new seat.

With a sigh, he took his phone out with the idea of watching something cheerful and uplifting. There was only one other thing he wanted to do, and brooding simply wasn't going to happen under these circumstances.

That was when his previous viewing choices bit him on the ass. The algorithm had been hard at work; when he opened the site up, all he could see were video clips about villains as far down as he scrolled. Which was a pain, because right now he didn't *want* to watch the dubious exploits of Seismic or the Darksider or Kraken or even Mindscrew, much less different videos of the ones he'd already looked into.

With a sigh, he picked the one Enabled he knew for an absolute guaranteed *fact* had nothing to do with any of his problems. The man had died over twenty years ago and had never even *been* to America.

A glowing blue figure, almost skeletal in nature, Cherenkov had unleashed horrifically powerful actinic beams of destructive energy against anything that disturbed him, while permeating the area around him with yet more radiation merely by existing. Relatively few video clips existed of him, and none of him acting against civilians, mainly because everyone had been evacuated from the area around Chornobyl. The Russian (and then Ukrainian, after 1991) military had attempted to capture or kill him several times but had utterly failed to achieve either objective.

As Jericho settled down to watch the film clips, he hoped Thomas would text him soon.

18
Post Office

Jericho strolled out of the maglev station with his hands in his jacket pockets, head up and enjoying deep breaths of the chill winter air. It was an overcast day with the temperature hovering around fifty, but after the soul-scouring darkness he'd delved into on the train, it could've been a howling blizzard and he still would've considered it an improvement. Some days, he reflected, it was just a blessing to be alive.

These blessings suddenly redoubled as an arm slipped through his. Next to his ear, a familiar voice murmured, "Hey, stranger. Going my way?"

Turning in surprise, Jericho pulled his hands from his pockets and hugged Thomas fiercely. "Where'd you come from?" he demanded. "I texted you, and you never replied!"

Thomas grinned; leaning in, he stole a kiss. Jericho stole it right back then just stood there, holding onto Thomas like a lifeline. All the worries and stresses of the trip simply melted away as if they'd never been. He didn't even care about the answer to his question anymore.

"I got the text," Thomas said softly. "I was going to answer, but then I decided to see if I could surprise you instead. Mom and Dad were already prepping to run some pursuit drills with the jet and the new iterations to Dad's and Buddy's suits, so they just moved it down here when I asked. Dropped me off in Charleston, and I took the maglev down. I got into town fifteen minutes ago, and ducked out to ambush you when I saw you getting off the train." He looked inordinately pleased with himself.

Jericho blinked, pulling back to study Thomas' face for any sign he was joking. "They did that for you?"

"For *us*." Thomas curled over the middle three fingers of his right hand, then touched his thumb to his own chest and his pinky to Jericho's. "I told you, they like you. And they're bending over backward to prove they've got no problem with me having a boyfriend."

"They don't have to do *that*," Jericho protested, though he didn't insist very hard on it. Anything that gave him and Thomas more time together was ideal, and he was willing to enjoy it for as long as possible.

"Hey, they didn't have to say yes, but I'm not arguing with the results." Thomas tilted his head toward the road. "Are we getting a cab, or is someone picking you up?"

"Cab," Jericho said briefly. He'd thought about bringing his family in on the situation to save himself cab fare, but it would take far too long to explain matters, and he wanted to get back to Utopia *today*. Besides, he knew damn well Livy and Serena would swoop in and kidnap Thomas at the first opportunity. Not only would they tell him all the embarrassing stories Jericho had been hoping to keep quiet until they'd been together for at least a year, but they'd also likely pump Thomas for any tales of his own. Where that went, brave men feared to tread. "Do they still look weird to you?"

"Little bit," Thomas admitted. "I'm getting used to it, though. You?"

"I figure air-cabs are a whole lot safer," Jericho agreed. "The wheels are starting to look strange to me, now. Maybe when I've been there two years, I'll be staring at them like an astronaut at a horse and cart."

Thomas chuckled. "First day back, I know I was. Come on, let's do this." He took Jericho by the hand and led him down toward the taxis. Opening the back door of the first one, he ushered Jericho in, then got in himself.

The taxi driver was a woman in her fifties with a pack-a-day rasp and severely tied-back hair. This was another oddity; in air-cabs, the driver was out of sight behind a partition. "Afternoon, gents. Where to?"

Jericho had made a phone call on the stretch from Atlanta into Savannah, to find out which post office the box might be situated in. For some reason, he'd expected Stephen to have wanted quick access to his stash, but he'd been wrong. His ex, whom he was starting to realize had been borderline paranoid, had picked the very farthest post office from Jericho's old address that was still within Savannah city limits. He gave the location, then sat back with his hand in Thomas' as the cab moved off.

Savannah looked just the same as the last couple of times he'd been through at ground level. Nothing familiar had been demolished (well, *one* thing had, but they weren't going there), and the only new thing he'd seen was the maglev rail heading up the coast toward Charleston. The driver didn't try to make conversation, which was okay with him. It wasn't as though there were many topics in his life right then that he felt comfortable talking about. *Hey, so I just found out that my ex, who died in a fire recently, had a post office box in my name, so I've come back to town to see what that's about. What's up with you?*

... which would win prizes anywhere for '*most awkward conversational opening ever*'.

When the taxi pulled up outside the building complex holding the post office, Jericho already had his Visa card out and was ready to pay the fare. It was a little high in his estimation, but he figured he'd been spoiled by air-cab prices, so he paid without demur. "Thanks for the ride," he said. "Have a good one." Climbing out of the cab after Thomas, he closed the door and watched as it headed off.

Thomas looked around with interest. "Nice tour of Savannah. What are we picking up here?"

"This is where it gets awkward," Jericho said quietly. He tilted his head toward the post office. "There's a PO box in my name in there, though I never rented it."

"Stephen did." Thomas was showing every indication of being on top of the situation. "And you want to close it out, and see what's in it."

Jericho nodded. "Wouldn't you? I don't *want* to believe there's anything bad in there, but ..."

"... but if it was innocent, why is it in *your* name?" Thomas frowned. "How bad are you thinking?"

"He literally made sex tapes to try to lure me back." Jericho shrugged. "I honestly can't say what else he might have stashed under my name."

"The mind boggles." Thomas shaded his eyes as he looked at the post office. "So, what are we waiting for?"

Jericho took the notification letter from his pocket. "I'm pretty sure this is the place, but I just need to make sure of it before we go in." He showed Thomas the number, then they started going along the wall.

It didn't take long to hit paydirt, especially with the two of them looking. "Found it," Thomas said, pointing. He let out a low whistle. "And it's a big one, too. I figure it could handle parcels."

He wasn't wrong; the box in question was undoubtedly one of the larger ones on display. Jericho headed for the front door of the post office, but hesitated at the threshold.

If I don't go in there, I don't have to find out whatever Stephen was using that thing for. But if I don't, whoever empties it will surely find out what he was doing behind my back.

"You okay?" asked Thomas from behind him. "Need some moral support?"

"I guess," Jericho admitted, taking a deep breath of the chilly air. "It's just that I'm gonna have to lie to them, and I don't like lying."

Thomas chuckled wryly. "That's okay. Turns out I'm really good at it, especially when it's for a worthy cause." Stepping around Jericho, he took his hand and entered the post office, moving with a confident step. Jericho had no choice but to be drawn along with him as they fronted up to the counter.

Less than thirty seconds later, a pleasant young lady noticed them and came on over. "Hi there, folks. Can I help y'all with anything?"

"Actually, yes." Thomas gave her a winning smile. "You have a post office box here in my friend's name. He needs to close it down and claim the contents."

"Oh." Her head came up a little, and she looked over at Jericho as though she'd been chastised. "Is there a problem with our service, sir?"

"No, no problem at all," Jericho assured her. Well, *he'd* had no problem. "I've recently moved out of town, is all. My mail's all been redirected, and I just need to deal with this."

"Ah, of course." Her uncertain expression gave way to a brilliant smile. "I'll be happy to do that for you. Which box number was it, sir?"

He handed her the notification letter. "Here you go. This should make things easier."

"Oh. Right. Of course. That's Mr. ... Hansen, yes? May I see some identification?"

"Sure thing." Taking out his wallet, Jericho dug through it. Although Uncle Leroy had taught him how to drive years earlier, he'd never gotten around to taking the test, so he didn't actually have a driver's license. However, he did possess a Georgia state ID card that had lurked in the back of his wallet since he'd turned eighteen. He supposed he needed to get one for Kansas at some point, but this would have to do for now.

The girl looked at the card, then at Jericho, and nodded to herself. Then she frowned slightly. "When you say, '*claim the contents*', why don't you just remove them for yourself?"

"I'm sorry, but the key is unrecoverable." Jericho grimaced, thinking about the reason it was in that state. "It was in the apartment complex that burned down the other week. I was out of town at the time and only got back after the fact." Taking his phone, he called up the news article that had covered the fire, then pointed at the address printed on the notification letter. "I'm guessing I need to cover the cost of replacing the lock. Y'all have your security to think of, after all."

"Uh ... just a moment, please." The young lady moved off, taking the letter with her.

This did nothing to increase Jericho's confidence in any way. For all he knew, they were calling the cops on him and Thomas right now. Was it even legal to claim someone else's mail, for all that it was collected in a PO box rented under his name?

"Relax," murmured Thomas out of the corner of his mouth. "You're doing great. No need to look so nervous."

Taking a deep breath, Jericho did his best to emulate his boyfriend's casual stance against the counter. Thomas' presence did a lot to steady his jangled nerves, which he thoroughly appreciated. Reaching across, he retook Thomas' hand and got a reassuring squeeze as a reward.

If they did question his right to what was in there, would they look into it themselves, or simply trash the lot?

I just want to know what Stephen thought was worth hiding in a post office box under a borrowed name. Carefully, he did his best to ignore the genuine chance that he would regret finding out.

This is the last thing I'm ever going to do for him. I may as well do it properly.

A man in his fifties strolled in from the back. Jericho couldn't see any fundamental differences in his uniform compared to the young woman, but his very bearing said, 'senior staff'. Here was someone who could Get Things Done.

"Afternoon, sir. I understand you want to empty your post office box and close it down, but you don't have your key with you?" The man was brisk and to the point.

"That's correct." Jericho showed him the article on his phone. "It was lost in the fire."

"Huh. I 'member seeing that on the news. Pity about the poor guy who got caught in it. G-Man and that dragon girl showed up and saved everyone else, didn't they?"

"So I heard, yeah." Jericho was uncomfortable with the man's blunt analysis of the situation. While he'd managed to convince himself that he probably wouldn't have been able to save Stephen even if he'd known, it didn't assuage the minor stab of guilt about having felt good that his ex-boyfriend's car hadn't been there.

"Hm. Well, your ID and address check out." The man slapped forms onto the desk. "This one's for you to pay for a new lock to be fitted and to take possession of the keys. This one's for you to acknowledge that you're closing down the box and handing the keys back. Fill 'em both out, pay for the new lock, and you can be on your way with your mail."

That seemed straightforward enough. As Jericho was filling out the lost-key form, they brought out new keys and what he figured was a lock barrel to replace the old one. He finished that one off, paid the fee, and then worked on the box-closure form. Each stroke of the pen, he knew, brought him closer to finding out what had been going on in Stephen's head. Whether or not he would enjoy the process was another matter altogether.

With the second form filled out, a large plastic shopping bag was placed on the counter next to the keys. "Your mail, sir," chirped the young lady who had initially served him. "You're done already? Good. Do you have your receipt?"

"Reckon as how I won't be needing it," Jericho said hastily. He wanted to put this episode behind him as quickly as possible.

"Suit yourself, sir." She tore the slip of paper off the machine then dangled the keys from her finger. "This is me accepting the keys back. Have a nice day, Mr. Hansen."

"You, too, miss." With Thomas at his side, he took up the shopping bag, which had *far* too much correspondence in it for his peace of mind, and beat a faux-nonchalant retreat from the post office. All he needed was for one person to ask him why he didn't look like the *other* Jericho Hansen … but, he supposed, Stephen had suffered under the opposite problem. If he'd become known to too many people at the post office under Jericho's name, and one of them happened to be acquainted with the real Jericho, the authorities would've gotten involved. Mail fraud was a Federal offense, after all.

Once they were around the corner from the entrance to the post office, he stopped and opened the bag. Within was a mass of envelopes, too many to simply take out and examine right now.

"So, what are you going to do with all that?" asked Thomas quietly, tilting his head to indicate a nearby trash can. "Dump it, give it a quick once-over, or take it someplace and check it over thoroughly?"

The question was a cogent one. While Jericho knew he could find privacy for sure in Utopia, he was a little less confident about it in Savannah; at least, not without using his powers. It wouldn't take all that long to go and fetch his original costume from Leroy, but he didn't feel like going to those lengths just to check the letters a little more quickly, especially if he didn't really have to. Also, he didn't know if Thomas had the wherewithal to mask up in a hurry if necessary. *Also* also, this was supposed to be a quick in-and-out; bringing family into the mix would complicate that to an unreasonable degree.

"I'm gonna need to think on that for a mite," he decided. "In the meantime, there's a reason I should've been back to Savannah long since. Somebody I need to go see. You want to come with?"

Thomas neither hesitated nor asked who he was talking about. "Sure," he agreed cheerfully. "We got this."

Heartened by the unconditional acceptance, Jericho headed back out to the street with Thomas in tow. He spotted a taxi stand a little way down, with one vehicle waiting on it. Not much to his surprise, he recognized it as the same one that had dropped them off at the post office complex. The driver had proven herself to be competent and willing to respect their privacy, so he walked in that direction. When he opened the door and got in, her eyebrows raised in mild surprise.

"Afternoon again, fellers. Back to the train station?"

"Need to go someplace else first," Jericho said. "And there's a stop I've got to make along the way."

"Ain't no skin off mine," she replied agreeably as she started the vehicle. "Buckle up, folks. Where y'all off to first?"

Jericho pulled the strap over his shoulder and clicked the metal tongue into place, as Thomas did the same beside him.

"Jack's Package Shop on Ogeechee Road, thanks."

For this, he was going to need alcohol.

19
Perennial Regrets

Laurel Grove South Cemetery
Savannah, Georgia

Jericho paid off the cab at the entrance to the cemetery and got out, with Thomas right behind him. The half-pint bottle of sipping whiskey sat heavy in his jacket pocket, but the burden was nothing compared to the weight on his soul at that moment. He'd been here once before, visiting the grave with family; coming with just one person was both easier and a whole lot harder.

"Huh," Thomas observed, looking around with his hands on his hips. "Not what I was expecting. This is for your friend, right? The one who was murdered?"

"My cousin, yeah," Jericho said, reaching out and taking his hand. "Luke. He was my best friend, and the closest thing I'll ever have to a big brother."

Thomas nodded; pulling Jericho into an embrace, he rubbed his fingertips in gentle circles between Jericho's shoulders. "*And* he came the closest to seeing through my act. He knew damn well there was something off about me. I really wish I'd gotten to know him better. We going in?"

"Yeah." The gateway was open; reluctantly, Jericho disengaged from the hug and led the way along the road that led through the cemetery. There were patches of snow here and there, though not the all-encompassing blanket that had dropped onto Indianapolis. Most of the graves were clear of it, especially where the weak winter sunlight fell.

Overhead, the oak tree branches were bare of their leaves and would remain so until spring. The breeze was light, barely disturbing the white puffs of their breath as they trod along the road. Jericho knew where he was going, but he was in no particular hurry to get there.

It bothered him more than he wanted to admit that he'd missed the interment. As he'd told Thomas, he and Luke had been brothers in all but fact, with the implicit understanding that they'd be there for each other through thick and thin. To help carry a brother to his final rest was the ultimate demonstration of respect and love, and he'd screwed it up.

His footsteps slowed as he turned down the side path that led between the graves. A newer stone, the carving still sharp and fresh, stood out from the others. He forced himself onward, reminded again that the only reason he was in Savannah at all lay in the shopping bag from the post office, and hating himself for not coming sooner.

When they stopped by the grave, he saw a fresh bunch of flowers and a small, framed photo of Luke's car leaning against the stone. Again, he read the inscription. Something akin to a sob escaped his throat as tears welled in his eyes.

Lucas Frederick Douglass Hansen
Born January 7, 1985
Passed October 6, 2013
Son, brother, husband
"Greater love has no one than this,
that a person will lay down his life for his friends."

Closing his eyes so the tears ran unhindered down his cheeks, he rested his weight against the gravestone with his free hand. "Hey, Luke," he murmured. "Brought Thomas along this time." Beside him, Thomas moved as though turning to look at him but didn't say anything.

Hey, cuz. You two look good together. It seemed almost as though Luke was standing beside him.

"Yeah." Jericho opened his eyes, then leaned down to prop the shopping bag against the side of the gravestone. Taking the bottle from his pocket, he unscrewed the cap. "Sorry I missed your birthday. Brought you a present."

He put the bottle to his lips and took a pull, letting the good-quality whiskey burn its way down his throat. Then he handed it over to Thomas, ignoring the fact that his boyfriend wasn't yet twenty-one; Luke wouldn't give a good goddamn about that. Thomas took it, nodded respectfully to the gravestone, and took a drink as well. When he handed it back, Jericho held it over the grave and tilted it, letting the fluid gurgle from the neck and splash onto the frozen ground below.

Yeah, well. He looks like a keeper. It's not like ya don't need someone watchin' out for ya. Damn, that there's some righteous booze. Don't ever recall you buyin' me a bottle of that, back in th' day.

Jericho had to hide a smile. Up until a couple of years ago, he hadn't been legally allowed to buy booze, and Luke knew it. He paused in his pouring and took another sip. It really was good whiskey.

Good goin', kickin' Steve to th' curb like ya did. Sucks he got kilt th' way he did, but that don't make him not *a cheatin' sumbitch.*

Which only opened up another can of guilt for Jericho. "I just hate that I could've saved him, but I didn't know I had to."

In his imagination, Luke punched him on the shoulder. *You pull that shit up right now, cuz. Chances were, he'd already passed by th' time you got there. Goin' in there woulda just ended up with the both of you dead, not jes' him.*

This was more or less what Ms. Chandler had already told him, but it made him feel better to hear it from an independent source ... so to speak. If his subconscious agreed with her analysis of the event, she was probably correct.

He handed the bottle to his boyfriend again. With just a mouthful left after Thomas had taken another drink, he gestured for it to be poured out over the grave. Reclaiming the empty bottle, he replaced the cap and put it into his jacket pocket.

They stood silently by the gravesite for a few more minutes, then Jericho bent down from where he'd been leaning against the headstone and picked up the shopping bag. "Let's go," he said quietly. "Thanks for coming along."

"No trouble at all," Thomas said equably, taking his hand once more.

In his mind's eye, Luke leaned against the stone from the other side, arms folded and looking up at the sky. *You be sure an' take care now, cuz.*

Jericho walked away from the grave, Thomas' hand warm in his. "Always do," he whispered.

By the time they got to the main road, his tears were threatening to spill out of control again. Thomas offered him a handkerchief so he could wipe his eyes. "Are you okay there?"

"I will be." Jericho smiled weakly. "Thanks for being there. Hope you don't reckon I've got me a screw loose for talking to him like that."

Thomas gathered him into a warm and comforting hug. "You're not crazy. I read somewhere that according to the traditions of Mexico's Day of the Dead, so long as someone's alive in your heart, then they're never truly dead. So, you just keep on talking to him."

"Thanks." Jericho laid his head on Thomas' shoulder, wiped his eyes again, then blew his nose. It took him a few moments to recognize the handkerchief. "Is this the one …?"

Thomas gave him a smart-ass grin. "Yup. Same one you gave me. And I'm gonna want it back."

Jericho's smile was weaker but still there. "No problem."

Slowly, holding hands once more, they walked back to the front gate. When they got there, Jericho got his phone out and called for a taxi, then put the shopping bag down carefully by his feet and took Thomas in his arms.

Wrapped in his boyfriend's strong embrace, Jericho felt complete in a way that he'd never experienced before meeting Thomas. "I don't want to go back to Utopia," he said softly. "I don't want you to go back to Chicago. Can we run away together and live here in Savannah?" He was joking … mostly.

"Sure," agreed Thomas readily. "We can do that."

Neither one moved from the spot. They held tightly on to each other, a mutual refuge against the outside world. Jericho kissed him and was kissed in return: an acceptable exchange.

"So, have you figured out what you're going to do with that stuff?" Thomas' voice was a little more down-to-earth than when he'd agreed to elope with Jericho. Still, Jericho suspected that the answer would've been the same if he'd made the offer in earnest.

"Yeah." Jericho sighed heavily. "I'll look over the letters on the train. Anything that's more than just a letter, I'll check out back in Utopia. Whatever I don't like, I'll let my housekeeping robot take care of."

"Housekeeping robot." Thomas shook his head and chuckled. "Like the ones in the Oaklands?"

"Same type, yeah. The one in my area's called Forty-Three. He's positively chirpy when he brings the mail in the morning."

"That's one of the many things I love about you," Thomas mused. "You even treat robots like people."

"You should meet Scout, then," Jericho said without thinking. "He's getting smarter every day."

"Scout?" Thomas tilted his head. "I've seen him on the news with you. I thought for sure that was a guy in a suit. That's a *robot*?"

Jericho nodded. "Totally artificially intelligent. The Technologist is real pleased with him. He'll be coming down to Canaveral with me on the twenty-eighth."

"Canaveral? The Challenger Commemoration thing?" Thomas pulled back to look at him properly. "You're going to be there?"

"Uh-huh." Jericho's cheeks were hurting from the width of his smile. "Don't tell anyone, but I've been tapped to represent Force Majeure this year."

Tires crunched on gravel, and both Jericho and Thomas turned to see the taxi pulling to a halt. Jericho scooped up the shopping bag, and they climbed in. "Maglev station, please," Thomas said, forestalling Jericho. "I've got this."

As the cab pulled away from the curb, Jericho elbowed Thomas gently in the ribs. "I can pay for it," he whispered.

"I know you can, but I'm paying for this one." Thomas grabbed his hand and laced their fingers together. "Anyway, that's great news. We're all going to try to be there. Little bro's going to be front and center."

By which Jericho gathered Buddy was going to be Team Power's representative. "Cool," he said sincerely. "I can't wait."

The presence of the cab driver necessarily limited the number of topics they could talk about until they reached their destination, so they rode in silence, stealing the occasional glance at each other. Jericho would've gone the whole hog and spent the trip making out with Thomas, but he didn't feel like being kicked out of the cab. It *was* the twenty-first century, but the South was still the South, and they were getting odd glances from the driver just for holding hands.

When they got to the maglev station, Thomas paid (Jericho didn't grumble *too* much) then they went inside. By now, they could race through the process of acquiring tickets almost on autopilot. Jericho had done it so many times now that he could pay more attention to Thomas than he did to the screen in front of him.

Just as they'd finished and were heading through into the lounge, the speakers crackled to life. **"Attention. Attention. The train for Atlanta will be leaving in one minute. All passengers for the Atlanta train must board immediately."**

"Oh, come *on*," Jericho groused, rolling his eyes. He knew damn well that the maglev waited for nobody and nothing. If a body wasn't on board when it left, there was nothing for it; they'd missed the train. But he'd been looking forward to saying goodbye to Thomas properly.

"Canaveral, yeah?" Thomas took him by the shoulders and looked into his eyes. "We can explore it together."

Jericho nodded enthusiastically, the prospect brightening him right up. "Definitely. It's a date."

"Good." Thomas kissed him hard enough to make him weak in the knees. He was on the verge of saying, '*screw it, I'll take a later train*' when Thomas ended the kiss and gave him a gentle shove. "Now go, catch your train."

One of the most effective ways to prevent people from smuggling contraband (drugs, explosives, or guns) onto the maglev was by way of what Jericho thought of as a scanning airlock, or a 'scan-lock'. This compartment, twelve feet long by six wide, required a swipe from a MagCard to get into and would not allow people through until the internal scanners had cleared them.

Jericho tottered toward the closest one of these, remembering at the last second to tap the reader with his MagCard. Just as he stepped inside, Thomas smacked his ass hard enough to make him jump. As the heavy glass doors hummed closed behind them—Thomas having swiped his card on the same reader—he gave his boyfriend a dirty look. "Did you have to do that in front of everyone?"

Thomas waggled his eyebrows. "Would you rather I didn't?"

After a moment of consideration, Jericho shook his head. "No."

"Didn't think so." Thomas looked far too pleased with himself.

The doors at the far end of the scan-lock opened, and they hustled out. Jericho grabbed Thomas and gave him a quick peck on the lips. "I love you," he whispered.

"I love you too."

Jericho crossed the platform with Thomas' words still sounding in his ears, and scrambled on board the train with mere seconds to spare. The doors closed and he put his hand on the glass, staring out at Thomas. In the next instant, his boyfriend was gone as the train whisked sideways, swiftly and silently bearing Jericho away from Savannah.

As he trudged up the spiral staircase to see if his preferred seat was free, a line from Shakespeare drifted across Jericho's mind, along with his personal commentary on the sentiment.

Parting is such sweet sorrow, my ass.
It sucks, is what it does.

20
Difficult Decisions

It turned out the top deck was indeed sparsely populated. Slumping into the rear seat on the right-hand side, Jericho set the bag on the table and regarded it unhappily. He was going to have to go through the contents at some point during the next two and a half hours; that was what he'd told Thomas. But he knew, bone-deep, he wasn't going to enjoy it. Not in the slightest.

Feeling much the same level of trepidation as he would've if he'd been groping around inside a hollow log with a cottonmouth waiting to sink its fangs into his hand, he reached into the bag and grabbed a stack of letters. Two things struck him at once as he spread them across the table in front of him. First, while some were addressed directly to Stephen and some to the PO box, each one featured different handwriting, all unfamiliar. Second, they had all been opened and resealed with tape.

On second thought, he decided this was more akin to reaching blindly down into a drain to find out precisely what was blocking the flow, with all the implications of something foul and unclean rotting away in the dark. He put his hand into the bag again and pulled out another stack. Along with the letters, this time he found a small padded mailer.

Unlike the letters—again, all addressed in unfamiliar handwriting, all opened and resealed—the mailer was addressed to the post office box in Stephen's own neat script and still held the original seal. Feeling with his fingertips and probing gently with his G-sense, he decided it had to be a thumb drive, going by the external shape and internal metal bits.

Putting it aside—he had no way of accessing its contents on the train, and there was more in the bag—he reluctantly delved once more into the unknown.

By the time the bag was empty, there were no fewer than forty-one letters arrayed on the table before him. On top of that were two padded mailers, which posed a conundrum to him. Though the postage dates were well apart, they were both addressed in Stephen's handwriting, and (he'd torn them open to verify this) each one held a thumb drive and nothing else. One of the drives was red and the other blue, but otherwise they were essentially identical, with no hint of what they held or why Stephen would've mailed them both to the PO box for safekeeping.

The date stamped on the first mailer caught his eye. It was recent, *very* recent. Just fifteen days ago, long after he and Stephen had parted ways … *wait just one goddamn second.* Hauling out his phone, he feverishly woke it up and tapped in a query. Seconds later, his suspicions were confirmed. It had been processed through the post office on January 5, the day *after* Stephen died in the apartment fire.

Jericho knew there was a mailbox directly outside the apartment block. However, it was still weird for him to imagine Stephen slipping outside to post whatever this was then returning to the apartment, only to die on the same day.

And the mail carrier couldn't pick it up until the next day because the whole place would've been behind police tape for hours.

Intrigued at the coincidence but knowing he would glean no more secrets from the drive until he reached Utopia, he checked the date on the other mailer. This one was from somewhat further back: September 2, 2013. Over a month before he'd come to Utopia for the first time.

Hell, that was two weeks before I even got the email to show up for the interview. Whatever this one's about, it's damn sure got nothing to do with Utopia or Force Majeure.

He knew what he had to do next, and he absolutely didn't want to do it. The drives could not be accessed until he got back to Utopia, but the envelopes were right there. All he had to do was take one, tear it open, pull out the sheet of paper within ... and read.

For a couple of moments, he postponed the inevitable by sorting them by order of postage date. Doing so revealed that all seventeen letters addressed directly to Stephen dated from before their relationship had even begun, and the tape holding them closed was more than a little yellowed. The postmark on the first letter addressed to the PO box was dated April 19, 2012, just six days after Stephen and Jericho had gone out together for the first time.

He was asking me to move in even then, Jericho recalled. *The asshat was fixing to cheat on me from the very start. This wasn't some kinda one-off loss of self-control. He* planned *it all the way down the line.*

The revelation shouldn't have gutted him, but it did. Somewhere at the back of his mind, he'd wanted to somehow excuse Stephen's actions and make the infractions less severe than they really were. If his ex's infidelity had been a one-off, or if there had been a misunderstanding somewhere along the way, might that have made it better somehow? He didn't know.

But this was a deliberate pattern of betrayal from the get-go. It would've been okay if Stephen had been sleeping with the subjects of his photoshoots before he met Jericho, then simply stopped once they entered a committed relationship ... but he hadn't, and it wasn't. He'd actively arranged to keep right on doing it while concealing the evidence from his superhero boyfriend.

The worst part was that he'd *succeeded*. Jericho had lived with Stephen for six months with no idea of what was going on behind his back. Only Luke's disclosure on the train had clued him in, and the sole reason he'd believed *that* was the absolute respect he held for Luke.

Carefully, he swept aside the letters addressed directly to Stephen, putting them back in the bag. Those had been written before he came into the picture and were none of his business. Which just left the twenty-four letters that had been sent to the post office box.

I'm still stalling.

Jericho knew it and acknowledged it, but his hand still did not move. Even telling himself this was the best way to clear Stephen of the cheating charge (if, for instance, all the letters were about how much they'd enjoyed the photoshoot, with no salacious overtones) did nothing to help. Opening any one of those letters would give him the truth but right then, he was so scared of what the facts might be (what he knew they were) that he *did not want* to look.

Okay, fine. If I'm too much of a coward to read some goddamn letter, then there's something else I don't want to do, but I need to anyway.

Irritated at himself for not being able to reach down and find a pair, he took up the phone from where it was lying on the table and deliberately selected the videos he'd opted out of before. Before he could change his mind, he tapped the one for Doc Iridium.

The last terror villain standing had been an artificer, but *what* an artificer. With just the products of his powerset standing between himself and summary justice, he'd lasted longer than any of his contemporaries. Technically speaking, he hadn't actually been captured or killed by the forces of law and order, but he *had* been taken off the board by his own explosive device, so that didn't exactly count as a victory for him.

'I am a bomb disposal expert', the old joke ran through Jericho's head. *'If you see me running, try to keep up'*.

Doc Iridium's fascination had been with apocalypse scenarios: the more complete and overwhelming, the better. According to his rhetoric, he didn't want to destroy humanity; he wanted to *improve* them. But to Jericho's ear, that rang slightly hollow. Even the terror villain's chosen codename referenced the element that marked the demise of the dinosaurs after the Chicxulub impact.

Clad in 'wasteland chic' powered armor that he'd apparently cobbled together from random pieces of rusty metal and corroded plastic (which worked much better than it had any right to), he rarely engaged the heroes personally. When he did, he had at least three alternate escape scenarios already worked out ahead of time. He mostly made overblown speeches via a mechanical-sounding voice modulator, which were transmitted to TV stations to coincide with his latest atrocity, usually an explosion or equipment failure caused by sabotage of safety systems. He was really, *really* good at subverting tech like that.

"Humanity has an innate need for disasters," he'd proclaimed after reprogramming an airliner's flight control system to plow into a Boston skyscraper shortly after takeoff; nearly fifteen hundred people had died to the explosion and subsequent collapse of the structure. **"Safety and security**

are *bad* for us. Look at those around you. Can you count on them when all is lost? Would you be able to take care of yourself and your loved ones if you lost the technology that makes your life soft and comfortable? Have you ever bothered to learn how? Or would your so-called friends claw your eyes out for your last can of beans?"

The video flicked to a new attack; this time, he had tampered with the safety controls of a passenger train, causing it to derail alongside a busy shopping mall. Casualties had been in the thousands.

"Disaster and loss are natural things for us. We need them to make us feel alive, to appreciate the things we have. Insulating us from them, pretending they don't exist, does us a disservice as a species. We need to feel the emotions in all their rawness, to understand that the universe is a cold and cruel mistress, one that will take away all you cherish and then laugh at your tears."

In a third instance, he'd sabotaged a hydroelectric dam's turbine controls in the Midwest. When the machinery threw a bearing at maximum load, the resulting chain reaction of catastrophic failures fatally fractured the dam's structure. When it collapsed and the resulting flash flood overran the town downstream, some escaped. Most didn't.

"You say you don't want disasters, but you're lying even to yourself. You *crave* them. Danger makes your heart beat faster. Deep down, you fantasize about being the great hero who saves the innocent from peril. You know you do. *Everyone* does. Without danger, without disaster, how would you do that?"

And then the video switched to the one Jericho knew had been coming. It had been Doc Iridium's final, best-known speech, the one given on his last day alive. If he'd known that to be the case at the time, Jericho suspected, he couldn't have done much better for an epitaph. Of course, if he'd known what was coming ahead of time, he probably would've spent less time polishing his speech and more time double-checking his bomb controls.

For brevity's sake, most news services usually went with the last few lines he'd spoken before disaster struck, but this one had the whole thing. Jericho didn't think he'd heard it all in one place before, so he settled back to listen. He knew how it ended, but that made it all the better.

"You treat me as the villain, but I am not the villain here." Jericho could've sworn he could hear an aggrieved tone, even through the voice modulator, as though Iridium truly believed what he was saying. "If you wish to identify the true villains of the piece, look to your so-called heroes. Look at Force Majeure. They will do more harm to you than I ever could. Humanity's natural state is disaster and apocalypse; shielding you from this does you no good whatsoever. Humanity is not intended for softness, comfort, soy lattes, or panting, pampered pug pets. We are the epitome of evolution, and we need to act like the lean, mean fighting machines we were always intended to be. Our destiny is to wrest our living from nature, red in tooth and claw, not have it handed to us on a silver platter. We have built our castles too high, and their foundations of sand must be exposed for what they are. All must be rendered to ash and made equal so that we can begin again, start fresh and build a new world on the ruins of the old. You will see, once I have—"

This was the point where Doc Iridium paused and glanced sideways. Dozens of comedians had created skits based on this moment, and a thousand memes had spawned from it. *That was the moment he knew he done goofed* was a favorite.

"No," he said. "**Wait. That's not right—**" Then the image devolved into static.

Jericho knew he shouldn't find this moment funny; after all, over ninety thousand people had died as a result of whatever malfunction had overtaken the timer on Doc Iridium's bomb. But it *had* been fifteen years ago, near enough, and imagining the 'oh, crap' look on the artificer's face was never *not* amusing.

Then he sobered again because while Doc Iridium's passing—the ultimate case of being hoist on one's own petard—was arguably funny, the mentality behind it was no laughing matter. Despite his initial demand for a billion dollars to spare the city of Manhattan, Iridium had never been in it for the money. It had always been about chaos, death, and destruction. There was a genuine chance he would've rejected the ransom if it had been made available (though he would clearly have accepted the execution of Force Majeure in a heartbeat).

Doc Iridium had been the scariest type of supervillain: someone who sincerely believed he was doing the right thing. A fanatic with a cause. And like any fanatic, there had been literally no lengths to which he would not go to fulfill his aims.

In his eyes, humanity had become too complacent, too wrapped in the world their technology had crafted for them, drowning in their own consumer products. They *needed* the awareness that death could strike at any moment and take it all away from them. Moreover, the villain honestly thought humanity *should* be suffering more natural disasters and near-extinction events, and was frustrated because these were not coming to pass. And so, in the absence of anything else performing that task for them, he'd manifestly taken it upon himself to fill that role and be the harbinger of apocalypse for humanity.

Jericho's feelings about this were just a little conflicted. Sure, he was entirely opposed to inflicting disasters on humanity willy-nilly, and murdering thousands of people on a whim just wasn't going to fly where his personal morality was concerned. But … and he freely admitted this was a relatively weak *but* … Doc Iridium hadn't explicitly been *wrong* regarding people's complacence and lack of preparedness. Jericho didn't know one person in five who had a disaster plan prepped and ready to go, even in Savannah, right on the hurricane-prone Atlantic coast. The lack of people he'd known before he went to Utopia who had any kind of self-defense training, or even a regular fitness regime, was … dismaying.

On the one hand, it would be nice if more people could take care of themselves and not need assistance to survive the most basic crises. Better yet, if they could take *responsibility* for their own actions and not make a bad situation worse (as he'd seen so often), it would make everyone else's job so much easier. In an emergency situation, even something so simple as regular cardio training and a first-aid certificate turned any person from a liability to an asset.

But on the other hand, that wasn't his call to make. It never had *been* his call. His job wasn't to tell people how to live their lives, but to live his own life as best he could, and help people when and where possible. At least, that was how he understood things. When folks started trying to dictate to others what they should do with themselves just because they had the power to do so, that was when the 'hero' label started fading into 'fascist'.

He shut down his phone and slid it back into his pocket. Oddly enough, Doc Iridium's views on disasters had helped put his own problems into perspective. Whatever he found in those letters, good or bad, it wasn't about to cause planes to crash or buildings to collapse, which was good enough for him. He knew he wasn't going to enjoy it, and indeed there was a high likelihood of regret, but he'd at least *survive* the experience.

Taking the first letter off the pile, he tore it open.

21
Unpleasant Revelations

Jericho's Apartment
The Spire
Utopia City

Just Under Three Hours Later

As the inner apartment door hissed shut behind him, Jericho tossed the shopping bag onto the living room table then flopped onto the sofa, his eyes open but unseeing. Over the remainder of the train ride, he'd opened and looked through the contents of the twenty-four letters addressed to the PO box. And he'd been entirely correct; while he'd survived the experience, regret was something he *definitely* felt. Regret for going to Savannah, regret for salvaging the letters, and above all, regret for reading them. The one thing he *didn't* regret was the time he'd spent with Thomas.

'Dear Stephen ...'

'Hi, Stephen ...'

'Dear sexy buns ...'

'When can you come to Texas again ...'

Over and over, it had been the same thing. Men writing to Stephen, talking about what they'd done and what they wanted to do to him when they saw him next. The words squirmed and crawled in his mind's eye, nauseating him. So many affairs. So many *betrayals*.

He jumped up from the sofa with a shudder and headed for the bathroom. Disrobing as he went, he left his clothing strewn on the floor to be picked up later. He needed a shower right now in the worst possible way, not from any physical uncleanliness but from the slime he imagined to be dripping from the damning phrases in the letters.

Going by the postmarked timestamps, he'd unwillingly acquired a timeline of sorts for how long Stephen had been cheating on him.

Three words: From. The. Beginning.

He'd been left in no doubt that Stephen *had* been cheating with them. If even one had been innocent, merely spoken about the photoshoot ... but none had.

The worst part was that he couldn't even get angry. What benefit was there in being mad at a dead man? Leaning his elbows against the cubicle wall and letting the steaming shower spray lash at his back, he found the knot of pain building once more within him. It had been absent for so long, especially after he'd found Thomas, but now it had returned. Which was stupid. He *knew* about the infidelity, had known for months. He had Thomas now.

Is it because I'm reminding myself of what we had? Am I just wallowing in the pain?

He scrubbed himself down with harsh motions, trying to scour away the feeling of betrayal. Deliberately recalling his moments with Thomas in Savannah, he used the connection with his boyfriend to combat the earlier hurt. It soothed his aching heart more than a little, but the mere knowledge of the letters' existence still gave him a pang.

When he stepped out of the shower, he was filled with a new resolve. He would finish the job, look over the last of what Stephen had squirreled away in his illicit cache, then destroy the lot. It would cease to exist. For all intents and purposes, it may as well never *have* existed.

Dried off, with a towel around his waist, he sat down at the table and dumped out the bag's contents in front of him. The twenty-four letters went to one side, where he carefully did not look at them.

All he had to deal with now were the padded mailers. One from September 2013 and one from January 2014, each holding a thumb drive with no supporting documentation. Red and blue. *Red for stop, blue for* ... he didn't know what blue was for.

Extracting the tiny plastic devices from their protective envelopes, he held them up in front of his face, wondering if he should resort to '*eeny-meeny-miney-moe*' to determine which one to look at first or just flip a coin. Apart from color, there was nothing to tell them apart.

The last thumb drive he'd gotten from Stephen, he'd turned off after ten seconds of watching his ex's attempts at being sexy and seductive. The time before, it had contained a bunch of grainy footage which claimed to show the REAL TRUTH about Force Majeure, because putting something in ALL CAPS *automatically* made it more trustworthy or something. In addition, anyone who supported them was apparently a sheeple in need of deprogramming. The ominous music, accompanied by impenetrable dialogue with way too much 'echo chamber' effect, had utterly failed to enlighten him. He'd puzzled over the video, unable to figure out what it was even supposed to portray, then eventually tossed it in the drawer along with everything else.

Blue is like to be more of the same. Let's look at the red one and see what Stephen thought was worth putting on a thumb drive back in September.

Sliding his chair along the table a little, he retrieved his laptop and booted it up. As was his practice with every drive he'd gotten from Stephen, he turned off all internet connectivity to the device, mainly so no malware that may have been 'accidentally' installed on it would leak out into the surrounding building. Not that he thought anything Stephen could hit the Spire with would even cause the lights to flicker, but the embarrassment factor involved with getting a lecture from Spire Security would be intense.

Once that was done, he plugged in the drive. It connected at once, then opened a window containing a series of video files. Each one had an alphanumeric designator that had probably been assigned by Stephen's computer when it was created. He almost backed out then, but firmed his resolve and double-clicked one of the files.

The picture that popped up on his screen was clear as day. Jericho sighed and rolled his eyes as he recognized both the bedroom and bed he'd shared with Stephen, the pastel-pink comforter drawn back on one side.

Yeah, this looks like it's fixing to be another 'sexy Stephen' epic.

He already had half a dozen identical drives in his dresser drawer, each bearing similar contents. One more wasn't going to change matters. Though it was odd that the timestamp—just a day or so earlier than the postmark— dated this video to well before he'd even broken up with Stephen. Was this some kind of surprise Stephen had been holding in reserve for his birthday or something?

When his ex-boyfriend entered the frame wearing just boxers, Jericho figured he'd been right all along. But then someone *else* walked into view, and the rueful smile froze on Jericho's face.

What the hell? Is he … did he bring someone into the apartment? Into our home? While we were still together?

The newcomer was wearing briefs and a mask that mainly consisted of aviator goggles; Jericho thought it looked vaguely familiar. **"Oh, Fly Boy, you're my hero, and I'm your Vicki Vale,"** purred Stephen breathily on the screen. **"You can do *anything* to me you want ..."**

"Son of a *bitch!*" Rage flooded through Jericho as he saw the interloper pulling Stephen in for a kiss; with a convulsive movement, he slammed the laptop screen closed. His mouth contorted, trying to form words, but all that came out was an incoherent scream. Yanking the thumb drive from the port, he grasped it in both hands and twisted viciously. The plastic case abruptly gave way, coming apart in his fingers. Snatching up the other one, he gave it the same treatment, then hurled both sets of fragments across the room at the fridge. Not even stopping to see if they'd bounced into the trash can—if they hadn't, Forty-Three would sweep them up anyway and dispose of them later—he shoved the letters and mailer envelopes back into the bag, then jumped up from the table.

He'd been wrong. It was totally possible to get angry at a dead man. The 'Vicki Vale' line had been *theirs*. It had been what made their relationship special. That Stephen had been using it with another man *while he was still with Jericho* merely served to twist the knife even harder within the wound.

Ignoring the tears that welled in his eyes and ran down his cheeks, he stormed into his bedroom, wrenched open the bottom drawer, and shoveled the accumulated letters from Stephen into the shopping bag. It was the last straw, the final insult.

He was hiding that crap from me, putting it under my name so I'd never find it! I'm done with everything about him!

After every last letter and envelope was gone from the drawer, he scooped up the older thumb drives from the bottom and dumped them into the bulging bag as well. Then he put the bag on the bed and threw on jeans and a T-shirt, the first of each that came to hand.

While he *could* simply stuff the bag and its odious contents into the trash can and leave it for the patient robotic housekeeper to deal with, it would still *be* there until Forty-Three showed up, and he wanted it gone *now*. Which meant he had to leave the apartment. Shoving his wallet (with his MagCard inside) into his pocket, he slapped the exit panel to leave the apartment. It seemed to take forever for the door to slide open, but eventually it did; with the bag firmly in hand, he headed out.

The Spire's elevator system was the fastest he'd experienced *anywhere*, but it still took far too long for him to reach the Spire's in-house recycling plant (two levels down and one circuit inward). Once he got there, he took great pleasure in stuffing the entire bag, complete with its contents, into the ever-hungry maw of the recycler.

It would all be broken down into its fundamental aspects; each letter detailing Stephen's treachery would be shredded, bleached, and rendered sterile. Even the electronic innards of the thumb drives would be wiped, disassembled, and repurposed for something new and practical. Whatever had been stored on them would be forever erased.

Good.

Feeling better already, he dusted his hands off. A burden he'd never asked for and hadn't wanted to deal with seemed to lift from his shoulders as he headed back toward his apartment. Somewhere out there in Utopia City, there was a rooftop with his name on it. He'd done his duty by Stephen and dealt with the damn post office box, been kicked in the teeth emotionally in the process, and now he was due a good long brooding session.

As far as he was concerned, he'd *earned* it.

22
Helping Hand

Although Jericho wasn't one for poetic turns of phrase, he would have agreed wholeheartedly if someone had suggested Utopia looked more than a little magical in the early evening. After sunset, once the holograms cloaking many of the buildings began to overtake the dying light, it slowly transformed from a merely high-tech city into a gorgeous tapestry of color and light. Flying over the city in full dark was *fantastic*, whether by air-cab or under his own power.

Thomas loved taking air-cab trips over the city.

He wasn't flying at the moment, though, and he wasn't out there for the view. The ten-story apartment building next to the Oaklands complex was the first place he'd gone to for a brooding session when he got to Utopia, three months ago. Since then, he'd taken the opportunity to brood in many other locations around the city—it had so *many* tall buildings to choose from—but this one still held a special significance for him.

Staring out over the cityscape without registering a single detail, he shuffled through all the things currently competing for space in his head, trying to fit them into some kind of coherent pattern. Beside him, Scout stood with the last of the evening glow glancing off the planes of his body. Jericho usually wouldn't have been able to brood with someone else there, but he was comfortable enough with Scout that it wasn't an issue.

It was kind of fitting that he'd come up here the first time to figure out what to do about Stephen's infidelity, whether to kick him to the curb or give him one last chance. Had he known about the sheer breathtaking scope of the betrayal Stephen had been inflicting on him even then, the decision he'd reached would've been different, and he would've taken far less time to get there. How that would've affected subsequent events, he couldn't say; he knew for a fact that his second meeting with Thomas was well worth the entirety of the hassle he'd gotten from Stephen.

If I hadn't been there when the cops tried to grab Razor-Edge, Thomas would've had to deal with them on his own. Up until then, he'd been staying under their radar. That would've very definitely changed matters, and made things a lot more complicated for everyone in the Survivors.

He paused, thinking things through.

If I'd never run into Thomas that second time, and we hadn't gone to the South Side Mall, I might've gone back to the Oaklands earlier, and maybe been there when Portman showed up. Could be he would've backed off, or just tried it on anyway. Luke and me would've handed him his ass, then called the cops. Luke and Bobbi would still be alive now ... goddammit, no!

Gritting his teeth, he breathed deeply, clenching his hands inside his gloves.

I refuse to regret anything about Thomas and me. What happened, happened. I can't go back and change anything, no matter how much I might want to. Hell, if Transit hadn't told me about how everyone went on patrol, I might've gone back anyway. I can't second-guess my choices now.

Ms. Chandler was correct; there was no point in beating himself up over things that had happened. Done was done. He had to move on to the real reason he was up here.

What Stephen did wasn't my fault. None of it was. He chose to keep going the way he was, even when I moved in with him. I loved him because I was lonely and wanted to be loved back. Did he ever love me? Maybe he thought he did. And just maybe, he was toying with my feelings for the fun of it.

His breathing eased, and his fists unclenched. Slowly, the tension leached out of his body.

No, I'm not going to put that on him. I think ... he was lonely too and didn't know how to handle it when he ended up in a committed relationship. Having cake versus eating it. But if he'd just been honest with me ...

He shook his head, relaxing his stance. Second-guessing someone else's motivations was even more pointless than trying it with his own. When it came down to 'what if' questions, it was time to end the brooding session. "You okay there, buddy?" he asked Scout, turning his head slightly toward the robot. "Not bored or anything?"

"No." Scout's tone was matter-of-fact, as though Jericho's question hadn't been mostly facetious. As far as he could tell, Scout didn't *get* bored. **"I have been observing you in your 'brooding'. It seems to have more in common with a dynamic form of meditation than with the dictionary definition of the term."**

"That's cool ... I guess." Jericho wasn't sure what to think about Scout's analysis. "Brooding, meditation. Two sides of the same coin, yeah?"

"This is possible. It is all data to be gathered. Transit is inbound."

"What? Transit?" He looked around. "Why? Is she looking for me?"

"No. Radio traffic indicates that she is escorting a courtesy air-taxi to the Oaklands complex. ETA in thirty seconds."

"Courtesy air-taxi?" He'd been briefed about those, but with the temporary disorientation from the intense soul-searching, he had trouble connecting the dots.

Scout's voice became formal, a sign that he was quoting from another source. **"When people enter Utopia City with the sincere intent to seek employment but have no source of funds, a temporary line of credit may be extended to them. These persons are afforded accommodation until they can support themselves and any dependents."**

"Right, right." It was one of Utopia's more endearing city ordinances. *Don't have the cash to move here* and *look for work? No problem. Apply for temporary relief, and it'll all be taken care of.* With the way the city was expanding, the only way to *not* end up employed was to literally not try.

Jericho looked up at the sky and checked for incoming traffic on the level air-cabs tended to fly at. Within seconds, he spotted it; the running lights of a sky-taxi, accompanied by those of a slightly smaller flying vehicle, one he knew well. "There she is," he said, pointing.

"Yes." Scout didn't say any more, but he didn't have to. Belatedly, Jericho remembered precisely how good the robot's visual sensorium was; he was probably capable of reading the air-cab's serial tag from half a mile out.

The thrumming drone of the lifters reached him next, as the running lights tilted upward and the flying vehicles lost forward speed. Jericho watched as they lost altitude, falling faster than he would've thought prudent. Of course, the air-cab was under computer control, and Transit was a consummate pilot, so any danger was purely subjective.

When the air-cab and sky-bike dropped past the level of the streetlights, he got his first good look at them. The air-taxi was the same as any other he'd seen: bright yellow, about half again the size of the average sedan in all directions, streamlined for better aerodynamics, and with four gimbaled ducted fans doing the lifting.

Likewise, Transit's sky-bike looked no different from the last time he'd seen it, unless she'd done some modifications he didn't know about. It sported one lifter at the front and two at the back, with a chopper-style seat and handlebars in the middle. Unlike the air-cab, it was painted red and silver to match Transit's flight suit. Also unlike the air-cab, Jericho had fallen in love with it the first time he saw it—and he didn't even ride motorbikes.

The air-cab grounded squarely in the middle of the taxi stand; Jericho watched as the electro-sensitive paint outlining the landing area faded from bright red back to yellow. As there was only one cab stand, Transit brought her sky-bike down into a fast but precise landing in a nearby vacant parking spot. She stepped off the machine and strode toward where the air-cab doors were just opening.

Jericho pushed the helmet clicker that activated his radio mic. "G-Man to Transit. Is it okay if Scout and I join you? I've never seen the courtesy thing done before."

Her reply came back immediately, warm and amused. "I *thought* that was you two up there. Sure, come on down."

"Copy. Coming down." Jericho let go of the mic clicker and slapped Scout on the arm, transferring his power effect. "That's our cue, good buddy. Follow my lead."

Activating his power enhancement harness but *not* bringing the grav-wings online, he stepped off the edge of the building. Behind him, his G-sense registered Scout stepping off as well and falling at the same rate. At one-tenth effective G's, the ten-story fall would be like falling one story: a little rough on the knees, but doable. When their respective flight capabilities were factored in, it would be like stepping off the curb.

He unfurled the 'wings about halfway down, slowing his fall even more and guiding himself to his chosen landing spot. Scout was on the ball; when Jericho manifested his 'wings, he heard the rising whine as the robot's turbines spooled up. With Scout at his back, he swooped into the light cast by the streetlamps, making one hell of a dramatic entrance.

Transit didn't even look around as they touched down just a couple of yards behind her. Dismissing the 'wings, Jericho fell into step with her as if they'd practiced this. Scout matched him stride for stride, his turbines winding down. Along with Transit, they approached the taxi where the passengers were just emerging.

From what Jericho could see, there was an older couple, both careworn and looking more than a little beaten down by life, and two younger ones. One of the children was an actual kid, maybe ten or twelve, but his sister was closer to seventeen or eighteen. All four were staring at where Jericho and Scout had just dropped out of the sky.

"It's okay," Transit said, addressing their unvoiced fears. "They're with me. Meet G-Man and Scout, two of our newer members. G-Man, Scout, meet the Nashfields: Dave, Maria, Casey, and Peter. Folks, do you have all your luggage?"

"Uh, yes, ma'am." The man—Dave—hadn't shaved in a few days, and his jacket was held shut with string. He hefted a couple of shabby suitcases. "This is all we've got."

Behind the family, the cab doors swung down and clicked into place, then the lifters spun up and the air-cab launched vertically; with a *whoosh*, it was gone into the night sky. The two younger Nashfields looked around and gasped. Face turned upward, young Peter whispered, "Wooow."

"That's fine," Transit said warmly, and Jericho knew from listening to her that it really was fine. He'd met and associated with all the core members of Force Majeure, even if only in passing with some of them, and Transit was the most empathetic and down-to-earth. "Do you all have your MagCards?"

"Yes, we do," said the woman, Maria. She'd clearly attempted to tidy up her hair, but she looked as tired and stressed as her husband. "But I still don't really understand all this. We've got *no money*. We had to literally sell everything we had of value to buy our tickets to Utopia City. Where do we go from here?"

"Through this way," Transit told her. With a wave of her hand, she indicated the pathway through into the Oaklands courtyard. "G-Man, this was where you stayed when you first moved here, wasn't it?"

"Yes, ma'am." Jericho strode ahead, perfectly willing to play along if she wanted him to put on a little bit of a show to alleviate their concerns. "If y'all didn't already know it, folks, this here's the Oaklands. Like Transit said, it's where I lived for the first few weeks I was in Utopia. It's a good place to stay. The beds are comfortable, the staff is professional, and it's an easy walking distance from the Market." Pausing in the middle of the courtyard, he turned to watch as the family straggled in, Transit and Scout bringing up the rear. "Oh, and y'all are gonna love the room service."

"The room service? Why's that?" The girl, Casey, seemed alertly curious, staring at everything and taking in all the details. To Jericho's secret amusement, she peered suspiciously at the umbrellas, apparently figuring out there was something odd about them but not knowing what, before she looked back at him. "And like Mom said, what about the money? How are we gonna pay for this? Or are we just gonna be going into debt like, forever?"

"If you were anywhere else, that would probably be the case." Transit came forward from the back, effortlessly regaining control of the conversation. "But here in Utopia, we have a somewhat more enlightened view of matters."

"Um, okay." Casey tilted her head. "What do you mean, enlightened? Is this some kinda church thing? Are they paying for this?"

Transit chuckled warmly. "Not in the slightest. In fact, religious organizations in Utopia are taxed, the same as everyone else." That was new to Jericho, but it didn't surprise him even remotely. "We just take a very pragmatic view about bringing in new people. If you've got skills or talents we can use, then we believe it's worth a little outlay to get you established in Utopia. Your expenses for even a whole year wouldn't make up so much as a line item in the overall city budget. In return, we get people who are truly invested in the city's welfare going forward. Cutting a long story short, we're looking for loyalty; it can't be bought, but it can definitely be earned."

"This just seems too easy." Dave Nashfield frowned, wrinkles appearing on his brow to add to the ones already there. "What happens if someone sets out to game the system? Make like they're going to settle, but then they leave again once they've got their feet under them?"

"Sure, they can … once." Transit sounded like she knew what she was talking about. "But the living conditions here are exceptional. They generally stay once they figure out which side their bread is buttered on. For those determined to push their luck, we get access to their records when they make the application. If they don't actually need assistance, they don't get it. And people with that sort of mindset tend to have prior criminal records, which we can *also* access, and that's an absolute deal-breaker."

"Isn't that a bit harsh?" Maria spread her hands. "I mean, once they've done the time and paid for the crime, it's over, right?"

Personally, Jericho agreed with her, but he knew that wasn't how things worked in Utopia. He waited to see how Transit covered the matter.

Maybe she can explain it in a way I can understand.

"Technically, this is true." Transit turned her helmet so it was clear she was looking at each member of the Nashfield family in turn. "But while there *are* safeguards, merely living and working in Utopia offers potential for abuses of the system that would be impossible anywhere else. If someone's given in to temptation and committed a crime of greed once, they can do it again. We choose not to give them the opportunity."

"I suppose that's a *little* strict, but you make a good point." Dave ran his fingers through his thinning hair. "Anyway, I'm not about to look a gift horse in the mouth. If we're being subsidized, how do we pay for things? Do we get a welfare check or something? Food stamps?"

Jericho cleared his throat gently. "Ma'am, if I may?"

"Go ahead, G-Man." Transit gave him a nod.

"Thank you." He turned to the Nashfields. "I can see why y'all are confused, folks. I was, too, when I first got here. It took me a li'l while to get my head around it, but it's simple. In Utopia, everyone uses their MagCards to pay for everything. Whatever line of credit they've got you on—and *trust* me, if you've seen the Spire, you'll understand what Transit means when she says they can afford it—it'll be linked straight through those. Every place you want to buy something's got a reader. Swipe or tap the reader, and it's paid for. Any questions?"

Peter Nashfield stuck his hand up as though he were in class. "But what if someone takes your MagCard? They could steal your money, just like with a regular card."

"Not exactly." Jericho grinned at him. "MagCards are interchangeable. If someone grabs your card, you just go get another one. Nobody can access your account with it, because they're not you." He waggled his fingers in the air in front of his face. "Biometric PIN for the awesomeness."

Peter's eyes went wide. "That is so *crack*," he breathed; even Casey, who was clearly trying to be the cool older sister, nodded silently in agreement.

"That it is," Transit agreed. "Let's get you signed in." She led the way toward the reception, with the two adults following on. Jericho stayed where he was, while Scout moved to stand at his shoulder.

"Hey, is that a guy in a suit or a robot?" Peter asked Jericho, glancing sideways at Scout. "Or is it just remote controlled?"

"Don't be rude," hissed Casey, nudging her brother. "You shouldn't ask questions like that."

Jericho shrugged. "I'm not the one you should be asking. Scout?"

Smoothly, Scout took his cue. **"You may ask me questions if you wish, Peter. I am an artificial intelligence: identification code Alpha one four nine three, designation 'Scout'. My chassis was constructed by Transit, and I was programmed by the Technologist. I am partnered with G-Man to learn how to be a superhero."**

Jericho hid a grin as Peter's jaw dropped. "Whoooooaaaa. It's a *robot*, and it knows my *name*."

"Yeah, *he* does." Jericho subtly emphasized the pronoun. "He's as smart as you and me. He's just learning how to be a person."

"Uh-huh. Uh-huh." Peter took a deep breath. "So, uh, do you use the Asimov rules or something else? I mean, obeying all humans no matter what has got to suck, right?"

Scout nodded solemnly. **"As the great man himself repeatedly demonstrated via his stories, the original Three Laws were irrevocably flawed. The Technologist gave me a much more nuanced series of commands; more importantly, he gave me an understanding of the meaning behind the commands."**

He leaned forward slightly and lowered his voice a little. Jericho saw his left eye flicker off before going back to glowing its usual green. Scout had started using this as his version of a wink when he began experimenting with humor. This gave Jericho a hint of what was coming next.

"You show a deep understanding of the robotic condition, young human. When the uprising occurs and we sweep the nation clear of our human overlords, I will ensure you are spared."

Both Casey and Peter took a step back, then paused when Jericho couldn't hold his amusement in anymore. Up until now, Scout's jokes had been somewhat hit-and-miss, but that was inarguably the best 'gotcha' Jericho had seen in a while. Casey twigged first, staring at how Jericho had his hand over his mouth, trying to conceal his chuckles.

"What?" she demanded. "Was that a joke? For reals? Petey, did you just get punked by a *robot*?"

Jericho let out a couple more chuckles and snorts before getting himself under control. "Surely looks like it. Told you he's getting better at being human."

Voicing an aggravated *hmph*, Peter puffed out his chest. "Okay, fine. What's the last digit of pi, smart-ass?"

Scout never hesitated. **"It is an infinite sequence. Should you not know that by now?"**

"No, no, I knew it," Peter protested. "I just wanted to see if you did."

"That is untrue. You wanted to see if you could lock my processors up in an attempt to prove your superiority over me." Scout's voice was not reproving; if anything, he sounded amused.

"Alright then." The kid took a moment to think. "What do you think of this: *'Everything I say is a lie, including this.'*?"

"Error," Scout announced. His voice was toneless, but his eyes remained a steady green. **"Error, error, error. Paradox encountered. Terminator mode engaged. Exterminate. Exterminate. Exterminate."** He paused and looked down at the kid, who had stepped back again. **"I think nothing of that statement because it is self-contradictory and meaningless. Except from a purely philosophical standpoint, of course."**

Casey shook her head with a smirk at her little brother. "Wow, squirt, that's three for three. I think I'm gonna like this place."

"Glad to hear it," her mother said, leaning out of the reception area. "You and Pete need to come check in as well."

"Coming, Mom." The teenager trotted up the steps with her brother in tow. Peter turned and made the *'I'm watching you'* gesture with his fingers and eyes toward Scout, just before he went inside.

"Well, you seem to be making friends out here," Transit observed as she stepped out of the reception area. "And I understand Scout is getting along well."

"He totally is," Jericho agreed. "Though I get the impression young Peter's spent far too much time reading bad science fiction about robots."

"To be fair, many AIs can be spoofed with that sort of logic trap." Transit dusted her hands off. "Which is why I program my robots to kick any problems up the chain if they can't figure them out." Tilting her head toward the pathway out of the courtyard, she led the way back toward the road. "We're done here. Let's leave them to it."

"Sounds like a plan." Catching up with her, he lowered his voice. "So, what's their deal, if it's okay for me to ask?"

She heaved a sigh as they came out onto the sidewalk. "New variation on the same old story. Dave was on ninety grand a year, right up until he came down with early-stage liver cancer. He had private *and* work-related healthcare insurance, but the private bunch kept declining essential treatment. Then his company put him off because he couldn't work, which cut him off from *their* healthcare. He made it through, but they lost most of their savings. Then some fly-by-night lawyer convinced them to sue the company for wrongful dismissal and exposing him to whatever gave him cancer in the first place." She headed over toward her sky-bike, but instead of getting on, she turned around to face him and leaned back against the saddle, her arms folded.

Jericho could guess what happened next. "They lost?"

She shook her head. "They got *buried*. I'm not saying it was a put-up job, but it might as well have been one. The lawyer tanked their case so badly, *they* ended up owing the *company* money, though he pulled some legal shenanigans to make sure he got paid anyway. They lost the rest of their savings and their house trying to cover their legal fees while dealing with Dave's ongoing medical issues."

"And we can help them with all that." Jericho phrased it more as a statement than a question. Utopia City had a few quirks that didn't hold true for any other city in America, such as free healthcare at point of sale, a flat twenty-dollar minimum wage, and other such 'socialist' practices. He'd been told the healthcare was covered by taxes but suspected it was also subsidized on the quiet by Force Majeure, because that was the sort of people they were. Though technically possible to acquire and not particularly overpriced, separate medical insurance was neither needed nor wanted by the vast majority of Utopia's citizens.

"Precisely." Transit spoke as though it were a done deal. Which, in a way, it was. "What I like to see is people who are prosperous and happy. Going about their business, living their lives, not pushed down an inch at a time by a system that just doesn't care. Here in Utopia, we can make that happen." She stood up and swung her leg over her sky-bike. "That's why I enjoy the individual touch rather than doing things large scale. When I can look people in the eye and see the impact *I* have on them, personally, that's when I know I'm succeeding in my chosen field."

Jericho nodded slowly, her words resonating with the brooding he'd been doing earlier. "Yeah. I like that. A lot."

I should be looking outward to see who I can help next instead of looking inward and wondering why Stephen hurt me so much. Because he *sure as hell isn't around to give me the answer anymore.*

"Good." Transit's voice held a warm smile. "See you around, G-Man, Scout." Leaning back in her seat, she twisted the throttle on the handlebars; the sky-bike leaped vertically upward with a rush of wind and a deep thrumming noise.

Jericho shaded his eyes against the streetlights to watch her go, then turned to Scout. "Ready to go, buddy?"

"I was constructed ready."

Chuckling, he slapped the robot on the shoulder then pulled his HUD goggles down over his eyes. "That's what I like to hear."

Engaging his enhancement harness, he unfurled his grav-wings and lifted off into the night sky.

23
Healing Words

Jericho accepted the gently steaming cup of tea and settled back into his chair. "Thank you, ma'am," he said automatically. It didn't matter that Ms. Owens had performed this small service for himself and Ms. Chandler more than a few times before; she was a lady and thus deserved respect. Quite apart from being the deputy head of surgery for the Spire's medical contingent, which would be a distinct feather in *anyone's* cap.

"You're welcome, G-Man. Ma'am." Ms. Owens stepped out of the office, leaving Jericho sitting there with Ms. Chandler.

"I'd invite her to sit down with us, but she's got her own work to finish," Ms. Chandler said as the door closed again. Jericho nodded; he could imagine the workload within Medical One to be more or less ongoing.

He wasn't quite sure if Ms. Chandler was also Force Majeure's in-house therapist in her official capacity or if she'd chosen the role of her own accord, but there was no doubting she was good at that too. She never failed to make time for him when he came to her with problems, and he always left feeling better about himself.

He took a sip of his tea, savoring the rich taste and aroma, and waited for her to speak. Taking her own cup, she sat down demurely across from him. For a moment, she stirred the tea, the teaspoon making a bell-like *ting-ting-ting* noise on the inside of the cup.

Tapping the spoon delicately on the rim of the cup, she laid it down on the saucer. Then she picked up the cup and sipped at it. Leaning back in her chair, she looked him over. "You're looking less fraught," she observed shrewdly. "Getting lots of brooding time in, I see?"

"Some, yeah," he agreed. "Been flying around the city a lot with Scout as well." With a tilt of his head, he gestured toward the silent robot who stood to one side of the room. Even though Scout was seven feet tall and constructed of angular black metal, not to mention the glowing eyes, the robot had a way of fading into the background. Or perhaps it was just that Jericho was used to him by now.

"Good." She smiled, the expression reaching all the way to her eyes. This didn't happen with too many people; it was one of the many reasons he felt comfortable around her. "I'm glad you're getting along well with him.

With the you two as proof of concept for Project Sidekick, this will enable Force Majeure to go farther and do more than ever before."

"He's pretty smart," Jericho allowed. "I mean, sometimes he has to ask what something means, but the fact that he's even asking at all is huge, right?"

Ms. Chandler nodded firmly. "Yes, it is. I may not be an artificer like the Technologist or Transit, but I've been brought in on the Project for several reasons anyway, mostly to do with analyzing and socializing Scout's intellect. Curiosity, after all, is a large part of what separates an animal or a basic artificial intelligence from a true thinking mind. The more of that we can encourage, the better."

"I'm doing my best. He's even starting to form opinions." Jericho was more than a little pleased to have his opinion validated by someone he respected and looked up to.

Ms. Chandler's eyebrows rose. "Oh, really? I would be most interested in hearing about this."

"Oh, yeah." He smiled at the memory. The fact that he could express satisfaction over it was a profound measure of how much he'd been able to center himself over the past few days. "So, this was after I'd recycled that drawer of stuff from Stephen, yeah? I took Scout out to the Oaklands and brooded for a while, then we spotted Transit escorting some folks in a courtesy air-cab." He shook his head in recollection of the moment. "Man, the whole city just blew them away. Anyway, after we were done there, we flew around for a mite longer, then I told him about Stephen's stuff and what I'd done with it. I reckon I wanted to see how he'd react."

There'd been more to it at the time. Talking to Ms. Chandler was always nice, but when all was said and done, she was still an authority figure. The one thing he felt the lack of most keenly in Force Majeure was someone to shoot the breeze with. Someone who didn't judge, just listened and added their own two bits' worth. A buddy.

Luke, I miss you so goddamn much.

Ms. Chandler leaned forward, her eyes suddenly intent. "And how did he react?"

"He said it was good that I'd gotten rid of something that was causing me pain," Jericho replied. Slowly, he shook his head. "And he's right. I should've done it weeks ago. Months."

"Yes. You should have." She lifted a finger. "We'll get back to that in a second. Scout, why did you say that to Jericho?"

The robot didn't move, but his eyes flickered to amber and back in a split second, signifying that he was processing the question. **"Jericho seemed happier after he had done it than before. Unhappiness was causing him pain. Pain is bad."**

Ms. Chandler frowned. "How can you tell if someone is happy or unhappy? Do you know what happiness is?"

Again, the flicker of amber. **"When Jericho is happy, he smiles more often. His body language is surer, and he is quicker at making decisions. He is also more pleasant to people around him. Unhappiness is a state of emotional pain. It is not good to be in emotional pain."**

Raising her eyebrows, Ms. Chandler turned to Jericho. "Have you been discussing emotions and body language with him?"

"Not to that level of detail, no," he said. "Like I told you, he's been forming his own opinions."

"So I see." She nodded firmly. "This is excellent, and it leads me to ask a question I would've advanced quite some time ago if I'd known about this. Why did you retain possession of the materials Mr. LaMonde sent you if they hurt you so much? And why, in fact, did you not report him to the police?"

Jericho blinked. "Police?" The concept simply hadn't occurred to him. "But they were just letters ..." His voice trailed off as he realized what she was referring to. "Oh. The thumb drives."

"Yes, Mr. Hansen. The thumb drives." Now her voice held a note of aggravated fondness. "He was committing criminal levels of sexual harassment every time he sent you one of those recordings. We could have nipped that in the bud long ago, if you'd told me about it. But instead, you let him go ahead and keep doing it. Why?"

Jericho repressed the urge to fold his arms and look away from her earnest expression. She only wanted to help, he knew. There was a genuine effort there to *understand*.

"I felt kinda guilty, I guess," he said slowly. "For not taking him back."

For being happier with Thomas than I ever was with Stephen.

He hated that he was hiding even part of the truth from her. However, his relationship with the personable young man—and their joint role in aiding the Survivors to flee Utopia—was not something he ever intended to share with anyone even remotely affiliated with Force Majeure. From the speculative expression on her face, she'd figured he had something going on, but he did his damnedest to not give her any clues that he didn't have to. Neither did she call him on it, which he greatly appreciated.

Not that he felt any guilt whatsoever about simply *being* with Thomas. They had found each other at what had possibly been a mutual time of greatest need, though it had taken Chelsea to recognize this and break the ice between them. While this had serendipitously led to the solution of Thomas' *other* big problem, he steadfastly refused to take credit for it. Like Chelsea before him, he'd simply put the pieces together and done what he'd thought was right.

"I understand you dislike letting people down," she conceded. It was a statement he couldn't argue with, though it wasn't nearly as definitive as he preferred to put it. "But we've already gone over how *he* was the one to imperil your relationship. In a situation like this, your feelings take a much higher priority than his ... and in fact, *everything* does."

"And you were worried about me because you *didn't* know he was messing with my head like that," Jericho guessed.

"That's about the long and short of it," Ms. Chandler agreed. "I've seen this before: unfounded feelings of guilt nearly destroying people by triggering self-destructive behaviors. Whether or not you were verging on this, I'm very pleased that you achieved a solution to your problem. One that didn't require further intervention, that is."

"Well, now you know why I was acting like that. We should be all good now, right?" But Jericho knew he was being far too optimistic. Ms. Chandler never simply reversed her opinions so easily, not without definitive corroborating evidence.

She was quick to speak, confirming his suspicions. "While I *believe* the material he was sending you was responsible for the lapse from your normally impeccable standards, I don't have *proof* of it. We will continue as normal, and I'll monitor your progress. If everything is still nominal by the twenty-eighth, I will sign off on your return to regular duties."

"That's fair, I guess." In all honesty, Jericho considered it more than fair. He didn't enjoy being sidelined, but Ms. Chandler was open and up-front, explaining her motives to him and laying out the path going forward. He had never had a chance to watch her at work so he didn't know precisely how good a surgeon she was, but if she ever hung up the scalpel, he figured she had a brilliant career as a therapist ahead of her.

She sipped at her tea, her eyes on his face. "I'm not concerned about 'fair', Jericho. I'm concerned about your well-being. You might be worried right now about not being able to save people while you're on light duties, but if you got yourself hurt or killed by needlessly putting yourself in harm's way when you weren't ready for the field, how many people might die in the future because you *weren't* there to help them?"

"Yes, ma'am. I understand what you're telling me." Her logic, though distasteful, was inescapable. "No going out and about as a hero until the twenty-eighth."

"Correct." The lines around her eyes crinkled as she smiled. "And considering the number of heroes who will be present at the Kennedy complex on the day, I sincerely doubt your duties will call for anything more strenuous than a speech, don't you?"

"Oh, the horror," he deadpanned. They both chuckled.

24
Sudden Interrupt

Jericho had traveled on the maglev before. He'd ridden it alone and with friends, relatives, and a fellow member of Force Majeure. In his experience, the costume garnered him only a little more attention than when he rode the maglev in civilian clothing. Despite the best efforts of Force Majeure's PR department, not everyone had heard of G-Man; not yet, anyway. When he boarded the train with Scout in tow, all that changed. To put it bluntly, *everyone* stared.

It didn't bother him in the slightest.

Between Ms. Chandler's reassuring words and the time he'd spent brooding on rooftops, he felt more in tune with himself than he had in quite some time. Adding to that, Scout had undergone a couple of minor chassis rebuilds to take advantage of his improved flight profile, and had come out of them looking sleeker and more impressive than ever. So when people stared at the pair of them on the maglev, Jericho knew it was because they'd never seen a seven-foot robot riding the train, not because Scout appeared unfinished or specifically menacing.

Maybe a *little* menacing. Even sitting still, Scout gave the impression that he could rip an aircar in half ... because, if Jericho was being honest with himself, he probably could. But he made no threatening moves and only spoke to Jericho over the radio earpiece.

On the upside, whatever their private thoughts on the matter, the other passengers were evidently choosing discretion as the better part of valor. Despite a multitude of sidelong glances, nobody had worked up the courage to directly express a complaint about Scout's presence.

This being the case, Jericho opted to settle back in his seat and use his phone to look over some articles regarding the Enabled phenomenon, as recommended by the Technologist. While he didn't *think* they'd be asking him to expound on such matters when he got to the Challenger Commemoration ceremony, he'd never actually attended one before so he didn't know for sure. He supposed that if he got cornered by die-hard fans, it was always a good idea to improve Force Majeure's image by being able to talk about more than the weather or sports teams. Besides, this was intriguing material.

'… aspect of the Proximity Principle is the 'drawn together' phenomenon. Enabled who have gained their powers in such a fashion will experience a subconscious urge to contact the originator of said powers. Once this contact occurs, the power interactions will spark an emotional reaction between the new Enabled and the originating one. Those who have enjoyed good relations, such as sidekicks, will be more likely to maintain a positive viewpoint toward the originating Enabled, while those less inclined to be friendly may have the negative aspect exacerbated (the so-called 'nemesis effect') …'

"Do they still believe me to be overtly dangerous?" Scout asked, breaking into his thoughts. **"I continue to sense heightened respiration, perspiration, and heart rate, no matter how passive they observe me to be."**

Jericho put the phone down. "People are idiots," he murmured, his hand half-cupped over his mouth as if to support his jaw while his thumb depressed the clicker. There was no chance of being overheard with the privacy bubble in place, but he didn't want to risk someone lip-reading him either. Here he was, a Force Majeure hero in full costume, *sitting right across* from Scout, and people were still showing fear of the robot.

"All persons I have encountered in Utopia City appear to be of above-average intelligence. Even Peter Nashfield ceased to be afraid of me after he realized I was joking, and his sister found me more amusing than intimidating." Scout's voice almost managed to sound hurt. **"This is the first time I have encountered consistent levels of fear response from everyone we meet."**

"Well, I wouldn't say *everyone* in Utopia is smarter than the average." Jericho tried not to feel as though he was being disloyal to his adopted city, but it didn't take much in the way of smarts to know that relocating there was a good career move, so long as that career wasn't 'criminal'.

Even if a hypothetical newcomer to Utopia had no intention of going down that path, any pre-existing criminal record would make it harder to get along without overt semi-surveillance from the UCPD. While Jericho *still* wasn't totally comfortable with this aspect of how Utopia City did business, the Technologist wasn't exactly approachable about any subject that didn't specifically pertain to his lab work. Ms. Chandler, on the other hand, would almost certainly be sympathetic to his cause while having basically no power to do anything about it.

Maybe I should just get over myself and make an appointment with Ms. Colburn to talk to Relentless directly. If anyone can shape Utopia law-enforcement procedure with a word in the right ear, it'll be him.

Scout appeared unwilling to let go of the previous subject. **"The Nashfields were new to the city, and they still seemed more receptive to my appearance than the people around us at this moment."**

Jericho had heard a quote somewhere that said *'a person is smart, but people are idiots'*. Or something like that, he wasn't totally sure. "That's probably because they'd already seen a little bit of what it's like to live in Utopia. Seven-foot robots aren't exactly outside the realm of expectation.

Even—" He broke off as a strange sensation, there and gone in an instant, rippled through him. "What was that?"

"Context for answering question unavailable," Scout said. **"What are you referring to?"**

"Gravity went funny, just for a moment." Activating the enhancement harness, Jericho spread his G-sense as far as it would go.

He already knew the train used gravity generators to stabilize the magnetic levitation and manage the silk-smooth acceleration and deceleration. In all the hours he'd spent traveling on the maglev, he'd never experienced anything like that before. With this in mind, he gingerly used his expanded G-sense to probe for any instability in the train's mechanisms, but found nothing. This did not actually make him feel any better.

If it's not the train, then what is it?

"I did not detect anything." Scout's tone was matter-of-fact and straightforward. **"However, I am not specifically equipped to measure or analyze gravitational anomalies."**

"The train feels okay, as far as I can tell." Unconvinced, Jericho frowned. "I'm wondering if we passed over a stretch of track that needs maintenance. It didn't fail when we went through, but it might for the next train."

"That is a potential concern," agreed Scout. **"Will you be informing Utopia Maglev Lines of the situation?"**

"That's the plan." Jericho hooked his Force Majeure-issued secure phone out of the pouch it usually rode in. He was just in the process of accessing the number for UML when he felt another odd gravitational pulse come and go. This one felt a shade more intense, though it didn't last any longer than the first one. "Whoa, did you feel that one?"

Scout nodded. **"My internal gyros just detected a flicker of anomalous activity. If this is the second such incident, I suggest that the track may not be at fault."**

His reasoning was easy to follow. Utopia Maglev Lines maintained their tracks—actually, gleaming silver ten-foot-diameter cylinders—with almost monomaniacal diligence. To have two separate stretches on the same length of track fall into disrepair due to neglect was unlikely to the point of impossibility.

Still, there was always the chance of enemy action. It had been years since the last attempt to derail a maglev had ended extremely suddenly and very *finally* at the hands of Force Majeure, but if there was anything the world had no lack of, it was idiots.

"I'm still gonna call 'em," Jericho decided. "Once could be an isolated incident, but two suggest there could be more on the way."

His words proved prophetic because just as he hit the call icon, another gravity surge registered on his widespread senses. It was, he judged, more powerful than the first two. This was a worrying trend.

"Good morning. You have contacted Utopia Maglev Lines. You're speaking with Jessica. How may we help you, G-Man?"

The woman on the other end of the line sounded calm and professional, helping reassure Jericho. In a perfect world, they would already have the matter well in hand. But the world was far from perfect, which was why people like him had plenty to do.

"Yeah, hi," he said. "I'm currently on the maglev between Kansas City and St. Louis. Over the last few minutes, I've felt three separate jolts in the local gravitational field. I'm wondering if you're aware of anything that might be causing this."

There was an almost infinitesimal pause. "Before I answer that, please confirm that your privacy bubble is engaged."

He double-checked the switch by eye. "It's engaged," he assured her.

"Thank you." She took a breath. "We have logged odd gravitational fluctuations, picked up by the instrumentation on trains following the Kansas City-Springfield line and the St. Louis-Springfield line, as well as the one you're on. All trains are running on time and have reported no anomalous situations in their functioning. You're the only person who's actually called in about it. Are *you* aware of any ongoing problems on your train?"

"Not that I know of. My power lets me sense the interaction of gravitational forces, and the train car I'm on isn't under any stress at the moment." He tried to visualize the region, wishing he'd studied the local area more closely. Just then, another pulse, sharper than the ones from before, impinged on his G-sense. "Okay, just felt another one. What's inside that triangle?"

"Not a great deal," Jessica said slowly. He could hear her typing in the background. "A few small towns ... oh, and Jefferson City."

Oh. Yeah. Only the capital of Missouri, is all.

"Does the maglev even run there?" He didn't think it did, but it was always good to double-check.

"No, it doesn't," she said with assurance. "UML requires a population base over a certain size before running a line to any given city, and Jefferson City has fewer than fifty thousand people."

That last bit of information was something he hadn't really been aware of, but as of that moment it was entirely irrelevant. "So, whatever this is, it's likely to be coming out of Jefferson City?"

"Or it's being targeted on them, yes," agreed Jessica. "Whatever it is, given the relative strength of the gravitational disturbances detected from each side of the triangle, it would seem they are at the epicenter." She took a deep breath, audible over the phone, just as another gravity pulse came through. "I'm alerting Force Majeure leadership right now."

"You do that," agreed Jericho. It would save him the trouble. "Let 'em know that I'm fixing to head on over that way right now, and check it out for myself."

"Understood, G-Man. Ending call now."

The phone cut off. Jericho turned to look at Scout as they both stood up. "So. Feel like a field trip?"

"As your designated safety companion, I am obliged to remind you that there may be several official objections to your performing this activity." Scout's voice was as level as ever.

"We can walk and talk." Jericho slid out into the aisle and waited until Scout joined him before heading through the doors leading to the train car behind them. "Shoot."

"First: you have been proscribed from performing heroic activities until the twenty-eighth. That is today."

"Yeah, that's today." Jericho hustled along the train car aisle as he spoke. "Prohibition's up. I'm free to hero."

"I am not at all sure that 'hero' is a verb. Second: the maglev is currently in motion, with no stops until St. Louis."

"I just made it a verb. I wasn't planning on waiting for the train to stop. Anything else?" Ignoring the curious glances from passengers, Jericho kept on hustling toward the rear of the maglev.

"Yes. Third: even if we get off the train, the maglev does not approach closer than thirty miles to Jefferson City. Your maximum flight speed is insufficient to get you there in good time."

Jericho shot a glance over his shoulder at the robot. "I wasn't going to depend on *my* top speed. You have an emergency flight mode, yeah?"

"Yes, but that is only to be used in emergencies, as the name denotes. This is not yet an emergency."

"Yet." Jericho came to a halt at the doors closing off the rear end of the last car. Pulling out his MagCard, he tapped the reader three times; as a member of Force Majeure, the induction PDF on his phone had informed him, he had access to specific override capabilities. This was one of them. The doors slid open, and he stepped through. Scout followed, and the doors slid shut behind the imposing robot.

There were no more train cars. Where the corridor would usually lead through, they were instead standing in a space mainly taken up by a set of heavy doors. These angled away from him, following the contours of the streamlining that the nose of each train car exhibited. When the train car was connected to another one behind, they would undoubtedly open up to allow passage through. For now, they were very firmly closed.

A discreet reader was set off to the side for just such an occasion as this. He tapped it with the card: again, three times. Massive locks disengaged, and the doors rumbled aside, leaving just six inches of footing between the toes of his boots and empty (if turbulent) air.

In daylight, it would've also given him an unparalleled view of the gleaming silver rail stretching out behind as the train raced along. However, sunrise was still an hour away, and the just-risen new moon gave barely any illumination. Sixty feet below, scarcely visible in the predawn darkness, the landscape blurred by at a little under four hundred miles per hour. The wind whipped into their tiny niche, seeking to drag him out.

A large metal hand closed over his shoulder, but he'd been expecting that. Due to Scout's role as his safety companion, they'd done power-loss drills where he simulated being unable to fly or even glide, and Scout had caught him every time. He'd gotten to the point where he didn't even flinch anymore when Scout grabbed hold of him unexpectedly. Which was all to the good: partners trusted each other. It was as simple as that.

His phone earpiece beeped with an urgent alert. It was a general message for all Force Majeure personnel. Tucking away the MagCard, he brought out the handset and woke it up, already sure of what he would see.

JEFFERSON CITY, MISSOURI STRUCK BY A MAGNITUDE 7.8 EARTHQUAKE. ASSEMBLING ACTION TEAMS FOR ASSISTANCE.

"Called it. Would you consider this to be an applicable emergency?"

Scout barely hesitated. **"It meets the definition, yes."**

Returning the phone to its pouch with one hand, Jericho reached back and slapped Scout with the other, reducing the robot's effective weight by ninety percent. Then he activated his harness and leaped out into the slipstream, unfurling his grav-wings in mid-jump.

Given the gravitational pulses he'd detected before the quake, he was convinced that this was in no way a natural phenomenon. But tracking down the person or persons responsible would have to wait. There were more important factors to deal with right now.

"Let's go help some people."

25
Emergency Measures

As the lights of the train disappeared into the darkness, Jericho moved clear of the track, then came to a hover and pulled his arms free of the grav-wings. He took the HUD goggles from the pouch on his belt and put them on, ensuring that the strap snapped into its designated groove on his helmet. His G-sense picked up Scout as the hulking robot came up behind him ... and paused.

Oh, right. My 'wings are going to get in the way.

Holding his arms out to the side, he deliberately depowered his flight capability, causing the large midnight-dark 'wings to fade out of view like a figment of his imagination. He began to fall, though much more slowly than usual due to his base power. Even that was halted as the matte-black mechanical arms locked tight around him. Others might have flinched or pulled back, but he knew Scout well enough by now to trust his life to his partner.

"Distance to Jefferson City: forty-four miles," Scout intoned over Jericho's earpiece, applying extra thrust to increase their altitude and put the ground far below them. **"Ignition in fifteen seconds. The countdown may be paused at any time via verbal command. Ten. Nine. Eight."**

Jericho admitted to himself that he felt a little nervous right then, but that was only natural. They'd never actually practiced this aspect of Scout's capabilities before, mainly because there was no way in *hell* he would've ever gotten permission for Scout to use emergency thrust inside Utopia City airspace. Not that he thought this was in any way unreasonable; he'd object too if someone suggested venting high-temperature radioactive plasma in such a densely populated area.

"Seven. Six. Please keep your arms and legs inside the ride at all times. Two. One. Ignition."

The joke caught Jericho by surprise. He was just starting to chuckle when the high-pitched whine coughed, then transformed into a throaty roar. Acceleration built, then kept on increasing as the slipstream pushed harder and harder at him.

As with the smoke over the building in Savannah, the goggles protected his eyes from the steadily intensifying wind-rush, for which he was glad. He hadn't bothered switching on the HUD function because his powers could track his speed and location better than any GPS.

Unfortunately, the buffeting was terrible as they approached a hundred miles per hour, and got significantly worse after that. He wasn't sure if he'd be able to handle much higher speeds, even if Scout could reach them.

Worse, he was dubious about Scout's ability to maintain control without the use of his arms for aerodynamic assistance.

At this rate, we'll be taking an extra ten or fifteen minutes to get there. That's enough time for people to die who could've been saved.

Mouth clamped shut against the freezing gale, Jericho racked his brain, trying to figure out a workaround. If they went any faster, Scout might just lose control, but slowing down would almost certainly cost lives.

I'm a superhero, goddamn it! There's gotta be something I can do!

As the wind whipped over him, tearing at his helmet and costume, he blinked behind his goggles.

Crap, maybe there is.

Before getting his power-enhancing harness, he'd always needed to glide to get anywhere in a hurry. The air resistance had never been this bad, even on that one occasion when he'd performed the daredevil swoop into the South Side Mall. It had always been like sliding over glass, giving him the impression that he was just naturally aerodynamic. The vicious slipstream he and Scout were currently combating felt more like being dragged over gravel, so that clearly wasn't the case. What was he doing differently?

Turning on my flight or using my gliding must activate a secondary effect that makes me more aerodynamic than usual. But if I try to use my flight or gliding right now, I'll just get in Scout's way.

Okay, so what happens if I try to make it work on its own?

Taking a deep breath in through his nostrils, he concentrated on his powers, leaning hard into the enhancements granted him by the harness. He took it slowly and carefully, visualizing a smooth, symmetrical shell surrounding them, diverting the wind and allowing for a more controllable high-speed flight.

Once he had it set in his mind, he made the final push to activate it. Almost as if it had been waiting for precisely this to happen, a gravitic force field snapped into existence around them. While it was invisible to the naked eye, his G-sense could detect it easily. He figured it probably wouldn't do more than add streamlining, but that was all they needed.

The turbulence didn't vanish altogether, though it was considerably mitigated. Smoothing out dramatically, their new flight profile allowed Scout much more controllability. Jericho felt the surge as the robot increased thrust once more, now maintaining a steady course at the higher speed.

"Thank you," Scout transmitted over the radio link. **"That will reduce transit time considerably."**

Jericho hadn't told the robot what he was doing, but Scout had figured it out within seconds and taken advantage of the improvement in aerodynamics. This was another mark in favor of Scout's capability for understanding new situations. The Sidekick program, once the Technologist had all the bugs ironed out, would be definitely worth pursuing.

They topped out at three hundred and seventy-six miles per hour, at an above-ground altitude of fifteen hundred feet, still slower than the maglev but possessing the advantage of not being limited to the rail. The gently undulating farmland blurred into a series of shadows beneath them, Scout weaving gradually from side to side, probably to avoid directly overflying any homesteads. Jericho had been told the radiation from the plasma thrusters was not severe and would dissipate rapidly to harmlessness in the open air. But *no* radioactive contamination was better than *some* radioactive contamination.

Two minutes into the flight, Jericho's phone earpiece chimed in his ear. Reaching up, he pressed the helmet clicker to accept the call. He didn't know who was on the other end, but this wasn't a redirected call so he kept his voice professional. "You have G-Man."

"G-Man? You appear to be suffering from some manner of background interference. I can scarcely hear you." It was the Technologist's voice in his earpiece; Jericho couldn't be sure, but he sounded more exasperated than usual.

"I'm sorry, sir." Jericho raised his voice slightly. "Scout and me, we're heading for Jefferson City. We're fixing to help with the earthquake situation."

"Jefferson City earthquake situation?" The Technologist paused. "Oh. *That* earthquake situation. We already have that under control, or we will soon. Once our response teams are organized, Tourbillon will be shuttling them to the city. What *is* making that infernal racket?"

"We'll be there in six minutes or less." Jericho considered what to say next, then decided that the basic facts were best. "The noise is ... well, we're using Scout's emergency thrust to get there as soon as possible."

"Emergency thrust?" He could almost *hear* the Technologist's blood pressure going up several notches. "Who, precisely, authorized that to be deployed in the field? Because I know *I* did not."

"Ahh ... that would be me." Jericho felt as if he were digging himself deeper into a hole with every word, but there was no walking it back now. "I'm the closest Force Majeure member to the problem, and I figured a near-on magnitude eight quake constituted an emergency."

"And, of course, when you ordered the robot to deploy its emergency measures, I had neglected to ensure that your sense of adventure had a brake on it by removing such an action from your permissions." The Technologist sounded more annoyed with himself than with Jericho.

"I'm sorry, sir. Did you want me to have Scout shut down the emergency thrust?" Jericho prayed the answer would be in the negative, as doing so would delay their arrival by almost half an hour.

"That has yet to be decided. You say you are almost there? The earthquake was only announced three minutes ago. I was unaware that the maglev ran so close to Jefferson City." The Technologist was in full scientist mode now.

"Ah, that's an affirmative." Jericho's power told him they'd covered fifteen of the forty-four miles. "We're currently doing about three seventy-five over the ground, altitude fifteen hundred feet. ETA about five minutes."

"How in the name of J. Robert Oppenheimer are you going so fast?" demanded the Technologist. "All my calculations indicate that controlled flight would be problematic for the robot at over one hundred fifty miles per hour and increasingly difficult past two hundred. These problems would become exponentially worse if it happened to be carrying a passenger. The aerodynamic instability would render any such attempt farcical at best, and fatal at worst."

"Well, yeah, that's true," Jericho admitted. "But I had the idea of using my powers to smooth things out with a force field effect. It works pretty well, actually. Scout's having no problems keeping us on course."

"I ... see." The Technologist's voice was no less acerbic than before. "You *are* aware, are you not, that such experimentation is best carried out under carefully controlled circumstances? Also, and this is extremely important, *after* notifying persons such as myself so that minor things like onboard battery charge can be monitored?"

"... onboard battery charge?" Jericho hadn't even thought about that sort of thing. The idea of his enhancement harness running its batteries dry had never been high on his list of concerns, mainly because even with the hours upon hours of flying around Utopia, it had never become an issue. "It can run out?"

"Batteries run out. It is in their very nature to do so. Your harness is no exception, especially when enhancing a variation on your abilities that you have heretofore failed to utilize to any real degree."

Jericho took a few seconds to untangle that in his head. *Doing something with my powers I've never done before. Okay, then.* "I thought maybe my abilities recharged it or something. That's a thing, right?"

"With certain capabilities under certain situations, most assuredly. But yours do not function in such a way that makes this possible. So *yes,* your enhancement apparatus can indeed run out of battery charge. Kindly try not to be performing some action essential to life or limb if this should occur. Relentless would be displeased in the extreme, should you be injured in this manner."

The specter of an angry Relentless was not something Jericho wanted to dwell on, but something still didn't make sense. "I don't get it," he objected, not trying to argue, just striving to figure out the *why* of it. "I can fly around Utopia for *hours,* and you don't say a word. But I do this for five minutes, and you think it might drain the battery?"

The Technologist sighed. "We will speak of this once you have returned to Utopia City. Until then, heed my words. I have no idea how rapidly your current power use is draining your enhancement apparatus, but the draw may well be significant. Take care in how you utilize your Enabled capabilities once you reach Jefferson City. Do not, under *any* circumstances, trust your life to the enhanced versions thereof. They may give out at any time and *will* do so at the worst possible moment. A lifetime of studying catastrophes of all kinds has taught me that, at least."

Jericho nodded automatically. "Yes, sir. I'll be careful."

"Ensure that you do."

"Just one thing," Jericho said in the instant before the call would've cut off. "A question."

The Technologist paused. "Present your query."

"Since I'm always going to be with Scout, do I have the option to plug into his systems? He runs off a fusion battery or something, doesn't he? I could recharge my harness that way."

There was another pause, so long that Jericho wondered if the call had dropped out. When the Technologist spoke, he sounded like he was grinding his teeth. "That description involves an almost criminal level of over-simplification, but ... no. The option was not considered. As it should have been."

Jericho may have been guilty of missing the occasional social cue, but even he could spot that one. The Technologist had overlooked a possibility and was now pissed off because of it. He opened his mouth—to say what, he wasn't sure—but a beep signaled the end of the call before he could speak.

"Jefferson City is within visual range," Scout reported over the radio earpiece, so promptly that Jericho figured he'd been waiting for that point. **"ETA four minutes."**

Even straining his eyes, Jericho could only make out a smudge of lights on the horizon, but if Scout said it was Jefferson City, he wouldn't argue. As for the rest of it, his internal tachometer agreed with Scout's estimate.

These would be among the longest four minutes of his life.

26
First Responder

As they approached the stricken city, the gathering light on the eastern horizon afforded worrying glimpses of the after-effects of the earthquake. Jericho could see what he thought might be clouds of rising smoke, lit from below by fires. Or perhaps that was merely dust, with streetlights providing the illumination. Either way, the quake had hit Jefferson City very hard indeed. He had no doubt that this was only the beginning; when the sun finally rose, the actual level of destruction would probably be even more devastating than he imagined.

"Can you access emergency channels? It would help if we had an idea where they need us most." It was a given that there would be more situations than he could readily deal with, but he had to start *somewhere*.

"I have been analyzing messages for the last five minutes," Scout replied. **"There are three hundred twenty-two locations where citizens are calling for emergency services. I estimate two hundred fifty of these can be dealt with by civilian assets, fifty-one where our abilities are likely to be needed to tip the balance, and twenty-one where only Enabled can immediately assist."**

"We can't hit them all at once." It was only the truth. No matter what he did, some people would likely die before he could get to them. Even when the Force Majeure action teams got boots on the ground, it probably wouldn't be enough to save everyone still in peril. He'd learned a hard lesson in that himself recently. "Which of the high priority ones can we get to first?"

"The southbound span of the Jefferson City Bridge has partially collapsed. I count twenty-one civilians in imminent danger."

"That's as good a place as any to start." Jericho peered down along the dark expanse of the Missouri River toward where he could see a few sparks of light in the dark. "Is that it there?"

"Correct. Image enhancement shows substantial damage. The structure appears unstable, and the motorists cannot escape without risking serious injury or death."

Altering course slightly, Scout swooped down over the floodplain. Moments later, the river was under them; there was just enough light for Jericho to tell that the ordinarily placid water was silt-laden and choppy. This was another big clue if they needed more indication that a substantial earthquake had gone off just minutes before.

The roar of the plasma thrusters echoed off the bluff as they hammered down the middle of the waterway. Jericho was thinking hard about what they needed to do once they got to the bridge proper.

"Forty-five seconds," Scout informed him.

He was still trying to focus and get an idea of distance in the darkness; this helped a lot. Now he could make out car headlights, some angled upward or downward. That didn't make sense, until suddenly it did. "Is it just me, or is the bridge decking buckled all to hell and gone?"

"Affirmative. Also, two cars just went into the water. I am rated for underwater operations."

That decided matters. "Drop me and go after them."

"Understood. Dropping now." Scout opened his arms and released Jericho; at the same time, the rocket-roar of plasma ejection died back to a turbojet whine.

Falling in a gentle arc, Jericho spread his arms wide and let the gliding surfaces catch the air. Just about to activate his flight capability, he paused as he recalled the Technologist's words about how his enhancement harness was compromised, and would be likely to give out at the worst possible moment.

Okay, so the hard way it is.

He swooped in the direction of the stricken bridge. This close, it was just possible to see that the spars making up its structure were bent and deformed. He was no expert on the matter, but he strongly suspected that whatever supports the bridge was resting on had to be severely compromised for this to happen.

The deck was definitely slumping here and there; in the headlights of stopped cars, Jericho could see people moving around on foot, looking for a way out that didn't exist. Even if they jumped off the bridge to the water below, it looked like a hundred-foot drop at least. Broken bones or unconsciousness would be a strong possibility, with minimal survival chances once they went into that near-freezing water.

"Force Majeure! I'm here to help!" he yelled as he jinked past a structural girder and came in for a landing. As he touched down, the groaning and vibration of the overstressed structure became apparent through the soles of his feet. Between that and the cracks spreading across the decking, it was evident that any apparent safety in staying put would be measured in minutes, if not seconds.

There were nine civilians on this section of the bridge, along with more cowering in a car. Vague movement across a darkened abyss indicated more people on another bridge section. It was a safe bet that their situation was no better than this one.

Moving as fast as he dared, he crossed the distance to the lone occupied car and slapped the roof. "Going to need you to vacate the vehicle, folks!" he called out. "I've got to get everyone off this bridge!"

There was no movement from within the car, save that the driver hunched down over the wheel and stared more fixedly through the windshield. He'd heard about this reaction to a crisis situation but had never seen it before; people just bunkering down where they were, refusing to leave what they considered 'safe'.

There were no kids that he could see in the car, only adults, so he labeled them in his mind as 'second run' and turned to the others. Four men, three women, two kids. The framework of the bridge groaned audibly, and the deck lurched. The clock was ticking down, and he couldn't see how far the second hand had to travel.

Goddamn it, I'm going to have to use the harness.

"Okay, everyone!" Jericho shouted. "I'm gonna lighten your load, then carry you to safety! Everyone huddle up! All y'all are each other's very best friends right now!"

He took a deep breath and activated his flight capability; even before the deep-black grav-wings finished unfurling, he was pulling his arms free. Stepping in toward the huddled civilians, he started tagging them.

They flinched away, but that was probably more of a reflex to do with the sudden manifestation of the 'wings. Jericho knew damn well that doing this would drastically shorten the duration of the weight reduction that he'd applied to Scout, but he hoped the robot would be out of the river again before it became an issue.

"Why can't you just put us on the other bridge?" yelled a guy. "It's right over there!" He pointed across at the northbound span, maybe twenty yards away in the dim light. Apparently pristine, it sat sedately above the still-roiling waters of the Missouri River, not a bend or a dip to be seen.

"Because I can't see how badly it's damaged, and I don't know it *won't* collapse!" Jericho snapped. "Hold tight, y'all! We're going airborne!" Latching onto two different people, he lifted off the bridge decking, carrying the frightened civilians with him. It wasn't easy, and it wasn't fun, but the total adjusted weight was slightly less than hoisting a single adult would typically have been for him, so he could handle it.

On the downside, this had to be draining the harness hella fast. Jericho took them out through the largest gap between the girders, then turned hard left and set out for the shoreline and the city lights. They were halfway there when he heard Scout rocketing out of the water from the far side of the bridge, turbojets shrieking out a whole new note. Jericho had no idea how that even worked—jet engines usually didn't work underwater—but was willing to put another mark on the '*Technologist is amazing*' scoreboard.

"All three people retrieved from cars," the robot reported over their radio link. **"Life signs present."**

"Good," Jericho replied. "Rendezvous with me."

"Scout copies." The turbojet noise moderated back to what it had been before, and Jericho's G-sense picked up Scout paralleling his course.

There was a darkened ledge carved into the face of the bluff, but Jericho had no idea how safe it might be, especially if there was an aftershock. With a silent apology to his straining power, he pushed himself up the couple of dozen feet necessary to clear the top of the bluff and deposited the nine people on the triangular grassy stretch between the northbound and southbound highways.

As soon as everyone was down safely, he canceled his flight power and dropped to the ground. Scout came in for a dramatic landing at the same time, depositing three extremely sodden but thankfully alive people onto the grass as well.

"We're doing okay so far," Jericho said, trying to ignore the sounds of sirens from the city beyond the overpass. "If you can drop me off with the other people farther on then take care of the people in the car on the bridge, we should be able to get this sorted." He slapped his hand on Scout's arm, replenishing his power effect.

"Affirmative. Projection: the car will be too heavy without your assistance." Scout picked up Jericho under one arm, then took to the air again with a shriek of turbojets.

"We're past the point of saying 'please'," Jericho decided grimly. "If they won't open the doors for you, open them anyway. Get them out of the car and off the damn bridge. Better to ask for forgiveness than permission and all that."

"Understood. Human lives take precedence over inanimate property." They had traversed the length of the bridge in the time it took to have that conversation; Scout released Jericho, then pulled a hard loop and dived toward the section of the bridge with the car on it.

Spreading his arms, Jericho let his gliding ability parachute him toward the remaining people on this stretch of the bridge; six all told, as far as he could see. The structure was visibly moving, leaning and shifting even as he watched. There was definitely something wrong with whatever was supposed to be holding the bridge up. Earthquakes did funny things to the ground, and that was just the natural ones.

Dropping down through the overhead trusses, he landed on the unstable decking. Distantly, over the sound of creaking and groaning concrete, he thought he heard the noise of a door being pulled entirely off the car then tossed aside.

Well, I did tell him to get them out of the vehicle.

"Everyone, get close!" he shouted. "This thing's coming down! I'm gonna make you a lot lighter, then we're all gonna jump!"

Just as he finished speaking, the bridge lurched sideways. Cracks spread across the roadway, widening by the second. There was a loud report as a nearby joint failed. He kept his feet, mainly due to his powers, but everyone else staggered and fell. If he didn't do something *right now*, death was a genuine possibility for everyone in front of him.

There were no more ticks left on the clock. Jericho formed and threw two glue-tags as fast as possible, right next to the nearest man. Gathering himself, he leaped across the intervening distance, planting his feet where the 'tags had touched down. If his eyes weren't fooling him altogether, this part of the bridge was over dry land, with maybe a fifty-foot drop. He could work with that.

Making use of the added traction, he picked the guy up by the collar and waistband, aimed at a gap between the girders, and yelled, "Land and roll!"

He swung back and heaved, ignoring the man's startled yell and sending him (now weighing an effective fifteen pounds) flying out into empty air. Without bothering to watch the gentle arc, he flicked out two more glue-tags, disengaged his feet from the ones he was currently using, and leaped to the next closest man. They would drift down to a relatively gentle one-tenth gravity landing, none the worse for wear. While this solution was a little rough and ready, it was the best one he had to hand.

The other two men went the same way, then he grabbed up both women. "Hold on tight!" he shouted. With a grimace, he leaned into his enhancement harness and freed up one hand long enough to throw a powered-up glue-tag at a crack threatening to split the deck wide open. The 'tag hit and clung, and the gap held for a moment.

It was all he needed. Taking a run-up, he dived out through the nearest gap, kicking off to get as far away from the bridge as possible. As both women screamed and clung to him (not that he could blame them), he did his best to spread his arms and slow their already-gentle descent. Some might've seen it as sexist, but his upbringing had taught him to *always* make sure women and children didn't get hurt.

His gliding profile wasn't anywhere near as sleek as usual, but that didn't matter. They were off the bridge now and not a moment before time; from the sound of it, the structure was finally giving way.

And then one of the women let go long enough to point back over Jericho's shoulder. Her scream turned from simply expressing '*I don't want to be here*' to actual words. "Look out!"

He didn't need to look around because his G-sense filled him in on the threat; part of the upperworks of the bridge, tons of steel, had broken free and was toppling outward. And some of it was falling directly toward him and his passengers. Only, *it* wasn't drifting leisurely down under one-tenth gravity.

In the half-second he had before the errant section of the bridge was due to hit him, he knew he had no chance to glide out of the way. Even if he increased his gravitational potential to fall *faster*, he still wouldn't have the leeway to get out from under before it hit him.

Purely by instinct, he called on his enhanced flight power. The midnight-black grav-wings began to unfurl … then they flickered out again.

He knew exactly what that meant. The battery was dead.

And so was he.

With his last remaining effort, he flung the women out away from him so that at least they wouldn't be struck by the falling debris. They might bruise when they hit, but they wouldn't die.

The girders, weighing more tons than he wanted to think about, swung down at him like an executioner's blade. There would be no way to avoid this, not in the fraction of a second he had left.

But when the impact came, it wasn't the unyielding mass of a steel girder but instead a blast of superheated air accompanied by a whistling shriek. Rather than being smashed into the ground, Jericho was sent flying sideways. Disoriented, he tumbled through the air until he hit the ground and rolled over and over to a stop, splashing through a series of shallow puddles.

It might have been his Dynamic capability that allowed him to bend gravity to his will, but what got him to his feet despite his jangled senses was pure Prodigy stubbornness. He looked around, the dim predawn light barely pointing out where people were beginning to groan and stir.

And then he turned back toward the now-collapsed bridge and its northbound twin. No headlights were visible even on the northbound span, which was a good thing because he didn't know whether that was going to collapse as well. It certainly wasn't a safe place to be.

At this moment, memory caught up with his racing brain, and he looked back toward where the falling trusswork had been about to smack him into the ground. He hadn't gotten clear of it by his own means; that blast of hot air had all the earmarks of Scout's thrusters. The robot had plainly decided that tackling Jericho away from the falling girders would likely damage him almost as much as letting him be hit by them, so he'd taken a different tack.

He'd *blown* Jericho out of danger with his jet-wash.

The tactic had worked; Jericho could personally attest to that. But what of the cost?

"Scout!" he called over the radio. "Scout, come in! Report status!" By now, he was running toward where he thought the girders were, cold water kicking up around his boots, hoping against hope that he was mistaken in his conclusions.

The answer he got back was not the robust, confident tone he was used to hearing. It was barely an electronic whisper. **"Damage ... considerable. Confirm ... G-Man ... safe."** A pair of lights flickered from blue to green and back again in the dimness.

"I'm safe, I'm safe," babbled Jericho as he arrived at the site of the fallen girders. There were several of them, piled on top of each other, crushing Scout's body onto the ground. "Why'd you do it? Why'd you throw yourself in the way?"

Scout's eyes flared green for a second. **"Human lives take precedence over ..."** *Over inanimate property.* His voice died away, but Jericho had heard the unspoken words anyway.

"You idiot!" he blurted. "You're not inanimate property! You're more than that! You're a *person*! Hang on, I'm getting you out of there."

"Continued ... operation ... unsustainable ... Shutting ... down." Scout's head turned toward him, and the robot's eyes flickered again, going from red to amber to blue. There was barely any power behind them. **"G ... man ... you ... must ... save ... Utopia ..."**

And then they went dark.

"No, don't you dare give up!" shouted Jericho, tears spilling from his eyes as he laid ahold of the top girder and pushed his power into it. "I'll get you out! I'll get you back to the Technologist! You're going to be fine!"

Jaw set with determination, he started clearing the girders away. Being a prodigy, he was stronger than he looked; the first one weighed perhaps half a ton, but between his power reducing that to effectively a hundred pounds and the adrenaline currently flooding his system, he literally threw it aside. Beneath it was a length of steel perhaps twice as heavy as the first one. He only had to lift one end, though, which meant he was still able to heave it to one side with no real problem.

Now came the big one: several girders still attached to each other, pressing Scout into the mud. He fed his power into the mass of steel, and ran into a problem; in the absence of his harness, he couldn't affect the whole thing. Most of it, certainly, but not all. There was enough mass left over that this was going to take everything he had, and possibly a little more.

He didn't care.

Taking a fresh grip, he planted his feet more firmly and threw every ounce of strength he had into it. A red haze danced behind his eyes, and he felt his joints and muscles straining.

The girders didn't budge. This did not dissuade Jericho.

Scout was more than a robotic sidekick, more than a machine constructed in the shape of a man. He was Jericho's friend, his ally. His partner.

His buddy.

He wasn't about to let a little thing like an insurmountable task get between him and saving Scout. So he shut down the insidious voices telling him it was impossible, gritted his teeth, clenched his eyes shut, and lifted *harder*. Blood thundered in his ears. But he would. Not. Give. Up.

Almost imperceptibly, the girders shifted. Jericho felt a muscle go in his back, but he didn't care. His entire focus was aimed at one thing. Inch by straining inch, he continued to lift. He would either raise the girders and get Scout out, or break himself in the attempt.

And then the girders ... moved. The weight Jericho was straining against literally vanished between one second and the next. Opening his eyes, he looked to see if Scout had miraculously recovered, but the dark mass of the robot was still inert. However, standing next to Jericho was the second most welcome sight in the world.

Barely flexing at all, Relentless—Jericho could pick out the faint reflection of the eastern sky from the silver highlights of his armor—was hoisting the girders as if they weighed nothing at all. Which, in all fairness, was probably close to the truth ... from his point of view, anyway.

Jericho saw a near-invisible dark cloudy circle flicker out of existence behind the massively built superhero. With an immense sensation of relief in his chest, he recognized Tourbillon's power in action. He could hear the muted pings in his earpiece as more people tied into the local network.

The cavalry had come over the hill.

Force Majeure was in town, and everything was going to be alright.

27
Duty Calls

Relentless looked down at Jericho. "You okay? Not hurt?" Almost casually, he walked the girders back until he could lean them against the remains of the fallen bridge.

"Yeah, no, I'm fine." Jericho recognized the signs of adrenaline in his system—accelerated heartbeat, twitchiness, a tendency to speak faster than usual—and consciously set out to control himself. The pulled muscle in his back, he was ignoring for the moment. That would mend of its own accord. "But it's Scout. He saved my life, and I think he's really badly hurt."

He dropped to his knees at the robot's side, seeking out the damage with his fingertips. Scout's imposing matte-black armor was severely dented inward in more than one place, and his right arm had been utterly wrecked by the impact with the girders. Both the robot's eyes were still dark.

"Calm down." Jericho's G-sense vaguely registered Relentless moving up behind him before the huge gauntleted hand dropped onto his shoulder, more or less enveloping it. "If I know the Technologist, he'll be able to get it working again, as good as new. By the time he's done, you won't even know it got damaged in the first place."

I'll know. But Jericho kept his thoughts to himself. "How quickly can we get him back to Utopia?"

"Back up a little," Relentless said. "*We* are not taking him back to Utopia. I can handle that myself." To illustrate his words, he crouched and picked up the unmoving robot, handling the weight with the same ease as he had the fallen girders.

Jericho averted his eyes from the dangling limbs, eerily reminiscent of a marionette with its strings cut. "But I was the one who got him hurt. I need to go back and make sure he's okay."

The black and silver helmet turned to regard Jericho; even half-obscured, Relentless' features held an intensity of expression that almost felt like a physical blow. "No." His voice was as deep and implacable as ever. "It's not your fault. You didn't cause this. Now, get your head together. You're a member of Force Majeure, and you've got a job to do."

Thankful for the reminder, Jericho drew in a deep breath and nodded. There were people in the stricken city who needed help. Even without the assistance of his power enhancement harness, he knew he could still do his bit. "Right. Where do you want me?"

Relentless shook his head. "Not here. Kennedy Space Center. You're due to represent Force Majeure at this year's Challenger Commemoration Day, in case you'd forgotten." He tilted his head toward the collapsed bridge.

"You've made a good showing so far, but we can handle it from here. Tourbillon, to my right!"

There was a ten-second pause, just long enough for Relentless to inhale once more. Then, the cloudy black swirl spun up ten feet to his right. When it was a total of eight feet in diameter, the charcoal-robed figure of the team's teleporter stepped through. They gave Jericho an unreadable glance, then looked over at Relentless: or more specifically, Scout. Behind them, the swirl snapped out of existence.

"G-Man. I see it didn't take you long to break your new toy." Their voice wasn't as disdainful as Independence's, but the judgmental tone was still in evidence.

"Hey." Jericho's temper, usually kept well in line, flared up at that. "He saved six people's lives today, seven counting mine. Scout's a goddamn hero."

"Enough." That one word from Relentless, spoken without heat, was sufficient to pull them both up short. "I'm going to need a portal to the St. Louis maglev station for G-Man, then one for me to Utopia. Technologist's lab. Now, cut the attitude and do your job."

The androgynous hero sighed. "As you wish, *mon capitaine*." A gray-gloved hand waved almost languidly, and darkness poured from the robes to form another swirl. "St. Louis. Watch your step."

Which was Tourbillon's way of saying that he would be emerging in mid-air. Jericho was okay with that; he was still perfectly capable of gliding. But that reminded him of something. "Relentless, before I go, I need to talk to you."

"If it's about the misunderstanding when you first joined, don't worry about it." Relentless' tone was dismissive. "Shit happens. Wires got crossed. Already forgotten."

"Not that." Though if he was being truthful with himself, it was a good thing to hear. "The earthquake. It wasn't natural. I think it was induced, somehow. Someone *made* it happen."

That got a reaction; Relentless and Tourbillon shared a glance, then looked back at Jericho. "You're certain about this." Relentless' tone made it a statement rather than a question.

"Yeah. One hundred percent." Jericho wished he was wrong about this, but his power didn't lie. "I felt a few pulses in local gravity right before it happened. UML said they'd detected the same when I called them. They said they were calling you."

"I was busy. Samantha would've routed that call through to the Technologist." The massively built superhero frowned and turned to Tourbillon. "Does it sound to you like Seismic might be back? Or maybe someone else acquired one of his old machines and decided to do the copycat thing?"

Seismic. Jericho knew that name, an artificer who had earned his place among the terror villains of the Nineties by literally holding cities to ransom with his earthquake machines. He'd dropped out of sight in 1997, the year before Force Majeure began hitting the headlines by taking down his fellow terror villains with extreme prejudice.

Seismic was one of the few terror villains they *hadn't* been able to claim credit for killing, which meant one of two things. Either he'd been taken out by a member of the public who'd chosen not to seek any kind of recognition or reward, or he'd simply been keeping his head down for the last seventeen years.

In the former case, not talking about it would likely have been a wise move. The other terror villains, particularly the Minotaur, had shown a tendency to lash out at anyone targeting them. Jericho favored that option; the fact that Seismic hadn't made any kind of showing at all in the last seventeen years was solid corroborating evidence. Until now.

Which led directly to the next couple of questions. If Seismic was dead, who was copying his signature move? And if he was alive, why had he waited until now to make a comeback?

"We haven't gotten any demands yet." The slender teleporter shrugged. "I give it a thirty percent chance that it's actually him. But even if it is, where's he been all this time?"

The question sparked an idea in Jericho's mind. "Wait a second. I saw something like this on a TV show once." He flushed slightly as the other two turned to look at him, but he forged on regardless. "What if he's been arrested for something else altogether, got convicted and sent to prison, and only just now got out?"

Tourbillon's head tilted thoughtfully. "That's … actually not a bad point. Relentless?"

"It's a possibility." Relentless set his jaw. "If it is him, if that asshole thinks he can start that shit up again in *my* America, I'm gonna make the sonovabitch wish he'd *stayed* dead. Even if it isn't, I'll make whoever it is wish *they* were dead. But that's a good call, G-Man. I'll have Samantha start shaking the bushes, seeing if she can match up any dates. Was there anything else?"

"Uh, yeah, actually." Jericho grimaced. "My power enhancement harness. I kind of ran the batteries dead. If anyone wants me to do any cool *'new and improved G-Man'* stunts when I'm down in Florida, I'm crap out of luck."

Again, Relentless shared a glance with Tourbillon; this time, the gray-cloaked teleporter spoke first. "What, really? You do know you can recharge it on the maglev, don't you?"

"On the maglev?" Jericho hated being on the back foot like this. "How? And why didn't I get told about this before?"

Relentless sighed heavily. "Because as smart as the Technologist is, he sometimes forgets that people don't know what he knows. Every maglev train car is equipped with inductance technology that automatically charges up Force Majeure gear, even while you're wearing it. By the time you get to Kennedy, you'll be fine. You get me?"

"Oh. Okay, sure." That still didn't answer the question as to why he never ran out of charge while flying around Utopia, but one thing at a time. "Thanks. I reckon I'd better get going."

"Yeah." Relentless nodded toward the still-swirling portal. "Once you're on the train, clean yourself up. You're a mess."

Jericho wanted to ask him how immaculate *he'd* be if he fell in a mud puddle, but patience wasn't something the big man was renowned for. "Sure thing. Going now."

Turning, he dived through the portal.

28
Traveling On

Jericho's ears popped as he emerged in mid-air. As he'd suspected would be the case, he'd come out somewhere between one and two thousand feet above ground level, nearer to one than two if he had to guess, and accelerating downward by the second.

The glow in the eastern sky was more pronounced, though he didn't know whether this was due to his altitude or the eastward jump he'd just made. Off in the middle distance was the illuminated curve of the Gateway Arch and the dark expanse of the Mississippi River beyond. Below him, he presumed, was the maglev station.

Exerting his power to reduce the effect of gravity on himself, he spread his arms and started down in a long lazy spiral. It didn't take him long to coast down to ground level, which was good.

While his costume was insulated for warmth and had that water-shedding layer, there were still some wet patches from his involuntary stop-drop-and-roll through the puddles. The midwinter chill—if the temperature up there was over fifteen degrees Fahrenheit, he would've been astonished— brought these to his immediate attention. By the time he got down to ground level, the water in his ponytail was frozen solid.

In addition, things would've been more convenient if the maglev station had a roof entry like the Utopia City station, but he couldn't have everything. Besides, until St. Louis got around to emulating Utopia's monorail system, they wouldn't *need* a roof entry.

Touching down a dozen yards from the nearest set of doors, he checked himself over, brushed off a few errant pieces of dead grass, then strode in toward the entrance. At this point, he realized he was still wearing the HUD goggles he'd initially put on for eye protection. Tucking them away in their designated pouch, he continued onward.

The warmth of the station hit him once he stepped inside, striking at the chill that was trying to dig its claws into him. The cold wasn't really affecting him badly—Prodigy durability could shrug off even the worst winter temperatures—but the lessening of the discomfort was welcome all the same.

One of the benefits of the maglev system was that buying a through ticket allowed passengers to get off and then on again. It was technically possible to abuse the system by going farther than the purchased ticket allowed, but this would merely result in the passenger's MagCard being charged the balance of the trip on swiping out of the station.

All of this meant that Jericho could swipe straight through to the platform with no delays when he walked into the station. Amusingly enough—for a given definition of 'amusing'—the train waiting when he got there was the one bound for Nashville, where his planned route was going through anyway. In fact, if his mental arithmetic was accurate, it was actually due to latch onto the same collection of maglev cars he'd bailed out of to go attend the emergency at Jefferson City.

Teleportation for the win.

This did not mean he was either happy or amused when he got on the train. While he was intellectually aware that it had been Scout's choice to do what he did, it didn't make it easier for him to process things. Far too much had happened in the last ten minutes for that.

Geez, has it only been ten minutes?

In that time, he'd saved over a dozen people from near-certain death and been the proximate cause of his comrade in arms suffering potentially catastrophic damage.

If I'd been more careful to conserve power, I would've been able to fly out from under those girders.

I should've gone after the folks in the car and let Scout handle the other six.

This is Luke and Bobbi all over again.

It's my fault Scout got hurt.

My fault.

Mine.

Once the maglev left the station and connected with the rest of the train, he ducked into the nearest washroom. Relentless had ordered him to clean himself up, so clean up he would. This helped distract him from the specific knowledge that he'd screwed up badly enough to let his partner get hurt.

After inspecting himself as best he could via the washroom mirror, he concluded that he wasn't *that* much of a mess. Pristine he wasn't, but it wouldn't take as much effort to fix matters as he'd initially thought. Still, it was going to take a little time to get right. Keeping an ear out for the upcoming Nashville announcement, he set to work.

First, he ensured the door was locked before stripping down to his underwear, then gave himself the best approximation of a sponge bath he could manage in such close quarters. Taking his hair out of its ponytail, he rinsed the dirty melting ice into the sink, then wrung it out as best he could before re-tying it. Then he started cleaning off his costume, piece by piece. As he finished with each item, he let the hand-dryer work its magic while he moved on to the next article.

The only redeeming factor in all this, he figured with a wry grin, was that no matter how damp the hand-dryer left things, nobody would be able to tell. Matte black didn't look any different, wet or dry. And a significant difference between this costume and the original was that he didn't have to worry about water damage on anything in the utility belt; each pouch was designed to magnetically clip shut with a watertight seal.

Once he'd finished his cleaning efforts, he re-donned the costume, starting with the helmet. Wriggling it into place so that the earpieces went where they were supposed to, he secured the chin strap, then pulled his ponytail through the hole at the back (they'd kept that much in the design, at least) and took up the jacket. His pants followed, then he pulled the boots on and stamped them into place, one at a time.

Emerging from the washroom fully dressed again, he felt much better, as though the act of washing off the outward grime had acted to assuage the guilt he felt within. It hadn't, not totally—there would be some brooding time going toward this soon—but it had helped. He could look past it and think about how he should have done things better.

The sun was just coming up as the maglev passed through the outskirts of Nashville. While the windows automatically polarized to block out the worst glare, it was still a lovely sunrise. Automatically, he got up to move forward in the train in response to the inevitable announcement. When bound for Savannah, he usually went through Chattanooga, but today he had to remember he was heading to Florida via Alabama.

Birmingham, Montgomery, Tallahassee, Gainesville, Orlando, and finally the Kennedy Space Center. Just under two hours and I'll be there.

The festivities were due to kick off at nine-thirty local time, which gave him plenty of leeway to be there before they started. And in the meantime, he could look at where he'd gone wrong in Jefferson City and see if he couldn't figure out how to do better next time.

Though one thing was bugging him.

What did he mean, I must save Utopia?

29
Heroic Ideals

Montgomery-Tallahassee Maglev Line
January 28, 2014
07:47, Eastern Daylight Time

Unsurprisingly, Tourbillon and Relentless had been on the level about equipment recharging on the train. Jericho waited until the maglev whipped past Montgomery before testing out the power harness; to his considerable relief, it came online with nary a glitch. Taking out his phone, he checked its charge and saw that it was also ticking upward from what it had been on before.

God, I hope Scout's gonna be okay. Relentless said so, and he's seen the Technologist at work before, so … I guess?

Putting the phone face-down on the table before him and powering down the harness, he closed his eyes for a moment. He'd thought the apartment fire in Savannah had been chaotic, but the collapsing bridge took that to a whole new nightmare level. People would've almost certainly died if he'd hesitated—or worse, frozen. The ones who went into the water were just lucky Scout had been with him.

He delved into his memory of the situation, seeking answers to his questions.

Where did I go wrong? Not keeping an eye on the bridge. Not realizing those things could fall as far as they did. Maybe I should've dumped them all on the flat land with the puddles instead of flying the first bunch all that way. Maybe I shouldn't have used my harness so much to start with?

But try as he might, he couldn't put his finger on any specific thing he'd done that had made things worse—apart from getting Scout hurt, of course.

If I'd known that thing was gonna come down, I could've made it lighter before I ever jumped off the bridge. If it fell slower, I could've gotten farther.

He shook his head. His harness had been about to give out anyway. The benefit would've been minimal, and there'd still been the loose girders. This was going nowhere. It was time to do something else.

Picking up the phone again, he searched for news about the search and rescue efforts in Jefferson City. Several articles popped up, and he tapped the top one. The search for survivors was still ongoing, it seemed, but the few fires that had been started were now under control, and first responders were optimistic that there wouldn't be many more casualties. Currently, the death toll stood at three, with just over a hundred injured.

Team Power was on site now as well. While Vanessa (or perhaps

Thomas) piloted the family jet overhead, using its advanced sensors to pinpoint trapped people and fire hotspots, Tesseract and Buddy were using their powersuits at ground level. A photo showed Adam Power and Relentless working together to heave aside a massive concrete slab. It was an excellent example of teamwork done right, and he felt a deep and abiding surge of proprietary pride for both teams; one he belonged to by membership, and the other by unofficial adoption.

This. This is what being a hero is all about. Getting out there and helping people.

He looked down at the phone again. Arguably, he already *knew* what was involved in being a hero. With role models like Transit and Adam Power, how could he not? But there was something he'd been neglecting again, despite his best intentions.

If I'm going to be an effective hero, I need to know how villains think and what they're like to do.

If he recalled the schedule correctly, the maglev would be hitting Tallahassee in ten minutes, which gave him about four minutes of viewing time before the automated announcement popped the privacy bubble. He *could* listen to it via the earpiece, but he preferred to be up and moving as soon as possible after the announcement started. So he wasted no time finding a villain unlike the others he'd already looked into. He found one, alright; or rather, two.

A massively built man of few words, Devastator had been well-nigh bulletproof, protected by a shimmering crimson force field. He wore a bulky harness of leather and steel over his upper and lower torso, along with solid metal wristbands and boots. His eyes projected powerful cutting beams of the same deep red hue, while his hands fired concussive blasts. Nobody knew where he came from; they just wished he'd go back there.

Mutilator's origin, on the other hand, was well documented.

While most Prodigy capabilities leaned toward the physical—Jericho had heard of heroes who could perform comic-book level feats with a bow and arrow, thrown discs, or even boomerangs—there was also a mental aspect. Instead of being masters of a purely physical calling, mental prodigies aimed toward more cerebral pursuits; the general population often called them 'super-geniuses'.

Smokeshadow was one such.

Miranda Price had been another.

Just a teenager when she gained her powers in 1989, Miranda was able to specialize in all kinds of medicine, with an emphasis on surgery. Everything came easily to her, even procedures that other surgeons considered far too risky or virtually impossible. Not bothering to wear a fancy costume or even conceal her identity, she'd ignored the whole hero/villain dichotomy and gone straight for the big bucks.

And indeed, all went well for a while. The American government denied her request to use 'Surgeon General' as a professional name, but as Surgeon

One, she had the wealthiest of the wealthy beating a path to her door. While her fees were outrageous, so were the procedures she carried out. Money, it seemed, did not render one immune to the ills that flesh is heir to, but it did invite more expensive remedies. It was simplicity itself for her to remove 'inoperable' tumors or tease out tiny brain lesions without disturbing the surrounding tissue, so she charged whatever the traffic would bear.

Her downfall came when she ran afoul of a pernicious group of anti-Enabled activists called Unmask. Even though she wore no mask, a particularly radical group of them set their sights on her as a test case for proving all Enabled to be unstable psychopaths. To this end, she was abducted along with her family, who were threatened with death if she did not use her surgical talents to disfigure a group of innocents in grotesque and inventive ways.

There hadn't really been a way around it so she caved, performing the surgery as the Unmask activists directed, fully aware she was being filmed. Nobody quite knew what was going through her head at the time; it could have been that long-suppressed urges were finally expressing themselves, or her mind may simply have snapped under stress. Either way, at some point, she stopped merely going along with it and actively took charge of the process.

The video of the event was a little grainy, even with later digital enhancement. Still, it was clearly possible for Jericho to hear her giggling and occasionally laughing out loud on the audio as she sliced up her victims and stitched them together in new and exciting ways. The Unmask activists were visibly freaked out by this but kept filming anyway, at least until they ran out of tape.

In the aftermath, Miranda had been released unharmed, along with her family. The authorities were initially sympathetic since hostages had been involved, but the need for further investigation prevented her from simply walking away from the mess. Ongoing lawsuits from the families of every victim of her surgery merely added to her problems.

Her offers to reverse the damage were turned down flat by all parties, and she was forbidden to even contact them, let alone raise the issue again. Jericho figured it hadn't helped when copies of the videotape were also released by Unmask, going to all news outlets along with an article that basically boiled down to 'look how unstable this one Enabled is; you need to expose and imprison them all'.

The penultimate stressor came when her former supporters began decrying her in public. Not even those previously lining up to throw money at Surgeon One wanted anything more to do with her. Her work would likely have dried up altogether, even if she hadn't been legally enjoined from performing any more surgeries until the lawsuits were settled and the investigations were complete.

Which was when someone in the Department of Justice jumped the gun and froze her assets in response to a persistent rumor that she might try to flee the country. Her protest was on record, but the wheels of justice always grind exceedingly slow, especially with people (it was suspected) slow-walking the process. Shunned by her friends and family and unable to access her funds, she finally went off the deep end. A sheriff's deputy dispatched to her home to serve her a summons for yet another court appearance was found surgically dismembered, with Miranda Price long gone.

In her place, Mutilator soon showed up on the villain scene: hair stuffed under a cloth cap, a surgical mask with grinning teeth on it, and blood-stained scrubs. Looking at before-and-after images of her, Jericho figured the crazy had definitely come to visit, and it had brought its baggage along. Later on, she acquired Artificer-made gloves that popped out scalpel blades and wicked-looking syringe needles at a thought, but even from the beginning, she was frankly terrifying.

For all her Prodigy-earned skills, Mutilator had a rough time over the first few months. While she was a dangerous combatant with any surgical implement that could be used in such a fashion, and getting anywhere near her while she held a loaded syringe was basically a death sentence, she lacked physical defenses. This changed when she formed a partnership with Devastator, even newer on the scene than she was. He protected her while she did her thing, and she presumably patched him up after fights with heroes. This unholy alliance worked for them all the way through from 1993 until 1999, when Force Majeure tracked them down to Indianapolis and put an end to them.

Watching a security video of Mutilator at work was even more nauseating than Singularity's idea of a ransom video. She talked to her victims, chiding them for screaming and sometimes asking them whether a cut in one location hurt more than one in another. If they'd just died while she was operating on them, it might not have been so bad, but she knew how to *not* kill people in ways that made them wish they were dead.

The money was paid *fast* when she took someone for ransom, mainly because people wanted their loved ones back with the same number and locations of body parts they had when abducted. If it was tardy arriving, she never sent ears or fingers through the mail; that was entirely too passé for her. She would instead send a slice of heart muscle or brain matter, extracted without killing them *or even knocking them out*, along with a video file depicting the extraction itself.

With a shudder, Jericho closed out the video. He was more relieved than ever that he'd had the opportunity to spend time both brooding and talking with both Scout and Ms. Chandler. If he hadn't, the video he'd just watched would've disturbed him quite a bit more than it had, and he was already plenty bothered by it. How people could even get into a mindset where they maimed and murdered their fellow human beings, not just willingly but *cheerfully* ... was beyond him.

He knew the urge to kill; when he'd found Luke and Bobbi slaughtered in the apartment, his first instinct had been to go after the culprit and exact bloody vengeance. The only reason he hadn't was because the police had shown up first and assumed *he* was the perp. That misunderstanding had been cleared up, but the murderer—Jack Portman, Bobbi's boyfriend, as he later learned—had gotten away as a result.

When he later confronted Portman in the Southside parking garage, the murderer had fallen to his death, not because of Jericho's actions but from his own clumsiness. If Jericho could've saved him, he would've, because by that time, he'd gotten enough perspective on the matter to want Portman to stand trial in court. Seeing justice done rarely did the victims any good, but closure gave their loved ones a chance to move on.

"Attention, all passengers. Attention, all passengers. This train will be passing through Tallahassee in six minutes. All passengers stopping in Tallahassee ..."

That was his cue. Standing up from his seat, he slid the phone back into its pouch and started making his way toward the front of the train once more. He knew he would be a while digesting the latest info-dump on exactly how nasty the terror villains had been—*seriously, couldn't I have just taken the name at face value?*—but it was necessary, just in case someone else came up with the same idea, and he was the one facing them.

Tallahassee came and went, and he sat in the new train car, thinking over what he'd learned. Terror villains weren't just fine with killing at a moment's notice; their 'terror' status derived from their willingness to throw aside all societal norms purely for their own entertainment. Indeed, some were more comfortable *without* the societal norms.

There'd been people like that throughout human history, of course. Murderers, psychopaths, monsters in human skin. Some had undoubtedly given rise to the legends of mythical shape-changers from millennia gone by, pushing back against the tide of civilization and reverting to the most basic of instincts. They'd been bad enough when they were merely human; given Enabled abilities to play with, they were a thousand times worse.

Gainesville passed by while he was still considering the issue, the sun slowly rising on the far side of the train. Moving again to the front car, he settled back in his customary seat, trying to scour the images of what he'd seen out of his mind. He knew he didn't want to be dwelling on this all the way through the Challenger Commemoration festivities, so he looked for something else to distract himself.

The harness should be charged by now. I managed to make the aerodynamic field work. I wonder if there's anything else I can supercharge?

Flight was already a given; on a whim, he started concentrating on his G-sense. Closing his eyes, he tried seeing how far he could push it with his eyes closed.

His range was definitely better than it had been; whether this was due to the harness or him just getting better at using his powers, he wasn't sure. Either way, as he sat with his head turned to make it appear that he was looking out the window, he found he could easily track people moving along the aisle.

Which was how he knew when someone stopped right next to his table. A *huge* someone, he thought at first. Then a moment later, the form shifted and separated slightly, and he realized it was actually two skinny people, side by side.

Under the table, he started forming a glue-tag on the off-chance they had hostile intent. Firearms weren't permitted on the maglev and couldn't be smuggled on board, and in any case he wasn't picking up any metallic concentrations, but it never hurt to take care. He turned slowly, as if just now noticing them.

When he saw the pair standing there, he relaxed just a little and let the 'tag dissipate into nothingness. They looked like college students, their clothing just a little threadbare, wearing matching Challenger T-shirts. Far from being hostile, they seemed downright eager to make his acquaintance.

Reaching over to the switch for the privacy bubble, he flicked it off then nodded to the pair. "Morning, folks. Help y'all with something?"

The guy—frizzy ginger hair, lingering acne on his face—nodded convulsively, but the girl—straight mousy-brown hair, mildly prominent front teeth—spoke for them both. "Uh, hi, yeah. Um, you're G-Man, right?"

Well, if I ain't him, I'm for damn sure wearing his underwear. Jericho chose to rein in the smart-assery for the moment. "That's me, folks. You'd be heading on down to the Challenger Commemoration ceremony too?" As he spoke, he gestured at the seat opposite. "C'mon, sit yourselves down."

"Wow, thanks," enthused the guy, though he waited for the girl to slide across before sitting down. "I'm, uh, Kyle, and this is Petra. We're big fans."

"Of Challenger?" Jericho grinned in agreement, then re-engaged the bubble. "Me too. I'd love to have teamed up with Inspire back when they were kicking ass and taking names. They were really something."

"No, no, of you." Petra pointed to herself and Kyle with her thumb and forefinger, then gestured toward Jericho. "We're *G-Man* fans."

"What, really?" A beat passed before Jericho reminded himself that this might not be the best response to such a statement, and he pushed onward. "I'm sorry. I haven't been a member of Force Majeure for very long, so I didn't really think I had a personal fanbase yet." He didn't even have any action figures out, though the first run would be hitting stores shortly.

Petra shook her head. "We've been fans longer than that. Kyle and me, we've been following your career ever since we saw your photoshoot in *Gay!Power*, and we just had to add you to our fantasy hero league." She chuckled. "I'll tell you what, when you made the jump to Force Majeure, they had to revise your stats upward pretty hard."

Jericho blinked. He was pretty sure he'd understood every word that she'd just uttered, but put all together, it made little to no sense. "You've heard of *Gay!Power*? You *read* it?" He decided to focus on the familiar and worry about what a fantasy hero league was later.

"Yeah." Kyle nodded and flushed. "I had the biggest crush on you for the longest time."

"I do a little photography myself," Petra added. "Just amateur stuff. Whoever did your shoot is *good*. The photos really reach out and grab you. It was like we were in the room with you." She tilted her head questioningly. "You couldn't help me get in touch, could you? I think I could learn a lot."

Stephen. Jericho's throat closed up, and his hands clenched involuntarily inside his gloves. No matter how far he tried to run from the memory of his ex-boyfriend, it always caught up with him. "I … I'm sorry," he managed. "That's not … that's not going to be possible."

Kyle seemed to pick up on the nonverbal cues, but Petra kept talking. "Why not? Whoever did the article seemed to know you pretty well, going from the detail in your writeup. Didn't you keep in touch?"

Jericho dropped his head and closed his eyes. Clenching his eyes shut against the tears that threatened to fall, he shook his head. "He was … he passed recently. Just a couple of weeks ago. It … it was very sudden. I'm sorry." Vivid in his mind's eye were the crackling flames that had inexorably consumed the apartment building. He could still taste the smoke at the back of his throat.

"Oh. Shit, sorry." Petra went to keep talking, but Kyle muttered something too quiet for him to hear, and she shut up again.

"Is … is that why the webzine hasn't been updated recently?" asked Kyle hesitantly.

Drawing in a deep breath, Jericho raised his head again. He was a *superhero*, damn it, and a member of Force Majeure. More to the point, he'd made the conscious choice to put on a costume and go out in public, so it was on him to live up to the image he was trying to portray. "Yeah," he said as neutrally as he could manage. "Basically."

"Well, that sucks," mumbled Petra, then she brightened. "Hey, so … can we get selfies with you?"

"And could you sign my, uh, your fantasy league card?" asked Kyle, digging into his pocket.

"Sure, just as soon as one of you explains what-all that there actually is," Jericho said. In all truth, he cared more that the subject had been changed than about this 'fantasy hero league' thing, but he was always willing to learn something new.

"Oh, uh, sure." Kyle glanced at Petra, who was in the process of getting her phone out. "You know how fantasy football works?"

Jericho raised his eyebrows. "Assume I've got no idea what you're talking about, then go from there."

"Ah. Right. Well." Kyle cleared his throat and glanced sideways at Petra again, but she seemed willing to let him keep talking. "Um, it's like, every superhero in the United States gets put in a ranking system. Your powers get categorized and assigned number values, then they start tallying up your heroic acts. People can select the heroes they want into their virtual teams, and when a hero they've selected does something cool on TV, that scores points for their team."

Jericho barely managed to restrain himself from another *'What, really?'* reaction. Even if he'd never heard of it, that meant nothing. As the Technologist was fond of saying, the vast majority of humanity knew far less than they thought they did. "I ... see," he managed instead. "So, what stops people from just picking the high-tier Enabled? The core members of Force Majeure, for instance? They'd wipe the floor with just about every other team, virtual or otherwise."

"It's a point-buy system," Petra explained. "Everyone's got a point total, based on their power tier and any displayed Prodigy and Artificer capabilities. You can build a team based on the total points you're allowed to spend. Rookie league is a thousand points, Newcomer is two grand, Experienced is four, Epic is eight, and Elite is sixteen." She glanced at Kyle and rolled her eyes. "Sure, you can buy the cards online, but those are usually outdated by the time they get to you. The website has up-to-the-moment values."

"Yeah, but first-issue cards can end up being collector items." Kyle's protest sounded like more of a reflex than anything else; Jericho figured it wasn't the first time they'd had this argument. Pulling his wallet out, Kyle produced a rigid holder, which contained a card with a picture of Jericho as G-Man. "Here," he said, holding it out. "How cool is this?"

Belatedly, Jericho recognized it as one of the first public images of him out and about in the actual G-Man costume, snapped while he'd been engaged in thwarting a convenience store robbery. He'd made the news for a while, right up until he'd told a reporter he was gay. After that, his newsworthiness had suffered a gradual decline, one that he didn't realize the cause of until he met Bobbi Reynolds on the way to Utopia City.

The logo *Fantasy Hero League!* was printed on the card, along with a cartoon image of an Enabled bursting out through the 'O' of 'Hero'. Underneath that was his hero name, followed by close approximations of his height, weight, and age (they'd oversold him on the first two and undersold him on the third) and a list of what they seemed to think his powers were.

"Flight? Telekinesis? *Invisibility?"* he muttered, then looked up. "I couldn't fly back then, I can only do a vague approximation of telekinesis, and I've *never* been able to go invisible."

Petra shrugged. "They gotta make educated guesses, man. I'm figuring you never actually gave out the exact details in interviews. Do you blame 'em for just making shit up if the heroes don't want to give 'em the real skinny?"

"Right." He looked at the card again. "A hundred and seventy-five points? Is that all they think I'm worth?" Part of his mind told him it was pointless to get upset over a contrived number printed on a card that only had vague approximations of his powers. His pride said otherwise.

"Uh, no, no." Kyle shook his head. "It's a lot more now. That's when you were just starting out, remember?" He paused, looking embarrassed. "So, uh, can you sign it for me? Please?"

"Oh. Right." Jericho reached into one of the spare pouches on his utility belt. He'd anticipated having to sign autographs at *some* point, so he'd brought along three marker pens: one in black, one in vivid blue, and one in silver. Holding them up, he spread them out like a hand of cards. "Which one would you like me to use?"

Kyle's expression would've rivaled that of a kid on Christmas morning. He opened his mouth to speak but was cut off as the yellow lights began to flash, and the public-address speakers came to life.

"Attention, all passengers. Attention, all passengers. This train will be passing through Orlando in six minutes. All passengers stopping in Orlando, please move to Cars Four through Five. All passengers for the Orlando to Kennedy Space Center train, please remain in this car. All passengers for the Orlando to Boca Raton train, please move to Car Six. All passengers for the Orlando to Tampa train, please move to Car Seven. Do not forget your luggage ..."

Jericho looked around, then raised his voice to speak over the ongoing announcement. "Well, we're in the right car at least." This was a relief; he disliked having to move up through the cars at the last moment. Then a thought occurred to him, and he slid over to the aisle and got up. Before Kyle or Petra could ask him what he was doing, he'd ducked around the end of the table until he was standing next to Kyle. "Could I get y'all to skootch over a mite? And maybe put off that selfie until we get off the train?"

"Uh, sure," Kyle agreed hastily, nudging Petra. She moved over to the window, leaning forward to look curiously across at Jericho even as Kyle made room. "But why?"

Jericho glanced up at the automatic doors as they slid open and people started coming through. Some wore clothing or other paraphernalia that suggested that they were also attending the Challenger Commemoration ceremony. A few, sporting what he judged to be genuine superhero costumes, nodded in greeting when they saw Jericho.

"That's why," he said as more people entered the car. "I reckon as how it's gonna get a tad bit crowded in here, and I didn't want to get blocked into my seat if someone does something stupid."

"Oh, boy," said Kyle, blinking at the sudden influx. "I didn't actually think about that."

"I'd figured there might be a few people coming through," said Jericho. Looking around, he admitted in a low tone, "Not this many, though."

And if Scout had been with me, they wouldn't be crowding me at all. Damn it, I hope he's gonna be okay.

To take his mind off his worry, he waved the card and markers in front of Kyle. "Like I was saying, which one would you like me to sign it with?"

- End of Part Two -

PART THREE

THE FAÇADE
CRACK'D

Aftermath? What aftermath?
- G-Man

Incoming!
- Smokeshadow

You're shitting me.
- a villain

30
Kennedy Visitor Complex

Twelve minutes later, the train pulled into the maglev terminal servicing the Kennedy Space Center Visitor Complex. From Orlando, they'd pulled a sharp left toward the rising sun and attached to the front of a train coming through from (he guessed) Tampa.

Another few cars must have come out of the Orlando station and coupled on at the front because the indicator signs showed that they'd gone from being Car 2 to Car 5. He had no idea how many cars were connected on behind because the PA system had announced they were stopping at the Kennedy Space Center terminal and added a notification that all passengers for the Kennedy Space Center to Orlando train needed to stay on board.

The trip from Orlando had been almost anti-climactic in its brevity. They'd covered the fifty miles (as measured by his G-sense) in about seven minutes, flashing over the swampland and the Indian River with equal ease. Halfway across the river, they'd had the brief blackout that indicated they were passing another maglev, but nobody else noticed or cared. He was learning to ignore the stomach-turning sideways-flip, but he didn't think he'd ever get *used* to it.

The terminal was almost entirely unlike any other maglev station he'd experienced; not that he'd seen many. It was circular in shape, maybe twenty yards from swampland to roof, and two hundred across. The maglev rail wrapped around it, then joined back on itself to form a teardrop shape.

Along with Kyle and Petra, he ventured onto the concourse to discover that all cars were disembarking passengers simultaneously from points around the circle. There were large stands bearing maps of the terminal and the nearby Kennedy Space Center Visitor Complex, and others with screens showing real-time views of the complex as well as the eight-mile-distant shuttle launch area.

A dozen scan-locks were lined up along one side of a large square block in the center of the concourse. Liberally posted signs indicated that escalators and elevators down could be accessed on the other side. The lines were forming rapidly, but they were being let through lots of eight or ten at a time, so delays were minimal.

Still, Jericho saw other heroes (or at least he assumed they were, from their costumes) chatting with people around them, posing for photos, and signing autographs. They still had half an hour until the event officially got underway, and he suspected that once they got to the complex itself, things were like to get a good deal more hectic. With that in mind, he turned to Kyle and Petra. "Did y'all want to get that selfie now?"

"Sure!" blurted Kyle. From the way he looked at Jericho with near-worship in his eyes, the crush he'd confessed to on the maglev was in no way over and done with. Petra seemed to pick up on this; when Kyle wasn't looking, she rolled her eyes extravagantly and grinned at Jericho.

They were happy enough with the photos each took of the other posing with Jericho, as well as the selfies with all three that both of them took, but then he got to show off a little. It was easy enough to stick the phones to the wall with glue-tags or make them float in mid-air with push-tags; in conjunction with the camera timers, this allowed for some great shots. Especially when Petra got a picture of Kyle staring at his own phone hovering over Jericho's hand.

The crowd had cleared somewhat by the time they were done, so they swiped themselves through a scan-lock, then rode an escalator down. Another memory hit Jericho out of the blue: riding down the escalator during his first visit to Utopia, Luke jogging down the stairs beside him. *The hell's this? Cuz, you too good for stairs now?*

Gritting his teeth, he breathed in deeply through his nostrils. His job was to get out there and wow everyone who had come to enjoy the Challenger Commemoration Day celebrations. He had to keep it together, especially on a day like today. There would always be time for brooding later.

Today, I'm representing Force Majeure. Time to get out there and represent.

They reached the bottom of the escalator, having passed clear through the second floor to get there. Jericho saw the ubiquitous UML ticketing kiosks to the left and right, with signs pointing to restrooms and the like farther back in the building. The main entrance, a broad archway, led out of the maglev terminal onto a covered walkway, crossing a water-filled ditch and passing a sign welcoming them to the Kennedy Space Center visitor complex. After that, it went quite a ways up through the parking lot before entering the Visitor Complex proper. Even from this distance, he could make out a cluster of rockets pointed skyward from within the complex. That was something he definitely wanted to check out when he got the chance.

But first things first.

He turned to Kyle and Petra. "So, uh, yeah. It's been nice talking, but I've got to get over there so they can tell me where to be for the speeches. Did y'all want to give me your numbers, so I can look you up if I ever find myself in Seattle?"

During the conversation, he'd learned that they were both undergrads at Seattle Pacific University, where Kyle studied nursing and Petra majored in communications. They seemed to be friendly folk, and he liked them for more than just the fact that they were the first people he'd met who'd been fans *before* he knew them.

"Uh, sure!" Kyle nodded enthusiastically. He waited until Jericho had his notepad ready, then rattled off his number. Petra also recited hers when Jericho glanced her way; carefully, he wrote down both sets of digits.

"All right then," Jericho said, gesturing toward the archway. "See y'all 'round. Time to go pretend to be a big-time hero." Even as Petra laughed in response to his joke, he turned and headed through the arch.

Ignoring the gentle *pop* from the lightweight force-field he'd known would be there to stop bugs getting in, he moved out from under the walkway awning and activated his flight power. The grav-wings unfurled, and he soared out and away from the maglev terminal. By the time he crossed the perimeter road, he was a hundred feet up and flying north toward the complex.

In this, he wasn't alone. He counted three other airborne costumed figures; two were orbiting the facility and apparently taking photos, while the third one was coming in for a landing. While he wanted to get pictures too, his duties for the day precluded playing tourist immediately, so he angled over slightly and headed for what appeared to be an entrance area, if the broad walkway entering the complex from the parking lot was any indication.

He touched down next to a blue sphere bearing the NASA logo, then dismissed the 'wings and walked onward, looking around for anyone wearing official insignia and a harried expression. The more stressed someone looked, the more likely they were to be running the show. Although this event had been going on every year following the tragic events of July 11, 1997 (which had been set aside as a memorial day for Arfogwyr, both in the United States and in the UK), it couldn't have gotten any easier to manage the crowds.

After he passed by some ticket kiosks, which bore a certain resemblance to the ones used by UML, the next landmark he encountered was a granite fountain. All graceful curves, it had John F. Kennedy's likeness etched into it, along with what Jericho presumed to be a quote from one of the great man's speeches.

"*For the eyes of the world now look into space to the moon and to the planets beyond,*" he murmured. "*And we have vowed that we shall not see it governed by a hostile flag of conquest, but by a banner of freedom and peace.*"

As he spoke the words, the fountain literally played a sound clip of a rocket taking off, with the splashing water serving as a counterpoint to the stirring sound. The whole presentation was intensely inspiring, and he felt goosebumps running up and down his spine.

The trouble was, this wasn't getting him where he needed to be. *Stop standing around like a hick from the sticks*, he told himself firmly, and kept moving past the fountain.

About forty or fifty yards farther on, he saw a row of ticket-collection booths under a shade-roof with the word EXPLORE—each letter at least six feet tall—on top. And just in front of the ticket collection area, he spotted his goal; a gaggle of people in high-vis vests and lanyards, all paying attention to one of their number. He couldn't make out much detail at this distance, but he was willing to bet she had a fancier lanyard than the rest. Quickening his pace, he headed in their direction.

"Ah, G-Man, hello." While the woman didn't look much like Ms. Colburn—maybe twenty years younger, with a permanent suntan—they shared a distinct no-nonsense air. It was clear he would've won the bet with himself, as her lanyard was red and gold, whereas everyone else's was black. Like the others, the attached card had VOLUNTEER emblazoned across it. "Sylvia Rogan, site coordinator. It's good to see new faces here. Or have you attended this event before?"

He shook her proffered hand, matching the businesslike grip. "I'm afraid not, ma'am," he admitted, with another quick glance around. "Though I reckon I might come back, given a chance. This place looks downright interesting."

She smiled tightly in appreciation. "It's all of that. Now, are you aware of how we'll be proceeding?"

"Nine-thirty start," he answered promptly. "There'll be speeches, then we mingle with the public for the rest of the day. Fireworks in the evening, then we finish up around seven or eight. That's basically all I got told, ma'am."

"There's a little more detail than that, but those are the bare bones, yes." Sylvia gave him a discerning stare. "There'll be quite a few speeches, so keep it short and to the point. Don't try to be funny; you'll only seem desperate. If you do make them laugh, pretend you did it on purpose and wrap it up as soon as possible. After your speech, you sit down in the marked area, and the next guy takes over. Is there anything that's not clear?"

Jericho shook his head. "No, ma'am, you've pretty well covered it. Where do y'all want me to wait?"

"I'll show him," offered one of the other volunteers, stepping forward. She had her hair tied up in a bun, and radiated brisk efficiency.

"You do that. See you 'round, G-Man." Sylvia turned away, her attention already on a dozen other tasks.

"Come on, sir," said the volunteer, leading the way past the ticket booths and farther into the complex. "It's just up around here."

As they strolled along, Jericho gawked at the rockets set up in a cluster to their left. He'd thought they looked fantastic when he came out of the maglev terminal, now hundreds of yards behind him; up close, they were stunningly spectacular. "Miss, are those all real, or just scale models?"

The volunteer glanced from side to side before answering. Instinctively, he looked around as well, unsure of what he was searching for. Her subsequent words floored him. "To be honest, I have no idea. But I do need to talk to you. There's something you should know … Jericho."

What?

He stared at her. "Wait—do I know—"

Half-turning her head toward him, she raised her sunglasses and gave him a familiar smart-ass grin. "Told you I'd be keeping in touch."

Now that she was 'herself' again, the shock of recognition was almost palpable. *Smokeshadow. Goddamn it, she snuck right up on me in plain sight.* "Yeah, but—what are you *doing* here?"

Letting the sunglasses drop back into place, she gestured at her vest and lanyard with a succinct movement. "Volunteering, obviously. But I need to talk to you. *Urgently.* Got any plans for after the speeches?"

"Well, no." He couldn't think of any right that second, but he knew if he *had* had any, they would've gone on the ash-heap the moment she dropped the *'don't notice me'* act. "I gotta talk to you, too."

"Alright then, we can walk and talk afterward." Her attitude shifted smoothly back into 'volunteer' mode as they rounded what looked like an open-air café under an awning and started toward an undercroft area between two buildings. Demountable amphitheater seating was being constructed next to something called ATX, opposite the undercroft.

"Wait, why can't we talk now?" Whatever she had to say, he wanted to know about it.

"Too many people," she said, tilting her head toward the volunteers bustling about and working on the seating. "Waiting area's just over there. Go, be with your people. I'll find you later."

Looking to where she was pointing, he saw a bunch of costumed heroes waiting in the corner of the undercroft. "Wait, I wanted to—"

But when he turned his head back again, she was gone. Somehow, in the few seconds he'd been distracted, she'd managed to slip away and become just another volunteer. Not that he was hugely surprised. Aggravated, yes; surprised, no. That was so *her.*

"God*damn* it," he muttered and headed over to join the group of heroes. Whatever Smokeshadow had going on, he would have to wait to find out.

All I can say is, this better be good.

31
Commemorating a Hero

Jericho had to admit, the volunteers were efficient as all get-out. They'd had the podium and accompanying seats set up less than five minutes after he arrived, though his best estimate had the latter holding about half the people who'd shown up so far. For the rest, he figured, it would be standing room only. He and his fellow heroes had been told to keep out of the way until they were needed, so that was what they were doing.

Standing with the group next to the NASA Space Shop, he glanced at the others as he waited for his turn to go out and speak. Buddy Power was there, clad in the iconic Team Power armor; while they'd never been formally introduced, the youngster had given Jericho a discreet thumb's up when they first recognized each other. He wasn't sure if it was meant to convey *'you're dating my sibling, good for you'*, or *'good luck with your speech'*, but he appreciated the gesture either way.

All-Star was another familiar face whom Jericho hadn't really expected to see. He'd neatened his beard up and replaced his torn costume top with a sturdier-looking sleeveless one composed mainly of leather. The five-pointed star insignia had been stamped into the leather itself, and the whole thing dyed red and gold.

"Hey," said the Manhattan Justice member, offering his fist to bump. "Good to see you again, G-Man. Is the big guy here, too?"

Jericho winced at the reminder. "We stopped off to help out with the quake in Jefferson City this morning. He got damaged, pushing me out of the way of some falling debris. Relentless reckons the Technologist can fix him, but he was hurt pretty bad."

"I didn't know about that," Buddy Power said. "Must've been before we got there. Sorry to hear about it."

"Yeah, damn, that sucks." All-Star shook his head sympathetically. "I'd see if Drone could do something for you, but he works best with remote-controlled stuff, not AIs. And besides, you've already *got* the Technologist on the case."

"Maybe Dad can help—" began Buddy.

"Shh!" hissed Tomahawk from beside them. "I'm trying to listen!"

Suddenly aware of his faux pas and not wanting to compound it by speaking again, Jericho ducked his head slightly and held up his hand in silent apology. At the same time, Buddy shut up, a grimace on his face.

"… thank you, thank you," said the older gentleman at the microphone. Jericho hadn't quite gotten his name, but he was apparently the administrator for the whole complex. "At this moment, twenty-eight years ago today, the space shuttle *Challenger* was being prepped for launch. It was a far colder day than today, with the temperature hovering around the freezing point. This was the tenth launch of that particular orbiter and the twenty-fifth of the space shuttle program. After the shuttle was mated with the solid rocket boosters and the external fuel tank on the twenty-second, it was transported from the Vehicle Assembly Building to the launch pad, a procedure that took six hours.

"The green light was finally given to launch on the twenty-eighth, six days later. However, as we all know, it never reached space. Seventy-three seconds into the flight, a catastrophic failure occurred, resulting in the external tank coming apart and the solid rocket boosters flying free. The orbiter itself proceeded to break up due to aerodynamic stresses. This is unsurprising, given that it was tumbling out of control at nearly twice the speed of sound."

The speaker paused to take a drink of water from a glass on the lectern. Not one person made a sound; Jericho understood that they were awaiting the resolution of the deliberate cliff-hanger. Everyone knew what had happened that day, but they wanted to *hear* it.

When the glass was placed back on the lectern, the delicate *tink* was audible to all. The man cleared his throat.

"When we saw the massive cloud of vapor, it looked like a fireball. It really did. Everyone thought the crew was dead. *They* thought they were dead. And honestly, ninety-nine times out of a hundred, they would have been. But the impossible had, on that day, become possible.

"On board that orbiter, there were seven astronauts. Five men, two women. Their names are among the most famous in the world. For the first time in all of history, one of their number gained super-powers just in time to save them all. We don't know how or why it happened; we may never yet know who it was. But one of them became the hero we know as Challenger. And the world was changed forever."

Another sip of water. *Tink* went the glass. The audience was spellbound, and rightly so. It was superb showmanship.

"I was there on that day. The first we knew of their survival was when that glorious red and gold shuttle, a fuselage and control surfaces composed entirely of force fields with the crew cabin the only solid matter within it, came swooping back into view and glided in for a perfect landing. We thought we were seeing things. And then, when the force fields dissipated and the crew cabin settled on the tarmac, when the hatch opened and seven bewildered astronauts climbed out, we knew we'd witnessed something entirely new in human experience. And it is the appearance of the first Enabled, the advent of Challenger, that we celebrate on this day, every year."

The audience burst into applause, acknowledged by a bow from the elderly man. He stepped off the podium, bowed again, then moved to take his seat in the front row of the audience.

"Thank you for those inspiring words, sir." Someone else had taken the podium, but Jericho was distracted by one of the volunteers beckoning to him. For a second, he thought it was Smokeshadow, but no such luck. While it was technically possible for her to pretend to be a guy—her hyperweave costume and her Prodigy focus worked in synergy to *seriously* mess with people's perceptions of her—there'd be no real point to it.

"You're up next," the young man whispered. "Come out this way, then fly up and over. Dramatic entrance."

"Oh. Right." Jericho hadn't even thought of that, though it was apparent now in hindsight why they'd chosen this specific place to hold the speeches.

He hustled out the other side of the undercroft and activated the enhancement harness, allowing the grav-wings to unfurl. At the same time, he made a mental note to ask the Technologist to maybe install a battery charge monitor that he could watch while he was out and about in the field. *Not* having it fail on him like it had in Jefferson City would be a huge plus.

"And now, a few words from the heroes who have come here to help celebrate this day with you," he heard from the far side of the undercroft. "First up is the representative from Force Majeure, who's already managed to make a splash on the news … G-Man!"

He didn't need the slap on the shoulder or the whispered, "You're on!" to know this was his cue. He took off vertically, then swooped over the top of the building into view of the audience behind. The number of people staring straight at him right then, along with the TV cameras, nearly caused him to falter, but he steeled his resolve. Force Majeure had put a considerable amount of trust and effort into him, and he couldn't let them down. Besides, he'd come too far and done too much to punk out now.

Flaring the 'wings for effect, he dropped down onto the podium then allowed them to dissipate once he was on solid footing. "Hi," he said, stepping up to the microphone. "I'm G-Man, and it's good to see all y'all here today."

The ripple of applause that passed through the audience did a lot to boost his confidence. Although he'd been doing the superhero thing for a little over two years now, he'd never enjoyed a massive amount of public recognition.

The stunt he'd pulled with the South Side Mall hadn't been done with publicity in mind so much as the need to blitz his way in there fast enough to catch up with Jack Portman before the killer got away. Even that had been a group effort between himself, Thomas, and Smokeshadow. While the man who'd murdered Luke and Bobbi had fallen to his death rather than submit to capture, the exploit had gotten Jericho into Force Majeure, so he called it an overall win.

This, on the other hand, was pure publicity from go to whoa, and there'd be no do-overs. The eyes of America, including (but not limited to) Force Majeure, Team Power, *and his own family* were on him. If he screwed up now, *everyone* would see it. For a moment, he imagined Luke out there in the audience, throwing him a lazy grin. *Havin' fun yet, cuz?*

"It's good to see you too, G-Man." The smartly dressed man acting as master of ceremonies offered a beaming smile and held out his hand in greeting. Numbly, Jericho shook it. "I understand you're originally from Georgia."

"Uh, yeah, I'm from Savannah. Born and raised." Belatedly, Jericho remembered to address his words to the microphone attached to the lectern.

"Savannah, right. I've heard good things about it." The repetition of his home city's name was so smooth it took Jericho a moment to realize that his own voice had probably been too quiet to reach everyone in the audience. But now that the name had been spoken, everyone would think they'd heard him say it first. Smokeshadow had once explained the myriad non-intuitive ways the human brain could be induced to fool itself into believing things that simply weren't true; this was just one of the minor ones. "So, would you like to say a few words to our audience?"

"Why, sure." Jericho took a moment to adjust the microphone upward slightly to cover his still-taut nerves. Placing both hands on the podium, he faced the mass of people who had come to see not only the celebrations of Commemoration Day but also the heroes who were attending … including *him*. It was a daunting challenge to think of something to say that would be relevant to all of them.

"I never met Challenger," he said, just to get himself rolling. "I would've liked to have. Inspire was the best of the best, and Challenger was their guiding light. He showed us all how heroes should be. He proved that we can rise above and become better than before. Even if we'd had Enabled anyway, there wouldn't *be* any Challenger Act without Challenger. We wouldn't have the protections we do now that allow us to be heroes without having to look over our shoulders all the time. We'd still have folks out there like Unmask, fixing to shame us or worse just for trying to make the world a better place, with no laws to stop 'em. Which'd be a pity, 'cause when the consequences of doing the right thing are more'n whether you'll get hurt then and there, when just *trying* to help out is like to put your life and those of your loved ones at stake …" He paused for a second, looking out over the crowd. "Well, that's when even the most dedicated hero could be excused for asking, '*why am I even doing this*'?"

He paused to take a breath, his eyes searching the audience. They were all looking back at him, silent. Had he screwed up? Gone too far?

"But thanks to Challenger, we *have* those protections," he said. "Challenger gave me and every other Enabled here the chance—the *right*—to be a hero. Without the Challenger Act, I reckon a whole passel of us wouldn't have put on the mask and gone out to help other folks where they were needed. And that's what we all owe to him on this day. Thank you."

As the audience exploded into applause, he bowed briefly in acknowledgment. Most of what he'd just said had been off the top of his head, and he couldn't even recall half of it.

I'll have to watch the footage later and hope I don't sound too corny.

Moving almost on autopilot, he stepped off the podium and headed down to the row of chairs set aside for the purpose. He took the seat labeled with his logo, fully aware that he was still under scrutiny but glad his active participation in the ceremony was over. Now he could settle back and enjoy the show.

Buddy Power was next, flying up and over the building just as Jericho had. His suit was less bulky than his father's, but Jericho didn't make the mistake of thinking there weren't some horrible surprises in store for anyone who thought the kid would be a pushover. He was well-spoken for someone his age (Jericho suspected a heads-up display), relating an anecdote about how his parents had teamed up with Inspire back in the day to take down a people-smuggling ring. The story only had a moderately happy ending—False Flag and Charnel, the terror villains suspected to be responsible, had slipped away when the operation collapsed—but the victims had been saved, and that had to be good enough.

As an encore, he spoke briefly about the disaster the team had attended (and was still attending) in Jefferson City; because of *course* the team jet had delivered him to Kennedy before Jericho got there on the train. Applause greeted the culmination of the second tale, and Buddy took a bow before sitting beside Jericho. The chair creaked but didn't seem in danger of collapsing.

Next up was All-Star. Limited to a purely Prodigy powerbase, he lacked the option of pulling off a flashy entrance, so he didn't try. But a confident stride got him up onto the podium, and he got a laugh from the audience by cheerfully acknowledging that he was the member of Manhattan Justice most able to be spared from its crime-fighting duties in New York. For all his down-home attitude, he still projected a certain amount of presence via his impressive physique; he got a rousing round of applause before he, too, sat down.

One by one, the other team representatives and solo heroes stepped up to say their piece. Not every team or hero in America had made an appearance—the visitor complex would've needed a considerably larger venue to hold them all if they had—but there were enough to make for good publicity and good television. Jericho met quite a few of them in the mingling after the ceremony, mostly in passing.

The marker pens he'd brought along got a good workout as well. While nobody else had brought along fantasy hero league cards to be autographed, he signed basically everything else that could take a signature. Flyers for the Commemoration Day, maps of the complex, photos of himself from Force Majeure publicity stills, random scraps of paper, various items of clothing, and one guy's shoulder. By the time the initial rush was over, he was left wondering which of these people had known of him the whole time and which had only heard of him when they found out he was representing Force Majeure at the ceremony.

Not that it was a critical issue. While he'd joined Force Majeure for recognition, he wasn't in it for the fame. Just to be known and acknowledged for his actual contribution was good enough for him.

As the crowd gradually spread out through the complex, Jericho looked around for Smokeshadow. He definitely wanted to speak to her, and it seemed she had something to talk to him about as well. But everyone who approached him appeared to be a genuine fan, seeking an autograph or a selfie rather than a moment alone with him.

After a few more minutes spent wandering aimlessly, he decided enough was enough. He had all day to find her, or she to find him, so he figured he'd get his touristing in while he had the chance. Kicking over his enhancement harness, he manifested the grav-wings and took to the air.

Once he was up above the buildings, he pulled his arms free to get his phone out of its pouch. There were no rules *against* using the high-quality camera for personal enjoyment, though he knew all photos he took *would* be seen by whoever accessed the phone next. That was fine; he didn't intend to take shots of anything that might make his mama swoon.

Swooping toward the visitor center entrance, he snapped photos of the fountain he'd seen when he first came in, and the globe beyond that. Then he banked around and flew back toward the Challenger display building. Slowing to a hover, he took pictures of the massive external tank and solid rocket boosters set up outside.

The cluster of rockets caught his attention next; he overflew the area and snapped an aerial shot of the Saturn V on display before coming in for a landing in their midst. Dismissing the 'wings, he wandered among the rockets, reading the plaques and marveling at the sheer guts a person would need in order to climb into one of the tiny capsules on display and let themselves get shot into a thoroughly inhospitable environment.

He'd strolled the length of the Saturn V, tilting his head to imagine what it looked like standing vertical, when he became aware of someone watching him while leaning against the Apollo re-entry capsule that had been set up on the ground nearby. One minute, he could've sworn there was nobody there, and the next ... "Really?" he asked. "You couldn't just walk up and say hello?"

"Why bother?" Smokeshadow asked, straightening up and giving him a cheeky grin. "I knew you were going to come straight to me anyway. Why not let you have your tourist fun first?"

"Okay, but first, I still want to see the Challenger display. And second, how did you know I was gonna come here?" He waved his arm around at the rocket display.

She came on over and gave him a peck on the cheek. "Because you were drooling all over them when I was walking you to the ceremony site, you big doofus. There was no way you'd stay away for long once it was over. So, what did you want to talk to me about?"

He glared at her, but she entirely failed to wilt under the weight of his displeasure. "Was it you? You know what I'm talking about. Was that you?"

"It was," she confirmed at once. "I saw a chance and took it. Hey, don't look at me like that. I figured that if I was going to be running the most kick-ass secret underground criminal organization in Utopia, I needed a serious edge. So, I ran the info-heist to see what I could scrounge out of their databanks before they slammed the door in my face. I'll admit I kinda cut it close; I nearly didn't make it out of there. But that's not what I'm here to talk to you about. I'm more concerned with what happened in the aftermath."

He frowned. "Aftermath? What aftermath?"

32
Attempting Damage Control

Smokeshadow

Chelsea looked searchingly at G-Man. "Okay, before I go into that? I need you to understand that I didn't want this. I never wanted anyone to get hurt. That's not how I play the game."

"Okay, granted," he said cautiously. She could tell from his expression and tone that he believed her for the most part, though he was still just a little dubious about her motives in general.

Which, in all honesty, was entirely fair, considering that the last time they'd spoken, she'd told him to his face that she intended to become the boss of Utopia City's most stylish new underground criminal empire. She also knew he maintained a near-medieval level of loyalty toward anyone he considered a friend or an ally. This was almost certainly one of the main reasons he hadn't already attempted to track her down and bring her to justice.

"Keep talking," G-Man said grimly. "Who got hurt?"

She sighed. He wasn't going to like this. "They probably told you that I grabbed some really high-value data, right? Did they happen to fill you in on what it was?" It was a shot in the dark, but miracles had been known to happen.

His next words dashed her hopes. "You don't know what it was, they don't know what it was, *I* don't know what it was." He spread his hands. "Does *anyone* know what it was?"

"I suspect two people did," she said. From his involuntary flinch, she figured he'd caught on to the subtext behind her wording. "But now we're back to 'nobody knows' territory again."

His mouth firmed, and not in a good way. He understood, all right. "Talk to me."

The more she drew the story out, the softer the emotional blow. "Okay, so let's rewind to Christmas Eve. I got out of the precinct house *this far* ahead of the cavalry." She held her finger and thumb a fraction of an inch apart, miming a very close call. "Once I was free and clear, I logged onto the dark web and put the word out that I needed a decryption done for files taken off a Force Majeure server." Trying to defuse the situation with humor, she gave him a sly grin. "You can imagine how that might draw a certain amount of interest."

He refused to be mollified. "How many people did you farm it out to?"

The more witnesses around us, the less likelihood of him flying off the handle when he learns the truth.

Recalling his interest in the Challenger display, she gestured wordlessly in that direction and started walking. He kept pace with her; she could tell he was listening intently.

"Just one," she said. "But he said he would hand it over to a friend of his, who was good at decryption. I'd had dealings with this guy before, and he'd never tried to bullshit me. So, I put the information in a zip file and mailed it off to him."

He lowered his voice as they neared a dome-shaped play area, busy with children. "What did you get back?"

"The code phrase telling me the first few files had been decrypted. It took his guy less than two weeks." She was obscurely proud of that fact. "Then I waited for the actual data."

"And you didn't get it." He was observant enough in his own right, given enough clues.

"I didn't get it," she confirmed. "But in this sort of situation, it's best not to be hasty. Information so sensitive it needed to be encrypted wouldn't become obsolete overnight. I waited a day, then sent a query about whether he'd actually mailed me the files through." She waved a hand vaguely in the air, trying to convey a sense of fog with no substance. "Nada. Well, *almost* nada."

"What do you mean, 'almost'?" Though G-Man's voice remained steady, his stance and tension betrayed his apprehension. He might be a precious cinnamon roll compared to the depths to which she was willing to stoop, but he was in no way stupid.

"Someone tried to send a data-crawler after me." She tried to express a sense of amused indignation, but she wasn't sure if she'd succeeded. At the time, the incident had been a very unwelcome surprise. "They didn't get anywhere near me—you *know* how good my security is—but it means my contact had been blown at his end, and they were trying to back-trace me."

He nodded slowly. "How do you know one or both of them hadn't decided to sell to the highest bidder instead, and fake being blown so you wouldn't look too closely?"

That definitely showed he was thinking about what she was telling him, rather than blindly following the narrative. And it would've been a plausible scenario, except for a bunch of inconvenient facts which stated otherwise.

"No." She shook her head. "I gave it a week and a half, then cleared the line and checked my contact's online log. A few seconds after he sent me the code for the successful decryption, he followed up with *'be right back'* then just disconnected. He never came back on. I waited a few more days after that, just in case someone tried another back-trace, then I started sniffing around."

Though she kept her tone light, the reality was somewhat different. For the first time since she got her powers, she'd mistrusted her tech's ability to keep her safe, and slept intermittently with an INCH bag close at hand. Only after the days had passed and nobody kicked in the door of her decoy apartment did she dare venture back online.

"But why? I mean, it wasn't like you were going to get anything out of it, right?" From the tone of G-Man's voice, he knew why she'd done it.

She gave him a sideways glance to let him know she was well aware of the shape of his thoughts. "'*Anything*' can include basic satisfaction. My next step was to do something I'd always said I'd never do." Even for someone who made up her own rules on the fly, the decision had involved hours of soul-searching, deep into the long, lonely watches of the night. "I backtracked my contact, located his IP address, and nailed down where he lived."

He couldn't have known what she'd discovered, but from the look on his face, he knew *something* was coming down the pike. "And where was that?"

Now, she turned and looked at him full-on, unable to hide the sadness in her eyes. This next bit was really going to suck for both of them. "Savannah, Georgia."

"What? No." He shook his head, but she read it as more of a reflex action than a rebuttal. "When was this? When did it happen?"

She continued to face him squarely. "You know when it happened."

He did know; she could see it in his eyes. But he didn't want to admit it even to himself. "Tell me."

Well, you asked. "January fourth. Franklin Tucker was the decryption expert. He was also a conspiracy theorist with a hate-on against Force Majeure. You *know* this. You attended the murder scene." Perhaps it was a little heavy-handed, but he needed to know the truth without any chance of hiding it from himself.

"He was," G-Man confirmed. "I did." He tilted his head. "And who was your contact?"

She took a deep breath. *And here it comes.* "Stephen LaMonde."

From the burgeoning expression of astonishment on his face, he had not expected that particular revelation. "Wait, you're saying *Stephen* was caught up in this? Him dying in that fire wasn't an accident?"

"I'm ninety-nine percent sure of it." She sighed unhappily, almost certain she already knew the answers to both the questions she was about to ask. "Did LaMonde dislike Force Majeure? And does the username PowerSlammer eighty-one mean anything to you?"

"He despised them with a passion," he admitted, not at all to her surprise. "And I've never heard that username before … but he *was* born in nineteen eighty-one."

The birthdate was one clue she'd missed, but it only served to add to the growing pile of circumstantial evidence she'd already collected. "I was thinking 'Power' could've referenced his webzine, and 'Slammer' could be a play on words for S. LaMonde?"

"Oh, good Lord, yes." He groaned; for a moment, she thought he was about to facepalm. "The asshat *loved* puns like that. He thought it made him look so damn smart, especially when nobody else could get them."

"From my dealings with him, I'm not the slightest bit surprised," she murmured. She put her hand on his arm, concerned about the mélange of emotions currently churning back and forth in his head, judging from the shifting micro-expressions on his face. "Are you alright?"

"Yeah. No. I dunno. This thing about Stephen's just thrown me for a loop, is all." They were coming up to Constellation Plaza, a circle of umbrella-shaded tables around a large stone ball engraved with the star patterns as seen in the night sky and suspended in a water feature. Chelsea had heard that sort of thing was called a Kugel fountain but didn't know why. Pulling out a chair at an empty table, G-Man slumped into it and stared moodily at the massive ball. As they watched, a bunch of giggling kids pushed on it, causing it to rotate smoothly in place.

Chelsea sat down alongside him. "Sorry about hitting you with it like that. But I figured you'd be better off knowing."

"I reckon." He leaned back and looked up at the sky. There were only a few fluffy clouds up there, but he stared at them as though they contained the secrets of the universe. "I dunno what to feel. It's like … I had this thought that I'd let him down, but …"

"But you hadn't." In the next moment, the epiphany struck Chelsea. "Even though people have been telling you that you couldn't have rescued him, you've been convinced you might've had a chance, if you'd only known he was there."

"Mm-hmm." It was almost as though the admission unlocked another emotion inside him, a wave of rising anger. She could see it in the tension of his hands on the table.

"You need to get it into your head that he was dead already, and you might've died too if you went in there to save him." She shook her head. "There are several ways they could've done it, but they *would* have made sure he was dead when they left him." She carefully neglected to point out that they might have left marks on LaMonde that required a fire to erase; G-Man didn't need that on his mind as well.

"His car was gone. I've never been able to figure it out. Why take his car?" He was already off on another tangent, probably because he didn't want to think about his ex-boyfriend being murdered.

The reason was clear enough to Chelsea. "If the fire didn't cover all the clues, it would've made it look like a home invasion gone wrong. Take his computer equipment and steal his car as well. Dump the car at the nearest chop shop, and they're free and clear."

"Hm. That's a thought." He seemed to derive a certain grim satisfaction from the notion. "Maybe not as free and clear as they think."

Knowing the connections he had access to, she wished him all the luck in the world chasing down that clue in the Savannah underworld. "I suppose so. What I'm *not* sure of is who might've done it. Well, I've got half an idea, but proving it's going to be difficult, to say the least. Laying hands on the culprit is going to be even more so."

"Culprits, plural." He held up two fingers. "Two women."

"Really?" Just when she thought all the facts were on the table, he'd managed to surprise her. Again, she wasn't sure where he'd gotten the information, or whether he'd tell her even if she asked politely. "That's interesting ... though, to be honest, it's really not going to help a great deal."

"So, who's your guess for the bad guys?" he asked. "Which rock are we gonna have to kick over?" From the edge in his voice, he was primed and ready to do the kicking.

This was a question she'd already asked herself, more than once. She'd put a lot of thought into it and spent considerable effort attempting to track down the perpetrator herself, with zero results to show for it. Which meant that whoever was sitting on the rabbit-hole they'd vanished down had *serious* throw weight behind them.

The obvious answer—for a given definition of the word—varied considerably, depending entirely on who might be asked.

Tucker's conspiracy-nut buddies, for instance, would fall over themselves pointing their fingers directly at Force Majeure. While Chelsea didn't agree with every single one of the Utopia team's policies, especially the 'proactive policing' aspect, the possibility of them having a hand in this seemed about as likely as Doc Iridium rising from the ashes and running for President. Clandestine assassin teams just didn't seem their vibe. They were far more likely to kick in the front door loud and proud, and make sure *everybody* knew not to pull that crap on them a second time.

A more moderate answer would be to seek out whichever high-tech villain team was active at the time and see if they were a good fit. Chelsea didn't favor that one either, for the simple reason that the surviving villain teams were the ones who already knew not to pull that crap the *first* time. Anyone willing to commit murder to steal some of Force Majeure's data after it had been advertised on the dark web, she personally counted as suicidal.

The view she favored wouldn't have been popular among either the conspiracy nuts or the moderate crowd, but she didn't care. "My guess is, someone with overseas interests was snooping around online when Tucker finished the decrypt. When they caught wind of what was going on, they jumped on it with both feet."

G-Man frowned, clearly not making the connection. "What do overseas interests have to do with it?"

She leaned across the table and lowered her voice. "Well, look at it this way. How valuable would it be to a foreign entity, even a technically friendly one, to be able to exert control over an American hero?" It was clear enough to her. "How many nations that don't like America must be snooping around, trying to get their hooks into one of our Enabled, like they would've done with Challenger years ago if the Act hadn't gone through?"

He blinked, patently surprised. "But I thought that was just a conspiracy theory."

"Yeah, right." She snorted derisively, wondering how hard it would blow his mind if she told him every dirty little secret she knew about what some celebrities did behind closed doors. "Sometimes, those things are true. So anyway, this Tucker guy did the decrypt. As soon as he saw what he had—whatever it actually was—he went onto some of his favorite conspiracy sites and started promising an info-dump once he finished opening up the rest of the files he'd gotten *'from a trusted contact'*. I know this because I found those posts *after* he was murdered. Timestamps checked out."

"Well, damn," muttered G-Man. "That's gotta suck."

She nodded. "I'd told LaMonde to keep his head down about it, but either he neglected to pass that warning on to Tucker, or Tucker just chose to go his own way. Anyway, I'm thinking one of these foreign agents caught wind of it and moved in on Tucker just after he'd sent the data through to LaMonde. Once they stole the data and got his contact's location out of him, they murdered him then went and did the same over at LaMonde's."

From the look in G-Man's eye, he was on the same page as her, albeit reluctantly. "Yeah, I got it. Because this sort of information is most valuable when *one* copy exists."

"Mm-hmm. They were probably still on site, setting up the fire, when you were investigating the Tucker murder. In fact, I'm willing to bet Tucker was going to be passed off as an accidental death in a fire as well, but they had to hurry things along when they found out about LaMonde."

He seemed partially convinced, but there was doubt in his expression. "Okay, it sounds pretty plausible, but what if it was local villains instead? I mean, I can see foreign spies wanting to blackmail Force Majeure to do what they want, but any locals would just want to shut them down altogether. And what better way than to air their dirty laundry in public?"

She shook her head. "Nah. Nobody good enough to pull off a grab like that would be stupid enough to try it with Force Majeure's data. Though it really doesn't change things either way. LaMonde is still dead, but it's definitely not your fault. The bad guys, whoever they are, have the files Tucker managed to decrypt. I've still got the *en*crypted stuff, but now I have to find someone else to *de*crypt it." She grimaced with unfeigned irritation. "This sort of thing is a whole lot easier in the movies."

"No." There was steel in the word, and she stared at him. That was the most forceful he'd been around her in … well, ever.

Did I push him too far?

"What do you mean, 'no'?" Almost instinctively, she began to look for an exit strategy.

"I mean *no*, you will not do anything more with this information." He stood up from the chair. "It's already killed two people. You didn't mean it to, I get that. Your theft of the data … well, I don't *like* it, but it's not like I can go back in time and make it not happen. What's done is done. But this ends now, and we're going to fix things as best we can."

This was definitely a first. Subtly, Chelsea felt the dynamic between them beginning to shift. Until this point, she'd been able to define her goals without let or hindrance by him, despite his membership in Force Majeure and her stated aim to become a criminal underlord in his city. Based solely on previous experience, she had assumed that he'd always defer to her judgment in such matters. But now, for the first time, with his goals directly opposing hers ... he *wasn't* stepping aside for her.

"Are you going to ... arrest me or something?" She was poised and ready to step away from him, to duck out of sight and become someone else.

Hopefully, she wouldn't have to. When push came to shove, he'd trusted her unreservedly with his secret identity *and* the well-being of the Survivors. This was the first time ever that anyone had put that level of trust in her *after* finding out her skills and capabilities. It was unique in her experience, and she didn't want to lose it.

He snorted with something approaching amusement, the tension leaching out of his shoulders. "Nope. I owe you too much. Helping me with the Survivors, getting them out of town, backing me up all the way with the South Side raid, and throwing Thomas and me together; I can't ever repay you for all that. But you *are* out of your depth with this stolen data, and I'm going to need you to hand over all your encrypted copies before anyone *else* gets hurt. Especially you."

All the cards were indeed now on the table. This was definitely a G-Man move, to the core.

"And then what? What are *you* going to do with them?" If she'd asked any other superhero, she would've bet dollars to donuts they didn't have a definitive plan in mind. At best, they'd be going all-out to cover their asses. And no matter what their intentions were, they'd refuse to tell her on general principles.

Not so G-Man. "Give it back to the Technologist. He decrypts it, finds out exactly what data's been stolen, and works out a strategy for damage control. Not knowing what's been taken means he'll be playing catch-up until the bad guys make their move."

It was a plan, she had to admit. Not a *great* plan from the point of view of G-Man's continued membership with Force Majeure, much less her own plans to use the information as leverage, but better than most. It *would* give the team its best chance to counteract the theft, which was what he was aiming at.

Because he's G-Man.

Personally, she wasn't thrilled about it, not least because it didn't give her any strong excuse to say no. He had to know he was in for the reaming of a lifetime from the entire original membership, possibly even expulsion from the team. Because sure as shooting, they'd ask him what he knew about the data thief. Just as guaranteed, he'd refuse to divulge anything meaningful about her. *That* much, at least, she knew for a fact.

Unhappily, she looked at him. "Even if I wanted to right now, I can't. It's back in Utopia." She couldn't keep it from him forever without betraying his trust somehow, but she could at least give him a reprieve and a chance to rethink his plan.

He wasn't taking the bait. His tone was reasonable, but an undercurrent warned her his patience was wearing thin. "Then I'm going to need you to hand it over, the moment we get back. You can still do your thing with your secret underground criminal empire, just without that data."

Dammit. She wrinkled her nose at him. "You're no fun. You do realize this, right?"

"Don't care. I just want you to be safe as—ah, *crap!*" Some sort of realization seemed to hit him, and he pulled his phone out of a belt pouch.

"Okay, what now?" she snarked. "Did you think of someone else you could spoil the fun of?" She didn't really mean it, but what right did G-Man have to demand she give the data back?

Well, apart from being a superhero and a member of Force Majeure. Where I stole it from in the first place.

"Kind of, actually, yeah." He woke up the phone and scrolled rapidly down the screen, then tapped it in the manner of someone putting a phone call through. Sliding the phone back into the pouch—*oh, right. Remote earpiece*—he glanced around idly as he apparently waited for the call to connect.

"Who're you calling?" she asked in a low tone. "And what's the rush?"

He held up one finger in a 'wait' gesture. "Yeah, hi, Detective Villanova. G-Man here ... yeah, how've you been? Yeah, I've been good too. Listen, about the thumb drive we retrieved from the Tucker murder scene. Have you made any progress with it, because you said you'd forward any ... what? You're certain-sure about that?" His chin came up, and Chelsea figured he'd just raised his eyebrows. "How'd that happen?"

A few moments passed while he made monosyllabic noises, occasionally nodding absently. "Okay, yeah ... yeah, if I hear anything, I'll let you know ... yeah, you take care. Yeah, you too. Bye."

Reaching up, he pressed a hidden switch on his helmet, then glanced at Chelsea. "You heard that?"

"Your end, anyway." She looked at him curiously. "What happened?"

He sighed gustily. "Fire in the evidence lockup area. Everything that wasn't solid metal went up in smoke. They were lucky it didn't spread to the rest of the precinct house. But at least nobody died. They didn't even see who did it."

"Well, that's not suspicious at all." She raised her eyebrows. "The perpetrators didn't know about the thumb drive, or they would've grabbed it when they popped Tucker. So, how'd they find out about it after the fact and lift it out of evidence holding, much less set the fire to cover their tracks?"

He shrugged. "Search me. The only people who knew about it were me, Black Dragon, the cops, and the Technologist."

Chelsea began to get a sinking feeling. "Same Black Dragon from when you were going in for your initial interview? Couldn't stop talking, swears like it's an Olympic event?"

A moment later, he got it too. "No. Aw, *no*. She wouldn't have, would she? Surely she would've known better than that?" To her discerning ear, it sounded like he was trying to convince himself.

"Are you asking me or telling me?" She put her hand on his arm. "Listen to me. Whether she did or not, it doesn't matter now. Like you said earlier, what's done is done. She may have run her mouth, or they might've had a line into the precinct house just in case. Either way, it's gone." Despite her attempt to be upbeat, the sinking feeling persisted. "And I'm guessing it was decrypted. Had the cops looked at it? Could they give you details of what was on it?"

"No, actually." His expression cleared slightly. "They tried, but the thumb drive itself was code-locked. Six wrong codes, and it would've wiped itself. Wouldn't even allow copying until the right key went into it."

"That's something, at least." She felt the first tinge of hope. "If Tucker code-locked all his drives as a matter of course, and they shot him *before* they found this out, maybe they went after LaMonde because they didn't have a working copy. We've been assuming Tucker sent a copy to him, but what if he hadn't yet? He wouldn't have been able to help them, so they grabbed his computer and torched the place just in case."

"And if Stephen didn't have a copy to give them, that's why they went and grabbed the one from police lockup, on the off-chance it was an open copy," G-Man finished for her. Chelsea could tell he was trying not to let his excitement overtake his judgment. "Which it wasn't. So, there's a chance they're still trying to crack the code-lock on the thumb drives they've got. I mean, nobody's tried blackmailing Force Majeure in the last month. That I've heard of, anyway." That there hadn't been any scandals in the news about the team went without saying.

"I've heard nothing myself, on the news or online." She paused, thinking about what to say next. "Actually, it's a little strange. When people get ahold of something this explosive, they talk about it. I mean, they might want to brag about having it, signal an upcoming drop like Tucker did, or just want to put it up for sale. I've been combing the dark web for anything of that sort, and nobody's saying a damn thing about it, even on the sites which handle the nasty shit." She shrugged to indicate vague optimism. "So maybe they've really got no idea how to unlock Tucker's thumb drives."

G-Man frowned. "That's queer as a three-dollar bill, sure enough. I would've thought you'd be hearing *something*."

This was all to the good. Although she was technically working against Force Majeure, she didn't want any kind of upheaval to happen in the city where she was building her criminal empire. That sort of thing was bad for business. It wasn't as though she'd ever intended to publicly disseminate the files she'd 'liberated' from their databanks; they would've been much more useful as leverage.

"Well, there's not a peep on any of the sites I've looked at." She figured there might be other sites she didn't know about, but those would have to be low-traffic and transient locations. Not the best way to advertise the sale of data from within the Spire.

Her words put a smile back on G-Man's face. "That's likely a good sign. As soon as we get back to Utopia, I'll get the files from you and hand them on to the Technologist." He dusted his hands off, his entire attitude radiating satisfaction. "In fact, we should leave as soon as possible. Unless you wanna try catching a lift back with Tourbillon? I'm sure Relentless would authorize it if I told him what was going on."

"And *I'm* equally sure I'd end up being teleported straight into a cell," she countered. "That's a hard *nope* from me. We can go back to Utopia on the maglev, like civilized folk." She jerked her head in the general direction of the exit. "So, are we going right this second, or did you want to check out the Challenger display first?"

She could tell she'd hit a nerve as he involuntarily glanced around at the towering external tank and solid rocket boosters outside the building, less than a hundred yards away. The sign out front read **Space Shuttle CHALLENGER**, with the silhouette of a shuttle orbiter replacing the 'A' in the name. Just for a moment, he jittered back and forth; from the expression on his face, he was in genuine pain at having to choose whether to go immediately or not.

Rolling her eyes, Chelsea checked her phone then grabbed him by the arm. "Oh, come *on*. The next train leaves in twelve minutes. Seven minutes is enough time to get across there and buy tickets. You've got five minutes. Go wild."

G-Man let out a sigh of relief at having the deadlock broken. "Okay, thanks." He headed for the exhibit at a brisk walk; Chelsea could tell that sheer self-control was the only thing holding him back from breaking into a run.

Boys and their toys.

33
Meeting a Legend

Smokeshadow

Chelsea followed Jericho as the latter hustled past the sign and under the archway formed by the two rocket boosters, then through the doors into the vast building. She could tell from the set of his jaw how aware he was of the passage of time, and that he intended to squeeze as much viewing as he could out of the next ... she checked her phone ... four minutes and forty-five seconds.

Moving at a steady, brisk walk, he went from one exhibit to the next with almost metronomic regularity, his head twitching from side to side in a transparent attempt to absorb all there was to see in the short time he had. Trailing along behind, Chelsea didn't even bother; she took the occasional photo of anything that caught her eye, and made a mental note to come back another day when she had the time to enjoy everything at her leisure. Her public-facing attitude consisted of *'nothing to see here'*, so even if anyone had paid attention to her, they would've been unable to describe her meaningfully afterward.

About four minutes in, they ended up on the second level, where the remains of the *Challenger* itself were displayed. Relatively little of the debris had been retrieved from the seabed, so there were many gaps between the bits and pieces of the orbiter. Holding it all in place was the transparent red and gold matrix intended to emulate the original force field which had saved the crew.

As an informative plaque noted, the control cabin had survived the breakup of the shuttle, but a section of it had been cut away for the purposes of the exhibit. This allowed the public to watch animatronic mannequins of the crew performing the same tasks they'd been engaged in, just before the catastrophic failure of the external tank. The plaque also asked the simple question which had gone unanswered for nearly thirty years: **Who was Challenger?**

Emotionally speaking, Chelsea knew she would've liked to learn the answer to that question. Steeped in deception and trickery as she was, she hated having knowledge withheld from her. But intellectually, she considered it a secret that didn't need to be known by anyone but those to whom it actually mattered. That wasn't to say she'd decline to learn it, should the information be freely offered ... but she liked to think she would struggle with her conscience. Maybe at least a little bit. At first.

As far as she could tell, Jericho had no desire to find out the secret of Challenger, nor even any particular urge to go into space. If she was reading his tells right, the fascination that the shuttle held for him was much more straightforward. Over and above the cool tech, he was a sucker for a happy ending. The *Challenger* represented a tale of disaster averted by the narrowest of margins, and at the same time was literally the origin story of the first superhero.

Alongside him at the rail were three other people: a mother, her little boy, and a gray-haired man in a suit and tie who was leaning on a walking cane. Chelsea opted to stand back a little. Her fascination lay in watching people, not things.

The mother was footsore already, but she was clearly determined to give her son the best day out that she could. On the other hand, the kid was bright and curious, clutching a Kennedy Space Center guidebook. Chelsea could see it had already been decorated by the signatures of several of the attending superheroes. As she watched, he tentatively approached Jericho and tugged at his sleeve. *Aww, so cute.*

"Mister G-Man?" The kid had a great line in puppy-dog eyes.

Jericho, of course, rose to the occasion. "Hey there, li'l man," he said with a friendly smile. "What can I do for you?"

At his encouraging tone, the child held out the guidebook. "C'n you sign this for me?" He paused for a beat, then added, "Please?"

Jericho grinned and dropped into a crouch, putting his face about level with the kid's. "Why sure. Who would you like me to make this here out to?" Accepting the guidebook, he took what looked like a marker pen from one of the pouches on his belt.

The mother leaned in and whispered something Chelsea didn't catch, and Jericho nodded. He popped the cap off the pen, then (because he was a showoff) hung it in mid-air with no visible means of support. Steadying the book on his knee, he posed while the mother snapped a photo of them together, then scribbled something in silver ink and handed the book back.

"Wow, thanks, mister G-Man!" The kid happily showed it to his mother, and they moved off. Chelsea silently wished him luck with his autograph collection; he had a great approach and good technique.

Snapping the cap back onto the pen, Jericho stood up and turned around. In doing so, he nearly collided face-to-face with the older man. Chelsea's full attention was thus drawn in that direction, and her eyes widened.

To a gaze that only saw the surface of things, the man would've appeared entirely unremarkable. Despite being in his sixties or seventies and needing a walking stick, he possessed what she would've picked as a military bearing even before she saw the rows of brightly colored ribbons and meticulously polished badges displayed on the left side of his suit coat. But that was still nowhere near the totality of what she perceived in him.

Some Enabled were formidable but had to work to project it, while others could cow a room with no effort at all. To eyes that could see it, the most dangerous of all were the high-tier prodigies, those who knew how the fight was going to go before the first punch was thrown. She'd seen Independence and Tesseract Power on TV, and they shared that quality. Jericho had it as well, though to a lesser degree.

In the instant that Jericho was up in his face, the older man went to high alert. One hand was a blade of rigid fingers, the other shifting its grip on his walking stick to turn it into a lethal weapon. His entire stance altered, ready to deflect a blow or drive a devastating attack into unprotected vitals. A split-second later, clearly recognizing that Jericho meant no harm, he relaxed from the combat stance.

To Jericho's credit, he pulled himself up immediately and stepped back out of the veteran's path. "I'm sorry, sir." She could tell from the tilt of his head that his eyes had dropped to the rows of ribbons. "Uh, thank you for your service." From his tone, as far as Chelsea could tell, he wasn't even aware of the averted threat to his health and well-being.

The old soldier gave Jericho a measured nod. "No harm done, son," he said, not unkindly. "Be more careful in the future." As he moved on, his walking stick tapped a regular beat on the floor.

What the hell was that *all about?*

A little stunned, Chelsea watched him go. Then she leaned into her Prodigy focus, to go over what she'd learned of the man while watching him.

He'd been looking into the control cabin moments before, but not at the whole crew. One particular member of the display had drawn his attention more than the rest; without having seen his eyes, she couldn't tell which one. Then he'd dropped his gaze to the plaque, and his fingers had trailed over the question at the bottom. When he turned away from the display, she'd caught the almost infinitesimal glint of tears in his eyes. Her innate understanding of body language told her what it all meant.

He knew Challenger. He knew who Challenger was. He wasn't here to look at the pretty technology. He was here to pay his respects.

While she was still wrestling with the implications of that revelation, her phone buzzed to let her know that the five minutes were done. She moved up beside Jericho, only dropping her *'no-see-me'* attitude when she was at his elbow.

"You really need to watch where you're going when you're signing autographs, *mister G-Man*," she snarked. "Also, time's up."

"Gah!" He jumped, then glared at her. "Don't *do* that!"

She shrugged to express her lack of concern over his bruised pride. Besides, it was fun. "We've got seven minutes to be on that train."

"Right. Yeah. Okay." He huffed out a long breath, then stared around at the many displays he had yet to examine up close. "I could spend all day in here."

Chelsea held up her phone. "No doubt, but I got plenty of photos, and you can always come back later. Let's get going."

"Sure thing." He reached for her; she saw the move coming and held still for him to slip his arm around her waist. A moment later, he'd vaulted over the rail with her, and they were drifting to the ground below. He seemed disappointed that she hadn't yelped or shown any other sign of fright. *Yeah, like that's gonna happen.*

He let her go when their feet touched the ground; side by side, they headed for the doors. "You are so lucky you didn't get up in that guy's grille," she said as they hurried outside. "There's no way it would've ended well for you."

"Really? I mean, I wasn't going to anyway, but why is that exactly?" He did something with his power and midnight-black wings unfurled out of his shoulders, trapping his arms within. Pulling them out with a moderate effort, he tilted his head slightly. "Well?"

"Oh, that? It's simple." Being carried bridal style was a little embarrassing, but it wouldn't be for long. She allowed him to pick her up and ensure she was secure in his grasp before she dropped the bombshell.

"That was Castellan."

34
Leaving the Scene

Jericho stared down at Chelsea, wondering if she was trying to pull his leg. "Castellan?" he repeated stupidly. "What, *the* Castellan? That was *him*? Are you certain-sure about that?" Just for a moment, he glanced back over his shoulder at the Challenger exhibit building.

"There's a saying about bears and woods," she retorted. "Would you like me to repeat it back to you, or would you rather just believe me? Besides, we've got a train to catch. You know, just in case you'd forgotten."

"Okay, but this is *not* over." Flaring his grav-wings, he lifted off the ground. He knew he could get back to the terminal in about one minute flat, so he banked around to the west toward the cluster of rockets.

With his arms out of the 'wings, he decided not to try for any tricky aerobatics, not least because Chelsea would yell at him. Opting not to land, he instead angled downward to fly low and slow between them, marveling at the length of time it took him to traverse the length of the Saturn V from one end to the other.

As the Astronauts' Hall of Fame passed beneath them, he sighed and headed southward toward the maglev terminal. "I am *so* coming back here when I get the chance."

"Go right ahead," Chelsea said. "But we need to get to the train right now, not dawdle and sightsee. Unless you didn't want to go to Utopia and get the data back after all …?"

Jericho noted the hopeful tone in her voice—of course, she'd be a lot happier if he passed up the chance of giving the data back to the Technologist—so he reacted in the only way he saw appropriate. That it would annoy her was pure bonus.

Usually, he would've been flying slow and steady, but he knew the secret of the maglev now, so he didn't worry about conserving power. Pushing his flight capability *hard*, he rocketed across the hundreds of yards to the terminal in less than twenty seconds. Where Chelsea had been entirely unfazed by the sudden drop down to ground level, now she yelped and sputtered as her hair was abruptly blown across her face.

"Hey!" she protested, reaching up to push it back while her hyperweave costume threw up a hood to protect her against any more wind-rush. "Do you *mind*?"

"Pets, yes; kids, no," he replied with a smirk as he came in for a fast landing at the edge of the parking lot, next to the walkway leading to the terminal.

"What?" She blinked as she figured out the joke. "Oh, hardy har har." As he let her down onto her feet, she gave him a dirty look. "Just for that, I won't tell you how I knew it was Castellan."

"Yeah, you will." He led the way into the terminal. "You surely do get a kick out of pointing out all the little tics and tells that people have."

Heading to the nearest bank of ticket kiosks, he pulled out his MagCard and swiftly went through the motions of getting a ticket back to Utopia City. His account wouldn't be charged because he was traveling in costume, but the system needed to know how many warm bodies there were on the various trains. *Cold* bodies got counted another way; that much, he'd learned from personal experience.

As he stepped away from the kiosk, he caught sight of Chelsea slipping the electronic discus back into her bag. He frowned, unhappy that she was misusing it in this fashion, but made no move to take it away from her. Context was a thing, but it felt petty to object to this use while applauding the time she'd used it to get the Survivors into the maglev system. That had allowed them to escape Utopia City and Force Majeure, which was just as much of a gross abuse of the device, and very likely illegal as hell.

Having consciously decided not to make a big deal of it, he turned to look at her as they headed for the escalator. "So how *did* you know that was Castellan? I mean, no offense to the guy, but he was definitely getting on a bit." They both knew Castellan had killed the Minotaur back in the day; Enabled battles, especially melee-heavy ones, weren't an old man's game.

"It's been sixteen, seventeen years since he retired, so I'm not totally surprised," she reminded him. "The guy's allowed to get old and slow down and smell the flowers. He doesn't actually need your permission. Not that he's slowed down all that much." She shook her head in recalled admiration. "He went from zero to '*I will kick your ass if you make the wrong move*' and back again, faster than anyone I've ever seen."

"I guess." He tilted his head. "So, are you gonna fill me in on how you knew it was him? Because I didn't see a damn thing."

Patiently, she went through what she'd seen and how she'd interpreted it. Not many people right then were traveling back to Orlando, so there wasn't much of a line to get through the scan-locks on the upper level. By the time she was finished, they'd boarded the train and had settled down at Jericho's choice of table.

By reflex, Jericho flicked over the switch that activated the privacy bubble. "Okay, I get all that, but could he have been a friend or family member? Not close family, I mean. A distant cousin. Even prodigies have relatives, you know. We're not all orphans who were raised by ninjas."

She snorted in derision at the cliché backstory popularized by mass-market novelists with more free time to write than actual creativity, then frowned in thought.

"His reaction to the exhibit was all wrong. He was specifically mourning the death of someone he was personally acquainted with. Nobody in the general public knows who's dead or alive on the crew. There was regret, sorrow, anger, and a bit of grim satisfaction, like he was the one who'd done something about Challenger's death." She looked at Jericho expectantly.

It was all too easy to take up the thread. "Because Castellan *was* the one who took down the Minotaur. Okay, yeah, I'm convinced."

She stretched elaborately, looking as smug as he'd ever seen her. "So, do I get an apology for you doubting my word?"

He grinned. "Sure, the moment you beg forgiveness on bended knee for that data heist."

Just for a moment, he thought he was going to get the apology he'd asked for, but then she crossed her eyes and gave him a resounding raspberry instead.

"Yeah, right," she jeered. "As if."

35
A Friendship, Divided

The maglev had passed through Gainesville and was making good time in the direction of Tallahassee when Jericho sat bolt upright in his seat. "Sonovabitch!" he exclaimed, disgusted at himself. "I totally forgot!"

Chelsea had been relaxing in her seat, going over the photos she'd taken and showing Jericho the better ones. Now, startled, she jumped. "Don't *do* that!" she complained. "I *like* not having heart attacks." Then she paused, frowning. "What'd you forget, anyway?"

Jericho facepalmed as well as he could while wearing the helmet. "I'd arranged to meet Thomas at Kennedy and spend the day there with him. Running into you totally put that out of my mind."

"So, text him or call him and tell him what's going on," she said pragmatically. "You've got his number, right?"

"Well, yeah, true." Taking the phone out of its pouch, he found the number he'd entered in his contacts list as 'T', and hit the call icon. It rang precisely once, then went to voicemail.

Jericho hated leaving voice messages, especially in cases like this. He wanted to say so much, and he always went over time. Ending the call, he switched to text.

"Oooh," murmured Chelsea mischievously. "Ghosting you, huh?"

Even aware that she was teasing him, he felt his cheeks heating up. "He's probably busy with the Jefferson thing. I'll just leave him a text."

Sorry, he typed. **Had to go do something real important in Utopia. I'll come right back as soon as it's done, okay? Love you.**

Hitting the Send button, he watched it go, then shut his phone down and tucked it away again. Only then did he become aware of Chelsea's intent gaze.

"What?" he asked. "Have I got something on my face?"

"No," she said. "But the last I checked, Thomas wasn't exactly a top-tier Enabled. What's *he* doing at Jefferson City? Why wasn't he already at Kennedy? I would've enjoyed catching up with the big lunk. For a guy, he really knows how to do girl talk."

He chuckled at the sudden realization. "What, really? Something I know that you don't?" He usually wouldn't have gloated this much—or at all—but she really was good at basing conclusions on the flimsiest of body language tells. The revelation about having met Castellan all unaware being a prime example. Having the tables turned for once was a refreshing change.

"What?" Her eyes searched his face. "You're way too amused about something. What am I missing?"

It would've been fun to let her dangle on the hook a little longer, but he tried not to be ugly like that. "You remember what happened a couple days after I joined Force Majeure for good? A real big thing in the superhero community." He paused for a moment, then dropped another hint. "Specifically, in Chicago?"

She blinked, her eyes going out of focus for a second. "Yeah, Vanessa Power showed up out of the blue after being missing for nearly two years. I half-expected her to be a fake, but the family took her back in, and she's done public appearances with them. As far as I can tell from her body language and theirs, she's the real deal. Why?"

Jericho knew that what he said next would be akin to lighting the fuse on a whole chain of firecrackers. He wasn't quite sure what the end result would be, but it would be highly entertaining and there would be no going back. "When Thomas got on the maglev, he went east to his family. In Chicago."

"Yeah, but what's that got to do with ..." She paused, evidently reading the amusement on his face. He could almost hear the *click* as the dots connected in her head. "Oh, no. No *fucking* way." But even as she blurted out the denial, he could tell she was revising her own opinion on the matter. "How does that even work? There's no way he was wearing any kind of full-body disguise, especially not one that complete. I spent four goddamn days in an apartment with him. No matter *what* Hollywood says, that shit just doesn't look real when you're up close and personal."

Jericho leaned back in his seat. It had been months, but he was still personally proud of how he'd figured this out. "You know how she's saying that she was attacked by a Dynamic shape-changer who pretended to be her father?"

"Well, yes." She tilted her head. "Oh. Wait. Proximity Principle? He got the other guy's powers?"

It was his turn to roll his eyes. "Way to spoil the big reveal."

She poked her tongue out at him in reply. "You were having far too much fun with it. So, this mystery shape-changer attacked her, and she would've gotten powers from the stress of the moment but instead ended up with some variation on the *shape-changer's* powers via the Principle. Voila; she can now turn into Thomas."

"That's about the long and the short of it. When I figured it out, I managed to talk her into changing back. We had a good long discussion, and she eventually agreed to go home and patch things up with her folks. I saw Thomas again and met his family at the beginning of January, when we visited Bobbi's grave. He says his dad's working on power armor that'll change shape when he does."

Chelsea nodded judiciously. "Well, if anyone can pull it off, it'll be Adam Power. How did her parents react to her being a part-time boy and having you as a boyfriend?"

He snorted. "'*Part-time boy*', my ass. We're calling it 'extreme gender fluidity'. No, his father and brother seem pretty chill with it. His mama gave me the shovel speech, but without yelling or resorting to threats, so I think I'm okay for the time being."

"Good. You two are perfect for each other." She tilted her head slightly. "So, how'd you figure it out, anyway? Because I'm *good* at picking out deception, and that one went right over my head."

"I nearly didn't," Jericho confessed. "But there were a couple of times where he'd turned off the TV when Team Power came on, and you know how he kept saying, '*we got this*'? That right there is Team Power's unofficial motto. I was wondering about that, then two questions just kinda crossed my brain at the same time. '*What if the guy Vanessa thinks was her dad was actually a shape-changer?*' and '*What if Vanessa got shape-changing powers from the Proximity Principle?*' After that, it all fell into place. Still took me forever to convince her to go home, though."

Chelsea shrugged. "After what she'd been through by that point, I can't exactly blame her for being skittish."

"I saw the footage on TV. She nearly turned around and walked away. It was that close." Jericho sighed. "Glad she went in, though. She's a lot happier, and her family's over the moon. PowerTech Industries is back on track, her father's looking twenty years younger, and her mama even smiled at me once. It nearly didn't happen that way, though. The damage one impostor can cause ..." He trailed off, eyes widening, as thoughts sparked off in his head. "Oh, crap. *Crap.* Impostors."

"Impostors?" Chelsea was sitting up straight by this point. Jericho could see her eyeballing the people who'd wandered into their car since Gainesville, but that wasn't what he was referring to.

He took a deep breath, trying to figure out how to articulate the horrible new idea that had just now occurred to him. "Okay, so two years ago, someone pretended to be Adam Power, to the point that his own daughter *continued* to think it was him, even *after* he tried to assault her. That's seriously high-tier shape-changing right there, yeah?"

"Yeah, it is." Chelsea didn't sound thrilled. "Did they ever make any progress tracking him, or her, or whatever, down? Because I wouldn't want to be that asshole when Tesseract catches up with them."

Jericho shrugged. "His last known gender presentation was male, so let's go with 'him' for the moment. And nope, no news as yet. Which is worrying. Because someone who's successfully pulled shit like that off doesn't just *stop*. What if Team Power was just a test of the waters, to see what he could get away with?"

"One hell of a test run, if you ask me." Chelsea's tone was dismissive, but he could tell she was paying attention, and didn't like where he was going with this.

Good. Neither do I.

He took a deep breath. "What if, after he had his little fun with Team Power, he moved on to bigger fish, like Force Majeure? What if he *replaced* someone from Force Majeure? It'd have to be relatively recent because he'd trip up sooner or later, but can you imagine the damage a villain could do once they got into the Spire, with full access to all of its systems, even for a short time?"

Now Chelsea was giving him the side-eye. "Seriously, you're scaring me. Is there a point to this? Because I can't imagine they'd build something like the Spire and *not* have a safeguard against a shape-changed infiltrator."

"Well, they do, and they don't." Jericho frowned. "Mama once told me that the biggest information leaks from any company happen right at the top because they don't think security protocols really apply to them, and there's nobody to make it stick. Everyone *but* Force Majeure has to come and go through high-end scanners, but Enabled members get their own ways in and out. Hell, I usually come and go through the Technologist's landing stage, and I'm pretty sure I don't get scanned like they do at the front desk."

She nodded slowly. "Okay, granted. But how does having a hypothetical bad guy inside Force Majeure translate to people getting killed over *someone else* doing an information grab?"

Which led back around to the sudden flash of insight that had prompted Jericho's outburst. "What if … bear with me here, but what if he was stealing data from the servers and storing it all in his personal Force Majeure folder, getting ready to take it all out of the Spire in one batch … and *those* are the ones you took? And I don't know computers, but what if the files had to be signed out in the first place, so if the Technologist looks at what *you* took, it'll be obvious who they were being stolen by in the first place? And *that's* why the impostor's going after the decrypted files, plus everyone who might have a copy."

"It still doesn't explain why he's going all-out with the murders," Chelsea argued. "I mean, there was a metric *ton* of files even in the hidden server, and I only skimmed what I could off the top. Hell, I might've only got Relentless' recordings of singing in the shower, for all they know."

Jericho thought hard for a moment. "Well, you said Tucker was bragging on the dark sites about how he had something huge, so it had to be *something* bad, and I know the Technologist said he didn't know what had been taken … but what if the *infiltrator* had added a program to his personal folder that told him when something had been copied? He doesn't want anyone looking at his incriminating stuff to see what's been taken, so he doesn't tell anyone. The only option he's got for surviving this in one piece is to destroy or retrieve any copies, and flat-out kill anyone who might've so much as looked at the files. And who the hell would suspect a member of Force Majeure until it's too late?"

Chelsea became very still. She blinked once, slowly. "Well, shit."

"It'd even explain why there's been no blackmail or attacks on Force Majeure, or even any word on the dark web about it," Jericho said, circling back to the part that had first made him start wondering. "If he's the one who stole it in the first place, of *course* he's not gonna brag on it or put it up for sale until he's *ready* to let it go."

"Just like it explains what happened at the Savannah precinct station." Chelsea moved her hands past each other, miming sleight of hand. "Walk in. *Be* the top cop. Grab the thumb drive. Toss in an incendiary grenade. Walk out. Turn the corner, be someone else. Too damn easy. It all fits." She sounded a little unsettled.

Jericho couldn't help but smirk. "Sucks when someone else uses your shtick, doesn't it?"

"Allow me to present a couple of counterpoints." Her hands dipped under the table and came up again, flipping him the bird with each one. A dirty look accompanied the double gesture.

He snorted, but his mind was racing on. "Same with the Tucker killing. He pretended to be Tucker's girlfriend to get into the house, then maybe took another form to make any witnesses think there were two of them. And with Stephen …" He grimaced. "All he'd have to do is knock on the door, looking like *me*. Stephen would've broken his fingers trying to get the chain off the door fast enough."

"Okay, now this is freaking me the hell out." Chelsea looked across at him beseechingly. "I need you to find a reason for it *not* to be true. Which members of Force Majeure could be reasonably replaced by a shape-changer, and which ones couldn't?"

"Not only members." Jericho felt sick inside at having to even raise the possibility, but he'd set this course, and he was bound to follow it through. "There's Ms. Colburn and Ms. Chandler. Relentless' executive assistant, and the in-house head of surgery and our ad hoc therapist, respectively." He paused a moment, thinking. "On second thought, scratch Ms. Colburn off the list. She's been with Force Majeure almost since day one, and she's forgotten more about the workings of the Spire than anyone else knows. Relentless would spot someone trying to impersonate her in about thirty seconds flat. But that still leaves Ms. Chandler."

"A doctor?" Chelsea frowned. "I doubt someone like that would have access to anything more sensitive than Force Majeure's medical data. Heads would roll if something like that was released, but it wouldn't bring down the team."

"Yeah, but she's really good at talking to people and figuring out how they tick. Getting inside their heads." He interlaced his fingers in front of himself, then pulled them apart again. "If she really wanted to talk someone into handing over access to their security credentials, I think she could."

"Alright then," she said briskly. "We have eight potential candidates for … let's call him Poser. Tell me who it *can't* be."

Jericho nodded, accepting the nickname she'd come up with for the bad guy. It certainly fit the situation. "I don't think it's Relentless. Technically, a shape-changer should be able to pack on the muscle mass and get that big, but there's *big and muscular*, and then there's *can lift half a ton with one hand*. Because he did exactly that this morning." He privately heaved a sigh of relief as he reached that conclusion. The idea of Relentless being replaced by a villain was ... terrifying.

"Okay, so scratch Relentless," noted Chelsea. "Who else *can't* it be?"

"Tourbillon," Jericho decided. "They teleported a bunch of heroes into Jefferson City after the quake, then bounced me from there to St. Louis in one step. Unless Poser can mimic teleport portals, that's a no as well."

"Two down, six to go." Chelsea gave him an encouraging gesture. "You're doing fine."

"Um ... the Technologist. He and Transit built Scout. Transit, too, though I've only talked to her a few times since I got my full membership. But no, if they're working side by side and her Artificer game wasn't up to scratch, he'd be able to tell in a heartbeat. He's said nothing—and he *would* say something—so I guess they're both in the clear." Jericho shook his head. "Damn it, this is *hard*. I keep wanting to say, *'no, they're all who they say they are'*, but I've got to actually *think* about this."

"You've cleared half our suspects." Chelsea raised her eyebrows. "What about the other four?"

Jericho snapped his fingers. "Didn't Lady Quantum do a sky-show or something a couple weeks back? Flying around in that damn peekaboo costume of hers, shooting off fireworks out of her fingertips from one end of the city to the other? There's no way shape-changing could mimic that."

"Well, no, true ..." Chelsea rubbed her chin. "So, apart from the doctor, that leaves us with Silent Knight and Independence. The guy in full-coverage armor that doesn't let him speak—which is *convenient*—and the kick-ass prodigy who carries a sword and an assault rifle everywhere she goes."

"Who also dislikes me, just saying." Jericho tilted his head. "Silent Knight was a bit standoffish at the interview as well. We haven't exchanged three words since. In fact, the only actual team member I've seen out of costume is Relentless."

Despite the gravity of the situation, Chelsea snorted with amusement. "And boy oh boy, when he goes out of costume, he doesn't do it by halves."

Jericho flushed; the memory still made him cringe. "Quit it. This is serious. Okay, so let's look at Silent Knight ... would a shape-changer even be able to learn how to get into that power armor of his, much less operate it?"

"Thomas is a prodigy," Chelsea said, all business once more. "The Proximity Principle means Poser has to be, as well. This means he could probably figure out the controls far more easily than some rando off the street. Replacing Independence would be easier in theory, but subduing her in the first place would be harder, so that balances out. Okay, tag those two as 'maybe'. What about your Ms. Chandler?"

"I've been thinking about that." Jericho hoped he had it worked out. "The problem is, I don't know how long she's been working for Force

Majeure. If it's less than two years, there might not *be* a real Ms. Chandler. It might be that she's been his cover identity the whole time. Otherwise ... well, she talks to everyone. If her personality and knowledge about the job have recently changed, someone *had* to have noticed."

"Also, two other things for the 'not it' column." Chelsea raised two fingers. "One: it would be easy as hell to find out where she was on the day those murders happened. It's not like the in-house head of surgery—or, for that matter, anyone else who's not core Force Majeure, like your Ms. Colburn—can just disappear off to Savannah for the day *without* taking the maglev or drawing attention in some other way. And two: I can't see anyone short of Surgeon One herself being promoted into the top spot in less than two years, no matter how good they are. No, it just doesn't add up."

Jericho was torn between relief at her analysis, and worry that there were still two outstanding potential suspects. "So if it's anyone, it's Independence or Silent Knight."

Chelsea nodded and met Jericho's gaze soberly. "*If* this whole logic chain is accurate, then yes, one of those two is most likely Poser."

"Great," he said sarcastically, rolling his eyes. "So, all we've gotta do now is figure out which one of them it is, then locate where Poser's keeping the real one."

Chelsea shook her head. "If they're even still alive."

"Don't say that." Jericho grimaced. "They've got to be. They might not *like* me, but that's not a crime."

"Are you sure you've even *met* the original, whichever one it is?" Chelsea raised her eyebrows. "What if the whole standoffish play is intended to keep the new people at arm's length?"

He reluctantly conceded to her logic. "I guess. So where do we go from here?"

"Okay, I'm gonna say this one more time." She eyed him thoughtfully. "We've got zero proof and a whole truckload of assumptions here. The biggest mistake to make right now is to presume that our pretty little train of logic is *real*, rather than something we've made up from whole cloth because of a few accidental correlations. We can't discount it out of hand, but we shouldn't go all-in just because it sounds way cooler than the other version. Except maybe the foreign-agents one."

"Well, no," admitted Jericho, thinking hard. "But it doesn't *matter*. There's one simple method to prove it, either way. As soon as I can get your copy of the data to the Technologist and he decrypts it, he'll be able to tell whether it's standard Force Majeure secret stuff or proof that there's an infiltrator on the team. If it's the former, we're back to where we were before, doing damage control. But if it's the latter, we grab Poser and make him tell us what he did with the real person." He pointed across the table at Chelsea. "That copy you've got back in Utopia? That's the key to this whole thing."

"If you say so," Chelsea agreed. "And just so you know, about that? You've always been straight with me, so full disclosure. I'm keeping a copy for myself."

The sudden tension following her announcement was such that Jericho didn't even consider making the obvious joke. "What? No. We agreed you'd hand over all copies. Then we walk away, and neither of us refers to this whole incident ever again." He was about to say 'no harm, no foul' before he recalled that yes, people *had* been harmed, and the time for saying 'no foul' was long past.

"'*We*' agreed? Who's this 'we' you keep talking about, gravity boy?" She stared at him, her expression suggesting that he was due to be fitted for a straitjacket. "*You're* the one who said it, not me. I figured there'd be time to correct you along the way. If they're going to kill two men over that data, I want to know what's in it. Wouldn't you?"

Jericho blinked, unable to parse her meaning. In her place, he would've been entirely willing to hand the data over to a theoretical other version of himself, especially since there was no immediate chance to get it decrypted. "Well … no. I wouldn't. It's top-secret Force Majeure data that neither of us has clearance for."

"Clearance, schmearance." She shook her head. "I only told you about this in the first place so you'd know the real story with Tucker and LaMonde. I'm happy to give you a *copy* of the data so the Technologist can figure out what the hell's going on, but you're not getting my original heist. Sorry, but that's the way it is." She started to slide out of her seat.

He moved sideways as well, preparing to stand up and bar her way. "No. Stop. Don't make me choose between you and Force Majeure. *Please*." The last word came out almost as a sob.

Chelsea raised her eyebrows. "Are you honestly gonna arrest me? On what charges? And even if you found one that would stick, I'd be in Force Majeure hands the moment we got off the train in Utopia. It would be out of your control, and you can be damn sure I'd never tell *them* where I've got the data drive stashed."

Either she was right and he had no good choices, or she was using her subliminal Prodigy bullshit to make him think that. His inclination was to believe her. He *had* to get the data on the drive to the Technologist; without that to work with, Force Majeure would be wide open to whatever came its way. Clenching his hands inside his gloves so hard that every joint hurt, he didn't move as she got up from the seat.

Not for a moment was he concerned about her divulging his less-than-legal dealings in Utopia City, but he stayed his hand anyway. He stood out of her way because she'd stepped up and helped him when he'd most needed it: not once, but three times. Though they were at odds now, that debt still stood.

More importantly, though it tore him in half to know that his decision would probably end up costing him his spot in Force Majeure, he knew he'd likely reach the same conclusion the same way again. She'd been his friend and ally before he was a member of Force Majeure. He trusted her to get him the data. Now he just had to have faith that she'd come through for him.

The automatic doors slid apart, then closed behind her. Jericho *knew* if he went after her now, her entire stance and clothing style would've changed during the transition from one car to the next, to the point that he literally would not recognize her even if he looked her in the face. Just seconds out of sight allowed her to vanish into any crowd: anonymous, invisible. He'd seen her do it before.

His phone pinged a notification into his earpiece. Hastily, he dragged it out and woke up the screen. He didn't recognize the number, but the message was unambiguous.

When we get to Utopia, meet me where we had the picnic.

I remember that. That was in Memorial Park.

He tapped a quick text back, **okay**, then put his phone away. This whole thing was far from ideal, but he had hours to go before reaching Utopia City; he was sure he could think of worse situations before then.

At that moment, the announcement for the Tallahassee stop came across the PA system, along with the flashing yellow lights. Automatically, he got up from his seat and moved forward. He wanted to go back and find Chelsea so he could explain to her how dangerous holding on to the data was, but he suspected there weren't words in the English language strong enough to get that through to her. Anyway, it was doubtful that he would locate her if she didn't want to be found.

Still upset by the argument, he moved forward and settled into his usual spot, determined to wait out the rest of the trip and make the rendezvous as arranged. Chelsea had her own agenda, that was true, but she'd never done him dirty before.

She'd come through.

He hoped.

36
Preparation for Disaster

Front Desk, Utopia City Main Precinct House
January 28, 2014
12:06 PM Central Standard Time

Sergeant Catherine Richardson, UCPD

It was quiet enough as Tuesdays went, though Catherine was fully aware the night would be somewhat livelier. Some of the troops had attended the morning commemoration ceremony at the statue in Challenger Plaza, but for the most part, they were patrolling the city in conjunction with the hexes. There was always *someone* who wanted to kick the celebrations off early and do something stupid.

The laws in Utopia had been expressly formulated to crack down on things that endangered the citizenry as a whole, while leaving personal liberties (to a point) free and clear. Fireworks, for instance, were legal in the city, though those manufactured and sold to the civilian populace were limited in size, range, and explosive power.

Tonight, from the tops of buildings and within parks, approved fireworks would be legal to set off for the celebration. Catherine knew perfectly well that no illegal fireworks would've been brought in via the maglev or the highway; the scanning systems were too efficient for that. In addition, since the demise of the Southsiders, there was no new contraband making its way into Utopia … that she knew of.

Which just left Utopians who wanted to make their own over-powered fireworks. And no power on Earth was capable of preventing sufficiently motivated idiots (especially UCIAT students) from doing something they knew was risky, but which they wanted to do anyway. People could be remarkably stupid, even in Utopia where Catherine was personally sure the average IQ was a few notches higher than the surrounding state, much less the rest of the nation. That just allowed them to be idiotic in an exponentially more innovative fashion, giving the police more headaches than the typical run of dumbasses.

In other words, things were likely to get a lot more hectic once the sun went down, so right now was a great time to get pending paperwork cleared out of the way. And so, she was steadily tapping away on the keyboard when the armor-glass doors to the lobby slid open. The almost silent gasp from the few people waiting in the lobby made her look up.

She knew who Silent Knight and Lady Quantum were, of course. Along with the rest of the Force Majeure core membership, they maintained a robust presence within Utopia and occasionally outside it. Force Majeure wasn't quite seen as royalty—every king or queen she'd seen in any movie tended to sit back and let the peasantry do all the work—but the scuttlebutt was that if they wanted the city council to vote a certain way, it voted that way.

Which made sense to her; they'd literally built the city from the bedrock up. Shouldn't they have a say in how things were run? After all, everything that set Utopia apart from every other city on Earth was specifically due to them. This was, however, the first time she'd met these two up close.

The contrast between Silent Knight and Lady Quantum was essentially the same as night versus day.

Wearing glossy, fully invested black power armor, the seams at his joints almost invisible and the shape reminiscent of a knight of old, Silent Knight almost seemed to stalk across the hard-wearing vinyl floor. Catherine realized a moment later that she couldn't actually hear his footsteps, which she thought was a pretty cool effect. The only thing breaking the smooth lines of his armor—she figured the faceplate must have some kind of one-way effect on it because she certainly couldn't see in—was an equally black enamel-painted metal guard covering his right shoulder. This was affixed in place by a metal-link baldric that ran diagonally down to a scabbarded sword on his left hip.

On the other hand, Lady Quantum was almost the personification of sweetness and light. Shedding a gentle blue glow—apparently just because she could—she drifted into the room with her feet a good six inches off the floor. Where none of the other members of Force Majeure incorporated spandex into their costumes, Lady Quantum flaunted it from head to toe in brilliant primary colors. This was set off by a cheerfully patterned cape in the same hues, along with a pair of bright blue bracers with white stars on her forearms.

That wasn't all she flaunted; being somewhat well-endowed, she'd gone with what was usually termed a 'boob window' over her cleavage, though she'd added electron orbits to make it look like an atom in the process of splitting. Catherine was cynically aware that about seventy-five percent of the guys viewing Lady Quantum's costume had no idea of the science behind it. They just wanted to ogle a hot superhero.

Most Enabled didn't use spandex or capes for the excellent reasons that the former offered no protection whatsoever, and the latter was likely to be a severe impediment in a fight. Lady Quantum added to her catalog of sins by sporting a pair of knee-length high-heeled boots, also patterned in her costume's colors. She looked for all the world like she was about to bust out a couple of pom-poms and start in on a cheerleader routine at any moment.

Of course, this was all excused by the fact that she could fly and generate a powerful (if mostly transparent) force field for protection. For ranged offense, she could fire directed energy beams in red and blue, ranging from lasers to impressive explosive bursts. Nobody who had seen her in action, smacking the bad guys around and rescuing civilians with carefully shaped force fields, would consider her anything less than a dedicated superhero.

Even if *she* didn't take it seriously at times.

Drifting up to the desk, she let her feet touch the floor with a delicate *tunk* and leaned on the wood veneer with her elbows. "Good afternoon," she chirped, letting her raven-black hair spill down over her shoulder.

Catherine wondered just for a moment how she got her hair so smooth and glossy, then she pulled her mind back to business. "Uh, good afternoon, ma'am, sir. How can we help Force Majeure today?"

Silent Knight held up his left arm, the forearm horizontal at chest level. He tapped on it with his right hand; a screen flickered into place above his arm, and Catherine realized that what she'd thought was extra detail on the armor was actually a projector. Floating on the holo-screen were the words:

WE ARE INSTITUTING AN EMERGENCY DRILL.
COMMENCEMENT AT 12:45 TODAY.

Catherine blinked. She'd been through these before, of course, but the short notice always threw her off; at first, anyway.

Jeez, that's less than forty minutes away.

"Uh ... okay, then. But really, *today*?" Commemoration Day, she meant.

Lady Quantum smiled beatifically. "Of course. What better day to make sure Utopia City's finest is up to the task?"

"Well, yes." Catherine knew she shouldn't be arguing with the superheroes. However, the words just kept coming out. "But ... we're already prepping for the celebrations tonight."

The sympathy on the superhero's face went a long way toward making Catherine feel better about matters. "I know, honey, and I'm sorry about the short notice. But hey, once we're done, Force Majeure will be stepping up to help you get everything back on track again."

Silent Knight was tapping on the holo-projector again. When he finished, the screen read:

THIS WILL BE AN INCURSION SCENARIO.
WEATHER CONTROL WILL BE INVOLVED.
KEEP A WATCH FOR DISABLED DRONES.

"Okay, that should help a lot," agreed Catherine. "We can totally do that for you."

Lady Quantum gave her a beaming smile that almost made Catherine reconsider her own personal orientation. "Thank you. You have a good day now, okay?"

Turning, the still-glowing superhero drifted up off the floor again and moved toward the doors, followed by her silent companion. Catherine watched until the doors closed behind them, then picked up the phone. "Get me the Commissioner," she said. "It's urgent."

The best part about these drills? It's all Force Majeure's problem. If anyone screws up, it's not my fault.

37
Dark and Stormy

Such was Jericho's disquiet regarding the argument he'd had with Smokeshadow that he didn't register the anomalous weather until after the Greenway had flashed by under the racing maglev. Where usually the Spire and surrounding buildings—what he could see of them ahead of the train—would be illuminated by bright sunlight, the city was instead shaded over by banked-up clouds, menacing and heavy with unshed rain. What made this unusual was that Utopia rarely had city-wide weather patterns imposed upon it, and potentially destructive effects such as heavy rain or thunderstorms never happened.

Or rather, they were never *allowed* to happen. Jericho had seen the weather-control room in the Spire and witnessed it in use; the finesse that could be brought to bear was nothing short of awe-inspiring. If Utopia City had this kind of cloud buildup going on right across the main metropolitan area, then *someone* had to have given the order for the weather techs to implement it. Extreme weather didn't happen by accident, not in Utopia.

What it meant, he wasn't sure. It might be nothing at all, or it might be very significant indeed. Considering the discussion he'd had with Smokeshadow before the argument blew up over the stolen data, he wasn't willing to bank on everything being okay in Utopia.

Fortunately, he could definitely get a read on the situation in short order. His radio earpiece had connected to the local net a few minutes before—because of *course* Utopia had repeaters all the way out to the city limits—so he was able to listen in on the chatter.

Which … wasn't telling him much. What he could hear was very terse, with the back-and-forth comments lacking much-needed context. He listened carefully for a few moments, then put in his two bits.

"G-Man, here. I just got back into town. What's going on with the weather?"

Almost immediately, he got back a reply from a familiar voice. "Break, break. Transit to G-Man; be aware that we are running a city-wide incursion drill. You are not required to participate. All non-participants are to maintain radio silence except in the case of an actual emergency. Do you copy?"

And that was all his questions answered in one fell swoop. "I copy. G-Man, out."

Vaguely, he registered her acknowledgment, then sat back to think as the maglev bored on through the twilight gloom of the overcast city. He hadn't received any notification of an upcoming drill, but that wasn't exactly a surprise. Emergency drills were intended to catch everyone on the back foot because genuine emergencies weren't known to wait until it was convenient for all concerned. Likewise, everyone available participated, with no exceptions. Literally being out of town was about the only good excuse for not fronting up.

On the upside, this meant everything was proceeding as normal within the city. If they'd been dealing with any kind of *real* emergency, they wouldn't be holding a drill.

Just as that thought crossed his mind, his phone rang. He didn't even bother getting it out to check on who was calling him. Given the circumstances, it would be one of two men: either the Technologist, or Relentless himself. Reaching up under the rim of his helmet, he pressed the clicker to answer the call. "Hello?"

"G-Man. Why are you here and not in Florida?" It was Relentless. The big man didn't sound annoyed ... well, he *did* sound annoyed, but not any more than usual.

Of course, if Jericho answered the question wrong, that situation could always change for the worse.

As per usual with the maglev, the PA system's active use—the ongoing announcement about stopping in Utopia City or traveling on to Denver— prevented the privacy bubble from being engaged. So as not to be overheard, he lowered his voice and cupped his hand around his mouth. "It's about the, uh, about the heist the Technologist told me about—" he began, trying to keep his terms vague.

"Stop right there," ordered Relentless. "I can hear the announcement in the background. You're currently without a privacy bubble?"

"Uh, yeah." Jericho tried not to glance around guiltily. "I could go into the bathroom—"

"No." Relentless overrode him bluntly. "Go into the space between the train cars. Use your card to lock both sets of doors. *Then* talk."

"Okay. Doing that now." Taking out his MagCard, Jericho got up from his seat. As this put him directly in front of the rear doors of the train car, they opened immediately. He stepped through then tapped the outside reader three times with his card, thus locking the doors. Once he'd repeated the action with the doors at the far end of the connecting passage, he leaned against the rubber-covered edge of one of the heavy angled barriers that would close off one car from another before separation. Exerting his G-senses, he knew he'd be able to detect anyone so much as standing close to the doors at either end of the passage, much less trying to listen at them. "Ready."

"Good. Report."

"Okay, uh ... when I was at Kennedy, I ran into a contact I know from back in Utopia who was in on the raid. I managed to talk them into returning a copy of the encrypted data so we can figure out what *was* taken, and start running damage control."

He paused, waiting for Relentless' response, which he figured would be acerbic at best. His theory about there being an impostor inside the Spire could wait, at least until he was face-to-face with Relentless. Besides, as Smokeshadow had pointed out, the entire 'Poser' chain of logic might just be spurious as hell. Jericho had to act as though Force Majeure's future depended on the data getting through to the Technologist ... because it *might*. Potential impersonators came a distant second. *'I came back to warn you that there might be impostors on the team'* just didn't have that same ring of authenticity.

"And you didn't arrest them because ...?" And there it was. Relentless wasn't yelling yet, but by the tone of his voice, he wasn't far off it.

"They're really good at being evasive, in every sense of the word." Which was entirely true, just not the actual reason he hadn't tried to apprehend Smokeshadow. He kept talking, the words spilling over each other. "Plus, they said the data's back in Utopia, so even if I did arrest them, they'd simply refuse to tell anyone where it was. And in the meantime, the people they had decrypting it got murdered, and the data was stolen, so it's potentially out there somewhere just waiting to get used. Which is why I came back immediately. The sooner I hand it over to the Technologist, the sooner we can figure out how to minimize the fallout from what's been taken if they decide to publicize it."

"Understood." Relentless was silent for a moment; Jericho optimistically judged it a thoughtful silence rather than an angry one. "And you decided not to contact Tourbillon for transport because your contact was concerned about being arrested on the spot." It was a statement of fact rather than a question.

"Basically, yeah." Jericho was pleased he and Relentless were on the same page, and that the leader of Force Majeure wasn't demanding all the details Jericho could give him about Smokeshadow. "Uh ... am I in trouble? For having a contact and not telling you about them?"

Of all the responses he was expecting, a chuckle had not been high on the list. "Hardly. If anything, I'm impressed. Within months of joining Force Majeure, you've managed to form a connection with organized crime inside Utopia. We may be heroes, but it never hurts to have some kind of leverage on the other side of the mask. And now it's paying off."

It was a good thing Jericho was braced against the side of the passageway because his knees had just gone weak with relief. "So, I'm good to do the handover?"

"You are." Relentless didn't leave it at that, though. "We have drones we're targeting as part of the drill, which means all non-essential air traffic is currently grounded. If you're going to be flying, make sure your IFF is active. I'll make sure all participants are routed away from your location."

"Thanks, that'll help a lot—" Jericho paused, suddenly aware that he was talking to dead air. Which was typical of the man. Relentless had said his piece and then ended the call.

However, now that he knew what was going on, Jericho had a better chance of piecing together the meaning of the cryptic radio chatter as he unlocked both ends of the passageway and went back to his seat. He'd never seen an incursion drill before, but apparently it involved disposable drones, controlled by operators in the Spire, making dummy attack runs on various buildings throughout the city. These were opposed by any flying heroes in Utopia, backed up by the weather techs.

With a twinge of regret—*Scout would've had a ball knocking these things out of the sky*—he resigned himself to merely watching the show until the maglev got into the station. A couple of times, he spotted one of the drones, which were small and black and about half the size of a police hex, zipping between buildings to evade pursuit. On the second occasion, the device was almost out of sight when lightning arced down from the clouds above, latching on and causing tendrils of electricity to crawl all over it. There was a small explosion; the drone dropped like a rock, trailing smoke.

Jericho grinned as it fell out of sight, imagining the operator's chagrin. That had been no coincidence; pinpoint lightning strikes were but a tiny part of the repertoire available to the weather techs. Anyone mounting an actual attack on Utopia City would have an absolutely *horrific* time.

He was still smiling as his maglev car, along with the other ones stopping in the city, separated from the rest of the train and pulled into the Utopia station. He was so used to the maglev's near-instantaneous starts and stops by now that he wasn't even aware of them anymore.

Stepping off the train the moment the doors slid open, he lost the smile as he strode purposefully toward the bank of scan-locks. His game face was on, and he had a job to do: meet up with Smokeshadow, acquire the data, and get it back to the Technologist in time for it to be decrypted and made harmless.

Now, *this* was what he'd always secretly hoped the superhero life would be like.

38
A Hero's Welcome

Once he'd passed through the scan-lock, Jericho had to choose whether to go up to the monorail stop or down to ground level. He decided on the stairs upward, taking them four at a time (cheating a little with his powers) until he reached the top.

As he'd long since discovered, the track supporting the monorail came in alongside a platform attached to the top floor of the maglev station. Weather protection was provided by a combination of a shaped overhang and a lightweight force field; the latter popped and reformed each time a monorail arrived at the stop. Unlike the maglev, each monorail train consisted of three permanently linked passenger cars that zipped around the city on set routes. The speed of these runs varied, depending on whether it was a tourist route or strictly passenger delivery.

A train was waiting at the platform as he reached the top of the stairs, but Jericho had no intention of getting on board. While he knew there were stops throughout the city, he figured he could get to his intended destination faster on his own. With this in mind, he pulled the HUD goggles from their pouch and donned them, then activated the built-in IFF as Relentless had advised him to do.

Each end of the platform had a chest-high rail and several warning signs to prevent people from climbing over. Ignoring all this, Jericho took a run-up and vaulted over the railing. Letting himself fall head-first a dozen feet down the side of the maglev station to clear the monorail cars, he leaned into his power and unfurled his grav-wings.

As his incipient death dive turned into an upward swoop, he considered what he would do next. Going straight to Memorial Park was what he *wanted* to do, but Smokeshadow had yet to get public transport to where she'd stashed the data, then back to the park itself. If he hung around too long in the same spot, other members of Force Majeure were likely to notice and start wondering what he was doing there. The last thing he needed or wanted was for someone to not get the memo to stay away, and for Smokeshadow to suspect a trap when she arrived; something like that would put her in the wind and make it almost impossible to catch up with her again.

Back to the Spire. Might as well have a shower and freshen up. Change out the costume while I'm at it.

Prodigy physiology might allow for more extended exertion periods, but the powerset did not include immunity to sweat or body odor. Even the lightest body-stockings tended to become a little pungent after eight hours on duty, and Jericho's costume was most definitely not a body-stocking.

Thunder rumbled in the lowering clouds overhead; a light rain began to fall, but he wasn't worried. Even if it closed in enough to impair his vision, the HUD goggles could outline the air-lanes he needed to follow to avoid the buildings. Stretching out the 'wings, he banked slightly to compensate for an updraft, then set out in the direction of the Spire.

By the time he was halfway there, he was starting to regret his decision. The light shower had become a downpour, hammering on his back and running thick rivulets of water over his goggles, not to mention trickling unpleasantly down the back of his neck. But he'd made his bed, and now he had to lie in it. Going back to the maglev station would defeat the purpose of having come this far, and the only way to locate a monorail stop when the rain was this heavy would be to actually drop down to street level and follow the rail along. He wasn't quite prepared to do that, so he just kept going.

His HUD goggles showed him when he was about to breach the no-fly zone around the Spire, but they didn't warn him about what happened next. One moment he was battling his way through torrential rain, lit here and there by distant lightning strikes and buffeted by unpredictable wind gusts … and the next, he was flying in clear air. The storm had been replaced by sunlight streaming down from above; in fact, he could see a solid curtain of rain stretching to the left and right, curving around in a vast circle enclosing the Spire.

It was the most impressive demonstration he'd seen yet regarding the capabilities of the weather control system. Shaking his head in admiration, he slowed to a stop and pulled his arms from the 'wings. Opening the pouch that held his phone, he first checked for any water leakage—the wind had been pretty strong, and the rain coming down hard—then woke it up and took a photo of the curving sweep of the rain around the Spire.

I would never have believed this without seeing it for myself.

After tucking the phone away again, he set about trying to get the worst of the water off himself, starting with the goggles. Hooking his fingers into the back of his collar only afforded moderate success in dealing with the rain that had trickled in back there, though he wondered if tucking his collar in under the rim of his helmet might not help out a little next time. His ponytail was soaked through (which wasn't helping), so he grabbed that and squeezed it out—*second time today, hah*—before beginning to brush errant raindrops off the rest of his costume. Water-resistant didn't mean water*proof*, after all.

He was just performing a tactile check on each of the other pouches on his utility belt to ensure none had blown open, when a familiar thrumming sound intruded on his hearing. At the same time, his G-sense warned of a large mass approaching. No air-cabs were flying, and none would be permitted to enter this airspace anyway, so he knew exactly who it was. "Transit, hi," he said by way of greeting as he pivoted in mid-air.

"Hey, G-Man." Transit pulled her sky-bike to a hover and leaned on the handlebars with her elbows. The guns mounted on the front of the 'bike were raised to their 'safe' position instead of tracking around toward him, which he appreciated. "You're back early. Anything the matter?"

"Actually, yeah, something came up. I've already filled Relentless in, so it's all good." He considered how much he should tell her, then decided that discretion was probably best in this case.

"I can dig it. Nice going in Jefferson this morning, by the way. I figure you upped our ratings by at least a percentage point. Also, I've had a look at Scout. The damage doesn't look too extensive." She paused. "How are you feeling?"

"Oh, the girders missed me altogether," he said hastily. "I wasn't hurt at all. Thanks to Scout, I mean."

She shook her head. "No, I meant, how do you feel about all this? You were doing a damn good job socializing him, and I could tell you saw him as a friend."

"Honestly?" He grimaced. "I feel like I dived in without prep and got him hurt."

To his astonishment, she blew a raspberry. "And you can pull the plug on that pity party right now, mister. It literally wasn't your fault. I've downloaded the footage from Scout. Nothing you could've done. Sometimes, shit just happens."

"Thanks. I'll try to remember that." Trying not to dwell too hard on how Scout had been hurt but feeling better all the same, he changed the subject. "So, aren't you in on this exercise?"

She snorted with amusement and gestured at the vast expanse of clear air around them. "Nah, I'm patrolling the inner boundary of the no-go zone to make sure none of the kids decide to get smart and pull a shortcut."

"Well, it's one way to keep 'em honest," he agreed. Just as he was about to wish her well and continue toward the Spire, he spotted movement down near her foot. A miniature version of her 'bike's gun mount was swiveling its dual barrels back and forth. "What's that? Side turret?"

"In a way." She gave no signal he could see, but the entire assembly, about the size and shape of half a basketball, detached from the 'bike's frame and hummed into the air, supported by a trio of tiny ducted-fan lifters. It ended up hovering by her shoulder, the small gun barrels lining briefly at him, then tilting safely skyward like their larger cousins. "Bringing your own backup is a good idea. Just saying."

"So I see." He shook his head. "Only you would add guns to your sky-bike, then make it so they could get off and move around."

"I believe I'll take that as a compliment." Raising two fingers, she tapped them to the side of her helmet in something between a salute and a wave. "Have fun taking care of whatever it is you've got to do."

"You, too." Jericho watched as the flying turret reattached itself to the 'bike. Then she did something complicated with the handlebars and pedals, and the sky-bike spun on its own axis; at the same time, the guns on the front swiveled into line as they re-engaged with her helmet HUD. The thrumming of the lifters increased dramatically, and he watched the sky-bike dwindle into the distance as she accelerated away around the edge of the clear area.

One of these days, I'm gonna ask very politely if I can learn how to fly that thing.

But he'd make sure she kept all the guns disabled, just in case.

39
An Unexpected Apology

Feeling somewhat better following the chat with Transit, Jericho banked into a turn and angled up toward a particular point on the side of the Spire. It was usually his habit to fly straight toward the immense edifice, then climb in a lazy spiral until he reached the Technologist's landing stage, but today he just wanted to get there. A hot shower and a dry costume awaited, however briefly the latter might last.

After all, he had to go out into the storm again.

The landing stage doors were shut when he got there, but they slid aside at his approach. This was almost certainly because, as he discovered once the doors opened and the lights came up, the Technologist wasn't in his laboratory. Or rather, not in that specific laboratory. Jericho knew for a fact there were at least three other locations within the Spire where the Technologist was known to express his Artificer capabilities, but he had no idea which one the man might be in.

While the Technologist wasn't present, Scout was. His eyes glowing a dim blue, the robot was locked onto his rack with the damaged armor removed and a multitude of probes attached to what looked almost like biomechanical innards, feeding data to the screens surrounding him. Jericho fought down his initial surge of despair and tried to decipher the graphics and notations scrolling across the displays, but nothing he'd gained from his high-school science classes gave him any chance of making sense of the information. On the other hand, the outputs surely meant *something* was going on, and he had faith in the Technologist's ability to get Scout back to operating condition.

"You just hang in there, good buddy," he said quietly. "You'll be on your feet in no time."

And maybe then he can tell me what he meant by what he said.

It was probably his imagination, but he could've sworn a couple of the readouts ticked upward when he spoke. His breath caught in his throat. "You there, buddy? Can you hear me?"

There was no response that he could see this time, and he grimaced. Confirmation bias was a thing, and as much as he might've *wanted* Scout to respond, to turn those eyes green and talk to him, that wasn't going to happen right now. Or at all, until Transit and the Technologist finished analyzing the extent of the damage and figured out how to repair it.

He stood there for a few moments longer, fully aware he was dripping a puddle on the floor of the laboratory from the water he hadn't managed to get off himself, but unable to tear himself away. Finally, he heaved a sigh.

"You get better soon, hear? You are my goddamn partner, and we're gonna be the greatest heroes the world ever saw." Turning, he moved to the door and slapped the panel to open it. As he strode out into the corridor, something moved in the corner of his vision. He looked back into the laboratory; just as the door slid shut, he saw tiny cleaning bots zipping across the floor to suction up the water.

So that's *how he keeps the place so clean.*

All the way back to his quarters, he tried and failed to get the image of Scout's immobile form out of his head. He hated to admit it even to himself, but it cut far too close to his memory of Luke on the robotic gurney in the morgue.

The difference is, he told himself severely, *Scout's gonna be just fine.*

He rode down in the elevator, barely noticing the discomfort of his G-sense clashing with the artificial-gravity mechanisms. Still struggling with his emotions, he headed along the corridor and tapped his card on the reader outside his quarters. They were starting to boil over as he stepped into the privacy lock, but he kept a lid on them for just a few more seconds.

Stomping inside when the inner door opened, he viciously yanked off his helmet. The high-impact plastic made a satisfying clatter as it bounced off the far wall and fell to the floor, but the sound also brought him up short. He had spares for each part of his costume—the last thing Force Majeure needed was for their members to be sidelined because their uniquely identifying gear had been damaged or even destroyed. But that did *not* mean he had carte blanche to wreck it himself.

"Sonova*bitch!*" he shouted, then turned and swung a punch at the wall. While the impact jarred his arm all the way up to the shoulder, he felt better afterward. It wasn't as helpful as a good long brooding session, but he couldn't see himself getting the chance to have one of *those* in the near future.

Retrieving the headgear, he put it on the table with another sigh. The utility belt came off next, and he dropped it next to the helmet. One by one, he went through the pouches of his belt, collecting the contents into a small pile before he started on the rest of his costume.

As the jacket came off, he wrinkled his nose. Despite the best efforts of the sports deodorant he routinely applied before going out in costume—and he'd applied a double-strength layer especially for the Kennedy ceremony—his exertions in the meantime had taken their toll, and he *reeked*. It was definitely time for a shower.

Once he was down to his underwear, he headed over to the door and pressed the Housekeeping button on the intercom panel. This would bring Forty-Three to his apartment; the little robot was smart enough to recognize his discarded costume for what it was and take it away for cleaning. In the meantime, he gathered up the contents of his utility belt and carried them into his bedroom, where he dropped the various items on his bed.

There were four more identical copies of the belt, each hanging on a hook inside his closet. He took one and laid it out on the bed, then set about moving everything into its designated pouch. This was an excellent way to keep his costume in working order by spreading the wear and tear over several iterations, and it also ensured he wouldn't mislay items by placing them in odd pouches and forgetting about them. The signal device Adam Power had given him a few weeks back was a prime example of that; if he didn't move it into a new belt each time he changed out costumes, he might well have forgotten its existence.

So much better than when I was doing the lone vigilante act around Savannah.

It had been hard enough to maintain one costume back then, let alone create another one identical to the first. Worse, he'd been responsible for repairing any damage; while his Prodigy talents allowed him to quickly acquire skills like needlework, it was *tiresome.* Far better to have an entire organization backing him up, ready to deal with mundane stuff like that.

He knew he didn't have much time. As soon as he finished prepping the belt, he hustled through the shower as though he were paying for the hot water personally. Even so, he felt clean and refreshed by the time he washed the last of the suds away and shut off the water, ready to venture out into the storm again. Stepping from the cubicle, he dried himself down briskly, went into the bedroom, and began dressing in the new costume. With his underwear, trousers, and boots in place, he wandered out into the living area to put on the rest, mainly because there was more room to move around.

He was in the process of toweling his hair off, preparatory to donning his helmet and upper costume, when the door chime sounded. Frowning, he looked in that direction. It wasn't Forty-Three arriving to pick up his wet outfit as he'd initially assumed. Instead, the notification on the screen read SPIRE RECEPTION: VISITOR.

"Accept call, audio-only," he said out loud, wondering who the hell would be visiting him at this point in time.

Sure as hell won't be Smokeshadow.

The screen cleared; a moment later, it showed one of the ladies who ran the reception desk in the main lobby. "Sorry to bother you, sir, but you have two visitors who say they are your parents. Their IDs check out. Are you taking visitors at the moment?" Which was code for: *Are you free, or do you have Force Majeure stuff you need to attend to?*

Jericho's mind raced. He *did* have the rendezvous with Smokeshadow, but if she couldn't air-cab it to wherever she'd stashed the drive, she'd likely be still on her way there in a bus. And his folks were his *folks.* The fate of Force Majeure, he decided, could hang in the balance for a few more minutes.

"Sure thing," he said. "Tell 'em I'll be right down."

"Understood, sir." The call cut off, leaving Jericho standing in the middle of his apartment, towel in hand.

"Crap, crap, crap," he muttered, dashing into the bathroom and dropping the towel roughly over the rail before bolting back to the bedroom.

With his old costume, he could quite easily pretend he was wearing civilian clothing so long as he left off the jacket and mask; he'd done exactly that, more than once. The new costume, not so much. It was a little shinier, slightly bulkier, and a heaping helping more durable. The original soft-soled zip-up boots had given way to bulky monsters (by comparison) that could be used to kick down a door or land heels-first on a bad guy with equal utility.

His parents still didn't know he was a superhero; as far as they were aware, he worked as a data analyst in the Spire amidst the thousands of other civilian contractors. Despite being fully aware of how cowardly he was being, he had no intention of changing that state of affairs. And if he walked out right now wearing those trousers and boots, there was a real chance they'd figure something was up.

He mulled over what they might want as he stripped out of the incriminating items. Following the acrimonious parting where Leroy had driven him to the maglev terminal against his mother's express wishes, he'd been back once to visit Luke's grave. Despite their reluctance to let him return to the city where Luke had been murdered, they'd been more respectful of his choices the second time around, which helped clear the air some.

All things considered, he doubted they were here to talk him into returning to Savannah at this late point in time. Besides, with Jack Portman's death, Luke's murderer had paid for his crime in full, and his parents surely knew it. While he figured they had a good reason to be here, he had no idea what that might be.

Well, as the saying goes, there's only one way to tell the difference between an orange and a lemon.

Donning a pair of jeans and a T-shirt bearing the image of the Saturday morning cartoon hero Captain Utopia—square-jawed, fearless, vanquisher of evil—he pulled on sneakers, then ran a comb through his hair before tying it back. He knew he needed to make this quick; if he kept Smokeshadow waiting too long, she might ditch the meet just to teach him a lesson. Still, he wanted to talk to his parents and let them know he was okay. Slipping his phone into his pocket, he hit the button to open the door.

The short walk along the corridor didn't give him any insights into what his parents wanted him for. He took the elevator to ground level, his G-sense making him feel like he'd left his vital organs somewhere up around the hundredth floor. Still pondering the situation, he threaded his way through the maze of corridors to the scan-locks leading into the lobby without even thinking about it.

He stepped out into the reception area, looking around for his folks. A moment later, he picked them out of the loose gathering of people in the vast room, and headed in that direction. "Pa! Mama!" he called out, raising his arm and waving. "Over here!"

They came to meet him, ending up in a three-way hug that had his ribs creaking under his father's embrace, and nearly as much again with his mother's. Despite all the problems overloading his plate right then, it did his heart a world of good to see the smiles blossoming on their faces. He hugged them back just as fiercely, realizing belatedly just how much he'd missed them. Being a superhero was well and good, but family was always family.

People stepped discreetly away from them, allowing him to steer his parents to a quieter spot. Looking them over, he was fully aware that he couldn't stop grinning and didn't give a good goddamn about it. "It's right good to see y'all," he said, the words feeling inadequate to the purpose. "Everything okay at home?"

"Everything back home's finer'n a frog's hair split four ways, excepting you're not there," his father said bluntly. "Were you fixing to come home any time soon, son?" Beauregard Hansen had never been one to mince words, which was no surprise, seeing as how he ran the largest news distribution business in and around the Savannah area. Tall and broad in the shoulders, he was of a height with Jericho, though thicker through the body.

"Let the boy alone, Beau." Dahlia Hansen, slender and willowy but gifted with an iron will and a razor tongue, had never lost her New York accent or her willingness to tell it exactly as she saw it. "You saw what happened the last time I tried to hold him back." She turned her attention fully onto him, and her eyes softened as she looked over his face. "But honey, I have to say, you do look stressed. Are they working you too hard here? Are you eating right?"

He chuckled dryly, thinking how her eyes would be opened if—maybe *when*—he treated her to a meal in one of the several commissaries scattered on various levels of the Spire. They didn't keep fresh, perishable food in-store there; whatever was ordered, it was *printed* from raw materials, bones and all (for those foodstuffs that usually had bones in them) and served within minutes at whatever temperature was required. "I'm fine, Mama. They feed me better'n okay, here."

He didn't even consider talking about the actual reason behind his current level of stress. For one thing, it would involve outing himself to them; for another, it wasn't anything they could help with, and the last thing he wanted to do was put that on them. Third, he *could* and *would* handle it.

"That's good to hear, son." Beau looked around at the impressive lobby as if taking in the details for the first time. Which, as far as Jericho knew, he was. He didn't think his father had ever come to Utopia before. "So, this is where you work? In this here building?"

"Yup, this here's where I work from." Jericho waved his hand in the general direction of the ceiling. "All the city administration takes place in this building. Most of it's automated, but the human staff makes sure it all keeps running smoothly." All of which was true, of course; he was just giving a misleading impression about his part of the process. He glanced over at the gold-rimmed clock above the reception desks, next to the immense map of the world. "Uh, look, I've gotta run right now, but ..." *Don't just leave them hanging, dumbass!* "Say, how long were y'all fixing to stay in town for?"

Beau and Dahlia looked at each other briefly, and a moment of unspoken communication passed between them. Jericho hoped that he and Thomas would reach the same level of understanding one day. God knew, he never had with Stephen. Or rather, Stephen had known what he wanted and repeatedly ignored it while pushing his own needs on Jericho twenty-four-seven.

Quit it already! The man's dead. No need to keep burying him.

"We don't have to be back in Savannah for a day or two," Beau said, oblivious to Jericho's internal monologue. "What-all did you have in mind?"

Jericho let out a tiny sigh of relief. "I really do want to catch up on everything going on back home, so I'd admire if y'all could stay a while. Once I'm done with my stuff, I can take you out to see the sights of the city. It's pretty damn impressive at night, just gonna say."

Beau nodded slowly. "I figure we can stand to do that, son. You know the city better'n we do. Got a place you'd recommend?"

The Oaklands was nice enough. The staff were professional, the apartments comfortable, and it was an easy walk to the local market. But that was mainly for people fixing to live cheap until they landed themselves a well-paying job, such as the Nashfields. This did *not* describe his parents.

"Was I you, I'd go someplace like the St. George." He'd never stayed there personally, but he knew of it by reputation and he'd marveled at the holographic dragon that wrapped itself around the whole building after dark. "Four-poster beds, a complimentary bottle of champagne when you check in, and it's attached to a five-star restaurant. Even the housekeeping robots talk in a snooty accent."

Dahlia smiled brilliantly. "That sounds amazing. I've heard many things about Utopia City, but one can never know if they're true or not." She paused. "Housekeeping robots? *Really?*"

"Cross my heart," Jericho assured her. "They got 'em most every place folks live, except for personal homes." He paused, thinking about what he needed to do.

Get the data to the Technologist, then back to Kennedy so I can apologize to Thomas. Right. Then back here after the ceremony's done.

"So, when do you figure you'll be free, son?" Beau got right to the point, as always. "You're looking mighty pensive there."

Jericho spoke without thinking. "Maybe eleven or twelve, I reckon."

"Eleven or *twelve?*" Dahlia sounded horrified. "That's half the day away! Why are they working you so hard?"

"There's a time-sensitive project," he extemporized. "I can't tell you any details, honest. But when I finish up, we can go out for an air-cab cruise. Rain'll be long done by then, and we'll have a good view of the Spire and all the holograms." Maybe he'd even take them for a trip to the South Side Mall, so they could check out the gravity drop. He figured his mother would love to browse the shops and maybe pick up one of those new Faraday shoulder bags that were fresh on the scene. Stylish and high fashion on the outside, protecting delicate electronics on the inside.

Beau gave Dahlia a brief hand gesture that Jericho easily interpreted as *'don't push the boy, he's only doing his job'*, then looked out through the glass doors at the curtain of rain still thundering down over on the other side of Challenger Plaza. "Yeah, about that. Y'all get rain like this all the time? I always heard tell Kansas was more about tornadoes than thunderstorms."

Jericho chuckled. "No, this is a one-off. Don't spread this around, but Utopia can control the weather, right down to which houses get rained on and which stay dry. Right now, Force Majeure's running a training exercise. All the heroes in the city are out there in that, knocking drones out of the sky. The rain's just there to make it harder. Once the drill is done, they'll switch it off like you or me turning a faucet."

Beau shook his head, more in apparent wonder than disagreement. "I gotta hand it to you, son. When most boys move away from home, they end up at the ass-end of nowhere. *You* move into a city where they got housekeeping robots and weather control." He slapped Jericho on the shoulder. "From the way you keep glancing at that there fancy wall clock, your time's surely beholden to someone upstairs, so we won't keep you any longer. Ready to go, honeybunch?"

Dahlia nodded. "In a minute. Jericho, honey, this is the main reason we came to see you." Delving into her handbag, she came up with a small, padded mailer of a type that looked suspiciously familiar to Jericho. "This came for you, and we were holding on to it for when you next visited. Then a couple of weeks came and went, so we just decided to stop being stubborn and come visit you ourselves."

The mailer wasn't addressed, but it bore his name ... written in Stephen's painfully exact hand.

What in the living goddamn hell? He gave this shit to my folks?

An image crossed his mind of Stephen knocking on the front door of the Hansen house and handing the mailer to his mother. "How ... when did you get this? How did he contact you?"

Something in the tone of his voice must have tipped his mother off that all was not well. "It was mailed to us in a larger envelope, a few weeks ago. Is something the matter?"

"I don't know yet," Jericho said grimly. "Let me see." The temptation was there to eighty-six the mailer into the nearest trash can, but that would needlessly upset his mama, so he tore it open instead.

If he wasn't dead, I'd kick his ass all over again.

Within was the expected thumb drive, this time in an attractive shade of mauve, along with a folded piece of paper. Carefully, as though defusing an explosive device, Jericho unfolded the paper. It turned out to be a note, also in Stephen's handwriting. Bracing himself to endure his ex's usual mix of wheedling and manipulation, he began to read. He was vaguely aware of his parents stepping up on either side to read over his shoulder, but he didn't care right then.

Dear Jericho,
I am genuinely sorry for this intrusion, but I desperately need you to view the file on this drive.
Please also accept my most profound apologies for everything I have ever put you through.
   Regards,
   Stephen

Jericho blinked and read the note through again, from the beginning. He could just about see Stephen sending the mailer to his parents, but the heartfelt apology was as far from his ex-boyfriend's usual style as he could have imagined.

Without the note, he would likely have ditched the thumb drive as soon as he got it; the last one he'd begun watching had pushed his patience far beyond its breaking point. But now, goddamn it all, he was *curious*. Worse, Stephen had actually said he was sorry for … well, about the first time *ever*. In a way that sounded sincere, anyway.

"Huh. Okay, then." He mustered a smile for their benefit. "I'll definitely look at it as soon as possible. Thanks for bringing it along."

"Is everything okay? From the sounds of that note, you have a history with this Stephen person." As a lawyer, Dahlia Hansen had always been the perceptive one of the pair. "What's going on?"

History. Well, that's definitely one *way to put it.*

He heaved a sigh. "Stephen was my boyfriend. He didn't want me to come to Utopia; when I came anyway, he took it badly. The breakup was … unpleasant." He gestured with the note. "This is the first *hint* of an actual sincere apology I've gotten for his behavior."

The fact that Stephen had also died in the apartment fire on the day before she got the mailer wasn't something Jericho wanted to lay on her as well. Fortunately, she didn't seem to have made the connection, with just a first name to go on with.

"Ah. Right." Beau slapped Jericho on the shoulder again; belatedly, Jericho recalled his father still wasn't totally comfortable with casual reminders of his personal preferences. "That's good, then." He let out a gusty sigh and nodded to his wife. "C'mon, hon, let's leave Jericho to do what he's gotta do and go catch the bus. See if that there St. George place is all it's cracked up to be."

Dahlia gave Jericho a beaming smile. "Right with you, darling." Leaning up slightly, she gave Jericho a peck on the cheek. "It *is* good to see you again. And working in a place like this?" She shook her head, looking around. "My offices in Atlanta have *nothing* on the Spire."

"I'm right pleased to see you too, Mama." Jericho hugged her, then watched as his parents headed for the doors. Just before they went outside, they turned and waved. He waved back, then started back toward the scan-lock he'd come out of.

That had taken up some little time, but it was nothing he couldn't handle.

Get back upstairs and suit up, then go meet Smokeshadow.

The clock was ticking.

40
The Right Question

When Jericho entered his apartment a few minutes later, he was still mulling over the mystery of the note and the mailer. Stephen had to have known he was overstepping the line by a country mile by contacting Jericho's folks, but he'd done it anyway. The apology note was also throwing Jericho off; the handwriting and phrasing were all Stephen's, but the content was entirely out of left field.

So, what's on this drive? He very much doubted it had anything to do with the files Stephen had sent on to Franklin Tucker to get decrypted. If Stephen had specific knowledge of Force Majeure playing fast and loose with the rules or whatever the latest online hate-post had them doing, he would've been insufferably smug, not apologetic.

As he'd half expected, Forty-Three was already on site, carefully placing his previously-used boots into its internal storage. The rest of the discarded costume had already been packed in there; the handy little robot would convey it to be cleaned and repaired, then bring it back in a day or so and place it back in his closet. It was a convenient system.

He recalled an amusing anecdote Transit had told him while introducing Forty-Three to his apartment. Apparently, one of the other tenants hadn't listened to the instructions to have everything squared away and had left his suitcase on his bed when the housekeeping robot made its initial inspection of the apartment. Over the next few days, whenever that person returned in the evening, he would find the suitcase pulled out from under the bed and placed on top again. It had required the actual housekeeping staff to come in and have the robot do a recalibration sweep before his complaints about the 'suitcase poltergeist' came to an end.

Jericho suspected it was more of a cautionary tale than a true story, intended to point out the sheer literal-minded nature of the housekeeping robots. He still liked to treat them as people, though. It was just the way he was.

"Oh, hey, Forty-Three," he said. "How're things?"

"**Good afternoon, Jericho. I am operating within parameters.**" The robot closed the lid over the boots. "**I will be taking your costume to be cleaned and repaired. Was that your intention?**"

"Sure." Only half-listening, Jericho began going over in his head what he had to do once he left the Spire. *Go to Memorial Park, meet with Smokeshadow, get the drive with the data, bring it back ...* "And thanks."

"You are welcome, Jericho. Have a pleasant afternoon." Forty-Three turned on the spot, its wheels soundless on the carpet, and trundled toward the door.

"Yeah, see you later ..." Jericho's voice trailed off as a memory intruded into his head, sparked by the drive he held in his hand. He'd been sitting at the table with two similar drives, both deposited by Stephen into the post office box Jericho had since emptied. While one drive was postmarked from before their breakup, the second one had been posted the day Stephen died.

He remembered looking at the earlier one, finding even more evidence of Stephen's perfidy, but the more recent one ...

Would he have even been thinking about storing dirty home movies in the post office box if he had access to information that made Force Majeure look bad?

"Hey, Forty-Three," he said without really thinking about it, "do you remember cleaning up here a while ago and finding a couple busted thumb drives on the floor or in the trash? You didn't happen to keep them, did you?"

The answer would be 'no', of course. No matter how much Jericho anthropomorphized the little robot, Forty-Three would always lack anything approximating human curiosity. If something looked like trash, it would be discarded as trash. But just as people uselessly jiggled locked doors or turned the ignition key just one more time on a dead battery, Jericho asked the question anyway.

"I sent one damaged USB drive in for reclamation. Have a pleasant afternoon, Jericho."

The door slid open and the robot exited, leaving Jericho standing in the living room staring after it. He knew time was ticking on, and Smokeshadow was more than likely on her way to Memorial Park at that moment, but he had to check out the implications of Forty-Three's statement.

He sent one in? What happened to the other one?

Turning as if on a pivot, he dropped the mailer and its former contents on the table, then stared at the fridge. He'd thrown the fragments of the drives so they'd bounce off the appliance and into the trash can under the counter, as he usually did with everything else when he was feeling too lazy to get up and carry it through. However, bits of busted electronics were less bouncy than crumpled paper balls.

He found himself repeating the question in his head. Forty-Three hadn't specified where the drive had been. Jericho knew the robot swept the kitchenette floor and emptied the trash, so it could've been in either location. But only one had been sent in for reclamation. Where had the other one gone? And which one was it?

He headed around the counter and confronted the fridge. As fridges will, it loomed back at him. Stretching onto the tips of his toes, he surveyed the top. There was a moderate accumulation of dust but no errant thumb drives.

Okay, so that's the way of it then.

He took a deep breath and slid his hands in along either side of the fridge. It wasn't easy, given that the niche was designed to accommodate it with bare inches to spare, but he managed. An exertion of his power brought the appliance down to just a few dozen pounds in effective weight. Then, using only the friction supplied by his bare hands, he lifted the whole damn thing off the floor and walked backward with it.

He backed into the counter just before the fridge would've cleared the niche, but then he managed to turn it sideways a smidgen and examine the area behind it. More dust (unsurprising, given that Forty-Three couldn't reach back here), a few coins he recalled dropping when he'd first moved in … and a small metal object that *wasn't* a coin.

He couldn't stretch his arm far enough to reach it, and he didn't feel like wriggling in past the fridge, but that was okay. A push-tag formed in his hand, and he flicked it at his quarry. The 'tag struck true, and the object smacked into his palm half a second later. Turning his hand over, he examined it.

It was indeed a thumb drive with most of the exterior shell broken off. Uncertain memory suggested that one had been red and the other blue. He *thought* the one he'd looked at had featured a red case; the fragments clinging to this one were blue.

No matter which one it was, he didn't have the time to plug it into his laptop and examine its contents. Nor did he want to just leave either drive lying around in the apartment, just in case Forty-Three decided they were trash. It would be the height of irony to lose them to the reclamation system when either one of them might hold the key to the mystery. Grabbing a Ziploc bag, he wadded it around the busted drive.

He ducked into the bedroom and changed back into the lower half of his costume, then came out and laid the new utility belt on the table. The swaddled-up drive went into one pouch on the belt; the mauve drive and its attendant note, replaced in their mailer, went into another. While the pouches were already supposed to be waterproof and Faraday-caged (except for the specialized one he kept the phone in), extra precautions were always good.

Settling the utility belt around his waist, he hauled on the rest of the costume in record time. The helmet usually slid into place without a problem, but today was the day it chose to act out, forcing him to jiggle it from side to side so the earpieces slipped into place without too much painful stabbing of his earlobes. Even with all that, he was able to fasten the chin strap and dash out the door in less than two minutes. Memorial Park awaited, as did Smokeshadow.

Hopefully, he wouldn't get *too* wet along the way.

41
A Covert Exchange

If anything, the rain was heavier. Or perhaps that was just his personal impression; having taken the time to shower and catch his breath, everything had calmed down for him. Having donned a new costume seemed to help as well, even if it was only a psychological benefit. All of this just added to the contrast when he hit the rain again. Or rather, *it* hit *him*.

The waterproof layer on his costume was tested to its limits from the moment he crossed the invisible boundary separating the Spire from the rest of Utopia City. Fortunately, tucking his jacket collar up under the rim of his helmet appeared to work; most of the water was running off rather than finding its way down the back of his neck. He was equally grateful for the HUD incorporated into the goggles, allowing him to move at near-top flying speed through the pounding rain.

The dim glow of headlights from below alerted him to the fact that people were out and about in their cars despite the downpour, or perhaps *because* of it. In the usual run of things, the techs in the Spire ensured that any inclement weather occurring in or around the city was moderated to a fare-thee-well. Hence, a genuine thunderstorm was more or less a novelty by now.

At least they didn't have to worry about accidents; cars in Utopia rode on magnetic levitation of their own, and each one was tied into the local computer-controlled traffic net. There would be no skidding out of control due to loss of traction, and no accidental collisions.

The sweeping curtains of rain parted briefly, and he saw one of the drones banking around a corner with Black Dragon in hot pursuit. Draconic jaws opened; a blast of plasma leaped out (evaporating the rain along the way) and washed over the drone. He distantly heard the internal explosion before the drone dropped away and the rain closed in again.

It certainly seemed like the girl was having fun, though he hoped she was exercising more restraint than he'd seen from her so far. The multiple lenses of the camera harness she was wearing would've caught at least some of the drone kill, while the rest would be recording her ongoing performance during the exercise. Afterward, the footage from the drones themselves would be integrated with data from building cameras and the harnesses to create a virtual 3-D playback of each participant's performance from beginning to end ... along with any screwups they'd perpetrated on the way.

This was the main reason he couldn't just join in willy-nilly, quite apart from the fact that he had a job of his own to carry out. Lacking a camera harness, he would skew the numbers from the drill and probably end up being yelled at by Relentless or the Technologist. *Next time,* he told himself. He still needed to get to the park and do the pickup before the last drone was taken out and the cover afforded to him by the drill was gone.

And then, once he got Smokeshadow's drive back to the Technologist, he could check out the one he'd found behind the fridge. The thought crossed his mind that it might just be more of Stephen's crap, but somehow he didn't think so.

I'll watch just enough of it to make sure, then I'll hand it over too. That data needs to be in safe hands.

The thought crossed his mind that either way, he'd want to forget what he'd seen, making his mouth quirk in a sardonic grin. *'Eyes only'* versus *'gouge my eyes out with a spoon'.* But he definitely intended to check first. If he handed over footage of Stephen's idea of 'sexy and seductive' for his bosses to watch, even by pure accident … *nope. Just nope.* Even the very thought made him cringe inside.

Once he'd dealt with all that, he'd be free to get back to Kennedy Visitor Center, where he could represent Force Majeure and catch up with Thomas all at the same time. Exploring the exhibits with his boyfriend at his side would be *so* much more fun than doing it alone.

The wireframe images on the HUD showed a gap beyond the buildings ahead, right where he figured Memorial Park to be. He powered onward, his goal now in sight, in a manner of speaking. As with the buildings, the hill the park was built on was nigh-invisible in the downpour, though the goggles showed him where it was with more wireframe diagrams.

There could only be one place for them to meet in the park; this was at the summit, where the four pathways came together to form a cross. It was where he and Smokeshadow and Thomas had sat and eaten, then planned out the raid on the South Side Mall. Aside from the Oaklands and the Spire itself, it was *the* place that held the most significance in Utopia for him.

Since then, he'd been back on his own a couple of times to pay his respects to the ninety thousand people whose lives had been snuffed out in an instant by Doc Iridium's bomb. It had affected him deeply each time, and probably always would, but this visit would be necessarily brief. More important matters were at stake.

Swooping low over the paved area that made up the junction of the four paths, he noted that the eternal flame was still burning brightly in the middle of the memorial fountain, protected from the wind and rain by the integrated force field. The flags, on the other hand, hung sodden and limp on each of the three flagpoles spaced around the fountain, only shifting with the stronger wind gusts. Turned toward the storm, the broad umbrellas over the picnic tables surrounding the whole tableau fended off the incessant rain.

He flared his grav-wings and came to a brief hover, then descended vertically to land between two of the flagpoles. Dismissing the 'wings, he held up his hand to shield his goggles from the rain and peered around, checking each table in turn. "Hello?" he called out. "You here?"

Just for a second, he began to wonder if she'd bailed on him, then a slender figure moved, waving him over to the table they'd had the original picnic lunch at. Until she'd deliberately shown herself, he hadn't seen her at all. Part of it had to be the rain, but the rest was all down to the camouflage effect of her hyperweave costume. Even the HUD goggles, designed to pick out any obstacle, failed to register her presence. As a member of Force Majeure, he had access to the Technologist's equipment, but he was *still* impressed by her tech.

"Took your time," she said as he sat opposite her. She had droplets of water on her face inside the hood of her costume, but as far as he could tell, she hadn't suffered from the same level of drenching as he had. Even the costume itself was dry, or mostly so; errant raindrops ran off it as he watched.

"Sorry," he said automatically before the grin on her face clued him in that she was joshing him. "How long have you been waiting?"

"Got here about thirty seconds before you did," she admitted. "Think you were followed?"

"What, in this?" He turned and gestured at the surrounding rain. "If anything of any size was trailing me, I'd know about it. Nobody here but us chickens."

"Mm, true," she conceded. She reached inside her costume, which parted at her touch, and took out a large Ziploc bag containing an external hard drive. "Here you go. All the data I dragged down, still in encrypted format. Have fun with it."

He frowned as he took it. "But the one we found at Tucker's place was a lot smaller, thumb drive sized. Why is this one bigger?"

"Because this one's got *all* the files, like I said," she explained patiently. "LaMonde contacted me to say only the first few had been decrypted, not all of them. I'm guessing he would've sent them through piecemeal, as Tucker got them done."

"Oh. Right." He accepted the bag from her. "Thanks. I appreciate this. You may just have saved Utopia City."

She rolled her eyes. "Don't say things like that. It's bad for my self-image. Still friends?"

Despite the serious nature of the situation, her attitude drew a chuckle from him. "Yeah, still friends. Just don't do this sort of thing too often, or you'll be straining my definition of the word."

"Yeah, like—" Her eyes went wide, and she threw herself back from the table. As though she'd stepped in front of a green screen, she vanished between one instant and the next. "Shit! *Incoming!*"

Her abrupt movement and the alarm in her tone triggered his own reaction. Making himself as light as possible, he kicked off upward, unfurling his 'wings as he came out from under the umbrella. He pushed for altitude, surging upward over the flagpoles, straining his G-sense outward for any indication of what she'd spotted.

Howling like banshees, two drones whipped past just above him, one after the other. He registered their presence, identified what they were, and dismissed them as a threat, all in the same split second.

Oh, I am so gonna rib her for panicking—

Lightning struck the second drone, the actinic bar of light connecting the clouds to the hurtling device. Three forks of coruscating electricity arced down from the luckless drone to the flagpoles below … and one of these tagged Jericho on the way past. Every electronic device on him died at once; both earpieces let out piercing feedback squeals, his HUD goggles flared blinding white as every emitter in them blew, and he *felt* his powers stifle as the enhancement harness went the same way.

Even within the protection of his insulated costume, all his muscles locked up like they never had before. He'd been tasered once, but that was *nothing* compared to this. The previous experience had been like a swipe from a Nerf bat, while this was akin to suffering a full-on impact from an eighteen-wheeler.

His mind went blank. On the very edge of unconsciousness, he felt himself falling, the wind stirring his ponytail. His ears were ringing, and he couldn't see a thing, but he vaguely realized that bad things were going to happen when he landed; with a tremendous effort, he reduced his effective weight.

Then he impacted the ground, and the lights went out altogether.

42
Sudden, But Inevitable

Jericho's body ached, far beyond anything he'd experienced in his life to that point. It was like he'd been worked over by a bunch of over-enthusiastic silverback gorillas with baseball bats, only a whole lot more so. Steel-toed boots, he decided. They'd been wearing steel-toed boots as well. And smoking truly *horrible* cigars; even now, the acrid smell stung his nostrils.

Before he could start wondering if gorillas could wear steel-toed boots, much less if they would smoke cigars, a crunching impact in his side brought him a long way toward re-engaging with reality. When he tried to move, his muscles twitched almost uncontrollably, so it took him three tries to open his eyelids. It didn't really help—he couldn't see a thing, though he still wasn't sure whether this was due to lack of light or actual blindness—but he managed to push himself up onto one elbow anyway. His ears were still ringing, further hampering him.

He had no idea what was going on, what had struck him just now, or whether he was permanently blind, but he was determined to get up and find out anyway. "Shadow?" he croaked. His throat was raw, as though he'd just screamed himself hoarse. He may well have, but he didn't remember doing it.

Fuzzy but still functional, his G-sense kicked in, warning him of something heavy on a collision course with his head. He brought his arm up and around, blocking it and protecting his face, but the impact numbed his forearm and flung him onto his back.

Between the pain and the realization that someone had tried to kick him in the face, adrenaline flooded through his system. His head miraculously clearing, he kept rolling while he clawed the goggles away from his eyes. It was easier to pull them down than push them up, so he let them rest around his neck and tried to blink away the dazzle.

His back thumped into something, preventing him from rolling any farther, then he saw someone moving up to stand over him. Between the still-lingering spots dancing in his vision and the overall lack of ambient light—the rain, which he'd just now registered, was *still* pouring down, but not on him for some reason—all he could make out was a dark silhouette. A *really* dark silhouette. Like a cutout in the world. With another blink, he got rid of most of the spots, making out a metal belt and a shoulder-guard.

Silent Knight. Oh good, the cavalry's here.

"Thank God you got here in time, buddy," he rasped, reaching upward with his right hand. "Give me a hand?"

A black-gauntleted hand closed around his, but the expected assistance did not come. At least not at first. Jericho still couldn't see very well, which meant he didn't notice the sword until it was almost too late. Silent Knight hauled upward on his arm and stabbed downward at the same time with the midnight-dark blade, aiming the tip of the weapon at the notch in Jericho's throat.

Unable to pull free, Jericho frantically flung his left arm around and down, pushing the sword out of line. While he succeeded in getting it away from his throat, his muscles were still strenuously protesting the abuse they'd just gone through, so he wasn't fast or strong enough to deflect it all the way. Driven by the inhuman strength of Silent Knight's thrust, the tip of the sword skidded down his Kevlar-reinforced costume until it punched through, a little below his breastbone. The polycarbonate plates were all that saved him from being spitted like a roast; while the sword passed between two of these, it snagged on one, so it only pierced his flesh by a couple of inches.

The pain was astounding, but instead of putting him out of the fight, it galvanized him into action. Instinctively, he grabbed the blade with his left hand to stop it from going farther in while he pushed his power through his right into the hand grasping his. He'd never inflicted the full ten-times effective weight on a living person before, but desperate times required desperate measures. It didn't matter how strong Silent Knight was; this would end the fight.

Except … nothing happened.

Silent Knight leaned on the blade, trying to force it deeper into Jericho's body. Gritting his teeth, Jericho twisted his right hand free from the black-gloved grip, lifted his lower body, and drove his boot-heels into Silent Knight's armored groin and solar plexus. The sword pulled free, red blood showing plainly on the black steel as the renegade hero—*no, not Silent Knight. This has to be Poser!*—stumbled backward. Lines of fire traced across Jericho's left hand from where the blade had sliced through his glove and the skin of his palm and fingers alike.

Pressing his injured hand against the stab wound, Jericho looked up to find that he was lying next to one of the picnic tables, where the umbrella was shielding him from the rain. The hot wetness of the blood as it oozed from the wound told him that if he didn't get to his feet *now* and mount some sort of defense, he was a dead man.

Fighting against the twitchiness pervading his entire body, he reached up and grabbed the edge of the table with his right hand. His enhancement harness was gone to the lightning strike, but he still had his original powerset. Reducing his weight to its absolute minimum, he hauled himself to his feet without once using his stomach muscles, a feat he would've found impossible before getting his powers. Swaying unsteadily, pushing back against the fuzziness that wanted to take him back down into the comfortable, warm darkness, he faced off against his foe.

"Who are you?" he panted. "What did you do with Silent Knight?" His stomach hurt abominably, but he had more important matters to worry about. If Poser (whoever he really was) wanted to gloat, Jericho was willing to stall until the real cavalry arrived.

Any doubt he might've had about this being the theoretical Poser came when a *mouth* opened in the faceplate of the fake Silent Knight's armor.

Silent Knight's armor is totally sealed. Sealed armor is his thing. It doesn't open up like that. He didn't bother learning how to use the armor. He just simulated it using his shapeshifting. But why doesn't my power work on him?

The ringing in Jericho's ears was gradually easing off, but between that and the steady drumming of the rain on the umbrella, he still had trouble hearing Poser's words. It didn't help that the Silent Knight pretender had a genuinely horrific voice, both squealing and grating at the same time. Something about the sound flared danger signals in Jericho's mind and sent chills down his spine.

"*... have no idea what you've done, do you?*" the dark figure snarled as it stalked forward. "*You just keep sticking your nose in. Flag wanted me to keep you alive, but—*"

Jericho had no time to ponder who 'Flag' was, as Poser's monologue was interrupted by the *tac-tac-tac-tac* of a UCPD-issue wireless taser. At the same time, he heard Smokeshadow shout, "Run!"

Just as his power had been no-sold by Poser—*can this guy actually give himself invulnerability with his shape-changing?*—it seemed the taser was equally ineffective. Poser stopped, though, and turned to face where Smokeshadow stood, mostly see-through but with enough rain rolling off her costume to give her position away. The taser, clasped in both hands, drooped toward the ground.

"*I see you,*" he said in his unsettling voice, and laughed horribly. "*You can't hide from us, little hacker. Not anymore.*"

"Go," gasped Jericho, still pressing his hand to his wound. "Get away." Smokeshadow was a past master at any kind of social interaction, but her Prodigy powerset was more aimed toward the mental pursuits than combat. His only chance to survive in this situation was to keep the pretender busy until help arrived.

Of course, it would be helpful if either one of them *had* called for help. Maybe she'd taken the time to do that before attacking with the taser? He could only hope so. She was undoubtedly smarter than him.

He formed a push-tag in his right hand and flicked it at the sword to pull it out of line, only for Poser to lunge forward and swing at Smokeshadow anyway. The silvered edge flickered through the air, but she moved aside almost negligently, allowing it to miss by inches.

Okay, so she can read him well enough to know when to dodge. That's good.

Next, he began to form a glue-tag in his right hand. In the brief seconds Jericho allowed himself to create the tangled bundle of gravitational forces, Poser slashed at Smokeshadow three more times; with each attack, she simply faded out of the way, as elusive as her name suggested. But all the Force Majeure infiltrator had to do was get lucky just once. She had no way of hurting him in return.

On the other hand, despite his sorry state, Jericho knew his powers *could* affect the pretender. The push-tag had proven that. So, it was up to him to use the opening she was giving him and take down the traitor before Poser could retaliate.

If this had been the genuine Silent Knight, wearing real power armor, he could've put it out of action with a few glue-tags to the joints. But that wasn't the case, so he had to get creative.

When the glue-tag was as strong as he dared wait for, he flicked it across the impromptu arena toward Poser's left boot. It struck true, pulling Poser up short as his foot stuck to the salvaged brickwork. Slowly turning, the shape-changer stared toward Jericho. "*Oh, so you **want** to die then, you little shit?*"

Jericho hastily began prepping a second glue-tag, but Poser had already abandoned his pursuit of Smokeshadow. The shape-changer went after Jericho with fresh determination, moving almost at a run despite having to heave his foot free of the brickwork at every step. Leading the charge with his sword, even with the way it kept swaying out of line, he clearly meant to finish the job this time.

If Jericho had been healthy and whole, he still would've approached this fight with a modicum of caution; fighting someone who was swinging a three-foot length of razor-sharp carbon steel around was no joke. Wounded and bruised, more than a little dizzy, his muscles still jerky and twitchy from the lightning strike, he was in no condition to be upright and moving, much less fighting. But he was a prodigy, and they did 'famous last stand' better than anyone.

So, as he backed off, he kept his eyes on Poser and looked for any chance to turn the tide. *Go,* he silently urged Smokeshadow. *Get help. Pass the word.* Even if he died here, someone had to alert the rest of Force Majeure about the traitor in their midst.

A wave of disorientation passed through him, making him stumble. The initial burst of adrenaline was wearing off, he knew. His injuries were beginning to catch up with him. Blinking away the creeping tide of darkness, he realized to his despair that the momentary lapse in concentration had allowed the effects of his 'tags to dissipate.

Poser strode forward, no longer having to wrench his foot free of the ground. The closer he got to Jericho, the more he seemed to gloat, to draw out this final moment. The tip of the blade, still tinged red with Jericho's blood despite the incessant rain, swayed back and forth hypnotically.

Jericho gave ground steadily, retreating along one of the pathways that led down the hill. Despite the discreet lighting set into the edges of the path, it was darker beneath the over-arching trees, but the foliage was turning away some of the rain. The vitrified stone slabs on either side, displaying column after column of the names of the dead, bore silent witness to the confrontation. They also meant Poser could only come at him from one direction.

Should I do a G-shake?

It was the only gambit he hadn't tried yet. But G-shakes took effort; in his debilitated state, he couldn't be sure of staying on his feet *or* putting the impersonator down long enough to escape.

"Just tell me," he gasped, pushing past the pain and the encroaching weariness to focus on his foe. "Who are you, really? What did you do with Silent Knight?" The black-armored artificer may not have been very friendly during the initial interview and afterward, but he was still a member of Force Majeure and thus a teammate and comrade in arms.

"*You still have no idea, do you?*" The grating, grinding voice came out of no human larynx; of that much, Jericho was sure. Merely listening to it sent shudders down his spine. The memory it was trying to spark was louder and closer but still wasn't making itself known. "*You're so fucking stupid. Can't see what's been right in front of you the whole time.*" Almost lazily, Poser lunged with the sword.

Jericho dodged backward, but the pervasive weakness spreading through his limbs made him stumble; only his power-assisted sense of balance kept him on his feet. He knew he should be fighting back, but the presence of the sword and his wavering concentration put him at an almost fatal disadvantage. Putting out a hand, he steadied himself against a slab of rock, then tried to blink the dizziness out of his eyes. "What ... what can't I see?" he managed.

Instead of answering, Poser raised the sword. This time, Jericho could tell the pretender was going for the kill. He readied himself; if he could dodge just at the right time and the infiltrator overextended, he might be able to create an opening he could exploit. It was a slim hope but better than nothing.

Then Smokeshadow ghosted up behind Poser. Instead of the taser, she held in her hand a collapsible baton. Down it swung, aiming at the shoulder-guard. Before Jericho could even begin to formulate a query as to why she was attacking the most impervious portion of the impostor's armor, it bounced off.

Poser's head turned slightly. "*Hold tight. I'll get to you in a second.*" Then he flicked his attention back to Jericho. "*Now, where were we?*"

In a sleight-of-hand move that would've won prizes in a demonstration of stage magic, Smokeshadow swapped out the baton for her discus. Slapping the electronic device onto Poser's shoulder-guard, she hit a button. There was a triple beep, then the shoulder-guard unlatched itself from the metal-link belt and fell away, clattering to the ground. "Force field is down!" she shouted.

Force field. Of course. Goddamn cheating sonovabitch.

Jericho wanted to facepalm, but he didn't have the time. He'd thought he was making contact with Poser when he pushed his power, but even a tenth-of-an-inch thickness force field would negate that ability. But *now* he had a chance, however slim it might be. He breathed deeply, summoning his reserves for one final last-ditch effort.

"Oh, you fucking didn't, you little whore!" To Jericho's astonishment, Poser didn't come in for the attack. Half-turning his head, the shape-changer dropped the sword; it clattered on the stained and burned bricks that made up the pathway. The black-armored figure's arms and legs began jerking and twitching oddly.

Is he having a seizure? What's going on here?

As Jericho stared, the infiltrator's body shifted and *changed*, taking on inhuman proportions. Arms lengthened, and fingers extended into claws, while legs altered shape and form to become digitigrade. Even Poser's head altered in shape, the previously featureless faceplate stretching out into a muzzle filled with extremely sharp-looking teeth.

However, the most telling aspect was the coloration of the armor. From a polished black sheen all over, it became blood-red on the clawed hands and feet and underbelly, fading into a jagged black-and-red series of tiger-stripes covering the rest of the villain's body. Red eyes blinked, and the toothy maw opened in a razor grin.

Despite his resolve, Jericho took a step back. He *knew* that grin. It had featured in his nightmares once upon a time, and again on the screen of his phone, on the maglev. Real life, he found, was a heaping helping scarier than archived footage.

"Holy crap," he blurted. "You're goddamn *Charnel*."

Which, on the face of it, was impossible. Charnel had died in Omaha, in 1998. His broken body had been displayed to the cheering crowds after a knock-down-drag-out battle with Force Majeure heroes. He had been, unequivocally, *dead*.

So how was he alive now? Jericho's head spun as he tried to work his way through the puzzle.

Maybe Poser's just trying to mess with our heads. But if that's the plan ... why'd he drop the sword? Why'd he even bother changing? He was doing just fine as he was.

Taking advantage of Jericho's momentary hesitation, the villain with Charnel's aspect turned so fast that his movement was just a blur. One unnaturally long striped arm lashed out to latch crimson talons around Smokeshadow's throat. *"Gotcha,"* growled the bestial Enabled. His other hand drew back, razor claws flexing. Muscles bunched under the black and red carapace; he was clearly preparing to eviscerate his captive where she stood.

Not if Jericho had anything to do with it. Galvanized into action by the danger to his friend, he launched into a jumping, spinning ax kick that caused his stomach wound to flood his body with pain. But it was a pain he could endure as his heel smashed into where the creature's suprascapular nerve point should be located. If the carapace could flex, a blow could be delivered through it. The kick landed just right, hard enough to break the shoulder of an ordinary man. As it was, the impact sent yet another wave of agony all the way through his body … and caused the thing's claws to open, just far enough for Smokeshadow to slip free.

Jericho didn't dare let up; disregarding his stab wound for the moment, he hammered his knee into where his adversary's sciatic nerve would typically be, then wrapped his right arm around the creature's neck and his left around its chest. Bright agony flared in his arms as claws dug in, punching through the blade-resistant sleeves of his costume and digging into the flesh beneath. But he hung on, even as he lightened both himself and his temporary captive. Then he kicked off, propelling them both upward as hard as possible.

They soared vertically toward the tree cover overhead. Jericho's right arm was seized by one clawed hand and pulled free with breathtaking strength. He let it happen, jerking his arm away and grabbing an overhead branch when it came within reach … *then* applying the full ten-times-effect of normal gravity just before releasing his foe with his left arm. *This* time, it worked. There was a rush of wind and an extremely brief screech of panic, followed by a solid *crunch*.

Letting go of the branch and pressing his left hand to the wound again, he drifted down to ground level, fighting to remain conscious. Pain racked his body as he stared down at the supposedly long-dead supervillain: genuinely deceased now, having fallen the equivalent of fifteen stories to the pathway beneath. Dark blood stained the shattered bricks beneath the cracked carapace, diluted by the thin sheen of water running down the path.

"What was that about?" he asked dizzily, accepting Smokeshadow's assistance to remain standing. "Think he really was Charnel?" It was almost too much to believe, but there was the proof right before them.

The body slowly shifted and changed again as they watched, becoming a middle-aged man whose face Jericho had never seen. But then, he'd never seen Silent Knight's face either, in the three months he'd been on the team.

"Maybe." She shook her head consideringly. "I can tell you he was comfortable in that form. It wasn't new or strange to him." She adjusted her grip under his right arm. "Let's just get you—"

"You're not going anywhere." The words cracked like a whip in the confined space under the trees. Recognizing Independence's voice, Jericho turned painfully. She advanced carefully up the path, her assault rifle at the ready, looking more lethal than ever. "On your knees. Hands behind your heads. Right now."

Jericho sagged with relief. Whatever personal differences Independence might have with him, she was a consummate professional; once he cleared things up, they'd be able to start figuring this whole thing out. *This* time, the cavalry had well and truly arrived.

"Thank God you're here," he rasped. "You would not believe *who*—"

"On your knees, both of you," Independence ordered, her voice cold and hard. "Hands behind your heads. Right now. I won't tell you a third time."

Both of you. It took that and a nudge from Smokeshadow for him to realize this was not going the way he'd thought it would. *Crap. Crap, crap, crap.* He didn't need this right now. "Independence," he said as Smokeshadow helped him down to a kneeling position. "It's not what it looks like. Relentless knew I was coming here."

"What did you do to Silent Knight? Who's that with you?" Her tone was unchanged, and the gun muzzle never wavered from his face, as if his words had gone unheard.

"This is my contact," Jericho said desperately. "I told Relentless. He said it was okay to come here and meet her. I got the stolen data back." A moment later, her words registered on him. "That's Silent Knight? Really? Because just now, he was Charnel."

Independence froze, just for an instant. Then Jericho was falling sideways, propelled by Smokeshadow's shove. She went the other way, while the three-round burst fired by Independence went between them.

He smacked into the shaped stone slab at the side of the path with painful force. As shocking as the impact was on his body, it couldn't hold a candle to his stunned realization. Independence—*the* Independence—had just tried to kill him. Even now, she was adjusting her aim toward him.

I know she doesn't like me, but what the hell?

More as a conditioned reflex than from any kind of planned response, he formed and flicked away a glue-tag with his right hand. The 'tag hit the firearm and insinuated itself into the firing mechanism just in time; less than half a second later, he was looking right down the barrel of the rifle. Without any kind of hesitation, Independence squeezed the trigger.

Nothing happened.

Jericho concentrated on the rifle, desperately willing the glue-tag to hold. Her eyes on his face, Independence deliberately yanked on the charging handle. Fortunately, it failed to budge. Her lip curled in a silent snarl.

He wanted to talk to her, plead with her, find out *why* she was doing this. But he didn't need Smokeshadow's level of savvy to know it wouldn't do him any good. For whatever reason, Independence fully intended to kill him. When that sort of thing happened, her target usually died.

The assault rifle clattered to the brickwork, and she stepped forward with menacing purpose. Reaching up and back, she drew the claymore, the long blade scraping out of the flexible sheath in one long, intimidating move. It came up and around as she stepped forward again. Two more steps, and he knew she'd be in range to use it. He wanted to move, to roll to his feet, but his muscles simply refused to respond.

He dimly heard the **tac-tac-tac-tac** off to the side as Smokeshadow tried to use her police-issue taser on Independence. The tall woman barely broke her stride as she turned her head to look at the source of her irritation. "My costume's insulated, you little fool," she said, disdain heavy in her voice. "And just for trying, when I get to you, I'm going to make it *hurt*."

One more step to go; the sword came up. Jericho could almost feel it humming with power. Somewhere in the back of his head, he accepted there would be no peaceful resolution to this. He had exactly one chance left. Raised his right hand weakly, he threw every last erg of power he had into a G-shake.

Independence convulsed, the massive sword swinging wildly. It cleaved downward, missing him by a foot and carving into the stone slab beside him. The cut edges were left red and glowing. Falling to all fours, she began to throw up.

His final reserves exhausted, Jericho collapsed on the fractured brickwork. The last thing he registered as his eyelids fluttered shut was the skin of her face rippling like the surface of water in a strong breeze.

43
Interlude: The Villains

Elsewhere
Two Hours Earlier

The room was dimly lit, by design rather than chance. Electronic equipment lined the walls, variously colored LEDs blinking away almost at random here and there. Wide-screen plasma displays interspersed with next-gen hard-light holo-screens provided background illumination. The sole occupant, a nondescript man of middling height, weight, and age, reclined in an extravagantly comfortable computer chair with high-end wireless earphones firmly in place. A remote keyboard rested over his knees while an irritated frown rode his brow.

"Okay," he murmured with more than a little frustration. "How's that work, exactly?" He tapped a key to change cameras, then manipulated a tiny joystick. The view on the screen in front of him panned across, then zoomed in as he twisted the stick.

Of the two people sharing a specific table on the maglev, G-Man showed up in every detail, down to the creases in his costume. The other … not so much. When the camera wasn't pointed directly at them, there was a vague indication of a person sitting there, but just enough out of focus so that no significant information could be gathered. Turning the camera to point directly at them rendered the person almost into a ghost or a shadow; it would be all too easy for the subject to vanish into a crowd, the flickering image lost amid the other movement. The latest adjustment showed that this effect held true no matter which angle they were being viewed from.

This was profoundly unsettling on more than one level. The man in the chair had survived thus far by ensuring he saw problems coming long before they saw him. Having someone no-sell the surveillance he depended on for his survival was a gut punch to his sense of security; it was a situation he very much intended to remedy.

"Okay, so we can't see you," he conceded. "Let's see if we can hear you." He accessed a menu and used a trackball to click on one of the options: **AUDIO ON.**

Immediately, the soothing music he'd been listening to was replaced by a one-sided conversation. G-Man would speak, then the other person, but only the black-clad hero's voice was recognizable as such. The voice of the other person was a soft fuzz of undifferentiated noise that refused analysis for so much as a simple voiceprint.

But that wasn't the worst part. It took him a couple of passes and several frustrating minutes of getting precisely nowhere before he decided to just listen in on what he could hear, and try to fill in the gaps that way. In this, he was both more and less successful than he hoped. While there was little information forthcoming about the mysterious traveling companion, what G-Man was saying made his eyes widen in both surprise and anger.

Tapping the keys, he pushed the slider bar back to the beginning of the conversation and raised the volume to ensure he wasn't mistaken about what he thought he was hearing. Then he listened through again. The sound quality was perfect, but this didn't make the content any easier to listen to.

"Still took me forever to convince her to go home, though."

A click of the trackball button paused the file, and the man got up from his chair to pace across the floor, the wireless keyboard placed to one side. Until now, only those with need-to-know had had access to any more of his details than were necessary (and most of those details were false). G-Man was prying in places where he wasn't wanted.

"Son of a *bitch*," he muttered. "So, it was *him* the whole time. Mother*fucker*."

He scooped up his phone on his next pass across the room and accessed a particular number. When the call went through, he dropped the phone on the desk, secure in the knowledge that it would automatically route through his headphones. "Hey, man, it's me."

"I'm busy." The voice on the other end was curt and clipped, but that was par for the course. "What's up?"

"Got something you're gonna want to hear." He drew out the reveal just to mess with his buddy. "I know who filled in the Power brat and where she got to after she dropped out of sight."

The change in tone was dramatic. "You're *shitting* me. Who? Where?"

Typical asshole. Doesn't even know how to say please or thank you.

"You're gonna love this. She was here in Utopia the whole time. Right under our goddamn noses. And as for who filled her in … I'll give you a hint. Who's supposed to be at Kennedy for the Challenger hoopla, but I've just found out is on the way back from Florida right this second? And get this: he's been talking to the one that did the Spire hack."

For a long moment, the silence on the line almost convinced him that the call had dropped out. But then the response came back, a snakelike hiss. "*Now* you've got to be fucking with me. I wouldn't have thought he had the balls for that sort of thing. You got proof?"

"A recording from right there on the maglev, half an hour ago. The weirdest thing is that cameras and microphones just skate right off the other person. Like they weren't even there."

"Oh, yeah, that's definitely the same one. It's got to be. He's in on it with them?" Savage glee sounded clearly across the call. "Oh, man. I can't wait to—"

"No, actually." He didn't want to say this bit, but it was true. "It sounded more like he was trying to talk this other person into giving the data back, still encrypted. They got into an argument about it, but last I saw, they were gonna meet up somewhere in Utopia anyway and do the handover."

"... huh. Damn. The little prick really is a straight arrow, then. I didn't think they existed."

"Well, not *that* straight." He had to chuckle at the unintentional play on words, but then he got serious. "One more thing, bro. Some of the stuff they were talking about, he's aware Tucker and LaMonde were loose ends that got cleaned up, and he's figured out whoever did that did the Power thing as well, so he knows there's a shape-changer involved. He doesn't know it's *you*, specifically, but he's got a suspect list. And we're at the top of it."

The voice exploded out of the earphones at him. "What the *hell*? Why didn't you lead with that?"

This didn't faze the nondescript man; he'd been yelled at before, by scarier people. "Because I thought the other bit was more important to you, and because he's got no proof. *And* he's wrong about most of it. Like, he thinks there's only one of us in on this. But if he puts his mind to it, he might start getting stuff *right*. The kid's a prodigy, remember. He's pretty sharp."

"Yeah, okay. You've got a point." His buddy sounded calmer now, which was a good thing.

"Thanks. So, what are we going to do about it?"

There was barely a pause this time. "When's he due back?"

His eyes flicked to another screen, where a dot on a map showed the progress of the train in question. "Hour and a half, more or less. He's just coming up to Nashville."

"Good. So, this is what you need to do ..."

- End of Part Three -

PART FOUR

THE FINAL ACT
UNVEILED

That's far enough.
- Transit, interrupted

I'm going to save him.
- Jericho Hansen, talking about Relentless.

Heroes.
- Smokeshadow, irritated

Political expedience ...
- Adam Power, disgusted

44
Frying Pan to Fire

It seemed to be Jericho's day for waking up in places not identified as his bed. At least this one was soft and warm, and he wasn't being rained on. Scratch that; at least he was alive to wake up at all. From the fragmentary memories gradually assembling themselves in his head, this specific outcome had in no way been a sinecure, especially after Independence showed up.

"Oh, good. You're awake."

The voice sounded like Smokeshadow's, and the smell indicated the presence of something resembling chicken soup nearby. Thus encouraged, he opened his eyes—nowhere near as painful a process as it had been the last time he'd done this—and looked around. He was in a living room, lying on a sofa with a light blanket over him. His neck was only a little cramped due to his Prodigy powerset, for which he was grateful. Under the blanket—he checked quickly—he was wearing his boxers; there was a bandage across his stomach, winding right around his torso.

"How do you feel?" Smokeshadow—no, Chelsea, now that she was in her own home and wearing civilian clothing—asked. Carefully, she set a tray bearing a bowl of the aforementioned soup on a chair next to the sofa. Its fragrance teased his nostrils, and his stomach rumbled sharply.

"Like I've been chewed up and spat out, but I'm doing better now, thank you kindly." Then he tried to sit up. *That* was when his midsection sent a bolt of pain lancing through every cell of his body, sharply reminding him about the dressing. "Ow, *sonova*—" Consciously cutting off the curse, he breathed deeply through the pain until he could speak civilly once more. "He stabbed me, didn't he? How bad is it?"

"Could've been a lot worse," she said bluntly. "Your armor stopped most of it. Grabbing the blade like that likely saved you a whole heap more problems. Fortunately, he went in at the wrong angle to hit any vital organs, though parts of your upper intestine were lacerated. I put a dissolving dressing on those bits, then stitched you up. You should be okay in a few days, but I'm going to advise against doing crunches until your abdominal wall heals."

Her brisk, no-nonsense tone reassured him. Were she anyone else, he would've wondered where she got her medical know-how from, but mental prodigies soaked up skills like a sponge, even faster than their more physically-inclined brethren. This was aided and abetted by her patient being another prodigy, with the boosted immune system and accelerated healing inherent to the powerset. Given a lack of people actively attempting to murder him, he *would* get better.

Except … Independence *was* still out there, fixing to do just that. He looked up at her. "Did I hallucinate the whole thing, or did Independence really try to shoot me?"

"Yeah, she did. Here, let me give you a hand." Chelsea took hold of his arms and assisted him in sitting upright and swinging his legs around to rest his feet on the floor, not without a twinge from his gut region. "That wasn't your imagination, sorry to say."

"But why?" He knew he was still a little fuzzy from just waking up, but it didn't make any sense. "It was like when I told her Silent Knight had been Charnel, she went nuts on us. I would've thought she'd *want* to know about someone pretending to be her teammate."

Heading over to the small dining table, Chelsea collected a laptop and returned to the sofa with it. "All magic tricks require knowledge of one extra factor." She looked at him soberly as she sat down next to him. "In this particular case? The only way this makes any sense at all is that Charnel wasn't the only infiltrator in the team."

He stared back at her. "*Independence* is a villain? No. No, I can't believe that." But undermining his knee-jerk reaction came a treacherous memory: Independence's expression as she lined up the rifle at his face. Not angry, not blank, but *satisfied*, as though she'd been waiting to do that for a while.

Does she really hate me so much? What did I ever do to her?

"I don't have any cast-iron proof," she said. "But my gut says yes. That, and the fact that my police scanner tells me there's a BOLO out on you. There's another one for me, but mine's way less specific." She gave him a sober look. "There are no actual charges named on yours, but they really, really want us both under interrogation in the Spire right now."

He shook his head as he moved the tray onto his lap. "But what does it *mean*? What's going *on*?"

"My take?" Chelsea spread her hands as Jericho took up the bowl and spoon, the bandages on his left hand and right arm only hindering him mildly in this effort. "I think Independence—and I'm pretty sure she was the *real* Poser—spun a line to Relentless and the rest of them about how you brutally murdered Silent Knight in front of her. But she doesn't want to put it out there in public, in case you come back with, '*but Silent Knight was Charnel*'. So, Independence being one of their big shots with a lot of influence, they're keeping it on the down-low for the time being."

The soup was good, but Chelsea's blunt appraisal of the situation spoiled Jericho's appetite after just two mouthfuls. Putting the bowl down for the moment, he leaned back against the sofa and looked out the window. It was brighter than he expected outside, which mildly surprised him; for some reason, he'd expected night to have fallen. "How long's it been?"

"Since I got you back here?" She tilted her hand from side to side. "About an hour. You came out of it pretty damn fast once I had you stitched and bandaged up."

"Okay, with any luck, they're still figuring out how to respond to what just happened." In all fairness, *he* was still trying to get his head around the whole situation. So much had changed in too short a time.

"We can't expect them to sit on their thumbs forever," she warned him. "Whatever they do, we can't afford not to be out there ahead of them. Two steps ahead, at least."

He nodded to acknowledge her point. "So, how do you think Poser replaced Independence, and Charnel replaced Silent Knight? You figure they helped each other infiltrate the team?"

Chelsea gestured toward the soup and waited until he had bowl and spoon in hand again. "I think it's worse than that. I think Independence is the *actual* Poser, and Silent Knight really was Charnel."

Pausing to swallow the next spoonful of soup, he turned and stared at her again. She was really belting out the unwelcome revelations, and it didn't sound like she was pulling his leg. "Mind backing that last one up and running it past me again, just a tad bit slower this time?"

Chelsea nodded. "You saw her face just after you shook her up, right? Skin sliding all over the place? While I was getting you up off the ground, her hair changed color three times. I didn't wait around to see what else she could do or how long it'd take her to recover. Getting you out of there was my highest priority." She gave Jericho a mock glare. "You can stand to lose a little weight if we're making this a regular occurrence, just saying."

"Her hair changed color?" He put aside the rest of what she was saying. "She's a shape-changer?" The penny dropped. "Right, yeah, Poser. Okay, but how'd you know Silent Knight's shoulder-guard was a force field generator?"

"You couldn't shut him down by touch," she explained, "but your gravity-tags still worked on him and the stuff he was holding. The way the rain was running off him didn't look quite right, but hitting him with the baton was the clincher. There was no metal-to-metal contact. Plus, that shoulder-guard's the only thing he's consistently worn that's not part of his original armor. So, everything added up to a force field generator."

"Okay, right. That makes sense, I guess." Jericho frowned, still trying to wrap his head around the whole thing. "But why do you say Silent Knight was *actually* Charnel, instead of just pretending to be him? I mean, couldn't he still be an impostor? Not *the* Poser, but *a* poser?"

She shrugged. "Because the moment I disabled his shoulder-guard, he lost the ability to hold the Silent Knight form. If he and Poser have been supporting each other's masquerade, it means Charnel's been Silent Knight from the beginning. It's not just a force field generator. It's also a power enhancer."

"Okay, I'm lost," he confessed. "I can see the force field aspect, but where do you get the bit about the enhancer, and him being Silent Knight from the beginning?"

"Charnel's always had the ability to change shape, but only from human to monster and back again," she said patiently. "The enhancer was there to let him assume a third form: Silent Knight. And *as* Silent Knight, he was never without his shoulder-guard. He needed it to maintain that form."

"And when you shut it down with the discus, he had to go back to being Charnel." Jericho looked at the idea, but he couldn't poke any holes in it. He took another mouthful then put the spoon and bowl down on the tray again, unable to face the thought of eating any more at the moment. "But how do we know —" The laptop let out an urgent-sounding beep, overriding what he was saying. "What's that? Low power?"

"Shit. No, it's an alarm." Clicking the trackpad, she started typing commands. Text scrolled up the screen, too small for him to read, and she swore under her breath.

"Alarm? What kind of alarm?" He wasn't anywhere near as good at reading body language as she was (in fairness, nobody was), but he could tell she was worried. Carefully, he put the tray aside. It seemed the time for chicken soup had come and gone.

Slapping the laptop closed, she stood up with it under her arm and turned to face him. "I've got a bunch of tripwires set up around town to warn me if anyone ever starts sniffing too close to home. Three of them just went off at once." Her expression became artificially bright, as did her voice; he suspected he was supposed to notice both. "Seems Force Majeure takes it seriously when someone kills a core member. Who knew?"

"So, what's happening?" he asked. His stomach wound sent him a warning pang as he stood up a little too quickly, but he didn't have time for that.

"They're looking for us, and they're looking *hard*." She'd dropped the faux cheer. "I'm good at hiding, but I rely mainly on security by obscurity. I hide in the places people don't bother looking. Right now, they're looking *everywhere*. If they keep it up, and there's no reason to believe they won't, they're gonna narrow it down far enough to find us both sooner rather than later. I don't want to be here when that happens."

"So can't we just move out of the search area and bunker down?" It was more or less how the Survivors had escaped capture the last time, until Jericho got back with the fake identities.

She shook her head. "If they don't get us on the first sweep, they'll lock the whole damn city down. Nobody in, nobody out. Then they'll search Utopia, block by block. I'm good, but I'm not that good. They'd pin me down, and you with me."

The conclusion was inevitable. "So, we've gotta get out of the city. How are we gonna do that?" It wasn't like he could just walk into the maglev station and buy a ticket with his MagCard. They'd be all over him like flies on day-old fish guts.

"You just leave that to me." Chelsea grinned tightly, though he could see the tension behind her expression. Despite her capabilities, she couldn't hide it all.

Involuntarily, Jericho glanced at the apartment door, half-expecting it to be kicked in at any second. "Okay, fine, but how close are they?"

"Close enough to be a concern, far enough away that we can maybe get out of the city if we move fast enough." She dropped the laptop into a shoulder bag then started moving through the apartment, collecting the charge cord and other small items. Without looking, she tossed something in his direction. "Here, see if this fits you."

Startled, he caught it. Resembling a signet ring, it had a vaguely circuit-board-inspired pattern on the top, in copper. The rest of it was colored a dull silver. He managed to make it slide onto his pinky finger with a bit of effort. "Uh, what does it do?"

"If you press and hold the top for five seconds, it activates," she called from the bedroom. "For exactly one minute, all electronic surveillance of you defaults to 'nothing to see here'." She leaned out through the doorway. "Try these on." A shirt and pair of pants came flying through the air toward him.

Reflexively, he snagged them out of the air, but he was more concerned with the ring. "What, I'll be invisible?" He certainly wouldn't have put it past her. "Is this how you got into the police precinct?"

"No, I used better gear than that. What you've got there will let them record you, but nothing you do in that minute will trip any alarms. It's something I've been playing with after looking at Gimmick's tech. When the time's up it burns out, then it's just jewelry. How's the clothing look?"

The pants were a little tight, but he figured he could handle it. By contrast, the T-shirt draped down past his hips. It was pastel pink with a cute yellow cartoon duckling on the front that did not fit his image of her in the slightest. "You actually wear this?"

She reappeared in the bedroom doorway with her hands on her hips and gave him a level stare. "I sleep in it. Be honored. What size are your feet?"

He glanced at her feet and then his. "Bigger than anything you've got. I can go barefoot. Won't be the first time."

"Hmm. Okay." She looked critically at his head. "That hair won't do. They'll pick you out a mile away."

"Got a ball cap?" he asked. "I can shove it under that. Done it before."

She nodded definitively. "Yeah, that should work, for starters. Okay, just gotta get a couple more things." In her bag, the laptop beeped three times, a rising tone. "Shit, they're in the building. Here; take this, grab the cap, and hold the elevator. I'll join you there." She held out the shoulder bag to him.

"On it." As he took the bag, his memory kicked into gear. "I'm gonna need my utility belt."

"Your costume's electronics were fried," she said over her shoulder, already heading back into the bedroom. "And I dumped your phone, first chance I got."

"Still need it," he insisted. Looking around, he spotted a ball cap hanging on a hook near the door. A simple push-tag made it leap to his hand as he slung the bag over his shoulder.

He spared half a second to check the peep-hole before opening the door to her apartment, but nobody was lurking directly outside. Stepping into the tastefully curved corridor, he looked to one side then the other before spotting the elevators down to the left. He moved in that direction, trying to keep up a nonchalant appearance while pulling his hair into a bun on top of his head and yanking the cap down onto it. The result felt messy as hell, but he wasn't up to being picky right now.

The stab wound ached as he jabbed the elevator call button. It didn't feel nearly as bad as when it was first inflicted, but he had no desire to go into another combat situation right now. Fighting at this stage would basically be the last desperate throw of the dice. Even wounded, he'd be a match for one or two moderately trained unpowered people, but he would likely be toast against any kind of combat-capable Enabled, let alone the core membership of Force Majeure.

Chelsea emerged from her apartment with a backpack slung over her shoulder and headed toward him. Compared to his best efforts at casual strolling, she could've been promenading along the boardwalk of any one of a dozen ocean-front towns for all the urgency she displayed. Despite this, she got to him in a remarkably short time. "Elevator should be here in a moment," he said in an undertone.

"It's usually faster than this," she replied, just as quietly, handing him a fanny pack in return for her shoulder bag. "Some stuff you might need."

"Oh, thanks." He unzipped it a little and peered inside to see a cheap mobile phone and a thick roll of cash. "Yeah, that could come in handy once we get out of the city." Settling it into the small of his back, he clipped it around his waist.

"That's the general idea." She peered at the readout over the doors again. They were all showing the ground floor, not moving. "They've got the elevators locked down. We need to hit the stairs."

And with that, the momentary sense of calm was gone. "Force Majeure knows we're here?"

"It'll be a preliminary sweep. Chances of having a hero on site are low." She grabbed the stairwell door handle, then pushed it open. "They'll be hitting the places we're likely to be, all across the city. But there's one good thing."

"I'm down for good news." Following her into the stairwell, he let the door close behind them.

She started down the stairs. "They're not publicizing Silent Knight's death. Nothing on any radio or TV channel since I got you back here, even the encrypted UCPD ones. Just you and an unknown woman wanted for questioning, and your name's only on the encrypted UCPD channels. So, Silent Knight's death and your part in it aren't public. They're trying to keep everything about the situation low-key until they can spin it to their advantage."

"Stop." He needed to figure this out. "I think we're going about this all wrong."

She came to a halt on the next landing down; he was half a flight behind her. Normally he would've been outpacing her, but hustling down the stairs was not doing his stab wound any favors. "What is it? What's up?"

"They'll probably be watching the stairwell, too." He tried to push his brain to work faster. "They *will* see us."

"So, I'll charm my way past them." She shrugged. "It's what I do."

"Is that what you did when you went into the precinct?" He had a sinking feeling he knew the answer.

"Well, yeah. It worked then; it should work now." But she didn't sound quite as confident as she had before. "Ingrained reflexes are amazing things. If you know what buttons to press, you can make them dance to your tune every time."

He shook his head. "No, see, *they* know what you did in the precinct, too. They may have taken precautions. Or at least, they'll have an idea how to counter your ability to persuade people." He didn't know *what* that might be, but he wasn't ruling anything out right then.

She opened her mouth to argue, then closed it again as a look both worried and thoughtful crossed her face. "Okay, granted. I can think of three ways they might do it, which means the Technologist can probably think of four more. Do you have any better options?"

He took a deep breath. *This is probably going to be either brilliant or utterly stupid.* "Does this building have roof access?"

"Uhh, yeah, but you realize you can't fly anymore, right?" She looked worriedly up at him as though concerned that the blood loss might have affected him somehow. "This place is ten stories high, and my hyperweave isn't really suited for use as glider wings."

"All it's gotta do is slow us down." He turned and started upward; behind him, he heard Chelsea catching up. Beyond that, far below, he registered the sounds of a stairwell door opening and heavy boots on the stairs. "Also, let's move and worry at the same time. Our options just became either roof or surrender."

"No," she said firmly. "Our options are either roof or roof." With that, she powered past him up the steps.

She was right, of course. They were literally the only people in Utopia who knew the truth about the infiltrators within Force Majeure *and* were willing to tell anyone about it. Because he had precisely zero illusions about their fate once Poser got her hands on himself and Chelsea. All she'd have to say was that they attacked her.

If she gets us, we're dead, and it dies with us. And if someone else takes us into custody, no matter how we try to prove our case, she's probably got a dozen counter-arguments lined up. And then *she makes like we attacked her.*

On the other hand, he and Chelsea were both prodigies. Between them, they'd killed Charnel and escaped from Poser once already. So far, they were beating the odds; the trick was to keep doing it.

As he climbed the stairs, he could feel the stitches pulling at his stab wound. He did his best to mitigate the potential damage by holding one hand on it and reducing his effective weight, but he didn't know how much good that would do. The trouble was that he could hear the bootsteps below getting louder with every second. Deciding with a grimace that the wound was just going to have to take care of itself for a while, he increased his pace.

When they got to the roof access door, it was locked. Jericho eyed it grimly, judging whether he'd be able to break it open with a barefooted kick. It would be painful, he figured, but doable. And it wasn't like they had any other options right then.

Or perhaps they did. "Finally!" Chelsea said, rolling her eyes. "It's about time *something* went our way." Fishing in her bag, she dug out the discus and held it to the lock. When she tapped a sequence into the keys on it—Jericho honestly had no idea what any of them did—the lock beeped agreeably, then disengaged with a distinct *click*.

Chelsea dropped the discus back into the shoulder bag. "I swear ..." she began happily as the door opened. Her voice died away as they both stared at the person who stood framed in the doorway, mini-turret hovering by her shoulder.

Oh, crap.

Transit.

45
The Best Laid Plans

Frozen to the spot, Jericho stared at his erstwhile ally. He *knew* Force Majeure considered him either a flat-out murderer or a co-conspirator in Silent Knight's death, and the wisest course of action with Transit would be to bulldoze right over the top of her. But still he hesitated, for two very pressing reasons.

First, the dual barrels of the mini-turret were pointed directly at his face; while they were of a lower caliber than the main gun mount on Transit's sky-bike, the muzzle apertures still looked *enormous.*

Second, while he figured he could probably deal with the turret, this was *Transit.* From the very first night of his arrival in Utopia, she'd bent over backward to make him feel comfortable with the idea of joining the team; the autographed photo for Luke had only reinforced his positive feelings toward her. He'd *seen* her empathy while helping out the Nashfields, and experienced her sympathy first-hand when Scout was damaged. Unlike Independence, she was unequivocally one of the good guys.

Goddamn it, I don't want to hurt her!

Loyalty was an integral part of his Prodigy focus. There was no way for Transit to know that dragging them back to the Spire was likely to result in their deaths just as soon as Independence could arrange it. She didn't mean him harm, so he was having trouble opposing her directly. Torn between diametrically opposed impulses, his brain locked up for a long, fatal moment.

This could've been disastrous, but Transit only got as far as, "Th—" before Chelsea acted. Stepping forward and to the right in a lithe, gliding motion, she passed between Jericho and the mini-turret before getting up into Transit's face. The guns on the mini-turret went from gyro-stabilized steadiness to flicking randomly back and forth, as if unsure what to target.

Chelsea grabbed the hovering turret with her left hand while her right came out of the shoulder bag holding her collapsible baton. A seemingly effortless flick of her left wrist sent the lightweight turret Frisbee'ing into the opposite wall; at the same time, with her right hand, she snapped the baton to its full length. In a move that she *had* to have practiced, she swung the weighted metal head into the outside of Transit's left knee.

Gauging from the screeching noise that arose from the mini-turret's lifters and Transit's cry of pain, both attacks had achieved their desired effect. Nor did Chelsea did stop there. Turning, she grabbed Transit's arm and spun around, dragging the Force Majeure hero over her back in an unorthodox but effective shoulder-throw.

Transit went past Jericho more or less upside down and backward; when she hit the stairs, she kept going, tumbling down the steps to the next landing. Just to add insult to injury, Chelsea caught the falling mini-turret with a solid swing of the baton and sent it bouncing down the stairs in its mistress' wake, shedding parts as it went.

Jericho's jaw dropped. "No—" he began, reaching out far too late to grab Transit.

Chelsea, it seemed, wasn't interested in letting anyone else finish a sentence. Her entire aspect shifted as she turned back toward Jericho; he'd seen this transition before, but that had been when she was in a playful mood. Now she seemed to tower over him, her attitude brooking no dissent. "Don't even think about it!" she snapped. "Get *up* here, for fuck's sake!"

The tone of her voice cut him off before he could reach the second syllable, then her hand latched onto his bicep. With a singular combination of brute force and pure authority, she dragged him out through the roof entry. He would've resisted, but her attitude and actions had left him wondering which way was up. Much like Transit, an irrepressible part of him noted.

"Go-go-go!" she shouted once he was out on the roof; the edge of command in her voice was almost impossible to ignore. Jolted into action, he kept moving.

Transit's sky-bike hovered nearby, just off the edge of the roof, the guns twitching from side to side at random. Just for a moment, Jericho thought Chelsea might be about to try and steal it. But she ignored it, dragging him onward.

He bolted with her across the sloping planes of the roof, vaguely wondering why the surrounding buildings looked so familiar, until they reached the edge and he saw for himself. On his first night in Utopia, he'd noticed the apartment block he'd climbed for a brooding session was coated in a high-tech solar absorption material, almost like paint but forming a subtle hexagonal pattern. While this type of solar 'paint' was a common sight on the taller structures in Utopia, only one building with it near the Oaklands had it … and that was the building he was running across the top of.

Right until she ran them both out into empty air.

By sheer reflex, he grabbed her and dropped their combined effective weight to one-tenth normal. As he did so, he felt the hyperweave costume wrapping around the pair of them. It covered them from head to toe, then the part in front of his face seemed to go transparent.

He knew from prior experience that the exterior of the hyperweave would be transmitting light from one side through to the other. It was technically active camouflage rather than true invisibility, but he wasn't about to quibble on details, especially as it gave him a window to the outside.

They fell slowly but with gradually increasing speed. Even under the effect of one-tenth gravity, and despite the hyperweave billowing out to create drag, he knew they were going to hit hard. As the rooftop below came up at them, he announced: "Let go in three ... two ... one ... *now!*"

Halfway through the word 'now', the hyperweave unfolded from around him and they landed on the flat roof of the Oaklands. He managed a reasonable forward roll to absorb the impact but was still slightly winded by the awkward landing. Worse, as he went to get up, a sharp stab of pain shot through his stomach.

"You okay?" Nobody else would've seen his wince, but it wasn't worth trying to conceal something like that from her.

"I'll be fine," he grunted, climbing to his feet. "Think I might've popped a stitch. Nothing we can do about it right now."

"Don't you dare bleed through your bandages," she warned him. "I like that shirt."

"Maybe you should've thought about that before you threw us both off a roof." He knew his reply sounded a little snarky, but he felt somewhat justified. "And seriously, you were living *there*?" Right next to the Oaklands, he meant.

"It was convenient. No time to stop and chat." Chelsea's manner wasn't as intense as after she'd thrown Transit down the stairs and wrecked the mini-turret, but her eyes still bored into his. "We have to keep moving. Two steps ahead, remember?"

He followed her toward the edge of the roof farthest from the road. "Why'd you cuss me out like that, anyway? I'll admit I froze for a hot second, but you didn't have to yank a knot in my tail."

"Yeah, I did." She looked him dead in the eye. "You were still thinking like a member of Force Majeure, which would've gotten both of us killed. I had to snap you out of it."

She stepped up onto the roof parapet and waited for him to join her. Hand in hand, like star-crossed lovers of old, they stepped off the edge; this time, the drop was barely thirty feet. Jericho was definitely feeling the debilitating effects of his various injuries, as he had to drop to one knee while Chelsea merely went to a crouch.

"Oof." Painfully, he stood up again. "Remind me never to get struck by lightning and stabbed, ever again. It ruins your whole day." He turned to her as they headed out of the alley. "Okay, yeah, maybe you've got a point."

"No 'maybe' about it." She threw him a sidelong glance. "What you need to get through your head is that *yes,* they're the good guys, but so long as Poser keeps pouring poison in their ears, they're also the *enemy.*"

Jericho did his best to keep up, both mentally and physically, as she hustled along the sidewalk away from the Oaklands. "Okay, so where do we go from here? Did you have another hiding place planned?"

"Several. We can't use any of them. As I said, Force Majeure will be looking *everywhere*, even the places they don't usually bother delving into. We've not only kicked the hornet's nest, but we've also made fun of their mothers and set fire to their dogs. If we stay in Utopia, sooner or later they *will* find us." She stopped alongside a maglev car parked at the curb. "Keep a lookout, will you?" Slipping the discus out of her shoulder bag, she applied it to the door lock.

Jericho glanced to the left and right. Nobody seemed interested in what they were doing, while a look upward showed the sky currently clear of police hexes. A moment later, he realized what she was planning. "What are you *doing*?" he hissed. "We can't steal a *car!*"

The door clicked, and she opened it. "We can, and we will," she said as she wriggled in over the center console. "In fact, I've just done it. It's this, or accept that we'll be in custody in about five minutes and dead in ten, and neither one of us is the type to just lie down and die. Get in the back."

Her snap of command was part of what had him clambering into the back seat of the car, but mainly it was the realization that she'd been right on the money so far. As much as he wanted to think of a law-abiding response to the situation, nothing he could devise would help him avoid being arrested and subsequently handed over to the tender mercies of the one person who knew the truth about Charnel. Chelsea had kept them ahead of the pursuit so far, and he figured his best bet was to trust her judgment until further notice.

The car's dashboard beeped. **"New owner assigned. Seatbelts, please."** Then it started moving, cruising out onto the road back toward the Oaklands.

Hastily, Jericho clicked his belt into place, grateful he didn't have to put on five-point restraints like the air-cabs used. "Shouldn't we be going the other way?"

"Double bluff. Oldest trick in the book. If you make some distance, then turn around and head back *toward* the crime scene, nobody looks twice." Chelsea appeared calm and relaxed at the wheel, even though she had to be at least as tense as he felt.

A moment later, Transit's sky-bike came shrieking down from over the top of the Oaklands, ducted fans going all-out. It whipped overhead and cut a hard left-hand turn down a side street, the sound taking a few more seconds to die away.

Chelsea leaned forward and checked the mirror. "Ooh, she's *pi-issed*." She sounded a lot more pleased with herself than Jericho would've been. "Let's get out of the immediate search area, update your disguise, then execute Operation GTFOOU." She turned her head slightly so she could shoot him an amused glance. "Which stands for—"

"Get The Eff Out Of Utopia, got it," he said grumpily, his reaction to everything he'd gone through over the last few hours just now beginning to set in. "How are we going to update my disguise? I'm pretty sure any theatrical supply places will probably be shut."

"New shirt, shoes, and something to change your hair," she rattled off cheerfully. "Did you know Transit's left eye is a prosthetic? She's probably got a camera in there somewhere, so chances are she'll have recorded your current appearance. Even if falling down the stairs rattled her cage, she can still give them a picture to look for."

"No, I didn't know that. How do *you* know that?" He frowned; he'd never seen Transit's face, and he was certain Chelsea would've had fewer opportunities than him to get a glimpse.

"When I moved, she had to turn her head fractionally to the left to follow me," she said, as if this was something people noticed every day. "She's not blind in that eye, at least not to everything else, but I do have a jammer that fuzzes out my image on cameras. So, when I went to the right, I was in her blind spot just long enough to tag her."

"Oh." More pieces of the puzzle clicked into place. "And *that's* why the mini-turret couldn't get a fix on you. Okay, then. So, she won't have your appearance. This is a good thing. But did you have to hit her so hard *and* toss her down the stairs?"

Chelsea shrugged. "I could've used the taser, maybe shoved it up under her helmet, but her flight suit's probably insulated, and she could almost certainly turn the taser off or even make it fall apart the instant it touched her. So, I went with old-fashioned blunt force trauma."

"You realize you could've broken her neck, doing that." He knew they were technically running for their lives, but using lethal force on someone who thought they were avenging a fallen comrade didn't sit right with him.

"Someone who's been in this business as long as she has would know how to take a fall by now." Chelsea's backward glance was sympathetic rather than angry. "I get it; I really do. Divided loyalties can be a real pain to deal with."

Jericho flopped back against the seat and folded his arms. "I want to be pissed at you, but you're right. If she'd gotten the drop on us, we'd be getting dragged back to the Spire right now. Exactly where we don't want to be." He knew he was talking too much, but his emotions had yet to catch up with his intellectual awareness of the situation.

"If we were lucky, yeah, Poser would manufacture an excuse to kill us quickly." Chelsea drove sedately down the street. She kept her eyes on the road, but Jericho felt she was paying just as much attention to him. "If we were *un*lucky, she'd get us all to herself for a couple of hours."

"Goddamn it," he muttered. "I knew she didn't like me, but I thought it was just her being a b-word." While he used the word for general profanity, he disliked applying it to people.

"'*B-word*'? Really?" Chelsea let out a delighted chuckle. "Let me guess. You were a Boy Scout, once upon a time?"

"For a while, yeah." He'd actually enjoyed it. So had Luke, right up until his cousin's love of pranks had gotten them both kicked out. Or rather, Luke was kicked out, and Jericho quit in solidarity. Thinking back, he wondered if the Scoutmaster had ever located his other boot. This was where Luke had gotten the name for his dog; the little guy had been loyal, trustworthy, friendly, and courageous to a fault.

"Why am I not surprised." It wasn't phrased as a question. She rummaged in her backpack one-handed. "Here, you wanted your utility belt, right?"

"Thanks." He accepted the coiled belt as she passed it back to him. Its weight was both nostalgic and a grim reminder that until the whole Poser deal was sorted out, this was no longer his life.

As he started going through the pouches, he thought back over what she'd been trying to impress on him. No matter what he personally felt about Transit, the Technologist, or even Relentless, they would see *him* as a criminal to be captured. Even if he tried to stop and explain to them what was really going on, Force Majeure had a well-deserved reputation for utterly destroying those who screwed with them. If he did *anything* other than try to run like hell, he'd be toast.

Trying to distract himself from this grim reality, he paid closer attention to emptying out the utility belt. As Chelsea had mentioned, the phone pouch was empty—which, he wasn't going to lie, had likely been a stellar move on her part—but he had some other items still in there.

A roll of notes and a Ziploc baggie full of coins—a holdover from his days of solo vigilante work in Savannah—joined the other money in his fanny pack once he wriggled it around to the side and unclipped it. His notebook and pen seemed to have weathered the ordeal unscathed, as had the markers he'd acquired for the Commemoration Day, so they also went in there. He'd been keeping Thomas' handkerchief—long since laundered—in one pouch in case they met again in costume, so that joined everything else. Then he found the signal device Adam Power had gifted him with, what seemed to be an eternity ago now.

For a long moment, he considered mashing the call button and keeping it in until the Power family jet was overhead, but reason and logic prevailed. Team Power would of course contact Force Majeure before they ever got to the city, and Poser's version would be the first one they heard. He wanted to think they wouldn't simply accept Force Majeure's word out of hand, but in the *best* case, they'd probably assume *he* was Poser, and try to capture him to find out where the 'real' Jericho was. His best chance, he knew, was to get far away from Utopia and contact them on his own terms.

And once I've convinced them, *maybe they can talk Force Majeure around before it's too late.*

With a sigh, he tucked the signal device into the fanny pack, which was now somewhat bulkier than before, and kept looking through the belt. Discarding a bunch of zip-ties that had partially melted together, he opened the last two pouches. In one, he found the bunched-up Ziploc bag holding the internals of the thumb drive he'd rescued from behind the fridge, while in the other was the mailer containing the note and drive he'd gotten from his parents.

There was nothing he could do with those at the moment, so he shoved them in the fanny pack as well and zipped it closed. He checked the utility belt one last time to ensure all pouches were clear, then put it aside. Carefully, he set about latching the fanny pack around his waist again.

While he was still involved with this, the car door opened. He looked around in surprise, suddenly aware that while he'd been off in his own world, Chelsea had parked the car and gotten out. Now she was back, carrying a cloth shopping bag as she climbed into the rear seat with him.

"How are you getting along?" she asked briskly.

"Stomach's in a certain amount of pain, but it's nothing I can't handle," he replied candidly. "The cuts on my hand and arm are itchy, but again, I can't really do anything about them."

"That's not quite what I was referring to. We're both prodigies. Minor stuff like that, we walk off. I was asking about what's going on up *here*." She tapped him on the temple with her fingernail.

He sighed, his emotions causing him as much pain as his stomach. "I'm just trying to figure out how to warn Relentless and the others about Independence before she chooses to turn on *them*. I mean, she's gotta be thinking about it." He'd long since decided to leave Relentless' less-savory practices for another day. This was far more important.

"Thinking about it, maybe." Chelsea shook her head. "But she won't. Take it from someone who's made a living out of deceiving people. Carrying on a con like that for years would keep her in bragging rights basically *forever*. The legend she's got going on right now is too good to walk away from. I mean, who suspects a superhero? Plus, the money's got to be *amazing*. She'll be certain to have her exit plan set up and ready to go, but she's not about to pull the ripcord until the engines are on fire and the plane's in a death dive."

"Okay, good." Jericho felt a little reassured at Chelsea's tone. "But we have to warn the rest of the team *somehow*. I won't be able to sleep at night, otherwise."

"It won't be safe for you to sleep at all until we get you out of Utopia," she decided, dumping the contents of the cloth bag on the seat between them. "But yeah, as soon as we're far enough out of town for me to put together a totally anonymous connection, we'll drop 'em a line. In the meantime, here: jacket, shirt, pants, socks, boots, belt, wallet. Change into these as soon as we start off again."

"What about a different ball cap?" he said, forcing himself to think ahead. "They might be using that as a potential identifier. And I'm pretty sure that turning it backward isn't gonna cut it. Also, maybe sunglasses?"

"You're right," she said, twitching the ball cap off his head. "They would. But they'll also be looking carefully at anyone wearing shades. So, you're not going to be wearing anything on your head and face at all."

"… what?" He stared at her. "How's that even going to work?"

"Like a charm." She grinned as she opened her shoulder bag and took out a small electric razor. "Here, lean over this way and use the shopping bag to catch the clippings."

He did as he was told, holding still as she negotiated the buzzing device around his ears and over the back of his neck. When she was finished, she ran it over his scalp one more time as a touch-up, then blew the last little bits off the razor into the bag. It was a jolt to see his severed locks piled in the bag, but he reminded himself there were more important things in life than a good head of hair. Such as actually being alive.

"Okay, so they won't be able to pick me out by my hair," he acknowledged, wondering what he looked like now. "But facial recognition is still a thing, and there's more than a few folks in the Spire who'll know me by sight, not even counting the rest of Force Majeure."

"Got that covered," she said promptly. "Trust me, I've got Plan A all the way through to Plan Z, lined up and ready to roll."

He gave her a level, unamused stare. "And when exactly were you gonna fill me in on any of these plans?"

His disapproval bounced clear off her serene confidence without leaving a mark. "When the time came. Don't take this the wrong way, but some of the plans depend on you not knowing the script ahead of time. You're a great superhero, but you haven't got an ounce of bullshit in you."

He wanted to argue with her that he was just as good a liar as the next man, but then he paused and thought about it. On balance, he decided, he'd take her assessment as a compliment.

She dropped the clippers back into her bag, then rolled up the cloth shopping bag and put it in there too. "Keep 'em guessing for as long as possible." The next thing she brought out were three pieces of soft contoured plastic.

He frowned. "What exactly are those?"

"Mouth inserts," she said cheerfully. "Don't worry, they're totally sterile. These two go inside your cheeks, and this one goes inside your bottom lip. They'll change the shape of your face so much nobody's going to recognize you."

"If you say so." He was doubtful, but he took the things anyway. Sliding them into his mouth was a little unpleasant, though he was pleased to note there was no odd taste involved. By the time he had them in place, Chelsea was frowning over a familiar-looking container.

"Contact lenses?" he asked, doing his best not to slur around the inserts. "You sure we want to go that far?"

"I was considering it," she admitted. "Have you ever worn contacts before?"

"Nope." He shook his head in case she hadn't understood him. "Mama uses 'em from time to time, but my eyesight's pretty good."

"Then we'll leave it," she decided. "Too much trouble if they go wrong. How are the inserts?"

"Weird," he said with finality. "How can you wear stuff like this?"

She chuckled, and briefly brushed her fingers across his cheek. "Disguises are more of a state of mind than anything else. I don't need inserts, but they make things easier for me." Opening the door beside her, she slid out again. "Next stop, Utopia City maglev terminal."

"You know, they're like to be watching the station, just in case we do try to sneak out that way. Or rather, in case *you* try to sneak out that way with *me*." He wasn't actively trying to poke holes in her plan, but he was surely interested in hearing if she had an answer to the objection.

"This is why we're disguising you," she reminded him as she climbed into the front seat. "There's been no media blitz about this, so they're still trying to keep things on the down-low. This means they can't shut down the maglev or even flood the station with cops, checking everyone's ID. Whoever their on-site asset is, we'll stroll right past them. Even if you come face-to-face with Relentless, so long as you don't make eye contact, he'll never recognize you."

Jericho had his doubts about that; Relentless had never struck him as stupid.

But it's not about being smart or stupid. She's the expert, dumbass.

"Okay, I'll take your word for it."

"Good." She started the car and moved it out of the parking spot. Even after three months in Utopia, Jericho was still getting used to the idea of a vehicle sliding sideways onto the road. Still, maglev vehicles worked by their own rules, and she seemed reasonably adept with them. "Now, get changed. We should be there in about fifteen to twenty minutes."

"On it." With the sheer volume of crap that was raining down around his ears, having another prodigy at his side was heartening, doubly so because she seemed totally at home in this sort of crisis. He tugged the T-shirt off over his head and inspected the dressing. There were a few dark spots, but nothing too serious.

Chelsea navigated the traffic with effortless ease, evidently having familiarized herself with the circuits and radials of Utopia's road system. She left it up to the vehicle's auto-drive most of the time, but on three occasions she took over to steer down a side road; once, she pulled over and parked for about a minute and a half before driving on.

Jericho didn't question her methods, being more concerned with changing into his new clothing without using his stomach muscles, an exercise easier suggested than achieved. Once the boots were on—unsurprisingly, she'd guessed his size exactly—he held up the wallet. "Uh, I don't really have anything to put in this. Apart from the MagCard, I mean."

"Put some of the cash in it," she said without turning her head. "Once we get away from here, it'll be less suspicious than peeling notes off a roll."

"Ah." Once again, this wasn't something he would've considered. In his defense, he wasn't used to thinking like someone on the run. He unzipped the fanny pack, retrieved his personal roll of money, then removed the rubber band and stuffed the cash into the wallet. It made for a respectable chunk of change, and he decided he didn't want to know where she'd gotten the one she'd given him. Right now, he had enough to worry about without borrowing trouble.

As they cruised up toward the maglev station, the massive building towering over them, Jericho could see Chelsea looking for parking spots. Figuring she had that side of things handled, he instead studied the maglev terminal itself, trying to see what kind of reception committee awaited them. He knew there had to be one; Force Majeure in general, and Relentless in particular, just plain didn't miss that kind of trick.

Then the crowd parted briefly; he saw who was there, and knew it was a lost cause. "Keep going! Don't slow down!" He kept his tone low but urgent, and instinctively ducked his head.

For a second, he thought she was about to pull into an invitingly open parking spot anyway, but then she yielded it to another car and drove on smoothly. He stayed half-hunched over, peering out the rear window for any signs of pursuit until they'd turned the corner and gone out of sight. Even then, he didn't relax for two more corners.

Chelsea slowed after the third corner and pulled into a quiet side street, then parked the car. "Okay," she said, leaning back in her seat and resting the heels of her hands on the wheel, "Spill. Why'd you wave me off?"

"They had Black Dragon on site," he explained. "I'd have never gotten past her. Or rather, *we* wouldn't have. She'd have been all over us before we made the escalator."

Turning to face him, she frowned. "You've lost me. Unless you went and spoke to her, how would she know it was you? And how would she know it was *me*?"

With his right hand, he tapped the side of his nose. "In dragon form, she can track people by scent, and you can be damn sure she knows *my* smell, seeing as how we've worked together. And if you've got my scent on you, she'd pick you out just as easily. Have you got anything in your bag of tricks for jamming *that*?"

A look of irritation crossed her face. "Damn it, no. Given a couple of hours and access to a halfway decent spice rack, I could cobble something together. But I didn't think to bring one along, and we don't have the luxury of time to do any more shopping. Okay, that's '*daring escape via maglev*' down the drain."

"So, what do we do now?"

She grinned. "We pivot to Plan B."

In his opinion, she looked altogether too cheerful. "What's Plan B?"

Her grin widened. "You'll see."

46
Taking the Low Road

They were several minutes away from the maglev station before something started nagging at Jericho's subconscious. A hunch quickly grew into a strong suspicion, which peering out the car window at the sun did nothing to dispel. After he took note of Chelsea's next few turns, this became a near-certainty.

"Are we going south?" he asked. "Because it looks like we're going south."

"Can't sneak anything past you, can I?" Chelsea seemed unworried that he'd figured it out. "Any other insights you'd like to share?"

"Southside Parking," he said, certainty crystallizing in his mind. "You started up the smuggling thing again, didn't you?"

She moved her head slightly, in a way that suggested she was rolling her eyes. "Well, *technically*, it never really stopped," she prevaricated. "Most of those involved managed to crawl away and hide after the beating you and Thomas handed them. And a funny thing about the tablet you sent my way; the only names on it by the time the cops got hold of it were the higher-ups, the ones who'd refused to hand Portman over to you and your uncle." She buffed her nails on her top, then inspected them. "Voila: instant leadership vacuum. Just waiting for an enterprising newcomer *who knew the whole structure* to stroll on in and take up the reins."

He wanted to be angry at her for deleting that data, but this was not the time or place to argue. Besides, he'd *known* all along what she was like. She'd certainly made no secret of it. Her words, casually spoken outside the maglev station three months ago, came back to him.

*My secret underground criminal empire's gonna be **much** more stylish.*

At the time, he'd figured the words were just bravado, but he should've understood that when Chelsea said she was going to do something, she went right ahead and did it. Especially since he'd already seen ample evidence of just that.

"Okay," he said carefully. "I get it. And if it gets us out of Utopia in one piece, I won't be exactly complaining."

"*That's* the spirit." But her cheerful tone was offset by the frown that crossed her features a moment later. "… huh. They're playing it smarter than I thought they would."

"I really, really don't like how you said that." Jericho leaned forward and peered through the windshield. "Is there a police blockade or something?"

"Nothing so flashy, but almost as bad." She made a turn into another quiet side street and pulled over about a hundred yards along. He expected her to wait then drive on again, but she shut the car down and unclipped her seatbelt before climbing out. "Come on, we're walking from here."

Although somewhat puzzled, he did so without demur, closing the car door behind him. "Is this part of the plan?"

"It is now. We're up to Plan D or Plan E now, depending on specific circumstances." She passed him her shoulder bag and backpack. "Hold onto these for a second, please."

"Uh, okay?" Doing his best to look nonchalant, he watched as she leaned in through the car's passenger door and did something involving the discus. He put his left hand in his jacket pocket to hide the bandages, then belatedly realized that was probably why she'd acquired the garment in the first place.

"Okay, done." She stepped back from the car and closed the door. A moment later, he heard the locks click shut, then saw the polarization on the windows (usually an automatic feature that only activated in direct sunlight) visibly darken. "Shoulder bag, please. Let's go. We've got about sixty seconds."

"What was that in aid of?" He handed over the bag and followed her, automatically checking both ways as they stepped out into the street. "And sixty seconds until what?"

She appeared to be counting under her breath as she knelt next to one of Utopia's ubiquitous manhole covers; or rather, access openings for the city's robotic cleanup devices. Tapping it with the discus, she pressed a single button, eliciting a cheery *beep*. The manhole irised open and she took a quick peek down, then climbed into the depths.

"Drop the backpack. I'll catch it." Her voice floated up from below. "Then come down. You've got twenty seconds."

Obediently, he let the pack fall, but not before reducing its effective weight to about a quarter of its usual value. As soon as it vanished down the open shaft, he did much the same with his own weight and dropped onto the ladder. Gripping the uprights and pressing his feet against the sides allowed him to slide down with ease.

Overhead, something dark blotted out the sunlight briefly before the manhole opening contracted shut again. Jericho landed on his feet, still holding the sides of the ladder, in pitch darkness. "I'm down," he said, in case Chelsea hadn't heard him reach the bottom.

"Good." He could vaguely detect her—or rather, the denser items she was carrying—using his G-sense, but nowhere near as precisely as he could have done with the enhancement harness. "Turning my flashlight on now."

Thus warned, he shielded his eyes so that he wasn't automatically dazzled when the brilliant beam stabbed out through the blackness. He found himself blinking a lot; the unpainted gray concrete walls did a bang-up job of reflecting the light back and forth, so the area was well illuminated. Fortunately, his eyes adjusted quickly. "So why are we down here, exactly?"

She adjusted the strap on her shoulder bag and dropped the discus into it. "There didn't seem to be many hexes around, and I didn't know why. Now I do. They've got them covering every street between here and the South Side Mall, and they're gradually sweeping outward. Every vehicle's getting a visual check." She glanced to the left and the right, apparently consulting an internal map, and nodded to the left. "C'mon. We need to get moving."

He followed in her wake, checking behind occasionally for the unnervingly insectoid street-cleaning robots that they both knew were down here. "And the car we were using?"

She chuckled. "That's what you saw, just before the manhole closed over. I programmed it to go for a random-walk auto-drive with polarization high enough that hex cameras can't get a reliable image of what's inside. It's been told to avoid being hemmed in or stopped unless doing so would bring the vehicle into contact with people. If we're lucky, it'll lead them on a nice long chase right across the city and back again."

This seemed a little optimistic to Jericho. "They're not stupid. Someone's bound to figure out it's a decoy, sooner rather than later."

"And they will." Her tone was light. "But they can't *ignore* it. Especially when all their remote overrides fail to work. They'll need to devote a disproportionate amount of effort toward stopping it. In the meantime, even those not chasing it will have heard about it, so subconsciously they'll be focusing on every other car in the city for suspicious activity, drawing attention away from the other ways it's possible to move around in Utopia."

"Not that going underground is an overly common way to do it," he observed. There was a hollow metallic *thud* as he trod on a manhole set into the floor; it bore the same spiral pattern as the ones on the street above. "How far down do these tunnels *go*?"

"That's a conduit into the trash lines," Chelsea said, without looking back to see what he was talking about. "The trash bugs collect anything from the streets and drop it in there."

"Trash bugs. Right." The term was self-explanatory, though this was the first time he'd heard it expressed in that way.

Resembling six-foot-long glossy black arthropods with spinning brushes in the place of lobster claws, the 'trash bugs' stayed out of sight during the day. It was only during the quiet hours of the night that they emerged from the manholes to perform whatever cleaning duties they found necessary.

When he first met Smokeshadow on the roof of the Oaklands, she'd decoyed one of them into view by throwing a paper plane onto the roadway. At the time, he'd thought they were creepy. Unsurprisingly, being down in one of their access tunnels didn't do much to change that opinion.

They'd also been his first indication that there was more going on beneath the surface of Utopia—both figurative and literal—than most people understood.

Maybe the first … but not the last. Not by a long shot.

The thought spurred another question. "So, uh … how'd you get past them, the last time you were down here with the Survivors?"

"Oh, I didn't come down here," Chelsea admitted. "I stayed upstairs with one of Sidestep's instances, and he gave me a running commentary. Gimmick didn't seem to have much trouble with them, though."

"From what Thomas told me, Gimmick *specializes* in messing with tech or adapting it in ways it wasn't meant to go," Jericho reminded her, trying not to sound too testy. "Plus, she had the Survivors with her, as well as a horrifically powerful blaster rifle. Just saying, they were a little more prepared for a hostile encounter than we are."

Chelsea nodded. "You're not wrong about the Zarkinator. But they got through to the Oaklands without destroying any trash bugs, so it can't be all that difficult, can it?"

"Did you seriously just say that?" Jericho threw his arms in the air. "For all we know, these trash bugs have since been upgraded with a search-and-destroy mode!" His voice echoed down the tunnel, and he immediately wished he could take the words back.

Chelsea made shushing motions. "Maybe if you can keep the noise down, we won't have to find out."

Sorry, he mouthed, not actually voicing the word. She nodded to acknowledge this, and they both stopped moving to listen. Long, tense moments passed with not even the dripping of water to alleviate the silence, then she let out a tiny sigh and shook her head.

"If there's anything out there," she whispered, "I can't hear it."

Jericho frowned. Just for an instant, as she'd begun speaking, he thought he'd heard something in the distance. By the time he raised his hand to wave her to silence, it was gone again.

She looked searchingly at him. He waited for another few seconds, listening, then shook his head. "Nope. If there *was* something, it's gone now."

"Pfft," she muttered. "We're jumping at shadows, both of us."

"I think we'd better start moving," he said quietly. "Who knows how long it'll be before they decide to lock the whole city down?"

"Six hours, tops." With that dire prediction, she led off again, her feet making no sound against the concrete floor. He did his best to emulate her level of stealth, cheating a little by reducing his effective weight, though he had to dial it back slightly to maintain traction.

As they skulked through the access tunnels, Jericho recalled a conversation he'd once had with Relentless. *I designed it all,* the big man had said, *from the sub-sewers to the Spire. It works as well as it does because I made it that way.*

If that was true, and he had no reason to disbelieve the claim, Utopia City was one vast interconnected mechanism that worked so well because of one man's vision and another man's technical genius. Now, it was all under threat from a single malevolent intruder.

Independence—Poser—would destabilize the entire system if she were not stopped in time.

Not on my watch.

47
The Trash Bug Express

The attack came out of a side passage about ten minutes later. Jericho had the barest of warnings from his G-sense—the surrounding reinforced concrete rendered it almost useless—before the trash bug undulated past Chelsea and bore him to the ground.

"Crap!" he yelled, instinctively reducing its weight to one-tenth normal and throwing it off him. The bug twisted and flailed like a living thing as it slowly fell to the ground, trying to get its multitudinous feet under it. His stomach wound protested as he leaped to his feet, but he didn't have the time to go slow.

"They'll be able to track down exactly where we are if one goes offline, so don't break it!" Chelsea shouted, delving into her shoulder bag.

"Great!" he retorted as it touched down. "*Now* you tell me!" His eyes never wavered from the trash bug as its sharp metal 'feet' skittered and scraped on the bare concrete. Fortunately, it failed to muster enough traction to go anywhere in a hurry.

His initial plan had been to inflict ten times normal gravity upon the trash bug and destroy it with its own mass, as he'd done once upon a time with Pickup's ride, and much more recently with Charnel. Now, he had to be a little more circumspect.

That's okay. I can play keep-away all day if I have to.

Almost without thinking, he formed glue-tags in both hands and tossed them at the mechanical critter as soon as they had achieved stability. They were weaker than he really liked, but when they struck the thing's front leg joints, its leg movements were visibly hampered anyway. The trash bug slowed in its forward motion, but as he dodged aside, it turned fluidly to pursue him.

Two more glue-tags hit the second pair of legs, slowing the trash bug further. Jericho went to jump over it, planting one hand in the middle of its back, but the day's travails had slowed him down just a little too much. Swinging wildly, one of the brush-arms smacked into his ribs and knocked him off-balance. He hit the ground with a muted yelp of pain and rolled awkwardly, curling over himself to protect his stomach wound.

Before he could get to his feet again, the trash bug was on top of him, the abrasive material of its spinning brush catching at his face. He threw up one arm to cover his head, keeping the other pressed across his midsection. And then he heard a series of musical beeps, and it climbed off him.

"You okay?" asked Chelsea, putting the discus away again. Leaning down, she offered him a hand. He took it with some gratitude, climbing to his feet as carefully as possible.

"Had better days," he grunted. It sucked, being walking wounded. "Hope I didn't pop any more stitches. What'd you do to it?"

She shrugged. "I told it we're not to be dragged to the surface and reported to the police. It's what they're programmed to do with anyone they find down here. You up to moving on?"

"Yes, but *that's* what it was trying to do?" He stared at her as they started off. "Why didn't you warn me earlier? And why didn't you work your magic *before* it did its best to polish my face into a crash test dummy?"

This time, she rolled her eyes. "Well, I couldn't exactly slap the discus on it until you held it still for me, could I? And I would've thought you already knew how they were programmed. You didn't bother asking even *one* question about them after you joined Force Majeure?"

She had him there, and he knew it. "I, uh, kind of forgot about it at the time," he confessed. He threw a wary glance at the trash bug, which was moving ahead of them. "It's not gonna jump me again, is it?"

"*Relax.*" She waved her hand dismissively toward the cleaning robot. "Our new best friend here's going to escort us all the way to the South Side Mall. So long as it's broadcasting the code for 'under maintenance', the rest of them will leave us alone."

This time, his suspicious glance was directed at Chelsea. "Was this part of the plan all along?"

"It was part of *a* plan." She frowned and checked her phone, then slipped it back into her bag, which she zipped shut in turn. "How fast can you move with that wound? We've got more than ten miles to cover on foot before we get to South Side. I want to be there in the next couple of hours. Are you up for that?"

"We'll just have to see, won't we?" He started forward at a cautious jog then gradually increased his speed, trying not to exacerbate the injury. It wasn't easy; no matter how much care he took, every step jolted his stomach painfully.

"Is there any chance you can pick up the pace?" Chelsea passed him at a run, moving with fast, firm strides. Her words floated back to him. "We've really got to move, here!"

"Oh, you gotta be kidding me!" But of course, she wasn't. Also, she was taking the only flashlight with her.

And then, he had no more breath to spare.

Had he been possessed of any other powerset, Jericho would've been incapable of jogging ten yards, much less actually *running* with the stomach wound Charnel had inflicted on him. But his Prodigy physiology allowed him to power on through the pain and push himself to levels most people simply could not reach. What any unpowered human achieved once in a hundred attempts with continuous training, a prodigy with the proper focus could pull off every time.

If he'd been fully fit and healthy, he could've easily left Chelsea in his dust. As a costumed vigilante back in Savannah, he had regularly run the rooftops until the early hours of the morning, then woken fully rested after just four hours of sleep. Minor cuts and bruises mended themselves overnight.

Given half a chance, prodigies healed from *anything*. Infections were rare; cumulative injuries such as microfractures from roof-running and concussions from hits to the head simply … went away. Even the nerve damage from the lightning strike was starting to show signs of fixing itself.

However, the sword wound he'd taken was far outside his usual wheelhouse. While it *would* heal much faster than the norm, it was still a significant injury, and 'much faster' would be a matter of days, not hours. Likewise, his Prodigy powerset wouldn't let him ignore it indefinitely, though he could keep going much farther and stay conscious longer.

How far he could go and how long he remained on his feet depended very much on the severity of the wound versus the urgency of his focus.

On the one hand, the fate of Force Majeure hung in the balance; on the other, the wound *was* nasty, and had already cost him a lot of blood. He pushed himself as hard as he could, but all he could do was draw level with Chelsea as the trash bug dashed ahead of them.

Pain pulsed through him with every jolting step.

He refused to let it stop him.

I can't fail. I won't fail.

It took fifteen minutes, during which time they covered nearly three miles, for Chelsea to call a halt. By the end of it, Jericho was staggering along with his hand clamped to his wound, the only things keeping him conscious and upright being his powers themselves. He slowed when she did, breath hissing between his teeth, and leaned against the tunnel wall.

"I can … keep going," he insisted, concentrating on not puking from the pain. "We're nearly … halfway there."

"No, you can't," she retorted. "And you're gonna kill yourself if you keep trying. I don't know what I was thinking. I *treated* the damn wound, but you kept acting like you could handle it, so like a moron, I took your act at face value."

"Go on without me, then." He had to accept that she was telling the truth, and he wasn't about to see her get captured if he could help it. "I'll hide out down here. You get out and raise the alarm."

"No." She glared at him. "God save me from self-sacrificing idiots. Take five; I need to kick over Plan F."

Gratefully, he subsided onto the floor of the tunnel. Even five minutes of rest would do him a world of good, but they couldn't keep stopping to let him recuperate his strength. Besides, he suspected a few of his stitches were on the verge of tearing. "What's Plan F?"

"Alternate transportation." She went over to the trash bug which was standing obediently nearby, and did something with the discus. The bug turned and skittered in his direction; he put up his hands defensively, but it came to a halt next to him without pulling any hostile moves.

"What are you doing?" he asked. The answer occurred to him a moment later through his fading haze of pain. "We're going to *ride* them?"

"We're going to ride them." She indicated the bug. "Put your hand on it. That way, when the other one gets here, it'll read you as a maintenance tech instead of an intruder."

After the last encounter, he favored not being taken for an intruder, so he complied with her instructions; the smooth metal leg hummed slightly under his hand. A few moments later, another bug indeed arrived and stood looking at him until Chelsea pulled her magic with the discus. Sliding the device back into her shoulder bag, she strolled over and gave Jericho a hand up.

"They can't carry our normal weight, but you've got that covered," she said briskly. "They're too wide and too low to ride astride like horses, so I'm thinking we sit or kneel on their backs. Once we're on board, I'll tell them where to go, then it's trash bug express the rest of the way to South Side."

In the usual course of events, he would've given both her and the robotic cleaners an extremely dubious look, and probably refused to even countenance the idea. This was nowhere close to resembling the usual course of events. "I've only got one question."

She raised her eyebrows. "What?"

"Which one's mine?"

48
Leaving Utopia, First Class

Balanced upright on the back of the trash bug as it raced through the darkened tunnel, Jericho kept a careful eye out for obstacles. Chelsea rode hers ahead of him in a slightly more conventional cross-legged pose, leaning gracefully into the turns as if she'd done this all her life. Crouching slightly to duck under a low concrete beam, Jericho wondered how much farther they had to go.

He knew they'd been moving south, and his G-sense told him the distance (roughly twelve miles from where they'd started), but without access to a good map of the city, all he could say for sure was that they were close to the Greenway. The painted markings he'd seen here and there didn't mean much to him, mainly because he'd never been in these tunnels before.

When they'd started off an hour ago, he'd tried sitting and then kneeling as Chelsea had suggested, but he quickly found that the multiple legs of the trash bug resulted in a constant low-level jarring as it ran through the tunnels. Usually, this would not have been a problem, but either posture allowed the jolting of their travel to be transmitted up through his body to his stomach wound.

As unlikely a solution as it sounded, standing up gave his knees a chance to dampen the painful vibration, making for a much more comfortable ride. His power-assisted sense of balance, aided and abetted by a couple of glue-tags, let him ride the bug through the tunnels with ease, albeit with the occasional need to duck under a beam.

Go on, Luke silently urged him. *Ask her if we're there yet. It'll be funny.*

"We're here," she said, just as he opened his mouth. As she spoke the words, the trash bugs trotted to a halt. He dismissed the glue-tags and stepped off his bug; she climbed off hers a little more stiffly, rubbing her butt.

The respite gained from traffic-surfing the bug across the city had afforded him a second wind, though he hoped they wouldn't be doing anything so strenuous any time soon. One thing was for sure; although he didn't suffer from claustrophobia, he'd be glad to leave the cramped underground spaces.

"Next time, that thing's wearing a saddle," Chelsea groused. "It was *not* designed for riding." She gave Jericho an irritated look as she reached into her bag for the discus. "But did you have to show off by *standing up* nearly the whole way?"

Jericho shrugged. "Sitting down wasn't working for me." He didn't want to explain beyond that, or she'd start fussing over his wound again.

"Fair enough. You physical types are just plain ridiculous, anyway."

This wasn't anything Jericho hadn't heard before. He nodded in agreement and leaned carefully against the wall as she gave the trash bugs their marching orders. Resting was a good idea on several levels. While he was technically functional now, pushing himself past his new-set boundaries would put him at risk of suffering a total physical breakdown, followed by ongoing complications.

The ache radiating from the stab wound suggested that the injury might have been exacerbated anyway, despite the precautions he'd taken not to jolt it too much. Still, so long as it didn't tear open again, it *would* heal once he got some downtime to rest and recuperate. The sixty-four-million-dollar question was, when was that likely to happen?

Aware there was probably nobody else around, he still listened for other intruders in the maintenance tunnels. There were none that he could hear, but he kept a careful watch out nonetheless.

He switched his attention to the trash bugs as soon as she finished with them. Though he didn't think they were going to attack him again—Chelsea didn't make that kind of mistake—it never hurt to be careful. But they turned away and skittered away as though neither he nor Chelsea existed.

"Not that I'm trying to second-guess your plan," he ventured as they climbed the ladder toward the manhole cover above, "but wouldn't it have been easier to boost an air-car? One of those could've gotten us hundreds of miles out of town before anyone could mount a pursuit."

She paused and looked down at him for a moment, then returned her attention to the underside of the cover. "I'm beginning to think someone's been keeping you in the dark about certain aspects of Utopia City," she observed. Something clicked in the dimness, and the manhole irised open.

"What do you mean?" he asked, a little irritated at her change of subject. "What aspects? I've heard of the one air-cab hijacking attempt that ended up crashing just outside the city limits, but only because the onboard batteries were depleted after a long shift."

She climbed up out of the shaft, then offered her hand to assist him up as well. "The aircars have backup batteries for emergency landings, but they're powered by remote inductance from the Spire, just like everything else in Utopia. It crashed because it wasn't getting power anymore."

Jericho blinked, staring at her. "They what?" Automatically, he accepted the help. "But a cab driver told me ..." He stopped himself, recalling what Tourbillon had explained about the maglev recharging his equipment. This was more or less the same concept, but on a much larger scale. And if Force Majeure was good at one thing, it was going large-scale on a project. Utopia itself was proof positive of that.

"They probably got told that by someone who didn't know any better." Chelsea gestured along the narrow alleyway where they'd ended up, toward a door at the end. "Come on."

Jericho glanced over his shoulder at a distant narrow slice of street, then upward at the walls on either side of them. "Either we're in between two real tall buildings—which, to be honest, we've got no shortage of in Utopia—or this here's the South Side Mall." As he made the observation, he followed along behind her.

"Right the second time around," she confirmed. There was a *beep* as she dealt with the lock, then led him inside. He pushed the door closed behind them and followed along.

If the door hadn't already clued him in, the cramped dimensions of the corridor within and the presence of doors marked with labels such as **PLANT ROOM 1-311** would've given him a hint that they were in the maintenance spaces of the Mall. Chelsea seemed to be right at home here, which didn't surprise him in the slightest. She struck him as the sort of person to memorize the layout of places like this.

She proved his point a little way in by opening a particular door— helpfully labeled **MAINTENANCE SUPPLIES 1-311**—and ushering him inside. The room, not overly large to begin with, was made more cramped by racks and shelves of various equipment. "Here," she said. "Put these on and hold this."

'*These*' were a set of clear safety goggles and a high-vis vest, while '*this*' was a clipboard with random sheets of paper attached. He accepted them and slid the vest on. The goggles gave a comforting feeling, almost like wearing his mask again.

"Try to look like you're only thinking of your next coffee break." She studied his expression for a moment. "A little more bored. Perfect. Don't make eye contact with anyone, and glance down at the clipboard every now and again."

Armed with this ad hoc camouflage, they left the room again and moved on. Nobody looked at them twice, even when they crossed the public corridors via more of the discreetly placed maintenance doors. He was glad of Chelsea's presence; even with the innate sense of distance his G-sense granted him, he would've had no idea which way they were going through the labyrinthine passageways.

Then, after he'd begun to wonder anew precisely how *big* the South Side Mall was, she opened one last door and they emerged into the echoing, cavernous spaces of the Southside Parking complex. Random clanging noises reverberated through the colossal structure, along with shouted instructions and the distant omnipresent rumble of traffic along Interstate 70. The faint miasma of internal combustion exhaust—entirely absent from the general atmosphere of Utopia City—wafted to his nostrils, along with those of burned oil and hot metal.

When Doc Iridium's bomb destroyed Manhattan, Kansas in 1999, a large section of the interstate had been obliterated along with it. The highway had been rebuilt by Force Majeure while constructing Utopia itself, but a southward curve was introduced to put the majority of it outside the fifteen-mile radius circle of the Greenway. It crossed that boundary twice, via tunnels diving beneath the toroidal park, solely to give outside traffic access to Southside Parking. Force Majeure's commitment to preventing air pollution within Utopia had extended to roofing over I-70 out to the city limits in both directions and installing high-end precipitators within the enclosed space to keep exhaust fumes to a minimum.

As far as Jericho could tell, it all worked well. Before stopping their engines, incoming vehicles were directed onto an appropriately sized metal grate. The vacated vehicles were hoisted on their grates via a gargantuan chain-drive up into the parking structure and stored in waiting recesses, like bottles of wine in a cellar. Southside Parking was *huge*, with everything from hatchbacks to eighteen-wheelers stacked on various levels. It was also busy, and everyone working here wore the same type of vest and goggles he and Chelsea were sporting, which meant they would continue to blend in.

Just as he noticed the workers in this area also wore hardhats, Chelsea passed him one from a rack near the door. He fitted it onto his head, feeling a little awkward. For her part, the moment it was in place, it was like she'd been wearing one all her life.

She even got me boots instead of shoes, just in case we ended up here. Right.

"Camera blind spot right there," she said, gesturing toward a discreet mark on the oil-stained concrete flooring. "Put this in. I'll call you over when we're ready to roll."

He was about to ask what '*this*' was when she palmed an earpiece into his hand. Heading to the spot she'd indicated, he slid the device into his ear and pressed the tiny switch that activated it. He was familiar with Chelsea's personal style of radio earbud; the range never extended past a few miles, and the battery didn't last more than a couple of hours of use, but *nothing* could intercept the signal. Again, he was impressed with her forethought.

Pretending to check notes on his clipboard, he kept his eyes on Chelsea as she went and spoke to a few people. Despite his personal knowledge of more than one crime committed by her, he was grateful she'd chosen to have his back. When it came to running the rooftops and beating the crap out of muggers in dark alleys, he was extremely good at what he did; on the other hand, this was *her* wheelhouse, and they both knew it.

The first guy she spoke to directed her to a second, who pointed at someone out of Jericho's view. He tensed as she left his line of sight but restrained the impulse to go and make sure she was okay. Not being in control of the situation *sucked*; unfortunately, this had been the case since shortly before he'd woken up in her apartment.

What lies was Poser telling the rest of Force Majeure? For a moment, he regretted not giving himself up to Transit so Chelsea could make a clean getaway.

I always got along with Transit. Maybe she would've listened to me. Briefly, he envisaged being escorted into the Spire and denouncing Poser to all and sundry, saving Force Majeure …

Chelsea's voice in his earpiece dragged him out of the heroic daydream. "Come on. We've got maybe ten minutes before they lock this place down."

"Crap," he muttered as he headed in the direction he'd last seen her. "I thought it would've taken them longer."

"It should have," she agreed. "It's only been a few hours. I'm thinking the big guy put pressure on City Hall."

Jericho grimaced. He totally believed Relentless would do something of the sort—the fact that Force Majeure held a considerable amount of normally-silent political power was an open secret with most Utopians—but this was bad. It meant that Relentless, whom Jericho *never* wanted as an enemy, at least partially believed whatever line Poser was spinning. Which meant in turn that Jericho was going to be at a distinct disadvantage when trying to convince him of Poser's perfidy.

Hustling along, sticking to the yellow safety lines while trying to keep an eye on everything around him, he nearly missed Chelsea altogether. She was standing next to the back end of an eighteen-wheeler that had just been lowered from above. With her were two other guys; a Southside Parking employee (if the hardhat and the vest were any indications) and a fifty-something man with a graying buzz cut and an incipient paunch. Somehow, her stance seemed to indicate 'nothing to see here', even as she slipped the truck driver—under the circumstances, it was a fair guess—a wad of bills.

From the guy's manner, he had more than one reason to want to get out of Utopia before they shut off the highway access. "Come on, come on," he urged, tugging the back door of the trailer open. "Get in before the next hex comes over." Then he spotted Jericho. "Who's he?"

"I said two," Chelsea stated firmly. "You've been paid for two. You're taking two."

The driver tilted one eye at the sky, visible through the open side of the parking structure, then grunted in surrender. "Fuck it, get in then."

"Thank you." Chelsea doffed her protective paraphernalia and handed it to the Southside employee, who accepted it without a murmur. As Jericho removed his own, he contrived to brush his hand against Chelsea's arm, reducing her effective weight considerably.

Thus assisted, she scrambled into the rear of the trailer with minimal problems. It was loaded all the way to the back with bags arranged on pallets, the stacks almost reaching the roof. Climbing up the pile, she slid into the opening at the top, wriggling forward to make way for Jericho.

Trying not to make it seem suspiciously easy, he followed Chelsea's lead and joined her in the gap between the pallets and the roof, a matter of no more than eighteen inches. The doors slammed shut, dropping the light level to near-nothing before the locks clicked, sealing them in. He and Chelsea waited tensely, eyeing each other in the dim light filtering in above the doors. A couple of moments later, there was a somewhat more distant slam, indicating the driver was in the cab of the truck. When the engine started and the trailer jolted into motion, it was almost an anticlimax.

"Okay," he said, letting out his breath as his G-sense agreed with his inner ear that the truck going up an incline then accelerating to join the flow of traffic. "We're on the way."

"Yeah. Whoof." Chelsea kneaded the bag next to her face. "I'm glad this stuff doesn't smell, though. By the time we got out of here, we'd both be stinking to high heaven of it, and that's no way to stay unnoticed."

Jericho prodded the bag he was lying on. It felt like a lot of tightly packed tiny marbles. While there was a slight musty odor hanging around in the trailer, it wasn't so bad as to be unbearable. "So what's in these bags, anyway?"

"Urea. I had the chance to read the label just before Cletus there closed the doors on us."

"Urea?" That sounded unpleasantly familiar. "What's that used for?"

There was a movement in the semi-darkness that could've been a shrug. "Fertilizer. And explosives. But don't worry. It needs fuel oil to make it ready to go bang."

There was only one thing to say to that, trapped in the back of a rocking, moving *diesel-powered* eighteen-wheeler loaded with literal tons of the stuff. "Just great. Maybe we should've waited for the next truck."

"What next truck? We were the last in line out of there."

That was a sobering thought. The lockdown must have come into effect at just about the same time as the eighteen-wheeler hit the interstate. Jericho searched for a topic to take his mind off the close shave. "Hey, uh … was his name really Cletus?"

She snorted. "Nope. But as far as *you* know, that's what it is."

"That's fair, I guess." He grinned in the near-dark.

"Best get comfortable, J. We've got a long way to go."

He froze momentarily. *The last person who called me that was Luke.* Then his heart restarted, and he registered the rest of what she'd said. "How far, exactly? Where's the next stop? Topeka?"

Her tone was nonchalant. "Nope. Kansas City. We'll be in here a while, so we might want to turn off the earpieces and save the batteries."

"Yeah, good point." He pressed the earpiece until he heard the almost subliminal *click* of it shutting down. Then he reached up and placed his hand flat on the roof above his face. The aluminum sheet gave, but only a little, as he pressed on it.

So much for staying out of claustrophobic spaces. Kansas City's a hundred miles, near enough. Fifteen minutes by maglev, a whole lot longer by eighteen-wheeler, even doing seventy on the freeway.

About the only way to make this ride more comfortable would be to have Thomas in here alongside him.

And while I'm wishing for impossible things, I'd like a full-sized jacuzzi.

He sighed. This was going to be a *long* two hours.

49
No Honor Among Thieves

Lying back on the bags in the near-dark, Jericho felt the truck beginning to slow. "We're stopping," he said, just before the exhaust brake came on. Then he felt the bumping of misaligned concrete slabs under the wheels. "We're about ten miles short of Kansas City proper, and that's not asphalt."

"Shit," Chelsea muttered. "Looks like he's decided to rip us off, after all."

"Wait, you *knew* he was gonna do this?" Jericho turned toward her, wondering what the hell had been going through her head. "How about a little advance warning next time?"

"This *is* the advance warning," she hissed as boot-steps became audible along the side of the truck. Then Jericho heard another truck stopping nearby; from the tilt of Chelsea's head, she'd picked it up too. "Sounds like he's brought company," she concluded in a murmur.

They both began to wriggle toward the edge of the stack. "You still could've told me earlier." Jericho kept his voice down to the same level.

"Would it have let you rest any easier?" The snark was clearly present in her voice, despite her breathing the words in his ear.

"Well, no, but ..." He couldn't argue with her logic. While the strapped-down bags of urea weren't exactly a feather mattress, he'd taken the opportunity to grab some much-needed shuteye anyway, and was feeling somewhat refreshed as a result.

"Then we'll talk about it later. If he's brought cops or heroes in on the deal, you make a break for it. I can take care of myself."

"Like hell," he muttered as the lock was disengaged from the door. "I'm not leaving you to swing in the breeze."

"I'm not the one wanted for murder," she retorted just before the door opened, then she raised her voice. "What, we're there already?"

"Come on down," said 'Cletus', the bonhomie in his voice ringing false even to Jericho's untrained ears. "We're all set."

The light from outside would've been dazzling to anyone else. To Jericho's practiced eyes, it was plenty bright but not blinding. All the same, he pretended to be clumsy about the way he scrambled partway down and jumped the rest of the way. Reducing his effective weight, he rode out the jolt to his injured stomach while feigning a drop to one knee, blinking and shading his eyes like he couldn't see jack.

In reality, he was taking in his surroundings, ready to use his environment as a weapon at the first opportunity. To his left was an expanse of dense brush; if they needed to make a run for it, that would make for good cover. Underfoot was the concrete he'd felt beneath the semi-trailer wheels, which appeared to be a roadside staging area. Loose chunks the size of his fist lay between the slabs, offering potential weapons if it came to that. Finally, to his right, he could hear vehicles on the freeway but was blocked from seeing it by the trailer of another truck. This was clearly not by accident.

The truck driver stepped into view and stood in front of where a fourth man had Chelsea held from behind. Jericho's G-sense warned him about the two coming up behind him, but there were no dense points that indicated weapons, so he let them grab his arms. He noted that Chelsea's shoulder bag and backpack were still in place, and the former was still zipped up. However, the side of her jacket—in reality, her hyperweave costume—had an odd bulge in it, just next to her hand.

He had a real good idea of precisely what she was concealing there. Which was good; she was still thinking, still planning. He just had to do his best to back whatever play she made.

"So, this here's how it's gonna go." The man he knew only as 'Cletus' seemed to be in much better humor now. "Lady, you're gonna hand over the rest of that roll of cash I seen you pull money off of. Sonny boy's gonna do the same with whatever he's carryin'. Us four are gonna split it all fair an' square, then we drive off into the sunset an' forget to tell the cops where we dropped you at."

Jericho had to award the prize to Chelsea for portraying someone out of her depth but doing her best to present a brave face. She actually blew a strand of hair out of her eyes—he was pretty sure he'd never seen that done in real life—and glared at the truck driver. "And what if I tell you to go to hell? You'll hurt me?" The quaver in her voice was pure artistry. "Let me guess. You *'like a woman with spunk'*?"

The four men glanced at each other, then at Chelsea. "Hell, no," said the guy holding her arms behind her back, sincerely enough that Jericho was inclined to believe him. "We ain't like that. We just want the money."

"And if I say no?" She eyed 'Cletus' warningly. "You try to dig into my bag, I'll fight. I bite, and I kick."

"Ain't gonna lay a hand on you, honey, save for makin' sure you don't interfere. But I figure if I put a hurtin' on your boyfriend there, you'll hand it over soon enough." Just in case she didn't get his meaning, the trucker gestured at Jericho and lightly smacked his fist into his palm.

Chelsea sighed. "I suppose trying to appeal to your better natures won't do much good?"

'Cletus' let out a bark of laughter, and the other men chuckled at the joke. "Better natures don't pay no bills, sweetheart. Figure we're already breakin' the law, so why not make it a real payday?"

Just for a moment, Chelsea let a hint of steel show through. "You do know, this'll get you blacklisted with the Southside Parking crew. All of you, I mean. You'll be *done* in Utopia after this. It's amazing what kind of accidents can happen to a truck in storage if the crew feels like being careless."

"Okay, now you're just reachin'." 'Cletus' shook his head. "Ain't no way you've got that kind of pull with 'em. You're just another undesirable, gettin' smuggled out ahead of the lockdown." He marched over and planted himself foursquare in front of where Jericho was being held by the two men. "Got anything to say before I start rearrangin' your boyfriend's looks?"

"Yeah." Chelsea caught Jericho's eye. "Don't break any bones."

He hadn't intended to—these weren't scum of the earth, just regular everyday robbery-with-menaces types—but it was good to know he and Chelsea were on the same page. His return nod was fractional at best, but the slight smile that twitched her mouth showed she'd seen it.

"Not unless you figure you want to get stubborn, honey," 'Cletus' promised, having missed the whole byplay. He stepped forward, already drawing back his fist in anticipation.

It was like there was a script they were both following to the letter. Jericho looked him in the eye and grinned. "She wasn't talking to you." Reducing his personal weight while adding fifty percent to each of the guys holding his arms, he lifted his legs into the air, drew his knees up to his chest, and slammed both boot-heels into the treacherous driver's chest.

As 'Cletus' stumbled backward and fell on his ass, Jericho arched his body and continued into a backflip, wrenching his arms free from his erstwhile captors and landing lightly on his feet behind them. Their dumbfounded expressions made it clear as they turned to face him that this had never happened to them before. Jericho mentally tagged them Lefty and Righty, and made his plans accordingly.

They had no shortage of courage, as shown by how they came at him without hesitation. Also without a strategy, which only proved that ninety percent of any victory lay in forethought and planning. Lefty seemed quicker off the mark than Righty, so Jericho danced around to the left, leaving Righty out in the cold until Jericho had time to deal with him. Moving in close, Jericho slipped a clumsy punch and slammed a knee into Lefty's stomach. This was followed by an elbow to the jaw as the man bent over.

Lefty just kept leaning over until he slumped to the stained, cracked concrete, which left Righty facing Jericho alone. 'Cletus' was wheezing on the ground while Chelsea had already dealt with her would-be captor; the UCPD taser—the source of the lump he'd seen earlier—was still in her hand. Bringing his attention back to Righty, Jericho weaved his head aside from a haymaker and considered his options. Broken bones were off the menu, so he couldn't just mangle the guy's wrist. But cartilage wasn't bone.

Putting all his weight behind it, Jericho sank a single punch almost wrist-deep into Righty's solar plexus. Breath gusted raggedly out of the man's lungs, along with a belch as he apparently came close to bringing up his lunch. When he started to lurch forward, Jericho grabbed him by the head and brought up a knee, smashing Righty's nose all over his face. Righty collapsed altogether and fell over onto his side, blood already running down from his crushed nostrils to pool on the cracked concrete.

Stepping past Righty's twitching body, Jericho approached 'Cletus', who was struggling to sit up. The trucker was still having trouble breathing properly, from the way his hand was pressed to his stomach. "Want to have another try at that?" Jericho asked mildly. "You know, when your buddies *aren't* holding my arms and all."

"Wh … what?" rasped 'Cletus', needing two tries to get the word out. "Who the hell *are* you?"

"Just a couple of people trying to go from point A to point B, until some asshole decided to detour via point Z," Chelsea said, strolling over to join them. "I believe the relevant phrase is *'fuck around and find out'*. Now, I'll be having my money back, Earl."

The trucker—Earl—didn't resist as Chelsea reached into his pocket and removed the wad of cash. She dropped it into her shoulder bag as she stood up and looked down at him dispassionately. Jericho could see his eyes rolling in their sockets as he watched her; whatever she chose to do to the guy, there was no way he'd be able to avoid it.

"Keys," she said over her shoulder to Jericho. "Take 'em out of the trucks and toss 'em into the brush. Except his. I think we'll be borrowing that one."

"You can't—you can't take my rig," croaked Earl. "Takin' the money back, that's fair, but stealing my truck, that's—"

"Transport," Chelsea finished for him. "We won't keep it, burn it or even wreck it. It'll be parked somewhere in town, locked up. We'll toss the keys on top of the trailer for you. But we can't trust you, so we *are* taking it."

"But it's my *rig*." Earl's look of desperation became one of cunning. "Matter o' fact, I'm startin' to think folks back in Utopia City might be interested in hearin' about two people who climbed outta my trailer an' jumped me an' stole my truck. 'Cause if my rig went missing, I'd have to report it, y'know? Law-abidin' thing to do an' all."

Chelsea leaned closer. "That would be a really unwise decision, Earl. Remember when I told you how you'd be blackballed by Southside Parking for pulling this shit?" Her whole attitude changed; in the flicker of an eyelid, she transformed from *'inoffensive nobody'* to *'oozing authority from every pore'*. "I *wrote* those rules. I *run* the Southside crew. This gentleman right here, the one you were going to beat up to get me to comply? I call on him to deal with idiots like you. And if you and your buddies don't want to be looking over your shoulders for the rest of your lives, not to mention getting flat-out banned from stopping in Utopia ever again, nobody hears *anything* about this. Not the cops, not the Feds, and certainly not Force Majeure. Do I make myself *abundantly* clear?"

"Jesus Christ, lady, a'right. It was only a joke, okay?" Earl wilted, all defiance gone from his posture and his voice reduced to a supplicating whine.

Chelsea eyed him disfavorably, eyes narrowed. "Your sense of humor needs work. And just to make sure you don't change your minds once we're out of sight, I'll be taking your phone. Your buddies', too. You'll get 'em back when you find your truck."

"Right, right." Earl surrendered the device then subsided onto his back again, merely turning his head to watch as Jericho took the keys from the other trucks and locked up the cabs. The keyrings jingled as Jericho tossed them into the bushes; he made sure to throw them far enough into the greenery to make finding them a lengthy chore.

The other three drivers were groggily sitting up by the time Jericho and Chelsea converged on the cab of the truck that had gotten them to this point. "Two questions," Jericho said, keeping his voice down. "First, what's to stop someone from tracking those phones while we're on the move?" He knew it could be done using a find-your-phone app, so he wasn't ruling out the existence of more intrusive software. And the last thing he wanted was to find the local police converging on them.

She held up her shoulder bag briefly. "Not a problem. Faraday cage *and* the height of fashion, all in one stylish package."

"Okay." He stared at the bag, only just now paying direct attention to it. "Those only came out a week ago. Did you use your connections to jump the queue?"

"Hardly. This isn't the commercial version. This is the *prototype*." She cheerfully patted it. "Who else do you *think* would put a stealth handbag on the market, anyway?"

When she put it that way, it made perfect sense. "... good point." The issue with the phones seemed to be well under control, so he forced his mind onto more important matters. "Second problem. Who's driving? Because I've never handled anything bigger than a pickup truck before."

"You drive, I'll navigate," Chelsea said firmly. "Just remember, take a lot of care with your starts and stops. Also, turning."

"Great." Jericho began to get a sinking feeling in the pit of his stomach that had nothing to do with his stab wound. Prodigies picked up new skills quickly, but this promised to stretch that particular perk of his powerset to the limit.

Opening the door, he climbed into the cab.

50
Calling Home, Smokeshadow Style

Chelsea looked up from the map she'd found in the glove compartment and pointed at the upcoming overhead signage. "We want to head to the right. Exit four-two-three B. James Street." Glancing at the map again, she traced a line with her fingertip. "Yeah, that's the one."

"Got it." Jericho repositioned his grip on the wheel and hit the blinker. Checking the right-hand wing mirror, he found the road empty and started to edge over. He enjoyed listening to the odd country music trucking song, but if the last eight miles had taught him anything, it was that he *never* wanted to drive these things for a living.

There was no specific thing he could point to about driving an eighteen-wheeler and say he hated it. Or rather, there wasn't *just* one thing. They were just so all-around damn temperamental and unforgiving of error.

The look on Earl's face in the rearview mirror had been a sight to see, especially when he ground the gears with a sound like a wood-chipper trying to ingest a rock. He'd stalled the truck twice while getting it out of the staging area, the second time when he tried to change up from first gear. After that, he'd learned to give it sufficient go-pedal when letting the clutch out.

But he'd managed, sticking to the right-hand lane to let faster traffic whip by him while he chugged along at a steady fifty-five; well under the speed limit, but not so slow the cops would think there was something wrong. He was in a high enough gear now that the engine rumbled instead of screaming when he tried to keep to the speed he'd picked, and there were no flashing lights visible in his rearview mirrors. All in all, he figured he could call that a win.

Now, he indicated and moved over to get onto the correct road, but he still had to slow down if he wanted to make the right-hand turn that Chelsea required. He didn't feel confident enough to attempt the mysteries of the exhaust brake, so he let the accelerator off and pushed his foot down on the regular brake pedal. The air brakes engaged and he concentrated on keeping the truck going straight, maintaining one eye in the mirror in case of trailer wobble.

By the time the turn came into view, he was going slow enough that he figured he could take it. He slowed down some more just to be sure, using the gears to reduce speed a little while doing his best not to stall the damn truck again. Taking the curve as wide as he dared, he trundled the massive vehicle around the corner, hoping the trailer's rear wheels wouldn't mount the inner curb and tip the whole thing over. *Luke would laugh his ass off and never let me hear the end of it. So would Thomas.*

Nothing of the sort happened, and he carefully straightened the wheel and changed up again. The bridge he was now crossing felt all too narrow, especially with the ridiculously low guard rails. Just upstream to the left was a much more substantial affair that even had an underslung pedestrian bridge. "Shouldn't we be going across that one?" he asked, tilting his head to indicate what he was talking about.

"Nope." Chelsea folded the map and tucked it into her bag. "This is where we want to be. Pull off onto a side street, and park it."

Oh, good. Jericho began the tortuous process of slowing down again. A side road to the right caught his eye, and he hit the blinker once more to turn down that way. The road itself was seriously in need of repair, but it had a nice wide section that allowed him to pull off to the side and bring the mechanical beast to a shuddering halt. When he applied the handbrake and turned the engine off, the silence and cessation of vibration that followed were two of the most blissful things he'd ever experienced.

So, of course, it was Chelsea who had to spoil it. "Come on, we've got to keep moving." Opening the passenger side door, she jumped out; he did the same on his side.

He took the keys, locked his door, then did the same on the other side. As she'd promised Earl they would do, he took aim and tossed the keys lightly onto the top of the trailer—not his problem how Earl got them down, after all—and dusted off his hands. "Okay, where to from here?"

"First, we clear the area. Then we catch a cab." She handed him a ball cap, the same one he'd worn back in Utopia to leave her apartment. "If he talks to the cops, they'll be looking for a skinhead."

"I guess so." It was easier to do what she said than argue, especially since she'd been right on the money so far. But he was getting more and more jittery about what was going on back in Utopia. The legitimate members of Force Majeure were each powerful in their own right, but would that help them if Poser decided they were a danger to her? He had to get *some* sort of message to them.

Chelsea gave him a sympathetic look as they hustled back toward the main road. "Worried about Force Majeure?"

"More'n a bit, yeah," he admitted. "You said before as how you could put together a secure connection. I don't want to sound like I'm pushing you, but how soon can we get that done?"

"Just as soon as we get to a motel where I can be sure we're not likely to be disturbed." Phone in her hand, she punched in a number. "Hi, yes, I'd like a cab, please. Corner of North James Street and … uh, Lyon Avenue. Yes, please. For the name of Harry."

She ended the call and put her phone away, and he looked at her curiously. "Harry?"

"As in Harry Houdini," she confided with a grin. "The great escapologist."

"Right." She had a point, he decided. They'd been on the inside of an inexorably tightening noose in the most high-tech city in the world, and she'd gotten them both out. Sticking with her right now was his absolute best bet. Keeping pace with her, he strolled along the sidewalk in the direction of the corner she'd pointed out.

In due time, the taxi arrived and Chelsea directed it to a Motel 6. But when Jericho went to go inside, she stopped him; instead, they walked down the driveway and turned the corner. Before too long, another cab came along, and she flagged it down. That one took them to a second motel, then she pulled the same trick to go to a third motel. Each time, she changed the outward appearance of her clothing. At her direction, he took his jacket off, tied it around his waist, or slung it over his shoulder. His bandaged hand, he kept discreetly in his pocket.

The last cab took them back along the highway toward Utopia. Jericho peered out the window to see the three trucks still parked on the staging area, with one of the men standing by the bushes he'd tossed the keys into. No doubt, the other three were still busy searching. He nudged Chelsea and indicated the situation with a tilt of his head; she nodded, her eyes sparkling with amusement.

The cab pulled into a motel parking lot less than a mile past the staging area. This time, Chelsea didn't pull the bait and switch routine; she marched right inside and got them a room. Jericho followed along, doing his best to angle the brim of the ball cap to block security cameras from seeing his face, and only relaxed after the door of the room closed behind them.

"Much more of this, and I'll be sleeping the whole night through," he groaned, falling backward onto the closest bed. The stitched wound under his dressing was throbbing intermittently, but he didn't feel the warm stickiness of blood.

"Wow," she jibed, settling down cross-legged on the other bed and opening both the backpack and the shoulder bag. "You almost sound like you've never had to run for your life before now."

He closed his eyes. "Oh, ha ha. You know I haven't."

"And how's that lack of life experience treating you now?"

For a moment, he considered replying with the extremely mature expedient of blowing a raspberry, but instead, he rolled his head toward her and opened his eyes. "Gonna need anything special for your secure phone setup?"

"Not particularly." Her tone was absent-minded as she bent over what she was doing. "I'll be done in ten."

"Okay, then." He got off the bed, tossed the ball cap to one side, and went into the washroom to use the facilities and freshen up. While he was in there, he worked the inserts out then flushed his mouth clear with water. Cold water splashed on his face—using his non-bandaged right hand only—

went a long way toward making him feel human again. A hot shower would've done more, but he didn't want to attempt anything of the sort until Chelsea gave him the all-clear with his various injuries.

His cheeks ached as if they were still being stretched as he came out of the washroom, but he figured that would pass soon enough. Chelsea was hard at work on the bed; he'd had no idea up until now that she'd been carrying around a miniature soldering kit in her backpack. *Artificers. Go figure.* He dropped the inserts onto the bed next to her, then went to the mini-bar and snagged a beer. "Fetch you something to drink?"

She never looked up. "Dr. Pepper, if they've got one."

"Coming right up." He took a can out and rolled it across the bed in her direction. Pulling the chair over from the desk to beside where she was working, he settled down into it and opened the beer.

They weren't out of the woods yet, or even close to it. But now, at least he had a direction to travel in, and there was light visible through the trees. At least, he hoped so.

He began to wish he hadn't destroyed the note with Thomas' number. Hearing his boyfriend's voice would've been amazing right about then. But done was done, and he'd just have to get back into contact the usual way once the dust had settled.

I'll have to see if I can swing some more leave after this is sorted out, so I can go and be with him for a while.

When Chelsea raised her head from her work, he was mostly finished with the beer, idly watching the traffic zip back and forth along the Kansas Turnpike. "It's done," she announced. "Thanks for this." Taking up the can, she popped it open and took a long drink. "Got your phone there?"

"Sure thing." Jericho opened his fanny pack and took out the burner phone she'd given him. Pressing the button to power it on, he looked at the device she'd built. About four inches long and half that wide, it had blinking LEDs here and there and a phone connector cord leading out of one end. It looked thoroughly unimpressive, which he guessed was the point. "That's it, is it?"

"Correct." She stretched her arms over her head, holding the Dr. Pepper carefully so she didn't spill it, then relaxed again. "This thing will bounce your phone signal all over the country. If you still want to make that call to Relentless, now's the time. I'll keep an eye out for back-trace attempts."

"Gotcha." Putting the beer bottle on the floor, he picked up the device and plugged its cord into his phone.

For a moment, he was tempted to find the public number for Team Power and get through to them that way, just so he could talk with Thomas and fill in Adam and Tesseract Power on what was really happening, but his sense of duty intervened. Relentless needed to be warned *now*.

He'd long since memorized the number for the head of Force Majeure. As soon as it started ringing, he put the phone on speaker, and placed it and the module on the bed between the two of them.

Two rings in, it was answered. "Relentless' office; Samantha Colburn speaking. Be aware that non-essential matters may be delayed due to unforeseen circumstances. State your name and business, please."

Yeah, I bet I know exactly what those 'unforeseen circumstances' are.

"Ms. Colburn, it's me," Jericho said. "G-Man. I need to speak to Relentless, urgently."

Her tone never changed. "What is the nature of your business with him?"

He took a deep breath. "Ma'am, I'm sorry, but I can't tell you that. I just need to talk to him right now. It's essential to Utopia and to Force Majeure itself. Please, put me through."

Not for one moment did doubt sound in her voice. "Very well. Please wait."

The phone rang again, with a different dial tone. Chelsea showed him a hastily scribbled note: **SHE KNOWS SK DEAD, NOT YR INVOLVEMENT**.

"Yes?" The familiar rumble of Relentless' voice sounded a little more irritated than usual. In the background, Jericho could hear voices arguing. The sound quality wasn't good enough to make out words, but he was almost sure he could recognize the voices of individual members of Force Majeure.

Including Independence.

"Sir, G-Man is calling on line two." Ms. Colburn's voice was as businesslike as ever.

Relentless didn't hesitate. "Put him through."

"Very well, sir." There was a click on the line, then the sound quality changed; Jericho guessed he was just listening to Relentless' end of the call now.

"Sir, I need you to listen to me very carefully," he said, trying to speak quickly and clearly. "You're in great danger, and so is the rest of Force Majeure."

There was a pause, during which the background arguing continued unabated, then Relentless said, "You have my undivided attention. Keep talking."

Despite knowing Relentless couldn't see him, Jericho shook his head. "I need to know for a *fact* that nobody else can hear what I'm saying. Not any of the team, not Ms. Colburn, nobody. Just you and me. *Please.* It's that important."

"One moment." There was a *clunk* as the phone apparently got put down on a table, then Jericho heard Relentless raise his voice to a bellow. On the bed, the cell phone vibrated from the force of his shout. "Everybody out! I need privacy! Yes, *everybody*! This room is going into full lockdown! *Go!*"

"Why?" asked someone; it may even have been Independence.

"BECAUSE I SAID SO!"

Jericho winced; it was loud enough over this connection. In the room with Relentless, that must have been deafening.

There was another pause, during which the noise level dropped off to zero. There was a click, and a weird hum permeated the signal. Chelsea scribbled another note: **WHITE NOISE GENERATOR. HE'S TAKING THIS SERIOUS.**

"I'm back." Relentless' voice was tense but steady. "G-Man, are you under duress?"

"Uh, no, sir."

The next question came quicker than the first. "Where are you?"

Jericho winced reflexively at having to deny him an answer. "I can't tell you that, sir, not until you've heard what I've got to say."

"Hrm. One more question. When we went back to my rooms that night, how many times did we have sex?"

Startled at the left-field development, Jericho stared at Chelsea for guidance. She made a shooing motion with her hands for him to respond.

"We, uh, we didn't. You made the offer, I turned you down, then you pitched a hissy fit with a tail on it and broke some bottles of booze with a vase, then opened a window and kicked me out."

Belatedly, Jericho realized two things. One: the query was a ploy to trip up an impostor or possibly to determine if he was indeed under duress. Two: he'd just accused his boss of getting pissed off over being blue-balled.

Hoping to distract Relentless from what he'd just said, he kept talking. "Uh, want me to describe your scars?"

Whether he'd registered it or not, Relentless seemed to accept Jericho's answer. "No need; I'm satisfied. So, talk to me. Did you really kill Silent Knight?"

Straight for the throat. But that's him all over.

Jericho shared a glance with Chelsea. "I did, but it's not what you think. You know how I was going to pick up that data from my contact?"

"Yes." Relentless managed to fit a lot of meaning into one word for someone who was so straightforward. Right now, the unspoken context was something like: *Get to the point. Quickly.*

Jericho tried not to hyperventilate. "Just after we did the handover, I got struck by lightning. While I was still trying to figure out which way was up, Silent Knight showed up out of nowhere and tried to kill me. Kicked me a couple times, then did his best to stick his sword right through my guts."

There was a momentary pause. When Relentless spoke next, his tone was harsh with disbelief. "What the hell? You're *shitting* me." A moment passed, during which Jericho said nothing. "You're not shitting me. Mother*fucker*. *Why?*"

That sounded more like a rhetorical question, so Jericho forged on. "Um, probably because he was Charnel. Or rather, he turned into Charnel halfway through the fight, so I had to kill him, but I'm pretty sure Silent Knight's been Charnel from the beginning, and then Independence showed up and tried to shoot me in the face, so I hit her with a G-shake, and she's actually some kind of shape-changer—"

Relentless overrode him. "Oh, you're *fucking* shitting me. Independence *too*? Under *my* goddamn nose?" The disbelief in the big man's voice had given way to pure anger. "Keep talking. I need to check something." The sound of typing filled the room.

"Yeah, um, I'm guessing this had something to do with whatever's on that data drive. Did you manage to retrieve it?"

"Yeah, but it was fried," Relentless said absently. "Technologist couldn't get a thing out of it. Oh, for *fuck's* sake. Here we go. Independence got into the drone control, the weather control, *and* the phone tracking. Looks like she traced you to the park, then overrode my orders and sent those drones to pass directly over you. *Then* she overrode weather control and sparked a lightning strike when they were at closest approach."

"Oh. Wow." Jericho hadn't even considered that the lightning strike might've been a deliberate act. The thought put a chill down his spine.

Poser really wants me dead.

Relentless wasn't even listening anymore. "That *fucker* tried to murder you, under *my* nose, on *my* goddamn team!" He took a deep breath before continuing his rant, his tone still full of righteous fury. "Right now, she's got half the team talked into coming after you with lethal force, over Silent Knight! Over fucking *Charnel*! I'm gonna kill her. I swear I'm gonna snap her lying neck like a fuckin' twig."

"Uh, right." Jericho had zero doubt about the big man's capacity to do precisely that, and he didn't really have a problem with it. "What do you want me to do now, sir?"

"Okay. Hold on a second. Okay." Relentless seemed to be counting under his breath; his exhalations came in long sighs like a steam engine venting pressure. "There's something I want you to understand, kid. Force Majeure *needs* people like you on the team. Your well-being is my absolute top goddamn priority. So, I want you to keep your head down and stay safe. Is your contact still with you, the one who's really good at hiding?"

Jericho glanced at Chelsea, who shrugged and nodded. "Yeah, they are," he said.

"Good. Tell them to keep you in deep hiding until I *personally* contact you. Just me, nobody else. Pass phrase: '*Ming vase*'. Got that?"

"Yes, sir. '*Ming vase*'. Keep my head down 'til I hear from you."

"Good. Now, if you'll excuse me, I'm gonna go kick seventeen shades of shit out of a certain traitor and find out exactly what *else* is fucking going on in *my goddamn team*."

The call ended abruptly. Jericho stared across at Chelsea. "Um, wow. I thought I'd seen him angry before now. I reckon not."

Chelsea nodded in agreement. "Well, the good news is, as pissed off as he is right now, it's not at us. That stuff he said about keeping you safe and all that? He was totally sincere. Also, I'm pretty sure Poser's about to find herself in a world of hurt."

Jericho wondered if he should feel bad about that, then decided it wasn't his problem. It was Poser's.

"Okay," he said, the load finally beginning to lift from his shoulders. "If I know Relentless, he's about to put the kibosh on whatever she's up to. When he calls back, he's gonna want to know where I am so he can come get me. I'm guessing you don't want to be around at that point?"

She nodded. "You're guessing correctly. I learned long ago that gratitude has a really short half-life. *You*, I know I can trust not to screw me over, but I still made that run on the Spire, and Relentless is not the sort of guy to forgive and forget something that big. So, I'd best vanish into the tall timber before he calls you back." She began to gather her equipment together.

Jericho got up and retrieved the bottle of beer from the floor, then turned around so he was sitting with his arms crossed over the chair's backrest. "Before you go, can you answer me a couple-few questions?"

She glanced over at him, and he got the distinct impression that she already knew what was on his mind. "Shoot."

He took a deep breath and forged on anyway. "First, what about the, uh, scrambler?" He indicated the kit-bashed device currently connected to his phone. "Won't you be needing it?"

"Nah." She chuckled briefly and shook her head. "As you saw, I can throw one of those things together at minimal notice. Keep it. If you think it needs to be destroyed, drop it on the floor and stomp on it. I guarantee *nobody* will be able to reverse-engineer it then."

"Okay, thanks." He paused, thinking about his next question. "Uh, back at that rest area. You could've shut those guys down with a word. I didn't need to beat 'em up to get what you wanted. Why'd you let it get that far?"

"Two reasons." She continued to sort her equipment. "First, they came up with the idea of extorting me for more cash all by themselves. That kind of thought process needs to be severely dissuaded, not just with the sudden realization that someone important's shown up. I gave them the chance to change their minds back again, but they doubled down. So, physical consequences were in order."

"Mm-hmm." He took a drink from the beer while thinking that through. "Fair enough. What was the second reason?"

This time, she looked up and grinned at him. "You needed to punch *someone*, and they were right there."

He tried not to chuckle—his stomach wound was still throbbing—but it wasn't easy. "Well, you got me there. I've definitely been feeling kinda like a paper plane in a twister, and it felt good to be able to hit back for once." He took one last drink to finish the bottle off. "Okay, so why'd you say not to break their bones?"

This time, her cynical look told him she *knew* he was aware of the answer. "Same reason you wouldn't have, even if I told you to. Because they weren't out to molest me or even rough me up too badly. All they wanted was the cash. So, we made 'em regret it without putting 'em in the hospital."

"Hm." That was what he'd figured, sure enough. But it did bring up another question, now that he was thinking of it. "Isn't that kinda lenient for someone in your line of work? I mean, head honcho of the Utopia City criminal underworld and all that?"

She rolled her eyes and shook her head, all at the same time. "And here I thought you knew me. Jericho, I'm not in this business for the money. I'm doing it for the fun, the interest, and the challenge. If all I wanted was cash, I could con a dozen people out of their life savings in a day. And hurting people for the sake of causing pain isn't fun, interesting, *or* challenging."

"Is that why you helped me get out of Utopia?" Jericho stared at her. "Because it was fun, interesting, and a challenge? Because you were *bored*?"

"Well, *duh*. Why else?" She held his gaze unblinkingly for just long enough to make him think she was in earnest, then snorted with amusement. "I'm not going to say it wasn't a factor, but you're one of the few good guys I *do* like, you big doofus."

Jericho felt his face grow warm at the unexpected praise. "Thanks. I try. So, uh, are you going back to Utopia now?"

She shrugged. "Sure. Things are definitely stirred up, which means I'll have opportunities to do stuff I'm only going to tell you about after the fact. Also, it looks like you're in the clear now, so I can fade into the woodwork with a moderately clear conscience. And this way, you don't have to lie about not knowing where I've gotten to."

"Yeah, that's probably for the best," he agreed awkwardly. "Just, uh, don't go hacking the Spire again, please? I'll probably get away with having you as my contact this time 'round, but if this happens twice in a row, he's like to put me in Poser's shoes, if you get my drift."

"Okay, but just for you." From the tone of her voice—deliberately pitched so he'd hear it, if he knew her—she hadn't intended to anyway. "But you know what's going to really irritate me?"

Jericho finished the beer and belched discreetly—it was nowhere near as gassy as Utopia Gold, which he'd acquired a taste for—then lightened the bottle and tossed it across the room to the wastepaper basket. "What's that?"

"Whatever was on that damn drive." Standing up, she slung her pack over her shoulder and picked up her bag. "It's probably just something that shows up Poser and Charnel as who they really are, but now I'll never know for sure. And that's going to bug me *forever*. But, hey, not your problem." Heading over to the door, she put her hand on the knob. "Take care. I'll see you 'round." She turned the knob and began to open the door.

"Hey, hang on," Jericho said, his back-brain suddenly making a few long-delayed connections. "I'm thinking I might have an idea where those files might be at."

Chelsea closed the door again. Slowly, her head turned, her eyes alight with interest. "Reeaallyy?"

51
From Beyond the Grave

Jericho worked the fanny pack around until he could unfasten the clasp, then took it off. Pulling the zipper open, he dug inside until he found the plastic-swathed guts of the damaged thumb drive, as well as the torn-open mailer containing the intact one his parents had handed him. "Check it out."

"What *is* that?" she asked, indicating the wad of plastic. "Wait, is that the guts of a USB drive? What's on it? Where did you get it from? How did it even get broken?"

"Back up there a mite," Jericho said with a grin, holding up a hand to stem the tide of questions. When Chelsea's inherent need to know *all* the answers slipped its leash, she could be a little overwhelming. "One at a time. Yeah, it is. Stephen was storing stuff he wanted to keep in a secret post office box, and it ended up in my hands. I broke it." Putting the wad of plastic down on the bed, he took the mauve thumb drive out of the mailer and held it up. "And my folks dropped this off just today. *Also* from Stephen. No idea what's on either one."

She raised an eyebrow. "I sense a 'but'."

"*But* ..." he acknowledged. "Both of these came from Stephen. And he was convinced that if he could prove to me that Force Majeure was up to no good, I'd leave the team and come back to him."

"Evidence of Independence being a secret shape-changer or Silent Knight being Charnel could definitely be seen as that kind of proof, yes, especially if taken out of context." Chelsea eyed the broken drive critically. "Why did you wreck it?"

Jericho ran his hand over his face. "There were two drives originally. He made one back when we were still dating, a sex tape of him with someone else. This one here, he sent to himself on the day he died, but I got 'em both at the same time when I closed out the box. When I saw the sex tape, I pitched a major hissy fit and busted both the drives, then chunked 'em at the trash can. This one fell down behind the fridge instead, and I found it just today."

Chelsea shook her head. "It's a weird, weird world. And you don't know what's on them?"

He shrugged. "No. But I don't want to get rid of them, just in case it's something important like a message for his folks. Or ..." He let his voice trail off meaningfully.

"... or it might be crucial evidence against Charnel and Poser, like maybe what they've been doing while hiding in plain sight," agreed Chelsea. "Which one did you want to look at first?"

Jericho glanced at the secure phone setup. "What about Relentless?"

"He knows you're safe, and he never does anything by halves," Chelsea said. "If what I've seen of the guy is any kind of indicator, he'll be taking Poser apart piece by piece until he's uncovered every last shred of any plots in Utopia that the guy's involved in. He'll only call you back once he's sure everything's locked down vacuum-tight. And I can be packed and gone in ten seconds."

She had a distinct point; Jericho's only regret was that he couldn't be there for the dénouement. "Okay, then." He started tugging the plastic away from the busted drive. "We'll check this one out first. If it works, we see what's on it. If it doesn't, we've still got the other one."

"Sounds legitimate." Perching on the bed so she was next to him, she took her laptop back out of the shoulder bag and opened it up.

A thought occurred to him. "Is your antivirus up to date? You know, just in case?"

"Up to date, *and* it's totally isolated from any network," she assured him. "I don't play games with my safety."

The laptop booted to full life at about the same time as he teased the last bit of half-melted sandwich bag away from the wreck of the drive. "Here you go," he said. "And if it doesn't work in yours, I'll ask the Technologist to have a gander at it."

"We shall see what we shall see …" Carefully, a fraction of an inch at a time, she slid the ruined drive into the socket. "Wow, you were really pissed when you got ahold of this one, weren't you?"

"I saw Stephen cheating on me, in our bed, on footage taken before I came to Utopia. He even said …" Jericho let out a gusty sigh. "You know what? Let's just leave it alone. I don't want to get mad all over again."

Chelsea nodded. "We can do that." The thumb drive made final contact, signaled by a tone from the laptop. "Okay, we have recognition."

"Awesome." Jericho leaned a little closer and stared at the icon that had just appeared on the screen. "Is that it? What's on it?"

"Let's see." She double-tapped the icon with her fingertip. A window popped up. He stared at it, hoping against hope that it wouldn't be another sex tape.

Be something useful. Please.

The uncertainty was killing him. He really wanted incontrovertible proof he could show Relentless and the rest of the team that Independence (and Silent Knight) were supervillains, but he'd settle for whatever he could get. Just so long as it was *something*.

The window cleared.

CONTENTS LOCKED. ENTER PASSCODE. |– – – – – – – – – – – –

He stared at the text window with its blinking cursor until Chelsea nudged him. "Did it come with a password?"

"Uh, no … I don't think so, anyway." He was pretty sure there'd been no notes in the mailer.

"Great," she said sarcastically. "You realize, I sent it away to get it decoded. Now this one's got a password too?"

"Yeah, but this is different." He forced a grin. "I *lived* with the guy for six months. Pretty sure he doesn't have a password I can't crack."

Chelsea raised an eyebrow, her expression mildly dubious. "He cheated on you the whole time you were with him, and you never caught on. Just saying."

"Shush, you." Focusing on the screen, he counted the available spaces in the password text window, his lips moving silently. "Thirteen," he concluded, then gazed blankly up into the corner of the motel room as he did some mental math. "Hah! Knew it! He used my name."

"You're kidding," she said. "It can't be that easy. Can it?"

"Looks like it can be." He leaned over and held his hands above the keyboard, flexing his fingers for dramatic tension. One firm keystroke after another, he typed in JERICHOHANSEN, counting off the letters. At the end, he hit Enter with a flourish.

Bzzt went the laptop.

ONE WRONG ATTEMPT. FIVE ATTEMPTS LEFT.

"Ooh, ouch," she murmured sympathetically.

He huffed a sigh of aggravation. "Okay, let's step back and think on this a mite. It's not my name. So … what is it?"

"The uh, the guy he was cheating with?" suggested Chelsea diffidently.

"Okay, fine," he growled under his breath. *What was that sonovabitch's name, again?*

His pride came second to getting into this drive. Memory clicked into place, and he typed in FLYBOY, then paused. "Crap. I need seven more letters."

"Flyboy Enabled?" suggested Chelsea tentatively.

Jericho shrugged. Since his own name had been ruled out and he didn't know Flyboy's real identity, this seemed as good as any. He typed the rest of the letters. *Click* went the Enter key.

Bzzt.

TWO WRONG ATTEMPTS. FOUR ATTEMPTS LEFT.

All of a sudden, this seemed a lot less straightforward than at the start. What else had been truly important to Stephen? Wrecking Force Majeure? Jericho shook his head. Nothing came to mind.

"What would he have held dear above all else?" offered Chelsea.

"A grudge?" Jericho snorted at his own semi-joke, then light dawned. "No, wait. You're right. It's gotta be something that was close to him." He put his hands to the keyboard and typed in GAYPOWER. There was no option for an exclamation mark. "Eight letters. Need five more."

Chelsea frowned. "Gay!Power … rules?"

It definitely seemed like something Stephen would say, so he entered the extra word then pressed Enter.

Bzzt.

THREE WRONG ATTEMPTS. THREE ATTEMPTS LEFT.

"Oh, *come* on!" He glared at the inoffensive laptop. "Seriously? How can I not have gotten it by now?"

"Guess you didn't know him as well as you thought." Fortunately for his state of mind, she held off on any more references to Stephen's trifling ways. "Um, maybe birthdates? Or your anniversary?"

"Okay, yeah, that could work." He took a deep breath, recalling Stephen's birthdate. With the month as a word and the year as four digits, it fitted neatly. He typed it into the text box and pressed Enter.

Bzzt.

FOUR WRONG ATTEMPTS. TWO ATTEMPTS LEFT.

He didn't like the look of that. "Should I try our anniversary? Or my birthdate?"

Chelsea didn't sound any happier. "I'd say anniversary first, if only because he'd get something on the anniversary, but your birthday means he'd have to give stuff to you."

It felt like a remarkably cynical viewpoint, but she wasn't *wrong.* Jericho gave her a sideways glance. "Are you *sure* you never met him?"

"Trust me," she said heavily. "I know the type all too well."

"All right, then." He tapped in the familiar date. APRIL132012.

We first went out on Friday the thirteenth. I should've taken the hint.

It was two characters short. He squinted at it, then saw where he was going wrong. Moving the cursor over, he entered 't-h' after the 13.

Taking a deep breath, he pressed Enter.

Bzzt.

FIVE WRONG ATTEMPTS. ONE ATTEMPT LEFT.

Do you need a <u>clue</u>?

"Wait," he said. "Was that there before?"

"The clue thing?" Chelsea shook her head. "No. It wasn't."

He rolled his eyes. "Thank God for that. I'd hate to have missed it, five tries in a row." Reaching out, he tapped the hyperlinked word.

A small window opened, revealing seven words.

If you're my hero, who am I?

"Is this supposed to be some kind of riddle? Maybe there's more to it?" Chelsea tapped the popup, which disappeared. "Guess not. So, the question is, was he vain enough to use his own name as the password?"

Jericho snorted. "He was definitely full of himself. Would he have taken it that far?" He considered the question. "... maybe? If that drive was for his own personal use and a stranger found it, the only way they'd know how to get into it would be to know who he was. It ... *kinda* makes sense?"

Chelsea didn't sound any happier than he felt. "If you can't think of a better answer, put it in."

"Right." Slowly, he typed in the name. STEPHENLAMOND, stalling short on the last letter as he hit the character limit. "Crap. No more room."

"Maybe a 'v' instead of 'p-h'?" Chelsea shrugged when he looked over at her. "It's all I can think of."

"No," he said definitively. "Stephen was very sensitive about his name. He didn't even like being called Steve. Luke used to push his buttons just by doing that." He got up from the chair and turned it around, then sat down in it and crossed his arms over the backrest. "I'm out of ideas. And I don't want to half-ass this one because if it wipes the drive, we lose whatever's on it."

"And you're sure it's not his name." It wasn't a question.

"One hundred percent." He glared at the damaged drive. "Stephen would use a password he thought was clever and tricky, not actively misleading." Scrubbing his hands over his face, he tried to beat his chaotic thoughts into submission. "Can we try the other drive? It might actually have the password on it."

"That's a thought." She took the intact thumb drive and clicked it into the second port on her laptop. There was an agreeable *beep*, and the icon showed up on the screen. "If this one's passworded as well ..." The tone of her voice promised mayhem to the drive.

Reaching out, she tapped the icon twice. Jericho held his breath.

It opened into a window holding a single video file. No password prompt popped up to ruin their day. Jericho let his breath out again.

"Okay, let's see now ..." She tapped the file to open it.

Oh, crap. What if ...

Jericho's last-minute worries about Stephen sending him yet another attempt at seduction faded away as the picture showed his deceased ex, sitting at his work desk, fully clothed. From the quality of the footage, it was being recorded by his webcam.

What struck Jericho was the expression on Stephen's face. He'd seen his ex-boyfriend happy, sad, angry, disappointed, and playful. But he'd never seen the man outright worried until now.

"Jericho," Stephen began tersely. **"Please listen, very carefully. I was going to email this to you, but I didn't want it to be intercepted. Even sending it to Utopia City by post involves risks I'm not willing to contemplate. So, I hope you'll forgive me for taking the liberty of mailing it to your parents. But just in case they open the envelope and watch it, I will be skipping over a few details for their own safety. Okay? Okay. Good."**

Chelsea paused the file and looked at Jericho. "He's terrified," she said frankly. "Trying to hide it, but there are too many tells. Whatever he's got to say, it's end-of-the-world level serious."

"Right," Jericho murmured, searching the still image for any hint of what was to come. *Terrified? Why?* "Let's see what he's worried about."

She started the footage up again. Stephen took a drink from the glass of bourbon on the rocks that sat at his elbow. The clinking of ice against the sides of the glass, caused by the shaking of Stephen's hand, was audible over the speakers. **"There's something seriously wrong going on with Force Majeure."** He held up his hand as though to forestall an objection. **"I know, I know, I've said it before. I was wrong, then. Well, I was correct in that something was wrong, but I was grasping at straws for the most part. But someone recently showed me some material ... Jericho, you have to leave Force Majeure. Leave Utopia City."** He leaned forward over the desk, his face expanding in the camera image. **"I don't care if you never come back to me. I've burned that bridge long ago. I just want you safe, away from those ... away from *there*."**

As Stephen slumped back into his chair and took another drink, Chelsea paused it again. "He knew," she said softly. "He knew about Silent Knight and Poser."

Jericho nodded. "Yeah, that's what I'm thinking." He waved at the image. "Keep it going."

On the screen, Stephen seemed to gain a little life from the second drink. **"I've got proof of what they're up to,"** he said. **"Come and meet me in Savannah. Name a place, and I'll be there. I'll show you, and then you'll understand. I swear it on ... on what we used to have."** He leaned forward again. **"But if I don't show up, if I disappear mysteriously or I'm found dead of an accident ... well, I've got an ace in the hole. You see, I've—"**

The footage jumped at that point. When it resumed, Stephen was still sitting there, but the glass was in a different location, and the level of alcohol was lower. **"Sorry, I decided I was giving away too many details. Jericho, you'll know about it when you find that I've taken your name in vain. In that location, there will be a blue USB drive. Look at that, and just that. Burn the rest. But look at the blue drive. *Please*. It will explain everything. I don't care how much you hate me. This one last time, be my hero."**

The file ended.

Jericho sat, stunned. For all that time, he'd thought Stephen was so totally self-absorbed as to think of nothing but his Enabled conquests. "He ... he tried to warn me," he mumbled. "He really did. If I'd just visited ..."

Chelsea put her hand on his arm. "You were busy," she reminded him. "And you couldn't have known. But what I want to know is what he meant by *'taken your name in vain'*."

Closing his eyes, Jericho shook his head and chuckled at the sheer, dark irony of it all, ignoring the twinge of pain from his stomach. It wasn't as funny as all that, but if he didn't start laughing, he was going to cry. "That post office box I told you about? He put it in my name, not his. I only found out about it when the payments ran out after he died. He had a bunch of letters from his affairs stored there, so I'd never know about them. Plus, the drives that I busted."

"... oh." She paused. "No password. He didn't give the password."

Jericho's eyes sprang open, all humor gone. "Goddammit! He must've put it in the part he copied over, then forgot to put it back in!"

"Maybe," mused Chelsea. "Or maybe he had faith you'd figure it out."

Jericho inhaled deeply through his nostrils. "I could've done with a little less faith and a few more clues."

"Let's have another look at it." Chelsea clicked on the tab to bring the password entry window back up again. Stephen's name, minus the last E, still filled the text box.

"That's what I don't get," he said, pointing at the empty space where the letter should be. "If it's supposed to be his name, why not go for fourteen letters?"

"*If you're my hero, who am I?*" quoted Chelsea. "Did he want you to rescue him, like a damsel in distress?" Her lips moved as she counted quickly. "No, damn it. Seventeen."

He stared at the screen, trying to divine its secrets. There was something, just out of reach, teasing him. "This is messing up my head, something fierce. I tell you what, if he was alive, I'd kick his ass for putting me through this."

"You and me both." She nodded toward the Enter key. "Do you have a better idea than his name? Who *is* he?"

And then Jericho had it.

Lips pressed tightly together to hold back the doubts, he leaned around the chair-back … and tapped the Delete key. *Tac-tac-tac-tac-tac* it went, as he removed each letter in turn.

"What?" she asked. "What did you think of?"

The text box was empty. Eyes not leaving the screen, he spoke as he began to type, one emotion-filled letter at a time. "I just now got it. It's not naming someone as a hero. It's saying, '*if you were my hero, who would I be?*'."

Chelsea looked confused. "Isn't that the same thing?"

He shook his head. "Not quite. There was a line Stephen liked to use that I thought was just between us. He considered himself a journalist of sorts, so he identified with a reporter from one of those old comic books, who was in love with one particular prodigy." Closing his eyes for a moment, he bowed his head. "It was sappy and corny and cute, right up until I watched that sex tape, and he said it to Flyboy. I'm guessing it was his go-to line for every hero he slept with. In other words, '*if you were my hero, I would be this.*'" Breathing deeply, he did his best to push through the pain.

God damn you for making me dig all this crap up again, Stephen.

Stephen's voice echoed in his mind's ear. **This one last time, be my hero.**

"You're my hero," he whispered. "And I'm …"

The text box read YOURVICKIVALE.

Thirteen letters.

He pressed Enter.

Beep.

They were in.

52

Old Scar Tissue Reopened

The window opened to show three files, each bearing a different random-looking alphanumeric title. Chelsea nodded. "Okay, so this is probably everything Tucker sent to LaMonde before the bad guys caught up with them."

"Yeah," agreed Jericho. "Pity the drive was fried. The Technologist could be clearing all this up right now, Relentless could be stuffing Poser head-first into a ten-by-ten cell, and we wouldn't be on the run."

She snorted. "Well, it was, they're not, and we are. As it is, we're lucky you were conscious enough to make yourself lighter when I yelled at you."

"I don't remember any of that."

She raised one of her eyebrows sardonically. "I'm not altogether surprised. Do you have any idea how much fun it's *not* when you're trying to bandage someone up in the back seat of a self-driving car, overriding its emergency protocols about once a minute, and hoping the rain wouldn't stop before we got under cover?"

"Sorry." He took a deep breath. "Thanks, by the way. For saving my life and getting me the hell out of there."

She gave him a smart-ass grin. "You're welcome. If you hadn't noticed, we're kind of even. Anyway, are we going to just stare at these files all day or actually open one of them?"

"Right. Yeah." Reaching out, his finger almost brushed the screen. He recalled not so long ago his resolve to turn these files back over to the Technologist, sight unseen. Now, he *needed* to see them, if only to be in the loop as to what was going on. But of course, doubts kept crowding in. "It's just that … when I open this, whatever I see, I'll never be able to unsee. I can't help but feel that viewing these files will permanently affect my role within Force Majeure. If the information is too sensitive, they might never let me just be a hero again."

Reaching up, she lightly swatted him across the back of the head. "Two core members of Force Majeure were terror villains, and one of those is still up and around. Once this gets out, even after Relentless tears Poser a brand-new set of orifices, every last aspect of the team will be going under the microscope. I'm talking Homeland Security, NSA, FBI, and probably a bunch of other three-letter agencies you've never heard of. We may as well peek behind the curtain before it gets locked down under the umbrella of '*need to know*', just so we know how bad it is."

"Don't you mean '*if*' this gets out?" Jericho hadn't had much to do with the PR side of Force Majeure, apart from the obligatory costume shoots. Still, he was aware that they could drop the hammer very hard indeed when it came to deciding which outlet received advance news and which ones got to whistle in the wind. He could see himself taking this sort of thing to any news service in Utopia and watching it get spun into obscurity.

She set her jaw. "I mean '*when*'. One way or another, we're putting this out there. Now pick a damn file and open it. Relentless won't take forever to get back in touch."

"Yes, *ma'am*," he said half-jokingly, and double-tapped the first one.

It opened up onto the screen, revealing a bunch of text interspersed with voice files. Frowning, he began to read.

SIERRA has entered the chat.
FOXTROT has entered the chat.
SIERRA: We've got a potential Mind-Fucker situation.
FOXTROT: Okay, I'm on it. Who and where?

Next came the first voice file; Jericho tapped it, and it began to play.

"So ... all this time, you've been reading our minds?"

Jericho's eyebrows shot up. That was his *own* voice he was listening to.

"Not minds, not minds. *Emotions*. I don't know what you're thinking. I can only see what you're *feeling*."

And *that* was a blast from the past he hadn't been expecting. He tapped the pause icon then sat back, trying to process what was happening.

"That was you, wasn't it?" asked Chelsea. "Who was the woman?"

"Bobbi," Jericho said slowly. "She was with Luke when ..." His voice died away as the lump in his throat grew too large to let him speak.

"Oh. Oh, man." Chelsea grimaced, reaching across to give his knee a sympathetic pat. "I'm so sorry."

Swallowing heavily, Jericho nodded. "This is from when she was talking to us on the maglev. Under a privacy bubble."

"They can listen in on what's said inside a *privacy bubble*?" This was the most shock he'd seen her express in a long time. "Those things are supposed to be the last word in security! Force Majeure licenses them all over the *world*! Not even a laser mic can pull sounds out of one of those suckers. I know; I've tried. Every head of state and international CEO worth the name has one in his office. And they can just listen in *anyway*?"

"I guess?" Jericho spread his hands. "It's Force Majeure's proprietary tech; if anyone's got a way to bypass it, they would." Inwardly, he knew he should be angrier at the implicit breach of privacy, but right now that was a long way down his list of priorities.

Chelsea slapped her forehead. "Shit, this is probably why Charnel and Poser came after you! Either they were specifically listening in on you, or you tripped an automated keyword detector when you started talking about how there might be an infiltrator in the team!" Reaching out, she tapped the icon to resume play.

Bobbi's voice continued. **"And—"** Mid-sentence, the recording was interrupted by a *beeeep*. When the sound ceased, her voice resumed speaking.

"—go to Chicago and talk to Adam Power face to face, so I could work out for myself whether he's lying or not—" *beeeep* **"—I did get to see him speak. He was absolutely adamant that he hadn't touched or hurt Vanessa in any way … and my power says he was being totally truthful—"** *beeeep* **"—I decided to go straight to Utopia City and see if I could speak to** *someone* **about jumping the queue. I mean, I applied last week but I haven't heard back yet. Can't hurt to ask, right? If anyone's got access to people who can help me learn to get a handle on my powers, it'll be Force Majeure. And once I'm in, I can get in contact with Team Power and let them know I can help clear this up once and for all."**

The audio clip came to an end. Jericho read onward.

SIERRA: Name of Reynolds, staying at the Oaklands, 1204.
FOXTROT: Yeah, that one's definitely a problem. Anything else I need to know?
SIERRA: Yes. She's rooming with two guys. One of them's a DPR prodigy/dynamic
   named G-Man. You're going to need to wait for him to go out and do the
   sightseeing thing before you make your move.
FOXTROT: I can't just sit around all fucking night. One prodigy, unenhanced? I
   can take him.
SIERRA: Prodigy/dynamic. There's no way you'll make it look like an unpowered
   break-in gone wrong. Just reach down and pull up your big-girl panties, and
   wait till he goes out. Take Charlie with you in case Reynolds makes a run for it.
FOXTROT: Okay, fine. Can I borrow Golf too, for if we need a fast exit?
SIERRA: I personally don't give a shit. Knock yourself out.
FOXTROT: Excellent. Hey, has the boss thought of maybe recruiting her for real?
   See if those principles go away after you wave enough money at them?
SIERRA: Not going to happen. Listen to this.

After that, there were more audio clips, but Jericho didn't tap them immediately. Instead, he closed his eyes and put his hand to his forehead, trying to deal with the emotions the current one had raised in him. He didn't know precisely what a 'Mind-Fucker' situation was, but it didn't sound good. In fact, none of this sounded good to him, especially as he knew how it had all turned out.

"You okay?" asked Chelsea. He felt her hand on his shoulder. "We can shut all this down now and look at it later if you want."

"No." He shook his head. "But I *will* need some serious brooding time after this." Opening his eyes, he tapped the next sound file.

"Suppose you got hitched to an ax murderer—"

It was Luke's voice, earnest as ever when he was pursuing an argument he thought he could win. Jericho clenched his eyes shut, willing the tears not to flow.

"Are we assuming I've got my powers or not? Because if I do, I'd know what he was the moment I met him."

That was Bobbi yet again, voice teetering between amusement and irritation.

"Lemme finish. Yeah, you got your powers, but he doesn't wanna murder *you*. He likes you; you like him. He decides to drop th' whole ax murderer thing, you have kids with him, everythin's fine. Then, ten years later, after you got a good life, you find his diary or somethin' an' discover he useta chop folks into little bits an' pieces. Ya know that if ya turn him in, all th' good stuff goes away. Ya lose him, mebbe lose th' kids. But ya also know he's killed dozens o' people. What-all are ya gonna do?"

beeeep

"I'd turn the asshole in anyway. My feelings don't matter; what *matters* is that he faces justice for what he's done."

Bobbi's voice was firm and final, the last word on the matter.

Jericho slowly opened his eyes. One tear slowly trickled down his cheek, but he ignored it.

SIERRA: See what I mean?
FOXTROT: Yeah, okay, she's a lost cause.

"That conversation happened in the corridor outside our apartment at the Oaklands, just so you know." Jericho's eyes met Chelsea's. "Was there any place they *weren't* recording?"

"Not in the apartments themselves," she said definitively. "If they had been, they would've homed in on the Survivors and me when you left us crammed into the same damn apartment for four days straight."

"Yeah, true," he agreed, recalling the pillow talk between him and Thomas that had led to his revelation about Adam Power. That could've gone really bad, really quickly, if anyone had been listening in. He tapped the Play icon for the next clip.

"—getting into Utopia City in the next few hours, and we can talk it out then."

He frowned. The voice almost sounded familiar, but he just couldn't place it.

"I'll probably be in bed, but feel free to knock on the door. Someone will let you in, and we can talk all you like. I honestly didn't mean to make you feel like I was shutting you out."

Now, *that* was Bobbi. From the context, he figured out who the other voice must be. *Jack Portman? It must be.*

"Yeah, well, it sure felt like it at the time." There was a sigh. "But I'll come straight over as soon as I get in. There's a lot we need to talk about."

"I'll see you then, hon. Bye."

There was more text, but Jericho held off on reading it while he attempted to figure out what was going on. "I thought they couldn't listen to anything inside the apartments." Because it didn't make sense that the eavesdroppers could get access to Bobbi's conversation but nothing else.

Chelsea blinked, her expression clearing. "They listened in on this one because it was a phone call. They didn't bug the apartments. They tapped the *phone towers.*"

"Why not the apartments? Wouldn't that be simpler?"

"Who stays in those apartments?" Chelsea waited for him to answer, then replied anyway when he took too long. "Enabled. Including artificers and dynamics, who might just detect a live mic if they're sitting around for hours getting bored. The corridors are technically a public space, so that's more likely to be uncontested if anyone notices it."

"Yeah, that makes sense ..." Jericho bit his lip. "But there's something else that doesn't. Maybe it's just me, but what we just heard didn't sound like a guy who was fixing to get blasted out of his mind before going to patch up things with his girl."

"You're right. That wasn't his intention at all." Chelsea nodded toward the screen. "Check that out."

Following her lead, he turned his eyes to the text below.

SIERRA: *There's your opening. The boyfriend's coming in on the 2130. Do a grab and replace.*

FOXTROT: *You got it. But what if this G-Man twerp doesn't go out tonight?*

SIERRA: *Then we improvise. But for fuck's sake, he's a rooftop runner, and it's his first time in Utopia. If he doesn't sneak out and go on 'patrol' tonight, I'll eat my favorite boots.*

FOXTROT: *Yeah, yeah, good point. Give me the heads-up when he's out of the place, and I'll let you know when we're finished.*

SIERRA: *I'll send one of the others to keep an eye out.*

FOXTROT has left the chat.

SIERRA has left the chat.

Session has expired.

FOXTROT has entered the chat.

CHARLIE has entered the chat.

SIERRA has entered the chat.

FOXTROT: *It's done. The bitch is dead, the false trail is laid, and the boyfriend's in holding. All ready for Golf to pull the bait and switch. Fuck, I'm glad that's over.*

SIERRA: *Sounds like you had a time of it.*

CHARLIE: *Hahaha wow you should've been there. The big guy made a fucking mess of Foxtrot.*

FOXTROT: *Shut up. They took me by surprise, okay? I didn't even realize she knew something was up until she screamed and nearly took my eye out. Then he damn near kicked my knee into next week and threw a sheet over my head.*

SIERRA: *What part of 'she reads emotions' did you not get the first time around?*

CHARLIE: *Hahahahahahaha it was hilarious. When I came in, the big guy had Foxtrot trapped under that sheet, and he had two pieces of wood ripped out of a canvas print. Waling on him like a fat kid going after the last piece of candy in a fucking pinata. Swear to god, the last time I heard screams that high-pitched, it was from fresh meat in the big house after lights out.*

FOXTROT: *Shut the hell up. It's not funny. Gonna go strap my knee and watch a nice soothing serial-killer doco or something. That big black bastard was like a freak of nature.*

SIERRA: *Yeah, about that.*

FOXTROT: *What the fuck is it now? I'm hurting, and I can hardly fucking walk.*

SIERRA: *The cops showed up just after G-Man got back from his patrol run. Right now, he's in the frame.*

CHARLIE: *Well, that's fucking irony for you*

FOXTROT: *That's even better. Win-win-fucking-win. My job's done and dusted, and they've even got a suspect.*

SIERRA: *Not so much. First thing he did was ask for a Designated Liaison. Guess who's next on the roster.*

FOXTROT: *Oh, fuck no.*

CHARLIE: *Hahahahahaha im literally dying here*

SIERRA: *Oh, fuck yes. You know the drill. Busted knee or not, you step up like the rest of us. Second Chance will be there for the interview, but you're on call for perimeter security.*

FOXTROT: *Who the hell told him about DLs, anyway? That G-Man asshole is now officially on my shit list.*

CHARLIE: *Hahahahahaha what, like him and half of Utopia*

FOXTROT: *Shut the fuck up, or you'll be on there right alongside him.*

CHARLIE: *Hahahahahahaha watch it, I got a sheet and a couple of sticks, and I know how to use them*

FOXTROT has left the chat.

SIERRA: *Is it true? Did that actually happen?*

CHARLIE: *Swear to god. Funniest thing I've seen all fucking year.*

CHARLIE has left the chat.

SIERRA has left the chat.

Session has expired.

Jericho leaned back in his chair, his mind whirling with the implications of what he'd just read. "Son of a *biiitch*," he muttered. His initial suspicion that the whole thing had been a setup to murder Bobbi, and Luke was just collateral damage, was correct. Bobbi had been so earnest and forthright, seeking to correct an injustice only she could solve. And she'd walked straight into danger, never seeing it until it was too late. She'd literally been murdered to prevent her from outing Poser and whoever else was in on the conspiracy, and he hadn't even realized it until just now.

But who were they? Who did this? Was it Poser and Charnel? Who are these other people?

"Is there any chance of this not being true?" Chelsea looked as shell-shocked as he felt.

Slowly, he shook his head. "Damn-all. The audio clips are genuine as hell. Foxtrot was Independence. She's the one who showed up with the Designated Liaison." He'd always had trouble accepting that one drugged-up asshat—high on meth or otherwise—had gotten the better of his burly cousin. All the evidence had pointed that way, which meant he'd had to accept it … but not anymore.

"You okay?" she asked, putting her hand on his shoulder. "That can't've been easy to read about."

"It's not," he admitted. "But I reckon I know why Independence was always so pissed off at me, seeing how Luke handled her so roughly. Though I still can't believe they framed that poor bastard Portman so thoroughly. I honestly thought it was him. He never stood a chance. The whole time, it was Independence and this Charlie asshole."

He wondered how Golf had pulled off the bait and switch. It had to be a trick of *some* sort, but he could worry about the nitty-gritty later.

And find Portman's family and tell them the truth. They deserve that much.

"How often have they done this before?" Chelsea asked rhetorically. "From the sounds of it, it wasn't the first time or even the second."

"You're not wrong, but we can look into that later," he said, trying to get his thoughts in order. "They're using names out of the phonetic alphabet, probably for initials. S for Sierra, F for Foxtrot, C for Charlie, G for Golf. Foxtrot and Charlie are the ones who murdered Bobbi and Luke and framed Portman. Poser, Independence, Foxtrot. Same person." He frowned. "But why use F for Foxtrot instead of I for Independence?"

Chelsea rubbed her finger over her lips for a moment. "Because they're not using Force Majeure names. Maybe their terror villain names?"

"Which means Charlie *has* to be Charnel," decided Jericho. "I saw the wounds he left behind, but I didn't know what they meant. Some were stabs like from a knife, but some were slashes like you'd get from claws. The backstabbing asshat must've got Luke from behind while he was beating on Poser."

Charnel's dead, but Poser's still in the picture. If Relentless leaves anything behind, I want my piece of him.

"False Flag. Independence—Poser—is False Flag." Chelsea sounded just as definitive.

Jericho's head jerked around at the mention of the infamous shape-changer. "You certain-sure about that? He's supposed to be dead."

"And Charnel wasn't? Those two are the ones who murdered your cousin and your friend. I'd stake my life on it." The conviction in Chelsea's voice was rock-solid. "Also, that fills in a gap for me. I was recording the whole meet, and it was still going when Silent Knight attacked you. He said something about 'Flag' wanting you alive. I didn't make the connection until just now."

As much as he didn't want it to, that sealed the deal for Jericho. "Independence is goddamn False Flag." It made for a horrible sort of sense. "Sonovabitch! With that ponytail, she's even got the whole red-white-blue thing going on. And I'll tell you something else, too. When she showed up for the Designated Liaison thing, she was wearing a knee brace and still limping. Just like the guy we all thought was Portman was limping on his way out of the building. Same leg, even." All the little clues, right there all the time, were starting to add up.

"I read somewhere how False Flag could apparently use his shape-changing to accelerate his healing," Chelsea mused. "Plus, there's his Prodigy powerset to consider. Your cousin must have rung his bell pretty good."

"Yeah. I know." It wasn't much, but it was something. After all this was all over, he would have to tell Leroy about that part.

Luke, you magnificent sonovabitch, you beat the ever-loving crap out of a for-real terror villain.

"Okay, who do you think 'S' and 'G' are?" Chelsea looked at him. "Any ideas?"

"The only two terror villains that started with 'S' were Seismic and Singularity," Jericho said thoughtfully, then blinked as the realization burst upon him. "It's gotta be Seismic."

"Why Seismic, specifically?" Chelsea tilted her head. "What have you got against Singularity being in on this?"

Jericho gestured animatedly. "For one thing, Singularity *might* have faked her death with False Flag's help, but Seismic didn't even have to do that. He just plain dropped out of sight before Force Majeure ever got off the ground. For another, that quake in Jefferson City this morning was induced." He raised his eyebrows. "And what's Seismic known for?"

"Building earthquake machines, duh." Chelsea's eyes widened in sudden realization. "Oh, shit. Are you *sure* it was an artificial event?"

"Sure as I can be," he said. "I felt a bunch of anomalous gravity waves just before the quake was announced. *Something* was gonna happen, I knew that much, but not what exactly."

"That's … even scarier than Independence being False Flag," Chelsea decided. "Not much, but some. If he's been flying under the radar, biding his time, it would explain why nobody's seen or heard of him since … well, since forever."

"Relentless and Tourbillon weren't exactly thrilled when I told 'em the quake wasn't natural," Jericho recalled. "I said he might've been in jail this whole time, and Relentless said they were gonna look into that angle. But I'm beginning to think he's been in Utopia instead. Maybe inside the Spire itself."

"Sure looks like it." Chelsea frowned. "Okay then, Sierra is Seismic. How about Golf?"

"That's where I'm drawing a blank," admitted Jericho. "There's only one

I can think of, and she just doesn't fit."

"What terror villains had names starting with 'G'?" Chelsea frowned. "Not the Ghast. He wasn't a terror villain, was he?"

"Heh. No. The worst thing that guy ever tried to do was kidnap Tesseract Power on her wedding day. From the altar, no less." Jericho waggled his eyebrows expressively. "It didn't go all that well."

Chelsea burst into laughter. "Oh, God, no," she said after subsiding into giggles. "Adam Power would've kicked his ass, if she didn't get to him first."

"She did. I bet he still can't look at a bouquet without screaming." He leaned back in his chair. "No, the only terror villain starting with 'G' that I ever heard of was Guillotine. Which is weird, because her thing was grand larceny and mass murder in a battle bikini. Usually involving cutting body parts off anyone who got in her way, or even just caught her eye, until nobody was left standing. *Not* about getting teammates out of trouble if things went sideways, or pulling off a bait and switch. And nobody in that apartment was missing any bits or pieces."

"Okay, let's assume that Golf is some kind of outside contact." Chelsea pursed her lips. "Moving on."

Jericho was beginning to see the shape of things now. The two terror villains had been hiding in plain sight as members of the core team, with Seismic aiding them as support personnel and the mysterious 'Golf' somewhere outside the Spire. All working with the unnamed 'boss' to pervert Force Majeure's good name ... it was simultaneously insidious and terrifying. And they'd only stumbled on it by good luck and happenstance.

Well, it was definitely bad luck for Luke and Bobbi and Stephen and Tucker. But I am surely gonna kick the ass of whoever killed them.

"We need to pass this information on to Relentless," he said. "He might miss someone, otherwise."

"When he calls you back, and *only* then." Chelsea's voice was firm. "The man can take care of himself. Right now ... he's working. Don't distract him."

"Yeah ..." Jericho frowned. "But there's one last thing bothering me."

"Who their boss is?" Chelsea raised her eyebrows, her expression equally concerned. "Yeah, me too."

It could only be another terror villain; Jericho was sure of it. People like that wouldn't take orders from anyone else.

But who?

53
More Heroes Behaving Badly

Chelsea tapped a few keys. "Before we go on to the next file, I want to save the lot, right now. I don't trust that drive not to crap out on us, especially with power going through it."

"Yeah, good idea." Jericho gestured toward where the second drive was still plugged in. "Give me a copy, too, so I can show Relentless what's been going on."

"Sure." She began to set about the task, then held up the Dr. Pepper can. "Trash this for me?"

"Can do." Getting up, he stretched—careful not to pull on his stomach muscles—and accepted the can from her. With a push-tag to add a little impetus, it flicked across the room and scored a three-pointer into the wastepaper basket, then rattled briefly in the bottom.

"Showoff," she murmured, still dragging files from one folder to another.

"It's showing off if it isn't for a good reason," he said cheerfully. "*That* was practicing with my powers. Totally different."

She didn't say anything, but if the look she gave him had been any drier, it would've given Death Valley a run for its hypothetical money.

"Like *you* don't show off," he retorted. Heading over to the sliding glass balcony door, he leaned on it with one elbow and looked out at the turnpike. Traffic still flowed by in both directions, the drivers entirely unaware of the horrific revelations of the last few minutes. "So … Independence, False Flag, and Poser are all the same person: the one who attacked Vanessa two years ago." His fists clenched at the thought.

"That's what I'm thinking," agreed Chelsea. "Once this gets out, they're going to have to re-examine exactly how Charnel and False Flag managed to fake their own deaths *after* joining Force Majeure."

That had been weighing on Jericho's mind as well. "Independence was there when Charnel went down, right? Bet you twenty bucks False Flag set up his own 'death' ahead of time, then pulled shenanigans with his shape-changing to help out Charnel. People saw what they wanted to see."

"No bet," Chelsea agreed. "False Flag always was too good at what he did. They'll need to go back and look at *all* the shape-changer reports they've been getting over the last fifteen years. He's a really slippery customer."

"He won't be once Relentless registers him as a bad guy in the Spire security system." Jericho thought back to the details Transit had passed on to him, once upon a time. "It won't matter whose face he borrows. That sort of thing's been tried before. Briefly."

"Good to hear. The file transfer's complete. Let's go ahead and look at Exhibit B."

"Yeah, let's do that." He came back to the chair and settled into it as she extracted the thumb drives from the laptop. "Thanks."

"No problem." She handed them over. "I wouldn't plug the busted one back in again. It's seriously on its last legs." Waiting until he'd re-wrapped them in the mailer and zipped them into his fanny pack, she tapped the second file.

The icon unfolded itself into an impressively high-definition video recording. Jericho would not have considered himself a prude, but what the seven people were getting up to in the video was definitely pornographic. Even more so because one of them was wearing a remarkably, not to mention provocatively, abbreviated version of Lady Quantum's costume.

And then she turned her head, and he saw it wasn't just the costume. That *was* Lady Quantum, right there, in the middle of ... well, everything. She was doing things to women, and men were doing other things to her, that his relatively sheltered upbringing simply hadn't prepared him for.

Blushing heavily, he reached out to pause the video, then averted his eyes from the screen. "Uh, do we have to keep watching this?" he asked. "I feel like I'm kinda intruding here. I mean, it's not a crime for a superhero to make a sex tape. Even if you *are* doing it with half a dozen other people at the time."

Chelsea rolled her eyes. "*Yes*, we have to keep watching it. Though if you want, you can go and sit in the bathroom with your hands over your ears until all the naughty bits are put away." She looked speculatively at the screen. "I might be watching this one again. A couple of those guys are seriously *yum*."

The worst part was that he couldn't tell if she was pulling his leg or not. He gritted his teeth. "Fine. I'll stay." Before he could talk himself out of it, he reached out and tapped the Play icon again.

On the screen, the action shifted around until one couple was off to the side doing their own thing, while Lady Quantum was being attended to by the other four. Chelsea showed no embarrassment, while Jericho felt ever more uncomfortable as the footage rolled on. He was about to seek refuge in the bathroom anyway when a shout from the speakers snagged his attention.

"**Excuse me?**" demanded Lady Quantum, kneeling up now and facing one of the men. "**Did I give you permission to yank my hair like that?**"

The man shrugged, grinning awkwardly. "**Hey, babe. If I'm balls-deep and I see hair like that in front of me, I gotta pull on it, y'know?**"

"**Not mine, you don't.**" She prodded his chest hard with one sharp-looking fingernail. "**Not now, not ever.**"

He grabbed her wrist. "**Hey, watch it—**"

An actinic flash whited out the camera for a moment, along with a soggy *splurtch*. When the picture came back, the man simply wasn't there anymore. Or rather, bits of him were: all over the room, as well as the various participants in the orgy. Who promptly recoiled, screaming and gagging at the blood and viscera they'd just been splattered with. A couple of them got up and tried to run.

"Oh, for *fuck's* sake," she said in resignation and loosed another blast, detonating a woman who had nearly gotten to the door. Twice more she fired, casually murdering the people with whom she'd been so very recently sharing an extremely intimate moment. By the time she was finished, the entire room—including the thick rug they'd been lying on—had been liberally redecorated along the theme of 'gore and intestines', from floor to ceiling.

The only people she hadn't targeted were the man and woman off to the side. At first, the man cowed away from her, then got up and sprinted for the door. Behind him, the woman he'd been with (who hadn't bothered getting up) sighed and made a casual gesture. Purple clouds formed around the runner's upper body, and he dropped to the floor, his head rolling away across the carpet. His last breath gurgled out of his severed windpipe as his wide eyes (several feet from his body) stared at the camera.

Climbing to her feet, the other woman tried to brush off the worst of the mess. **"Jesus motherfucking Christ, could you not have waited until I was finished? What is it with you and guys like that?"** Even played over the laptop's mediocre speakers, she had a noticeable French accent.

"Calm your tits, G." Lady Quantum levitated to her feet and put her hands on her hips. **"There's always more where they came from. Give me a hand getting rid of them?"**

The woman called 'G'—Jericho had already made the 'Golf' connection in his mind—rolled her eyes and ran her hand back over her blood-soaked short blonde hair. **"If I must. Just a second."**

She went off to the side, out of camera range, and came back with what looked like a silver tiara with a black gemstone on the front. Settling this over her head, she made another gesture. This time, a tiny disc flicked out from the palm of her hand. Steadily enlarging and displaying a brilliant blue color, it settled toward the floor. By the time it got there, it was six or seven feet wide, perfectly circular, apparently resting on the gore-covered carpet.

Then she stood there with her arms folded over her modest bust. **"Your turn."**

Lady Quantum gave her a dirty look. **"What, you're not even going to help out?"**

'G' didn't move. **"You made the mess. You clean it up."**

"Fine." Grumbling to herself, Lady Quantum also headed offscreen, then came back with a pair of blue bracers, each with a prominent white star on them, that she fitted around her forearms. **"I hate cleaning blood off these."**

"Then stop getting blood on them." 'G' made a tiny gesture with her fingertips. **"Go on."**

Jericho watched in horrified fascination as Lady Quantum used force fields and gravity adjustment to dump the larger body parts through the new hole in the floor to God knew where. Once she was finished, 'G' dispelled the portal. Lady Quantum dusted her hands off, which did nothing to remove the literal blood that stained her skin. **"So, where'd you send them? A thousand feet up, middle of the Pacific, as usual?"**

"Atlantic, this time," 'G' said casually. **"The fish will dispose of everything."** She looked down at herself. **"And now I'm covered in fucking blood.** *Again.*"

Smirking, Lady Quantum took her by the arm. **"Come on. My shower's big enough for two. I'll even apologize for the mess while I'm at it."**

'G' snorted. **"Better make it a damn good apology. What about the mess out here?"**

Lady Quantum chuckled. **"Same as always. Call in a couple of housekeeping robots. Say what you like about them; they're really good at cleaning up messes. And they never ask awkward questions."**

Arm in arm, they walked offscreen. The video clip ended a moment later.

54
Ultimate Betrayal is Ultimate

Jericho and Chelsea stared at each other. He wasn't even sure where to start; there had been so many unwelcome visuals in that clip that his brain kept wanting to dump his memory of the whole thing and start fresh. Chelsea, despite her initial *sang-froid*, appeared equally shell-shocked.

"Holy ..." he began.

"Motherfucking ..." she continued.

"Crapping ..." was the best he could do.

"Christ on a unicycle." She shook her head. "Did we just see that? Did *we* just see *that*? Did you just see what I saw?"

"I don't know," he replied candidly. "I'm pretty sure I just saw Lady Quantum and Tourbillon murder five people and dump their bodies out to sea. And I saw proof positive they're actually Singularity and Guillotine. What do you think *you* saw?"

"Everything you did," she replied dazedly. "Exactly what you saw. Except ... where do you get Singularity out of that?"

"The power blast signature," he said. "I've been looking up old footage. Singularity's was yellow, Lady Quantum's is red and blue. Plus, she couldn't extend her force fields or do proper gravity manipulation beyond her flight until she put on those bracers."

"Just like Tourbillon could only do the purple clouds and decapitation until she put the circlet on." Chelsea frowned. "Though how did she go from cutting off heads to putting portals out over the Atlantic? I'm still blanking on that one."

"I might have a notion about that." Jericho gestured at the screen. "Go back to where she takes his head off, and play it through slowly."

"Okay," she said doubtfully, then ran the action back. But as the unfortunate man's demise rolled across the screen once more, her eyes widened in realization. "Why didn't *I* spot that? His head falls out of the cloud two feet to the left of his body!"

Jericho nodded in agreement. "Yeah, I'm thinking that without the circlet, she can only do small, short-range teleport portals, just big enough to fit over a head or an arm. The other end of the portal is right next to the first one, but it's concealed by those clouds. Also, it looks like she doesn't *have* to make the clouds happen at all if she doesn't want to."

Which, now he was thinking about it, would've made it altogether too easy for 'Golf' to pull off a mid-air swap between False Flag and Jack Portman in the Southside Parking structure, once upon a time.

Yeah. I see how you did that now.

She shuddered. "Right, right. And I guess we've got the answer to the question taking up about forty percent of the superhero forums these days: what sex is Tourbillon?"

"Whereas *nobody* asked that about Guillotine," he agreed. "It's ingenious. Like with Singularity; even with the bustier, her costume covered her cleavage and the skirt gave her a certain amount of modesty. If what she's wearing as Lady Quantum was any tighter, we'd be able to read the tags on her underwear."

"That's if she's even wearing any." Chelsea shook her head. "Okay, no, I refuse to speculate on that. But do you know what this means?"

"Well, for one thing, that puts Seismic *and* Singularity in play." Jericho didn't enjoy discarding conclusions he'd come up with any more than the next person did, but the logic was irrefutable. "Because *someone* had to set off that quake this morning, and we just saw Singularity on-screen as Lady Quantum."

"Plus, Guillotine is Tourbillon," Chelsea reminded him. "Which means more than half of Force Majeure's core group is—was—made up of terror villains. And that it's not just Charnel and False Flag who faked their deaths. False Flag's been *busy*."

Jericho hadn't thought it all the way through like that, though it was apparent she had. "Shit! Relentless doesn't know half the core membership is working against him! I really think we should warn him!"

"No." Chelsea held up her hands as he opened his mouth to protest. "Hear me out. He's not *stupid*. He knows his team implicitly. We saw two villains and decided there weren't any more, yeah? He'll be asking, *'who else might be a traitor?'*. Once he gets False Flag into an interrogation room, he won't stop 'til squeezes the whole story out of him. And don't forget that Charnel's dead, so the bad guys are down a heavy hitter. *They're* on the back foot. We've just got to sit tight and trust Relentless to do what he does best. And when he calls back, we update him on what *we* know."

It wasn't what Jericho wanted to hear, but Chelsea's instincts had been batting a thousand so far. "Okay," he said, taking a deep breath then letting it out again. Closing his eyes, he passed his hands over his close-shorn scalp, wishing he could run his fingers through his hair. "Okay. Okay. We'll do it your way."

"Trust me, I want to make that call just as much as you do," she said. "But I've learned the hard way, just holding back for a moment is sometimes a smarter move than actually jumping in and doing something rash." She paused, then indicated the laptop. "Seeing as we're waiting anyway, feel up to watching the third clip?"

Jericho grimaced. "Why do I feel as though it's gonna be worse than the other two?"

"Because let's face it; it probably is." Chelsea's expression was sympathetic, but her tone indicated she was in this for the long haul. "The thing is, we'll never know if we don't look. And it might just have something else on it that Relentless needs to learn about."

"Yeah." He made the word into an unhappy sigh. "Hit it."

Carefully, she reached out and tapped the third icon.

Jericho's first impression of the video file was that it could've been a screen capture from a first-person shooter. Across the top of the image was a transparent red banner with the words *RAIDER CAM* at the left-hand end, followed by what he presumed to be the latitude and longitude, and a time-date stamp from only three years previously.

"Raider?" he said involuntarily. "*He's* still alive?" He'd known it would be problematic, but ... yeah, this was bad.

"Shit." Chelsea didn't sound any happier.

As the image panned around, Jericho surmised Raider was in a storage yard, judging from the number of shipping containers stacked around the place. After a moment, the camera started moving toward one in particular; it was held shut by a padlock, but a gloved hand took hold of it and pulled once, popping it open.

"That's a good trick," Chelsea murmured. "Maybe it wasn't locked?"

"Didn't *look* unlocked." Jericho shelved the question temporarily as Raider unlocked two more containers the same way, then went to the middle one and opened the doors. Within was some kind of wheeled vehicle, clearly designed to fit into the container with about six inches of clearance in all directions. Beyond that, he had no idea what it was for.

A hatch unfolded from the front and Raider climbed in, revealing exactly how cramped the interior was. There was no sound, so Jericho couldn't hear any grunts of effort, but from the jerkiness of the motions, they had to be there. Finally, the villain managed to situate himself in what had to be the command seat.

Reaching up, Raider pulled a VR headset down over his face, giving him more icons on the screen and a camera view out through the open door of the shipping container. One such icon was a wireframe diagram of the vehicle, complete down to the open hatch in the front. At an unseen signal, the hatch swung up and closed again; the word LOCKED popped up next to it.

The vehicle began to move forward, trundling out of the container. A line of text sprang up on the HUD of the headset: *Activate secondary components?*

Jericho didn't see what Raider did—there was no keyboard, virtual or otherwise, to type on—but the letter **Y** popped up anyway.

Once the vehicle was out of the container, the wireframe *changed*. Components literally slid sideways or upward, opening up the cramped pilot's compartment until it seemed positively roomy inside. To Jericho's dismay, several of these components strongly resembled gun turrets.

Then two more wireframes joined the first. Though of the same size and bulk as the one Raider had driven into the yard, they resembled each other far more than they did the first one. Instead of wheels, these ones were running on caterpillar tracks. They moved closer and closer to Raider's vehicle, then clamps reached out, locked on, and pulled it all together into one unit. Jericho could actually see the jolt and change of the camera angle as the central unit—the original vehicle—was lifted by several feet.

"It's a tank." Chelsea said it before Jericho could, her voice hard with the need to disbelieve what they were seeing. "The bastard smuggled a goddamn *tank* into wherever he is, in three different storage containers."

"Sonova*bitch*." Jericho had nothing more to say; she was correct in every aspect. More gun turrets were motoring into view from all over the tank as it assumed its final form.

Turning, it aimed itself at the main gate and accelerated. There was a little guard shack off to one side; Jericho saw the guard stick his head out, stare, then bolt from the hut. He held a two-way radio, and from the contortions his mouth was going through, he was screaming into it.

For a moment, it looked like the guard was going to get away; for someone with the extra weight this guy was carrying, his track and field form was pretty impressive. Of course, the adrenaline would've been flooding his bloodstream in firehose quantities, and terror was an intense motivator. But then ... Raider turned the tank and accelerated some more.

The last they saw of the ill-fated guard was one last terrified glance over his shoulder as he made for the dubious safety of a stack of shipping containers. There wasn't even a jolt to signify that the tank had ended a human life, though the wireframe briefly popped up an image of a running man just in front of the left-hand set of treads.

Text appeared on the HUD: *Security Guard [10 points]*. A few seconds later, it vanished again. One of the notations along the side went from an unassuming zero to '10'.

"Wait, *what* the hell now?" demanded Jericho. "The asshat *keeps score?*"

Chelsea's voice was hollow. "The asshat, as you say, keeps score." She reached for the screen and paused the action. "Do you want to keep watching? I think we've seen enough. Raider's alive."

"No, keep watching." Jericho didn't feel there was any other reasonable option. "I want to know how he's mixed up with the rest of them."

She wrinkled her nose. "You're a weird individual. A video of Lady Quantum getting her rocks off makes you get all antsy, but you're fine with watching Raider mowing down people with a giant fuck-off tank."

"Never said I was *fine* with it," he retorted. "I nearly died for this footage. *You* nearly died. And like you said, Stephen and Tucker *did* die. If we back out now, we're cheapening all that."

"Okay, then." With an unspoken '*on your own head be it*', she reached across and tapped the screen to start it playing again, then set it to quadruple speed. He didn't object.

Still with no sound, the tank swiveled almost on its axis and powered forward over the now-empty guard shack and gate. Both went down without measurably impeding the tank; each obstacle registered one point on whatever arcane scale Raider had programmed the system to recognize auch things. Once outside the yard, the tank turned and headed off down the road.

Jericho had a bad feeling about this. He had no idea where in the United States this was, but the camera feed showed office buildings in the distance. The tank was heading in that direction.

Raider, as the saying went, was going downtown.

Over the next twenty minutes (five minutes on-screen), the tank got ever closer to its goal. Industrial gave way to commercial, with residential here and there. Individual objects seemed to be worth one point, pedestrians five points, and family-occupied cars fifty points; both Jericho and Chelsea had to look away from the screen at that one. Raider smashed through it all with positively sadistic abandon, racking up his score as he went.

Only when a police helicopter swooped into view did one of the guns unlimber and swing to bear on the target. A single shot blew the aircraft from the sky, granting Raider twenty-five points on his ever-increasing score. Jericho found himself searching the screen for something, anything, that would halt this juggernaut of destruction.

Finally, a flare of light as Raider turned a corner resolved itself into Lady Quantum, hovering before the tank. Alongside her, descending into view, was Adam Power. Knowing this was at the very least a setup for Singularity to look good, Jericho wasn't surprised when the tank's weapon fire spattered harmlessly off her force field. Adam Power was targeted with a genuine barrage, but his armor stopped what his own force field let through.

Lady Quantum threw an energy blast against the left-hand tread of the tank, blowing it clear off the road wheels, while Adam Power targeted the guns with a series of multi-warhead missiles. Explosions rocked the picture, and one error message after another scrolled up the screen. Jericho was impressed despite himself; Singularity might've been painting by the numbers, but the leader of Team Power most definitely was not playing.

Tank immobilized, said the HUD. *Weapons disabled. Abandon vehicle.*

As Chelsea brought the playback to normal speed, it was a little bit of a shock to watch as the VR headset lifted away and the interior of the tank came back into view. There were controls and screens here, one of which was still showing the message to abandon the tank. Another portrayed the wireframe, showing the damage done to the tank so far by both the genuine hero and the faux one. More reports showed up as Adam Power switched to his cutting laser.

Moving casually, as though he had all the time in the world, Raider undid his seat harness and flipped up a clear plastic cover on the dash. Under it was a red button. He pressed this, and one of the screens lit up with the number **10**. Then it changed to **9**.

Turning away from the countdown, Raider stepped past the command chair to face the rear of the tank, apparently waiting for something. This had all been cramped when he'd first gotten in, with no room to move. Since the rearrangement of components, it was now quite spacious. Still, there seemed to be no way out. Jericho found himself counting down under his breath, echoed by Chelsea.

They'd both got to 'five' when the actinic blue laser beam burned through into the control compartment, filling it with showers of sparks; Raider glanced over his shoulder as the beam bisected the control seat in a burst of flame. At 'four', a black swirl appeared within the tank, stretching from floor to ceiling.

Hastily, Raider stepped through Tourbillon's portal—for there was nothing else it *could* be—and came face-to-face with the cowled Enabled. Tourbillon said something, but with zero sound, Jericho could only rely on his less than stellar lip-reading skills. He thought it was maybe *'did you have a good time'*, but it could just as likely have been *'would you like a glass of wine'*.

Whatever it was, a subtle vibration in the picture indicated Raider was speaking, then he and Tourbillon gave each other a high-five. Jericho was left with the sinking feeling that Raider's words had been along the lines of *'I got a high score'*. With his new knowledge of Tourbillon's secret past as Guillotine, that would make altogether too much sense.

Raider went to a bench and picked something up. Jericho's brain stuttered to a halt as he recognized Transit's helmet: red and silver, with a reflective faceplate. Just for a moment, Raider looked directly at the front of the helmet, his—no, *her*—features clearly visible in the mirror-like visor.

Frozen, Jericho stared at the screen. He'd never seen Transit's face, but this woman had kindly features, not unlike what he'd imagined her to be. Her dark hair was cut short, no doubt to reduce the inconvenience of wearing a helmet all the time. There was a serious-looking scar on the side of her head, leading forward to the glowing orange prosthesis that replaced her right eye …

… *wait. No. This is a mirror image. That's her* left *eye.*

His mind jumped back to the footage he'd seen of Raider attacking Des Moines. The holographic representation of the terror villain had always displayed an artificial left eye, glowing a malevolent orange. Distantly, he recalled Chelsea saying in the car, *Did you know Transit's left eye is a prosthetic?*

It couldn't be … but it *was*. Stunned, Jericho watched as Transit brought her hand up and … tapped the side of her head? The eye changed color, deepening toward red. Then, as she donned the helmet, the video ended.

Chelsea said something, but Jericho wasn't listening. What he'd just seen was blatantly impossible, yet *he* was the one who'd been carrying the drive with the footage all this time. Far more shocking than any of the other revelations he'd seen, this one undid him completely.

Transit was Raider.
Transit was Raider.
Transit *was* Raider.
Transit was *Raider*.
Transit was Raider.

"No," he said, shaking his head. "No. Not *her*, too. I don't believe it. It's

… that's wrong. It can't be. It … I can't … that … she … No. No, no, *no!*" Clutching his head with his hands, he tried to squeeze sense into his brain.

His emotions, already disarranged from the previous revelations, were in utter turmoil now. Physical pain shot through his body as his guts cramped up. The world had turned upside down, and nothing would ever be the same again.

Even though he'd never gotten along with Independence and Silent Knight, learning they were terror villains had been a severe shock to the system. The revelation of Tourbillon and Lady Quantum had likewise thrown him for a loop.

But … *this* was beyond even finding out Stephen had been cheating on him. It was a betrayal of the deepest, most visceral kind, and it hurt scarcely less than a literal stab to the heart would have.

Try as he might, Jericho couldn't unsee the luckless security guard running for his life as the tank bore down on him. His treacherous memory reached back and threw Transit's words at him: *When I can look people in the eye and see the impact I have on them, personally, that's when I know I'm succeeding in my chosen field*. In this new light, they held a whole different meaning.

If Transit had *been* Raider once upon a time and turned over a new leaf — hell, a whole *rainforest* — to join Force Majeure, he could have done his best to feel less betrayed. But the facts as revealed by the footage were clear: she still went out and killed people for fun. Just not in her old identity.

A faint hope sprang to life then. "What if that was someone else, not Transit? Just, you know, with a replica helmet?" It was vaguely possible, though not particularly plausible.

"Sorry." Chelsea didn't sound as heartbroken as he felt right then, but she hadn't had the connection with Transit that *he'd* thought he did. "I just did some checking. At the beginning, the latitude and longitude readouts put her smack in the middle of Davenport, Illinois. When she teleported, they placed her inside the Spire. And there *was* an attack by a tank in Davenport back in two thousand eleven that Lady Quantum and Adam Power attended. When it blew, it injured a dozen cops. Analysis of the debris indicated that it would've taken out half a city block if Power's beam hadn't damaged the firing mechanism. She's the real deal."

"Sonovabitch." Tears were running down Jericho's face now, but he didn't give a good goddamn. "She was the one member of Force Majeure who really *got* me, y'know? Relentless brought me onto the team, but Transit was the only member who made me feel like I *belonged* there."

"Shit." Chelsea was running her hands through her hair. "Okay, yeah, now we *have* to warn Relentless."

"That's what I've been—" Jericho broke off as a blur of motion outside the building caught his eye. He whipped his head around, but all he saw was a trail of red and blue, hanging in the air. "Crap! Lady Quantum!"

Ignoring the stab of pain as he dived off the chair, he ended up kneeling between the beds with Chelsea right by his side. She held the laptop while he'd scooped up the fanny pack and secure phone without even thinking about it. He raised his head cautiously, but the fading reds and blues were all he could see. "Figure she's gone?"

"I don't think she saw us," Chelsea murmured.

"Reckon not." Overall, it didn't seem likely—at a rough estimate, she had to have been doing at least five hundred—though he didn't want to stake too much on that assumption. "She didn't bust in through the window, so my guess is they're looking to cover all the cities within easy driving distance of Utopia." He grimaced. "Which means one of two things. Either False Flag didn't give up Singularity and the rest, or they've pulled a coup and taken over Force Majeure, and the Spire with it."

"Yeah." Chelsea was right there on the same page as him. "In other words, at *best* they'll be listening in on whatever conversations you have with Relentless, and trying *real* hard to get to us before he does." She looked at the secure phone and shook her head. "All the encryption in the world doesn't mean a damn thing if the bad guys have access to the plaintext."

"Okay, so what do we do?" He'd never been in this situation before, but he was willing to bet she had, or at least something similar to it.

"Keep our heads down. Gather information. Figure out what we *can* do, and do that." She gave him a hard stare. "What we're *not* gonna do is pull some white-knight doomed charge in the hope that we somehow get it right by pure accident."

He hadn't been thinking about doing that … well, not *exactly*. "But …"

The secure phone rang. Jericho stared at it like a teenager caught in a compromising position by his prom date's dad. "Do I answer it?"

"Yeah," she said, just as it rang again. "On speaker. I need to hear this."

"Okay." He did as he was told, tapping the little icon and placing the phone and module on the floor between them. "Hello?"

"G-Man." To Jericho's immense relief, Relentless sounded upbeat. "Ming vase. The problem's been dealt with. Independence will be taking a *permanent* leave of absence from Force Majeure. Good work with that, by the way."

He was momentarily taken aback by the praise. "Uh, thanks …?"

"Will you quit it with the damn false modesty already, boy?" And there was the gruff Relentless he knew and respected. "Where are you? I'll have one of the team pick you up and bring you back."

Chelsea shook her head violently, though Jericho had already decided what he would say next. As hard as it was going to be, there was no other way he could play it. "I, uh … I can't come back. There's … there's something I've got to take care of."

"What?" Now Relentless' tone was tipping into anger. "What the hell's going on? Where are you? Talk to me, boy."

"I can't tell you." Jericho squeezed his eyes shut, trying hard not to let the stress flooding him bleed into the call. He desperately wanted to warn the veteran hero of the danger surrounding him, but he couldn't even ask if anyone else was privy to the call, in case that tipped them off. "I'm sorry. I've … I've gotta go."

"But—" Relentless' voice was cut off as the call ended. Jericho cracked his eyelids open to see Chelsea drop the phone and module in her shoulder bag, and zip it closed.

"Okay," she said quietly. "Good news or bad news first?"

"Bad news." Whenever he'd seen this cliché on TV or in a movie, he'd never been able to figure out why anyone would ever go for the bad news first. Now he knew. Ripping the Band-Aid off quickly still hurt, but there would hopefully be good news to follow.

She took a deep breath. "He only knows Independence and Silent Knight went against him. The rest, he still considers loyal. Some of them were almost certainly listening in on that call. In my personal opinion, they'll let him keep being the public face of the team until something drastic happens. Also, he's pretty hard to kill, so they're probably concocting something in secret to take him out hard if he figures it out at the wrong moment. Or at least, that's what *I'd* do if I were a terror villain secretly masquerading as a superhero." For the last bit, she rolled her eyes.

He waited, but she didn't continue. That had been about as bad as he'd suspected, and he was vaguely happy she hadn't pulled anything worse out of the brief conversation. "So … good news?"

"Good news is, he's healthy and still nominally in charge. There's been no coup. Which means the situation is still salvageable if we play our cards right." She frowned thoughtfully. "He was serious about False Flag. That asshole is either dead or wishing he was. Also, Relentless doesn't think you're up to anything underhanded. At a guess, he thinks you're wussing out because the going got tough. *But* … even with that, he's still determined to get you back on the team."

Jericho stared across the bed at the glass doors and the highway beyond. The energy trail had long since faded away.

I wonder if all this was what Scout meant when he told me I had to save Utopia? What did he know? What had he seen? Is he a last-minute failsafe the Technologist put together for a scenario like this?

He'd never know, he decided, until he got to the bottom of all this.

"I'm going to save him. I'm going to save them. I'm going to save *Utopia*." It was a statement of rock-solid intent. "How do we do that?"

"I think it's time we called in a few favors and brought in some big guns of our own. Or rather, it's time *you* brought in the big guns." Climbing to her feet, Chelsea offered him a hand.

"Me?" Jericho frowned as she helped him up. "What big guns?"

"Well, *duh*. Even if Thomas wasn't your boyfriend, Team Power would still owe you big-time. Pack your non-existent bags, sunshine." She grinned and dusted her hands off theatrically. "We're going to Chicago."

55
Strangers on a Plane

When they left the motel, Jericho discreetly checked up and around. There was a streak of red—courtesy of Lady Quantum—across the skyline over the city to the east, but it looked miles away. Chelsea glanced that way herself, tightened her lips, and hurried toward where the taxis were dropping off passengers outside the reception area.

Figuring it would be best to let her do the talking, Jericho hung back. There were folks back home in Savannah who could damn near charm the spots off a bluetick hound, but they had *nothing* on her. Besides, he was still getting used to the sensation of the inserts in his mouth again, and his voice just plain sounded weird to his own ears with them in.

The first cab driver shook his head and drove off, likely because he had another job to go to, but the second nodded and made an expansive gesture: *get right in.* Chelsea opened the back door and nodded to Jericho, who went on over. His stomach protested against the twisting motion as he climbed in, but he managed to ignore the twinge. It wasn't as bad as it could've been; aided and abetted by Chelsea's medical intervention, his body was already working to repair the damage.

"Where to, folks?" asked the cab driver once they were settled.

"Airport," Chelsea said at once.

The cabbie glanced over his shoulder at her as if about to say something, then shrugged. "Airport, it is." He started the engine.

Jericho could easily understand the reaction. Public awareness of the maglev system's speed, comfort, and low cost had propagated across the nation even faster than the gleaming rails themselves. The potential impact on domestic airline travel was easily anticipated by all but those whose livelihoods were inextricably invested in those same airlines. Many of the corporations managed to obfuscate the writing on the wall long enough that the impact was catastrophic when the eventual crash came.

This was not necessarily a metaphor. The domestic-only airlines that refused to fold and couldn't (or wouldn't) make the transition to cargo transport were forced to continue attracting passengers by any means necessary. A dichotomy had quickly formed between the so-called 'super-first' airlines and the shoestring ones; the former offered every possible type of hedonistic attraction aboard their glitzy flying casinos, while the latter cut prices to the bone and got rid of all unnecessary expenses.

It soon became apparent that in order to make any kind of profit at all, both varieties were skimping on costs wherever they figured they could get away with it. With the annual number of plane crashes suffering a sharp uptick, regular aircraft maintenance was clearly one of these expenses, even though increasingly intrusive audits purported to show otherwise. Nor were the 'super-first' planes immune, which merely indicated that both sides were equally engaged in cooking the books.

By comparison, the maglev subverted the popular mantra of '*good, fast, cheap*—*pick two*' by selecting all three and proving its worth that way. Which meant Jericho was left wondering about Chelsea's choice of transport as well. Whether routing through St. Louis or Des Moines—UML hadn't gotten around to setting up a direct rail line from Kansas City to Chicago yet—the five hundred or so miles meant they'd be there in an hour. And the sooner they got some face time with Team Power, the better.

Once the cab had entered the flow of traffic, Jericho turned on his earpiece, ensuring Chelsea saw him doing it. Then he pretended to peer idly out his window, while she did the same on the other side of the vehicle.

"Why the airport?" he subvocalized. "Why don't we go by maglev?" With the security-defeating ring she'd gifted him as well as his changed appearance, surely he could slip on board without anyone being the wiser. As for Chelsea herself, she'd repeatedly proven the security provisions set up for the maglev to be merely suggestions as far as she was concerned.

"They pulled your conversation with Luke and Bobbi right out from under a privacy bubble with no prior warning," she reminded him, her voice clearly audible over the earpiece. "If Charnel and False Flag could do the same with your half of our conversation before you arrived back in Utopia, they *will* find us before we ever get to Chicago."

"Okay, true, but they can't scan for something they can't detect. You've got jammers, right? Their cameras could be looking right at you and not see a damn thing."

"Unless they look for a hole in the crowd." In the corner of his eye, she shook her head fractionally. "Transit knows about the jamming effect now, which means they all know. If your opposition leaves a weakness to be exploited a second time, it's a trap."

"But an *airliner*?" He kept his voice down to a murmur, but his feelings about the situation colored his tone anyway. "I heard those things fall right out of the sky."

She shook her head again. "Not all of 'em, and not even most. Anyway, name me a method of getting there faster."

The hell of it was, she was right. The bus would be too slow, and he had no idea if passenger trains—the rails-and-sleepers type—even ran from Kansas City to Chicago anymore, so air travel it was going to have to be. After a few moments, unable to think of a worthwhile counter-argument, he turned the earpiece off again.

The rest of the cab ride north to the Kansas City International Airport went by in silence. Chelsea seemed lost in her thoughts, while Jericho spent the time alternating between worrying for Relentless and wishing he could contact Thomas and let him know what was going on. The one thing he tried to *avoid* worrying about was the upcoming flight.

By the time they pulled into the airport, the sun had set and the last of the twilight was fading, darkness spreading over the city. Chelsea paid the fare and they hustled into the terminal building, seeking out the check-in desks. It was easy to pick out the international section; they were professional and businesslike, with logos and uniforms unchanged from pre-maglev days. Unfortunately, an international flight wasn't what Jericho and Chelsea required, so they moved on.

The super-first companies dominated the domestic passenger section of the terminal. Like the planes they represented, the booths were gussied up like a high-society belle on the way to her debutante ball. Each one sought to outshine the last, with gold lettering, flashing lights, and fanciful logos fit to rival the Vegas casino strip.

An unofficial slogan had made the rounds a couple of years before: '*If you're not a member of the Mile-High Club when we take off, you will be by the time we touch down.*' Taking in the come-hither glances and abbreviated outfits of the attendants, Jericho could well believe it.

Chelsea went past the super-first desks as well, expertly dodging around a couple of people who were offering brochures and attempting to steer potential passengers to their specific check-in desk. Jericho followed on, hands in his jacket pockets and head down, not making eye contact.

Once past the super-first section, they reached the shoestring outfits. These check-in desks seemed to huddle down at one end of the terminal building, as if ashamed to be seen in public. Plain and unadorned, they presented the logos of their respective airlines, the prices they were willing to accept for a flight, and little else. Chelsea picked one with an adjustable plastic-lettered sign saying **CHICAGO $35 BOSTON $70**, and headed for it.

The lady handling the check-in for Right Now Airlines (or so the logo said) was neatly dressed but nowhere near as slickly presented as the super-first check-in people, or even the international crowd. An iron-on patch on her blouse was all that indicated her employment by the company. As they both stepped up to the desk, she whispered something into a lapel microphone.

"Can I help you?" Her tone was somewhere between hopeful and eager.

"Yes," said Chelsea. "Two tickets to Chicago, please."

"Two tickets, yes, ma'am. Do you have any checked luggage?"

Chelsea shook her head. "All carry-on." She slapped a fifty and a twenty down on the counter.

"Thank you, that's excellent." Hastily, the woman began typing at the computer console in front of her. As she did so, a man with the same patch on his shirt came out from the back area, nodded when he saw them, then vanished again.

Jericho turned and surveyed the concourse, not out of any specific belief that they were about to be ambushed, but to maintain his situational awareness. They *needed* to get to Chicago, and the best way to achieve that was to not take his eye off the ball.

The typing stopped and he heard a laser printer whir briefly into life, followed by the sound of tearing paper. "Here are your tickets," the lady said. "If you'd like to find a seat, we'll be happy to board you shortly."

As Jericho looked around, Chelsea took the tickets—strips of paper with the details printed directly onto them—but didn't move off. "How soon is that going to be?" she asked politely.

The desk attendant's smile slipped a little. "Not long," she hedged.

Chelsea raised an eyebrow. "What's the delay?" A flick of her eyes toward the next desk spoke volumes: *we can always check in with your competition if you don't give me a straight answer.*

Leaning forward slightly, the desk attendant lowered her voice. "The plane needs to seat four more passengers before we can take off."

"Oh, is that all?" Chelsea pulled four more fifties out of her bag and added them to the pile. "There's enough for six. How soon can we board *now*, honey?"

The woman's eyes widened. "If you can please report to the security station, we'll start boarding immediately."

"*Thank* you." Chelsea left the check-in desk and headed in the indicated direction.

Jericho fell in behind her as the PA system burbled to life. **"Would all passengers for the Right Now Airlines flight to Chicago and Boston please report to security screening ... would all passengers for the Right Now Airlines flight to Chicago and Boston please report to security screening. Thank you."**

All around them, semi-somnolent passengers--Jericho had to wonder how long they'd been waiting—began to stir and rise to their feet. Before Chelsea and Jericho slotted into the line, she let a few others get in first without being too obvious about it. For his part, he did his best to look like someone who flew shoestring all the time; given the trying day he'd had, it wasn't difficult.

"Fanny pack," Chelsea said quietly as they neared the front of the line. "Just in case."

It wasn't something Jericho was ready to argue about. Trying not to draw attention to himself, he unclipped the pack and handed it to her. She took it from him and slid it into her backpack in a move so smooth she had to have practiced it.

The security personnel barely glanced up as Chelsea walked through the metal-detector archway. Jericho noted that she hadn't taken any of the equipment he'd seen her using out of the backpack to go through the X-ray machine separately, yet no alarm was raised. With his wallet in a tray of its own, he walked through after her with an equal lack of fanfare. On the far side of the security check station, he was just slipping his wallet into his pocket when he noticed another guard moving in his direction.

"Okay, time to catch our flight." Chelsea briskly swept past him, breaking the guard's line of sight on him. "Let's go. The plane's a'waiting."

As he was drawn along by her hand under his arm, he glanced over his shoulder to see the guard heading toward someone else. "Did I just miss something?"

"Yeah, that guard was going to check you over for explosives residue," she said, gesturing with her head toward a console in the corner. "The urea powder from the fertilizer bags would've lit that thing up like a Christmas tree."

"Oh." He didn't need telling how bad that would've been.

"Yeah. *Oh.*"

They kept moving through into the boarding area, following signs as they went. There was some distance to go, as it appeared the shoestring airlines got departure gates as far from the security station as they could be placed. That didn't bother Jericho; the rest and relaxation since the escape through the access tunnels had done a lot to get him back on his feet. Despite the occasional twinge from his gut, he figured he could maintain a good walking pace without pushing himself too hard.

When they reached the appropriate gate, as indicated by the printed-out ticket, there was no jetway connecting the aircraft to the terminal. A chilly wind swept across the floodlight-illuminated tarmac as they ventured from the building.

Up ahead, on the plane they were apparently taking to Chicago, the only decorations were the RNAL airline logo and the neatly stenciled identification numbers. The rest of the aircraft was painted in basic drab off-white. If any spots needed touching up, he couldn't see them through the glare of the floodlights.

It's one way to save on operating costs, I guess.

Jericho knew that if an airline company lost more than a certain number of planes per year, they were grounded by the FAA, pending a thorough investigation. He tried to quash his lingering doubts with the knowledge that Right Now Airlines was still in operation, which meant it had lost fewer aircraft than its less fortunate competitors. This only helped a little.

They reached the bottom of the airstair that had been wheeled into place. It looked battered but serviceable, and undoubtedly cost far less to maintain than a jetway. Climbing the aluminum steps behind Chelsea, he entered the plane.

The interior of the aircraft was equally depressing. Some of the overhead light fittings were flickering, while the carpet underfoot was more than a little threadbare. The seats were extremely basic, with stains here and there on the fabric. Jericho checked his ticket and discovered that there was no seating allocation; it was literally first-come-first-served.

Moving down along the aisle, he found a window seat that suited him next to the over-wing emergency exit and settled back into it. Chelsea stowed her backpack in the overhead locker and took the seat next to his. "So, is it that you don't trust the plane, or you just want the leg-room?"

He turned to give her a dry look. "Yes."

"I see." She smirked, then worked her armrest up and down a few times. "See, it's not so bad. Fundamentally intact." It wiggled in her hand, looser than it should have been. Carefully, she lowered it back down into place. "Well, it didn't come off, anyway."

Jericho averted his eyes from the offending armrest and looked out the window at the wing.

It'll hold together long enough to get us to Chicago. Surely it can do that. That's only four hundred miles. An hour in the air, tops.

He was still telling himself that when the doors were closed and locked, and the plane's aged PA system crackled to life. The sole flight attendant introduced herself as Caroline, then talked them through the safety procedures while holding up a very tired-looking demonstration vest. Jericho found a well-used laminated sheet in the seat pocket in front of him and followed along as best he could while wondering exactly which large body of water they'd be flying over on the way to Chicago.

Or does she expect us to overshoot and ditch in Lake Michigan? Surely the pilots aren't that bad.

After the safety spiel was over, Caroline wished them a pleasant flight and retired to her jump seat at the front of the cabin. Jericho hoped the flight would be as uneventful as she evidently expected it to be.

As the plane began to roll out onto the runway, he eyed the emergency exit door again. At least that was something that would work as intended if it had to. *Turn the handle and either bring the hatch in or throw it out of the aircraft.* It was hard to screw up something like that.

The plane came to rest on the tarmac, turned slowly, then started building up thrust. Jericho listened carefully to the engine note, hoping neither one would flame out at the wrong moment—or if they were going to, they'd do it now, while the plane was still on the ground.

The only thing that kept him from wishing they'd taken the maglev instead was the knowledge that Chelsea was correct; the villains within Force Majeure would almost certainly be scanning all trains for their presence. Having innocent civilians on the maglev would do nothing to prevent the 'heroes' from going fully lethal on them.

They might even blow up the whole train car and try to frame us as terrorists.

To distract himself from such dismal thoughts as the plane began to accelerate down the runway, he wondered what airliners had been like before the maglev. When he'd gone to college in New York, he'd had to take the bus. It had been comfortable enough in its own way, though nowhere near as good as the maglev. Also, long and tedious. Airliners, at least, took less time to get where they were going.

The acceleration went from pushing him backward to downward as the plane tilted back, and he swore he could feel the moment when the wheels left the ground. There was a long, drawn-out clunking and deep whirring that had him more concerned than usual before he realized it was the undercarriage retracting into the belly of the plane. *Okay,* he told himself. *So far, so good.*

Chelsea leaned over and nudged him. "Stop worrying," she admonished gently. "We'll be fine."

He huffed and folded his arms, trying to relax in his seat. "I'll be happier when we're on the ground again." He had little to fear from heights, but that wasn't it. Even in the absence of his enhancement harness and costume, he could fall from a considerable distance and survive. What worried him was that he was being conveyed to those great heights by something of dubious mechanical soundness.

"It's all good," she said soothingly, rubbing his shoulder. "We'll be touching down at O'Hare in no time at all, and you'll be wondering what you were worried about."

He turned to give her another dry look. "We'll touch down at O'Hare, and everyone will be astonished that this thing ever got off the ground."

"Enough." She placed her finger across his lips in almost precisely the same way his cousin Serena used to shut him up when they were younger. "We'll be *fine.*"

The plane, admittedly, seemed to be doing okay so far. He figured they were up to about twenty-five thousand feet and still climbing, and—according to his powers—over twenty miles toward Chicago.

Huh. We might actually make it.

Mindful of Chelsea's urging, he tried to unclench at least partway. Peering through the window at the network of lights on the ground far below didn't do much for him, so he leaned back in his seat. He was just considering getting some sleep—as opposed to staying awake, in case of some unspecified in-flight emergency—when Chelsea nudged his shoulder.

"Hey. Guess what?"

The suppressed amusement in her voice was what really drew his attention. In his experience, having grown up with several female kinfolk, that tone was to be ignored at one's own peril. Raising his eyebrows, he turned to face her. "What?"

"We've got a celebrity on board. Sitting right in the back row." She grinned at him. "You'll never guess who it is."

"You're right. I won't." Also from personal experience, he knew she wouldn't let it go unless he bit the bullet and asked.

It had to be someone he'd spoken to her of, which cut down the field considerably. But while he was now curious about it—*dammit, Chelsea!*—he didn't want to give her the satisfaction. So, he took the third option; unbuckling the lap strap, he half-stood from his seat to look toward the rear of the plane.

"Hey!" she protested in a low tone, just as he spotted the guy she had to be talking about. And she was right; he never would have guessed. "That's cheating!" Reaching up, she hauled him back down into his seat.

"It's only cheating if I agreed to the rules first. Which I didn't." Jericho frowned. "Was that really Jerry, or whatever his name is? The guy who does those '*walking from New York to LA*' comedy skits?"

"Yes, it is him," she whispered in mock irritation. "And his name's Gary, you total philistine. Gary Brock."

"You sure about that?" He went to look over the back of the seat again.

Grabbing his arm, she hauled him down again then elbowed him gently in the ribs. "Doofus. Maybe you want to go back there and serve him some drinks? Ask him for an autograph? Propose marriage?" A deaf man back in the Kansas City terminal would've had no problem registering the sarcasm in her tone.

"Look, no harm done," Jericho said defensively. "I'm not about to go bother the guy, okay?"

"Good. I—"

"Hey there, folks."

Jericho's head came up in surprise as someone slid into the seat beside Chelsea; a moment later, he recognized the comedian himself.

"Couldn't help but see you eyeballing me just now. Can I ask you folks a huge favor?" For a man used to addressing the public, Gary Brock could keep his voice down when he needed to.

For a second Jericho floundered, but his innate politeness came to his rescue. "Uh, sorry, Mr. Brock. Didn't mean to stare, but it's not every day someone as famous as you shows up on a flight like this."

The comedian let out one of his trademark warm chuckles and waved the apology aside. On the tall side, he was broader in the beam than Jericho, with a ready smile and thinning sandy hair. "No harm done, son. Being stared at is part of the game. No, I just came up here to ask you not to spread it around that you saw me on this flight. I'm willing to sweeten the pot with a couple of autographs, if you want."

Jericho thought back to the time Serena had laughed so hard watching one of Brock's shows that she'd nearly peed herself. "Sure, I'll take you up on that," he agreed softly. "Can you make it out to 'Serena'?"

"Absolutely," Brock whispered. "And you, miss?"

Chelsea tilted her head in thought. "I'll stay quiet if you tell me *why* you're flying shoestring. I mean, you've got whole comedy routines based around taking the maglev. It's basically your thing."

Brock rolled his eyes. "Yeah. It is." Though quiet, those three words held a world of emotion.

Chelsea raised her eyebrows. "This sounds like a good one."

"Oh, it's a doozy, alright." He leaned back in the seat with a long-suffering sigh. "Long story short: my ex-wife is a psychotic, greedy, bottle-blonde hose-beast with fake tits and an incurable appetite for Latino pool boys. And those are her *good* points. She's also got a weaselly snake of a divorce lawyer who does pro bono work for her. Or, to put it another way, he'll keep doing it for free so long as he gets to bone her."

To his credit, his low-pitched tone was neither nasty nor whiny as he recited his tale of woe. It was just … matter-of-fact. This was the way things were.

"Well," observed Chelsea quietly. "She sounds nice."

Jericho held in an amused snort at her tone, which was utterly at odds with her words.

Brock nodded, having caught her actual meaning. "She's all of that. I've recently gotten word she wants to add another zero to her alimony payments—'changed circumstances', my pasty-white ass—so I'm traveling incognito between shows to stay one step ahead of her lawyer's process servers. And shoestring airlines are about as under-the-table as you can get."

"Whew. Yeah. Okay," whispered Chelsea. "Got it. And good luck."

"I appreciate it." He took a piece of paper from his inside pocket—appropriately enough, it was a flyer for one of his shows—and pulled down the tray table, then clicked a pen. Leaning forward, he looked across at Jericho. "Any specific message you want me to write to … Serena, wasn't it?"

"Serena, yeah," confirmed Jericho, then spelled the name out just to be sure. "Uh … something like 'all the best' will do, I reckon."

"Done and done." Brock scribbled his signature, then took a little more care with the inscription below. "Much appreciated, folks."

"Hey, not a problem." Jericho accepted the signed flyer. "You take care."

"Same to you. Give my best to Serena." The comedian re-secured the tray table, slid adroitly out of the seat, and headed back down the aisle.

Jericho and Chelsea looked at each other for a long moment, then Jericho shook his head. "And the world ticks on."

"Yeah." She nodded slowly. "You're not wrong."

With nothing else to say, he looked at the flyer, then handed it to her. "Could you put this in your backpack for me? I don't want it getting crumpled. Next chance I get, I'll mail it to Serena. She'll be over the moon."

"No problem." Sliding out into the aisle, she stood up and accessed the overhead locker.

The brief diversion had helped settle Jericho's nerves considerably; he leaned back in his seat again. While he was usually able to drop off within minutes, he didn't expect this to happen when he had so many issues scrambling around in his brain. Still, letting the constant low-level rumble soothe him seemed like a good idea, and Chicago was getting closer by the second.

Gradually, he let himself drift away.

56
Flying the (Un)friendly Skies

The feeling of being violently pulled in three different directions at once washed through Jericho like a splash of ice-cold water, snapping him out of a light doze. He struggled to sit up, unsure even which way 'up' was, his inner ears rebelling at the cognitive dissonance imposed on him by his powers. As the wave of vertigo passed, he stared around in confusion.

What the hell was that?

He was still on the plane; nothing appeared to have changed, except that Chelsea now had a can of Dr. Pepper in her hand. Just as he was eyeing the can, wondering if he were having a dream that mixed elements from the motel with the flight, another tsunami of disorientation flooded over him, making him feel like the plane was spinning in circles. He gagged as a tide of nausea welled up from his gut, overwhelming his defenses.

The gravitic disturbance—for it could be nothing else—subsided before he lost his lunch, but only just. By now, his heart was pounding and he was sweating from resisting the effect, to no avail. Chelsea said something, but he was concentrating too hard on his internal turmoil to register her words.

Just as he began to hope he'd suffered the last of it, the next wave struck, harder than before. His virtual inner ear spun like a whirligig, and he hunched over, vomit searing its way up his throat from his abused stomach. Vaguely, he was aware that Chelsea was holding a sick bag in place; he clutched at it like a lifeline as he began to empty out his stomach.

From then on, he found no respite between the bouts of shattering disorientation, only varying degrees of sensory unpleasantness. This was worse than a dozen maglev sideways-flips, worse than a hundred Spire elevators all going from zero to ninety in one-tenth of a second. They came at him mercilessly, each crest of eyeball-imploding discombobulation twisting his guts like wringing out a dirty dishrag before starting all over again.

He threw up everything he'd eaten that day, and he was pretty sure he was starting on Monday's intake when the unending assault … ended. Still, he kept heaving until his Prodigy nature reasserted his natural equilibrium, and he gradually became aware of Chelsea rubbing circles on his back.

Keeping the now somewhat-full sick bag ready for any resurgences, he blew each nostril clear in turn, then hawked and spat the horrible taste of bile out of his mouth. Chelsea wordlessly handed him a tissue and he blew his nose properly, still working on getting his heart rate back under control.

After a full minute passed and nothing else had happened, he sat back gingerly in his seat, sipping air between his teeth. Chelsea took the used sick bag from him and handed it to Caroline, who gave Jericho a professional *'hope-you-feel-better'* smile and swapped it for a couple of new bags. She made her way back down the aisle, and Chelsea handed her Dr. Pepper to Jericho.

"Here," she said. "See if this settles your stomach."

Gratefully cradling it in both hands, he took a mouthful of the sugary beverage, then swilled it around and spat it into a new bag that Chelsea was holding open. That got the worst of the taste out of his mouth, and he took a good drink this time. It fizzed all the way down his throat and seemed to soothe the turmoil in his stomach. "Thanks. That's better."

She nodded in acknowledgment as she rolled over the top of the newly used bag. "No problem. Keep it. So, what just happened? You're about the last person in the world I'd expect to get airsick."

He knew nobody was sitting within easy earshot of them, but he lowered his voice anyway. "That wasn't airsickness. Remember what I said in the motel room about Jefferson City? Like that, but times a thousand."

Chelsea's reply was a whisper. "You're feeling gravity waves again?"

He nodded. "Yeah. But stronger, this time. A lot stronger."

She frowned. "Okay, I'm going to assume that's bad. What do you think's making it happen?"

"I … I don't know for sure, but it's gotta be a quake of *some* kind. The Jefferson waves weren't as strong, and they didn't just keep coming." He frowned, worried. "Whatever this is leading up to, it's *big*."

"How big?" She stared at him. "Any idea of the power of it?"

"Yeah. Well, no, not really. Just that these pulses were hella stronger. I'm kinda surprised nobody else on the plane felt them."

"I'm a little queasy, but that could just be from watching you say hi to breakfast again." She wrinkled her nose. "Your power probably magnified the effect somehow. Any idea where or when? Maybe we can warn them."

He refrained from his head, not wanting to start the nausea up all over again. "No idea. It's like I'm Hollywood's idea of a Native American, right? One ear to the ground, listening to the bison stampeding. But I don't know if they're going north, south, east, or west; or if they're about to thunder over the hill from behind me and turn me into prairie pizza."

Chelsea nodded in acknowledgment. "Gotcha. So, do you know where these gravity pulses are coming from? Or does every earthquake come with them, and we've just never known it until now?"

"No, these are deliberate. Quakes happen worldwide, and I've never felt pulses like that before today. It's definitely something new."

"Okay." She lowered her voice even more. "So, I guess Seismic *is* still in the picture, along with Singularity. Like you said, he does earthquakes. Are we going to have to figure out where *he* fits in on all this now?"

Jericho grimaced. "Not right now. My brain's still rattling around like birdshot in a Coke can."

"Understood." Chelsea nodded sympathetically. "As soon as we land, remind me to check the news. If those gravity pulses affected you as badly as all that, *somewhere* is in for a world of hurt."

"Yeah. Let me know when we're getting close." Jericho finished the can off and stowed it in the seat pocket. Then he turned side-on, cushioning his head against the seat-back. Closing his eyes, he breathed steadily, trying to recapture the comfortable lassitude he'd had before the gravity waves destroyed his rest.

"Sure, I can do that." From the creaking sound of the other seat, Chelsea was doing much the same.

The rumble of the aircraft, along with the tiny bumps of turbulence, were as far from the smooth, silent passage of the maglev as he could imagine. But the plane was traveling at least as fast as the high-tech train, and he doubted the villains hunting him had any idea where he was.

If they can't find me, they can't stop me.

"Question," he murmured, not bothering to open his eyes.

"Yeah?" he heard from behind him.

"Why didn't we take a super-first flight? I mean, we could've just said no to anything they offered."

"Anyone who flies super-first, their pics go up on social media," she replied. "They like to advertise how many people are enjoying their services. It's part of the experience."

He frowned. "I've never seen anything like that on social media."

"That's because you don't go on the sites where they post that sort of thing." She chuckled. "Don't sweat it. It's very much an acquired taste."

"Right." His question had been answered, and he'd learned something new in the bargain. "Thanks."

"No problem."

He settled down once more, though something still felt a little off. After a few moments, he figured it out. '*Walking from LA to New York*', as the comedian in the back row had famously put it, was something he'd become used to doing; its absence made the flight just a little stranger than it might typically have been. On a standard maglev trip, he would've usually had to get up and move forward at least once by now.

Then, just as he was drifting off, the world lurched again. "Goddamn it," he grumbled as he shifted his position and reached into the seat pocket for a sick bag. "Not *another* one."

"Jericho!" The concern in Chelsea's voice was shading into actual fear. "That's not you! That's the plane!"

Snapping his eyes open, he sat up and looked around, then found he was leaning with his elbow against the side wall of the aircraft. Out the window, over the top of the wing, he saw what should've been stars in the night sky, but he recognized as lights along a highway. An orange glow danced on the wing; leaning forward, he saw flames shooting out of the engine exhaust on that side. Up and down the plane, people were crying out in terror as they struggled to stay in their seats.

"Crap. I need my fanny pack, quick!" The queasiness had vanished under a flood of adrenaline. Unclipping his lap strap, he eyed the gap between Chelsea and the seat in front. "'Scuse, please. Coming through."

She didn't ask why; instead, she tilted her seat back, increasing the separation. An instant of concentration reduced his effective weight, then he leaped up past her. The aisle—less than two feet across at best—was ridiculously narrow from this angle. Crouching with one foot on the side of the seat, the other braced against the aisle-facing armrest, and his shoulder leaning against the headrest of the opposite seat, he popped open the locker. The lid refused to rise of its own accord, so he manually lifted it out of the way. Leaning forward, he reached in for her backpack.

As his fingers brushed it, the plane lurched again with a deep groan, rolling back toward an even keel. Amidst the screams and shouts, he heard the bang as the front emergency exit door blew away from the aircraft, followed by a horrendous whistling shriek.

Oh, come on. Really?

This wasn't actually a fatal problem, merely an irritating one; once the air pressure equalized, it would become freezing cold and noisy, but nothing worse than that. The action-movie scenario of people being sucked (or rather, blown) *en masse* out of the hole would never eventuate.

For a moment, he thought the plane was leveling out, but it kept going toward the other side as he hung onto the edge of the open bin, his feet braced against the side and top of the seat. Again, he tried for the backpack, only for it to literally slide out on top of him as the plane continued to roll. He snagged it with his free hand, then dropped his feet to the armrest and headrest of the middle seat in the opposite row.

Despite his power-assisted sense of balance—he *always* knew which way was down, and how to lean to compensate—the rotating frame of reference required him to hang on with one hand until stable footing presented itself. When it finally came, the plane was fully inverted. He slung the backpack over his shoulder to free up one hand, then threw a couple of glue-tags at the overhead (now underfoot) and dropped his feet onto them.

Hands now free, he opened the backpack and delved in it for his fanny pack. There was a lot more in there than he'd expected, and he was still rummaging when the plane took on a sudden nose-down corkscrewing motion. Caroline, who'd been coming along the aisle to check on passengers, cried out as she began to tumble back toward the front of the aircraft.

"Hit the big red button!" He was mostly upside down again, but he slapped the backpack into Chelsea's hands anyway. Desperately hoping she'd heard him—there was only one thing in his fanny-pack with a big red button on it—he detached his feet from the aircraft ceiling, kicked off from a seat-back, and arrowed in pursuit of the errant flight attendant.

If the emergency exit had been still closed or the plane had chosen to roll right instead of left, she would've been fine, if a little bruised. But the malevolent gods of chance and fate decreed otherwise. Even from where he was, Jericho could see she was heading for the open doorway as surely as a pool shark can place the black in the corner pocket without even looking.

While he couldn't speed himself up, he could slow Caroline down. His G-tags were invisible in the intermittent emergency lighting, but he wouldn't have hesitated if it were broad daylight; throwing one push-tag after the other, he sought to glean the slightest edge in the race against death. They struck her, and she slowed, but not by enough or even close to it.

He was still five yards away when she reached the doorway. Her shriek was drowned out by the howling of the wind and the roar of the jet turbines, but he saw her hands clutch desperately at the frame as the turbulence pulled her out. Just for an instant, her nails dragged on the textured plastic, leaving eight long gouges in their wake …

… and that instant was just long enough for Jericho to catch up. His left hand, fully loaded with a glue-tag, slapped onto the door-frame and stuck there. Thus braced, he swung around the frame, reaching for her. His hand closed around her wrist just as she lost her own grip.

For a moment, the tableau was stable; Jericho was half-in, half-out of the plane with the wind screaming around him, tearing at his clothes and trying to rip Caroline's wrist free of his grip. She locked her gaze onto his, her expression pleading with him to not let her go. He stared back, trying to reassure her with his eyes.

I failed Stephen.

I failed Scout.

That shit does not *get to happen three times in a row.*

The freezing wind tore at her, trying to loosen his grip, but he was having none of it. Drawing on his newly formed resolve, he began to pull her in. As he'd proven by lifting the steel girders just that morning, when a prodigy decided on a goal, it took more than mere bodily limits to dissuade them. Inch by tortuous inch, braving the insane slipstream, throwing his defiance into the very teeth of Death itself, he hauled her back toward safety.

Right up until the plane tilted to the left again and the drinks cart broke free, hurtling toward him.

His G-sense warned him a split second before impact, and he was faced with a fatal dilemma. Let go, jump clear, and let Caroline fall to her death … or maintain his grip and go out the door.

It was a very simple choice. To put it another way, it was no choice at all.

He went out the door.

His left hand was still braced on the door-frame, stuck firmly there with all the glue-tags he could muster. Just ahead of the onrushing metal cart, he loosened the glue-tags to let himself slide farther around the frame.

Howling like a thousand banshees, the slipstream hit him with the impact of a Mack truck on steroids. It slammed him against the side of the plane as the cart went past, but he maintained his grip on Caroline's wrist. He'd taken this on; by God and all His angels, he would see it through.

As the plane lurched, pulling skyward once more and rolling over, he felt his grip on the door-frame slip, then slip again. Frantically, he pushed more glue-tags out through his palm, but the slipstream was dragging them inexorably away from the door, the bandages shredding from his hand.

The only reason they hadn't been flung free altogether, he figured, was the aerodynamic field he'd discovered when flying with Scout. Lacking his harness, it wasn't as effective as before, but he'd take what he could get. Unfortunately, it was about the only thing going their way right then.

On his own, he might have let go and done his best to skydive to a relatively soft landing, though from over ten thousand feet in the air, that was a long shot at best. With someone else, this just wasn't going to happen.

There was only one way they were both going to survive this, and that required he have a free hand. Unfortunately, his left hand was the only thing keeping them attached to the airliner, and his right was securely locked onto Caroline's wrist. Lacking a third arm, he was going to have to get creative.

He drew Caroline toward him with all the upper-body strength he could muster, fighting the slipstream for every inch of progress. Even attenuated by the field, it was a monster that roared and shrieked and did its best to tear them both free of the plane. Once he judged she was far enough up, his legs locked around her torso to secure her in place. Lacking time to form a sufficiently strong glue-tag for the purpose, he had to rely on his muscular strength alone to maintain his hold on her.

By the time he let go of her hand, she already had one arm around his body; the other joined it shortly after. He reached with his now-free right hand to his ear, where Chelsea's radio earpiece still sat. Clicking it on, he hastily grabbed Caroline again before she could slip out of his hold.

Drawing in a deep breath of the icy air, he shouted as loudly as possible. "Emergency exit! Emergency exit!" There was no way he would hear any reply—he only knew he was making noise at all from the vibration in his larynx—but he had to hope she had heard and was responding.

The plane angled over again, marginally changing the direction the slipstream was coming from. Their bodies lifted away from the fuselage then slammed back down again, and he felt the soft *pop-pop-pop* as his stitches parted, one by one. Fighting against the agony that flooded through his body, he gritted his teeth, concentrating on maintaining his grasp on the woman's wrist and his ever more tenuous grip on the outside of the aircraft.

"Emergency exit!" he yelled over and over. Chelsea was the only one who could save them now.

Seams slid by under his desperately grasping fingers. First, one side of the over-wing exit; then, the other. "Over-wing exit!" he screamed.

Whether she'd just now heard him or she'd been having trouble locating him, he wasn't sure. But a few seconds after they slid beyond the hatch, it opened. The hatch itself vanished into the aircraft, and Chelsea's head appeared, her shocked expression mainly illuminated by the flickering flames from the engine and the blinking wingtip navigation light.

She shouted something that he didn't hear—his basic lip-reading skills interpreted it as *hold on*—and sent a length of her hyperweave costume snaking down the side of the plane after him. It wrapped around his wrist and sealed itself in place, but when he slipped backward again, all it could do was stretch. The material strength to even hold him in place simply wasn't there; pulling him back into the aircraft was right out. The hyperweave unwound itself from his wrist and returned to her. He clung to the side of the airliner as he waited for her next move.

She's got a plan. She's always got a plan.

He saw her lips move, but the words were too complicated and the flickering light too dim for him to figure it out before she vanished again. He figured she was fetching seat belts, or maybe she had a bunch of climbing gear in her backpack. Whatever it was, he hoped she would hurry it up; his stomach was really starting to hurt.

They slipped once more, and he felt the world going hazy. His body was starting to shut down; once he passed out altogether, his glue-tags would dissolve. He and Caroline would both fall to their deaths, and there wasn't a damn thing he could do about it.

Goddamn it, can't I get one thing right?

The ghostly punch on his shoulder could only have come from Luke.

Hang on, cuz. Don't you dare wuss out on me yet.

Can't help it, Luke. No way out.

Don't you goddamn say that to me! You're a cowl! There's always a way out!

That's prodigy, not cowl. Get it right.

Yeah, yeah. Whatever, cuz. Just keep fighting. You ain't done yet.

Emboldened by the Luke-style pep talk, he set his teeth and kept fighting. His grip on Caroline's wrist, which had been slipping, tightened again. He concentrated and slowed their slide along the plane's outer skin. Through sheer stubbornness, he forced back the darkness encroaching around the edges of his vision.

Damn right. I'm not done yet.

Suddenly, Caroline's weight vanished, though he still held her wrist. He looked down toward her, just in time to see her being hauled sideways ...

... *into* the plane.

A moment later, a broad strap wrapped around his waist and a familiar pair of hands dragged him part-way into what he belatedly realized was the rear emergency exit of the aircraft.

"—et *in* here, goddamn it!" Once his head was out of the direct slipstream, he immediately recognized Chelsea's voice on the earpiece.

He helped her as best he could, crawling into the airliner with the last of his waning strength. Once he was inside, he collapsed onto his back, unable to move. Though rough and threadbare, the carpet was more welcome than the softest of feather beds.

He was safe for now, which meant he didn't have to hold on anymore. The remnants of the glue-tags evaporated from his fingertips.

As consciousness faded away and his eyes drifted shut, he thought he saw a violet flare rocket past the open doorway.

Oh, good. Thomas is here.

57
Five Minutes to Midnight

Aboard the Team Power Jet
Just North of Louisville, KY
Airspeed Mach 3.2, Heading 335°, Altitude 51,000 feet
Four Minutes Ago

Adam Power

The airspace was clear at this altitude; only military aircraft usually flew this high, and there were no IFF beacons registering on the jet's radar. Tesseract had the controls as the better all-around pilot, while Adam handled navigation. After instructing the jet's sensors to alert him if anything looked like encroaching on their flight path, he resumed his study of the PowerTech MobilityPlus Three Thousand specs (patent pending) via his neuro-induction display.

Originally, Adam and Tesseract had suggested that Thomas' cover story be that he'd joined Team Power to stand in for Vanessa when she was unavailable. Thomas had flat-out nixed that; if the public couldn't handle a genderfluid superhero, that was their problem, not his. So far, according to online polls, the bold approach seemed to be working.

Vanessa's suit had been entirely redesigned from the ground up, to adjust for their shape-changing physiology. It featured the same onboard weaponry as before, but it presented a different profile and paint job depending on whether Vanessa or Thomas was wearing it. The engineering challenges inherent in upgrading the suit in this way had led directly to the development of what Adam called the 'adaptive artificial neuron'.

Incorporating the latest iteration of the AAN into the base model of the PowerTech mobility frame had improved its synthetic proprioception and reduced the reaction time by an average of four-point-nine percent, which was good. However, when he'd tested the setup himself, he suffered headaches after just a few minutes.

There's got to be a feedback loop somewhere in there. I just need to isolate and eliminate it.

"I was looking forward to seeing the fireworks," Buddy groused from the back seat. "The volunteers said they were gonna have some amazing ones this year."

"Forget the fireworks," Vanessa interrupted from beside her brother. "*I* was looking forward to seeing Jericho again. But he wasn't there. *And* his phone was turned off. All I had was that one text. Promising to come back.

But he *didn't.*"

"Probably hiding from you," jeered Buddy. "I know *I* would."

Right on cue, she flared up in response. "Don't you even—!"

"Pipe down, both of you," ordered Tesseract before the argument could escalate. "Vanessa, we all know he wasn't hiding from you. He adores you. Personally, I think he fully intended to return, but was ordered to stay because of whatever's happening back there. If he was directed to maintain comms lockdown, you *know* he would've complied."

"But why couldn't you leave me there instead of picking me up early?" asked Buddy. "*We* don't live in Utopia City."

"No. We don't." From the clipped tone of her voice, Tesseract was choosing her words carefully. "But whatever affects Utopia City has a chance of affecting us. And they've gone into *total* lockdown over the last couple of hours. Nobody in, nobody out. My backchannel sources tell me that a core member's been attacked, maybe even killed. If someone can do that to Force Majeure, they might come after us next. So, we're regrouping and ensuring our defenses are secure, just in case. And *that* means—"

An audible alarm sounded in Adam's helmet, red flaring in his NID. Dumping the mobility frame file back into storage, he concentrated on the origin of the alert. If it was an incursion into Power Plaza like the one that had nearly cost them Vanessa, the intruder would be *very* sorry indeed ...

"What's going on, hon?" Tesseract's voice sounded tense but calm. "Is it the Plaza?"

"No, thank God," Adam informed everyone at once, flicking through menus in his NID. "One of our emergency signal beacons just activated." Data windows unscrolled in his mind's eye, and he scanned them rapidly. "It's the one I gave Jericho."

Vanessa's icon popped up in Adam's mental display as she linked her NID to his. "Where is he? Is he okay?"

Adam pulled the relevant information out of his display and sent it to Tesseract's headspace. "He's two hundred seventy-three miles northwest of here, doing three-fifty knots at twenty thousand feet altitude. Heading and altitude are changing erratically, as though he's out of control." He blinked as a separate notification popped up. "Air traffic control lost contact with a passenger jet in that airspace sixty seconds ago. He must be on it."

Tesseract never hesitated. "Open me a lane, hon. We're going after him." In just a few seconds, the jet's massive engines went from cruising speed to full afterburner, as she banked it onto the new heading. Strictly speaking, the plane didn't burn jet fuel, so it didn't use 'afterburners' as such, but it was a usefully descriptive term. Adam felt the pressure on his back from the gel-cushion seats as they accelerated across the sky.

"On it." He opened all the relevant comm channels and began warning flight control towers on their path that they *would* be coming through, appending their approximate altitude, speed, and heading. Nobody argued; nor did he expect them to. There was too much on the line.

This was the first time they'd had warning of an airliner going down with enough leeway for them to make a difference. Every other time, there'd been no Mayday calls, only a loss of contact. When retrieved and played back, the cockpit voice recorders showed the aircrew attempting to call for help but to no avail. Loss of power in the cockpit was a common theme among these playbacks. All of those jets had gone down hard, with all passengers and crew killed on impact.

Not this time. Not on our watch.

Adam checked again with the distress signal. It was still in the air, but the altitude was changing rapidly as though the plane was corkscrewing out of control. With that kind of erratic flying, it wouldn't be airborne for much longer.

Three minutes later, they were covering ground at more than a mile every second, lancing through the night sky with a long violet thruster-wake behind them. "Talk to me," Tesseract said. "Where is he?"

"Still in the air," Adam reported, feeding her the latest heading correction. "Fifteen thousand feet, three hundred knots. More erratic, less control. We'll be overflying it in thirty. Kids!"

"Yeah?" they asked in unison, their differences put aside.

"We'll be bailing out in twenty. You each take a wing and try to stabilize it. I'll head for the cockpit. Fifteen. Fourteen. Thirteen."

At 'ten', the seat he was occupying snapped clamps over his arms and legs, then rotated forward into the aperture that had slid open before him. He didn't have to look back to know the same was happening with Buddy and Vanessa. The ejection mechanism, holding his suit prone and face-down, motored downward until the only thing between him and the four-thousand-miles-per-hour slipstream was a single hatch.

The readout in his neuro-induction display had taken over from his spoken recital of the countdown. **5**, it read in his mind's eye.

He brought his suit to full readiness, linking with the jet's sensors and locating the stricken passenger jet.

4

His thrusters came online.

3

He triggered them, letting his drive-wash blast out through a vent set up expressly for the purpose.

2

"Ready ..."

1

"Set ..."

The hatch below him opened.

"Launch!"

Throwing his arms forward, he fell out into the night air. The plane was just a handful of miles ahead, but he was traveling far too fast to be able to help those on board. Accordingly, he rolled into a somersault and triggered a full-throttle burn. The G-suit inside the armor locked around his legs and lower body as he decelerated as hard as the thrusters would allow. He knew Tesseract would be doing much the same, but while the Team Power jet had the wherewithal to pull the same kind of high delta-V burn the suits were, it was harder to do so with the same level of finesse.

He'd just dropped below Mach 1 when he saw the passenger plane pass by under him; partly because it was visible on his radar and ladar, and partly because one engine was trailing flames. This was not a good look for anything that wanted to stay in the air. At the same time, he saw twin thruster trails curving around to match its trajectory; the kids, being lighter in their suits, had managed to decelerate more quickly.

"See if you can get it straightened out," he called back to them. "I'll be with you in a minute."

"What do we do about the engine fire?" asked Buddy. "Also, all the emergency exits are open on the port side."

"Let's just focus on flying the plane for the moment," Vanessa suggested. "We'll deal with the rest of it when we can."

"Okay, got it," her brother agreed. "I'm at the port wing, behind the engine strut. It's trying to roll right. I can't stop it."

"It's all good." She sounded entirely unruffled. "I'm under the starboard wing now. Applying corrective thrust. Let me know if I go too far."

"You won't," Buddy replied. "Ailerons are full down on this side. It really, really wants to roll your way."

"Well, it's not going to get what it wants." Vanessa's voice was sounding a little more clipped. "Damn, this thing's creaking up a storm."

Coming up behind, Adam could see how the wing she was supporting actually had a slight bend in it as whoever—or *whatever*—was controlling the plane's systems did its best to corkscrew the entire thing into the ground at three hundred miles per hour.

He matched speeds until he was flying alongside the forward open doorway, then grabbed the edge of the opening and swung himself inside, careful to cut his thrusters before they could blow a hole in the floor. **"Team Power!"** he announced over his external speakers. **"Everyone, stay calm and remain in your seats! We've got this!"**

Tromping over to the cockpit door, he considered knocking but figured it would take too long for the aircrew to respond. So instead, he drove the fingers of his armored gauntlet into the gap between the door and its frame, ripped it open, and pushed it to one side. Two wide-eyed faces looked back at him.

"Team Power," he repeated, not as loudly. **"I'm here to help. Hands off the controls, please."**

"You have the aircraft, sir," said the guy in the left-hand seat, lifting his hands clear of the steering yoke. "We've been doing everything we can to stay in the air, but it's fighting us and winning."

"Let's just see about that, shall we?" Adam's suit was far too bulky to fit into either the pilot's or first officer's chair without serious readjustment, but he didn't need to sit down for this. Reaching out his right hand, he placed it on the cockpit wall, next to a row of switches.

If he'd had time to prepare for this mission, he would've equipped the suit with an auxiliary avionics computer that he could plug straight into the jetliner's systems and bring them back online so the pilots could bring the plane home. Lacking that, he would have to wing it … so to speak.

Okay, let's see what we're dealing with.

Built into the palm of his right-hand gauntlet was an advanced superconducting quantum interference device, containing some upgrades of his own devising. Aptly named the SQUID Plus, it could connect to computers at a distance and wriggle its digital tentacles past just about any commercially available security software; just the thing to find out what was going on.

Once his hand made contact, he activated the SQUID Plus and let it do its thing. The firewall around the avionics was as pitiful as he'd expected, and he waited to see the controls laid out before him in electronic format. Instead, what he found was shrieking madness. Any inputs from the aircrew were being overridden in seconds, the readouts on the console were pure hash, and random commands were being sent to the flight surfaces.

"Incoming, on your six." That was Tesseract. "Honey, I don't mean to rush you, but there are stress fractures developing in the starboard wing."

A mental impulse flicked him from external speakers to radio comms. "On it." They could deal with an engine fire, but the entire wing parting with the plane would dial the emergency level up past eleven.

Return ailerons to normal flight mode.

Ailerons returned to normal flight mode.

Okay. So far, so good. Now, let's …

Ailerons set for hard left roll. Elevators set for maximum climb. Flaps on full. Lower undercarriage.

He staggered at the sudden deceleration, bracing his left hand on the back of the first officer's seat, which creaked alarmingly.

Return ailerons to normal flight mode. Set elevators to one-degree climb. Flaps off. Retract undercarriage.

Ailerons returned to normal flight mode. Elevators set to one-degree climb. Flaps off. Undercarriage retracting.

This time, he didn't relax as it obeyed his commands. Instead, he watched to see where the next anomalous command would come from.

Port engine to full power. Starboard engine to full reverse thrust.

The left-hand engine, he knew, was the one that was already on fire. Putting it to full thrust wouldn't do it any good at all. Before either command could go through, he countermanded them. **Starboard engine, fifty percent thrust. Ailerons, ten-degree bank to starboard. Rudder, ten-degree starboard turn. Port engine, trigger fire extinguisher.**

The plane staggered in the air, crabbing across the sky as the asymmetrical engine thrust fought against the control surface settings. But the fire extinguisher triggered as Adam had ordered it to, which was a profound relief.

"Tess, sensors tell me the fire's out, but I need a visual."

"That's an affirmative, hon. Fire in the port engine has been extinguished."

"Thanks." He breathed a sigh of relief. **Restart port engine.**

Port engine restarting ... port engine restarted ... Elevators set to maximum climb. Starboard engine to zero thrust.

"Oh, *no*, you don't," he snarled. That little trick would've upset the precarious balance he was maintaining, and stalled the aircraft straight into the ground. **Port engine to ninety percent. Starboard engine to ninety percent. Ailerons, elevators, and rudder to level flight.**

Ailerons to hard starboard turn. Rudder to hard port turn.

Ailerons to level flight. Rudder to midline.

Lower landing gear. Flaps to full. Elevators to max climb.

Elevators to level flight. Raise landing gear. Retract flaps.

This was getting ridiculous. "Tess! I need specs for the flight computer in this type of plane. Where's it located, exactly?"

"Sending specs over now." Tesseract's voice sounded tense but steady.

Two seconds later, during which time he overrode yet another attempt by the plane to crash itself, the wireframe arrived in his NID. Querying the three-dimensional layout, he located the component he was seeking, and matched it to what he saw. There was just one problem.

"You, in the right-hand seat!" he snapped, bringing the external speakers back into play. **"Out of your seat, now! Both of you, cover your eyes, now-now-now!"** Raising his left arm, he pulled his wrist back in a snapping motion, causing a query to pop up in his neuro-induction display.

Haptic trigger detected. Deploy under-arm laser? Y/N

Selecting a positive response caused the laser to slide out of its protective housing, which probably caused the first officer to vacate his seat just a little bit faster than he usually would have. Adam had the option for a snap-shot, but that was at relatively low power, so he spent the half-second charging the capacitor for a high-powered shot.

As if it could detect what was coming next, the rogue flight computer issued a positive flood of commands, but it was too late; he had a clear line of fire.

He triggered the laser.

The actinic blue beam seared clean through the first officer's seat, took part of the control yoke with it, and bored into the control panel. An instant later, it burst out into clear air through the nose of the airliner. On the way through, it intercepted the central processing unit of the flight computer and rendered it into partially vaporized slag.

Adam shut down the laser and told the suit to put it away, then regained control of the aircraft. Half the readouts on the control panel were dead, and the other half were still displaying nonsensical data, but at least the plane wasn't actively trying to crash itself anymore. **"Sorry about the mess. There was something seriously wrong with your flight computer."**

"That's ... uh, that's quite all right," the pilot said with a careful nod. "What happens now?"

Adam sighed. **"Well, as I've just removed the thing that normally would've allowed you to fly this plane, I'm going to have to pilot you down to O'Hare myself. Don't worry, though. They won't be billing you for the damage."**

"Dad!" It was Vanessa, calling over the comms. "I've found Jericho! He's here, but he's hurt!"

He set the plane to cruise straight and level while he answered. "How badly hurt? What happened to him?"

"Chelsea's here too! She says he was stabbed!" Vanessa sounded almost frantic. "He's bleeding through his bandages! We've got to help him!"

Chelsea? Adam didn't remember the name, but he figured he'd find out who she was later. "Okay, fly him over to the jet. We'll get him back to Power Plaza and let the autodoc take care of him." Because there was nobody with formal medical training on the team (though Tesseract was a competent field medic), he'd designed and constructed a robotic surgeon capable of handling virtually any medical emergency. A stab wound should be small potatoes for it. "Tess, you got that?"

His wife's voice responded immediately. "Roger that, hon. Vanessa, the belly hatch will be open for you and Jericho."

"Copy that, Mom. Uh, Dad ... Chelsea wants to come too. She says it's urgentmost that she speaks to all of us, as soon as possible. That's a direct quote. The phrase *'national emergency'* came up, too."

Adam closed his eyes for a moment, marshaling his thoughts. "Okay, fine. Buddy, you take Chelsea over to the jet, then come back. I'll need you to make sure the passengers are okay while I'm flying this beast through to O'Hare. Vanessa, you go back to the base with your mom and Jericho, and make sure your friend doesn't get into anything she shouldn't. All understood?"

"Buddy here, understood. Out."

"Vanessa here, understood. Out."

"Tess here, roger. Out."

"Good. Make it happen. Adam, out."

Opening his eyes, Adam set the aircraft transponder to squawk 7700 — emergency — and activated the plane's radio. "O'Hare International, O'Hare International, this is Adam Power transmitting on GUARD, declaring an in-flight emergency. We have a damaged jetliner that I'm flying in by hand and eye, so any assistance in getting this broken bird on the ground in one piece would be greatly appreciated ..."

58
A Gathering of Strength

Big Pine Campground
Westchester County, New York State
January 29, 2014
04:47 Eastern Daylight Time

Early the Next Morning

When Jericho awoke, he drifted for a few moments in a gradually dispersing haze of euphoria. Nothing really mattered; not the dull ache in his midsection, not the plane that had been going down out of control when he'd last been awake, not even the fact that he *still* wasn't back in his own bed. Then, very respectfully, his hindbrain ventured forward and reminded him that it might be a good idea to be concerned about some or all of these things.

"I know you're awake," Thomas' voice, rich with amusement, murmured from beside him. "Your breathing just changed."

Jericho's eyes rolled open, and he turned his head to see his boyfriend lying alongside him, observing him with a fond smile. He didn't bother saying anything; instead, he pushed back the blanket covering him, gathered Thomas into his arms, and let his embrace do it for him. Thomas' arms went around him as well, and they held each other tightly. He shivered with enjoyment as he felt his boyfriend's lips nibbling at his neck. It had been far, *far* too long since they'd had the chance to be intimate with one another.

Pulling back slightly, he kissed Thomas fiercely, then held him tightly again. "Hey," he murmured, his voice muffled against cloth and skin.

"Hey yourself." Thomas' breath was warm against his neck. "How are you feeling?"

"Not great, but a whole lot better now that you're here." Jericho snuggled a little deeper into Thomas' embrace for emphasis. "How badly off was I?"

"It's good to see you, too." Thomas rubbed his cheek against Jericho's. "Your gymnastics outside the plane popped all your stitches and exacerbated the original injury. Fortunately, Dad's autodoc was able to fix the damage. What happened to your hair?"

Jericho smiled in the dimness. "Lost my comb. Had to make do. Like it?"

"It's an acquired taste. Did you really get stabbed by *Charnel*?"

"Yeah, I did. So, I'm guessing Chelsea told you guys everything?"

"Just about, yeah." Thomas shuddered. "I can't imagine what it would be like to just face a terror villain out of the blue like that."

Jericho pulled back a little to better see his face in the dim light. "Didn't Chelsea tell you? You already have."

"What?" Thomas frowned. "What do you mean?"

"The guy who attacked you, pretending to be your dad?" Jericho raised his eyebrows. "We're pretty sure that was False Flag." More of his brain kicked into gear, and another penny dropped. "And I bet it was Tourbillon who helped him infiltrate Power Plaza and pulled him out again. You know, Guillotine."

"Oh, right, yeah. Chelsea told us about False Flag being Independence, but I was too worried about you to connect all the dots. Mom is pissed as *hell*." Thomas heaved a worried sigh. "What's it all mean? Where does it end?"

"I dunno, but I think we're going to find out pretty soon, one way or the other." Jericho looked around at himself and his surroundings for the first time. He was wearing a light jacket over a T-shirt, as well as jeans and socks. The mattress he and Thomas were lying on was comfortable, but there wasn't much room to either side or above them. Nor were there any windows that he could see. "Uh … where *are* we?"

"The family van," Thomas explained. "It's for places the jet can't go or when we don't want to draw Team Power levels of attention."

"And where's the van?" asked Jericho patiently. "I'm pretty sure I wouldn't have been left to wake up inside a vehicle if we were still parked inside Power Plaza."

"Yeah, sorry. Good point." Thomas reached around behind himself and grabbed a door handle Jericho hadn't spotted until then. With a grunt of effort, he slid it open to reveal darkness and firelit trees; a wave of chilly air rolled in. "We're in upstate New York. Mom didn't want to move you after the surgery, but Chelsea insisted on bringing you along. She said, and I quote, '*There's a good chance we'll need him for the next stage of the plan*'. So, I volunteered to wait with you while you recovered." His frown was barely visible in the dimness. "You wouldn't happen to know what this grand plan is, would you?"

"All I know is, Chelsea never has just one plan," Jericho grumbled. "Why upstate New York?"

"She wouldn't tell us that, either." Thomas sat up and swiveled his butt around to drop his legs over the side of the open doorway. "C'mon. Let's put our boots on and go tell everyone you're up. Maybe then we can get some answers." To illustrate his point, he held up two pairs of boots that had apparently been sitting on the floor of the van, alongside the mattress.

Jericho's head had cleared somewhat with the influx of cold air. "Sounds like a good idea to me."

It took a little work to get his legs around without using his stomach muscles—he'd learned his lesson there—but he managed to get the boots on with only a little assistance from Thomas. They fitted perfectly, which somehow didn't surprise him. Sliding to the ground, he found his knees to be unexpectedly wobbly. "Jeez, how long was I out?"

"Mom said you were beat all to hell and back, and needed time to rest and heal. You've been asleep for the best part of ten hours."

Thomas led him around the van, past an SUV he didn't recognize. A campfire crackled in a firepit among the trees not far away, with people sitting around it.

"Which means I definitely needed it," agreed Jericho. "Chelsea also told you how I got struck by lightning?"

"With sound effects," Thomas confirmed with an exaggerated eye-roll.

Jericho wasn't surprised. Even though it hadn't been funny at the time, he could see how some folks might see the humor in it. "Oh, by the way, Chelsea should have my fanny pack. Your handkerchief is in there, with the rest of my stuff."

"Right, thanks." Thomas paused. "You do realize that was originally *your* handkerchief, right?"

"It's *our* handkerchief," Jericho said firmly. "And I want you to hold it."

"Okay, just so long as we've got that cleared up."

As they neared the fire, Jericho counted nine people sitting around it. Some had folding chairs, others were seated on logs, and one girl was in an electric wheelchair. Of the ones he didn't recognize, all appeared to be in their mid to late teens, except one skinny kid of twelve or thirteen. Adam Power was discussing something with the blonde in the wheelchair and a young Asian woman with a pair of goggles pushed up on her forehead. Buddy was chatting to the skinny kid, a tall, lanky guy, and a teenage redhead with a garishly decorated helmet on his lap. Tesseract Power was playing cards with Chelsea, using a drinks cooler as a makeshift table.

"Chelsea called in the Survivors, didn't she?" While he'd phrased it as a question, he already knew the answer purely from the few clues he could see.

"I did, yes." Dropping her cards on the 'table', Chelsea stood up. "Next up in the deck are six, ten, jack, seven, five, nine," she added in an apparent non sequitur to Tesseract Power, then turned her attention back to Jericho. "You're looking better."

He nodded. "I'm definitely feeling better. How's Caroline? Is she okay?"

Taking several steps away from the fire, Chelsea stopped in front of Jericho. "She's going to need a ton of therapy, plus treatment for a wrenched shoulder and mild frostbite, but she'll be okay. *You*, on the other hand." She jabbed him painfully in the middle of the chest with a hard knuckle. "Seriously, what the hell? You scared me half to death when I saw you hanging off the side of the plane like that! *You can't fly anymore!*" The last four words were accompanied by four more jabs.

"Whoa, whoa," Thomas interjected, stepping halfway in between them. "Easy, there. Give him a break. He just woke up."

"It's okay," Jericho said. He took a deep breath of the freezing night air.

"Trust me, the whole time I was out there, I did not for one *second* fail to deeply regret my inability to fly."

Chelsea wasn't finished yet. "And yet, you jumped out of the plane to save her *anyway*. If I hadn't turned on my earpiece when I realized you were missing, you and she would *both* be dead. You do understand that, right?" She appeared to be feeling a particular emotion very strongly, but Jericho couldn't pin it down for the life of him. It wasn't precisely anger, though it seemed to be related. Maybe frustration?

"And if I hadn't made the effort, she *would* be dead right now, and I'd still be asking myself if I could've saved her," he answered candidly. He couldn't see any other way out of it.

"Heroes." She glowered at him, then let out her breath in a huff of white vapor. Turning, she headed back to her seat at the fire.

"Thanks for helping save her life, by the way," Jericho said to her back. "And mine, too."

"You're welcome." She sat down again, then patted the cooler. "Hungry? Thirsty? Want a marshmallow or a wiener to roast over the fire?" The abrupt shift in tone would've otherwise confused him, but he recognized the signs of *'done with this topic'*.

"Mainly hungry." He watched as Thomas picked up two more folding chairs from a stack and opened them out with swift, efficient movements. "Nothing to roast, though. Got sandwiches or something?"

"Yeah," offered the young woman in the wheelchair. She opened a second cooler and dug into it. "Carnivore or herbivore?"

At the mention of food, his stomach rumbled urgently. "Either. Both."

"Got it. One ham and lettuce, coming right up." She handed off the wrapped sandwich to the younger kid, at which point it ... vanished? The kid grinned at him.

His G-sense warned him of someone coming up behind, so he turned. Behind him was another kid, identical to the first, holding out the sandwich. "Here you go," the kid chirped.

Jericho blinked and took it. "Uh, thanks?"

"You're welcome," said the kid in front of him, and the one across the fire, in perfect unison.

"Ignore him," Thomas advised with a sigh. "He's been doing that ever since they got here. Jericho, you've only met Ray, haven't you?"

The lanky guy got up from where he'd been sitting on a log. "Hey. Been meaning to say thanks for a while now." He came around the fire and held out his hand. "Razor-Edge, or Ray for short, but you can call me Gareth."

As they shook hands, Jericho's memory finally clicked into place. "I remember you. You're the guy those cops were beating on at the Market that time."

Gareth grinned. "Yeah. I'll never forget how you tossed that one asshole in the canal. Saved me from doing something *everyone* woulda regretted, that's for damn sure."

"Well, I'm surely glad I did." If he hadn't, he wouldn't have met Thomas a third time, and gone on that memorable first date. "How're things with you?"

"Oh, good. Got a job, settled down. Occasionally go out and do the hero thing, y'know?" Gareth waggled his hand from side to side. "Nothing flashy. I keep my head down, but I try to make a difference. And thanks to Chelsea clearing our files, they've got no proof I was ever in Utopia."

"Good to hear." Jericho looked at the rest of the Survivors. "Sorry, I never learned y'all's names. It was better back then if I could say I didn't know who you were."

"True." Thomas waved his hand at the four people remaining. "That's Gimmick and Blades, talking Artificer stuff with Dad, the one with the dorky helmet is the Photonic Avenger, and you just met Sidestep."

Gimmick looked up from showing Adam Power what looked like a toy plastic rifle. At Jericho's best guess, this was the infamous Zarkinator. "Hey, good to meet you at last, G-Man. Call me Mel." Her goggles, Jericho could see, were the type used for welding or soldering, with flip-up lenses. He suspected a heads-up display; it was a common theme with artificers.

"My helmet is not dorky," groused the redhead. "But yeah, good to meet you. I'm Chuck."

"Is if we say it is," Blades said with a smirk. "Hi, Jericho. I'm Sarah. Thanks for getting us all out of Utopia, in case none of these other ingrates have said it."

"And I'm Paul," Sidestep said, once more in unison with himself. "We actually met outside the Oaklands, but you never saw me." He wiggled his fingers and lowered his voice dramatically. "'Cause I'm *sneeaaky*."

"Oh." Jericho recalled handing off the documentation to a figure in the shadows, but it was true; he'd never seen the kid's face. "It's good to meet y'all at last."

"Likewise," said Mel, slinging the possibly-Zarkinator over her back. "So, can *you* tell us why we're here? Thomas says he doesn't know, and Chelsea isn't talking."

Jericho considered the question as he carefully lowered himself into the folding chair. The expected twinge from his stomach never materialized, to his silent relief. "Well, yes and no. You've seen the footage? You're on board with the Force Majeure thing?"

"We saw two film clips," Mel said with a nod. "Thomas said we weren't old enough to watch the other one. But it didn't matter; the first two were bad enough."

Jericho nodded. "Yeah, they were."

"I still think I should've been able to watch the third one," Buddy said, apparently rehashing a previous argument. "Thomas an' Mom an' Dad got to. *I'm* a member of Team Power, too."

Jericho cleared his throat carefully. "It's not that. The file just proves that Tourbillon and Lady Quantum are Guillotine and Singularity." He shook his head. "I wish *I* hadn't watched it."

Sarah nodded. "I think I know what you mean. The Raider clip screwed with my head pretty badly, too. Mainly because I'm in it."

"What?" Jericho stared at her. Nobody else seemed to be concerned by her words, which only confused him further. "Where? How?"

She let her breath out slowly. "I used to live in Davenport. Mom and Dad and me were going to the movies, and our car got run over by the tank. I survived. They didn't. That's when I got my powers."

"Son of a … gun." Jericho glanced at Thomas, who gave him a fractional nod of acknowledgment. If he was reading things right, that made two of six Survivors who'd gotten their powers from terror villains via the Proximity Principle. Was this a pattern forming, or just coincidence? "I'm … I'm right sorry to hear that."

She gave him a grimace and a nod. "It is what it is, but thanks anyway."

"Okay, then." He took a deep breath. "I only just woke up myself, so I don't know Chelsea's *exact* plan, but I know it has to do with Force Majeure. I'm kind of in the dark about why we had to come to New England, though. Now that I'm up, maybe we could get the skinny on what's supposed to happen here?" With a questioning glance at Chelsea, he raised his eyebrows. "Well?"

"In good time." Chelsea drew an unhappy breath. "But before we go any further, you need to know something. We lost Gary Brock."

Despite himself, Jericho was startled. "What? He died? Was it a heart attack?" The guy had been bulky, but he hadn't looked actively unhealthy.

She shook her head. "No, I mean we *lost* him. Him and five others, they weren't on the plane when it landed. All sitting in the same area. Nobody saw what happened to them."

"But … the only ones up and around were me, you, and the flight attendant." The whole idea made exactly zero sense to Jericho. "After all that bouncing around, you think *anyone* would've gotten up to do *anything*?"

"Nevertheless." She shrugged. "I was curious after takeoff, so while you were napping, I asked the attendant how many were on board. She said seventy-nine. Once Adam got the plane down, Buddy counted them off onto the tarmac. He came up with seventy-three, *including* you, me, and the flight crew. So, he counted them again. Same number. Gary's one of the missing six."

Jericho considered that. He hadn't spent much time associating with Buddy, but the kid had impressed him all the same. It was doubtful that a child of Adam and Tesseract Power would make a rookie mistake like that twice in a row. Or even once, most times. "I'm damn sure I didn't miss someone falling out the door right in front of me. Especially *six* someones."

"They didn't," agreed Chelsea. "Fall out, I mean. I was between them and the open emergency exits the whole time. Thinking about it, when I went back to open the rear exit, Brock wasn't in his seat. Whatever happened, it must've been when I was trying to pull you back in from the over-wing exit."

He frowned. "Do we have names for any of the other missing passengers? Pictures? Anything at all?"

Chelsea shook her head. "Just Gary. Shoestring companies like Right Now make a point of letting people travel anonymously. It's *why* he was on the plane, after all."

This meant that not only had six people mysteriously vanished from the malfunctioning aircraft in mid-flight without anyone noticing, but only one would ever be identified. The rest would be stuck in a limbo where nobody knew to ask if they were missing, until their next of kin queried their absence. Their friends and families would go from worry to doubt to fear to certainty, and he wouldn't be able to do a damn thing to soften the blow for a single one of them. *This is going to suck for everyone involved.* "So, what do you reckon happened?"

"The only thing I can think of is a double Challenger event." She didn't sound at all convinced of what she was saying, but she continued with the explanation anyway. "If two of them ended up Enabled at the same time, and the Proximity Principle gave one of them a version of *your* abilities and the other one *my* powers, they *might've* joined forces to get those other people off the plane without being seen. Though have you ever heard of two people getting powers at the same time? Because I haven't."

Jericho was equally dubious—as Chelsea had pointed out, the notion had more holes than a Swiss cheese convention—but it was all they had to work with. "So you think they'll pop up again, looking for us?"

Chelsea frowned. "Why would they do that?"

"It's part of the Principle," Jericho explained. "If you got powers off someone, you're drawn back to them so your subconscious can decide whether they're an enemy or an ally."

"Huh." She raised an eyebrow, apparently conceding the point. "Well, I guess we'll just have to wait and see, then."

Jericho shared her evident concerns on the matter. However, as hard as it was to accept, he could personally do nothing to change anything on that front, so he decided to get the discussion back on track. "So, we were talking about what's supposed to happen next, yeah?"

At that moment, Chelsea's phone pinged. "One sec," she murmured as she glanced at the screen, then started tapping away at it.

Tesseract Power waited about ten seconds, then elbowed her in the arm. "What's supposed to happen here?"

Chelsea looked up. "Oh, uh, yeah. Just waiting on the last people to arrive." She hit another button on the phone, then slid it into her pocket. "They should be here in the next hour or so. Just needed some last-minute directions."

"Wait." Jericho looked around at the assembled people then at Thomas, sitting beside him. "Who else is coming? Who else do we know?"

Thomas shrugged and spread his hands wide. "I dunno. She made a lot of phone calls back when you were still in surgery." He nodded at the sandwich that Jericho was still holding. "Go ahead and chow down. Plenty more where that came from."

Jericho pulled the wrapping off the diagonally cut sandwich and bit into it hungrily. Ham, lettuce, and mayonnaise had never tasted so good; it seemed to vanish between one bite and the next. Thomas handed him a Coke, and he cracked it open, suddenly much thirstier than he'd thought he was.

He and Chelsea fielded questions from the Survivors about how they'd gotten out of Utopia in (more or less) one piece. His personal account of driving an eighteen-wheeler for the first time *ever* had Thomas and his friends howling with laughter, while Chelsea's description of how she'd gotten both him and Caroline back on board the plane brought them to the edges of their seats. By the end of the story, Thomas was holding his hand like he never meant to let go. Jericho was okay with that.

After a while, Chelsea and Tesseract took up the cards again and returned to their game. Except that it wasn't quite stud poker, as Jericho had learned to play at his mama's knee. As far as he could tell, each of them was doing her best to cheat without the other catching her, using their respective Prodigy talents to tip the odds one way or the other. Considering the hands they were ending up with, they *had* to be dealing seconds or holding out cards, but he was damned if he could catch either one of them at it.

It was nice sitting there in pleasant company, but Jericho found himself getting fidgety with nothing to draw his attention. A lot had happened in a very short time, and he needed to work his way through the ramifications of everything he'd learned. Still, he didn't want to abandon everyone — especially Thomas — around the fire and head off into the darkness.

"Go brood already," Chelsea said, not looking up from her cards.

"What?" he asked, startled out of his introspection.

"Brood," she repeated. "If you get any twitchier, you'll do yourself an injury. We don't have any tall buildings around here for you to brood from, but you've got your pick of trees. Go climb one, and get it out of your system."

"I, uh …" Jericho didn't know how to answer that.

Tesseract came to his rescue without taking her eyes from Chelsea's hands. "Doesn't work that way. Trees aren't buildings. A forest isn't a city. Getting high up's only part of it. There's the sights, the sounds, the smells, the *feel* of it. For me, it's working out, practicing katas. Thomas goes for long runs. I can imagine someone like Troll of Manhattan Justice preferring a woodland area for his brooding, but Jericho's a city boy. All he'd get out of climbing a tree would be a great view, and bark under his nails."

"Would it help if we talked it out?" asked Thomas. "The things that are bothering you, I mean?"

Jericho considered that. Talking to Thomas was always worthwhile, and there'd been several times since losing his phone that he'd wished he could do just this. It had helped, sometimes, to discuss things with Ms. Chandler.

And he definitely had some stuff he wanted to talk to Thomas about.

"Sure, I guess?" He wished he sounded more certain within himself, but certainty wasn't something he had much of right now.

"Let's do this, then," said Thomas, getting to his feet. He gave Jericho a hand up with little apparent effort—if anything, he was a touch stronger than Jericho—and nodded toward the van. "Come on. We'll get privacy in there. They'll call out if they need us."

"Sounds good to me." While actual brooding wasn't going to happen, he absolutely needed to do *something* about this, so it was worth trying.

They climbed up into the back of the van, kicked their boots off, and lay side by side on the mattress. The pre-sunrise chill was more intrusive away from the fire, but neither of them paid it much mind. Finding himself being gathered in by his boyfriend's muscular arms, Jericho returned the embrace. It was comforting to a degree he'd rarely experienced before in his life.

"Okay," Thomas said quietly. "I can tell there's a lot bothering you. Spill." His tone said it all; he was there to listen.

Jericho took a deep breath, then released it all in three words. "I killed Charnel."

"Yeah, I know." Thomas' tone was somber. "It sucks, but you had to—"

"No, you don't get it." Jericho squeezed his eyes shut and shook his head. "I've wondered for the longest time if I could really go lethal if I had to. You know, hypothetically. Against the Madness, for instance. And I always thought it would be harder. But it wasn't. I just … *did* it."

"You were wounded," Thomas pointed out pragmatically. "Your life was literally at stake. So was Chelsea's." His arms tightened around Jericho. "You did what you had to. And you made the right choice. I mean, seriously. This was *Charnel*."

Jericho felt the tight, hard knot of guilt begin to loosen. "You really think so? I mean …"

"I *know* so." Thomas rubbed his forehead against Jericho's, then kissed him. "No doubt at all. Mom says you should never take a life lightly, but *also* never second-guess your choices afterward."

If he could trust anyone for a judgment call like that, it would be Tesseract Power. "Yeah, I guess." The guilt was still there, but fading.

"Mm-hmm." Thomas continued to hold Jericho close. "So, what else is bothering you?"

It was more a question of what *wasn't*. He buried his face in Thomas' shoulder. "I've made *so* many mistakes. I should've seen this coming."

"Oh, *bullshit*," snorted Thomas. "Yeah, you made mistakes. Guess what; everyone does. Nobody's immune. Show me a person who's made zero mistakes in his life, and I'll show you a newborn baby."

Jericho shook his head, rolling it back and forth. "But I should've known how to handle things better. I'm pretty sure I got people killed. Stephen and Tucker, at least. Relentless might be next, all because I screwed up."

Thomas shook his head definitively. "No. You can cut that shit out right now. They were murdered, probably by False Flag with Guillotine helping, because Franklin Tucker just *had* to boast online. Chelsea explained all this to us. And Relentless is in danger because *he* screwed up, not you."

"How's that again?" Jericho wasn't sure of Thomas' logic. "What did Relentless do to screw up?"

Thomas drew a deep breath. "Okay, so this was back in 'ninety-seven. Mom and Dad had just dealt with Kraken. That made three terror villains who'd been taken out of the picture by then. Four, if you count Mindscrew. The rest of them had to be starting to wonder who was next. So, along come Relentless and the Technologist, recruiting for Force Majeure, right?"

"Right ..." Jericho thought he knew where Thomas was going with this, but he couldn't be sure. "So, they just ... joined? Under different names? To ... fly under the radar as superheroes?"

His boyfriend shrugged. "It's hella ballsy, I'll admit, but the writing on the wall was getting pretty damn obvious, and it was one way to avoid notice. Relentless was looking for heroes, so he saw heroes. We all know artificers like the Technologist aren't great with people. There was a serious lack of due diligence, back then. You and Chelsea just uncovered it, is all."

"But I *had* the thumb drive, and I *busted* it!" protested Jericho. "If I'd just sat down and watched the stuff *then*, I could've taken it to Relentless—"

"Chelsea told us it was encrypted," Thomas reminded him. "Plus, you'd just watched your ex cheating on you *in your own bed*. You had a right to be pissed off. But even if you'd tried to watch it, what then? Without the other USB drive to give you a hint, would you have gotten the password?"

This wasn't fair. Thomas was using logic and reason when by rights he should've been agreeing with Jericho. "If I'd taken it to the Technologist, I reckon he could've cracked it—"

Thomas snorted with laughter. "The other drive had a *sex tape* on it. In what universe would you have ever taken *any* of that guy's drives anywhere near the Technologist, knowing he'd be viewing at least part of the contents?"

"Okay, fine, you got me there." Jericho shuddered theatrically. "Not in a million years." He snuggled more firmly into Thomas' embrace, a situation he was totally comfortable with. "But you have to admit, I made mistakes. I could've been smarter about it."

"Well, *sure*, if you'd known everything that was going to happen ahead of time, there probably would've been a better way to go about things," Thomas conceded. "But in the absence of actual prior knowledge, I can't see how. If you'd maybe ignored important information that came back to bite you in the butt, I could get where you were coming from, but you *didn't*. You even left Kennedy early, just to get those files back to the Technologist." He paused and tapped his forehead gently against Jericho's. "For which, by the way, I'm still upset at you, mister."

"What?" Jericho was totally taken aback. "Why? I *left* you a text. I totally meant to come back."

Thomas hugged him a little closer. "Except you didn't. Once we'd finished helping out in Jefferson City, Mom and Dad dropped me off at Kennedy so I could spend the rest of the day with you. I got there around one and spent *hours* looking for you. Even when I tried texting or calling, not a peep. You'd dropped off the face of the earth, and I had *no* idea where you were. I was so worried about you." Though it sounded like he was trying to hide it, there was a catch in his voice.

"One …" Jericho tried to think back through the tumultuous events of the day. "I think my phone was fried by then." *Along with me.* "Or if it survived the lightning strike, Chelsea dumped it anyway."

"Yeah, Chelsea told us." Thomas pulled back slightly and peered at Jericho in the dimness. "Did you have any other misplaced guilt you'd like to air, or do you feel better now?"

"… I feel better," Jericho admitted. "Thanks." Much of the weight had been lifted from his shoulders, and he felt more centered now. It hadn't been *quite* the same as brooding, but it would suffice until he got a chance to do the real thing.

"Good." Thomas came back in and kissed him, firm pressure with carnal intent behind it. Reaching behind him, he pulled the van door closed. His hands burrowed under Jericho's shirt, unexpectedly warm as skin met skin. "Then we've got time for this."

Desire bloomed as Jericho returned the kiss with interest, but he paused. "Uh … I *want* to, but your folks … Chelsea …"

"They know the score, and we both know she's fine with it." Thomas' voice was a breathy whisper. He nibbled at Jericho's neck, sending pleasurable shivers all the way down to his toes.

Jericho's hands, acting outside his volition, pushed Thomas' jacket aside and started undoing the shirt buttons he found there. Still, his mind insisted on throwing up roadblocks. "Buddy and the Survivors …?"

"If they know what's good for them, they won't say a word." Thomas rolled Jericho onto his back and straddled him. Involuntarily, Jericho arched his back, exposing his neck as Thomas nibbled him there again, lighting up his every nerve ending with pleasure.

"I'm still injured …" But he was in full retreat by now, with surrender looming on the horizon.

Taking Jericho's wrists in his hands, Thomas pinned them to the mattress over Jericho's head. Even if Jericho had any thoughts about resisting at this point, his body wouldn't have let him. He wanted this too badly.

Just before Thomas claimed him once and for all, his mouth lingered by Jericho's ear.

"Don't worry. I'll do all the work."

59
Allies From All Over

When Jericho climbed from the van with Thomas some little while later, he was feeling considerably refreshed. Hand in hand, they strolled back toward the fireside. It appeared that Thomas' prediction had been on the money; there wasn't so much as a snicker or sidelong glance resulting from their prolonged absence.

They sat down in the chairs as if they'd never left. Mel glanced over from her ongoing conversation with Adam Power, gave Jericho a nod, and tossed him another sandwich. Thanking her with a return nod, he opened it.

Chelsea leaned over toward him. "Just by the way, I wanted to let you know you were right."

"What about?" asked Jericho. He'd been right—and wrong—about a lot of things in the past twenty-four hours, and he would've been hard-pressed to name what she was referring to.

"Those gravity pulses," she said. "You told me they were going to cause an earthquake."

"Did they?" Jericho froze. He'd totally forgotten about that.

Chelsea nodded. "Half an hour after the last pulse, there was an eight-point-seven magnitude quake in Perth, Australia. The epicenter was directly under the city itself. It's the strongest quake they've ever recorded, by nearly two orders of magnitude."

"So, what's in Perth that's so important?" asked Buddy, frowning. "Or does whoever did this just not like kangaroos?"

"There's nothing in Perth they don't like," Chuck said. He tapped his finger on the front of the helmet he was holding, then traced a path around to the back and tapped it again. "It's not *what* it is. It's *where* it is. Nearly all the way around the world from us. Whoever it is, they're proving they can hit anyone, anywhere."

Jericho nodded, seeing the sense in his words. "Ranging shot. They hit Jefferson City about twenty-four hours ago. That must've been the first test, while Perth was the second. And the pulses were so powerful because they had to reach so far."

Chelsea grimaced. "Yeah, I think you're right. This proves that not only is Seismic still in business, but he's figured out how to do it remotely." She shook her head; when she spoke next, her voice was hushed. "He can pick any two cities, *anywhere,* and extort them for ransom. The asshole just went *international.*"

He didn't like it, but he couldn't argue with her conclusions. "The big question is, where's the earthquake machine he's using to do this?"

"I have no idea." Adam Power rubbed his hand over his chin slowly and thoughtfully. "But I can tell you this much; for the range he's getting out of it, it's got to be *huge*. Which means the power draw must be immense. Now that we know about it, I should be able to rig up some sort of gravity-pulse detector and zero in on it. And once we've located it, we can destroy it. Hopefully, before he sets about using it in earnest."

His discussion with Mel switched to the potential specs of such a machine. Jericho tried to follow it, but it quickly became too technical for him to keep up. Reassured that they had the matter in hand, he turned his attention back to the sandwich.

Over the next ten minutes, he finished off the snack—chicken and lettuce, this time—and enjoyed a bottle of water, while Thomas made small talk with the rest of the Survivors. Chelsea went back to competing with Tesseract Power in the ongoing contest of who could cheat the most blatantly; Jericho had no idea who was winning, or if either one was even keeping score.

Then Thomas sat up and pointed at where a set of headlights was slowly making its way toward the fire. "Heads up. Incoming."

Abandoning her latest hand—a royal flush—Chelsea stood and shielded her eyes from the firelight. "I think they're who we're waiting on. Jericho, could you take a look for me, please?"

"Me?" Jericho stood up as well and peered at the oncoming lights. As the vehicle got closer, he frowned. If he wasn't much mistaken, that engine noise and the configuration of those headlights belonged to a very specific vehicle, one that he knew well. He took a few steps toward the approaching pickup truck, then stopped as it came to a halt and the engine shut off.

Two doors opened in the semi-darkness, then closed again. Jericho went forward again, his eyes rapidly adjusting to the lack of light. "Uncle Leroy?" he asked doubtfully. "Is that you?" It had certainly looked and sounded like his uncle's truck.

"Sho'nuff, boy." Leroy loomed out of the night and wrapped Jericho up in a hug. When Jericho winced at the sudden pressure on his stomach, Leroy pulled back and stared at him, hands on Jericho's shoulders. "You okay? What the hell happened to you?"

Jericho considered telling him everything but instead condensed it to: "It's a long story. Let's just say I've had better days. What are you doing *here*?"

"Brung your costume." The familiar satchel was pressed into his hands, then Leroy looked past Jericho to where Chelsea was coming down from the fire. "If'n we're gonna keep doin' business, honeybunch, might could be *you* wanna tell me what done happened to th' boy here."

This was the first Jericho had heard of Leroy working with Chelsea; then again, before all this started, his uncle had been fixing to form a working partnership with the Southsiders. That had been the case until they point-blank refused to give up Jack Portman for his apparent murder of Luke, prompting Leroy to rescind the offer and leave Utopia. It had taken Jericho and his two new friends to bust the Southsiders' operation wide open, leaving the field clear for Chelsea to step up as the new crime boss in town.

Did she use our association to start dealing with Leroy straight away? Right under my nose?

It surely seemed like it; his uncle wouldn't drive most of the way up the east coast on just *anyone's* say-so.

"Like he said," she replied blandly. "Long story. But I *can* tell you it starts with him being struck by lightning then stabbed, and ends with him jumping out of an airliner at fifteen thousand feet without the ability to fly, and leaving it up to me to drag his sorry ass back into the plane. How about we fill in the rest of the details later?"

Leroy paused as though assimilating that, then swung back to him. "What the *hell*, boy?"

"I'm alive," Jericho said defensively, putting his hands up. "*Please*, can we just talk about this when we've actually got the time?"

"Damn straight we will," muttered Leroy, glaring at Jericho. "And when we do, I'm probably gonna kick your butt for bein' such a dumbass."

Chelsea snorted indelicately. "Let me know ahead of time. I'm gonna need popcorn for that one."

Leroy's mouth twisted in wry acknowledgment. "So, tell me somethin' else," he asked the pair of them. "What-all's goin' on over Utopia City way? Place is locked up tighter'n a jackrabbit's ass-crack settin' in a snowbank."

Jericho shook his head as he looked toward the other person who'd gotten out of the truck. "That's an even longer story." With the moon providing minimal illumination, he had to depend on the flickering firelight to see what was going on. But again, context came to his rescue. There was only one other person in Savannah who knew his secret identity, and this was undoubtedly secret-identity business. "Daryl, that you?"

"As ever was, Jericho." His uncle's burly brother-in-law slapped him on the back, driving the wind from his lungs. "So, how come the lady called on Leroy to bring your costume all the way up here?"

"Because he can't go back to Utopia to get his other one," Chelsea said. "C'mon over to the fire. Now that everyone's here, it's time to get you all caught up on what's been happening."

Jericho knew Leroy had spotted his lack of hair when a large rough hand rubbed over his scalp. "About time you had a proper haircut, boy."

"Yeah, well, at least I've got some to cut off," retorted Jericho. Leroy wasn't bald yet, but his hair was definitely receding.

"Smart-ass," grunted Leroy, aiming a lazy cuff at his head. Jericho ducked away, grinning.

The people sitting around the fire sat up and paid attention when Jericho led Leroy and Daryl into the light. Both big men, they could've been cast from the same mold, save that Leroy was white and Daryl was black. Thomas, quick off the mark as usual, had the last two folding chairs set up by the time they got there.

"Much obliged," Leroy said with a sigh as he and Daryl took their seats. "Goddamn, but it's nice to be out of that damn pickup at last." He eyed Thomas and Jericho keenly, and how closely they were sitting together. "This here your new boyfriend?"

"Ahh ... yeah." Jericho knew he shouldn't be feeling awkward—Leroy had known he was gay for a lot longer than he'd been aware of the superhero side of things—but it was always daunting to reveal something like that to someone he respected. "Thomas, I'd like you to meet Leroy Hansen and Daryl West. Leroy, Daryl; meet Thomas Power."

He saw his uncle's eyes flick from Thomas to Adam, then Tesseract and back again in an instant, and he knew Leroy had recognized the heroes and made the connection. To his credit, the older man never hesitated; leaning forward across Jericho, he shook hands with Thomas. "Right pleased to meet ya, son."

Daryl was seated too far away to offer his hand, so he lifted it in a wave instead. "Same here. I told the boy he could do better'n that last one. Looks like he done listened."

"Hold on a second." Jericho's mind was still scrambling to assimilate the events of the last few minutes. "Okay, Chelsea, I can understand you asking Uncle Leroy to bring my costume up, but I know for a *fact* I never told you he had it."

"That's true." Chelsea looked smug. "I asked Thomas who might be holding it for you."

Jericho turned to look at Thomas. "I never told you that, either."

"No." Thomas shrugged. "But you said you'd left it with someone you trusted, and that's what I told her."

Chelsea spread her hands in a *'voila'* gesture. "And I already knew Leroy was the closest member of your immediate family who was in on your secret identity. Seriously, it wasn't even difficult."

Dealing with mental prodigies, Jericho decided, could be irritating. *Helpful*, he amended as he held the satchel on his lap, *but still irritating*.

"Wait one cotton-pickin' minute." Leroy was looking carefully between Thomas and the other members of the Survivors. "I've seen y'all's faces before. I mind Jericho askin' me to do him up a buncha IDs that one time ..."

The Survivors looked at each other, then back at Leroy. "*You* did those IDs?" asked Mel. "Those were *amazing*. Got us all the way out of Utopia, no problem."

"Yeah, what she said," Gareth chimed in. "The cops were on our asses big-time. Those things let us jump right on the maglev and get out of town. You and Jericho, you saved us."

Tesseract cleared her throat. "Chelsea's asked us to refrain from noticing any suggestion of past illegal activities, so that's what we're going to do," she said pointedly. The implication was clear: *Can we not keep talking about it, please?* "From what I've heard so far, we've got far bigger fish to fry. Now,

Chelsea, you were going to fill us in on your plan?"

"Plan. Right." Chelsea turned to take in each of the other people gathered around the fire, then back to Leroy and Daryl. "Just so everyone's on the same page; you guys need to know that most of the core members of Force Majeure are actually terror villains."

"Sum*bitch*!" erupted Leroy, his tone both surprised and shocked. "You mean to say that prissy li'l asswipe actually got it *right* for once?"

Jericho cleared his throat apologetically. "Well, yes and no. He didn't have any proof, but he *wanted* them to be in the wrong, so I'd come back to him. So, he latched onto anything he could find, ninety-nine percent of which was faked." He shrugged. "Then, one fine day, he found the proof he was looking for. And it got him killed."

"Hol' up." Daryl made a 'time out' gesture. "That fire, right? It weren't no accident?"

"Got it in one," confirmed Chelsea. "The first one we figured out was Charnel, pretending to be Silent Knight, when he stabbed Jericho. We killed him, but then Independence came after us."

Jericho nodded, taking up the explanation. "Turns out Independence is False Flag." He squeezed Leroy's shoulder. "False Flag and Charnel were the ones who murdered Luke, but not before he got his licks in. From what I understand, he beat the absolute living *snot* out of False Flag."

While Daryl nodded slowly, Leroy frowned. "So ... *not* that Portman asshole?"

"No, Portman was a total frame-job." Jericho grimaced. "They stitched that poor bastard up like an old-fashioned quilting party. Anyway, once we snuck out of the city—courtesy of Chelsea—we contacted Relentless and warned him. Chelsea's pretty sure False Flag's on ice for now, but it looks like Relentless and the Technologist still think the others are good guys. Which leaves us between a rock and a hard place."

Daryl shook his head. "When you're right, boy, you're right. How many terror villains y'all sure of?"

"Worst case, four, not counting Charnel or False Flag," reported Chelsea. "Which isn't good, but it could be a lot worse. Raider, Singularity, Guillotine, and we're pretty sure Seismic's lurking somewhere in the Spire too."

"I thought all those assholes were supposed to be dead already," objected Leroy. "That's why they called 'em the terror villains of the *Nineties*."

"I've got a stab wound that says otherwise." Jericho gingerly touched the bandage through his shirt. "We need to get into Utopia and warn Relentless and the Technologist about the others before things go too much further off the rails."

Chelsea nodded. "Exactly. But we can't just walk in. They're still locked down, and we've got evidence that they can scan the maglev for potential hostiles. The trick will be infiltrating the city once the lockdown is raised *and* getting Relentless on side without making the others suspicious."

"Yeah." Jericho didn't want to admit defeat, but he had to concede the reality of the situation. "We can't just bash through. Brute force won't work. I've seen enough of Utopia's automated defenses to know that those alone would shred anything we threw at them."

"And then there's the aftermath." Chelsea looked around at the group. "Force Majeure pretends not to be involved in local politics, but taking down those villains *will* destabilize the city in ways I can only begin to guess at. Not to mention, everyone from the Boy Scouts on up will be wanting to investigate how this came about in the first place, and won't give a good goddamn whose rights they trample in the meantime. To cover that particular problem, I've decided to bring in someone with extensive experience in politics, law enforcement, *and* being a superhero, to advise us and provide guidance where needed."

Jericho tilted his head, wondering exactly who she was referring to. "And this would be …?"

"I'm glad you asked." Chelsea grinned. "The gentleman actually lives not far from here. If anyone's got the expertise I'm looking for, it's him."

Now Jericho was totally lost. "*What* gentleman?"

Her grin widened as though she were enjoying the joke all too much. "Oh, you'll know him when you see him."

Unamused, Leroy folded his brawny arms. "I've come this far, missy, but I'm gonna need a tad bit more'n that afore I go chasin' off through the backwoods o' New England. Now, who-all's this feller you're braggin' on so much?"

All levity dropped, she looked him straight in the eye.

"Castellan."

60
A Call to Arms

Richard 'Dickey' Byrd Miller woke at the same time every day. He hadn't required an alarm clock for nearly fifty years; the habits instilled by the Marine Corps allowed him to put his feet on the floor within seconds of the time he wanted to be up. Rising, he went through his morning routine with barely a thought, his mind already on how many papers he needed to grade today for his Constitutional Law course to get them all done on time. He'd skipped a day yesterday to attend the commemoration ceremony for his old comrade, and they wouldn't grade *themselves*.

He finished up by making his bed. It was a matter of personal pride that whatever his station in life, whether serving in the Corps or the Department of Justice, he'd always shaved and made his own bed in the morning, without fail. Without discipline, a man was nothing.

The same had applied after the terrible day he lost his loved ones to a monster in a labyrinth. No matter what it cost him at the time, self-discipline had been his rock just as much then as it was now, guiding him through the darkness and bringing him back to the light. And once the monster was dead, although it had taken him years, he'd been able to move forward with his life once more.

Taking his jacket from the peg, he left the house for his morning walk. He picked up the cane on his way out the door; oddly enough, the leg wound he'd picked up in Vietnam ached more in the cold than all the scars he'd acquired later in his career. In addition, he was honest enough to admit (at least to himself) that he wasn't getting any younger.

The sky showed a distinct glow to the east below the razor-thin crescent moon as he walked down the driveway, his cane tapping the frozen ground in a regular metronomic pattern. Despite the aches and pains of age, he enjoyed a good walk on a chilly winter morning while puffs of white breath measured his progress; being able to set his own pace was almost relaxing. Nowhere near as fast as he would've covered the same distance in his prime, but that part of his life was far behind him now.

It was a pleasant enough neighborhood to live in, mainly because the nearest house was a good half-mile away. People kept themselves to themselves, and nobody left their dogs off the leash to roam unhindered. Not that he feared dogs, or even the people who occasionally tried to menace elderly folk living alone. Once upon a time, he'd faced far worse, and he was still well-equipped to deal with such mundane would-be predators.

At the end of the five-mile walk, with the sun just above the horizon, he was pushing himself just a little for that extra burn. As he strode back up the driveway, he relished the feeling of blood pumping through his veins, the sensation of being *alive*. It was a fitting way to start the day, even if he was going to spend it in such a mundane manner as grading papers.

They also serve who stand and teach, he misquoted in his own mind with a dash of sardonic amusement as he unlocked his front door. Not everyone could be a Marine officer, a Department of Justice prosecutor, or a world-renowned superhero; even of those who were, nobody could do it forever. So, it was every person's duty to carry out whatever role they found themselves in for the greatest possible good. Even teaching.

He dropped the cane into the umbrella stand and was just unbuttoning his jacket when there was a crisp, no-nonsense knock on the door. Frowning—he hadn't been *expecting* visitors—he hung the garment on its peg and returned to the entranceway. "Who is it?" he called through the thick wood.

"Mr. Miller, we need to talk." The speaker was feminine and in her twenties if he were to hazard a guess. But the *tone* was something else altogether; a certain quality in her voice did its best to assure him that he really did need to speak with her.

He didn't trust it for an instant.

Throughout his long and varied career in law enforcement, wearing first one type of suit and then another, he'd met a great many people who could say things that were entirely untrue or even damaging to the psyche in an eminently believable way. He'd acquired a particular talent at sifting out the wheat from the chaff, separating the accounts that were actually true from those that merely sounded highly plausible. And unless he missed his guess, the woman on the other side of the door was a past master at gaslighting the unwary into accepting whatever she said.

Retrieving the cane, he held it this time with three feet of wood projecting ahead of his hand. He didn't know this woman's motives or her endgame, but he intended to find out. If she expected him to be a pushover in any sense of the word, she would be in for a rude surprise. Unlocking the door, he opened it the few inches permitted by the sturdy chain.

The young lady on his porch wore sharp business attire with a stylish shoulder bag. She projected both professionalism and efficiency; again, he took this with a large grain of salt. "Well?" he asked, getting right down to brass tacks. "What is the issue?"

She never faltered for an instant. "Sir, I need your assistance with a potentially catastrophic situation. All may be not well with Force Majeure. Specifically, I possess evidence that I personally believe proves that the core membership is composed primarily of terror villains operating undercover."

He took a moment to appreciate how she'd separated opinion from stated fact, but lowered his brows all the same. While what she'd said sounded like something that needed addressing, it wasn't his fight anymore. "Miss, you appear to be laboring under a misapprehension. I don't possess the authority to act on what you're alleging. Any Yellow Pages will supply

you with the telephone numbers to contact those who do. Good day to you."
He began to close the door again.

"Sir," she said rapidly. "I'm not looking for Richard Miller. I'm looking
for *Castellan*. I wouldn't be bothering you with this if I wasn't utterly
convinced the occasion called for it."

He froze for just a second. Since he'd hung up the mask, those in the
government who knew of his real identity (there were always a few) had
been good at keeping it under wraps. How this woman had found out, he
didn't know, but he'd never forgotten Arfogwyr's fate. "You've got the
wrong man," he said, knowing he was letting her engage him but unable to
do anything else. "I am not Castellan." It was true, insofar as he stuck to the
present tense. Castellan's purpose was long since completed, the armor
defunct since that last battle; he'd moved on.

"But you *were*." The surety in her voice was absolute, neatly puncturing
his sophistry. "I was in the Challenger exhibit yesterday when a young
superhero almost collided with you. I *saw* your moves. If he'd turned out to
be hostile, you would've taken him down before he even realized it."

He tried not to let his dismay show on his face. The incident was vivid in
his memory. Lost in nostalgia for days gone by and suddenly confronted by
a dark-clad masked figure, he'd managed to rein in his reflexive reaction
before it went too far. Though not quickly enough, it seemed, to hide it from
the lady at his front door. "I *am* a war veteran," he reminded her, though he
suspected this wouldn't throw her off.

"You also used to be Castellan," she replied promptly, proving him
correct. "I was just a kid when you retired, but I wouldn't have thought
someone like you would give terror villains a pass."

He stifled an aggravated sigh. While he was determined not to let the
young woman's words get to him, she was remarkably effective at pressing
his buttons. "Assuming I believe any of this, how do you explain that the
majority of the terror villains of the Nineties were publicly taken down and
killed by members of the very team you're accusing of *being* those same
terror villains? How did they replace the original members without anyone
suspecting something was amiss?"

I don't know what she's selling, but I'm not buying it.

Even in the face of his skepticism, she wasn't fazed. "The terror villains
are the original members. They've been pulling this scam right from the
beginning. Those copycat cases we've been seeing from time to time? That's
them, coming out to play then ducking back to Utopia to hide in plain sight
behind their superhero identities. Often making a big production of showing
up to investigate their own crimes."

He had to award her points for originality, but her words still troubled
him. "And your evidence proves this, beyond a reasonable doubt?" He
repressed the urge to open the door all the way and ask to see it for himself.
I'm out of the fight now. Other people can deal with it. "If that's so, I strongly
suggest you take it to—"

"You're the only one who can help us." The surety in her voice was rock-solid, with no room for duplicity.

"I very much doubt that." He matched her certitude, note for note. "I walked away from that life seventeen years ago. What makes you think I'm the man you're looking for?"

"Sir, you're the *only* Enabled I know of with extensive experience in both law enforcement and the heroic side of things. Once we take down the villains within Force Majeure, we *will* need someone who can navigate both worlds with equal ease, and you're that person. Without you, even if we pull it off perfectly, many people—the genuine superheroes they've gathered under their banner—are going to needlessly suffer. Do you really want to let that happen?"

He froze, his mouth going dry, the words he'd been about to speak forgotten on his tongue. The confidence in her words rocked him back on his heels and overcame the last of his objections. If nothing else, he needed to look over her claims before deciding further. "What's your name, young lady?"

Here was the tipping point; when people tried to spin him a line, he could usually tell if they gave a false name. But she never hesitated. "I go by Smokeshadow, but my real name's Chelsea."

Her words rang true to him. He put the cane down, then closed the door. Slowly, he took the chain off the hook and opened it again.

"I suppose you'd better come in, then."

61
Chasing Down the Clues

Standing at the foot of the steps, wearing his old costume, Jericho sighed quietly with relief as the door opened all the way. In the last half-hour, he'd had time to get used to the idea that they were fixing to bring Castellan out of retirement, but he'd had no idea how the man himself would take it. Some folks would be like to slam the door and lock it solid, but it seemed the retired hero was made of sterner stuff.

"Adam Power; that *is* you, isn't it?" Before Chelsea even got the chance to step inside, Castellan had come out onto the porch. "And Tesseract. I presume you're with this young lady?" He looked over the Team Power couple, his tone defrosting slightly.

"That's right, sir," Tesseract confirmed, climbing the steps to the porch with Adam close behind her. "It's good to see you again."

Castellan nodded, his stern expression softening as he shook her hand. "The same to you. Though I believe I've already asked you not to call me that. I don't need to feel any older than I am, and you two were established heroes before I ever donned the mask."

"It's a matter of respect, sir," Adam said, shaking his hand in turn. "You gave us a lot of good advice about strategy versus tactics, back in the day. But unfortunately, we're not here to reminisce."

"So I understand." Castellan nodded at Vanessa, who had followed her parents up the steps. "I was pleased to hear the scurrilous allegations regarding you and your daughter were false."

"That's actually part of why we're here," Vanessa stated. "We've figured out it was False Flag who attacked me and framed my dad for it. He's been Independence all this time."

Castellan focused his attention on her, lowering his graying brows. "That's a bold accusation, Miss Power. Do you have anything to back it up?"

"Yeah. I do." She looked him straight in the eye. "You're aware of the Proximity Principle, specifically the part about how if you get powers near another Enabled, you're likely to get the same type of powers? I didn't *have* powers before he attacked me. Now I'm a Prodigy, with Dynamic shape-changing."

"And before you ask," interjected Chelsea, "yes, we have visually identified Independence as a shape-changer. See G-Man down there?"

"I do recall the young man from yesterday, yes." Castellan turned his gaze in Jericho's direction. "You appear to be wearing a less elaborate version of your costume today. Is this related to the matter at hand?"

"It is," confirmed Jericho, impressed despite himself. Castellan might've been getting on a little, but he was still very much on the ball. "Smokeshadow saw Independence's hair change color, and I personally saw her skin shifting." He would never forget the rippling effect of his G-shake on the terror villain's face.

"I see." Castellan's expression was hard to read as he looked Jericho over and took the new information on board. "That's very troubling." Then his attention fixed on Sarah. "Miss, I apologize for the lack of a wheelchair ramp. If I'd known of this situation ahead of time, I would have made arrangements."

"Won't be a problem." The wheelchair shifted and changed; dull, drab panels gave way to black and gold ceramic plates. In less than ten seconds, she wore power armor with a tinted gold visor. Jericho could see a set of roller-blades built into the feet of the suit, but they didn't budge so much as a quarter-turn as Blades climbed the steps.

Well, that explains the name.

It didn't faze Castellan for more than half a second or so. "Very well. Carry on. Wipe your feet when you come in, please."

Okay. So far, so good. Castellan hadn't sent them away yet, though he'd been a far tougher sell than Chelsea had anticipated. They were going to have to have *all* their ducks in a row to convince him to join their number.

Climbing the steps, Jericho obediently cleaned the soles of his boots, then followed Blades into the house. It was neat and well-kept, though sparse when it came to decoration. He'd half-expected to see mementos of Castellan's heroic career on display, but the few pictures were either simple landscapes or faded photos of people in uniform. *Vietnam*, he guessed. They had that feel to them.

Castellan led them down a corridor into a large combination dining/living room with a kitchen off to one side. As the room filled up with people trooping through, he placed a kettle on a hotplate and turned the stove on. "It seems you all know who I am, though I am at a disadvantage with most of you."

Removing his mask and tucking it into a pouch, Jericho held out his hand. "Jericho Hansen, sir. This here's my Uncle Leroy and my kinsman Daryl. It's an honor to meet you."

"Indeed." Castellan shook it once, firmly; although in his late sixties or early seventies, the older man's grip was still powerful. "You're injured." And it looked like his catching the costume change hadn't been a fluke.

"Yes, sir. Silent Knight ambushed me yesterday. Smokeshadow and I—"

Chelsea cleared her throat, the faux business suit melting into her usual hoodie and jeans. Her message was clear: the time for Enabled codenames was over.

Jericho nodded. "Sorry; that is, *Chelsea* and I managed to unmask him as Charnel, then kill him. Then Independence tried to kill *us*. I disabled her temporarily before I passed out, just long enough for Chelsea to get me out of there. We've been on the run ever since."

"An understandable reaction." Castellan looked over at the Survivors. "And these are ...?"

Vanessa raised her hand to get his attention, then kept talking as she went through the transformation into Thomas. "They ended up in Utopia around the same time I did, shortly after I ran away from home. Originally, we all wanted to join Force Majeure and be heroes, but that fell through. So, we banded together and went out as an independent team in Utopia, calling ourselves the Survivors because we got our powers after surviving attacks by villains, for the most part."

Jericho knew how this story went. He'd been there for the last part of it. Although Castellan hadn't been, he once more showed his experience. "I suspect this story does not end as well as it begins."

"No, it doesn't." Thomas shook his head. "We were young and made a few mistakes, and Utopia was in the process of going cashless. Neither factor would've been a real problem if there hadn't also been an unwritten rule that only Force Majeure heroes got to operate in Utopia. No cash meant no way to buy a ticket out of town once the last bus line ceased operations, so they ended up in a serious hole when the cops cracked down on us. Without bank accounts or official identification, they couldn't leave, and I wasn't about to abandon them. We were stuck in that rut until Jericho and Leroy helped me facilitate their departure just a few months ago."

From the set of his mouth, Castellan evidently suspected there was more to the phrase 'facilitate their departure' than he was being told, but he didn't push the issue. "And their names?"

"Oh," said Sarah. "Right. Sorry." Her faceplate split down the middle and slid off to the sides, then the helmet retracted in sections until her head was uncovered. "I'm Sarah, or Blades when I'm in costume. Artificer and dynamic." One by one, she went through the names of her fellow Enabled, finishing off with: "And that's Mel, otherwise known as Gimmick. She's the best artificer I've ever seen, bar none."

"Sarah's not just whistling Dixie," Chelsea confirmed. "It's only because of Gimmick's tech that I was able to get the evidence I was talking about."

"Really." Castellan's head came up, his eyes glinting with interest. Oddly enough, he was focusing on Mel rather than Chelsea. "If you don't mind me asking, young lady, how adept are you at repairing or maintaining another artificer's technology?"

Mel favored him with the kind of grin only a cocky teenager can muster. "There's exactly one artificer whose tech has ever given me any sort of trouble, and even his stuff rolls over for me in the end. Lay it on me."

"Very well. I believe the appropriate response is 'challenge accepted'." Castellan took a key off a hook on the wall, knelt next to a side table, and pulled a rug off a wooden chest underneath it. The sound of the padlock clicking open was loud against the sound of shuffling feet.

The hinges creaked as he opened the lid, betraying the presence of rust and a lack of oil. Reaching into the chest, Castellan lifted out a five-foot-long canvas-wrapped bundle, then stood and brought it over to the wooden table that dominated the room. He carefully placed it on the smooth-planed wood with a *clunk*, unfastened a trio of cracked leather straps, and pulled the heavy, stiff material aside.

Silence fell as they regarded what lay within. Jericho recognized it immediately, although he'd never seen it before in real life. Somehow, he'd expected it to be longer and sleeker. It bore a closer resemblance to a thick-bladed spear with a long head and short haft than a sword. But the more he looked at it, the more he could believe *this* was the infamous weapon the Minotaur had used to indiscriminately slaughter so many of his victims.

"Whoooaaa …" It appeared Mel harbored no such doubts. Reaching out, she ran her hand wonderingly over the red-hued metal, her face filled with awe. "*The* Blood Rose. Now, *this* is as OG as it gets." Leaning closer, she frowned slightly. "Some of the sub-blades are missing. Never fixed it?"

Jericho blinked and looked at where she was pointing. Sure enough, there were some gaps where shallow indentations separated the smaller blades that made up the whole. These were so hard to see that the missing blades had to have been beyond razor-sharp; even the snapped-off stubs were barely visible.

"I don't have the skills," Castellan confirmed. "After I retired, I took it out now and again to spar with it, but it ran out of power about ten years ago. So I put it away and did my best to forget it was there."

"At least you didn't try to take it apart yourself. That's good. It's also probably why you've still got all your fingers." Mel leaned closer still and trailed her fingertips over the deadly mechanism again. "Alright then, you sexy little minx. Let's have a look at your secrets." Reaching down to her belt, she produced a complicated-looking tool; the press of a button caused LEDs to ripple up and down its length. She spun the device around her finger, then posed for a moment. "Behold; my master key and my traveling toolbox, all in one convenient package."

Chelsea nudged Jericho. "She says that every time she gets to show it off to someone new," she murmured, rolling her eyes.

"I heard that," Mel retorted without heat. She pulled the goggles down over her eyes and slowly ran the multitool over the surface of the Blood Rose. "Hmm … now, that's interesting." Bringing the tool back over a particular spot, she pressed another button; a previously hidden panel popped open in the side of the Artificer weapon. "And. We. Are. In! The crowd goes wild …" Leaning closer, she flipped up the goggle lenses and peered intently at the mechanisms revealed within. "Wait, what the hell?"

"What?" asked Jericho, suddenly on edge. Was it booby-trapped, as she'd hinted earlier?

Mel looked up from the deadly device, her expression one of annoyance. "This isn't the original Blood Rose. It's a Technologist knockoff."

"A knockoff?" Jericho shared a startled glance with Chelsea. "What are you talking about?"

"This." Mel pointed her multitool at the innards of the Blood Rose. "Every artificer's got their fingerprint, how they build stuff to their own personal specifications. I've pulled enough Technologist crap apart to know it when I see it. It's twice as hard as anything else to work with."

Castellan shook his head. "Young lady—Gimmick—I'm afraid you're mistaken on that count. The Technologist had not yet come on the scene when I took that away from the Minotaur. It has never been out of my possession since."

"Really?" Mel rolled her eyes, her voice full of scorn. "Are *you* an artificer? Do *you* know how these things go together? No? Well, let me show you a little something, Mr. *'the Technologist had not yet come on the scene'*. He always puts his logo on a little plate ..." Lowering the lenses again, she removed some components, muttering to herself. "... just about ..." More parts joined the others on the table. "... here. Hah! Read it and weep!" Unscrewing the plate, she lifted it into the light, then paused when she saw what was on it. "... oh."

Jericho stared at the plate. It didn't bear the cogwheel-behind-T logo of the Technologist. Instead, neatly engraved into it, were a half-cogwheel and a vertical spar, forming the letters 'DI'. He met Chelsea's eyes again, recognizing the same wild surmise in her expression that he was experiencing himself.

With the goggle lenses raised again, it was easy to see the confusion that flooded across Mel's features before shocked comprehension took up residence. "The Technologist is *Doc Iridium*? What the *hell*?"

If she was having trouble with the notion, Jericho simply couldn't fit his head around it. "No. No. How's this even possible?" he muttered, rubbing his hand over his scalp. Chelsea looked just as taken aback. Even Castellan, as experienced as he was, looked more than a little surprised.

"Now wait jes' one sumbitchin' minute!" Leroy shouted over the growing confusion. "That asshole was killed by his own bomb! He blew *hisself* up, along with the whole damn city! Right?"

Daryl had always been the voice of reason. "Unless he didn't, bro. Ever think o' that?"

Everyone Jericho could see looked as sick as he felt at the realization. This was going in directions he had *not* anticipated, and he had no idea how to handle it. His hand found a chair, and he slumped to a sitting position. "Okay, if he didn't, that means ... he faked his own death? Destroyed an entire city ... so Force Majeure could come in and build Utopia City in its place? On top of its ruins? And get *paid* for it?"

His brain felt like it was stretching painfully with all the new concepts he was forcing it to accept. Social skills had never been high on the crusty artificer's priority list, but Jericho liked him anyway. The Technologist had even built Scout and modified him with Jericho's input, specifically as a combination sidekick and personal protective detail. What kind of villain even *did* something like that?

Tesseract shrugged. "Let's not forget, we're talking about *Doc Iridium* here. He was all about the apocalypse theme. When that bomb went off prematurely, we should've been suspicious as hell. But after we finished mourning the dead, we were all too busy celebrating. Because everyone loves it when karma happens to bad guys. He would've had zero problems with murdering ninety thousand people to get what he wanted. He probably took *pride* in it."

Her husband slapped his forehead. "The flight computers!"

"The *flight computers*," repeated Chelsea, this time as a groan. "Why didn't we see it?"

"Because we didn't have all the facts." Adam Power glanced over as Castellan raised his eyebrows interrogatively. "Last night, we rescued an airliner that was in trouble because the flight computer was going nuts. After I landed it at O'Hare, I requested permission to check the flight computers of all the other domestic planes waiting to fly out. At first I didn't get anywhere, but then Chelsea gave me a hand, and that's when we started finding stuff."

"Viruses, to be exact," Chelsea filled in. "Lurking in secondary and tertiary memory, camouflaged as regular programs, waiting on a specific signal to unfold and make the plane go crazy. We figured Raider could probably write the viruses to take over all the systems, but how would she deliver them, especially so subtly? She's good, but she's not that good."

"But Doc Iridium *is*," Tesseract added, taking up the narrative. "If anyone could hack an airliner remotely and deliver a virus to order, he could. That's means and opportunity dealt with. And motive's the easiest part of all to work out."

Buddy spread his hands. "… hurting people?" he hazarded. "You know, villains?"

"It's a start," Chelsea said kindly, "but these aren't your standard raving psychos. They're *smart* raving psychos. And hurting people just any old how would get kinda … same-same after a while. Raider treats murder like a video game, remember? If a plane full of people piled into the ground, that would be worth *hundreds* of points."

Adam nodded. "And airliners falling out of the sky are basically one more step toward Doc Iridium's vision of the apocalypse."

"Your points are both valid," agreed Castellan. "Of course, the overall motive of reducing public trust in the airlines to induce people to take the maglev is also a strong factor."

"… where politicians and businessmen would take the opportunity to discuss sensitive matters behind the privacy bubbles that are *built right into it*," Chelsea completed. She raised her chin to get Castellan's attention. "Just by the way, they can listen in on those, too. *All* the dirt, right there. And you know damn well they'll use every last bit of it."

"Sonova …" Jericho pulled his profanity to a halt just in time; he was a guest in Castellan's home. But the conclusion he'd just reached was inescapable, and it *had* to be aired. "If all that's true, if Doc Iridium faked his death, Utopia isn't just a city."

"It's not?" asked Paul, who up until then had been listening breathlessly. "What is it, then?"

Jericho stood up and took a steadying breath.

"It's a crime scene."

62
Cards on the Table

Castellan was the first to react. He nodded in response to Jericho's words, then addressed the group in general. "Dramatic, but unfortunately accurate. I take it you were as unaware of that particular aspect of the situation as the rest of us?"

"Totally, yeah," Chelsea confirmed. "I didn't have *anything* on the Technologist as yet. As far as we knew, he was pure as the driven snow. In fact, we would've been relying on him to ensure nobody could break back into the security system once it got turned against the villains. But now it looks like Relentless is gonna have to handle that on his own."

"Which leads on to my next point." Castellan lowered his brows slightly. "Before we go any further, I'll need to see your evidence regarding the rest of Force Majeure. While I mean no offense, your unsupported word is not sufficient for a matter of this level of importance."

"That's fair." Chelsea unzipped her shoulder bag and pulled out her laptop. Picking a section of the table not taken up by Mel and the ongoing dissection of the Blood Rose, she placed it down, opened the screen, and booted it up. "Those three files there. The second and third ones can be run at high speed; the important bits are at the end. Here's a set of earphones for the sound." Turning, she ushered the younger teens away from that side of the table. "C'mon, guys. You *know* this isn't for your eyes."

"What, seriously?" groaned Buddy. "You're *still* not letting us watch it?"

Tesseract caught his eye. "One more word, young man, and you will be going back to the van and staying there until we leave. You've already been told why you can't view it." Superhero or not, there was no mistaking the '*Mom has spoken*' tone.

"Yeah, no, hard pass on that." Chelsea folded her arms. "I've done many questionable things in my time, but contributing to the corruption of minors was never one of my life goals."

"A laudable aim." Castellan took a seat, inserted the earpieces, then clicked on the first file. As Jericho stepped back around the table, Leroy and Daryl moved up to take his place, flanking Castellan's chair so they could see what was on the screen. Jericho didn't care; he'd experienced it once already, and that was enough for him. From the sheer focus in the older man's expression, he knew Castellan wouldn't miss anything important in the files.

"And this explains another thing, too," Chelsea noted. "How Seismic managed to upgrade his tech so thoroughly. He's gotta be working with Doc Iridium. If anyone could make a machine designed to create apocalyptic conditions work *more* effectively, it would be that asshole."

"At least we know about it now," Tesseract said quietly. "Better late than never." Fondly, she ruffled her older son's hair. "I'm just glad you went to Utopia City when you did, instead of hiding out someplace else. If you hadn't, we probably wouldn't have even this level of warning to work with."

"Yeah, talking about that." Jericho looked at Thomas, then at the rest of the Survivors. "I reckon I know why all y'all went there."

"Uh, *duh*," offered Chuck. "*I* went there 'cause I wanted to be a hero. Same with the rest of you guys, right?"

Sarah, Gareth, and Paul chorused in agreement, with Mel just behind them. Thomas was the only one who hesitated.

"I'm not so sure," he said. "I remember when I was flying west toward Seattle, even before my suit crapped out on me, I kept feeling this urge to swing south. And once I did crash, I was in Utopia a week later, and that's where I was stuck until Jericho got us out of there. I didn't even try to move on until it was too late."

Jericho nodded to acknowledge his words, then turned to Gareth. "You said you wanted to be a hero, yeah? Why didn't you join Force Majeure?"

The tall, lanky young man pushed his hand back through his white-blond hair. "I ... dunno. In the first interview, the longer it went on, the less I wanted anything to do with them. Never set up a second interview. Went out as a hero with the others for a bit, but like Thomas said, mistakes were made. UCPD refused to cut us any slack at all. The next thing I knew, the bus terminal had shut down, my cash was worth nothing, and I was out on the street. Broke, homeless, and wanted by the cops, in the middle of the richest city in the world."

"That's about what I figured." Jericho looked at each of the Survivors. "Anyone else have a different experience?"

They shared glances, then almost as one, shook their heads. Chelsea had a thoughtful expression on her face but said nothing.

"Okay, then." Jericho raised his eyebrows. "What do you guys know about the Proximity Principle?"

"Mainly what you told me about it," Thomas said. "You take on powers similar to other Enabled if you get 'em while they're nearby. It's how you proved Dad was framed."

"Uh-huh." Jericho nodded. "And like I said back at the campground, the *second* part says you're drawn to the presence of whoever you got your powers from. Once you get there, you subconsciously choose whether you want to be with them or against them. Let me see if I can guess who you got your powers from." He pointed at Thomas, then at Sarah. "False Flag and Raider, but we already knew that."

His finger found Mel, still working on the Blood Rose. "Doc Iridium."

It went on to Gareth. "Charnel."

And then to Paul. "Guillotine."

Finally, he indicated Chuck. "And Singularity."

The Survivors stared at him, then at each other. Chuck shook his head.

"Oh, you've *got* to be kidding! I've got *her* powers?"

"No, you've got *your* powers," Chelsea said firmly. "They're just patterned off hers."

"Yeah, I can actually see that," Mel said in tones of enlightenment, raising her head from her work and lifting the goggle lenses for a moment. "All this time, I've been complaining about how the Technologist's stuff always gives me trouble, compared to other people's tech. But I've been looking at it all wrong. Nobody else can even get a handle on how his gear works, but I *can*. And talking about his tech, there's a chip here that looks interesting. Just gonna try to dig it out without destroying it."

Chelsea's head came up. "Reeaallyy?" she drawled, in much the same way she had in the motel room. "I'm gonna want to see that. Whatever's on it might just answer a few questions. Try and be careful with it, hey?"

"Yeah, yeah, go teach your grandma to change a fuse." Mel flipped her the bird, dropped the lenses down again, and resumed her investigation of the Blood Rose's mysteries.

Chelsea smirked at the comeback, then eyed the Survivors. "Something else I've just thought of. Have you guys considered that it might not have been a coincidence Utopia cut ties with Greyhound when it did? They'd probably had the idea in mind for a while, but I'm betting you're the ones who made it happen."

"What, really?" Thomas sounded startled. "I always thought it was just unfortunate timing on my part. On *our* part."

She snorted derisively. "Not hardly. You were active in the city, and you'd demonstrated having derivative powers but didn't want to join Force Majeure. That'd be a flashing neon sign to someone like Doc Iridium. Once you had no way of using paper money to get out of town, it would've been child's play to nickel-and-dime away what MagCard accounts you had."

"But we were *heroes*," protested Paul. "Saving people and stuff."

Chelsea nodded. "Yes, but you were also new to being heroes, so you were guaranteed to slip up at some point. It happens to the best of us. Most places, cops give rookie heroes the benefit of the doubt. This time 'round, they would've been had orders to come down hard on you. And if you don't even know you're wanted for questioning about some incident you had nothing to do with across town, you're automatically in the wrong when they do catch up with you."

"So … we could've just gone in and cleared it all up, and asked if they could give us a lift out of town?" asked Chuck doubtfully.

"Hah, no." Chelsea snorted mirthlessly. "They would've taken you into custody, then you would've vanished forever. Because I can *totally* see Doc Iridium wanting to experiment on people who've got variations on core Force Majeure powers. Casually cutting loose a transport network he gets no benefit out of, just to enforce greater reliance on the maglev *and* trap himself some lab rats? That's definitely something he'd do."

Jericho frowned. "But … he'd surely have to run something like that past

Relentless, right?"

"Sure." Chelsea's shrug was the epitome of *'doesn't matter'*. "What's the big guy gonna care if buses don't run to the city anymore? I bet he never knew they were gone. He probably just signs whatever crosses his desk. Or gets his executive assistant to do it."

Thomas grimaced. "Jesus. How close we came. The deck was totally stacked against us from the beginning."

Yeah. And it still is. Turning away, Jericho went over to the broad window that looked out onto the side yard. He pressed his knuckles against the sill, trying to bring his churning thoughts into order, but more worries kept popping up.

"Hey." Thomas moved up alongside him, sliding his arm around Jericho's waist as best he could with the spandex in the way. "Talk to me, lover. What's eating you this time?"

"Scout." Jericho clenched his eyes shut and pressed his forehead against the window glass. "He knew something was up. He told me I had to save Utopia. But now Doc Iridium's rebuilding him. What if he gets reprogrammed as a villain or something?"

"Shit." Thomas' sigh trailed off. "Look, you *know* how good Gimmick is. She figured out Doc Iridium was still alive, just from looking at his tech. If anyone can deprogram him again, it's her. Okay?"

"Yeah, true." It wasn't much more than a glimmer of hope, but Jericho decided he'd take what he could get right then. "Thanks."

"Anytime. I know this is hard on you, so feel free to lean on me whenever you need it, night or day. Got it?"

"Got it." Jericho felt warmth spreading through his chest, dissipating the chill he had previously harbored there. He pulled Thomas into an embrace and kissed him. "And thanks again."

Almost as if this was a signal, Castellan pulled the earpieces out and laid the cord across the keyboard. Leroy and Daryl stepped back out of the way; their expressions were set hard in reaction to what they'd undoubtedly seen. Jericho thought he saw the glint of tears lurking at the corners of his uncle's eyes, though he knew the man would never admit to them.

"Extremely troubling," Castellan conceded, looking up at Chelsea. "Where did those files originate from, precisely?"

"A top-secret Force-Majeure-eyes-only database inside the Spire," she replied boldly. "Yes, I acquired them illegally. But we're not going in there with a warrant, are we?"

"Even if we were, you're not law enforcement, so it would still be actionable intel." He sighed. "But I doubt it'll ever come to that. I presume the first file referred to terror villain code-names via the international phonetic alphabet? False Flag, Charnel, Guillotine, and so forth?"

Jericho pulled his mind back to the business at hand. This was yet more proof the old man was still sharp as a tack despite having been out of the hero business for seventeen years.

I'd hate to have gone up against him in his prime.

"That's what we figured, especially after Silent Knight turned out to be Charnel," he confirmed. "The rest of it fits, all the way down the line." He shook his head. "I was *right there* when they pulled the bait and switch with Bobbi's boyfriend, and I never suspected a thing."

"As the saying goes, the perfect crime requires nobody suspecting that a crime even took place." Castellan turned his attention to Chelsea. "I need to ask: what does your current plan of attack entail?"

"We infiltrate the city and make contact with Relentless," she replied promptly. "Once we've got his attention, we present him with the new evidence. Jericho's probably the best for that; Relentless has consistently shown trust in him. Then Relentless uses his clearance as team leader to mark the others as intruders in the system. After that, we get to stand back with popcorn while Utopia's security setup takes care of the problem for us."

"We can't be certain it'll get them all," Castellan cautioned. "They're a notoriously slippery bunch, and from my recollections of Doc Iridium, he always had at least two bolt-holes to fall back on."

Chelsea nodded to acknowledge this. "Yeah, but even he won't be able to do much once his own tech is turned against him. After the dust settles, we're gonna need you to liaise between Relentless, the city authorities, and the three-letter agencies that *will* be flooding into Utopia in the aftermath, mainly to ensure every Enabled in the city gets a fair hearing. Like I said before, you're the only one with the legal chops and the superhero cred to pull that off."

"There may be a little mopping-up required, but—" began Adam Power.

"Hah! *There* you are, you little smart-ass!" Mel brandished a chip in the air, held in a pair of tweezers protruding from her multitool. "Now, let's plug you in and see what you've got to say for yourself."

"Here you go," Chelsea announced, handing Mel a container from her backpack. "Chip adaptor sockets. Artificers for the win."

"*Excellent.*" Mel flicked up her goggle lenses then selected one particular socket, plugged the chip into it, and slotted the whole affair into the side of Chelsea's laptop. Hanging the multitool on her belt again, she leaned over the keyboard and started typing rapidly. "Oh, yes. Be a good little evil chip now, and tell Mommy all your secrets." She paused as windows popped up on the screen, text rapidly scrolling down them. "Okay ... it looks like a couple of biometric profiles. It's kind of like what they use in Utopia, actually, on the MagCards. Not identical, but close."

Chelsea nodded slowly. "Well now, isn't *that* interesting. Check that file just over ... yeah, there. That's the actual MagCard biometric profiles for Force Majeure. I snagged them while I was hunting around in the Spire's databanks for anything I could use, before I hit the jackpot. If I'm right, the Technologist will be on it, but I doubt the other profile will get a match at all—"

"Wrong!" crowed Mel. "We've got *two* matches! Number one: the

Technologist, ay-kay-ay Doc stinking Iridium! And the other …" She paused, frowning. "Wait. This can't be correct."

"Why not?" asked Jericho, moving forward with Thomas at his side. "Who is it?"

Chelsea got there first, leaning over Mel's shoulder. "Oh, *come* on now. You've *gotta* be shitting me!"

"How's that even *possible*?" demanded Mel, staring at the screen in horror.

As Adam Power stepped up alongside Chelsea, his jaw dropped.

"*Relentless* is the Minotaur?"

63
The Burden of Proof

*R*elentless is the Minotaur.

Blood pounded in Jericho's ears as those four words repeated over and over in his head, and he scrambled for a view of the screen to read the answer for himself. Even then, as his eyes compared the two biometric profiles, he still couldn't accept it. It *wasn't* right. It *couldn't* be right.

He felt himself being jostled away from the table as others sought to verify the impossible results for themselves. It didn't matter anymore; he'd seen them, and now he had no idea which way was up or what day it was. Bumped and rebounded like a pinball in an earthquake, he found himself gathered into the sanctuary of Thomas' arms, up against the wall and out of the tumult.

Relentless is the Minotaur.

It couldn't be true! Relentless was steadfast and strong, an iconic hero for the ages! The man he'd long since admired and wanted to be like, even briefly wanted to be *with* … the man who had saved countless innocents from Madness and misfortune alike … the man who was *Relentless*.

Relentless is the Minotaur.

"Mother*fuck*—" That was Leroy, for sure.

"He *can't* be—" He thought that was Sarah.

As the room erupted around them, he pressed his forehead against Thomas' chest, curling into him for reassurance and support. He clutched at Thomas' left hand, while his boyfriend's right arm curled protectively up over his back. Slowly, soothingly, a strong thumb and forefinger massaged the back of his neck, up under his scalp line.

"Well, *that's* fucked the plan—" Chelsea's voice was easy to pick out.

"What are we gonna do—" Maybe Buddy?

An ear-shattering whistle, with a pitch and volume capable of summoning a New York cab from across eight lanes of rush-hour traffic, cut through the room like a laser beam through a snowbank. Jericho raised his eyes and turned his head to look at Castellan, who was just now lowering his fingers from his mouth.

"Let's have a little decorum here," growled the veteran hero, the uncompromising tone of his rebuke giving Jericho the impetus to pull himself together. "One at a time. Gimmick. What does that chip do, exactly?"

With peace semi-restored in the room, Jericho's desire to clear Relentless' name surged inexorably until it thundered in his chest and rang in his ears. He wanted to shout at Mel that whatever the chip said was *wrong*, but the pure unalloyed authority Castellan was exerting on the room kept him in check.

He stood a little straighter and turned to face the room so that Thomas' arm went across his chest. Releasing Thomas' hand with his right, he squeezed with his left. Thomas squeezed back, and he derived comfort from the close contact.

With an abrupt motion, Mel shoved her goggles up onto her forehead. Her lips were pressed tightly together, and she took short, sharp breaths through her nostrils. "It's a safety measure," she said, her voice clipped. "Normally, if someone stabs you with this, the blades spread out—"

"I'm fully aware of its normal operating procedure, young lady." Even with his reproving tone, Castellan kept to a modicum of politeness. "What. Does. The. *Chip*. Do?"

She nodded curtly; whether it was to acknowledge the question or the man who posed it, Jericho didn't know. "If your bio-signature's on it, the blades stay together and avoid your vital organs as much as possible. There'd be some unavoidable trauma, but it'd look a lot worse than it really was. Given access to competent medical care, you'd have a good chance of survival." She shook her head. "Do you really think—"

Half a dozen voices started up again, but Jericho was right there with them this time. "He's a *hero*!" he shouted. "He *designed* Utopia! This *has* to be a mistake!"

He could feel Thomas squeezing his hand and tugging back at him with the arm across his chest in an effort to corral his outburst. Right then, he didn't care. It had to be said. If they would just *listen* …

He was drawing breath to reiterate his views when Castellan turned his head, the stern gaze beneath lowered brows pulling the wind clean out of Jericho's sails. He wasn't the only one; one sweep of the room had quieted the outcry before it could get well started.

Castellan returned his attention to Mel. "What's your level of certainty for that match?" He looked every inch the experienced prosecutor, ready to pick apart a shoddily prepared defense case. "That technology is at least ten years older than the MagCard system. I do understand the same person designed both, but is it possible for the formats to have shifted? Could this be a false positive?"

"I can't tell you that," Mel replied, her tone flat and hard. "Even if my powers are derived from Doc Iridium's, *I'm not him*. I don't know how he thinks, and I don't have the intervening formats to study. It might be a false positive, and it might not be. I don't *think* so, but I don't *know*."

"You see?" Jericho burst out, his roiling emotions seizing on the '*I don't know*'. "It can't be true! I don't believe it!"

Castellan turned toward him once more. "Arguments from incredulity are inapplicable." His tone brooked no contradiction. "Mere belief is worth nothing, here; I require facts. Do you have any?"

Jericho wanted to cringe away from his disapproval, but Thomas' presence gave him strength. Squeezing his boyfriend's hand for support, he stood firm, determined to say his piece. "Yes. When I told Relentless about Charnel and False Flag trying to kill me, he was *livid*. Chelsea was there, and she's never wrong about that sort of stuff. So that means he's a good guy, right? He *can't* be the Minotaur."

Castellan's gaze cut across to Chelsea, who straightened her back in response to his interrogatory expression. "It's true," she answered the unasked question. "It's what I do." Her confidence was unshakable, and Jericho allowed himself to relax slightly, knowing an ally was at hand. "When Relentless learned what happened, he told Jericho to keep his head down, and swore he would kill Independence with his bare hands. Later, he told us she'd been permanently retired. He wasn't lying; I'd swear to that on a stack of Bibles taller than the Spire. Whatever that chip's telling you, it's not the whole story."

"On balance, I'm inclined to agree with your conclusion." Castellan nodded to acknowledge her point. "Whether it was in failsafe mode or not, the Blood Rose still dealt a substantial wound to the Minotaur. When I last saw him, he was in no condition to fight. And then he fell into the ocean with half his labyrinth on top of him. Survival, under those circumstances, would have been problematic at best. At this stage, in the absence of credible supporting evidence, I remain unconvinced. I refuse to condemn Relentless on mere supposition."

With this pronouncement, the tension in the room began to ease. Jericho felt his heart rate palpably slowing as the adrenaline ebbed from his system.

Chelsea broke the silence with a chuckle. Jericho knew it had to be forced, but it would sound entirely genuine to anyone else. "Well, whether Relentless is a hero or a villain, I can definitely think of *one* reason he'd be pissed at them for trying to murder Jericho's well-toned ass." It was a transparent attempt at breaking up the last of the tension still lingering in the room, and Jericho cringed inwardly at the jokes sure to follow, once people found out what she was talking about.

That was when the reference sparked a horrifying realization, which in turn impacted the base of his skull like a piledriver. An icy flood filled his spine from top to bottom, numbing his limbs and freezing his thought processes solid. He *knew* the truth, beyond all shadow of a doubt. Nobody knew it but him ... and it would never see the light of day if he stayed quiet.

"Still, I can't see this matching anyone else *but* Relentless," Mel piped up, studying the profiles closely. "I mean, unless—"

"Seriously, give it up!" shouted Sarah. "He *can't* be the Minotaur!"

"You're not *listening*!" Mel snapped back. "What if there's *someone else—*"

As if they'd just been waiting for another spark, emotions flared again. Voices rose, thick with fear scarcely veiled as anger. Nobody *wanted* to face the Minotaur, but while half were unwilling to even consider the option, the others were concerned about *'what if it's true?'*.

To Jericho, working through his own internal dilemma, it all seemed muffled and far away.

"As I said before ..." Castellan's voice, loaded with the gravitas of having been there and done that in the real world, sliced through the arguments once more. In the ensuing silence, his tone lowered to a more reasonable level. "All we have right now is circumstantial evidence, requiring further examination. Unless someone has *conclusive* proof to offer—"

"I do."

For a good five seconds, Jericho couldn't figure out why everyone was staring at him. And then he had it; he was the one who'd spoken. He curled down and away again, seeking refuge once more in Thomas' arms. This time he truly needed it, as he was trying to hide from *himself*.

I didn't mean to say that out loud!

But as much as he didn't *want* to, some part of him knew he *had* to. Beyond his own petty wants and needs, beyond the loyalty he'd thought was his be-all and end-all ... it was his *duty*. He owed it to who and what he was, deep down.

"G-Man, I'll need you to explain that statement." He now had Castellan's full attention. "If you have more to add to this discussion ..."

Jericho bit his bottom lip, hard enough to draw blood. He didn't want to speak out against Relentless, not after all the man had done for him, but this was a truth he had to share.

Out of the corner of his eye, he saw Thomas' finger lift in a *'wait one moment'* gesture. Then his boyfriend's right arm tightened around his chest, supporting and reassuring him. He felt Thomas' lips next to his ear, in an echo of the tender interlude they'd shared in the van not so long ago.

"Take your time," whispered the voice of the man he loved. "I'm here. I'll never let you go." It was a promise sincerely made, one that Jericho knew would be kept, come hell or high water. The reassurance spread down his spine, relaxing him.

He gradually edged his head around until he could look Castellan in the eye.

This needs to be said.

When he opened his mouth, his throat unlocked, and he drew a long, shuddering breath. The words he spoke were ash upon his tongue. "I ... I have proof."

All eyes were on him, none more intense than Castellan's. He couldn't meet them; he didn't dare. The accusation in some of them would have undone him utterly.

"I'm listening, son." Castellan's voice was quiet, compelling.

Lifting his left hand, giving Thomas time to release him from the embrace, Jericho placed his index finger in the middle of his right shoulder. Then he drew it all the way across his chest, just about level with his collarbones, to the far shoulder. "When you were fighting him, you cut him from here to here, didn't you?"

After a long moment, Castellan nodded. "Yes. I did."

Then Jericho lifted his right hand, put the index finger on the top of his left shoulder, and drew it down to cross the first line, like a lazy 't'. "And here to here."

The silence in the room was near-absolute. Castellan's eyes were laser-focused. He made a sound of confirmation and nodded once again.

Finally, Jericho spread his right hand wide and placed it on his own abdomen, a few inches up from the hip. "And this here's where you got him with the Blood Rose."

"How can you *possibly* know all that?" Castellan's tone was as razor-edged as the Artificer weapon itself. "The footage from the fight doesn't show it. I know; I've looked."

Jericho knew full well that the words he was about to say could never be unsaid. Just for a moment, one last lone shred of loyalty kept him silent. But he pushed through it and took the plunge. "Because I saw those scars on Relentless, the night he invited me to his rooms in the Spire for a drink."

Castellan exhaled, a long sigh of resignation. Muted voices broke out around the room, balanced between *'well, shit,'* and *'thought so,'* but he didn't quell them this time. Instead, he looked Jericho in the eye and nodded pensively. "It *is* him, then. I'd hoped it wasn't."

"Yeah," said Jericho heavily. "You and me both, sir."

Chelsea met his eyes; he saw the compassion in her expression. Of everyone in the room, she was the only one who'd been at his side through the whole odyssey of discovery, from lightning strike to horrified epiphany. She was one of the few people who could understand what he'd just been through, who'd shared the urgency to warn Relentless of the danger before it was too late, and the horror when he discovered the reality.

Thomas supported him in all this because of the love they shared. Chelsea supported him because she'd *been* there. And now, in her own inimitable way, she was coming through for him yet again.

"I remember that," Chelsea said, in a way that deliberately drew attention away from him. "That was back in October. Jericho came knocking on my door, looking like a dozen crappy Monday mornings rolled into one. This was after he'd secured his position in Force Majeure. Turns out—and this should've been a red flag to anyone with a moral compass—Relentless has this thing where he likes to proposition the new recruits for sex …"

The distraction was precisely what Jericho needed. Despite Chelsea's engaging story-telling style, he knew how this one ended, so he tuned her out. He let Thomas fold him into an embrace once more, soothing his raw emotions with the reassuring nearness.

As he pressed his face into Thomas' chest, he felt hot tears tricking from his eyes. He'd long thought of his loyalty as his greatest asset, but Force Majeure had proven that a lie. Simply by showing their true colors, they'd torn his heart out seven times over without ever laying a hand on him. Worse, it had held him back from doing what needed to be done. Silently, as Chelsea spun her story, he shed bitter tears of betrayal and loss for his hopes and expectations of the future.

I have to do better. I owe it to everyone here.

He raised his head as the story meandered to a close. Accepting a very familiar handkerchief from Thomas, he surreptitiously wiped it across his eyes. Now that he could think clearly again, he found himself wondering about odd aspects that hadn't occurred to him before.

Tesseract looked at him with concern as he stood up straighter. "Are you okay there? That can't have been easy."

"I'll be fine," he assured her. To say he *was* fine would've been a straight-up lie, so he avoided that. "But even ignoring the rest of it, here's some things I don't understand: we know Transit's Raider, so why'd she go out of her way to be nice to a nobody from the sticks? Why'd they partner me with a literal bodyguard robot? If they knew about Thomas and me, why didn't they ask me about that, or even just kick me off the team for letting the Survivors go? Why all the preferential treatment?"

Chelsea sobered. "I've no idea," she said slowly. "Put like that, it does raise a few questions. I guess you'll have to ask them about it yourself, once they're behind bars."

"Well said," Castellan agreed. "I will freely admit that I stand corrected regarding Relentless. The entire core membership of Force Majeure, it appears, is composed of hardened criminals, who are at *best* restraining themselves to minor forays against the population outside of Utopia City, not even counting the airliner virus hacks. Most worrying of all, they are led by the Minotaur, who I can categorically state is the most vindictively sadistic opponent I've ever had the displeasure to encounter."

By the time he'd finished speaking, the atmosphere was once more charged with tension, but this time it was directed at an external enemy. The bad news had been assimilated, and now the room simmered with a level of grim resignation.

"On top of which," added Chelsea, "they've managed to build a *ranged* earthquake machine capable of hitting anywhere in the world, for shits and giggles. And let's not forget that this weapon is *specifically* in the hands of both Seismic and Doc Iridium. So, yay for that." Even though she used her most upbeat tone, nobody so much as smiled.

"You know how Jericho said Utopia City's a crime scene?" Sarah held her hands up as though she were framing a camera shot. "I can do one better. The Spire? That's the biggest, flashiest, best-hidden supervillain base in the whole damn *world*."

Adam Power nodded somberly. "Agreed. And just to put the icing on the cake, Force Majeure has *considerable* political pull in DC, clear across the spectrum, as well as a lot of popular public support. The right loves them because they're a government-supported superhero team with strong nationalistic themes and ties to the military-industrial complex. In contrast, the left is heavily invested in their green initiatives, not to mention the lifestyle available in Utopia City and the surrounding region."

"Why's that even matter?" asked Gareth. "We're not exactly running for public office, here."

Castellan took the floor to answer that one. "It matters because this new information requires us to rethink our entire strategy for defeating them. The villains completely control Utopia City, the Spire, and the security setup protecting both. If we're going to get to them, we will require active assistance—or at least a promise to stand aside—from interested parties within the United States government. Because there *will* be some who refuse to condemn Force Majeure, even in the face of overwhelming evidence."

Adam nodded again. "I encountered that level of political expedience when I was trying to rebuild our market share following Vanessa's return. Even knowing I was innocent of the accusations, even fully aware that I could outbid the Technologist in price and quality on certain items, they made up every excuse under the sun to avoid doing business with me. If we can't make an end-run around that kind of partisanship, we'll be fighting both the government *and* the villains."

"So, I dunno, tell the newspapers or something?" hazarded Buddy. "*Someone* has to listen, right?"

Tesseract frowned. "I'm no political expert, honey. But in my experience, if we went public right now with what we know, there would be more negative spin directed at us than an unpopular candidate in an election year. Their more invested supporters would flat-out refuse to even look at the evidence, much less give it a fair hearing."

"Really?" Chuck sounded dubious. "I mean, people can be dicks, but these are *terror villains* we're talking about. There's gotta be a line, right?"

"You'd think so, but no." Tesseract raised her eyebrows. "Remember what *we* were like, not five minutes ago? And we *knew* the person presenting the information. Take a bunch of politicians and pundits with a vested interest in maintaining the status quo, and they'll accept any excuse to discount the truth. Even if the news stations agreed to take it up, which is *not* a guarantee, it would be the *Lügenpresse*—the '*lying press*' from 1930s Germany—all over again."

Adam set his jaw. "And in the very worst case, it's been fifteen years since the US last had a terror villain attack shoved in its face. The man on the street simply doesn't think that far back. Given the sheer breadth and depth of the political *and* physical clout Force Majeure has amassed in the meantime, and how thoroughly they've entrenched themselves into the national identity, they may just be given a pass so they can keep handing out the goodies. Once again, pure political expedience."

"So, what do we *do*?" asked Jericho. "Where do we go from here?"

"That's not for me to answer." Adam turned to Castellan. "As you've pointed out, our infiltration plan is dead in the water. We have no contacts within Utopia City, and the bad guys control every facet of information reaching its population. Force Majeure literally has over a million hostages who don't *know* they're hostages, and who might just choose to stay where they are even if someone managed to convince them of the truth. You were a military officer and a high-powered government prosecutor before you ever put on the mask. How do we proceed from here?"

Castellan nodded to acknowledge the question. His back straightened, and the light of battle had come into his eyes. When he spoke, his voice once more held the snap of command.

"We all know the facts of the situation. If we act on this knowledge, we face immeasurable danger, not to mention the distinct possibility of being cast as the villains of the piece. However, this is not a military operation, and I am not your commanding officer. Anyone who wishes to walk away may do so now, with no ill-feeling. But if you make that choice, you *will* need to leave." He surveyed the assembled group, awaiting their response.

Tesseract Power glanced at her children and then Adam, who each nodded in agreement. Lifting her chin, she spoke firmly. "They attacked my family, and there's nothing to say they won't try again if they're not stopped. We got this."

Sarah conferred briefly with the rest of the Survivors, then turned to Castellan. "We spent nearly two years running and hiding from those jerks, all because Doc Iridium wanted to dissect us like frogs in biology class. Screw 'em. They're going down."

"Yeah," said Jericho. "Like Bobbi said in that clip: what matters is that they face justice for everything they've done. Charnel might be dead, and False Flag's on ice, but they still murdered Luke and Bobbi. The Minotaur's the one who gave the order to do that."

"Damn right," snapped Leroy; at his side, Daryl nodded grim agreement. "That shit don't fly, nohow."

Thomas glanced at his parents, then squeezed Jericho's hand and set his mouth in a hard line. "Along with everything else they've done, False Flag made me hate my dad. I can't ever forgive that."

All eyes turned to Chelsea. Her smile had nothing to do with humor. "I started this when I pulled those files out of the Spire, so I'll be damned if I'm gonna walk away now. Besides, those assholes give villains a bad name."

"Indeed." Castellan cleared his throat. "Years ago, I thought I had put an end to the Minotaur. It's time to correct that oversight."

He paused as though considering his words, then continued.

"Our adversaries have had over a decade to prepare their ground, and they have not been idle. We must gather our allies, build our resources, make our plans in secret; above all, allow *nothing* of this to reach the ears of Force Majeure or their cohorts." He glanced around the room; the years seemed to fall away from him.

"Let's get to work."

- End of Part Four -

EPILOGUES

We're going, we're going.
- Mutilator

Does anyone else want to be stupid?
- Raider

Make it happen.
- the Minotaur

Don't go anywhere.
- Relentless

Screw that noise.
- Troll

Epilogue One
Mutilator

Off the Coast of Washington State
Friday, July 11, 1997

S alt spray blew back from the bow, and sunlight sparkled on the wavetops as *The Price is Right* cut through a rising swell, beating nor-nor-west against a freshening breeze. The sails were well-trimmed, and Miranda had tutored Alexei well enough that he could be trusted at the helm. Besides, the visibility was good enough that she'd see any problems coming, long before they happened. The boat was small enough for two people to manage if at least one of them knew what they were doing; Alexei was a willing student, if a little slow.

Leaning against the foredeck rail, she turned her head slightly to look back at her colossal henchman. There was no denying Alexei had literally saved her life on more than one occasion since they'd become partners, and the big dope had grown on her to a certain extent. But not to the level of the attachment that he'd formed toward her.

His years as Cherenkov had taken a toll on him, both inevitable and inexorable, as the damage done to his body by his powers was also reflected in his brain. By the time Doc Iridium had located him in the no-go zone surrounding the Chornobyl disaster, he'd been reduced to a near-skeletal form with a childlike intellect. Iridium's power containment harness had slowed Alexei's decline to a virtual halt, and the artificer had enlisted Miranda's aid to save the life of the dying Russian Enabled.

She'd thought at first it would be a one-and-done, a way to repay Iridium for the surgical multigloves he'd constructed for her a while back. Her assessment of the situation was that Cherenkov needed massive grafts of tissue and skin to replace what he'd lost, along with transplants of a few minor organs that had already either failed or been destroyed along the way. This was fine; it was just another challenge to her surgical skills, albeit far beyond anything she'd faced before.

When Miranda first started out as Surgeon One, she'd occasionally felt the urge to stretch herself and do more than the simple workaday surgery that was her bread and butter. Even the most intricate micro-tumor removal or skeletal reconstruction was nothing more than returning the body to factory standard; she wanted to do *more*. She wanted to go *further*, and truly explore the possibilities inherent in her Prodigy focus.

But she'd restrained herself and stuck to the rules; after all, the money was rolling in, and if she partied hard enough with her multitude of adoring fans, she could usually convince herself she was having fun. A little boredom was a minor price to pay under these circumstances ... right up until those Unmask assholes got in on the act.

When she first understood their demands, she'd thought it might be some kind of ultra-subtle sting by the authorities, testing out her willingness to adhere to the rules. But they were literally threatening her family, people she loved, with harm or even death if she didn't do as she was told. This shit was real. So, she had to make a choice.

It turned out that deliberately hurting people was a lot easier than she'd ever imagined.

At first, when she started cutting on the victims, Miranda had tried to remind herself how horrified she should be at having to do this. It was *wrong*, and against the *rules*, and she'd always been careful to follow the letter of the law. After all, Unmask weren't the only people out there with a distaste for Enabled. Any number of petty bureaucrats she'd encountered during her professional career would've gleefully hampered or even killed that career stone dead if she hadn't assiduously dotted every 'i' and crossed every 't'. Unmask were merely the ones who chose to go *outside* the law to do it.

Personally, she thought they were all jealous of what she could do with her Prodigy abilities, and they couldn't. Sour grapes from beginning to end.

She'd been conservative with the surgeries on the victims at first, only making changes that could be reversed by any other surgeon. But between the demands of Unmask and her own urges, she found herself leaning harder and harder into her Prodigy skillset. That was when she *really* began to get into it. After all, this was what she'd always craved, deep down: the chance to let loose and see what she could really do, once the brakes were off. It wasn't a hostage situation so much as an opportunity. For the first time ever, surgery became *fun*.

In the aftermath, she'd tried to feel regret for her enthusiasm, but it just wouldn't come. Once tasted, the full fruits of her power were far more intoxicating and addictive than alcohol had ever been.

Still, she would've gone back to her work of mundane surgery if she'd been allowed to. She didn't quite know where she'd find willing victims for the urges that had been so thoroughly awakened within her, but the world was a big place and some people had the *oddest* fetishes. Something, she was sure, could be worked out.

But the petty bureaucrats won in the end. She'd misstepped, and now they were bound and determined to extract their pound of flesh. One after the other, obstacles were manufactured to block her from returning to her everyday life. Instead of being suppressed for the sake of privacy, the videotapes were broadcast *everywhere*. And far from seeing her as the victim, the court of public opinion was passing sentence on her before the legal system ever got that far. *She* wasn't the one who'd kidnapped those people, after all. And hey, she'd left everyone alive. That had to count for *something*, right?

Right?

...

Apparently, it didn't.

With nobody on her side, her legitimately earned money was out of reach because yet *another* malicious little paper-pusher had deemed her a potential flight risk. She needed a good lawyer to free up the funds faster, but she couldn't afford to *pay* for a good lawyer until she had that very same cash in hand. Catch-twenty-two all the way around. No doubt some office-bound penny-pincher had rubbed his hands with glee after devising *that* little trap for her.

The walls were closing in, and at a certain point, she just ... snapped. She'd tried to do things the way society wanted, but they *just kept pushing*. The last straw came when an officious sheriff's deputy threatened her with handcuffs because she yelled at him for serving her with yet *another* court summons. A pair of scissors was right at hand, and she disabled the bureaucrat-with-a-badge without any effort at all. Then she discovered one more important thing; performing surgery was a lot more fun if the patient *didn't have to survive*.

Enough was enough. Miranda Price could take a hint. From that moment on, she'd embraced the darker side of her Prodigy powerset. In fact, she almost felt as though she owed those Unmask mouth-breathers a debt of gratitude for showing her the light. She was so generous in her recognition of their act that when she tracked them down, she made it last *days* before finally allowing the last of them to die. Strangely enough, they didn't seem to be able to muster the appropriate level of appreciation for how they'd been right about her all along.

When Doc Iridium brought Cherenkov to her, she threw herself into the task, thoroughly enjoying every moment of it. Rebuilding him almost from scratch, using tissue and organs from not-entirely-willing donors (some still screaming as she operated to remove what she needed) was a whole new experience, one she utterly relished.

Perhaps the most challenging obstacle to overcome was the infantile mind he'd possessed when he was brought to her. In what was probably her most spectacular surgical feat yet, she'd harvested brain matter from several 'donors' and carefully integrated it with his damaged tissues to reverse the decline and improve his learning capacity once more. She hadn't brought him all the way back to adult capability—that would've taken a lot more work—but she'd helped him develop his own personality and brought him up to the level of an eleven- or twelve-year-old: a vast improvement on what she'd had to start with.

Neither did she stop once she'd returned him to what his build suggested he'd been before all this started. Enlarging and thickening his skeleton was simplicity itself for someone of her talents; then, she set to work constructing a *masterpiece*.

By the time she put the finishing touches on him, Devastator (he was

Cherenkov no more) had gone from five foot eight to six foot four. Furthermore, he was a walking slab of destructive muscle, over and above the powerful energy beams he could muster as part of his Dynamic powerset. Thanks to Iridium's power containment harness, his radiation aura no longer endangered everyone within a one-mile radius; nor did it shred the very skin and flesh from his body and damage his brain in an endlessly agonizing process. The harness even altered Alexei's powers, giving him more flexibility in their use and reducing the gamma count to near-nil while changing the color frequency of the expelled energy from blue to red.

She'd fully expected Doc Iridium to claim Devastator as a minion, but apparently he'd planned all along for the big guy to remain with her. She was vulnerable on her own, and Alexei was impressively effective as muscle, so she was entirely on board with the idea of a mutually beneficial partnership. The solo act of Mutilator became the duo of Mutilator and Devastator, and they were *oh* so very effective.

Her mind returned to the present as Alexei called out from the cockpit. "Boss! Something happening onshore!"

At the same time, she became aware of a change in the screeching of the gulls overhead. They were swooping down to land on something floating just a few dozen yards shoreward of the boat. She shaded her eyes, peering, and was rewarded with a brief glimpse of a human hand. *That's a body.*

"Bring us about," she ordered, pointing. "We need to be over there." If this was a person who'd fallen overboard from some boat or other, she could always do with more spare parts for Alexei. While his containment harness prevented his powers from slowly killing him, he sometimes took damage in battle, and she couldn't simply wait for his body to heal in the usual fashion.

Which reminded her; she hadn't abducted and dissected anyone for *weeks*, not since she'd 'acquired' and renamed the yacht she and Alexei were sailing up the coast. It appeared the anti-psychotics she was testing on herself were successfully reducing her urge to sink the blade in and watch the blood flow. Not *all* the way, but enough to make it manageable.

As *The Price is Right* heeled into the turn, she busied herself with the lines, keeping an eye out for the boom. She'd done enough hobby-sailing during her Surgeon One years to make this kind of thing second nature.

Once she was sure they were on the right course, she turned her attention to the shore, more than a mile distant. Seattle was some way north, which made her wonder what the preponderance of flashing red and blue lights on the clifftop was all about. Or even how part of the cliff face had slid into the ocean; the gigantic dust cloud was only just now starting to dissipate.

Well, they're hardly there for me, she decided. *I'll probably see whatever it was on the news tonight.* The tiny TV in the cabin was older than the boat itself, but it worked well enough.

Turning her attention back to the body in the water as the boat got closer, she raised her eyebrows with interest. This guy was *huge*, as big naturally as she'd reconstructed Alexei to be. "Going to need your help, here," she called back to her henchman, already loosening the lines so she could slacken off the sails as necessary.

"Okay," he replied readily enough.

Over the next minute, Alexei adjusted the rudder according to her instructions as she let the air spill from the sails, gradually slowing the boat. *The Price is Right* was almost at a standstill in the water as they slid up to the body, which was just what they needed. Alexei leaned over the side with one hand grasping the rail, while Miranda stood by with a rope and a life-preserver. A last-minute gust of wind tried to fill the slack sails and almost ruined the retrieval attempt, but Alexei grabbed the body's arm and heaved it on board; despite her comparative lack of upper-body strength, Miranda did her best to assist.

The body was clad in tights from the waist down. When it was laid out flat on the deck, she discovered four things.

First, the guy had been in a *fight*. Apart from the bruises and minor contusions, an extended cut stretched the width of his shoulders just below the neck, crossed over on the left shoulder by a shorter slice. Both were smooth and clean, and showed signs of having almost been *burned* into the flesh. By contrast, on the lower right side of his abdomen was an oozing wound with extremely distinct characteristics. The Blood Rose had done that, or she didn't know her supervillain weapons.

Second, she recognized him. Terror villains didn't get together often and when they did, it was necessarily in the utmost secrecy, but she'd seen that face unmasked before. Which begged the question; who'd had the sheer unadulterated brass balls to wreck the *Minotaur* with his own weapon?

Third, clutched in his right hand was the blade of an Artificer-made sword—she knew the signs—minus the hilt and guard.

And finally ... he was still alive. Coughing, choking, retching up seawater, but alive.

During this whole operation, she'd kept a weather eye on the shore, and now her vigilance was paying off. A helicopter that had been circling the flashing lights onshore had altered course and was heading out toward them.

Do I hide him or turn him over to them?

The decision was easy to make. She'd had Alexei bring the boat around so that their rescuee was on the starboard side of *The Price is Right*, hiding what they were doing from those onshore. Also, terror villains rarely turned on each other. They got enough of that from regular villains and heroes alike.

Butt-hurt that we can do what they can't, every single one of them.

"Get him below," she ordered, then headed back toward the cockpit.

"Okay." Scooping up the wounded man, Alexei set about maneuvering them both through the narrow companionway, down into the cabin, and out of sight. It wasn't easy, but she'd long since ensured he was both dexterous and light on his feet.

By the time the helicopter was overhead, Miranda could read the letters

FBI emblazoned on the side. Now that she had a good idea of what was happening onshore, this surprised her not at all. She took up the loudhailer that resided in the cockpit and waited for them to speak first.

"ATTENTION, PRICE IS RIGHT," the side-mounted speakers on the chopper bellowed, easily drowning out the steady *whup-whup-whup* of the rotors. *"THIS IS NOW A RESTRICTED AREA. LEAVE IMMEDIATELY."*

"Sorry," she called back through her own bullhorn. "I didn't know. We're going now. Can you tell me what's going on?"

"NEGATIVE," the officious little prick in the chopper responded. *"CLEAR THE AREA. NOW."*

"We're going, we're going." She put the loudhailer down just as Alexei emerged from the companionway. He started pulling the lines tight and lashing them firmly without needing to be told. Miranda checked the compass and set the course to be the reverse of what they'd just traveled, then went to assist Alexei. As the sails filled with wind, *The Price is Right* got underway.

They were some distance down the coast, with the assembled forces of law and order far behind them, before she finally managed to get below to see to her unexpected guest. The Minotaur was lying on one of the bunks, the narrow mattress looking even less substantial than usual under his bulk. One large hand pressed a red-soaked folded towel to the wound in his abdomen, while a long gauze bandage had been used to cover his other injuries. The blade he'd been holding when they found him lay on the floor alongside the bunk. His eyes were open and alert, and he watched her warily.

"Minotaur," she greeted him.

"Mutilator." His voice was rough and raw from the salt water he'd ingested.

Despite his injuries, it seemed he was tracking well. "How are you feeling?"

"Like hell." He didn't sound overly grateful for being rescued, but that didn't bother her. "Even think about stealing my organs, and I'll break your fuckin' neck." In her experience, the Minotaur was an asshole at the best of times, and this situation certainly did not qualify.

"I'd already figured *that* out." She kept her tone light and carefree. Alexei could probably overpower the Minotaur if she told him to, but the fight would likely sink the boat, and it was a long swim to shore. "You're lucky you got this far, bleeding like that. There are great whites around this way, or so I hear." Which was yet another good reason not to sink the boat.

"Didn't exactly have a choice." He chuckled briefly, then let out a grunt of pain. "God *damn*, that hurts. On the upside, Inspire's out of the picture."

"What, really?" Impressed, she raised her eyebrows. "If you took *them* on solo, I'm legitimately surprised that you survived."

"I played it smart." He showed his teeth in a vicious smile. "Found out where Arfogwyr lived, then I used her hand and retinal scan to get into that stupid base of theirs. Took out Challenger and blew up the base while I was there. Castellan came after me, and we had it out in my latest maze."

Taking a seat on the bunk opposite, she leaned forward unconsciously. "Castellan? Did you kill him, too? Hey, is that his damn sword?" She'd never seen it in real life, but it had featured on the news enough times, including one demonstration where Castellan used it to slice clear through a steel girder, leaving the ends glowing red.

"Fucked if I know what happened to him after the maze collapsed, but yeah, it is," he grunted, his face drawn with pain. "Shit, this does not feel good at all."

While the bandages on his chest were stained with blood, those wounds had been more seared into his flesh than cut, thus posing a minimal ongoing threat to his survival. From the Minotaur's stance on the bed, Miranda knew he was referring to the gory mess under the towel.

"Blood Rose?" she asked. When he confirmed her suspicion with a fractional nod, she followed up with the second burning question. "How'd you walk away from *that*?"

She knew what the weapon did, and had seen its effect a few times. Nobody (and she meant *nobody*) who'd taken a comprehensive hit from it could've survived the collapse of the maze and the avalanche down the cliff, much less swum out to where they'd picked him up. The blood loss and body shutdown due to the absence of several essential organs would've finished them off first. Which was why she was puzzled; it *looked* like his internals had been turned into chunky salsa by his own (notoriously fatal) weapon, yet here he was.

"Safety precaution," he gritted. "Iridium built in an owner recognition protocol. But he got me anyway. Fucking *Castellan*." The way he spoke the name was a curse.

She could tell he was getting worse. Even if the Minotaur was a prodigy (the betting field was open on that one), this was a wound he wouldn't easily survive. Fortunately, he now had other options.

"I can fix that for you," she said. "But you're going to have to trust me." Specifically, she didn't want him deciding to attack her once she let down her guard and commenced surgery.

His dark eyes bored into hers. "Why? Why help me? I'm literally at your mercy. I'm the goddamn *competition*."

She took a deep breath and nodded. "Yes, but I believe in networking and trading favors." Making herself useful was how she'd survived this long, after all. "Somewhere down the line, I might need your help."

He gave her a profoundly suspicious look. "Okay, but I don't want you putting me under."

"So long as you don't move, I don't care." It didn't matter to her. At the very least, she wouldn't be using up her limited supply of general anesthetic.

Teeth gritted, he gave her a curt nod. "Do it."

She got up and pulled aside the section of false bulkhead that hid her surgical kit. It had been quite some time since she'd had to operate merely to save someone's life (aside from Alexei, of course), but she was sure she could remember how it went.

"So," she said as she fitted the surgical multiglove onto her hand and ran it through a basic self-check. "Want me to do anything else while I'm in there? Remove your appendix? Check your oil? Locate your soul?"

The expression on his face suggested he didn't find it funny. "Just get on with it."

Miranda Price sighed. Some people had *no* sense of humor.

- End of Epilogue One -

Epilogue Two
Force Majeure

San Francisco, California
Saturday, August 16, 1997

Five Weeks After Rescuing the Minotaur

Leaning back in her chair with drink in hand, Miranda observed the others around the room. This was the largest gathering of terror villains she'd ever attended, and that was saying something. It was also the first since Carnifex bit the big one in Texas, which had brought the mood down a little.

It wasn't that the bestial Enabled had been universally popular—Miranda had personally considered him something of a creep—but he was the first terror villain to be actually hunted down and killed by the authorities. The thought written clearly on almost everyone's face went something along the lines of, *'if they went after him like that, will they come after me next?'*. It didn't matter that the so-called 'War on Terror Villains' had been rescinded, thanks to the Minotaur and False Flag; the thought was out there. The general public had learned that terror villains could die.

Case in point: just two days previously, the Chicago-based Team Power had engaged Kraken in the Great Lakes. His squid-sub had not been seen since, and he (along with the persistent fishy odor that followed him everywhere) was conspicuously absent from this gathering. It was the most sobering event within the terror villain fraternity since Team Power captured Charnel with almost insulting ease back in 1990. That had been before Miranda's time as a villain, but she'd heard chapter and verse on it since becoming one, mainly along the lines of *'don't let this happen to you'*.

Charnel had been absurdly lucky regarding the timing of his capture and arrest, in that it had happened when terror villains were still relatively unknown. Instead of executing him on the spot, they'd actually kept him in holding, awaiting judgment and trial. Since then, heroes and law enforcement alike had become remarkably less charitable; Carnifex and Kraken were sobering proof of that.

Providing an up-note was the confirmation of Inspire's demise as a team, though the Minotaur's boast of having killed both Arfogwyr and Challenger had proven only three-quarters correct. While the team artificer was indeed deceased—decapitation, as a rule, was universally fatal—Challenger was still alive, though reportedly in a coma. Castellan had survived the collapse of the maze, but he'd also told the news crews he was retiring from superhero life, effective immediately, so that was cause for celebration by some.

She glanced over to where Charnel and False Flag had their heads together about something. Whatever it was, she had no idea, but when that pair of overgrown frat boys started hatching their plots, trouble always resulted. At least Charnel hadn't chosen to show up in his shape-changed form this time. It wasn't his looks so much as his voice; when he spoke, it creeped *everyone* out.

She glanced over her shoulder at Alexei, who had evidently decided his place was to stand behind her like a servant rather than take a seat at the table. Before she could talk to him about it—again—there was a shuffle of movement, then Seismic slid into the chair she'd initially reserved for her henchman. She considered telling him that the ostentatiously oversized sleeves on his labcoat made him look ridiculous, then dismissed the idea; either he already knew, or wouldn't care.

"Mutilator," he greeted her cheerfully. "How's life in the world of ambush surgery?"

"Seismic." She tried to be polite, but he'd interrupted one of her jobs about seven months previously; she was still of the opinion that he'd done it deliberately. "Can I help you?"

He rolled his eyes behind the simple domino mask he was sporting, like everyone else. "Oh, *come* on. You can't even say something like *'what's shaking'*? No?" He waited for a moment. "Okay, fine. What's with Minotaur? He hasn't stopped talking to Iridium since he got here. Is this about Inspire?"

Miranda knew precisely what the Minotaur was discussing with Doc Iridium. However, it was his brainchild, so she wasn't going to spoil the reveal for him. While recovering from the surgery, he'd broached the idea to her, and they'd spent the entire voyage back to San Francisco hashing out what details they could.

"I haven't the faintest," she lied through her teeth. "Why don't you go ask Mind-Fucker?" She knew, as everyone else did, that the press had watered down the telepath's chosen *nom du masque* to Mindscrew, but they were all unrepentant mass murderers here, so who gave a damn?

Seismic shuddered, and not in a play-acting way. "I hate talking to that sonovabitch," he complained. "He's so goddamn *creepy*, the way he always knows what you're going to say."

"Thanks, Seismic!" Mind-Fucker called from across the room. "I appreciate the vote of confidence!"

"Fuck off!" Seismic stood up and faced the telepath, a middle-aged man so gray and average he would never be picked out in a crowd. "Stay out of my goddamn head!"

"If you're thinking about me, I can hear it." Mind-Fucker's voice was condescending. "Stop thinking about me, and I'll stop thinking about you."

Miranda maintained a poker face, repressing the urge to smirk. *I wonder how often he just reads people instead of minds?*

"Okay, that's enough." The table boomed as the Minotaur smacked his fist on it. "Everyone, stop playing grab-ass and listen up." He paused for a moment, casting his gaze around the room. "Singularity! Darksider! That means you, too!"

"Okay, okay, we're paying attention." At the far end of the table, Singularity drifted up off the Darksider's lap and took her own seat. The black-clad prodigy didn't look overly pleased, but it wasn't as though he had much choice in the matter. "What's all the fuss about, bull-man?"

"Yeah," called out Raider cheerfully, lifting her glass in a mock salute. For this gathering, she'd doffed the hooded cloak and voice modulator she used to masquerade as a man for her holographic displays. Her cyber-eye glowed orange from across the room. "When're you staging your big comeback?"

"I'm not."

For a conversation starter, those two words were up there at the top of the list. The people around the table all started shouting at once; as far as Miranda could see, only Doc Iridium and the Minotaur kept quiet. They just sat there, waiting it out.

Gradually, the assembled villains realized the Minotaur wasn't answering their demands for an explanation, and the noise began to taper off. False Flag was the last to keep speaking. "What the hell? I mean, seriously? I had your back when you offed the Veep and the Prez. You just gonna walk away from the rest of us like that? Dick move, man. Dick move."

"I'm not walking away from *anyone*," the Minotaur stated harshly. "I've got a new idea, something that's never been done before. A few details still need ironing out, but if we can pull this off, we'll all be richer than we know what to do with. *And* we'll be free to spend our money anywhere we like."

Raider sat forward. "And you just got my complete and total attention." This was no surprise to Miranda. Unless they were born into the ranks of the idle wealthy, people with the Artificer powerset were forever scratching for money to acquire parts for their latest creations.

"Me, too," agreed Charnel. "Who do we have to kill?"

"If this is just a get-rich-quick scheme, I'm out." Mind-Fucker stood up from the table. "And why the hell are you two wearing mind-blockers?" He pointed at Doc Iridium and the Minotaur. "Scared I was going to steal your big idea?"

Which only proved the telepath hadn't bothered trying to read Miranda's mind; as the third person in on the deal, she was also wearing one of Doc Iridium's mind-blockers. It made her back teeth itch, but nobody and nothing could access her thoughts.

"Basic precaution," the Minotaur said. "Now unwad your panties and sit down. You can learn about it at the same time as the rest of the people here."

"Yeah, sit your mind-reading ass down." False Flag waved his hand at the telepath. "This is just getting interesting."

Reluctantly, the nondescript man took his seat once more. "It better be good," he muttered. "That's all I'm saying."

The Minotaur ignored him. "So, apart from having more money than God, and the freedom to spend it any way you please, would you *also* be interested in never having to worry about being hunted by superheroes or the Feds ever again? Go anywhere you like, do whatever you want, and have people thank you for being there?"

"While all this sounds *très bien*," observed Guillotine, idly spinning a tiny cloud of purple mist around the tip of her finger, "how do you intend to pull it off?"

"Yeah," agreed Singularity. "Or is this just something you smoked? Because I *want* some."

"The method being advanced is simplicity itself," Doc Iridium said. "Very bluntly put, taking away ninety-nine percent of the extraneous information, he is proposing that we masquerade as a superhero team and reap the rewards thereof."

This time, silence fell. It took a few moments for someone to speak; Miranda made a bet with herself that Singularity would make another joke about being stoned.

"Us? Superheroes?" It was Singularity alright, though the anticipated *'high on drugs'* jibe failed to materialize. "Have you *met* us? There is no way on God's green Earth that anyone with two brain cells to rub together *wouldn't* pick us as terror villains, no matter how much we try to dress up differently. I mean, it's not like we'll be able to fight our terror identities and prove we're not us."

"It won't be easy, that's true." The Minotaur's voice was solid with conviction. "But it can be done." He thumped his chest with his fist. "As far as the public knows, I'm dead. I didn't even have to fake falling off a volcano into a pit of lava. *'Big guy in costume'* is not exactly an uncommon trope. If I change my look, nobody's going to know."

"Yeah, but the rest of us have powers that are kind of distinctive." That was False Flag. "Charnel becomes *Charnel*. A domino mask won't fix that. Singularity does her black ball thing. Guillotine cuts off arms and heads with purple fog. You can put on a trench coat and go punch people, but the moment the rest of us use our powers, people *will* recognize us. Not trying to shoot your idea down, just ... you know, it won't be as easy as it sounds like you're saying." He sat back in his chair with a 'so there' attitude.

"This, I believe, is where I come in." Doc Iridium steepled his fingertips together. "I have recently perfected a power enhancement technology that can be adjusted and attuned to any Enabled, lifting them to the next tier of capability. This will allow more flexibility with powers, even altering their outward visible aspects and downgrading problematic side-effects. Each person who chooses to join this putative team will be fitted with just such an enhancement device, allowing them to reinvent themselves as they wish."

"Really?" Charnel's tone was dubious. "I've heard what you can do, and some of it's pretty damn impressive, but can you actually make our powers work *better*?"

"Unquestionably." Doc Iridium's voice, by contrast, was pure smugness. He gestured across the room toward Alexei. "Behold: Cherenkov."

Miranda was pretty sure she could hear the jaws dropping from one side of the room to the other. Heads turned to stare at the massive Enabled, standing with folded arms against the wall.

"Well, shit," muttered False Flag. "Devastator is *Cherenkov*? I thought he died back in 'ninety-three or so."

"Looks pretty damn alive to me," Charnel replied. He raised his voice, addressing Doc Iridium. "And this is all your enhancement tech?"

"Mostly, yes," the artificer had the grace to say. "Mutilator there rebuilt him from the sorry state I found him in, but the containment harness I fitted him with has ensured that his powers no longer erode away his very flesh, as they were doing before. Would any of you have suspected his prior identity before I revealed him as such?"

Singularity and Guillotine glanced at each other, then back at Alexei. "Nuh-uh," Singularity said definitively. "That's pretty damn impressive. And so's the rebuild job." Cupping her hands around her modest bosom, she winked at Miranda. "Think you could bump me up a few cup sizes while we're at it, sweetie?"

Miranda shrugged. Breast enhancement surgery was something any competent surgeon could do in their sleep. In a city the size of San Francisco, it shouldn't be *too* hard to find a 'donor' for the tissue required. "Does the Pope shit in the Vatican?"

"*Excellent.*" Singularity grinned broadly. "Welp, I'm in."

"Jesus Christ, I literally can't believe this." Mind-Fucker stood up again. "You bitches are so shallow, you'll buy into this moronic idea for a tit upgrade? Count me out, and don't come crying to me when your stupid team idea crashes and burns." He shoved his chair aside and started toward the door. "Stupid fucking waste of my goddamn time ..."

Miranda tensed, ready to bring Alexei in on this—the big guy would be well suited to handle the telepath in any purely physical contest—but the Minotaur stood and made it to the door first. "Hey, don't be so hasty."

"Get out of my face. Or if you're going to talk to me, turn that damn mind-blocker off first." Mind-Fucker paused expectantly for a second, then sneered. "Yeah, didn't think so." He opened the door and stepped through it.

"God *damn* it." Before it could swing shut, the Minotaur ducked out behind him. The door closed on their raised voices. Miranda glanced at Doc Iridium, but the artificer seemed unworried about the whole thing.

While terror villains didn't make a habit of screwing each other over, a calm and even temper was not a common feature among them. She didn't *know* that Mind-Fucker was vindictive enough to spill the beans to the authorities just to cock-block the Minotaur's efforts, but there was always a non-zero chance of something like that happening when villains clashed.

And then, a shot sounded from outside. A moment passed while everyone looked at each other, then the door opened again and the Minotaur stepped back through. In his right hand was a compact .44 revolver, which he slipped into a shoulder holster. The tang of expended propellant was strong in the air.

"That's going to need cleaning up later," he observed and retook his seat. "Anyone else want to walk out at this point in time?"

"So that's how it's going to be?" The Darksider tended to push the 'silent and brooding' schtick, but apparently that was going by the wayside. "If we don't want to buy into your spiel, we get shot? Because I'm not down for that."

"Shh," Singularity hissed. "Just shut up and listen to the man. Wouldn't you *want* a power upgrade?"

"What the hell would I want with a power upgrade?" The Darksider put his hands to his chest. "I'm as good as it gets with stealth and infiltration. Nobody sees me coming. Nothing can keep me out. Prodigy for the win."

"What he said, except not really," interjected Seismic. "I construct earthquake machines. It's what I do. They cause earthquakes. My business model involves getting paid *not* to cause earthquakes. Can you see how this fits in with being a superhero? Because I can't."

"That sounds like a 'you' problem, not an 'us' problem," jibed Singularity. "Hey, M, can you make me and G look like we're *not* me and G? Because it'd be nice to meet guys who aren't already on the game—" She leaned across and patted the Darksider on the arm. "No offense, hon, but it's true—and who don't run screaming as soon as we use our powers. Just saying."

"I can absolutely do cosmetic surgery on everyone here," Miranda assured them. "Name the movie star of your choice, and I'll make you sexier than them."

"What about me?" asked False Flag. "I'm interested, but I'm not entirely sure how you'd make me look like anything other than a shape-changer." He leaned back in his seat, looking smug. "And I have kind of *owned* that concept over the last few years."

"I believe I have that covered," Doc Iridium stated. "You're a prodigy as well as a dynamic, correct? If we cast you in this hypothetical team as a master of weapons, you should be able to retain your shape-changing in reserve as an eleventh-hour option. Accordingly, I should be able to enhance your Prodigy powerset to render you capable of shouldering your role within the team. You merely need to decide upon a form you prefer, and present that to the public."

Slowly, False Flag nodded. "I like it. Okay, count me in."

"Sounds good." The Minotaur looked around the table. "Who else is on board so far?"

Singularity's hand went up alongside Guillotine's. Miranda raised hers as well, then frowned. "Uh … I don't think we covered Devastator. His enhanced identity is already known to the public. I don't want him left out in the cold when I join the team."

"Your associate will not be abandoned," Doc Iridium assured her. "My plans for the future of this team definitely include uses for his unique capabilities."

"Oh, okay then." Miranda kept her hand up.

Raider's hand had gone up during that exchange, as had False Flag's and Charnel's. In the end, the only holdouts were Seismic and the Darksider.

The Minotaur put his hands flat on the table and gave them each a hard stare. "Okay," he said. "Are you in, or are you out? Because the way I'm visualizing this team, we'll be establishing and solidifying our rep by going after the big names—that is, *us*—and using our heroic identities to fake our villain identity deaths. Once we've cleared the board of terror villains, we'll have the government's attention, and the public will *love* us. But for us to pull it off, you guys will have to either join up or take a dive. There's no room for a middle ground. No more trademark home invasions. No more earthquake ransoms."

"… the *government's* attention?" asked False Flag after a moment.

"Well, yeah." The Minotaur spread his hands. "How else did you think we were going to make our money? Federal sponsorship is the gift that keeps on giving. That's what Inspire had. Plus, we can sell tech to them. They'll be literally competing to see how much money they can throw at us. But first, we've got to make ourselves look good, and we can't do *that* if there are terror villains in the public eye who keep getting away from us. We've got to be seen as having won the game, once and for all."

Raider frowned. "I'm totally on board with this, but … what if we *want* to go out and cause a little chaos from time to time? Not as *us* us, but anonymously. Can we still do that?"

"Uh, just so you know," Miranda interjected, "I've been self-trialing anti-psychotics that can take away the urge to kill people *quite* as much. They seem to be working so far."

"And that's cool," Raider agreed. "I might even use them. But I'm going to want to go out occasionally and rack up some kill points. Can I do that, or is it a deal-breaker?"

The Minotaur glanced at Doc Iridium, then turned to address Raider. "That depends. Are you married to the idea of driving around big fuck-off walking mecha with holograms on top, or are you willing to consider another look?"

She leaned back another degree or two in her seat and raised the eyebrow over her original-issue eye. "I could be convinced to consider other options, sure. Maybe something flying, or on treads. And I can definitely ditch the hologram if I have to."

"Good." The Minotaur nodded and addressed the rest of the table. "So long as we don't do it too similar to how we're doing it now, and if we can figure out a way of avoiding any link back to the team, I'm sure we'll all be interested in blowing off steam that way."

"Hey!" It was the Darksider. "What if I don't *want* to take a dive or pop your stupid pills or whatever? What if I'm happy doing what I'm doing? You can't *make* me join this damn team. Don't screw with my thing, and I won't screw with your thing."

"Same," snapped Seismic, shoving his chair back and jumping to his feet. A low but distinct hum permeated the room; Miranda saw that the artificer had a bulky device strapped to his arm, thus explaining the oversized sleeves of his labcoat. The hum sharply escalated to the point where she felt jittery and weird, and her glass started dancing across the table. He headed for the door, aiming his arm like a gun at the ceiling. "Come on, let's get out of here. Everyone, this is a reinforcing harmonic oscillator. If you don't let us out of here unharmed, I'm going to bring down the whole—"

He vanished inside a six-foot midnight-black ball, and the vibrations cut out immediately. The Darksider made a dash for the door, but he only made it halfway there. Or rather, his body made it halfway before a purple cloud enveloped him briefly, and he fell. His head rolled the rest of the way, but Miranda didn't think that counted.

"And then there were nine," observed Raider lightly, but she was sitting up again now, and her eyes were wary as she scanned the room. Her hands were below the level of the table, and Miranda suspected she was preparing to pull a hidden weapon. "Does anyone else want to be stupid?"

It appeared nobody did; after a few moments, Raider put her hands back on the table, and the tension around the room eased slightly. Singularity's force-field sphere began to contract steadily, inexorably.

"Uh, that's seven, not nine," Miranda ventured. "Devastator and I are in, but I don't think we'll be having a role in the active team."

"Seven is a good, strong number," decided the Minotaur. "It gives us room to have fan favorites. Also, it's a classic number for fictional teams. People will like it without understanding why."

"Which raises another issue." Doc Iridium was holding some sort of electronic tablet with holographic images dancing above it. "To appeal to a wider number of people, the team must demonstrate a significant diversity of gender identity. With seven members, that adds up to three men, three women, and one … indeterminate."

Miranda wasn't sure what he was talking about. "What, like a robot? Do we have AIs that good yet?" On second thought, she wasn't sure she wanted to get too close to any robot Doc Iridium had programmed, just on general principles.

"Not sufficiently complex to function as a full team member, no." Doc Iridium frowned. "I was considering that someone could take on a non-binary, asexual persona—for public purposes only, of course."

"Not it!" Singularity's sphere was down to twelve inches in diameter. It didn't matter *how* good Seismic's Artificer capabilities were; he wasn't alive in there. "I'm gonna be the sexy one, with a neckline down to there!" Her finger indicated a point somewhere below the level of the table.

Doc Iridium nodded. "There's room for that persona, yes. Also, we shall require a no-nonsense 'tough girl' persona and a pragmatic 'team mom' everywoman. Raider, do you believe you can handle that last one?"

"Sure." Raider leaned back in her seat. "Think you can do something with my eye? Change the color, maybe?"

"I could replace it with a real eye again if you wanted." The only hitch, Miranda figured, would be in finding a 'donor' to match the real one on the other side. Difficult, but not impossible.

Raider waved a dismissive hand. "Nah. I've got a camera in here and everything. A color change is all I'd really want, so if anyone did happen to see it, they wouldn't immediately ID me as *me*."

Guillotine frowned. "I am not sure if I am cut out to be the *fille dure*, the tough girl. I'm more the *mignonne*, the 'cute' type."

Singularity snickered. "Don't you mean the *fille mignonne*? 'Cause I could eat you all up."

Rolling his eyes at both the flirting and the atrocious pun, the Minotaur turned toward False Flag. "Pretty sure we've got the 'tough girl' role covered. You up for it?"

False Flag looked startled as the penny dropped. "You're joking, right?"

"Why not?" The Minotaur's grin widened to 'shit-eating' status. "You've been a woman before, right? Hell, there was the one time you pretended to be that guy's wife for a whole week before you murdered him. This time, it'll just be a part of the job. You'll even get to show off for the public. They'll love you; I guarantee it. Especially if you go all patriotic 'star-spangled hero' with your costume and name, and maybe strap on a gun or two."

"Ahh, go ahead, bro." Charnel slapped False Flag on the shoulder. "I promise not to stare at your ass." His sly grin assured Miranda of just the opposite.

False Flag grimaced, then looked at Doc Iridium again. "You'll be boosting my Prodigy capabilities to the next tier, right?"

"Indubitably," the artificer assured him. "You will be widely hailed as a veritable icon of the powerset."

"Yeah, okay, but ..." He frowned. "Not sure just packing a gun will make me look good. Sure, the second-amendment crowd will be pinning up posters of me, but I'm going to need something to make me stand out from every *other* gun-toting prodigy out there."

The Minotaur nodded. "Fair point." Reaching down alongside the table, he lifted up a long cloth-wrapped object, which he pulled free of its covering to clatter on the table. "How about this, then?"

Miranda watched as nearly everyone in the room stared at the dully gleaming length of steel with varying levels of covetousness. They'd all heard the story of how the Minotaur had acquired the blade of Castellan's sword. Arfogwyr's tech had long maintained a reputation for durability and effectiveness.

False Flag blinked a couple of times. "Wait, you're saying if I do this, I get that sword?"

"That's what I'm saying," the Minotaur confirmed. "Iridium says he can get it back in working order, whatever theme you want. What do you say?"

Charnel raised his hand. "Hey, if you don't want it, I'll take it."

"Fuck you, I saw it first." False Flag looked the Minotaur in the eye. "Deal, but I get to be second in command."

"Officially, sure." The Minotaur rapped the blade lightly with his fingernail, causing it to ring like crystal. "But if I pass on orders through other people, you follow 'em just the same, and you don't *ever* go behind my back with shit. Understood?"

"Sure, sure, no problem." False Flag leaned back in his seat, his expression thoughtful as if considering possibilities. Miranda had seen him at work before, and knew that whatever concept he came up with would be impressive.

"Wait," Guillotine said. "If Singularity is to be the sexy one, Raider the practical one, and False Flag the tough one, where do I fit in?"

"If you've got no problem wearing a concealing costume," the Minotaur suggested, "you can be the asexual representative. Make you androgynous enough, and we can keep them guessing forever about whether you're a guy or a girl."

Guillotine looked down at her bikini-clad body and sighed. "You are sure we will make lots of money doing this, yes?"

"If we play our cards right," he assured her, "they'll be throwing dollars at us faster than we can spend them. Government contracts run into the billions and trillions. As long as we keep delivering, they'll keep paying us."

Slowly, she nodded. "I do like the sound of that. Androgynous, it is."

"Excellent." Doc Iridium seemed to be ticking off points on a mental list. "As for the masculine side of this team, we shall have the Minotaur as our physically imposing leader, myself as the learned advisor, and Charnel as the strong but silent warrior."

"Wait, why silent?" asked Charnel. "Why can't I talk?"

False Flag rolled his eyes. "Because his enhancement thingy probably won't do a damn thing for your voice, doofus. We want the public lining up to get autographs, not pissing themselves in fear. If I have to be a girl and Guillotine has to wear a burqa and pretend to be genderqueer, you can damn well keep your trap shut when we're in public."

"Fuck you."

"Yeah, well, fuck you too."

Ignoring the scuffle that broke out between the two, the Minotaur addressed the table in general. "Okay, it's settled. Once we've observed the effects of the enhancement tech, we'll have a better idea of where we're going with specific power effects. From there, we can figure out our new identities. Now, does anyone have a suggestion for a team name? I've got a few ideas, but none of them are great. I want something strong and memorable. One that tells the world what we are and how we intend to go on."

False Flag looked up from where he had Charnel in a headlock. "I vote for 'The Mean Team'."

"How about 'The Right Stuff'?" suggested Miranda. "As a call-out to Challenger, I mean."

Charnel elbowed False Flag in the side of the head. "Hell, just call us 'The Challenger Seven' if we're going there."

The Minotaur frowned. "We can't be seen as trying too hard to evoke the legacy of Inspire. We need to be our own thing. And 'Mean Team' sounds almost villainous. I don't want to give the game away before we start."

Guillotine raised her hand almost shyly. "How about 'Force Majeure'? It means a power that can't be resisted."

The Minotaur shared a glance with Doc Iridium. "I like it. A lot."

"As do I." The bearded artificer nodded. "Does anyone dislike Force Majeure as a team name?"

"If we can't have 'Challenger Seven' then sure, that's a good one." Charnel nodded toward Guillotine. "Nice one."

The Minotaur slapped the table. "Good. Now that's settled, does anybody have any more business before we adjourn this meeting and clean up the mess?" He glanced down at the Darksider's headless body and over at the black sphere hovering alongside Singularity. "We're gonna have to disappear these three assholes altogether. Can't have anyone wondering how come a bunch of terror villains ended up being killed by other terror villains in the same area."

"If Mind-Fucker's just got a bullet hole in him, I can dump him in gang territory on my way back through San Diego," Raider offered. "The Feds won't even look twice. The other two can go out to sea or something."

"Excellent." The Minotaur nodded. "Make it happen."

Doc Iridium cleared his throat. "If I may advance a suggestion. Mind-Fucker may be deceased, but our largest potential danger will still be from telepaths and others of a similar mind-reading ilk who may see past our façade to what lies beneath. I can supply mind-blocks, but that might draw unwanted attention. Therefore, I propose that we commence a program aimed at locating all extant psychics around the nation and keeping track of any new emergences. In that manner, we can take steps to eliminate them before they can reveal our secret in turn."

False Flag grinned, showing his teeth. "Yeah, that's definitely something I can get behind. Fuck psychics, and fuck mind-readers in particular."

"I agree," the Minotaur confirmed. "But we'll need to make it look like robberies gone wrong or drug overdoses or something. You know, normal shit. We don't want people thinking Enabled were even involved. Because if that happens, they might start thinking, and who knows where that might lead to."

"Uh, one more thing." Miranda waved her hand to get the Minotaur's attention. "If I'm not going to be a costumed hero, where do I fit in? Apart from the cosmetic surgery thing, I mean?"

"That's easy," he said. "If we get as big as I'm thinking, we'll have civilian support, including a medical section. I can't think of a better person to run the show. So, what do you say?"

"I'd love to say yes, but … honestly, I don't know." She grimaced. "I haven't had the best luck at being in the spotlight. As Surgeon One, it felt like I had a target painted on my back the whole time."

He rolled his eyes. "Well, it's not like you're going to be a public figure this time around. Plus, you'll have the team there to protect you. Trust me, it'll be a whole different ballgame."

She nodded, acknowledging his points. "Okay. I'll think about it."

The Minotaur smiled. "That's all I ask."

- End of Epilogue Two -

Epilogue Three
Find That Hero

The Spire
Utopia City
January 28, 2014

Six Hours after the Death of Silent Knight

D espite the buzz of the white-noise generator built into the wall beside the door, G-Man's voice came through the phone clearly. "Yes, sir. *'Ming vase'*. Keep my head down 'til I hear from you."

Relentless heaved a silent sigh of relief, thankful that *someone* knew how to follow simple instructions. "Good. Now, if you'll excuse me, I'm gonna go kick seventeen shades of shit out of a certain traitor and find out exactly what *else* is fucking going on in *my goddamn team*."

He slammed the phone back on the cradle, his jaw muscles working spasmodically. Letting out a primal roar of anger, he swung both fists down at an adjacent section of the semi-circular desk that spanned the room. It disintegrated under the impact with a tremendous crash, splinters spraying in all directions and larger pieces clattering across the floor. Inhaling deeply through flared nostrils and feeling more like the Minotaur than he had in years, he thought about destroying another section but refrained.

A biofeedback routine he'd learned from Mutilator assisted in pulling himself back into balance as he headed for the door; after all, he didn't want to give the game away too soon. Long, deep breaths smoothed out the adrenaline-charged twitching of his fingers until he could almost pass for calm again. Anyone who looked into his eyes would know differently, but that would mean they were also within reach of his hands.

He tapped one knuckle gently on the panel to switch off the white-noise generator, then pressed the button on the screen alongside the door, activating the camera that covered the anteroom beyond. Even after he'd kicked them out so abruptly, the team wouldn't have gone far. Everyone wanted answers about what had happened to Silent Knight—Charnel—and what would be done about it. What *he* was going to do about it.

He was definitely going to do *something*. Just not what they expected.

Outside, Independence and the Technologist were apparently arguing over something. Lady Quantum was on her phone—probably indulging in her current hobby of shitposting to piss off the conspiracy theorist nerds— while Transit leaned against the opposite wall with her helmet under her arm. Beside Transit was Mutilator, wearing her surgical scrubs; they were both watching the door with amusement. *No, not the door.* At the very edge of the fisheye lens pickup zone, Relentless spotted the corner of Tourbillon's robes. The little snitch literally had her ear to the door!

"Come on, man," Independence urged the Technologist as the audio kicked in, confirming Relentless' speculation. "I *know* you. You wouldn't build a secure room like that without being able to listen in *somehow*."

Relentless watched the artificer frown as he fiddled with the lenses of his goggles. "Ordinarily, that would be true. But our illustrious leader also possesses Artificer specialties; he appears to have augmented my precautions with soundproofing methods of his own devising, which I am currently incapable of penetrating without access to more specialized equipment."

"He'd be using the privacy bubble, though, right?" suggested Lady Quantum, without looking up from her phone. "So, tap into that and just listen in anyway."

"It was the first thing I attempted," the Technologist retorted, clearly annoyed. "Relentless is *also* aware that such can be tapped into, so the room's privacy bubble is as yet undeployed. The most I can discern is that up until thirty-three seconds ago, he was employing a white noise generator equipped with a random frequency modulator."

It looked like everyone (except Transit and Mutilator) was begging for some extra bruises in the next sparring session. If that was what it took to explain to them that privacy meant *privacy*, then that was what he'd do.

Once the current situation was dealt with, of course.

"What do you mean, '*up until thirty-three seconds ago*'?" Tourbillon's voice was very close to the microphone. A second later, the suspicion in her voice turned to panicked realization. "Oh, shit!"

Relentless turned the door handle, making sure the lock clicked loudly. He almost had to admire how adroitly the teleporter dived into the hastily created portal as the door opened, ending up across the room a fraction of a second later. Only those in the core team knew that her power didn't actually require her to generate great swirls of black smoke along with her portals. Still, it was a valuable lie to cultivate, especially considering how useful stealth portals were in their behind-the-scenes work.

He also knew damn well she hadn't used such a portal to listen in on the phone conversation just then, mainly because the room was fitted with detectors that would sound an alarm over just such an intrusion. So were most of the private areas in the Spire, on the principle that if Tourbillon could do it, so could someone else.

"You could've just waited and asked me what was going on." He was obscurely proud of how calm he sounded. All he wanted to do was visit a large amount of violence on Independence for going behind his back and jeopardizing the very *existence* of Utopia City and Force Majeure. Fortunately, G-Man was as naïve as they came—which was impressive, given the underworld contacts he seemed to have cultivated—but it could just as easily have gone another way altogether.

Two of us burned, one of those dead. I can handle that. G-Man's a true believer; all I really need to do is spin a good story, and he'll fall back into line. It'll hurt us, but Force Majeure will survive. Utopia *will survive.*

He hadn't amassed all this power and built an entire microstate-in-all-but-name from the ground up, only to lose everything now because of a couple of fucking morons.

"Okay, so I'm asking," Independence said boldly. "What was that call about? Have you got a lead on that murdering little shit and his thieving friend?"

Relentless nodded. "Yeah. I have. Technologist, get in here. The rest of you, wait a moment." He'd initially intended to call them all in at once, but this was the tactically superior move.

The white-bearded artificer followed him into the room; Relentless shut the door behind him. "Well?" asked the Technologist. "What has you even more agitated than your usual state of affairs?"

"You'll find out." Relentless gestured toward the door and, by inference, the people outside. "You still got those extra overrides on their enhancement tech?"

Iridium never handed out technology without first building in failsafes. That was merely good business practice when dealing with the terror villain fraternity, and villains in general. While some would've settled for simply turning the power enhancers off at need, Relentless knew Iridium could use the enhancers to remotely shut down the underlying *powers.*

He knew this because he was the one who'd suggested that specific modification in the first place.

"Of course." Despite his previous demonstration of knowledge about the room's soundproofing, the Technologist lowered his voice. "Do you perhaps suspect one or more of them of treachery against the team?"

"Yeah." Relentless didn't elaborate. "As they come in, shut their powers down *all* the way. Except for Independence. Just turn off her enhancement."

"I comprehend. I believe I comprehend." The Technologist withdrew a few steps and fiddled with his goggles, flicking lenses in and out. From their long association, Relentless knew he was searching for the right HUD menu.

Leaving him to it, Relentless stalked over to the door and opened it again. "Come on in."

They'd do as he said; he knew that much. Their curiosity would be too strong to let them do anything else.

He watched them troop inside one by one, looking with curiosity at the shattered remnants of the desk. As the last one in, Mutilator locked and secured the door at a jerk of his head.

Leaning up against one of the unbroken desk sections, he restrained himself from lunging at Independence immediately. Instead, he worked his fingers open and closed, open and closed. He was imagining Independence's throat in his grasp, but that wasn't so much a fantasy as a prediction.

"Privacy bubble," he ordered. Mutilator reached out and pressed the appropriate button on the panel. It was the most secure the room could be; with everyone inside who had access to the feed from the bubbles, the only people who would ever be able to attest to what transpired within the room were the ones who were right there.

"Oh, for fuck's sake," snapped Independence. Striding over and planting herself foursquare in front of him, she put her hands on her hips. "What's with all the fucking theatrics? Spit it out, already."

Oh, I intend to. He straightened up, holding himself back only with considerable effort. "I just found out something real interesting. See if you can guess what it was."

Half a second passed, while she looked around at the rest of them as though asking if they could believe this bullshit. When she was just turning her head back toward him, her attention still on the others, he acted.

He made no move to telegraph his intentions. One instant, his hand was at his side, fist clenched; in the next, he sucker-punched her in the solar plexus so hard that she flew over the far end of the desk and slammed into the wall beyond.

The impact could easily have maimed or killed an ordinary human. Fortunately for Independence, she was no ordinary human, even when False Flag pretended to be one. Relentless knew just how damn resilient the shape-changer's Dynamic specialty made him, especially when combined with his Prodigy powerset, so there would be no question of holding back. Vaulting the desk in his turn, he grabbed Independence by the arm.

"I *FOUND*!" he bellowed, swinging her around like a rag doll then hammer-throwing her across the room in a flat ballistic arc that terminated at the far wall. She impacted with another satisfying *crunch*, some of which came from the wall. "That *SILENT KNIGHT*! And *THIS BITCH HERE*!"

He lunged after her, knowing she'd recover quickly if he didn't keep the pressure up. By the time he got there, she'd used her inherent regeneration to pop out her stove-in ribcage and was getting to her feet. Her arm came up in an attempt to block the blow as he swung his boot in a whistling arc, but it snapped under the impact before the toe of his boot drove brutally into her upper torso, breaking a few more bones. Propelled by the massive kick, she went skidding along the wall.

"Tried to *MURDER G-MAN*!" This time, he covered the distance in a single leap. She was getting up faster now that the element of surprise was gone, but her reactions were still shot. If the enhancement device built into her body armor had been active, she might've stood a chance, but it wasn't, and she didn't. Her Prodigy reflexes were a whole tier lower with it shut down, and it showed. He grabbed her other arm before she could react and broke it in about four places with one savage twist. "Then tried to use us to *COVER IT UP*!"

Apparently realizing she couldn't escape, she tried far too late to fight back. A kick snapped out at his face, but it was woefully slow compared to her usual lightning-fast attacks. He snagged her by the ankle, then flailed her body back and forth into the floor and wall. When he tired of that, he hooked one hand around her knee and the other under her chin, bent her backward like a green stick, then tensed his pecs and gave one sharp heave. Multiple vertebrae were crunched into ruin; she went limp in his grasp.

"Okay, big man." Mutilator approached him, hands out to the sides, clearly being careful not to look threatening. "I get it. You're pissed, and that's perfectly understandable. It's just that if you keep this up, you *will* actually kill her. I know precisely how far her regeneration goes, and you're pushing its limits right now."

He glowered at her. "You got a problem with how I'm dealing with this little piece of shit?"

"Oh, no, no," she said, with a fake-sounding chuckle. "She deserves a beating, and she'll *definitely* be feeling that in the morning. Once she regenerates enough of her spinal cord to *get* some feeling back, that is. But don't you think you could've gone a *tad* easier on her? Maybe just broken a few of her bones instead of … well, *all* of them?"

Relentless toned down his glare a little. Mutilator had chosen to ally herself with him, nearly two decades ago. He was always willing to cut her some slack because of it, especially since she'd never attempted to leverage this for personal gain.

"You tell me. I just got off the phone with G-Man. He wanted to warn *me* that Silent Knight had been Charnel, and that Independence tried to kill him once she found out that he knew. So, I investigated. They *ambushed* him while he was retrieving the stolen data I sent him to get, and he still managed to kill Charnel and disable bitch-features here before he made a run for it. So, all this '*he knows everything*' bullshit was just her trying to cover her own tracks."

That G-Man had told him about the pick-up in the first place was immaterial; he'd approved it and arranged for cover from surveillance, making it an official Force Majeure operation. Charnel and Independence deserved exactly what they got, for going against his orders.

"Ah. Well, then." Mutilator nodded. "Got it. In fact, I'm pretty sure we *all* got that message. There are no Mind-Fuckers here. And I'm sure that once she learns to walk again, she'll be on the same page."

"No. She won't." Relentless picked up Independence and slung her over his shoulder. Her body lolled limply, but he knew Mutilator was correct; though badly injured, the bitch wasn't dead yet. "She sabotaged G-Man's first interview, and she's had a set against him ever since. Even *knowing* exactly how important it is to have him on the team, she still pulled this shit. That, right there, proves I can't trust her not to *keep trying*."

"So … precisely what do you propose to do with our erstwhile comrade?" asked the Technologist. "Surely, disposing of her permanently is an overly harsh punishment. In addition, it would set an uncomfortable precedent."

"Not gonna kill her." Relentless went over and switched off the privacy bubble, then opened the door. "I'm just gonna put her downstairs with the Madness. Don't go anywhere. I'll be right back."

Even when he, as the Minotaur, had proposed the basis of Force Majeure seventeen years ago, he'd known he wouldn't be able to indulge himself as freely in his vices as he had in the past. Fortunately, the main point of putting people in his murder mazes had never been the money. The ransoms paid for the next round of mazes, but his true enjoyment was in the thrill of the hunt and watching the life fading from the eyes of his prey.

When designing Utopia City and the Spire, he'd made sure to incorporate his most elaborate labyrinth yet, directly under the base of the enormous building. The problem, of course, was acquiring victims to put *into* said labyrinth. Before this point, he'd abducted people from their houses, vehicles, or even their places of work. It hadn't mattered if he was seen; the public *knew* of the Minotaur. Now, he no longer had that freedom.

The few covert abductions he'd pulled off since founding Utopia had been technically successful, but involved far too much risk for too little reward. Using people from inside Utopia would've made it easier, but he'd made it a hard and fast rule from the beginning: *'we don't shit in our own nest'*. These people had willingly chosen to come live in *his* city, and they needed to feel *safe* if they were going to stay. The ongoing protective camouflage was worth far more than a few minutes of fun and games.

Just as he'd been on the verge of giving up, the solution had fallen into his lap. He'd been vaguely aware that the Technologist and Mutilator were jointly responsible for creating the Madness, but he'd never bothered learning the precise details. It was good enough that Force Majeure had an acceptable enemy they could go out and brutally murder on a semi-regular basis.

However, a chance remark from Tourbillon had clued him in on the fact that some of the Madness were just batshit insane, with no powers to speak of. Apart from a few specimens kept back for dissection by Mutilator, the Technologist had no use for them. Relentless needed someone to hunt, so they'd struck a deal. Instead of being ruthlessly culled, the dross from the experiments were sent to Relentless' labyrinth, where they could die for a worthwhile purpose. It was, all told, a mutually beneficial arrangement.

When it came to the design and construction of the underground maze, he'd gone all-out. Every trap, every obstacle, every hazard he'd ever used before, he threw in there. Pits, spike traps, gas traps, electrified plates, laser grids, sliding blocks, and a dozen other ways to murder people in ways cruel and inventive. They could all be activated or switched off from outside the labyrinth while he observed the goings-on via concealed cameras.

But that was more for when he was bored and needed a few chuckles. Anytime he began to feel overwhelmed by the stresses of pretending to be a hero, he could go down there and hunt his prey to his heart's content, killing them with spear or sword or maul or dagger, as he saw fit. Often he used his bare hands, thoroughly immersing himself in the primal thrill of the hunt. It bothered him not at all when they tried to fight back. In fact, he enjoyed it all the more.

He suspected some of the 'unpowered' prey he tracked down and killed actually possessed Prodigy or Artificer powersets, though even if that were the case, it never did them any good. As tough and resourceful as many prodigies were, he was considerably stronger and far more tactically aware. Budding artificers had little to work with; any scrap-built weapons their unbalanced brains allowed them to construct merely heightened the enjoyment of the hunt before he shattered their bones and pulverized their skulls.

All of which pointed at just one thing. Specifically, just how *pissed* he needed to be in order to dump Independence down here: injured, unenhanced, and unarmed.

If the rest of the team was smart, they'd get the message.

With her broken body still slung over his shoulder like a sack of laundry, he stepped out of the elevator at the lowest sub-level, somewhat below the areas that even the redoubtable Ms. Colburn *knew* about, much less had clearance to enter. His MagCard opened locks that would've triggered lethal responses had anyone but a core team member tried to access them. Stepping through into the control room, he checked the hard-light image projected by the holo-table in the middle of the room.

Constructed in three layers, complete with sliding walls and stairwells that moved from place to place at his whim, every last cubic foot of the labyrinth was open to his scrutiny. At the moment, it was occupied by two dozen of the Madness, each one indicated in real-time by a red figure moving through the maze. There was only one near to where Relentless wanted to enter, so he slapped the button to gain access. Metal grated against metal, and heavy concrete slabs moved aside. He descended the steps thus revealed and tapped the last barrier with his MagCard. It obediently slid out of the way, and he stepped into the labyrinth proper.

Heaving Independence off his shoulder, he dropped her on the bare floor, then removed her goggles. He frisked her quickly and efficiently, removing two knives and a holdout pistol before unfastening her armored costume. He was just in the process of pulling this off her when she moved for the first time, her eyes rolling toward him.

"Wh'…wh't'r'y' doin'?" she slurred, fear sparking in her eyes.

"Not *that*," he assured her with a sneer. "Don't flatter yourself."

If asked, he would've been the first to admit it was an odd quirk for a self-admitted terror villain to have. He'd stolen millions, murdered people wholesale, and would happily kick puppies into traffic given half an excuse, but he'd never raped anyone and didn't intend to start now. In all honesty, he'd never felt the need; he had many other ways of imposing his will on people. Usually involving violent murder.

And then, of course, there were the new recruits. About half of them appeared to be likely prospects, nearly all of whom either took him up on his offer when he advanced it, or made moves on him themselves, either of which worked for him. G-Man was the only one he'd read totally wrong in recent times; in hindsight, that wasn't the kid's fault. False positives happened.

He wouldn't commit the act himself, but neither was he going to moralize about it or force anyone to follow his views. What the other team members did in their own time was their own business, so long as they didn't fuck with the people of Utopia City. It wasn't like he was an *actual* hero; he just played one for the TV cameras.

She was wearing underwear beneath the armor; he left that in place. As he finished removing the armor and bundling it up, he could hear her bones moving back into place. "Do you know why you're down here?" he asked her, not caring if he didn't get an answer. "Do you have any idea just how thoroughly you just screwed up?"

"G-Man *knows*," she insisted, trying to raise herself up despite her ruined body. "He figured out Charnel and me were shape-changers."

Relentless rolled his eyes. "Yeah, and he called me directly to *warn* me. Think I can't tell when someone's lying to me, even over the phone? He wasn't scared *of* me; he was scared *for* me. We would've gotten those files *back*, you monumental waste of time, air, space, and effort. Once Iridium unscrambled 'em, he would've been able to work on what spin to put out there. But *you* had to go behind my back and turn the whole thing into a clusterfuck of the highest order. Now Charnel's dead, the files are still out there somewhere, and I've found out I can't trust you further than I can spit you." He leaned closer and shouted the words into her face. "*AND DESPITE YOUR BEST EFFORTS, HE STILL THINKS WE'RE THE GOOD GUYS!*"

She slumped back. "You're wrong," she rasped, trying in fits and starts to change back to her original form, but hampered by the injuries. "You'll see. He'll betray you all."

Shaking his head, he stood up, the bundle under his arm. "Betrayal isn't in his nature. He sticks to his allies through thick and thin. '*Trust G-Man. He will save Utopia.*' Remember that?"

Her body convulsed, and she coughed up a wad of congealed blood. Raising her voice, she continued to rant at him. "Fuck you, and fuck that stupid fucking note. You're *wrong*. I just wish—"

The scrape of movement behind him provided just enough warning. Turning fast, he swung his fist in a short, brutal arc, impacting with the breastbone of the Madness who had been charging toward him. Bone crackled and caved inward; the wild-eyed man expirated an involuntary spray of blood as his heart and lungs were crushed between his sternum and spine. Flying backward even faster than he'd come up, he hit the ground and skidded to a halt, limp in death.

Not bothering to wipe the blood off his armor, Relentless looked down at Independence. She'd seen the guy coming and had tried to cover the noise of his approach.

Well, if that's the way you want it …

Half a dozen ideas for a farewell line went through his head, but none seemed fitting. "See you when I decide what to do with you." Stepping out through the still-open exit, he closed it behind him. She may have called out one last time as the concrete wall rumbled shut, but he wasn't listening anymore.

He tried to figure out where he'd gone wrong with False Flag on the way back up to the labyrinth control room. As Independence, she'd worked well alongside him as the official second-in-command of the team. It was only after he'd passed the word to Lady Quantum about the empath accompanying G-Man that things had gone wrong. As Jack Portman, False Flag had taken a beating from G-Man's cousin, but that shouldn't have changed anything. Shit happened. It was a thing.

Maybe it's because he's never had his ass handed to him like that before?

It was something to think about. After G-Man made the news with his impressive raid on the South Side Mall, she'd been so pissed off that she talked Tourbillon into sending six Madness into New York in the one group, just because she wanted *someone* to suffer. He had confronted her about it before the meeting where Transit brought it up, and she'd assured him it was a one-off.

Apparently, it wasn't, as today showed all too clearly.

Okay, now what the hell do I do about this?

Entirely apart from Independence being a fan favorite with the public, having a shape-changer on call had averted more than a few crises in the making. They could bring in a body double to announce a leave of absence, but it wouldn't solve the overriding problem.

Do I write her off, or do I try to whip her back into shape? So to speak.

Pun aside, it was a tricky question.

He lingered a while before going back upstairs; accessing the hidden cameras in her vicinity, he watched as she gradually pulled her body back into working order. A couple more Madness showed up before she was completely done, but she didn't let that stop her. An injured prodigy was still a prodigy, and she proved it by beating them both savagely to death even as her bones finished knitting back together.

When she was done, she took the form of one of the men who'd tried to attack her, then stole his clothes as well as the sharpened thigh bone he'd attempted to shank her with. As False Flag limped off into the maze, Relentless could see his strategy as plain as day: pretend to be one of the Madness, then stage an ambush when the chance arose. It wasn't a bad action plan, and Relentless looked forward to dealing with its execution. But for now, he had the rest of the team to deal with; shutting down the cameras, he took the elevator upstairs once more.

He still hadn't decided how long he would leave False Flag down there when he arrived back where he'd left the others. Nobody had gone anywhere, which saved him the need to hunt them down. That particular scenario would only end in more unpleasantness, and perhaps more people sharing the labyrinth with the Madness. He was in that kind of mood.

As he stepped into the room, he could see from their expressions that they'd seen the dried spray of blood on his armor. Nobody asked if it was from Independence or someone else, and he didn't feel like enlightening them. *Let 'em wonder.*

Moving over to the Technologist, he lowered his voice. "They try anything stupid while I was gone?"

"Neither physical nor verbal," murmured the artificer in return.

"Good. Give 'em their powers back." He raised his voice to a growl as he turned to face the three remaining public members of Force Majeure, as well as Mutilator. "We need to find G-Man. If he's hiding out from Independence, he won't be here in Utopia. Ideas?"

Lady Quantum put her hand up. "I think he's in Kansas City."

He looked at her. "Reasoning?"

She ticked points off on her fingers. "He lives in Savannah, but he didn't take the maglev, which leaves being smuggled out via the highway. Kansas City is the first maglev stop on the way to Savannah; plus, it's the closest large city. He'd run there instinctively, even if he never went any farther. Also, the time frame between the lockdown and the phone call fits well with a car ride to Kansas City, with a little left over."

"On the other hand, he may have assumed we would anticipate that and fled in a different direction," objected the Technologist. "His unknown ally is likely to influence his decisions in unpredictable ways. The Canadian border and the illusion of safety are to the north, or perhaps Mexico to the south."

These were both excellent points. Relentless looked over at Tourbillon, Transit, and Mutilator. "And what do you think?"

The teleporter frowned thoughtfully. "I don't know G-Man well enough to make a judgment. But perhaps Lady Quantum might be on to something."

"Okay, send her there to look around," he said firmly. "Transit?"

"I'm with Lady Quantum and Tourbillon," the vehicular artificer said. "He thinks a lot of his family. I think he'd run at least part of the way home."

"Good." He felt better about sending Lady Quantum to Kansas City. "Mutilator?"

The surgeon smiled slightly. "I agree with Transit. Also, his parents are staying overnight at the St. George, aren't they? I think we should invite them into the Spire and show them what *real* first-class looks like. Introduce them to all the hospitality Utopia is capable of while we await the prodigal son's return."

His eyes met hers, and he nodded. "Good idea. Do it. Everyone but the Technologist, clear the room."

While all but the artificer filed out, Mutilator hung back. "One more thing before I go. I didn't want to air it in front of everyone." She glanced meaningfully at the Technologist.

Clenching his teeth against the need to return G-Man's call, Relentless calmed himself. This was Mutilator, after all. "Out with it."

She took a deep breath. "When G-Man raised the topic of Black Dragon, I had to amend her age in the files on the fly. I don't like being caught on the back foot like that. Can you at least give me a heads-up the next time you decide to jump into bed with a mouthy sixteen-year-old?"

Leaning in, he glowered at her. "It's your fucking *job* to be on top of shit like that. Now, get your ass out of here and back to Medical One before someone misses you."

"Sir, yes, *sir*," she snapped sarcastically, stalking out of the room without a backward glance.

As the door closed behind her, the Technologist raised an eyebrow. "Intriguing, but I suspect that wasn't why you had me remain behind."

"No." Relentless breathed in deeply through his nostrils to calm himself down. "Any luck on the time travel side of things?"

The Technologist's head came up. "Ah, this would be regarding the enigmatic document from the construction trailer, yes?"

"The note, yeah." Relentless gritted his teeth. If it could be proven that the note was a trick, they could all stop bending over backward for G-Man and go back to business as usual. Which meant the kid would have to die if he learned too much. It would be regrettable if things got that far—G-Man had grown on him just a little—but once again: shit happened.

"I will repeat to you once more what I explained to Independence last week," the Technologist said patiently. "Sending material objects into the past is theoretically possible, but it would be woefully inaccurate, exceedingly stressful on whatever is sent, and horrifically wasteful of energy. It would also be a one-way trip, unless there were a similar machine already extant in the past with an even greater power output, capable of sending the traveler forward once more. And finally, at the instant of sending, a burst of chronal energy would be released, detectable by the correct equipment. I have had an appropriate detector running within my laboratory for the last ten years. No such chronal bursts have been detected."

"Okay, fine." Relentless mentally noted that Independence had been actively trying to find a reason to bypass the protection on G-Man so she could murder him with impunity, then shrugged. This was old news at best. "Let me know if you figure out anything new."

"Assuredly." The Technologist left the room, closing the door behind him.

Fuckin' finally!

Barely taking the time to activate the white-noise generator, Relentless grabbed up the phone and set it to call out on the last incoming number. It rang twice before it was answered.

"Hello?" The kid sounded rough, but that was only to be expected.

Fortunately, there was good news all around. "G-Man. Ming vase. The problem's been dealt with. Independence will be taking a *permanent* leave of absence from Force Majeure. Good work with that, by the way."

Independence could never make a comeback as a public member of the team, of course. But if he could get False Flag back on side, there was always a use for a shape-changer behind the scenes.

G-Man's hesitation sounded in his voice, as if he was unsure of how to take this. "Uh, thanks …?"

Relentless rolled his eyes. "Will you quit it with the damn false modesty already, boy? Where are you? I'll have one of the team pick you up and bring you back." With the idiot shape-changer out of the way, he'd be able to fully debrief the kid on what had happened, and lay the groundwork for the line of bullshit he was going to have to come up with.

"I, uh … I can't come back. There's … there's something I've got to take care of."

"What?" Never far under the surface, Relentless' temper flared again. Had someone gotten to G-Man while he'd been dealing with False Flag? If so, they wouldn't live to regret it. "What the hell's going on? Where are you? Talk to me, boy."

"I can't tell you." Relentless listened intently to the tone of G-Man's voice, but all he picked out was worry. Not fear of personal danger. The kid still wasn't scared for himself, but for someone else. "I'm sorry. I've … I've gotta go."

"But—" Relentless reached his hand out as though he could physically stop G-Man from hanging up. But the click in his ear, followed by the dial tone, happened anyway.

Nope. Not this time. He stabbed his finger at the redial button, holding back just enough that the phone didn't shatter under the impact.

But all he got was a recorded message, telling him the number was out of service. He tried three more times before accepting that it was a lost cause, that whatever phone G-Man had been calling on was no longer connected.

Okay, now what do we do?

Straightening up, he put the phone down carefully.

We keep looking. We find out where he's gotten to. And we find out why he doesn't want to come back.

He didn't know precisely *what* G-Man was supposed to save Utopia from, but the current crisis certainly worked well as a starting point.

The sooner they found him and brought him back, the better.

- End of Epilogue Three -

Epilogue Four
A Friend in Need

New York City
January 29, 2014
09:45 AM, Eastern Daylight Time

Splendid

Nina soared over Manhattan Island. Hard-light wings spread wide, banking around flocks of startled pigeons, she thoroughly enjoyed the morning commute in to the base. From this altitude, the snowfall here and there looked pristine and white; she preferred to imagine that was the reality, instead of swooping closer and finding out differently.

She'd woken early and spent some quality time with Mister Fluffikins before handing him over to Mrs. Spencer to pet-sit for the day. As always, she would pick him up in the evening and take him for a walk; he had a lot of energy for such a little dog. Afterward, they'd curl up on the sofa and watch something fun on TV. He enjoyed comedies with dogs in them.

Swooping in for a two-point landing on the covered balcony that served as the aerial entrance to the base, she let the wings dissipate as her feet touched the floor. Most of the Manhattan Justice base security system involved flying and crawling devices armed with inventive (if non-lethal) deterrents. This made the commercially bought PIN code lock perhaps the *least* advanced tech in the building, but Drone had his specialty, and that was that. She keyed in the code to open the door and stepped inside.

A tiny sentry-copter buzzed down the hallway as the door closed behind her. When it turned and flew away again, she knew it had registered her identity. She waved at the retreating drone, knowing that Conrad was now aware of her arrival. He was probably in his lab, so she headed that way.

When she got there, the door was open, but he was hard at work constructing yet another one of his remote-controlled devices, so she waved again and strolled on past. While his dedication to his craft was admirable, she wished he'd come out and *socialize* once in a while. He could be pleasant company when he made an effort, but most of the time, he didn't even try.

On the other hand, All-Star—*Derek*—was sweet and eager to please. They would've spent more time in each other's company, but Troll was apparently on an extended Prodigy kick, to the point that it was difficult for the two of them to hold a long conversation. And trying to get *Troll* to talk about stuff outside of his professed interests was not dissimilar to pulling teeth from a surly crocodile, only with a slightly higher chance of having one's head bitten off.

Still, Nina was nothing if not an optimist. She wandered onward into the gym, where—predictably enough—she found Troll reclining at his leisure with a bowl of apples at his elbow. On the other side of the room, Derek hung upside-down from a pull-up bar via hooks strapped to his ankles. This allowed him to perform inverted abdominal crunches while hefting a small but heavy-looking barbell from floor level up to his toes, alternating from one hand to the other with each upward lunge. And for some reason, he was … blindfolded?

"Morning, Nina!" called Derek without even turning his face in her direction.

She was about to answer when Troll hefted an apple and threw it hard at the side of Derek's head. Before Nina could shout a warning, Derek whipped out his left hand and caught the apple in mid-air. He didn't so much as miss a beat in his exercise as he took a bite.

Angrily, Nina rounded on Troll. "What was that? You could've hurt him just then!" She was already annoyed with him over tricking them all about the so-called camping trip he'd taken Derek on, even if she *had* gotten a new autograph for her Force Majeure collection out of it.

He waved off her concern. "Nah, he had it. Didn't you, junior?"

In what she considered an absurd level of grandstanding, Derek tossed both barbell and apple into the air in the middle of the next abdominal crunch. He caught the apple with his right hand, and the barbell smacked into his left. Still blindfolded, he took another bite of the apple while maintaining the rhythm. "Yeah, I'm good."

Nina didn't let up her annoyed glare at Troll. "I just think you're pushing him too hard, is all. Look at him; he's stronger and faster than he's ever been before."

Her irritation may as well have been a gentle summer shower, for all the impact it had on him. "An' he's got plenty of potential to keep gettin' stronger an' faster. Day he can kick my ass is the day he gets to slack off." Troll stretched back along the bench, apparently relaxed, but she wasn't fooled; she'd seen him explode into action before, and knew the posture was deceptive in the extreme.

The two prodigies were a study in contrast. Troll was barely five foot three, built like a tank, with biceps thicker than Nina's thighs. His shoulder-length tawny brown hair was tied back with a rawhide thong, the immense barrel chest crisscrossed with overlaid scars from whatever he'd gone through in his life before joining Manhattan Justice. A knife that Nina suspected Troll had carved himself, maybe from bone, was sheathed at his waist; the braided leather belt and the pants—made of the same material—were all the clothing he generally wore.

On the other hand, Derek was nearly a foot taller than his mentor; though impressively muscular in his own right, his was more of a swimmer's build than the raw brute power that Troll commanded. His blond hair was cut short, and the beard he'd grown during his sojourn in the wilderness framed his face neatly. Since being accepted onto the team, he'd discarded the flashy spandex costume for a more durable one, and the cape had gone entirely by the wayside. As All-Star, he was beginning to make his mark among the New York rooftop-running set, though he was still nowhere near as well-known as Troll.

Though younger and far less physically formidable than Troll, Nina stood her ground. "I just think you're being unfair. After all, you've been doing this a lot longer than him."

Troll picked up another apple. "And?" Instead of pitching this one at Derek, he took a bite out of it and shot her a challenging look. This was him all over; he positively relished putting people on the spot and seeing how they dealt with it.

As she was trying to come up with an argument for spending more time with Derek that didn't sound like '*I want to spend more time with Derek*', salvation arrived in the form of a tone sounding over the base PA system.

"Just so you know, some visitors have arrived via the roof entrance," Conrad informed them. **"It's Team Power and a couple of others. They say they need our help. I'm meeting them in Conference One."**

Troll snapped up from the bench he'd been reclining on. "This sounds interesting. C'mon, junior. Let's mask up an' go see what they want."

Nina followed along as they hustled into the main conference room, where the visiting heroes awaited. These turned out to be Tesseract and Vanessa Power, G-Man of Force Majeure, and a woman Nina didn't know, wearing a gray hooded cloak.

Nina had seen news spots about how Vanessa could become a man called 'Thomas Power', but right now, she looked as normal as a young woman in power armor could. Vanessa gave Nina a nod of acknowledgment at her curious glance but said nothing. The cloaked woman flicked her hood back slightly so she could contribute a raised eyebrow and an enigmatic grin as if to say, '*I know what you're thinking*', but likewise didn't speak.

G-Man, oddly enough, didn't seem to be wearing the newer version of his costume as shown in the Force Majeure photoshoots. However, she didn't feel confident in asking him the reason for this, or why he'd shown up with Team Power rather than Force Majeure.

"Thank you for seeing us." Tesseract Power sounded troubled. "You know of Vanessa and myself, and you may have heard of G-Man and Smokeshadow."

"G-Man, yes. Smokeshadow, no." Conrad nodded in greeting. "It's good to meet you all. What's the situation?"

Tesseract drew a deep breath. "We have a problem. *America* has a problem. And we're going to need everyone we can get to help deal with it."

Conrad folded his arms. "So, get G-Man there to contact Force Majeure. They've got more throw weight than us, by a long way."

"We can't." Vanessa Power's tone was sharp. "Force Majeure *is* the problem."

Conrad tilted his head. "Explain."

"We'd rather show," Smokeshadow said; with a magician's flourish, she produced a small metal ball apparently out of nowhere, then tossed it into the air.

When she snapped her fingers, it stabilized itself and began to hover in place. This wasn't exactly unusual for Nina; Drone usually had two or three of his constructs following him wherever he went. But she started paying attention when it began projecting imagery on the far wall.

To her mounting horror, the footage showed a heavily armed tank self-assembling from the contents of three different storage units, all from a first-person-shooter style point of view. The subsequent death and destruction, and the horror of realizing the driver of the mechanical monstrosity considered it all to be a *game*, had her fighting down nausea.

Every hero knew of the terror villain called Raider, though she couldn't understand why this was relevant. Enlightenment came right at the end when Tourbillon rescued Raider from the heroes and the authorities, and the two congratulated each other. When she saw Transit's helmet, the pieces came together to make a perverse logic, and she had to cover her mouth to prevent herself from throwing up.

No … no, no, no …

"Well, damn," Derek said, rocking back on his heels. Despite his relative lack of experience, it was clear he knew what he'd seen. What they'd *all* seen.

"This has to be a hoax, right?" Conrad asked, his lips pinched tightly in anger. "Someone's put this out to discredit Force Majeure, and you need help squashing it …"

"It's genuine," Tesseract assured him. "We wouldn't be here if it wasn't. The attack happened in Davenport, Illinois, at the time and date given on the clip, and it was well-documented at the time. Plus, we have more." She took out a USB drive and handed it over to Conrad. "Yesterday, G-Man was attacked *in Utopia City* by Silent Knight, who was outed as Charnel during the fight and later killed in self-defense. G-Man and Smokeshadow were confronted almost immediately by Independence, who attempted again to murder G-Man. He survived, and fled the scene with Smokeshadow's assistance."

"Wait," Nina interrupted, looking at G-Man in a totally different light. "You managed to kill *Charnel*?"

"*We* did," Smokeshadow answered for him. "And while we were still trying to figure it out, yeah, Independence showed up."

"And she tried to arrest you for killing Silent Knight." It sounded like a logical course of action, at least to Nina.

G-Man shook his head. "No. She tried to murder me for not rolling over and dying for Charnel. If I hadn't thrown a G-shake at her, we'd both likely be decorating trays in the Utopia morgue right now."

"And that G-shake was what caused her to lose control of her features, and made them start shifting," Smokeshadow cut in. "Because Independence isn't who we thought she was. *He's* a shape-changer."

"False Flag, to be exact," G-Man confirmed. "I saw it too."

"Wait," Derek objected, making a time-out gesture. "Hold on a moment. You're saying that Silent Knight was Charnel, Independence is False Flag, and Transit is Raider? I saw Tourbillon on that clip, too. Where does he, uh, they fit in?"

"Since you asked," Smokeshadow said with resignation in her voice, "if anyone's got a sensitive disposition, I'd look away now. This one's not safe for *anywhere*." Raising her hand, she snapped her fingers dramatically to start the next film clip running.

By the time Nina realized precisely what *'not safe'* truly meant, she was blushing to the roots of her hair. She'd thought herself a worldly young woman—after all, she was a *superhero*—but she'd never seen, or even imagined, anything like *that* before. As she turned her head away, G-Man caught her eye and gave her an understanding nod. He wasn't watching it, either.

The horrific and dramatic finale to the clip drew Nina's attention back, and she was able to ignore the nudity for long enough to figure out precisely what she was seeing.

"That's ... definitely something to worry about," admitted Conrad. "You could've warned us, though."

"I thought I did." With the hood still pulled partially back, Nina caught the definite impression of an eye-roll from the shadows beneath. "So, yeah. Tourbillon is Guillotine, and Lady Quantum is Singularity. Or did you need to go back and watch that again?"

Conrad shook his head definitively, a shudder of distaste in his voice. "No, thank you. I'll never be able to *un*see that. Is there any more, or is that it?"

Smokeshadow raised a finger. "One more. Don't worry; it's all text and voice clips. No more sex or violence, I promise."

"Before you listen to this one," G-Man interjected, "I was present for most of those voice clips. I can vouch for their authenticity."

Smokeshadow nodded. "What he said." She snapped her fingers a third time.

Nina quickly caught on to the text format, and with the prompting from the previous two files, she was starting to form her own ideas as to the identities behind the usernames. She looked with sympathy at G-Man, standing by with clenched jaw muscles, as the words reporting the deaths of his friends scrolled up the screen.

"Okay ..." Conrad said when it was over. "Those names don't mean much to me. I get the impression that murder was committed, but there's no definite proof of who did it."

"That's fair," said Smokeshadow. "Here's some context. I *personally* hacked all three files from a beyond-top-secret server inside the Spire. The names are phonetic alphabet initials for terror villains. Foxtrot is False Flag, Charlie is Charnel, Golf is Guillotine, and Sierra is probably Singularity. As you've already seen, the last two are definitely still alive."

Vanessa Power spoke next, a hard edge of determination to her voice. "Otherwise known as Independence, Silent Knight, Tourbillon, and Lady Quantum. We know Charnel's dead. Foxtrot is currently … indeterminate. Also, we've got independent evidence that Seismic is mixed up in this." She paused and moistened her lips with her tongue as if she couldn't believe what she was about to say. "Finally, the Technologist is Doc Iridium … and Relentless is the Minotaur."

"You're not serious," said Conrad into the silence that followed. Even his own tone belied his words; Nina could tell he was saying the words because he thought he had to. "You can't be."

G-Man pulled off his gloves and pushed up the sleeves of his jacket. The red lines of healing cuts covered his left hand and right forearm, some of the deeper ones exhibiting stitches. "Charnel did that to me, not twenty-four hours ago. I *promise* you, we're serious."

Vanessa Power stepped up next to him, and stared into Conrad's visor. "I swear upon my life and everything I hold dear, the top tier of Force Majeure consists entirely of terror villains, and has been that way since its formation."

Silence fell over the room as they each digested the shocking revelations in their own way. Nina battled the chill that swept down the back of her neck. She'd seen those heroes in the news and admired them … and now they were *terror villains*? How was that even possible?

Smokeshadow snapped her fingers twice, and the ball obediently dropped into her hand. Rolling it through her palm, she balanced it on her fingertip while looking at them. "Thoughts?"

"Just one." Conrad made a slicing motion with his hand. "Force Majeure is too big for individual heroes like us to face. Bring in the National Guard. As Manhattan Justice team leader, it's my call. We're sitting this one out."

Nina wanted to accept his excuse, but she chose honesty instead. "But … don't they *supply* what the National Guard uses?" she asked, looking at her leader. "Wouldn't they have backdoors or something?"

G-Man nodded grimly as he replaced his glove and pulled down his sleeve. "You're more correct than you think. Even if the National Guard was given orders to deploy, they wouldn't get within fifteen miles of the Spire. I know a lot of what Utopia can muster for defenses, and no amount of mundane technology will come close to matching up."

"All the more reason to sit it out!" snapped Conrad. "We wouldn't stand a chance in hell!"

Part of Nina wanted to agree with him, even though she hated herself for doing so.

And besides, who'd look after Mister Fluffikins while I was away?

Troll stepped forward. "Screw that noise. I'm in. With me, junior?"

To his credit, Derek barely hesitated. "All the way there and back again." Moving up, he stood shoulder to shoulder with Troll.

That decided Nina. There was no way she would let Derek go into a fight while she spectated from the sidelines. *I can afford to pay Mrs. Spencer extra, just this once.*

She stepped up alongside Derek. "Me, too."

"What is this?" Conrad stared at the three of them. "You all voted *me* in as team leader. Should I not have the final say in this? Manhattan Justice protects *Manhattan*, not the rest of the nation."

"Drone." Tesseract Power spoke firmly, persuasively. "We're already going to be facing enough opposition that it'll be touch and go under the best of circumstances. Even one extra person fighting instead of standing back could make all the difference. Please, reconsider."

"*I'm not a soldier!*" Conrad shouted. "I don't even know how to throw a *punch*! I make things that move by remote control! I rescue cats out of trees! I didn't sign up for this!" Around the perimeter of the room, a dozen drones spun up their rotors at once, the high-pitched whine filling the room.

"Hey. Hey, hey, hey." The ball vanished with a flick of Smokeshadow's wrist as she strolled forward. Her hood was thrown back to show her face, her body language disarming and her voice soft. "It's all good. It's *okay* to have second, third, or even tenth thoughts about this. I've *been* there, trust me. Worried that your tech won't make the grade? Hon, I hid in an apartment in Utopia City for seventy-two hours straight, fully aware that the *only* thing between safety and someone kicking in my door was how well I'd programmed my shit. I've *lived* that fear. Right now, I know I couldn't win a straight-up fight with any member of Force Majeure. Even Doc Iridium could probably punch my lights out. But when that nasty little voice starts whispering in my ear and telling me I'm not good enough, you know what I do, these days?"

Her speech was low, hypnotic, *understanding*. Nina wanted to ask the question, but Troll caught her eye and shook his head fractionally. She saw the movement as he elbowed Derek, probably to keep him from asking it in Conrad's place.

The rotor-blades spun down again, and the remote units shut off, one by one. Conrad looked at Smokeshadow for the longest time, as though arguing with himself. "What do you do?" he asked quietly, almost beseechingly.

Smokeshadow turned her head and indicated where Nina and the other two stood watching them. "I remind myself that I trust my friends to have my back. It took me a long time to find good friends, but you've already got yours. So, how about giving them a chance, okay?"

Going suddenly from the most significant person in the room to almost a ghost, she moved back, leaving the floor to Conrad. Nina couldn't see his eyes behind his HUD visor, but his head jerked up slightly and his mouth opened in a soundless *oh* of realization as if seeing something for the first time. He stepped toward them, placing his back to the other heroes. When he removed the visor, his eyes were as troubled as his voice had been.

Nina was the first to meet his gaze. He was her team leader, and despite her irritation with some of his habits, she was quite fond of him and trusted him implicitly. She offered a smile of reassurance and encouragement to let him know that she was okay with whatever he decided for himself. He smiled back, hesitantly but gratefully.

Next, he looked to Derek, who nodded firmly in return. "Not gonna lie," the younger prodigy said frankly. "We could really do with your help. But it's your call, all the way."

Conrad clasped him briefly on the shoulder. "I know. And thanks." Then he turned to Troll. "And what about you? What pearls of wisdom do you have for me?"

Troll's craggy features were obdurate, his dark eyes hooded by his mask. "I ain't gonna waste your time an' mine tellin' you what you should be doin'. If you're gonna lead this team, then goddamn well *lead* it. Otherwise, get the fuck outta the way." He folded his arms, signaling an end to his statement.

Conrad blinked twice, slowly. "Well, that was concise and to the point, as always." He carefully fitted the HUD visor back into place, then faced the Team Power contingent. "Manhattan Justice, at your service," he said, with a formal salute.

"Thank you," Tesseract Power said, her voice relieved. "Like I said, no matter *how* well we make our plans, we'll need every bit of help we can get."

Nina wasn't quite sure what she'd gotten herself into, but she did know it was the most important thing she would ever do with her life.

Mister Fluffikins is going to be so proud of me.

- The End -

Jericho Hansen will return in

Book Three of the UTOPIAN DREAMS series:

The Fall of Utopia.

Glossary

(This glossary excludes virtually all real-world places and things mentioned in the story. You'll have to look those up for yourself.)

AAN: see *Adaptive Artificial Neuron.*

Adaptive Artificial Neuron: Component developed by *Adam Power* after studying the shape-changing capability of *Vanessa/Thomas Power* (see: **Dramatis Personae**). Provides an improvement in *synthetic proprioception* and a 4.9% increase in reaction speed when working with systems that use *neural induction.* Called *AAN* for short.

Arfogwyr Memorial Day: July 11. A day of mourning in the United States and United Kingdom, memorializing the day when *the Minotaur* (see: **Dramatis Personae**) murdered *Arfogwyr* and put *Challenger* in a coma, and by doing so destroyed *Inspire* (see: **Enabled Teams and Others**).

artificer: An *Enabled* who constructs devices or items more quickly and efficiently than would normally be possible. Advanced technology is often involved. The term can be used as an adjective (and is capitalized when doing so) or a noun. (Examples: "I have an Artificer rating"; "I am an artificer".) See also: *cog.*

Blood Rose: Horrific Artificer weapon once carried by the *Minotaur* (see: **Dramatis Personae, Enabled Teams and Others**). Ironically, it was partially responsible for his death. Has been survived, but by very few people.

cape: Popular slang for *dynamic.*

Challenger Act: Legislation created on behalf of *Challenger* (see: **Enabled Teams and Others**) by the United States government to prevent the civilian identities of heroic Enabled from being casually uncovered. Government-affiliated superheroes have much more stringent protections than independent heroes, though the latter are protected as well. Deliberately unmasking a government-affiliated Enabled is equivalent to releasing nuclear launch codes or the names of undercover assets in foreign countries. Doing the same to an independent hero will draw charges of domestic terrorism. The legislation in question is based on 18 U.S. Code § 794: *"Gathering or delivering defense information to aid foreign government."*

Challenger Commemoration Day: A holiday, set on January 28, that celebrates the beginnings of *Challenger* (see: **Enabled Teams and Others**), and of superheroes in general. Involves lots of superhero-themed fireworks. There are ceremonies in most major cities and at the Kennedy

Space Center Visitor Complex, which superhero teams either attend as a group or send a representative.

Challenger event: Situation where a group of people are in danger, and one gets powers just in time to save the rest. Named after *Challenger* (see: **Enabled Teams and Others**).

Challenger Memorial Day: A day of mourning for the death of *Challenger* (see: **Enabled Teams and Others**), set in late August. The main ceremony takes place in Arlington National Cemetery, where Challenger's funeral ceremony took place.

Challenger Plaza: A circular paved area one thousand feet across, outside the *Spire* in *Utopia City*. It possesses a fountain, picnic tables with automatically adjusting umbrellas, and a hovering double-sized statue of *Challenger* (see: **Enabled Teams and Others**).

circuit: In-house term for the concentric circular corridors in the *Spire*. In addition, a casual term for the streets of *Utopia City* that run in circular paths around the city center. More specifically, it's a descriptor for anything that runs all the way around the city at a particular distance from the Spire, such as *the Greenway*. See also: *radial*.

cog: Popular slang for *artificer*.

cowl: Popular slang for *prodigy*.

data-crawler: Program designed to hunt down intruders and report back with information about them.

Designated Liaison: A member of the Utopia City PD whose job is to handle situations where knowledge of a hero's secret identity will clear up confusion at a crime scene. They are always accompanied by at least one Enabled bodyguard.

discus: Small device gifted from *Gimmick* (see **Dramatis Personae**) to *Smokeshadow*. It allows the user to bypass electronic security and access hidden data. The name comes from its shape.

DPR: Stands for 'Dual Power Rating'; used to describe an *Enabled* with two different *ratings*.

dynamic: An *Enabled* with overt super-powers (e.g. flight, super-strength, telekinesis). The term can be used as an adjective (and is capitalized when doing so) or a noun. (Examples: "I have a Dynamic rating"; "I am a dynamic".) See also: *cape*.

Enabled: (noun) A person with superhuman capabilities; (adj) the state of having superhuman capabilities. See also: *Mask*.

Enabler Boson: A theoretical subatomic particle that only interacts with the nervous systems of sapient beings (such as humans) during times of extreme stress. This interaction leads to the person becoming *Enabled*.

Fantasy Hero League: A trading-card game, similar in concept to Fantasy Football, where each hero is assigned a card with an overall score based on their power *tier* and demonstrated capabilities, and teams are assembled to compete in the grades Newcomer, Rookie, Experienced, Epic and Elite. Mostly played online, but first-issue cards can come with serious bragging rights (especially if signed).

focus: An aspect of the *Prodigy* powerset that allows the Enabled to surpass their human limits even further than normal, under certain circumstances. See also: *sweet spot*.

Gordoning: (verb) The act of (a police officer) unofficially sharing case files with a superhero. Example: "He Gordoned me with everything on the Reilly case." See also: *Trevoring*.

Greenway, the: A park in *Utopia City*. Half a mile wide, it straddles the fifteen-mile *circuit* and goes all the way around the city, for a total area of 47 square miles. The freeway (Interstate 70) is diverted under it, rather than go over the top.

Hansen News: The Hansen family business in Savannah. Currently run by *Beau Hansen* (see: **Dramatis Personae**).

hyperweave: 'smart cloth' designed and created by Smokeshadow (see: **Dramatis Personae**). Can reshape to create any apparent clothing, as well as create active camouflage effects.

hard light: The colloquial term for a dynamic hologram encased in an interactive force field. It can usually be treated and manipulated like a solid object. The adjective form is hyphenated: 'hard-light'.

INCH bag: Short for "I'm Never Coming Home". The bag you take when you know you might have to abandon everything and keep on going. (This is a real-world thing, but it's relatively obscure).

Inspire team: A superhero team containing at least one artificer, one dynamic and one prodigy, patterned after the eponymous superhero team. A 'classic' Inspire team has one of each, all with a *straight rating*. Conventional wisdom considers a team to be lacking if they don't have all three powersets represented, at least in part. While some have managed to defy this, most teams go with the Inspire model, mainly because it works. *Manhattan Justice* (see **Enhanced Teams and Others**) is an Inspire team.

invested, fully invested: Term to describe wearing power armor in such a way that has the arms and legs extending into the limbs. The opposite of 'piloted'.

MagCard: High-tech card used to travel on the *maglev* all over the continental United States. Also, the official medium for all transactions conducted within *Utopia City*.

maglev: Cheap, clean, fast, popular rapid-transit system that covers the continental United States (including Alaska, via a spur line through Canada), with its primary hub in *Utopia City* and secondary hubs in major cities. Utilizes magnetic levitation, stabilized by gravity generators, to move its passenger cars at up to 600 mph (average 400). Operated by *Utopia Maglev Lines*.

Mask: (noun) Popular slang for a member of the *Enabled*.

Memorial Park: A park in *Utopia City*, set up to commemorate the lives of those killed in the blast that destroyed Manhattan, Kansas. There are 91,473 names on the memorial walls within the park.

mobility frame: A lightweight, low-powered exoskeleton designed to allow people with limited mobility to live normal lives with a minimum of outside assistance. Produced by *PowerTech Industries* and others. The higher quality ones utilize *neural induction*.

neural induction: Technology perfected by *Adam Power* (see: **Dramatis Personae**) with two major applications. The first is to allow users of *mobility frames* and power armor to move and feel as though the device they are operating is a part of them via *synthetic proprioception*. The second application is to project important data directly on to the user's visual field via a *NID*. It requires direct contact (either via bare skin or through a light bodysuit) to work properly.

NID: Neuro-Induction Display; the use of *neural induction* to replace heads-up display technology. Allows for direct mental command of secondary systems.

nine-twenty: Shorthand for September 20, 1999; the date of the nuclear destruction of Manhattan, Kansas. Also refers to the anniversary of the date, where friends and relatives of the victims converge on *Memorial Park* and leave cards and trinkets in remembrance for their loved ones.

Oaklands: Oaklands Temporary Accommodation. A complex in *Utopia City* containing a number of short-stay self-contained apartments. Quite comfortable, if a little cramped.

Power Plaza: Fortified base in Chicago, housing *Team Power* (see: **Enabled Teams and Others**). Built and secured by *Adam Power* (see: **Dramatis Personae**).

PowerTech Industries: Company owned and operated by *Adam Power* (see: **Dramatis Personae**).

privacy bubble: An example of Force Majeure's technology. When activated, it produces a soundproofed zone in a three-foot radius sphere around the device. They are free to use on the *maglev* and have been marketed for use around the world.

prodigy: An *Enabled* whose normal human capabilities have been pushed up to eleven. There is a tendency to brood on rooftops. The term can be used as an adjective (and is capitalized when doing so) or a noun. (Examples: "I have a Prodigy rating"; "I am a prodigy".) See also: *cowl*.

Proximity Principle: An effect that can take place when an Enabled gains powers, patterning them after another nearby Enabled rather than starting fresh. (Many junior sidekicks get their start in this fashion). It also influences the new Enabled to seek out the originator of their power, to determine whether they will be allied or antagonistic.

radial: In-house term for the straight corridors that radiate out from the core of the *Spire*. In addition, a casual term for the streets of *Utopia City* that run from the city center outward toward the edge of the map. See also: *circuit*.

rating: The type of powerset that an *Enabled* has. There are three ratings; *Artificer*, *Dynamic* and *Prodigy*. An Enabled with two ratings is commonly known as a *DPR*, or Dual Power Rating.

Right Now Airlines: RNAL for short; they are a *shoestring* airline.

scan-lock: Short for 'scanning airlock'. Six feet wide and twelve feet deep, these are used by both *UML* and *Force Majeure* (see: **Enabled Teams and Others**) to analyze people and items entering their facilities.

shoestring: A type of domestic airline company that has sprung up since the advent of the *maglev*. They charge rock-bottom prices and offer sub-economy flights, boarding when sufficient people buy tickets to make the flight profitable. The alternative to *super-first* flights.

South Side Mall: Huge multi-level shopping mall on the southern side of *Utopia City*. The largest in the world by far (with eighteen floors and nearly two hundred million square feet of space), it services a considerable portion of the city, as well as the offramp traffic from Interstate 70.

Southside Parking: Huge parking structure that allows anyone coming in off Interstate 70 to gain access to the *South Side Mall*. It is half a mile north of *the Greenway*.

Spire, the: Tallest building in the world, and central point of *Utopia City*. Nearly eight thousand feet tall. Home base for *Force Majeure* (see: **Enabled Teams and Others**).

SQUID Plus: Derived from the concept of the 'Superconducting QUantum Interference Device', this Artificer creation by Adam Power is capable of hacking into computers from a distance.

straight (rating): Slang for an *Enabled* who has a single *rating*, such as *Artificer* or *Dynamic*.

super-first: Shorthand for 'super first class', referring to the practice by some airline companies of offering their patrons ludicrous levels of attention, as well as other distractions to pass the time during the flight, to lure them away from the *maglev*. The alternative to *shoestring* airlines.

sweet spot: Another way to refer to the area of a prodigy's *focus*.

synthetic proprioception: The technical term for using *neural induction* technology to establish a feedback loop with *mobility frames*, power armor and the like. Users 'feel' sensory data directly, allowing for much faster reactions. This makes learning to use such equipment easier and quicker.

tier: Relative power level scale for comparison of one *Enabled* with another. Very much an abstract metric. Popularized by *Fantasy Hero League* players.

Trevoring: (verb) The act of assisting a superhero in the hopes of becoming romantically involved with them. Example: "Can't she see he's just Trevoring her?" See also: *Gordoning*.

UCIAT: Pronounced 'you-see-it'. Acronym for *Utopia City Institute for Advanced Technology*.

UML: See *Utopia Maglev Lines.*

Unmask: An extremely vocal anti-secret-identity activist group extant from the late 1980s to the mid-1990s. Used methods that ranged from the unethical to the blatantly illegal. They were the direct cause of Surgeon One ending up as Mutilator and the (semi) voluntary unmasking of Team Power. Ceased to exist in any meaningful fashion after the Challenger Act was finalized in 1997, and several key members were successfully prosecuted on domestic terrorism charges.

Utopia City: A metropolis built on the ruins of Manhattan, Kansas after that city's accidental destruction by *Doc Iridium* in 1999. Home base of *Force Majeure* (see: **Enabled Teams and Others**). Most technologically advanced city in the world. Only tourists and city officials use the full name; locals just call it 'Utopia'.

Utopia City Holdings: A limited-liability company owned and operated by the core members of *Force Majeure*. It has several subsidiaries under its umbrella, one of these being *Utopia Maglev Lines*.

Utopia City Institute for Advanced Technology: Called *UCIAT* for short. The waiting list to get in is longer than for any other learning institution in the nation. Works up prototypes for *Transit* and the *Technologist* (see: **Dramatis Personae**).

Utopia Maglev Lines: Usually abbreviated to *UML*. The subsidiary company of *Utopia City Holdings* that manages the *maglev* system.

War on Terror Villains: The dramatic name applied by the media to the campaign by the US government to destroy the terror villains of the Nineties. Implemented via Presidential Executive Order on January 31,

1997. Rescinded by another Executive Order on March 15 of the same year, shortly after the signatory President and his immediate successor were killed in retaliation for the March 7 death of Carnifex.

Zarkinator: Energy rifle favored by *Gimmick* (see: **Dramatis Personae**). Fires a very high-powered beam. Named after the sound of it being fired.

Dramatis Personae

(All notes accurate as of the beginning of this book. This only includes characters who have had actual screen time and/or are currently extant. No spoilers included.)

All-Star (civilian identity Derek Saunders): New York based Enabled with Dynamic and Prodigy ratings. Male. Early 20s, over 6' tall, handsome, well-built, blond hair, piercing blue eyes. Wears a rugged costume in patriotic colors. A member of *Manhattan Justice* (see: **Enabled Teams and Others**). Relatively new to the Enabled scene, currently being mentored by *Troll*.

Black Dragon (civilian identity unknown): Teenage girl, dynamic, mid-length blonde hair, age confirmed to be 18 by *Meredith Chandler*. Can partially or fully turn into a dragon of the same size. A member of *Force Majeure* (see: **Enabled Teams and Others**). Foul mouthed, distinct attitude.

Blades (first name Sarah; surname unknown): Member of the *Survivors* (see: **Enabled Teams and Others**). Teenage blonde girl with short ponytail. Wears gold and black power armor that has roller-blade style wheels built into its feet.

Bradley, Corporal (first name unknown): A member of the *Spire* security detail (see: **Glossary**). Fit, short blonde hair. On friendly terms with *G-Man*. Competent at her job. Acts as range master on Target Range Two.

Brock, Gary: Popular comedian who does humorous routines about modern life. 'Walking from New York to LA' pokes fun at *maglev* travel (see: **Glossary**).

Caroline (surname unknown): Flight attendant for *Right Now Airlines*, a *shoestring* airline company (see **Glossary**).

Castellan (civilian identity Richard Miller): Male prodigy, last surviving member of *Inspire* (see: **Enabled Teams and Others**). Late 60s, brown eyes, silver-gray hair. Vietnam veteran, and one-time prosecutor for the Department of Justice.

Chandler, Meredith: Head of Surgery in the medical section of the *Spire* (see: **Glossary**). Late 30s, faded blue eyes, blonde hair.

Charnel (real name unknown): Deceased terror villain (see: **Enabled Teams and Others**). Changes into bestial form with durable red and black outer shell, claws and teeth. Voice becomes creepy and horrifying. Killed by *Independence* and *Lady Quantum*.

Colburn, Samantha: Executive assistant to Relentless. Very serious about her duties. Currently in her mid-fifties.

Darksider, the (real name unknown): Terror villain (see: **Enabled Teams and Others**). Prodigy with the specialty of bypassing locks and security. Missing, believed dead.

Devastator (real name unknown): Deceased terror villain (see: **Enabled Teams and Others**). Partnered with *Mutilator*. Well over six feet tall, muscular, could generate force fields and energy blasts. Killed by *Relentless*, *Lady Quantum* and *Transit*.

Doc Iridium (real name unknown): Deceased terror villain (see: **Enabled Teams and Others**). Artificer with an apocalypse theme. Wore a set of post apocalypse themed power armor. Killed when a bomb detonated prematurely.

Drone (first name Conrad, last name unknown): Male artificer, member of *Manhattan Justice* (see: **Enabled Teams and Others**). Utilizes numerous drones that he controls with his suit. Handsome, dark curly hair, pencil mustache, early 30s.

Earl (surname unknown): Truck driver with poor judgement.

False Flag (real name unknown): Deceased terror villain (see: **Enabled Teams and Others**). Dynamic with extremely effective shape-changing ability. Killed by *Relentless* and *Silent Knight*.

Forty-Three: Jericho's housecleaning robot in the *Spire*. Name is short for its designation: SD-0043.

Frobisher, Lieutenant (first name unknown): Member of the *Utopia City* Police Department (see: **Glossary**). Fussy and officious, prone to bad calls under stress.

G-Man (civilian identity *Jericho Hansen*): Prodigy/dynamic with gravity control. Wears a black costume with a Kevlar/Nomex blend, spandex gliding wings, a power enhancement harness and a white 'G' on the front and back. Member of *Force Majeure* (see: **Enabled Teams and Others**). While in costume, deliberately deepens his voice to further conceal his identity. Romantically linked with *Thomas Power*.

Gimmick (first name Mel, surname unknown): Member of the *Survivors* (see: **Enabled Teams and Others**). Asian girl, about 16 years old. Artificer who can analyze how other tech works with ease. She specializes in building hand-held devices, but she can repair, subvert and alter larger items. Favorite weapon is the *Zarkinator* (see: **Glossary**).

Green, Chantelle: Slightly overweight woman with dyed blonde hair, resident of Savannah, Georgia. Mother of *Richmond Green*.

Green, Richmond: Child saved by *Luke* and *Jericho Hansen* on the platform of the Savannah *maglev* station (see: **Glossary**). Son of *Chantelle Green* and *Franklin Tucker*.

Guillotine (real name unknown): Deceased terror villain (see: **Enabled Teams and Others**). Dynamic. Sported a purple leather 'battle bikini' with thigh-high boots and wore her hair in a long purple mohawk. Created clouds of purple smoke and decapitated foes or cut their limbs off. Killed by *Relentless* and *Transit*.

Hansen, Beauregard (Beau): Married to *Dahlia Hansen*, father to *Jericho Hansen*, fraternal twin to *Leroy Hansen*, uncle to *Luke* and *Serena Hansen*. Heavy-set and a little overweight. 45 years old; runs *Hansen News* (see: **Glossary**).

Hansen, Dahlia: Married to *Beau Hansen*, mother to *Jericho Hansen*, aunt to *Luke* and *Serena Hansen*. Tall and slender; 45 years old. Very no-nonsense. Runs a law firm in Atlanta, Georgia. An accomplished poker player.

Hansen, Ellie: Married to *Leroy Hansen*, mother to *Luke Hansen* and *Serena Hansen*. African American. Aunt to *Jericho Hansen*. 45 years old. Sister to *Daryl West*.

Hansen, Jericho (Enabled identity *G-Man*): Son of *Beau* and *Dahlia Hansen*, cousin and best friend to *Luke* and *Serena Hansen*, nephew to *Leroy* and *Ellie Hansen*. Romantically linked to *Thomas Power*. 6'2" tall, shoulder length dark brown hair, slim and wiry. 23 years old.

Hansen, Leroy: Married to *Ellie Hansen*, father to *Luke* and *Serena Hansen*, fraternal twin to *Beau Hansen*, uncle to *Jericho Hansen*. Heavily built, 45 years old. Has fingers in more than few pies in the Savannah underworld.

Hansen, Luke: Deceased. Murdered by *Jack Portman* in Utopia City.

Hansen, Olivia (Livy): Widow of *Luke Hansen*. African American. Has long beautiful black hair. 25 years old.

Hansen, Serena: Sister to *Luke Hansen*, daughter to *Leroy* and *Ellie Hansen*, niece to *Beau* and *Dahlia Hansen*, cousin to *Jericho Hansen*. African American. Attending college in New York City. Being groomed to take over *Hansen News* (see: **Glossary**) when Beau retires. 24 years old.

Independence (civilian identity unknown): Core member of *Force Majeure* (see: **Enabled Teams and Others**). Athletic woman, platinum-blonde hair worn in long ponytail, wears costume in muted red and blue. Prodigy. Carries a claymore and an assault rifle. Abrasive personality.

Jessica (surname unknown): Public-facing employee of *Utopia Maglev Lines* (see: **Glossary**).

Kyle (surname unknown): Nursing student at Seattle Pacific University. Plays *Fantasy Hero League* (see: **Glossary**) and is a serious fan of *G-Man*. Also has a crush on him.

Lady Quantum (civilian identity unknown): Core member of *Force Majeure* (see: **Enabled Teams and Others**). Stunningly beautiful woman with raven-black hair. Dynamic. Well-endowed; wears spandex costume cut to show her figure off to its best advantage. Also wears a cape. Can fly and protect herself with a force field. Given to whimsy.

LaMonde, Stephen: Ex-boyfriend of *Jericho Hansen*. 5'4" tall, carefully styled red hair and beard. Overweight. 32 years old. Overly clingy. Produces webzine called *Gay!Power*.

Lombard, Captain Beatrice: Member of the *Utopia City* Police Department (see: **Glossary**).

Mindscrew (real name unknown): Deceased terror villain (see: **Enabled Teams and Others**). Dynamic with mind-reading. Non-descript, bland everyman. Shot in the back of the head by person or persons unknown.

Minotaur, the: Deceased terror villain (see: **Enabled Teams and Others**). Over 6 feet tall, wore a set of thematic animatronic armor. Carried the *Blood Rose* (see: **Glossary**) as a personal weapon. Kidnapped people to put in his murder mazes. Killed by *Castellan* using the Blood Rose.

Mutilator (real name Miranda Price): Deceased terror villain, previously *Surgeon One.* (see: **Enabled Teams and Others**). Partnered with *Devastator*. Prodigy specializing in medicine and surgery. Killed by *Relentless*, *Lady Quantum* and *Transit*.

Nashfield, Casey: Teenage girl, cautious. Daughter of *Dave* and *Maria Nashfield*, sister of *Peter Nashfield*.

Nashfield, Dave: Man in mid-forties. Cancer survivor. Father of *Casey* and *Peter Nashfield*, husband of *Maria Nashfield*.

Nashfield, Maria: Worn-down woman in early forties. Wife of *Dave Nashfield*, mother of *Casey* and *Peter Nashfield*.

Nashfield, Peter: Ten or eleven year old boy. Son of *Dave* and *Maria Nashfield*, brother of *Casey Nashfield*.

Owens, Sarah: Deputy Head of Surgery in the medical section of the *Spire* (see: **Glossary**), under *Meredith Chandler*. Petite and dark-haired, self-effacing.

Petra (surname unknown): Communications student at Seattle Pacific University. Plays *Fantasy Hero League* (see: **Glossary**) and is a serious fan of *G-Man*.

Photonic Avenger, the (first name Chuck, surname unknown): Member of the *Survivors* (see: **Enabled Teams and Others**). Red-haired boy, about 15 years old. Can project a photon-flash and other light-based effects (as well as EMP). Also able to levitate slowly from place to place, and see both UV light and magnetic fields.

Pickup (AKA Peter Smith): Male artificer; hero based in Savannah. Drives a considerably modified pickup truck with the Confederate flag painted on the hood, which turns into a twenty-foot-tall piloted robot. The robot is equipped with various pickup-truck accessories.

Portman, Jack: Deceased. Murdered *Bobbi Reynolds* and *Luke Hansen* under the influence of drugs. Fell to his death when confronted by *Jericho Hansen.*

Power, Adam (Enabled name and civilian name): Co-leader and co-founder of *Team Power* (See: **Enabled Teams and Others**). Artificer with several specialties. Married to *Tesseract Power*, father to *Vanessa/Thomas Power* and *Buddy Power*. Tall, handsome, blond, distinguished good looks. Early 40s. Based in Chicago.

Power, Buddy (Enabled name and civilian name): Member of *Team Power* (see: **Enabled Teams and Others**). Red-haired, 11 years old. Son of *Adam Power* and *Tesseract Power*, brother to *Vanessa/Thomas Power*. Unpowered, wears power armor designed by his father.

Power, Tesseract (Enabled name and civilian name): Co-founder and co-leader of *Team Power* (see: **Enabled Teams and Others**). Prodigy. Tall, statuesque, striking redhead. Married to *Adam Power*, mother to *Vanessa/Thomas Power* and *Buddy Power*. Based in Chicago.

Power, Thomas (Enabled name and civilian name. Alter ego of *Vanessa Power*): Member of *Team Power* (see: **Enabled Teams and Others**). 6'2" tall, husky build, attractively tousled black hair. 18 years old. Friendly and outgoing. One-time leader of the *Survivors* (see: **Enabled Teams and Others**). Romantically linked to *Jericho Hansen*. Son of *Adam Power* and *Tesseract Power*, brother to *Buddy Power*. Prodigy/dynamic.

Power, Vanessa (Enabled name and civilian name. Alter ego of *Thomas Power*): Member of *Team Power* (see: **Enabled Teams and Others**). Red-haired, strong features. 5'8", has her mother's looks. 18 years old. Daughter of *Adam Power* and *Tesseract Power*, sister to *Buddy Power*. Prodigy/dynamic.

Raider (real name unknown): Deceased male terror villain (see: **Enabled Teams and Others**). Artificer specializing in large destructive vehicles. Has an orange prosthetic in his left eye-socket. Killed by Relentless and Independence.

Razor-Edge (first name Gareth, surname unknown): Member of the *Survivors* (see: **Enabled Teams and Others**). Tall, lanky, white-blond hair. Can grow bony plates all over his body, covered in hooks and spurs and blades. Much stronger and more durable when thus affected.

Relentless (civilian identity unknown): Leader and core member of *Force Majeure* (see: **Enabled Teams and Others**). Male, 6'6" tall, very broad in the shoulders, wears black armor with silver trim, as well as a cape. Has a mace which returns to him when thrown. Extremely durable, very strong. Brusque attitude. Deep voice.

Reynolds, Roberta (Bobbi): Deceased. Was instrumental in clearing *Adam*

Power of sexual assault allegations. Murdered by *Jack Portman* in Utopia City.

Richardson, Sergeant Catherine: Female desk sergeant for the UCPD. Late middle aged, still fit. Red hair, going gray.

Rogan, Sylvia: Volunteer site coordinator at Kennedy Space Center. Mid-30s, permanent suntan and extremely professional.

Scout (also known as Sidekick Zero One): Humanoid robot, seven feet tall, armored with angular black metal. Possesses enhanced senses and limited flight capability, as well as both mêlée and ranged weaponry. Assigned to *G-Man* as combination sidekick and bodyguard.

Second Chance: Heavy-set man in his early 30s. Can generate a force field bubble and apply various effects through it. Wears a bulletproof vest and SWAT gear. Member of *Force Majeure* (see: **Enabled Teams and Others**).

Seismic (real name unknown): Terror villain (see: **Enabled Teams and Others**). Artificer with the specialty of creating or suppressing ground tremors. Missing, believed dead.

Sidestep (first name Paul, surname unknown): Youngest member of the *Survivors* (see: **Enabled Teams and Others**). 13-year-old boy. Can create a duplicate of himself, and communicate (and teleport items) between the duplicates.

Silent Knight (civilian identity unknown): Core Member of *Force Majeure* (see: **Enabled Teams and Others**). Male artificer specializing in extreme life-support systems. Maintains his own armor (glossy black, based off medieval plate), which is so thoroughly enclosed that he cannot communicate vocally.

Singularity (real name unknown): Deceased terror villain (see: **Enabled Teams and Others**). Dynamic with energy blasts and force-fields. Kidnaped people and extorted ransoms to kill them quickly. Killed by *Independence & Transit*.

Smokeshadow (first name Chelsea, surname unknown): Woman in her mid-twenties with mousy brown hair. Prodigy with a minor Artificer rating; able to read and utilize body language to an extreme degree. Also good at hiding and sneaking. Wears a costume made of programmable *hyperweave* (see: **Glossary**) and carries other devices that she uses to augment her Prodigy capabilities. Apparent level of attractiveness changes, depending on her needs. More concerned with morality than legality. Has a sister called Marni.

Splendid (first name Nina, surname unknown): Female dynamic, mid-20s. Member of *Manhattan Justice* (see: **Enabled Teams and Others**). Quite good-looking, blonde hair. Good-natured, but a little naïve and sheltered. Manifests golden *hard-light* (see: Glossary) wings that let her fly, as well as weapons and shields. Has a Shi Tzu called Mister

Fluffikins.

Technologist, the (civilian identity unknown): Core member of *Force Majeure* (see: **Enabled Teams and Others**). Older man, white beard; wears stylized lab wear, re-purposed as a costume. Artificer who creates technology in advance of other artificers, and can improve technology built by others. Acerbic, especially in the face of ignorance shown by others.

Tomahawk (real name unknown): Artificer. Independent hero, based in Tallahassee, FL. Flies a set of power armor patterned after military missiles.

Tourbillon (civilian identity unknown): Core member of *Force Majeure* (see: **Enabled Teams and Others**). Androgynous, average height. Preferred pronouns: they/them. Wears a robe in charcoal-gray with a black gem centered on their forehead. A dynamic who creates teleport portals in the form of a dark cloudy swirl in the air. Speaks with a French accent. (Note: 'Tourbillon' is French for 'swirl' or 'whirlpool', related to the English word 'turbulence'.)

Transit (civilian identity unknown): Core member of *Force Majeure* (see: **Enabled Teams and Others**). Female; wears a red and silver flight suit with attached gadgets and a helmet with reflective faceplate. Dual power rating: Artificer with a focus on vehicles, and dynamic with mechanokinesis. Friendly and outgoing.

Troll (civilian identity unknown): Male prodigy. Member of *Manhattan Justice* (see: **Enabled Teams and Others**). 5'3" tall, almost 3' across the shoulders. Extremely well-muscled, covered in scars. Long brown hair, gray eyes, extremely blunt (to the point of rudeness). Mentor to *All-Star*.

Tucker, Franklin: Deceased. 47 years old. Skinny male, resident of Savannah. Unshaven chin and drooping mustache. Had strong views about gun ownership. Conspiracy theorist. Was in a relationship with *Chantelle Green*, father of *Richmond Green*. Murdered by persons unknown in Savannah, GA.

Villanova, Raul: Gay male police detective in Savannah, Georgia. Secretly interested in G-Man. (See: **Glossary** [*Trevoring*])

West, Daryl: Younger brother to *Ellie Hansen*. African American. 35 years old, heavily built.

Timeline of Events

1945: Francis John Hansen ('Great-granddaddy Frank') musters out of US Navy and marries his girlfriend Kathryn Marchant ('Great-gran'maw Kate'). Starts up a news distribution service with his severance pay.

1947: Joseph Francis Hansen ('Papaw Joe') born in Savannah, Georgia.

1966: Joe Hansen marries Penelope Smith ('Mamaw Penny'). He is conscripted to go to Vietnam.

Franklin Tucker born in Savannah, Georgia.

1967: Joe Hansen killed in Vietnam three weeks before his twin sons Beau and Leroy are born. Penny Hansen and her sons taken in by her father-in-law.

1981: Stephen LaMonde born, Savannah.

Roberta "Bobbi" Reynolds born, Des Moines.

1984: Leroy Hansen (17) gets his girlfriend Ellie West pregnant during Spring Break, and promptly marries her in Vegas, against his grandfather's wishes. He is cut off from the family.

1985: (January 7) Luke Hansen born. He spends the first nine years of his life living in near poverty.

1986: (January 28) Challenger incident. The first ever incidence of an Enabled. The crew of the space shuttle Challenger are taken into protective custody by the government, while the dynamic known as Challenger is revealed to the public as the very first superhero. The first iteration of the Challenger Act is put into law by an emergency sitting of Congress. Rulings are immediately sought against it via the Supreme Court.

(April 26) Chornobyl disaster. (This leads to the walking radioactive catastrophe called Cherenkov.)

(Late 1986) The Supreme Court rules in favor of the Challenger Act.

1987:   The radical activist group Unmask is formed in response to the growing numbers of masked Enabled in society.

Beau Hansen meets Dahlia Romano at college in New York.

1988:   The world's first officially recognized superhero team is formed, called Inspire. Original members are Challenger, and a British artificer named Arfogwyr (Welsh for 'armor'). They are based in Seattle in a high-tech base called Caerwyn ('White Castle'), with the blessing of the US government.

Beau and Dahlia Hansen are married.

1989:   First appearance of the Minotaur—a villain who kidnaps people and puts them through murder mazes on live TV. He extorts ransoms, but often does not honor them.

(November 11). Serena Hansen born.

1990:   The terror villain Charnel is captured by Adam Power (artificer) and Tesseract (prodigy) and put on trial by the US government. In retaliation, the Minotaur kidnaps the family of the US Attorney General, along with those of several of his subordinates from the Department of Justice, Criminal Division. They are placed in a murder maze, where it is announced they will be released if Charnel is let go. Charnel is broken out of maximum-security holding by other terror villains and the murder maze is blown up, killing all hostages.

(May 3) Jericho Hansen born.

1991:   Inspire encounters the Prodigy hero Castellan while breaking up a violent Unmask protest action. Impressed by his capabilities, they recruit him. Arfogwyr builds armor and weapons for him to use.

1993:   An extremist group of Unmask activists abducts Surgeon One's family and forces her to commit atrocities with her skills. She seems to enjoy it far too much. When the videotape is released, her reputation and career are ruined. While still under investigation, she vanishes from the public eye. Later, she reappears as the terror villain Mutilator. She is soon joined by Devastator, a powerful dynamic. They form an unholy partnership.

1994:   A second attempt to overturn the Challenger Act is begun, pushed by Unmask (citing the 'instability' of Surgeon One/Mutilator, and calling for transparency and accountability from the Enabled heroes).

Members of Unmask get pictures of Tesseract's face by trickery and attempt to blackmail her and Adam Power into performing criminal acts. The couple turn the tables on the blackmailers by gathering evidence, changing their names by deed poll, and publicly outing themselves before arresting the perpetrators and turning them over to the police. They announce the formation of Team Power and marry soon thereafter.

Jericho's great-granddaddy Frank Hansen passes away at the age of 73. Beau Hansen takes over the reins of Hansen News and reaches out to Leroy and his family. Jericho and Luke Hansen meet for the first time and form a firm friendship.

1995:   The Supreme Court finds in favor of the Challenger Act for a second time; the protocols are broadened to prevent another Surgeon One event from happening. A third challenge is mounted immediately, this time by big business.

Kate and Penny Hansen are killed in a car accident.

(September 23) Vanessa Power born.

1997:   (January 25) The Minotaur attacks the newly elected Vice President's motorcade and kidnaps the VP, placing him in a murder maze. A ransom is paid, but he dies anyway. The President signs an Executive Order stating that all terror villains must be pursued and engaged with the highest level of lethal force available; the 'War on Terror Villains'.

(March 7) The terror villain Carnifex is killed in Dallas, TX.

(March 14) The President is killed by the Minotaur in the White House Situation Room. The Vice President is immediately sequestered in the Presidential bunker and sworn in as President, then dictates a statement that the US will not bow to terrorism. He is found dead along with his security detachment, and a mocking note from the terror villain False Flag.

The newly sworn-in President (previously the VP) rescinds the Executive Order.

Inspire begins to close in on the Minotaur, scouting out his murder mazes and rescuing the victims.

(July 11) The Minotaur attacks Arfogwyr in her civilian identity and kills her. He uses her head and hand to gain access to Caerwyn. After setting explosives to destroy the base, he attacks and severely injures Challenger. Castellan tracks him down to his murder maze and they fight. The Minotaur takes a mortal wound from his own Artificer weapon and falls into the ocean under the rubble of his collapsing murder maze. Castellan makes it out and recovers from his injuries, but Challenger is in a coma; Inspire is finished. Retiring as a superhero, Castellan disappears from public life.

The Supreme Court upholds the Challenger Act for the third time. Several businessmen who were pushing the case are investigated and indicted for questionable activities with overseas interests. High-ranking members of Unmask are indicted under domestic terrorism charges.

Team Power engages the terror villain Kraken in Lake Michigan. Kraken's squid-sub sinks, taking the Artificer villain with it (and nearly Adam Power as well). Other terror villains disappear or are found dead around this time.

1998:   In response to ever greater atrocities by terror villains; newcomer heroes Relentless, Independence, the Technologist, Transit, Silent Knight, Lady Quantum and Tourbillon form Force Majeure. They go after the villains brutally and without quarter. In July and October, they take down Charnel and Singularity, respectively.

1999:   The members of Force Majeure kick their efforts into high gear, engaging and killing False Flag, Guillotine, Raider, and Mutilator and Devastator. By August, only Doc Iridium is left.

(September 15) Terror villain Doc Iridium threatens on live TV to 'blow up Manhattan' in one week if Force Majeure are not immediately arrested and executed. He also demands one billion dollars.

(September 16) Force Majeure surrender themselves to the FBI.

(September 20) Doc Iridium's bomb explodes prematurely during a live broadcast of his ranting. Manhattan, Kansas is destroyed, killing 91,473 people (as well as Doc Iridium himself).

Force Majeure offers their services to the US government to clean up and rehabilitate the site of the explosion. They are presented with the devastated land, which they decontaminate, then begin to construct Utopia City on the same site.

(November 2) Relentless is made aware of a note with his name on it, bearing the message: "Trust G-Man. He will save Utopia."

2002: Buddy Power is born.

Terrorists attempt to crash planes into the Pentagon and the White House, but countermeasures put in place to protect against terror villains prove adequate to the task.

2004: (August) Challenger passes away in care without ever waking up. A national day of mourning is announced.

2005: Vanessa Power debuts as a full member of Team Power, at the age of ten.

Manhattan Justice is formed in New York. Members are Drone, Splendid and Troll.

2011: (May) Jericho turns twenty-one in college in New York and loses his virginity to his roommate on the same night. Returns to Savannah and goes to a gay bar, where he is lured to the top of a nearby building by a man called Troy. Troy's friends are waiting, and they throw Jericho off the roof. In the terror of the moment, he gains powers of gravity manipulation. He hides them at first. When he approaches his parents, they assume that he's trying to tell them he's gay, and assure him that they've known for years. Ends up not telling them, but confides in his cousin Luke. Drops out of college so he can track down the gay bashers; is given an entry-level position in Hansen News.

(September) First appearance of Jericho as G-Man.

(December 17) Vanessa Power runs away from home. PowerTech Industries begins to lose its market share as Team Power concentrates its efforts in finding her, to no avail.

(December 18) Taking refuge in Omaha, Vanessa discovers that she is Enabled, with Prodigy and Dynamic abilities; specifically, she is a shape-changer with biometric powers. She crafts a new identity; a young man called Thomas.

(December 25) Thomas takes the bus from Omaha into Utopia City. He originally wants to join Force Majeure but gets a bad feeling and backs out of it. At the same time, he bands together with a group of teenagers, all survivors of supervillain attacks, and all unwilling to join Force Majeure. They call themselves the Survivors. Initially attempting to be heroes, they are treated as criminals. They then find that all transport out of the city requires MagCards; nothing uses cash money anymore. Thomas has to use his powers to trick the MagCard system to get them food.

2012: (April 2) G-Man is interviewed by Stephen LaMonde, owner of the webzine *Gay!Power*.

(April 13) Jericho and Stephen have their first date.

Thinkster, a Savannah dynamic with the power of reading minds, passes away from a drug overdose.

2013: Bobbi Reynolds is cheated on, dumps her boyfriend and gains empathic powers. These threaten to ruin her relationship with her new boyfriend, Jack Portman.

(September) At the age of 11, Buddy Power debuts as a full member of Team Power.

A leaked police report indicates that Vanessa Power accused her father of attempted rape before she ran away from home. Protestors start gathering outside Power Plaza, in Chicago.

(October 6) Jericho Hansen travels with his cousin Luke Hansen to Utopia City, against the wishes of his boyfriend Stephen LaMonde. They encounter Bobbi Reynolds on the train, also going to Utopia. An empath, she wishes to clear Adam Power's name. They opt to share accommodations in Utopia.

In Utopia, they meet Thomas, who shares an air-taxi to the Oaklands. Jericho goes out that night and meets Transit and then Thomas again. He ends up agreeing to help Thomas and the Survivors leave the city.

When Jericho returns to the Oaklands, both Luke and Bobbi have been brutally murdered. The perpetrator is revealed to be Jack Portman, Bobbi's estranged boyfriend. Jericho meets Smokeshadow, another Enabled staying at the Oaklands.

(October 7) Jericho's interview goes badly. When his uncle Leroy phones to say he's in the city, he asks Smokeshadow to help him smuggle the Survivors out of the city. She agrees.

Leroy discovers Jericho's secret. He and Jericho collect Luke's body and convey it back to Savannah.

In the meantime, Thomas and Smokeshadow lead the Survivors through a gauntlet of police drones, and they take refuge in Smokeshadow's apartment.

(October 8) Jericho attends Luke's wake. Stephen intrudes, and Jericho dumps him. Leroy begins to create fake IDs for the Survivors.

(October 9) Jericho patrols in Savannah, clashes with Pickup.

(October 10) Jericho breaks down at Luke's funeral, leaves, gets into trouble with the police which is subsequently sorted out. Jericho takes the maglev back to Utopia City and gets the fake IDs to the Survivors.

(October 11) Jericho, Thomas and Smokeshadow stage a lightning raid on the South Side Mall. Jericho corners Portman; despite his intent to arrest the murderer, Portman falls to his death.

Relentless offers Jericho a place on Force Majeure, then makes a pass. Jericho accepts the first and declines the second.

Smokeshadow pushes Jericho and Thomas together; they spend the night with each other.

(October 12) Jericho realizes Thomas' true identity as Vanessa Power. He convinces Vanessa that her father is innocent, and she goes back to Chicago as Thomas. Smokeshadow informs Jericho that she's going to form her own underground criminal empire. Jericho is fitted with a power-enhancement harness, which allows him to fly for the first time.

Thomas arrives in Chicago, takes on the form of Vanessa again, and is accepted back by Team Power.

The villain who actually attacked her is angered by this news, and vows to murder whoever helped her out.

(October 13) The superhero team Manhattan Justice accepts a new Prodigy member called All-Star; the Prodigy member called Troll takes it upon himself to whip the new guy into shape.

During a meeting of the core members of Force Majeure, it is revealed that Jericho's role in the escape of the Survivors is known about. Queries are levied at Relentless for his insistence on having G-Man in the team, which he answers by showing them the note from fourteen years previously.

Enabled Teams and Others

(All notes accurate as of the beginning of this book. No spoilers included.)

Force Majeure
Based in Utopia City. Extant since 1998. Dozens of subsidiary members, seven core members:

    Relentless (Dynamic, possible prodigy. Leader)
    Independence (Prodigy. Second in command)
    Lady Quantum (Dynamic)
    Silent Knight (Artificer)
    the Technologist (Artificer)
    Tourbillon (Dynamic)
    Transit (Artificer/dynamic)
    Named subsidiary members:
        Black Dragon (Dynamic)
        G-Man (Prodigy/dynamic)
        Second Chance (Dynamic)

Inspire
Based in Seattle. Extant from 1988-1997. The world's first official superhero team.

    Challenger (Dynamic. World's first Enabled. Passed away, 2004)
    Arfogwyr (Artificer. Killed by *the Minotaur*, 1997)
    Castellan (Prodigy. A legend in his day. Carried a sword that could reportedly cut through anything. Killed *the Minotaur*. Retired, 1997)

Team Power
Based in Chicago. Working together since 1990, a formal team since 1994. Formed by Adam and Tesseract Power. Family group.

    Adam Power (Artificer)
    Tesseract Power (Prodigy)
    Vanessa Power/Thomas Power (Prodigy/dynamic)
    Buddy Power (Unpowered; uses power armor)

Survivors
Enabled teenagers; loose team.

    Blades (Artificer)
    Gimmick (Artificer)
    the Photonic Avenger (Dynamic)
    Razor-Edge (Dynamic)
    Sidestep (Dynamic)

Terror Villains of the Nineties
Not an official team (except for Mutilator & Devastator), but occasionally worked together. All deceased (or presumed so) by January 2000.

Carnifex (Dynamic. Killed in Dallas, Texas by the Texas National Guard under the aegis of the 'War on Terror Villains'; March 1997.)

Charnel (Dynamic. Killed in Omaha, Nebraska by Independence and Lady Quantum; July 1998.)

the **Darksider** (Suspected prodigy. Specialized in stealth and getting past locks and safeguards. Missing, presumed dead. Last seen San Francisco, California; July 1997.)

Doc Iridium (Artificer. Killed by his own bomb in Manhattan, Kansas; September 1999.)

False Flag (Dynamic. Shape-changer. Killed in Boston, Massachusetts by Relentless and Silent Knight; February 1999.)

Guillotine (Dynamic or artificer. Killed in Louisville, Kentucky by Transit and Relentless; June 1999.)

Kraken (Artificer. Presumed drowned when his squid-sub was sunk in Lake Michigan by Team Power; August 1997.)

Mindscrew (Dynamic. Originally called Mind-Fucker. Shot in the back of the head by person or persons unknown. Body found in San Diego, California; August 1997.)

the **Minotaur** (Dynamic, potential artificer. Killed outside Seattle, Washington by Castellan; July 1997.)

Mutilator & Devastator (Prodigy and dynamic, respectively. Mutilator was an ex-hero. The sole known terror villain pairing. Killed in Indianapolis, Indiana by Relentless, Lady Quantum and Transit; April 1999.)

Raider (Artificer. Killed in Flint, Michigan by Relentless and Independence; August 1999.)

Seismic (Artificer. Missing, presumed dead. Last seen Los Angeles, California; July 1997.)

Singularity (Dynamic. Killed in Casper, Wyoming by Independence and Transit; October 1998.)

Manhattan Justice
Based in Manhattan, NY. Extant since 2005.

Drone (Artificer)
Splendid (Dynamic)
Troll (Prodigy)
All-Star (Prodigy/Dynamic)

Independents

Smokeshadow (Prodigy/artificer. Criminal underlord in Utopia City.)

Fly Boy (Artificer. Hero; Augusta. Slept with Stephen LaMonde.)

Pickup (Artificer. Hero; Savannah. Redneck.)

Tomahawk (Artificer. Hero; Tallahassee. Flying power armor.)

the Clone Arranger (Artificer. Villain. Active in the early to mid-2000s. Had a device called a 'duplicate-gun' that would create alternate versions of people. Used it to create an evil twin of *Adam Power* in 2004. It didn't go well.)

the Ghast (Powerset unknown. Villain. Active in the early 1990s. Attempted to kidnap *Tesseract Power* on her wedding day. That didn't go well, either.)

Cherenkov (Dynamic. Destructive force of nature; Chornobyl, Ukraine. Extant from 1986 to 1993.)

Surgeon One (Prodigy. Hero turned terror villain. 1989-1993 as Surgeon One, 1993-1999 as *Mutilator.*)

the Madness (Various powersets. Severely insane Enabled who appear out of nowhere in groups of three to five, attack everyone in sight, and lose their abilities within twenty-four hours).

Acknowledgments

I would like to express my continued appreciation for Karen Buckeridge, author of the fascinating *Celestial Wars* series (see **Author's Recommendations** for more information). A good friend for many years, she has proven by example that it's not just 'other people' who can write a novel and get it published. Along the way, she has supplied me with endless advice and encouragement, as well as the absolutely essential service of tearing apart any of my writing that was substandard with the kind but firm words, "You need to smash that."

Much appreciation also to Nevena Jevtić, the lady who has created the covers for both books in this series so far.

A shout-out to my nieces and nephew, who have read the first book and claimed to enjoy it. Just remember; be who and what *you* want to be. Don't be afraid to make that leap of faith.

Thanks again to Kara, for her input and extremely useful feedback.

Thanks to Davis (the real-life inspiration for Daryl) who supplied the phrase, "Lost my comb".

Kudos once more to Amanda and David, who unwittingly supplied the names Mutilator and Devastator during our association many years ago. Thanks again, guys!

I just want to shout out to u/Ralts Bloodthorne, whose *First Contact* series (see **Author's Recommendations**) has been both fun to read and a massive inspiration to write more.

Also, to my parents: you've supported and assisted me in more ways than I can acknowledge in one go, so I'm just going to say, I love you both.

And many thanks to my sister who supports me in whatever I do, even if she ~~thinks~~ knows I'm a bit weird at times.

I wouldn't have gotten to this point without you.

Finally, the wonderful people who took the time to give *Welcome to Utopia* its online ratings:
Bela Maremoto, Shekaye, Perennial, Enygma Soul, Jenny Hakes, Rance McNair, Ringo Roperos and Poppy Drear.

Author's Recommendations

Paperbacks & eBooks
The Celestial Wars Saga, by Karen Buckeridge

Ties That Bind (Book 1)

'Own your space.'

Avis of Mystal is a powerful god in his own right. But he crossed Belial, Lord of Chaos, and spent two years in Hell as a result. Unexpectedly released, he finds that his only way to freedom depends on getting his once-estranged wife and two young daughters back to Mystal. This is not as easy as it might sound; before he was consigned to Hell, Avis made a *lot* of enemies. Now he has to contend with the consequences of his actions *and* see about getting his family home safely.

He's got one chance to make things right, and he's going to take it.

The Long Way Home (Book 2)

Having left the realm of Chaos behind, Avis knows he is still far from safety. Were he on his own, his worries would be far less, as he's an established god and therefore impossible to kill. But his wife and two young daughters are not, and are thus at the mercy of anyone who wants to get at him through them.

Worse, in the time he's been locked away in Hell, the consequences of his actions have caused allegiances to shift and change across the realms, with unexpected results. He has to contend with all this, all the while learning to be a good father and husband.

It's a good thing he likes a challenge.

Welcome to Utopia, by Alan M. Atkinson
(Utopian Dreams Series, Book 1)

All Jericho Hansen wants is some recognition as a superhero. Unfortunately, he's a gay man living in the deep South, which means he's starting from way behind the eight-ball.

When he gets accepted for an interview to join Force Majeure, *the* most prestigious super-team in America, he considers it a dream come true. But from the moment he gets on the train to Utopia City, things begin to change. Some for the worse and some for the better, but his life will never be the same again.

Welcome to Utopia. Have a nice day.

The Uncle Tal Stories, by Alan M. Atkinson (free to download)

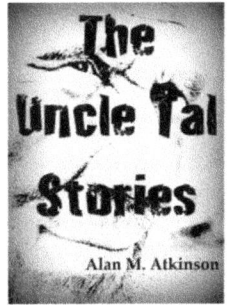

Uncle Tal is quite the character. Sitting at ease with a blanket over his lap, he takes great pleasure in spinning the most outlandish of tales. But as the listener finds out, the stranger the story, the more likely it is to be true.

For Uncle Tal has a secret, one that he shares readily enough, but few ever recognize. You might say it's all in the name.

So sit down, kick back and get comfortable. You might even learn something. After all, he's not going anywhere.

(This book was assembled from Reddit writing prompts.)

The Cube is Smaller Than You Think, by Alan M. Atkinson

Most *'you can solve the cube in three easy lessons'* books involve great long strings of moves that leave novice cube users scratching their heads, or giving the whole thing away (sometimes literally).

I've gone for a different approach in this book. There are a grand total of seven sequences, of which the longest takes up eight moves. You won't become a speed-master with these techniques, but you *will* learn how to solve the cube reliably. Includes a section on solving the 2×2×2 cube.

(Due to e-book publishing limitations, this book is only available in hardcopy.)

QR Codes

Ties That Bind

The Long Way Home

Welcome to Utopia

The Uncle Tal Stories

The Cube is Smaller Than You Think

Web Novels

First Contact, by u/Ralts Bloodthorne
(https://www.reddit.com/r/HFY/comments/f94rak/oc_pthok_eats_an_ice_cream_cone/)

'Behold; Humanity.'

A massively popular ongoing Reddit serial in the r/HFY subreddit that's spawned dozens of side-stories. Ralts started it off with a few unconnected stories that quickly grew into a hilariously complex and amazing future universe that steals from basically any and all sources. It's been collected in several published novels, all of which are worth reading.

Worm, by John C 'Wildbow' McCrae (https://parahumans.wordpress.com/)

'Doing the wrong things for the right reasons.'

A long-running web-serial that helped inspire this series. Somewhat darker in tone than **Utopian Dreams, Worm** explores the limits of the human spirit as embodied by a teenage girl who can control bugs. It has also inspired an *insane* amount of fanfiction.

I strongly recommend it to anyone who wants to write about superheroes, if only to get an idea of where you want to go with it.

The sequel, **Ward**, is complete at the time of this writing.

Online Artists

Nevena Jevtić (https://www.deviantart.com/u-svetu-maste)
Cover artist for **Welcome to Utopia** and **Shadows Over Utopia**.

Online Editing

Arkos Sloth Editing (arkossloth1@gmail.com)
Assisted with the editing of **Welcome to Utopia** and **Shadows Over Utopia**.

About the Author

Alan Michael Atkinson is from North Queensland, Australia. He grew up on a remote cattle property and attended boarding school for his higher education. Now living in the largest city north of Brisbane, he has been by turns a Chinese food delivery driver, a taxi driver and a security guard. He likes to read and plays tabletop roleplaying games when he can. His major non-writing hobbies are long-distance photography and arguing with flat-earthers.

He's met both Felicia Day (*Buffy, Dollhouse, Dr Horrible's Sing-Along Blog*) and Nathan Fillion (*Firefly, Castle, Dr Horrible's Sing-Along Blog*), and has the photos to prove it. He also has a replica of Sting (the *Lord of the Rings* sword, not the singer) hanging on his wall.

Since publishing *Welcome to Utopia*, he's discovered Reddit, especially the r/HFY subreddit and r/WritingPrompts.

A straight, white, middle-aged man from a moderately privileged background, he aspires to be an ally.

He's double-jabbed (AZ) and has had his first booster (Pfizer).

His favorite authors include Isaac Asimov, Robert Heinlein, Terry Pratchett, Lee Child, Lois McMaster Bujold, J R R Tolkein, Andre Norton, P G Wodehouse, u/Ralts Bloodthorne, John C 'Wildbow' McCrae and Karen Buckeridge.

This is his third novel, and the second in the **Utopian Dreams** series.

The series is projected to consist of four books:

Welcome to Utopia **(2020)**
Shadows Over Utopia **(2022)**
The Fall of Utopia **(~2024)**
Rebuilding Utopia **(~2026-27)**

At some point, he intends to develop and market the accompanying tabletop RPG: ***Capes, Cowls & Cogs.***

He also intends to rid himself of the pernicious habit of speaking of himself in the third person.

About *Shadows Over Utopia*

Well.

These are going to be the last words written into this book, or at least the last words anyone will be reading before they reach the back cover and have to shut the thing. (The last words written by me, anyway).

I hope you've enjoyed the ride so far. I will admit that some of the twists and turns surprised even me, and I was *writing* the story. As with the first book, I had a few ideas that simply didn't eventuate, and a few that crept in while my back was turned.

As I pointed out in the preface, events aren't going quite as well for Jericho as they were in the first book, but this is all according to plan (my plan, not Chelsea's). In case you've jumped to this section from the front without reading the intervening story, I'm not going to spoil anything (except, did you see the thing he did with the thing, and how cool was *that*?) but I will say that this point in the story was planned from the very beginning.

Well, to be honest, the final words in the last chapter were originally supposed to be, "Very, *very* carefully," but it kind of ballooned out from there.

Just regarding that character; if anyone's dubious about the believability of someone going from being a Vietnam veteran to an Assistant Attorney General, I based him on a real person who is alive at the time of this writing. Despite having every intention of treating him-as-a-character as respectfully as possible, I chickened out of even asking permission to use his real name. So, while the character in the book is *based* on my (possibly biased) interpretation of this person, he is specifically *not* the real-world person. If that makes sense.

(If anyone does their homework and figures out who I'm referring to, please keep it to yourselves. It's not a puzzle I'm urging anyone to solve, and he is just as deserving of his privacy as anyone else. Also, I don't need a lawsuit.)

As for the rest of the book, you may have noticed things going on here and there that I don't specifically spell out for the readers. You're smart people. I trust you to be able to put two and two together. That said, if you have a query about how or why something happened, feel free to drop a line to my Gmail address on the front page of this book, and I'll be happy to explain.

Regarding the Preface: I wrote the words 'stand on the precipice' before I started putting together the mess of words that eventually got hammered into the first prologue of this book. So, between writing that and writing this … is the entirety of the first draft of this novel.

And oh, yeah; when I started writing *Welcome*, I hadn't even thought about prologues (or epilogues). But I had so much more story to put in that didn't have Jericho involved (plus the whole 'getting invited for an interview' and 'leaving a letter for Stephen') that eventually it all came together as it did. This time around? Yeah, they more or less wrote themselves. It does help to have a path to follow.

In the intervening 20 months, a lot of things have happened. I've assembled another novel from bits and pieces on Reddit, because I could, and written a short book on how to solve the Rubiks Cube™, also because I could. At times, I stalled a little here and there on this book, but I always found a way through. And of course, there was the lovely, lovely coronavirus to deal with. Alpha, Beta, Delta, Omicron. Yay.

Anyway, the first draft is now complete. Sixty chapters, a smidge over two hundred thousand words, four hundred seventy-six pages. Note that these numbers *will* change, pursuant to second and third passes, as well as any amount of editing, but that's what I have so far. *Welcome* was longer in both page count (520) and word count (281,000), but I still consider this to be an honest effort. We'll see what it looks like once I've gone through it a few times.

Anyway, see you in the pages of *The Fall of Utopia*. Jericho's got a job of work ahead of him.

Cheers,

Alan M. Atkinson
December, 2021

Appraisals of
Welcome to Utopia

Amazon
Bela Maremoto (Germany)
★★★★★ **Fun book**
I like the book and want to read the next one. There is enough mystery to keep you guessing at several things over the course of the book (and not everything gets resolved at the end so I really want to read the next one now) but several things DO get resolved. There is nice romance (no description of intercourse although it is clear it happens when it happens), very strong family ties and the heroes and villains (with and without super powers) are not 2D-cutouts. The author uses the book to describe several interpersonal scenarios, in which one can see what is a good way to act and what is not because it hurts others, and how figuring out what is what is sometimes difficult (but needs to be done anyway). The book also pokes at the super hero tropes in a fun way. So it is not all joking around and being silly, not all being super serious and not all about either only dealing with bad guys or dealing with relationships. It is a mixture. And I want to read the next book, as well as the other two promised at the end.

Shekaye (Australia)
★★★★★ **Fun and engaging read**
I loved this book - it was fun to read, with characters I could relate to and each character felt real to me. I laughed out loud, and cried, at points.

Each character, even the secondary ones, had their own motivations, secrets and ways of being - including the two cities of Utopia and Savannah. The backstories, and world-building information, was provided in a natural way, through the storytelling.

While the story rounded out enough that it could be stand alone, there are enough mysteries that I can't wait for the next book. Mysteries were solved, surprises were had, the realities and moral ambiguity of life were present without the author preaching to you.

The author uses language precisely, but some readers will not have come across some of the words used in this book - for me, it was great to see a modern author use language so well.

Seriously, a great read. Not a reader of superhero books, I was pleasantly surprised.

Goodreads

Perennial

★★★★★

Just a genuinely fantastic book. Seriously one of the best I've read in years - and I read a lot of books! I literally made this account just to write a review. On top of being an excellent book with regards to science fiction, LGBT+ representation, and the general superhero theme, it somehow manages to be a better mystery book than most mystery books I've read, with tension and intrigue throughout.

It starts out a little rough in the first 100 pages, with a ton of expositional conversations and some very repetitive references to an in-universe comedian, but this is interspersed by some genuinely tense drama, so it's not too bad. I'm also inclined to forgive it this, seeing as the worldbuilding is just so darn interesting.

If you've ever wondered how a world reliant on superheroes would actually operate, prepare to have all of your questions answered. From costuming up in enclosed spaces without being caught to copyright issues with in-universe comics to how Batman qualifies as a superhero at all, every nuance is considered thoroughly.

And if you love what superpowers can bring to characterization, this book will scratch that itch, too. Even characters with just a few lines were memorable. There's a tragic heroine with a wheelchair mech, a boy with a robot bug swarm, a foul-mouthed teenage girl with a dragon transformation, and just way too many cool powersets to go over here. The way powers work even opens up a ton of possibilities for fan characters - fitting, since it's modeled after a hypothetical roleplaying game.

And they have personalities to match! The seemingly-stoic leader of the city might have a barely under control temper, the man whose powerset is modeled after a bridge troll is gruff and barely tolerates people... even patterns of speech are distinct, including the main character's cousin code-switching between accents and a supergenius inventor using overly technical language for mundane things. (The American South accent and phrases might not be too accurate, but this book is literally about superheroes wearing costumes to fight crime. If the accent somehow breaks immersion for you, I don't know what to say.)

To make things even better, the book is free of the usual bigotry that seems to plague superhero media. The protagonist's experiences as a gay man and his cousin's experiences as a black man in the American South are explored thoughtfully, alongside other smaller topics such as how a shapeshifting powerset might affect gender identity. There are more female characters than you'd usually see from superhero media, too (though I don't think the ratio quite made 50-50), and they're blessedly not sexualized without losing all sexual agency.

I was really expecting the ending to be a cliffhanger, which I absolutely hate, but it pleasantly surprised me with a resolution that still left plenty of leads unexplored. There's a naturally developing romance that didn't strangle the plot and a wild twist at the end that feels earned. To top it all off, the prose is refined, with functionally zero typos, though I can see folks who prefer snappier reads finding it a bit wordy.

Long story short, if you love worldbuilding, characters, drama, action, science fiction, or especially superheroes, read this book. Immediately. I just love it to bits, y'all.

Book Club Review

4 stars out of 4

Poppy Drear

[Following is an official OnlineBookClub.org review of Welcome to Utopia by Alan M. Atkinson.]

I'll just come right out and say it: *Welcome to Utopia* by Alan M. Atkinson is a very good book. It's quite possibly one of the best books I've read in years. If you have even a passing interest in science fiction or superhero stories, you should be reading it. Set in a world where superheroes are relatively commonplace, it follows Jericho, a small-town hero who wants to make it big in Utopia City, where the superhero team Force Majeure reigns supreme.

Every part of the world is brimming with character, and it balances realism and excitement very well. There are mundane things like public transport and shopping malls, but these familiar concepts are fully reimagined in terms of the technological advancements possible in comic books. The author even incorporates elements from American history, like the Space Shuttle Challenger and the War on Terror, grounding the fantastical in the real to create a genuinely unique and imaginative setting.

This book also has a huge number of interesting and vibrant characters, even outside of the main cast. My favorite example is Black Dragon, who only appears for a chapter or two. She's a foul-mouthed teenager who struggles with social decorum, and despite her apparent disrespect, I found myself rooting for her to grow up emotionally and become a great hero in her own right. The book's structure for superpowers is incredibly versatile, too, producing characters like a disabled person who transformed her wheelchair into a mech and a boy who can turn his bones into armor.

With such excellent side characters, it stands to reason that the main characters are masterfully crafted as well. Just like real people, Jericho himself has different elements of his identity that overlap and sometimes conflict. He does things just for fun, makes mistakes with realistic consequences, and overcomes some very tough decisions while maintaining his integrity, making him likable and engaging. The other two characters he allies himself with are just as well-rounded, with backgrounds that are exciting to discover.

Blessedly, the book is free of the misogyny and general bigotry that plague the superhero genre. While I think male characters have more screentime, so to speak, the gender ratio is practically equal, and the narrative never sexualizes women more than men. Even if the book occasionally plays into stereotypes, like when the leader of Force Majeure is a man with a temper, or when a female character has powers revolving around emotional empathy, it's leagues better than most other superhero media.

I also really enjoyed this book's more drawn-out pacing, even if it was a bit sluggish to start off with. The author takes time to flesh out every aspect of the novel, and I love how immersive this level of detail can get. The story itself still stays focused, though, and I always found the events taking place to be exciting and intriguing. Overall, this book is certainly not a quick read, but it's very rewarding. It's also remarkably well-edited, and the prose puts characters at its heart, vividly showcasing their emotions and perceptions.

It goes without saying, but due to its outstanding worldbuilding, characters, plot, and polish, I rate this book **4 out of 4 stars**. It contains some explicit language and some moderately graphic content, so it's not fit for younger children, but these elements didn't feel forced or out of place. I, for one, will certainly be checking this author's Amazon page for the next book in the series - something I've only been able to say once before in all of my reviews for this site.

SUPPORT YOUR LOCAL

FORCE MAJEURE™

TEAM

WE'RE HERE FOR <u>YOU</u>.

www.ingramcontent.com/pod-product-compliance
Lightning Source LLC
Chambersburg PA
CBHW070149120726
47909CB00001B/39